BY H. G. ADLER

The Wall
The Journey
Panorama

THE WALL

THE WALL

A Novel

H. G. ADLER

Translated from the German
by Peter Filkins

RANDOM HOUSE / NEW YORK

Translation, introduction, list of characters, and principal events copyright © 2014 by Peter Filkins

Published in the United States by Random House, an imprint and division of Random House LLC, a Penguin Random House Company, New York.

RANDOM HOUSE and the HOUSE colophon are registered trademarks of Random House LLC.

This work was originally published in Austria as *Die unsichtbare Wand* by Paul Zsolnay Verlag, in 1989. Copyright © 1989 by Paul Zsolnay Verlag, Vienna. This edition published by arrangement with Paul Zsolnay Verlag.

Grateful acknowledgment is made to HarperCollins, Publishers for permission to reprint an excerpt from *"Ars Poetica?"* from *The Collected Poems 1931–1987* by Czeslaw Milosz, copyright © 1988 by Czeslaw Milosz Royalties, Inc. Reprinted by permission of HarperCollins, Publishers.

Library of Congress Cataloging-in-Publication Data
Adler, H. G.
[Unsichtbare Wand. English]
The wall : a novel / H. G. Adler ; translated by Peter Filkins.
pages cm
ISBN 978-0-8129-9306-6
eBook ISBN 978-0-679-64455-2
1. Holocaust survivors—Fiction. 2. Exiles—Fiction. 3. Psychic trauma—Fiction.
4. Self-realization—Fiction. 5. Prague (Czech Republic)—Fiction. 6. London (England)—
Fiction. 7. Psychological fiction. 8. Jewish fiction. I. Filkins, Peter, translator. II. Title.
PT2601.D614U5713 2014
833'.914—dc23 2014003513

Printed in the United States of America on acid-free paper

www.atrandom.com

2 4 6 8 9 7 5 3 1

First Edition

Book design by Susan Turner

CONTENTS

TRANSLATOR'S NOTE

THE GERMAN TEXT FOR THE NOVEL IS TAKEN FROM *Die unsichtbare Wand*, published by Zsolnay Verlag in 1989. Although this title would translate as *The Invisible Wall*, H. G. Adler clearly intended to call the novel *Die Wand*, and only the publisher's concern about confusion with Marlen Haushofer's novel *Die Wand* prevented this from happening. Hence, I have chosen to restore the original title in translation.

I wish to express my thanks to the German Academic Exchange Service (DAAD) and the Deutsches Literaturarchiv for grants that allowed me to research Adler's letters and manuscripts in his archive in Marbach, Germany. I am also grateful to Bard College at Simon's Rock for a sabbatical and leave, and for the support provided by a residency at the James Merrill House, where part of the translation was completed. As always, I remain deeply grateful to my colleague Chris Callanan for his kind contribution in answering many questions on the German, and to Jeremy Adler for his patient and supportive response to queries throughout. I also wish to thank Susan Roeper for her faith and sustenance throughout the process, and Lindsey Schwoeri and Sam Nicholson, my editors at Random House, for their committed and generous support during the many months spent on the novel's translation.

INTRODUCTION

The purpose of poetry is to remind us
how difficult it is to remain just one person,
for our house is open, there are no keys to the doors,
and invisible guests come in and out at will.

—Czeslaw Milosz, *"Ars Poetica?"*

H. G. ADLER'S *The Wall* MARKS THE COMPLETION OF THE SHOAH TRILOGY that he began with the writing of *Panorama* in 1948 and continued with the composition of *The Journey* in 1950–51. Having finished a first draft of *The Wall* in 1956, and an extensive revision in 1961, Adler unfortunately did not live to see publication of the novel in 1989, a year after his death as a postwar exile in London. However, he considered it his crowning achievement as a novelist, and continued to make small changes to it well into the 1970s. Although he would also go on to write a social satire titled *Hausordnung* (*House Rules*), published in 1988, *The Wall* essentially marks the end of his career as a novelist, a remarkable run that saw the composition of six novels in ten years, beginning in 1946, as well as his seminal monograph, *Theresienstadt 1941–1945: The Face of a Coerced Community*.

Three of those six novels were never published, while the first two parts of the trilogy, *Panorama* and *The Journey*, were published out of their intended order in 1968 and 1962, respectively. After completing *The Wall* in 1961, Adler continued to write and publish short stories and essays, work on his other great study of the deportations, *Administered Man*, published in 1974, and privately write the poems that would eventually make up a collected volume of twelve hundred pages, published as *Andere Wege (Different Ways)* in 2010. Adler's last book, published in 1987, was a treatise outlining an experimental theology that he had begun writing in 1938 and continued to work on during the two and a half years he spent in Theresienstadt. Although Adler's career stretches across many disciplines—including literature, history, sociology, philosophy, and religion—there is something fitting in the fact that his last book is essentially the first he set out to write. Despite his having been deported from his native Prague and plunged into the nightmare world of Theresienstadt, then surviving no fewer than three concentration camps, including Auschwitz, as well as the loneliness and penury of forty years of exile in England, Adler's sensibility remains consistent and unified, a mien suffused with the powerful, extreme experience it had survived, and yet able, in the end, to stand outside of that experience and give it meaning and order.

The struggle and cost of the effort to remain a unified person alive to the present, despite the weight of the past, lies at the heart of *The Wall*, and, as with *Panorama* and *The Journey*, Adler clearly taps his own biography in the shaping of this epic tale. At the novel's start, we find Arthur Landau living in a "metropolis" that clearly mirrors Adler's postwar London, while the city he remembers from "back there" is a sure stand-in for Adler's native Prague. The fact that Arthur's first wife, Franziska, perished in the war also alludes to the loss of Adler's first wife, Gertrud Klepetar, to the gas chambers in Auschwitz. Similarly, the importance of Arthur's second wife, Johanna, in saving his life ties directly to the crucial role that Adler's second wife, Bettina Gross, played in getting him through the postwar years and beyond. Like Arthur, Adler also struggled to find sure footing in London, both economically and socially, despite the company of fellow exiles and friends, such as Elias and Veza Canetti, Franz Baermann Steiner, and Erich Fried. *The Wall* in fact functions as a roman à clef, for the portraits of

Professor Kratzenstein, the oddly named So-and-So, and Oswald and Inge Bergmann are indeed caricatures of Theodor Adorno, Steiner, and the Canettis, respectively, while lifelong friends and colleagues of Adler's also show up in various transformations.

But in several important ways this is where biography and fiction part ways, and even more so in *The Wall* than in the first two installments of Adler's trilogy. For one thing, Arthur has two children with Johanna, whereas Adler had only one son with Bettina. Arthur's work on his *Sociology of Oppressed People* certainly parallels Adler's work on *Theresienstadt 1941–1945*, yet by the time *The Wall* was completed in 1956, Adler had enjoyed extensive success and renown with the publication of his monograph, whereas Arthur still awaits publication while doubting that his talents will ever be properly recognized or employed. Last, though Adler suffered the difficulties of exile, throughout his postwar life he continued to return to Germany, Austria, and Switzerland on extensive reading tours and research visits, all of which complicated the nature of his experience as an exile. True, he never did return to his native Prague, but as a German speaker and writer he identified strongly with German culture and society. Though he stated that he could not live in a land where the corner grocer might once have been a Nazi, he nonetheless had no trouble whatsoever returning to it.

Hence, while *The Wall* undoubtedly has powerful ties to his own life, it is important to realize that Adler is also the one standing on the outside, shaping Arthur Landau's tormented psyche, rather than simply suffering it once again. Arthur may confess, "On the day they announced that the war was over, there was nothing left but a snakeskin, a dried, brittle skeleton that I could discern through tender self-regard, though I the living animal had slipped away, gone without a trace, no longer to be found," and this may indeed be a very real description of Adler's own state of mind in 1945, but the fact of its articulation argues that the author stands at a further, more stable remove. In this way, *The Wall* serves as the quintessential novel of the survivor's duress and guilt, for while Adler is the artist determined to shape it and give it meaning, his challenge is also to survive the seeming injustice of his own survival. Likewise, Arthur cannot help feeling that he is someone who has "ceased to exist, called it quits, [is] completely spent, the vestige of a memory of who I no longer am, . . . someone who can never find his foot-ing, never land in one place," but there is no reason to suppose that, in the end, the same holds true for Adler.

The Wall, like a symphony, is an arrangement of competing and in-terwoven themes, and Adler is the composer-conductor directing the en-tire opus. As a modernist montage in the same vein as the works of Joyce, Woolf, and Faulkner, the novel takes up and repeats a host of key notes: the loss of Franziska and the struggles of the war; the return to Prague and Arthur's hope of finding his parents alive; work in a museum that collects Jewish artifacts; Arthur's anxiety about crossing the border and leaving his homeland and his friends for good; his eventual arrival in the "metropolis" of London; the effort to reconnect with old friends there and find mean-ingful employment as a writer and an intellectual; the neglect he suffers at the hands of prominent intellectuals who spent the war in exile; the first encounters with Johanna Zinner among these circles; their eventual court-ship and engagement; the rearing of their two children; and, finally, Arthur's continual fantasy of being "that first Adam" expelled forever from Paradise. Add to this list the recurring nightmare of two pallbearers showing up on his doorstep to cart him off in a hearse while he's still alive, and the phan-tasm of Arthur's consciousness is complete.

Like any consciousness, Arthur's is a dense entanglement of past and present, fantasy and reality, daydream and meditation, hope and regret, tenderness and suffering, love and guilt—all of it occurring and recurring through the connected disorder of an extended chain of thought. However, because of the intensity and extremity of his experience, Arthur's conscious-ness threatens to bind him forever to the past, and the narrative strategy of The Wall is meant to mimic this conflict. By employing a kind of mise-en-scène technique—whereby Arthur finds himself thinking about life in Prague right after the war only to then find himself at a gathering of post-war intellectuals in London, or back in the Bohemian forest where he once walked with Franziska—the novel shuttles the reader between the past and the present without any clear sign that such a switch has occurred. In fact, the past is always present for us as readers, as it is for Arthur, for it lurks in the shadows, waiting to appear at any moment, whether as reverie or as nightmare.

The novel's nonlinear plot does at times make it difficult for us to know just what is going on or how we ended up in a certain locale or set of circumstances. However, such challenges are performative in nature and are meant to show how the duress of Arthur's past constantly informs the present, in much the same way that flashbacks occur to those suffering post-traumatic stress, or even how everyday memory constantly transports us between realms, surprising us with what pops up suddenly in the course of our thoughts. Whether it be the voice that threatens to expel Arthur as Adam, his haunting memories of Franziska, his nightmares of being carted away by the pallbearers, or the guilty visions he has of his dead parents, all of these function as eruptive dislocations that not only control Arthur's consciousness but define it. Therefore, the difficulty of the novel is really meant to engage the reader in the difficulty of being Arthur Landau, and to appreciate that is to appreciate the weight that extreme duress places on the imagination, as well as the imagination's inventive capacity to order and comprehend the past in the most fantastical of ways through memory.

Indeed, the "wall" that Arthur finds himself standing before and unable to penetrate is the past. Because of this, Arthur realizes, "I don't belong to human society. I and the wall, we are alone, we belong together; there is nothing else that I belong to." Arthur, however, is not willing to settle for this, and thus he continually strives to make some connection to the world and to find a place within it. Unfortunately, despite initial avid interest in his past on the part of his old friends and the new people he meets, little practical help comes his way. Instead, like the heaps of prayer books and dusty portraits of the departed that he helped collect and sort at the museum "back there" (as Adler himself did at the Jewish Museum in Prague right after the war), in London's "metropolis" Arthur is treated as a kind of exotic relic, interesting at first for the descriptions of the horrors he can provide, but ultimately dispensable as a fellow competitor for the limited opportunities available amid postwar privation.

All of this would make for a very dour novel, were it not for the fact that, in the end, *The Wall* is—surprisingly and paradoxically—a love story. Arthur's life with Johanna and their two children is crucial to his survival, and their home together on West Park Row remains the anchor of his life throughout the novel. There is an immediate attraction between him and Johanna when they meet at a social gathering, and their relationship is what allows Arthur to come to grips with himself and with the past. Johanna, in fact, sees the wall that he confronts quite differently from the way he sees it. "I honestly believe that the wall is your protection," she tells him. "It separates you from your past, from all the horror." Although Arthur does not entirely agree, he nonetheless adores his wife and confesses, "When I look at Johanna I am often happy, though sometimes also sad, yet always something is affirmed, and many fears are tamped down. What happens between us folds in upon itself and creates an understanding; we trust each other, there's no need to search for anything else."

Yet search he does—for his parents, for release from Franziska, for support for his writing, for meaningful intellectual engagement, and for a place in the world. Though Johanna provides emotional grounding while in some ways living his life for him, writing is the other means by which Arthur finds some kind of solace. Just as the novel continually returns to West Park Row and his family, it is in his study that Arthur is most at home while working on his *Sociology of Oppressed People*. The source of this work is his own experience of survival during the war, just as Adler tapped his own past in order to write his study of Theresienstadt. But, as was true for Adler, Arthur does not simply write a memoir of his experience; he studies it in a scholarly manner, in order to do full justice to it and to the many who perished. He does this in part because of the difficulty of holding on to his experience through memory: "I collected so much experience and carried it along with me, so much pressing deep into my memories, held there as I told myself I would need it, and now it appeared to me it was indeed lost, myself unable to find it any longer, Franziska's death and my survival having shredded the volume that gave the contents some kind of sense, all my stowed-away knowledge now covered in dust and ground down to a pulp."

Although Arthur admits, at first, that "all I wanted to set down was one word, and yet it all remained bottled up inside me," he does not give up. Realizing that "the less of a person I am because I am not allowed to exist, the more the world is closed to me," he nonetheless sits down to write a story titled "The Letter Writers," which appears about halfway through *The Wall*. This simple act somehow frees him, allowing him to give in but not to give up. . . . To slam into the wall as if it were not there, to flatter and play about with it, as if it would let itself be conquered, yet to acknowledge it and not doubt such knowledge of it, accepting that it's pointless to do so and will probably always be pointless. To exit the most secret depths with great vigor, as if victory were assured, and let myself be battered and defeated, pushed back, back into the hidden recesses! To hope for nothing and then to invoke the wondrous as if what I had never dared hope were already guaranteed.

Writing is what allows Arthur to exist, "to make a plea out of a continually obsessed conscience, a plea directed at someone beyond all borders," be they the borders of geography, history, memory, or even time. This plea is particularly urgent because it is not one made by Arthur alone. Through his experience at the museum while collecting portraits and artifacts left behind by "the disappeared," he comes to understand powerfully the burden of his responsibility as a survivor, as he tells his fellow curators:

We are remnant survivors, who are there for all who are not. That's true in general; the living are there for the dead, for their predecessors, and thus we also represent the history of the dead. How difficult it is, then, to exist as oneself when we are also history, so much history! But we are particularly there for all those dragged away by force and annihilated. . . . We are the history of the exterminated, the history of the shadow that consumed them. And we collect what was stolen from them, what we can store up of their remains. But that is indeed alive and really not history. It amounts to neither memory nor keepsakes; it is commemoration.

Arthur's experience and memory, then, are both singular and collective, and his effort to grapple with the past through writing is tied to a deeply felt need to commemorate the lives that were lost to it. For him, the past is both burden and sustenance, as it has formed his life in the present and is the only means by which he can find a way to the future.

However, what is most often missing from that past is particulars, Arthur admitting early in his courtship with Johanna that "there are only a few things that I recall precisely," and that what he really possesses is "a memory for the relationship between things, for the dense interweaving of experience." This also mirrors the narrative guise of *The Wall*. Rather than functioning as a memoir disguised as a novel, the book is a novel interested in the "interweaving of experience" and the performance of it. Given that the novel begins and ends with Arthur looking out his study window at two old women at a window across the street and the cat that walks nimbly along its sill, one might even entertain the possibility that the entire narrative takes place inside Arthur's consciousness in a single day, much like James Joyce's *Ulysses*, a novel that Adler deeply admired and read as early as the 1940s. Even if this is not the case, clearly *The Wall* encompasses the past and the present, and how both occur within Arthur's consciousness, while at the same time that consciousness is meant to serve those who did not survive the past. "Until everything is thought through and made clear, I cannot rest, let alone find peace," Arthur says to Johanna. "Thus there can be no escape." At the same time, however, "memory is something else altogether. It's the identification with the deportation and all its consequences, therefore with those who suffered extermination. That I can't do. At best I was broken, perhaps shattered, but, because I indeed stand before you, I was not exterminated."

This, then, is the paradoxical hell that Arthur inhabits: because he did not die, he cannot live, and because he is alive, he cannot properly commemorate the experience of those who died, for he did not share that experience in full. And yet he must go on, for only then can he write the works that will contain some part of the lives that were lost. Add to this classic formulation of survivor's guilt the fact that Adler also suffers the exile's plight of living a rootless and discontinuous life, and one sees the extent to which *The Wall* encompasses two great cataclysms of the twentieth century: forced deportation and permanent exile. "Whoever loses his home against his will, simply because he has been expelled by the powers that want to annihilate him," Arthur muses, "cannot return alone to the site of expulsion as one who happened to be saved from joining the fellowship of the murdered, no matter the reasons that move him." Given such duress, Adler's heroic journey is one that arrives at the barest of reconciliations, one in which he realizes, "I simply have to be, because I am." Paltry as this may seem, there is a certain victory in it, for though Arthur remains "a survivor, condemned to cling to a signpost in the deadly snowstorm of misery," he stands at that same post with his wife and two children while wielding the tools of his trade—namely words, which Adler, too, wielded (in novels, stories, poems, essays, and scholarly studies) in an effort to both invoke and stave off the demons that he had involuntarily been assigned by fate.

Czeslaw Milosz, another enduring exile of the twentieth century, ends his "*Ars Poetica?*" ironically by saying:

> *What I'm saying here is not, I agree, poetry,*
> *as poems should be written rarely and reluctantly,*
> *under unbearable duress and only with the hope*
> *that good spirits, not evil ones, choose us for their instrument.*

It is a sentiment that will also serve well the reader in approaching *The Wall*, for despite the anxiety and despair that so often suffuse Arthur Landau, threatening to derail his every foray into the unknown, he battles on in "the hope that good spirits, not evil ones," will choose him for their instrument. Indeed, Arthur may be "broken," but he knows, too, that "you have to be able to feel broken and yet not damn the world, to not become callous, not hate your neighbor, not the guilty, for they are your neighbors. You can't separate them from those who are not guilty. Doubt and lack of faith are two very different things. Beware the one who exchanges one for the other, or mixes them up!" In like manner, Adler's symphonic novel is composed in the faith that light will somehow prevail within such darkness, its source being the consciousness that binds together its major and minor notes, its themes and variations, its Kafkaesque poise amid inscrutable suffering before the wall of time.

PETER FILKINS
April 7, 2013

For Luzzi Wolgensinger

What is life? A trial?
We search, but never know;
Behold, your life alone
Becomes an enormous treasure.

THE WALL

A BLACK PLUME OF SMOKE FROM THE SQUAT CHIMNEY DRIFTS AT AN ANGLE over the factories, invading the neighborhood near MacKenzie's, where cars are overhauled and rebuilt, the smoke moving heavy and thick through the streets. Ron, the old ragman, thin with a pinched face, pushes his cart wearily along the sidewalk like a mobile cage and then stands awkwardly before our house as he has done each week for years, ever since Johanna gave him a huge box of old clothes, which delighted him, even though the weight nearly brought him to his knees, while we were happy to be free of that junk, he becoming our benefactor in taking it off our hands, rather than just a ragman. Santi, the aging yellow hound from Simmonds's vegetable stand, wanders lazily about, barks suddenly for no apparent reason, and then shuffles silently along. With shopping bags swaying, women from the neighborhood gather together, stand for a while and lose themselves in meaningless talk until they suddenly separate, parting with an unexplained sharp laugh that disappears abruptly. In the distance, where the train heads west into the countryside, a whistle blows, as if announcing the joy of any kind of journey away from here.

It all goes as usual and is familiar, for it's been more than seven years since we first settled here. Not in this city, and certainly not in this country, nor even really in this part of town, but just in the immediate surroundings of this neighborhood, here on West Park Row, where we live in a tiny single-family house, as well as around the corner on Truro Street and among the neighboring streets, corners, and squares with their open greens and playgrounds, all of it within a ten-minute radius. We know the entire area, but that which is closest and the most familiar is no farther away than twice the reach of a good strong voice. Here is where we live, adrift and tolerated, comfortable despite everything, almost well liked as old-timers, as they say, us not even knowing whether we have settled in a major city or a village. If anything, it feels like living in the countryside, for it's hard to imagine that distant neighborhoods are even attached to this same place.

There are several reasons for this. If you want to visit another part of the city, then you pull yourself together, say goodbye, hop into a car, or onto the bus, or even onto a train, and you are quickly whisked away from familiar surroundings. Because here on West Park Row and for miles around us, we are strangers; the few people who know something about us are no less than an hour away. We rarely see them, some of them never, others hardly more than once a year, and only a few more than once a month.

It's as if we were foreigners, as if we lived in a foreign country, although with each passing year more people in the neighborhood greet us and even know our names. Michael and Eva also play with children from the neighborhood. One might even think that we were almost on intimate terms with the people to the left and right of us, with the salesclerks where we buy our groceries and little daily items, and with a few others. Yet these relations don't reach very far and are certainly not that deep. There's us, then there's others. Maybe just a passing glance, festoons of particular greetings and intricately woven exchanges, certain rites that amount to simple human interaction, sometimes even full of warmth and fellow feeling, yet passed from mouth to mouth without consequence, one hand reaching out to another. It goes without saying that people in the neighborhood have their own ideas about us, and some of them share them with one another, but we cast a blind eye to it. For we don't think twice when we also talk about the neighbors and others in our own everyday terms, if only rarely, and in mere fleeting snippets of conversation fed by nasty gossip.

This is a humble neighborhood. For the most part, it houses workers and clerks who have no real wealth but are not at all accustomed to misery, people whose aspirations we might guess at but will never fathom, destinies that, for us transplants from afar, melt together indistinguishably among all that is foreign, no matter how unique or special they may actually prove to be inside the circles we are forbidden to enter. Two groups, however, remain clearly separate. There are the families on our side of the street, who, along with the abutters on Truro Street and farther on in that direction, make up a stretch of better appointed houses inhabited by more well-to-do solidly bourgeois citizens. Then there are the people across from us (to the left of MacKenzie's), who don't live in badly built and somewhat uncomfortable, yet indeed quite cozy, single-family dwellings like us but instead occupy two sprawling apartment complexes with smooth, spacious courtyards that, at first glance, look almost friendly and inviting but on closer inspection betray a cold, boxed-in, narrow feel. Most of the people over there, which must amount to nearly a thousand, probably don't make less than the heads of the families on our side, but no one here would consider them to be the same class. One has to admit, though, that the kids over there get up to much worse mischief than do our own. Many of the boys run wild, others hang about or sleep away their time, the children often running about filthy, the sucking of sweets and poisonous ice-cream treats never ending. Also, the language used in unattended courtyards and the noises that one hears there are different. For us, the tolerated, there is no reason to look down on these shiftless and nonetheless well-meaning folk, though we take pride in not wanting anything to do with the neighborhoods opposite us, where the sounds of family life and the blare of foul-sounding radios pressing through thin walls and down narrow hallways never allows you to escape your neighbors.

The village in which we live is neither beautiful nor charming, yet for us it's tolerable, because no one bothers us. Also, there is enough light, the chimney is not too noisy, and the area has open spaces to escape to, the largest being Shepherd's Field, an open space for romping around that is just a few minutes away from our house. In addition, there is available for both grown-ups and children four parks that offer, before they close at sunset, more freedom than one would expect in a major city. Our neighborhood—surprisingly, given that it's next to MacKenzie's—is almost free of traffic.

Only through Truro Street, where our only bus runs, do long lines of cars pass, West Park Row being more often abuzz with children's voices than from any other hustle and bustle.

Nonetheless, it took a while to settle in here. Johanna winced when, after some years in a much more well-heeled part of the city, she found something for us here, it being a place that didn't bewilder me like everything else in this country and also this city, where everything was new for me. No matter where I went, I was a newcomer who could make out only the basic outline of things, myself familiar with nothing, a stranger, acting whatever way I wanted, wrapped up in myself, though also pressing forth from my inwardness with the manner of a salesman who hawks the gaudy wares of his heart for all the world to see and who forgets that perhaps no one really wants them, though it never bothered me if someone turned up his nose at my treasures, for many others appeared eager to buy them. The world felt as if it stood behind glass, and I myself felt as if I were made of glass, but everything consisted of a delicate glass, alive and sinuous, yet fragile, everything peculiarly at odds with itself, subtly transparent, and yet also impenetrable, more to be looked at than comprehended, and nonetheless alien, alien, an inner trust at last slowly deducible only after dogged, constant efforts to feel it.

I was almost done in; there had to be a way out. Now I wanted to blossom. The mortal wound, from which I had not recovered, I either denied or assumed was healed, powerfully striding forth, though less sensitive men would have been frightened, but somehow I was protected from realizing that back then. Johanna, who was busy setting up the house and was otherwise busy with a number of things, looked at me with concern, but I seemed so carefree and relaxed that she yielded, more indulgent than concerned, to the all-consuming fits I would throw about all the useful and harmful borders set up by society, during which she would shrink from me without my noticing. However, daily items such as food, clothing, and shelter had become so precious and expensive, all I could do was be amazed, though I was never worried. I thought the money to pay for what we needed would somehow appear; even though there was no guarantee, if I just kept at it, then everything would work out. Johanna, meanwhile, offered up whatever she could as alms to purchase what we needed. She saw how happy it made me, and so she found inventive ways to make use of her meager funds and hard-earned savings. Thus my burdens were eased, and I enjoyed the feel of life blossoming again in what Johanna had done for us, and, with full wallets holding out to me ever more profligate promises, I could confidently let go of the idea of regaining a small bit of wealth preserved for me for many years in America.

I was constantly restless. Neither earlier nor later in life was it as easy for me to remain so consistently creative. I loved my work, for it was new and came to me so easily that it never occurred to me that others might not understand it or find it difficult or wouldn't agree with it. However, that's not quite what happened, and thus seeds of doubt were planted, for others listened quite attentively—or so at first it seemed to me—to what I had to say about my research and findings, but then I unfortunately did not realize that though they expressed amazement at what I had to say, they were not interested at all in what I had to say. My self-deception only grew as a result of the effect people had on me in the postwar years, as both the educated and the half-educated desired an affront to their own conscience, which is what I offered, whether I wanted to or not, for what I said felt like a shower of repentance flooding down upon them. Thus, people wanted to hear what I had to say and yet none had to take it seriously; they wanted to listen, but didn't have to think anything more about the content, which then made it easy for them to shower me with approval as long as there was no cost to them. People felt a deep guilt and lusted after the chance to whip their injured senses through a kind of filtered horror, even if, though it was not my intent, they did so in such a merciless, skillful manner through me.

The little house on West Park Row was like a little volcano that held me inside and felt good to me. There I could work and gather my powers until they overflowed. But should I erupt and through my actions cast raging fire and glowing ash upon people, then terror was let loose and others had to defend themselves. For who indeed dared to consciously provoke me? It was a vain, indeed sick new beginning! Yet I couldn't help myself, and, unfortunately, there was no one who could intercede between me and others. There was no such balance, and in the following years this sealed my fate. When today I look back at my life in this country, I have to admit that I am burned out, and the comparison to a volcano is somewhat close to the truth.

But in the end one should never think in terms of metaphors, for they can drive you crazy. Much has changed over the years, and I've carried myself differently for some time now. By now, most of them have forgotten about me, those for whom back then my existence was a sensation that caused a real stir. Now I'm only dormant. However, a monument to my past actions I am not.

Rather, everything around me, whether human or concrete, has become perfidious, everything and everyone—except Johanna, the blessèd and ever-devoted companion, the woman, the incomparable essence at the heart of it all. How can one such creature alone encompass, and I really mean encompass, so much inside herself? There is a bounteousness in her that hardly any one person could contain, something so multifaceted and rich, yet hardly comprehensible. What can I say? It's simply incomprehensible! When I really think about it, Johanna is everything I am, for I do not exist, only she does. She props me up and stands by me, she brings together many different sides of me, something that allowed me to exist again, that put me back together and taught me and gave me a name and made me whole.

It's unimaginable to me what would remain of Arthur Landau without Johanna, because I have ceased to exist, called it quits, am completely spent, the vestige of a memory of who I no longer am, maybe even a message from nowhere, someone who can never find his footing, never land in one place. Other people are just as dubious, I am at least aware of that, but I never even rise to the level of a dubious existence, the fragile bearing of a single nature, because I am homeless in every sense, belonging nowhere and therefore expendable, never missed, because no one knows anything about me. But, because of Johanna, how I think of myself is not entirely true. She moves about the house, works in the kitchen, places food on the table, suddenly says something that is wonderfully clear, and always then follows up the consequences of any particular incident with something that makes sense of it all, everything placed in meaningful order, and—what is really amazing—most of it somehow relating to me, affirming me and affecting me. Johanna speaks, the two syllables of my name rolling out from her lips, such that I hear it, look up, understand, and already, amid the emptiness of my potential existence, something is planted which I must acknowledge— namely, that I exist. This is what Johanna wants. She married someone and bore him two children who belong not only to her but also to someone else, whom she softly and innocently calls Father. Father, Father! Then I have to wake up and look around, as if I were coming out of a dream, in order to realize that I'm there. The harder it is to do this, the more I feel it is true, because in realizing that I am simply here at all I could even agree with the philosopher who boldly wished to conclude from nothing more than his own thinking that he existed. Nonetheless, it is not thought that returns me to this sense of wonder; indeed, it's not my own thinking at all, but rather a condition amid which one is conceived, and that one is me.

Johanna brought about this miracle. She took me in when I no longer even existed and before I reappeared. She took in something that lay among the fields of possibility, nothing that was certain and nothing that was real, but something she thought was there, which she had a feel for, and which to her was perceivable. She had an unshakable trust in the unreal she chose out of blind, hopeful courage, because she believed in the possible, in the promise of the future. That's how she was able to wrest her very being free from the times that hardly offered any hope, much less a future to believe in, tomorrow an improbability in itself in which everything begins anew and is again created anew, whereby one greets it with a powerful cry of an inner birth: You're alive! You're alive! She must have sensed the kind of exultant inner strength that within the shadow of a ghostly entity still feels itself to be real, such that it also feels incarnate through a palpable presence and is freed from all other apparitions with its limbs intact, a single being in an equally apparent space. That remains an incomprehensible feat, and even if I am nothing else, I am this feat or, better yet, I am the culmination of this feat, he who sits amid the security of what he's been given by this woman, who day after day does everything she can to assure my existence, so that I don't sink into the ever-present danger of the delusional and disappear into things and dreams that surround me with a steady, mildly disorienting, and abrasive whir, reminding me that I am among them, a subject among objects, a separate other amid the endless flood of so much existence, re-laxed and singularly composed amid an unfathomable network. Touched by such earnest effort, I cannot betray myself, or, at least, what I am. Thus my demise is avoided, such that I can feel alive. I hear laughter, and so I laugh along as well. Doubts creep up, but they cannot last for long on West

Park Row, for I do not succumb to them. To the neighbors, my background seems nothing special; I'm just someone from elsewhere. But no one asks where, no one asks at all.

It's good that I have been restored to life here. In the four rooms and the closets of the house, I don't need to think of the life I lost anymore than I do in the tiny yard that is squeezed in among other such narrow yards belonging to the neighbors and the fenced-off green field that stretches out behind them, where the children play, both the children of others and my own—what it means for me to be able to say that!—where fat cats stretch out and yawn among thistles and coltsfoot. Here I don't know my past, and everything is new, the foster home of one orphaned early, one who was once lightly told only in passing, "We brought you here from somewhere else far off when your father and mother perished. You were only a little boy then, so little that you can't remember, and no one knows anything about it, for it all disappeared long ago." Then I think hard, it lasting a while, myself serious, until finally I say, "Indeed, it must have been that way. Deep within there is a little room in my soul which I cannot enter, yet I see a faint shimmering that escapes from there, and then I finally know that there was a life, another life that must have belonged to me, and indeed it is my own life." Not only did my mother and father die early; I also died, but people forgot that I had, which is why they neither put me in a casket nor buried me, but instead left me to lie on the side of a road or on a shore, outside of any place where one would notice whether one was really dead or alive, and that is where I was carried away while sleeping, far, far away, until I finally awoke.

Then I looked around. Johanna stood there with the key in her hand and pointed to the door and said, "Here we are—I'm going to open it right up." We stepped in, the air damp. From every corner and crevice it was obvious that no one had slept here in a long time. Then we moved into the house. Beds, tables, bureaus, chairs, and boxes full of all the things needed to take care of our everyday needs were all carried in. I was tired and not of much use, the sweat of my own weakness breaking out on my forehead and neck. Full of worry, Johanna kept an eye on my struggles, taking me by the hand and leading me into the back room, where the sun poured in. She rustled up a chair, the window was opened, the barely stirring air pressing through the dormant old dust. I was ashamed that I was so incapable of being any help with moving in. Pleadingly I looked at Johanna to ask whether there was anything I could do, but she wouldn't hear of it, and instead stroked my hair, hurried out, and returned with a little something to eat.

"The men are much better at this than us. They'll take care of it all."

Johanna said that all she had to do was tell them where to put things and it would be done. Then I recovered a bit and realized that it was only because of me that nothing was being carried into the back room. Because I didn't want to linger anymore in the empty room in my chair, I felt stronger and considered how I could make myself useful. As I stood up to look at the workers, I still felt weak in my legs, so there was nothing I could do. I wandered over to the door that led to the little yard and pushed at it, it giving way only after some effort. I slipped out and stood in sleepy delight amid the overgrown grass.

This little garden, Johanna was pleased to see, returned me to my childhood. I know nothing about gardening, but a desire awoke within me to take pleasure in this little patch of garden. I began by putting in some plants, which resulted in a comical mishmash that any proper gardener would have laughed at. The soil is poor, nor before we arrived had it at all been taken care of: shards, bits of brick, rubbish, and rubble were intermingled with the paltry soil. But it was precisely this neglect that roused me. I culled the ugliest bits and in good spirits, which it certainly helped to bring on, I proceeded to fashion a modest measure of peace amid that patch of garden. Johanna was happy to leave me to it, for she knows nothing about gardening, nor did she have enough time to set everything aright out here. Thus I controlled my own little realm along with the children, to whom I granted a corner sandbox that I filled with fine-grained yellow sand, Eva and Michael a welcome presence as long as they didn't step on the flowers. Such a lovely little world it was, full of primroses, wallflowers, safflowers, vetches, cresses, and other wonders! It all took some effort, which I was surprised to find I could muster. Whenever I bend over the weeds, or pick snails off the lupines, or weed out some ribwort by applying lime, or tie up scarlet runner beans, or prop up noble delphiniums with stakes, or water the soil, I know for sure that it's all an unsuitable folly which anyone in the know would smile at. But I also know that a hopeless city boy is at play, one who remains clueless, and yet in no false manner has transformed his cramped little square into a realm magically aburst, and who now celebrates the victory of the guardian over a conquered land. None of this is what I intended. No doubt things don't run amok inside my little compound as they do beyond my lazy and broken fence, or the way that something wild shoots up in the middle of the city, unfolding its grayish green here and there among abandoned stretches and abandoned lots, where the realm of the meadow does not spread its protective cover across the earth through the densely packed soft grasses that blossom within it. Alas, such a realm is far off, whereas the abandoned lot is nearby. Still, it's not so bad so long as with my own hands I can try to get this ridiculous patch of earth to please us, the power of chance continuing to surprise me. Which is why I tolerate having the strawberries underneath the thorny rosebushes. No doubt the neighbors probably had a good laugh together over that, but it doesn't bother me, and the berries ripen beautifully.

I can't help enjoying the almost forbidden peace and comfort I cherish in this shrunken world in which I remain secluded from sharp-toothed fears and deadly misapprehensions, an island estate inside an archipelago for other landowners whose fate I do not share in the least. But the fact that I can live here means that I still have an almost invisible relation to our neighbors. Speaking to them, however, is not allowed, nor can I approach them; instead, I have to keep my eyes lowered, gazing only at my allotted ground, if only to show in understated fashion that I'm not up to anything suspicious nor do I have anything to hide. Whenever a greeting from the next little garden hops over to me, I have to answer in an unselfconsciously even tone, making sure to squash any urge toward a friendly smile. I don't have to suppress such gestures for long, for the good neighbors are satisfied and want nothing more from me, such that I can once again continue on inside the borders of my garden, and no one will dispute my right to do so. Thus I am transformed into a proprietor to whom belongs the tangible residue of his property, an owner who has paid for what he owns, this leading to the miracle of such freedom.

But how do I really feel, and what do I think about it all? I prefer to head inside and to my workroom. Johanna had arranged for me to have the biggest one, the front room on the ground floor, with the wide window behind which stands a narrow fringe of untended grass and a bushy hedge of evergreens that protects me from the street. Here I am left to myself, my misery is almost entirely protected from searching glances, one needing to be almost rude or have to dare to come up the tiled walk to the front door in order to look in at me at my desk. Thus I can carry on as I wish and no one bothers me. Many hours stretch out in which I need listen only to myself. Eva and Michael are in kindergarten and at school, or they cavort around outside; Johanna is busy somewhere else in the house or has gone off somewhere. Everything is well arranged, and yet I feel at sixes and sevens, and staying in my room makes me anxious. Outside, everything is quiet or just scurries by, unaware, having no idea that someone might visit me, someone who might seize the chance to speak to me.

"I know you. You got away from me and my clutches, but now I have found you again here behind your wall. Why have you tried to hide for so long? Do you mean to deceive me with your little family idyll? You stupid swindler! The wife and children don't belong to you; you don't even belong to you, for you are mine, mine! You are completely mine, for I am your destroyer. I let you get away in order to feed upon your powerlessness, as you helplessly and fearfully struggled to get away, as if there were some way to escape. Not a bad idea! But there is no cave in which you can hide, into which you can crawl with all your filth. You'll look suspicious no matter where you are, you old rat. A sweet, numbing scent rises from the sewers in which you must stow yourself. Just you wait, I'll smoke you out, in much the same way I always destroy your kind."

It's much better if no one visits and all the noises just rush by the house. If a policeman comes along, walking slowly and intently, I feel nervous. I have often told myself that he's making his rounds to protect me as well, and he means me no harm, but that's hard to believe when, behind the most harmless of miens, there still lurks a threatening presence that wants to do away with me, to abolish me. For when did I come by the right to be tolerated? Have I done so much good that I need no longer feel any menace? I take stock, realize that I am here, think of the legal principles that promise my safe existence, but I can never be certain that everything will turn out right.

Is it now two years or is it longer since Johanna and I were ordered to appear before the immigration police? It was an official, somewhat dutiful-looking little note done in the manner that is common to the local authorities here. The simple words seemed gentle and suggested nothing ominous. It just said that I should appear; the day was named, but the time was up to us. But what had I done that would cause them to want to see me? I searched inside myself, probing the deepest folds of my unrenounced feelings of guilt, but they were secrets that the police couldn't know about. I sighed and said to myself, "They want to know who I am." In spite of the good common sense and the helpful tone that Johanna kindly tried to instill in my own confused senses, there was little time to spare. My unknown past lay like a heavy weight inside me, the world around me opening up like a yawning abyss before any thought of escape, the rights of the tolerated guest about to be challenged.

The smartest thing to do would have been to disappear. Stupidly I let myself be led along, turning back toward that from which I had once fled, just like when I followed the call of my grammar-school teacher Herr Prenzel. As a schoolboy, I admired him and was gulled by the enticing letters with which he irresistibly lured me in. Before I knew it I was on the train, only a suitcase on the rack above. Soon we would be at the border. All the other passengers had already gotten off. Some had warned me to get off as well, while there was still time, before that sinister border gobbled me up. I pointed arrogantly to my passport: "This is all I need, it will protect me, nothing is going to happen!" People shook their heads and smiled skeptically or mockingly. Then they disappeared. But then it was too late to change my mind: with helmets, rifles, and pistols, the border police boarded both ends of the long train in which there was no one left but me.

As I saw the men noisily climbing onto the train, I retreated to my compartment and sat down on the hard seat. I needed to look completely harmless, a harmless traveler with a clear conscience. But already the men stood outside, one of them ripping open the door and pressing inside along with another, while the others stood stiffly outside the compartment. The two inside pressed so close that their legs rubbed against my knees. I could hardly move. "Passports, please!" growled one. He spoke in the plural, as if I weren't the only passenger there. Just as I was used to from earlier trips, I had had everything in order ahead of time—my passport, wallet, ticket, currency receipt, and whatever else was needed to assure that all was in order—but now I rummaged nervously inside my coat pockets and could find nothing, the disengaged impatience of the men unnerving me even further. At last I managed to produce my papers, but I was still nervous, my fingers unable to sort out the contents of my pockets, the passport falling from my hands and onto the dusty floor. A policeman bent down to get it, and though I tried to get it back from him while begging his pardon, he waved me off energetically with his hand as he lifted it up in triumph and began to pore over it with the others. He looked it over thoroughly with his colleagues, page after page, they whispering something to one another now and then that I couldn't understand because of my worry. Then they handed the passport to the men outside in the corridor. They studied the document in detail, marking it with red and blue ink in various places. But then everything suddenly seemed to take a turn for the better, as they pulled out their rubber stamp and pressed their hallowed endorsements onto the passport with satisfaction.

I now expected that at last I would be getting back my precious document, a huge hairy hand closing its cloth cover and stiffly holding it out to me. However, pressed between the policemen as I was, I couldn't reach out to get the passport. One of the policemen on my side took pity and reached for it himself, I myself almost feeling what it would be like to have it back in my own hands. Then one of the men who had seemed satisfied and had stepped back now said something, and once again it was decided that the passport needed to be inspected more closely. The policeman in my compartment, who I thought was accommodating, turned away so forcefully that his cartridge belt banged painfully against my knuckles, causing me to cry out.

"A wimpy little passenger, what a joke! And we want such a guest here in our country!"

"Forgive me, forgive me!" I called out fervently. "But I'm not traveling by choice; it has to do with written orders from my teacher!"

By saying this I had betrayed myself, doubly so, for I had not only revealed my reason for coming, but I had also spoken in my own tongue rather than speaking innocently in the language of the country from which the passport had been issued.

"What?" interrupted the man outside who had demanded to see the passport, and who clearly was the commandant, as he shoved his way into the compartment with the others. "What are you babbling about? You must be a spy!"

I yelled, "The passport is real. I paid for it with good money. I'm no crook!"

My earnest protest was met with scornful laughter from the surly men. They buried themselves once more in the document, leafing through it with licked fingers and throwing nasty glances toward me from time to time. Finally the commandant announced, "You're not a crook, we know that. Only spies have real passports these days. The poor devils who talk about it openly don't get to travel, or they try to sneak across the border with counterfeit papers."

I was defenseless and tried to think how I could make a bad situation a little bit better. It was hopeless, and so I decided to just wait and see what would be done with me, though I was smart enough to realize that the best chance I had was to remain calm and convince the men that I was a harmless passenger who deserved to be trusted. This proved correct, as my composed demeanor appeared to leave a good impression. The commandant looked more at ease and said that the passport and what was written inside it clearly allowed me to enter the country, and that as long as there was no contraband in my luggage there was nothing to stop me from traveling. The order from the teacher, the commandant explained with sharp civility, was nothing but an idle pretense in his considered view, but it was not his job to say if it was or was not, for if it were, half the government could be arrested. That said, he bowed in an officious manner and let my passport, my precious passport, disappear into a deep side pocket of his military coat. I was so struck by this terrible turn of events that I gasped.

"Sir, my passport! My good passport! I need it! Give me back my passport!"

"We're not a country for robbers and bandits. Here every citizen is safe. Foreigners need to list their place of residence with the police. You can apply to the border authorities for your passport."

"I want my passport back now!"

"As a visitor to our country, you must dutifully comply with our rules and regulations."

"I'm not a visitor, and I don't want to stay in this country any longer! I withdraw my request to enter and want to take the next train back!"

"It's not as easy as that. What are you thinking? Whoever tries to get in just doesn't walk away unless we deport him. But we've detained you. So you have to stay. Wasn't that your original intent? No? Then show us your ticket! Indeed, it's clear as day that you're headed for the city! The visa is good for four weeks. That means you can stay here for at least another fourteen days."

I tried to reason with them some more, but it did no good; I didn't get the passport back. Then my suitcase was rummaged through and my pockets emptied of their contents, though this procedure was carried out in a relatively quiet manner, something the authorities prided themselves on. I was hit with the requisite fine and handed a receipt. I was told that it had to do with an official tax on foreigners. The levy was high, which was regrettable, but the government, unfortunately, saw no other way to finance the high cost of the border patrol, especially as there had been substantially less travel in recent years. The government had decided not to allow citizens of this free state to travel outside it and face horrible oppression, for it would be inhumane to do so. There was certainly also no way that it could allow members of exploitative countries to be sent here, for under the innocent guise of business, visitation, or recreation, they did nothing but stir up trouble here and serve as spies, or, at the very least, spread nasty lies about the modern workings of this nation the moment they left.

"So you see, Herr Landau," said the commandant, having noticed my name, "you now have a worthy task. If we just let you go back, which, given the circumstances, I don't doubt will happen, at the border you'd have the chance to sign a pledge whereby you would be required only to state the truth about our nation, and avoid anything that would harm our reputation."

With this, the formalities came to a pleasant resolution as they wished me a safe journey, saluted, withdrew, and left me to myself. Then the locals were allowed to board the train. People entered my car, and soon my compartment was full. The train passed through several towns as I looked out the window or observed the other passengers, though I didn't say a word to anyone the entire way to the city, where my old teacher was waiting for me on the platform. We greeted each other warmly. Prenzel suggested that first I needed to have a closer look around the train station with him, which was fitted out more magnificently than ever, and which I'd see if we took a thorough tour of the building. I tentatively risked a countersuggestion and said that I was tired from the day's journey and worn out, and that after such a long time I was anxious to see the city where my parents had lived, and thus what I wanted most was to quickly get to my hotel, if only to have a bit of a rest. I invited Prenzel to accompany me and to join me for dinner there as my guest. I was then immediately informed that I must be from the moon or something, for my hotel was restricted to foreigners, and locals were forbidden to enter it, including Prenzel. When I asked, I was then also told that natives could not even enter the restaurant. I didn't inquire any further, but suggested that Prenzel meet me somewhere for dinner after I registered at the hotel. My teacher smiled obliquely and answered my remaining questions with single-word answers that explained little. Then I realized that after I left things had changed here much more than I had previously known.

Prenzel took me by the hand and led me from one end of the station to the other, passing many people, who timidly looked on with surprise, until—without my knowing just what had happened—he delivered me to the station guardhouse. Just like lost luggage, I thought to myself. As no one seemed to be especially concerned about me, I then whispered excitedly to my teacher, asking what this was supposed to mean. He timidly looked around. Once he ascertained that we were not being observed, he confided in me that my situation was relatively good, a couple of interrogations, maybe a couple of days of detention, but there was no need to fear for my life.

"Interrogations? Because of what? I've done nothing, Herr Prenzel. I only came because of you, since you invited me with such urgency and enthusiasm. I didn't come here just so the authorities could keep tabs on me. I just wanted to see the last teacher of mine still alive. You wrote me again and again that your last wish was to see me once again!"

"Certainly it is. For my part, I am deeply grateful that you have come. I was even given a special pass because of it, for they phoned from the border to say that you really had arrived. What a gentleman! Until now, not a single one of my students has returned from abroad to accept my invitation to visit."

"You've invited others . . . ?"

"Be quiet, young man. You don't know what you're talking about! Not even my smartest students were smart enough to get through."

"But I want to leave! I won't stay here. You've seen what my intent was—that's all I need, so I want to leave straightaway!"

"All I can say is good luck with that!" Prenzel replied in a strangely excited voice, adding more heatedly, "Landau, if you managed to . . ."

My teacher said nothing more. He pulled himself together, as we were approached by a uniformed youth, and politely addressed him.

"Comrade Assessor, I present you with a dangerous enemy of the state, along with his suitcase. I suggest you assess his political sympathies."

The Assessor of Sympathies waved mildly for my teacher to step back. As Prenzel bowed deeply to the young man, I saw for the first time how gray and thin the old man's hair had become. Without the slightest concern for me, he lowered his head and slipped out of the station guardhouse. The Assessor signaled to me to take my suitcase and follow him. I listened without a word and—despite all my distress—with no small hope that it was all a misunderstanding, that after an interrogation everything would become clear, and afterward there would be nothing to prevent my immediate departure. The Assessor prodded me down a badly lit stairway, though there were not many steps, then I was pushed into a garishly lit room, where a woman sat waiting in front of a typewriter. The Assessor sat down behind a conference table and indicated that I should put down my suitcase and sit on a low round stool. I noticed that it was a turn stool, like the ones you used to see in front of a piano. The stool was way too low for me, which is why I started to turn it so that it would go higher—a tiresome business, for the thing was not oiled and squeaked miserably.

"Man alive," yelled the Assessor of Sympathies. "Are you mad? Leave the witness chair alone for just a minute and sit yourself down!"

"Sorry, the stool is much too low. I'll almost disappear in front of your table."

"Just sit down there and be so nice as to not turn around. Understood? Later, we'll see if you can raise it any higher."

I gave in and sat down all scrunched up, no higher than the stool, with my legs crossed, since I couldn't stretch them out. It was exceptionally uncomfortable. The young man took no notice of how I sat there shrunken and only asked me to pull my legs in farther. There was nothing to do but cross them all the more tightly, such that the joints cracked. When I had finally attained the proper position demanded of me, the Assessor just took a cigarette out of his case and tossed a second one to the secretary, which she adroitly caught while saying thanks. There was nothing for me to do but shove my fingers into my pocket in order to fetch my own cigarette, though a sharp look told me immediately that I needed permission to do that. For a long time I was asked nothing, and I observed the Assessor carefully, but without fathoming the thoughts of my opponent. As soon as I moved, the Assessor tapped indignantly on the desktop with a pencil. The Assessor and the secretary stubbed out the glowing ends of their cigarettes, and, finally, the interrogation began.

"Arthur Landau, what is your mission in entering the country?"

"There is no mission—"

"We know there is. You can't deny it, though it's all part of the game played between the police and every criminal. But we have little time for such pleasant foolishness. Therefore, for both our sakes, make it short! Who hired you?"

"I came for my own reasons—"

"We know about that, too, a journey made for idealistic reasons. Who sent you here?"

"Who? No one? I only came to visit someone. I just wanted to satisfy the wishes of my old teacher."

"Fine! But you, of course, knew that Prenzel works for us?"

"I had no idea of that. You mean . . . No, an old teacher wouldn't serve as a snitch!"

"Snitch? That's a bit rude."

"Okay, then, a policeman."

"Of course he's a policeman. It's obvious that as a teacher he is also a policeman."

"When I was a student, it wasn't obvious to me."

"Fool! Not then! Now! My God, don't you understand anything?"

"No."

"But you are saying that you conspired with him? You are raising suspicions against a civil servant? You know, such testimony is a very serious matter, even if you're innocent!"

"I don't know anything. I suspect no one and have done nothing."

"Do you deny that you were born here?"

"No."

"Good. And do you deny that you were once hauled away from here, yet that still didn't keep you from returning after the war was over?"

"No, but—"

"There, you see, that explains it! That's all we need. You haven't done anything, that's correct, simply because we have stopped you before you could. And that's all we need. You needn't think yourself innocent, because there's no way you can be. No, you were looking to start something."

"That's not true."

"Quiet! You wanted to. Otherwise you wouldn't have tried to slip into the country."

"I didn't slip in. I'm legal, and I came on a regularly scheduled train—"

"And almost were arrested for violent resistance when our border police wanted to inspect your passport."

"That's not true."

"Really? And you didn't raise any kind of a stink when they wanted to hold your passport for security reasons? And you didn't give cause for suspicion on the day when you were not ashamed to demand a written receipt of your passport and assumed you'd get one?"

"Part of it isn't true; part of it is completely distorted. I wanted my passport, but I neither asked for a receipt nor was given one."

"So you're denying it even happened? I'm warning you!"

"I deny any kind of bad intention."

The Assessor and the secretary, who was typing hurriedly, shook with laughter.

"To us there is no one who, after having once emigrated, returns without bad intentions. You have to at least see how it looks to us."

"I wanted to see my teacher. That's all."

"Excellent. That's all we need. But let me remind you that to just take your high treason and all your bad intentions and just shove them onto your old teacher is obscene."

"Prenzel lured me into a trap?"

"Is that a question?"

"Yes."

"You don't ask the questions here. Besides, you should have thought about all that earlier."

"I've had it completely up to here with this visit, and I don't want to wait another day before returning to the country of my choice."

"You'll have to remain here, at least until we hear the decision handed down by the judge."

"Am I charged with something?"

"Not yet. First, you have to confess. Since you don't seem inclined to do that today, I'll give you a day to think about it. Later the jail time, if that's what you're given, will be a good deal longer—a month, maybe even a year."

"I object! I demand that I be allowed to contact my embassy immediately."

"If that's meant as a plea bargain, and there's no doubt about your culpability, then I can formally remand you for trial immediately. If, however—"

"It's not a plea! Not at all! It's a demand for human and legal rights!"

"Spare me your lousy, stupid speeches! You've already gone too far and made matters worse with your loud protests. There is, however, an honorable way out. . . ."

The Assessor of Sympathies paused and looked at me searchingly to see if I understood what he meant, waiting for me to give a sign that I understood. However, I had no idea and sat there unhappy on my stool. Since the Assessor gave no hint of what he meant, I tried hard to think of something smart and to come up with the right answer. Nothing occurred to me except to ask if I could raise my seat. That way, I would at least learn whether my situation had at all improved. The Assessor seemed not to have understood, for he completely ignored my request, saying instead that he was happy to hear that I was ready to collaborate with him, which took me completely by surprise. Stunned, I just muttered, "Collaborate . . . collaborate."

"Yes, of course, collaborate. That's something else altogether. If you go to work for us, I will drop the charges. You'll be let go in no time, the charges will not be filed with the district attorney. Understand?"

"Understand what, Herr Assessor?" I asked very quietly, confused.

Then he got mad and yelled at me with contempt, "That's really the best that such a stupid fool like yourself can ask from well-meaning folk who have a knife held to their throat by foreign degenerates!"

I wanted to say something quickly, and I was upset that I had passed up the chance to do so, but the Assessor ignored me and decided not to let me say another thing. He then rang a bell. A policeman appeared, and after some orders quietly and hastily whispered, which I could neither completely hear nor understand, I was led out of the detention room. I tried to reach for my suitcase, but I had barely grabbed hold of it when it was knocked from my hand. Then I was led higgledy-piggledy up stairs and down through a confusing labyrinth, though we never left the area of the train station. Several times I caught the unmistakable smell of the locomotives, and in passing I spotted a train from afar and once heard clearly the melancholy whistle of a machine, which then began to puff as it started to move. Finally, we arrived at a door with "Station Jail—Department of Espionage" written on it. My guard knocked, the door opened, and a jailer took me by the arm. "By special order of the Assessor of Sympathies. He'll likely be picked up tomorrow." This I heard the policeman say.

Then the door was closed behind me. With instructions that I couldn't make out, the jailer handed me over to an attendant, who grabbed my right hand painfully and dragged me off. He stopped in front of a cell, opened a low door through which a ten-year-old could barely walk upright, forced me to kneel down, and gave me such a swift kick that I fell facedown upon the slimy wet floor inside a cagelike room. It was no higher than the door that had already slammed shut behind me.

The cell was empty. I could only sit on the floor, unable to stretch out, because even diagonally the room was shorter than I was. There was nothing there to see except a quietly fluttering ventilator fan that was the only source of air, while from the ceiling a dull lightbulb hung at the end of a wire, barely bigger than the bulb of a flashlight. When I clumsily, but not too harshly, bumped the bulb, the light went out. Now it was dark, for the door was shut so tight that not even the barest of light got through any crack. I despaired that through my clumsiness I had robbed myself of the last comfort available to me in my dungeon, and so I tried with clammy fingers—for I was almost done in, and the thick air was miserably damp—to feel for the lightbulb, which probably wasn't burned out but had just come loose. Soon I held the glass bulb in my fingers and gave it a twist, but it didn't work. I grabbed the socket with my other hand, but with no success.

There was nothing to do but surrender to my misfortune, but the dark bothered me more and more, and I thought that if no other comfort was going to be supplied here the light, at least, should work according to prison regulations. All I needed to do was yell in order to get the guard's attention, and he would come and fix the light. It was to no avail; no one showed up. No one cared about me—no one brought anything to eat or to drink, no blanket to protect me from the cold and damp. Not one thing was provided for my needs. I listened intently for any kind of noise, naïvely imagining that I heard the jangle of a key chain, and, more serious, the cries of someone being mishandled. But nothing broke through the abysmal silence, not even the rumble of the distant train, it was that deadening. All that could be heard was the soft fluttering of the ventilator fan. Although that was not too bothersome, it got on my nerves, for it continued on so monotonously.

What I had had on me or in my pockets had not been taken away, nor had I even been robbed of my watch. There then arose in me the urgent need to find out the time. I had always been one to keep an eye on the time, but never before had I wished so hard to follow its secret unfolding. I was pleased to be able to take my watch out of my pocket, but I couldn't hear any ticking. I held it up to my ear, but there was no sound. No doubt it had broken when I was shoved into the cell. I couldn't feel anything wrong with it on the outside, but I wanted to figure out what was broken as best I could, and so I tried to get the light to work once again. When I reached for the wire, I discovered that there was something the matter with it, for I got an electric shock, which, because of the damp, was so strong that it caused me to sit up. I hit my head hard on the ceiling and was dazed, almost falling unconscious, as I sank back down.

I had no idea how long this woozy state lasted, but it seemed to go on for an endless stretch of time. Everything I knew was reduced to nothing; my memory was so worthless that I no longer even knew why I had been placed in custody. I couldn't account for the reason I was there. Fearful thoughts of being buried alive disrupted my sleep, and I never expected to see the light of day again. Deep pain bored into the hand that had suffered the shock. Certainly I had gotten a nasty burn that, if not cared for, would soon become infected amid all this filth. Perhaps the hand was lost, even if I was rescued. Indeed, there seemed little cause for hope, as, more than likely,

I would only be subjected to new and worse treatment, if not altogether abandoned here to languish in the dark.

Then I decided to change entirely; I wanted to be transformed, to stop being who I was. And yet such a total transformation was not in itself enough: I no longer wanted to be a human being. All consciousness had to disappear. For it was not enough that such a transformation should turn me into something other than a human being if that meant I still felt like a person who was full of memories of suffering that he could not bear.

I rocked back and forth inside my cage, banged against its walls, and became smaller and smaller as a result. I felt a buried strength within me, then I began to dig with my hands. The ground gave way and I touched small clumps of earth, but I could feel that they were breaking up and so I pressed on. It was dirty and tiresome work, but my limbs grew stronger the more I tried, my forehead and my mouth, especially, taking on incredible force. It eventually became clear that I had struck some small stones and roots, impediments that threatened to halt my progress. Yet my focus remained unshaken. By pummeling, scratching, twisting, and biting, I pushed through the mass in front of me and broke it into bits, so that I slowly, yet steadily dug on. As a result, I did not so much move forward as find that I was able to stand taller. It was the urge to stand up and possibly reach the light that spurred me on. I became ever thinner and more pliant, like a badger or a mole, but much more flexible. I had turned into a caterpillar.

At the moment I realized that I had turned into a caterpillar completely, I pushed hard through the dense gravel and was greeted by an unexpected shaft of daylight, which blinded me. Because of the glaring light, I pressed my eyelids together. Exhausted, I sank down. Then I blinked as I ventured to look around, though only for a few moments, because it hurt to do so. I then regretted renouncing all human feelings, though of course I knew that my crazy urge had not been fulfilled. I realized that one would rather die than forsake the roots of his human existence. I had not forsaken my human nature at all; it had just become wretched, my extremities reporting that I was nothing but a raw suffering hulk, and, above all, a body filled with sensations and thoughts that had never disappeared. Instead, they had balled themselves up quite densely, like clumps that had frozen together, simply because they could no longer be shared with others; nor was there another being to appreciate them. A person does indeed remain a human being, but the world around him no longer takes him for a human being when he is scorned by all groups, and he hardens as a result, concerned with himself alone, unloved and unrecognized.

Such desolate thoughts haunted me as, miserably, I failed to extricate myself from the earth. And so I thought back to everything that had happened recently. I knew that my effort to escape was probably fruitless, for I couldn't escape the reach of the police. In fact, I heard someone calling me from back in the cell, demanding that I respond and appear immediately. "Arthur Landau! Arthur Landau, report to interrogation! If he's hiding and doesn't crawl out right away, then drag him down here straight off!" I sensed the bloodhounds circling, and that my trick had come to an end. In my despair, I rallied all my strength and stood up with a sudden leap. I then shook off the earth and found my footing. And there I stood, in the middle of a garden. It seemed familiar to me as I rubbed my eyes and looked around me, blinking, for I couldn't believe what I saw. And yet there was no doubt— there I stood in the middle of my own garden. Johanna could not be far off. Magically freed, I wanted to give a fervent shout of thanks. But good as everything seemed to be, my voice had hardly any strength. Upset, I realized that I had celebrated too soon, for the house and garden were surrounded by police officers, their weapons drawn and pointed at me. Then I released a terrible cry, and Johanna shook me from my dream.

That was only one of the many dreams that plagued me, but this one returned again and again, though in slightly different forms. In my room, I bent over my books and writing and couldn't work, instead staring only at the request to appear before the immigration police, while my inability to shake the nightmarish imaginings that haunted me further undermined my sanity. Johanna wanted to phone the police in order to calm me. It bothered her to see me so intensely upset. Yet when she made such well-meaning suggestions, I was the one who would snap at her and point out that, no matter how insensible my fears were, any such inquiry with the authorities would only make us look ridiculous. Secretly, I also feared that perhaps a harmless disclosure that might be made in the process could lead to more serious trouble if further questions were asked. One should never ask an official anything if it can be avoided, for it will only lead to suspicion. Don't attract attention—that's the central motto of the hunted and the weak, and whoever has survived such persecution without losing his head should never risk having the earthly powers take interest in his activities and freedoms.

Finally, the day of our appointment came. We left Eva two doors down with Mrs. Stonewood, then dropped Michael off at school before riding twenty minutes on the city train. When we came up out of the station it was cloudy, and we walked along slowly. I smoked a cigarette, and every step that took us closer to our destination felt heavy. It was an older, somewhat ostentatious brownstone that we had been summoned to, not the modern building of the immigration department that I well knew stood in the middle of the city. Johanna took me firmly by the hand and pointed to the front garden: cowslips, snowflakes, and tender yellow plants, none of which looked afraid. I forced a smile and agreed that it was nice to have blossoms protected by the police. Johanna said something imprudent, but only with the intention of shaking me out of my stupor with her animated observation that one could be thankful for a country where even the police had not lost the appreciation of the good things in life. This well-meant attempt at diversion made me uncomfortable. The good things in life. A pompous term, which I found tasteless. "You mean flowers, sweet animals, and little children," I replied sharply. Indeed, the hardest of hearts can't help being softened by them. The authorities carry out their nasty business without restraint, and take joy in bringing any criminal under the protection of their legal powers. They are prepared for any horror and will murder, if they are allowed to, for they want to perpetuate the right to kill. But then they go all soft and wipe away a tear when they see a little cat that has hurt its paw. Pity is an abominable virtue when it's a cover for mean-spiritedness. I stood there and didn't want to move an inch, and spoke as loud as seemed appropriate. Angrily, I wanted to step from the walkway and trample the blossoms in the next bed. "What's gotten into you?" Johanna asked, and I couldn't bear the look she shot me, myself at last laughing over the miserable madness that I had yammered on about, feeling ashamed. Willingly, I let myself be led on.

We were shown to the first floor. A hall with huge windows and a balcony door served as the waiting room. At the smaller end of the room, near the entrance, a uniformed policeman presiding over a large battered table responded cheerily to our greeting, and asked to see our summons and papers. Then he pointed to where we should take a seat among the chairs lined up in wide arcs on three sides of the hall. Already many sat there waiting in what must once have been a very handsome room. All that was left of it was its height, the whitewashed silk coverings that were pulling loose from the walls, and the precious, though somewhat broken plaster on the ceiling that had also been whitewashed. Otherwise, it looked meager and barren, the floor covered with gray felt that had holes in it. Sadly the chairs stood there, one hardly matching another, many of them rickety, and not one of them without a stain. An unlit iron stove—it was good that we had coats with us—stood somewhat near the policeman's table, the exhaust pipe winding in a crooked fashion out through the lead-covered upper part of a window. Not on the table but rather on a chair near the door was a telephone surrounded by tangled wires, one of which led off through a door panel in order to make some unknown connection somewhere else. Originally, the hall had been larger. Now it was divided by a paper wall constructed of thin laths. This barrier wasn't quite square with the corners of the walls that ran lengthwise, such that the window side was longer than the other side. Oddly and irregularly, this offensive barrier infringed upon the cold, bleak room, slicing through the ceiling ornament as well.

Men and women of various ages who had been gathered there were tossed together and could see how they filled to bursting the badly arranged, miserable space. But they never came together as a single body. Each sat with his own thoughts and each had a different goal, each being from a different world, be it the fragile little mother, or the hefty young man with swollen cheeks and sullen eyes, or the nicely dressed young lady with dainty feet, or the pointy-nosed pale intellectual. There they sat all together, whether sour or concerned, apathetic or arrogant, good-natured or crude, nothing shared between them but the power of the immigration police, who had only to send off their brief notes in order to haul in little men and little women, this being how they were treated for a number of hours amid their daily business, brought together submissively from every quarter and every major city here in this waiting room, themselves the lost, who can be in the right only by meekly following orders in the hope that their always precarious good standing might last forever.

There was hardly any noise. Only the policeman up front dared say anything aloud whenever a new visitor entered and looked about at the others, clueless and dense. Our guard being good, he called out in a husky voice until the new arrival figured out what to do and was at ease, though still without hope, shuffling over to a vacant chair. Sometimes a second policeman, to whom our guard whispered something, got involved. Usually it was our man who called out the names—four or five at a time, as a rule—when people's turn came, butchering the foreign ones so badly that confusion would arise. That was harmless fun, pleasing the policeman enormously, for the time went by so slowly, and except for calling out the names, there was hardly anything else to do but now and then pour tea from a huge thermos into an ugly green cup or light a cigarette whose ashes he tapped into an old-fashioned inkwell.

Those waiting nodded their heads and dozed or chatted quietly. Most of them didn't know one another, but some ran into others they knew here, including married couples, while others had brought along their bratty children. Some crossed their legs, while others sat there stiff and upright, others bending forward or aslant, others fidgeting, while still others chose not to rest on a chair but instead stood up and, with large, energetic steps, paced back and forth, though only for a little while, for they soon discovered that it did no good, though no one said anything, not even the police. Women had planted their shopping bags next to them on the floor and worked away at their knitting needles, the slowly climbing threads of yarn rising up from the bags below. A student brooded over geometric figures and mathematical formulas, some other men burying themselves in rustling newspapers, while others read books. The few children that were there soon found one another out and began to play, running frequently to the window or straying toward the policeman, who had fun blowing smoke at them, their antics otherwise not bothering him at all, while nearby a young girl fed her doll a piece of chocolate.

Whoever was called got his papers back from the police, disappeared somewhat noisily with a cough, and was never seen again. An exit into the unknown. Anyone who had once waited never had to wait again. You were called, taken in, then spit out; no one knew what happened to you. I had to admit that all my anxieties had been uncalled for, yet I pitied those who were called up, who now had to fight their little battles, while, looking on, the rest of us felt that we had a much better chance of success if we would be allowed to mount a defense. What nonsense. For what good are such insights when no one believes in them or trusts them? In chopped-up segments, time passes by, while just before noon the last stragglers arrive, more and more of those having been called up by the police, the empty chairs soon looking thin and spiritless.

After remaining patient for more than two hours we were finally called up. The policeman said, "Seven," which was the room number where we had to appear. A sign said to enter without knocking. A small, somewhat wizened man in civilian dress and wearing glasses, no doubt a school warden in better times, greeted us in a friendly manner. We were offered a seat. After we hastily spread our papers in front of him on the desk, everything grew silent. The civil servant sank with pleasure into the contents of the documents. It seemed that for him everything was in order, the statements recorded in the valid passports were true, a world of doubt kept at bay by the neat entries made by civil servants. Born, entered, and approved—everything was in order; the picture is real once it's been stamped. As anyone who is trained to do so can read, passports reveal that the state attests to the validity of created beings. Whoever has documents that are in order, good for him—he is indeed alive and may go on living. Yet how pitiable the one who does not empty his pockets and offer up papers meekly with outstretched hands, like a desperate prayer to the civil servants, who, immediately touched by such gestures, take on much weightier matters. The ones asking, or who have been summoned to step forward, can relax and stretch out on their chairs, breathing easier through their noses with the patience of pure being, or play with their fingers, look gratefully at the floor, or boldly look wherever they wish, as long as they remain civil. But the best thing to do is watch with shy restraint the promising quiet proceedings of the official, always ready to respond to any glance with the right bits of information or nods of the head in order to assure someone that everything is on the up-and-up. As the official looks over the work of his predecessors and his colleagues, the one summoned is taken in, his fate almost suspended, for everything he is lies there in the written notes, his physical presence just a means in itself, a messenger delivering a message, an appointed courier of papers that grant him a complete sense of himself. So it goes for every person, especially if he is a foreigner, in order that he be certified.

The official took from a little basket a long handsomely printed form, spreading it out carefully on his blotter, and stretching it taut when the fold would not flatten out. Then the man took a pen and gracefully and skillfully wrote down the names and several other items that he found while flipping through the pages of the passport and visa. Johanna and I might as well not have been there, for potentially we could only provide wrong answers that would undermine what the documents already accurately attested to. Maybe I was mistaken, but it is difficult to know whether the questions that the official posed were necessary or whether he wished only to relieve our possible boredom. Or was he cleverly just checking to see what effort we had made to learn what was stated in the papers themselves? I was grateful to the man for taking as much care with the first page of his form as with those that followed, for it put me at ease. Only now and then did he stop to look over his entries. He seemed to be pleased with all of them, which boosted my confidence. When the process had gone far enough that it could no longer remain at just this orderly and comfortable level, the official looked up at me.

"Can you tell me, Mr. Landau, why you are really here?"

This was the last thing I expected to be asked, and so I was immediately shaken from my calm and got upset. Behind his glasses the official's eyes were neither threatening nor shifty; rather, his gaze appeared almost friendly. All I had to do was not disappoint him.

"No, I really have no idea. I was asked to come here. The summons gave no reason."

My answer was not bad, for the official smiled mildly, and I was happy that I had not followed his provocative question into the plummeting depths. I had been saved.

"I mean, why did you come to this country?"

"Because I love it. I wanted to get out. I wanted to be free."

The eyes of my examiner lit up. He sensed that I really meant it. He could tell from my voice just what kind of person was before him.

"Yes, a very good reason indeed. But why didn't you remain in your own country? Here you are a foreigner, who doesn't speak the language so well, and for whom things are not easy."

I defended myself and this country and offered a picture that explained why I had left there and come here. The official wrote down what I told him. He let me go on talking, only rarely posing a question in between that helped my story stay on track. It was all pleasant and easy. Finally, my examiner was satisfied; his form had been filled out. He nodded approvingly as he touched each line with the end of his pen while reading through them once more. Then, at the end, he looked at me again.

"Your case seems clear to me. I wish that matters were as simple with all foreigners. Now, just tell me off the record: how do you make a living?"

"I'm a freelance scholar. I do lectures now and then, write articles and reports. Sometimes I also have private support. Never public welfare."

"I understand. It's not easy. I really just wanted to know for myself."

Then the official turned to Johanna, who sat there respectfully.

"I don't need to hear much from you. You're a housewife. I can see that. It's obvious that is enough to do on its own. And as for your intentions? Certainly they are the same as your husband's."

With that we were dismissed and handed back our papers, the visas now having a little stamp upon them. That was the only thing that disturbed me a bit, for once such a symbol is entered it can lead to unforeseen consequences. I dared to share my thoughts aloud, but the official just smiled.

"That's just for our interior records. Now your stay in this country is at last officially legal."

I looked at the official questioningly, since I didn't understand. He smiled in response.

"When you first arrived here, you didn't inform us, and perhaps didn't yet know, that you wanted to remain as our guest. At that time, we didn't worry about it. We allow foreigners to visit, as long as there is no reason not to. Only when someone wants to stay do we look at the matter more closely. In the past few years, a good deal more have stayed. That's why we asked you here."

The official stood up, shook hands with Johanna and me, and led us to the door. Relieved, we headed off, Johanna seeming pleased, more so than I'd ever seen her. Indeed, she had always said that I had nothing to fear in this country and that I just had to be patient, and now I just had to chase away all my fears. I had to agree and felt ashamed. She looked at me seriously.

"Still so gloomy?"

"Everything is different, Johanna. We simply don't know. It's a good sign, but things can change in unforeseen ways. One should never be too sure. All you can do is try to do the best that you can, but then suddenly things can go wrong. It can all be taken away, even if, for now, something good is said on our behalf. All our success should teach us only that an infinite amount of prejudice lies behind any approval. But onward. I'm pleased and have no right to spoil a good day with my negative thoughts."

As we headed home, Johanna often looked at me gratefully. After our trip to the immigration office, my spirits were lifted. I say lifted, but not really better. After suffering doubts that had eaten away at me, I was now feeling somewhat more secure. Things were falling into place; the world around me was becoming more bearable. I listened to the voice inside me, and it said, "Try!"

Try was indeed what I had often heard, dull fleshly existence sunk in a judicial prison, as within death's waiting room I was not allowed to do as I wished. Try, even if you don't want to. "Next, please!" someone called, but was I the next? I looked around me to see if someone wanted to be the next, but no one indicated so, no one having set up an orderly line; instead, all were held together in a reeking lump of fear. Someone with a scraggly beard turned to me: "Don't they mean you?" No, they didn't mean me. How could I even step forward, since among the surrounding crowd there was no clear direction in which to go? Even if I were to try to press my way through, it would do no good. Above us rose the long arms of cranes that growled and rumbled as they rose slowly into the air. Sometimes an arm bent down with a sharp rattling as it snatched at the heap of fear and grabbed some bodies up into the air. "Next, please!" That was how many were hauled off, no one knowing where to. So how could I allow myself to be looked for if I couldn't allow myself to be found and there was nowhere to hide?

"Adam, where are you? Why are you hiding?"

A monstrous voice, grave and powerful, posed this question, a thunderous storm that drowned out the ever-wilder stomping to the right and left of the snapping cranes. I didn't move from my spot, but instead just tried to shrink and duck down, though someone grabbed me under my arms as if to hold me and force me upward so that I appeared taller. Again someone called for Adam, though no one replied. I said nothing as well. "Why don't you answer?" someone demanded. It wasn't the one with the scraggly beard but someone who looked like my murdered father, except without his voice.

"You are Adam. If you don't answer, things can go badly. Don't hold back, and the cranes will let these people go."

"I'm not Adam. How can I respond as someone I am not? That makes no sense and won't be tolerated, for it's not true."

"It is true, my son, for you are Adam!"

I had to laugh that this false father mistook me for another. I simply couldn't go along with his crazy notions.

"My name is Arthur, not Adam. You're wrong. I'm not Adam."

Then the other voice laughed, and many laughed along with him, for as far as they could see, I was lying.

"Adam and Arthur, they are the same. Go forth and do as you have been bidden to do."

No one told me what to do but had only called for Adam. Nor did I hear the thunderous voice again. Instead, the ghastly cranes fished out ever more victims from the heaps that somehow got no smaller, given how thickly packed together they were. Around me there was no end to calls for me to answer as Adam, but I could do nothing to stop them, as I had no authority. But I also didn't want the situation to continue to deteriorate because of an error.

"If I can replace Adam, I will," I shouted loudly.

"No, you can't do that!" replied the cool voice of a doctor. "Next, please!"

I was off the hook, let go with a single stroke, the patchy beard and the false father having disappeared. Soon I was forgotten and left, to my surprise, on the edge of the seething cauldron of flesh. I no longer believed that it had an end and that one could escape from it. Certainly I had saved myself because I didn't answer to Adam, but I didn't feel well, and the truth that I had spoken seemed hollow and base. The admonition to "Try!" lingered on the wind, because how could I exist if I didn't dare try to?

Then I was pushed more and more to the side until I could go no farther. Very high and gray stood the wall. What else could I do? My limbs grew weak, my will was drained and leaked away in wormlike, irresolute urges that powerlessly waited for me to say what to do next. "I can't do anything for you, really, because I can't do anything for me. I'm useless. My age remained indeterminate in the hours spent in that inconclusive trial." Sadly, I spoke out loud, but the wall didn't move, and I had grown too weak to try to push my way through it. Nor did I have enough left in me to try to move to the left or right or behind me. To take control of one's fate, I thought, is an audacious wish, and I had unintentionally done so with mine. No one likes me; he who does not exist cannot even die. Slowly memories began to bubble up, and I needed to climb up in order to avoid drowning. Higher and higher I climbed, but the wall remained the same. It was forbidden to rest, for my memories pressed hard at me and threatened to drown me in a flood.

I looked on at the children in the street on West Park Row and all around the neighborhood, my son, Michael, among them, particularly loud as usual, his voice even rising above the noise of his playmates. The day was heavy, and you could smell the sweet, rank odor from the sewers so badly designed that sometimes their disgusting discharge fouled the air of the entire area, creating a terrible nuisance nothing could be done about, since they had been poorly installed four or five decades earlier. There is no way to alter them without rebuilding them from the ground up, and the millions that it would take to do that are not available. Therefore things have to remain the way they are. The sanitation inspector assured me, hopefully and a bit sadly, that it would one day be taken care of, though he also felt that perhaps I was a bit overly sensitive, the rest of the neighborhood's inhabitants never having complained about it at all. Nonetheless, I could rest easy, for unpleasant as these odors may be, his nose confirms that they are certainly no danger to anyone's health, because in a sanitary and sound sewer system the sewage is disinfected and regularly monitored for its chemical and biological content. The man advised me to buy some Ozono, an odor-killing solution that had been shown to work most anywhere, only a couple of bottles placed in the apartment being required to guarantee relief. I took his suggestion, and ever since I've been freed from these miasmas, though out in the open I still have to put up with the stink when, at certain hours, the heavy air persists.

It doesn't bother the children; perhaps they are insensitive or they don't have such sharp noses. And so they blithely run around outside with the kids from the neighborhood. Who knows where they got hold of the tattered white pieces of linen that they chase after the first cabbage butterflies with, though they are too clumsy to catch one. A young band of foolhardy robbers, they have nothing to worry about; they have it all, they exist, and they have been allowed to feel self-evident and remain satisfied with that. Much presses at their souls, be it stirring passions, ambition, envy, tweaked cravings, burning greed, and yet it's all harmless, none of it doing them in, but instead only driving them on. They squat down on the ground and no longer care about butterflies or other animals, then they toss marbles, gambling for rolling loot. And so they fan out, insatiable cravings driving them on as they explore and roam about until they are dirty, tired, and hungry. Then they are waved in from doors and windows, the rowdy bunch hauled back into the houses or voluntarily heading home, the mothers already busy arranging and cutting what from the day's bounty no longer conforms to more modest restraints. Swallowed up by the house, hemmed in by protection and comfort, at night the children drift off into the secret world of sleep, renewed and enriched, until they burst forth from its capsule to enter a new day. But nothing bad happens to the children, for no matter how much they are cut or knocked about, or sometimes hurt themselves, their inner world is never depleted. They have themselves, no matter what happens; that which is self-evident does not betray them when illness or an accident consumes their life. For they have memory, full and complete; their worries are met head-on and do not rob them of the certainty of their being. Memory . . .

Whenever I remember, that's not the way it is for me. Instead, I am lost in confusion, I cannot form any picture of myself, I get no further than mere attempts to do so. I reflect and try very hard to seize hold of my past, but Father and Mother cannot be found; the image of them is unavailable to me, so that I don't even know if they exist. My own childhood, and yet how am I to access it? Bewilderment is all I know, as no actual memory is allowed. Johanna is all I can rely on, for she knows and tells me what is necessary, as if everything were all right. She talks to me and comforts me, pointing to things: "Look, look, it exists, it exists!" She points to my hand and says, "Hand," to my forehead and says, "Forehead." How wonderful this helpful denotation, this naming of names, and how through such invocation the multiplicity of all things manifest is gained. At night, she leads me to the little beds in the children's room and says their names again: "There they are. Just look at them—your son, Michael, your little daughter, Eva." The little slumbering bodies are gently covered, only the heads sticking out from the blankets that long to cover them, sometimes a hand as well, all rosy with five fingers folded together, maintaining a sure grip upon some dream or carefree oblivion, the children alive, their quiet breathing protecting them within a sleep lovingly observed, and from which awakening is promised. Your children—so Johanna confirms in a subdued monotone meant to disturb no one, though she also affirms that their sleep is deep; the children don't wake up even when roused. How wonderful this sounds. I have Johanna to thank for these children, little strangers who do not belong to me, who are cut off from me and, because of what I'm able to understand, separate. But indeed they are mine, though alas not mine, yet still my legacy, my gift to a memory that I myself cannot fully share, West Park Row in a strange city, in a strange land. Johanna stands between us, the go-between, who moves me to hidden tears, the guide who asks no questions but, instead, mercifully acts on my behalf. But how can I live up to such caring intervention?

Empty, the wall before me, empty, no way to know whether it is permanent. From the cracked-open sash of a window on the fourth floor of the apartment building on the other side of the street, two old ladies look out, their faces lit up by the sun, a hand scattering crumbs or scraps (it could easily be the crushed shells of peanuts) onto the street below. Black with a couple of white spots, its stiffened tail sticking up, the cat snakes its way between them, embracing this human domain made all the more secure by this housemate. Alas, these women, perhaps they are vexed by unfulfilled wishes, perhaps worries eat at them, but probably it's not so bad. They have the leisure to act so, for it is not just the cat that is wrapped in contentment; the women purr with satisfaction as well. I know very well they have reason to, because with shopping bags chock-full they head home from Simmonds's. Do the women remember? Certainly! They are comfortable in their own skin, the whisperings of the radio granting them confidence and a shine to their cheeks. Their mouths open, the lips flap away, roundabout talk that, even when not entirely taken in, is still understood. Like the children, these women have nothing pressing before them; they simply are, and that's the way it is.

Why must I rise above my own memories as they rise below me? And my own, what does that mean? Where is it that I stand? How free the view, the world open, but soon you bump up against the horizon's border, and once again you see that there is another border much farther off. No, there's no such border, it's only an idea, but not one that can be grasped; only the law identifies you, demands that you stop. But where the laws of heaven and earth do not hold sway you brush up against a command, a command that overshadows you, announcing that you may not, you may not do something. That's true for you as well, Johanna. It's true for all of you, though it rarely catches up with you, and therefore you rarely realize it.

Now both ladies are gone; they both left at the right time so that they didn't have to see it, having been warned, a task having called them away, they leaving behind the street where now they could not have helped seeing the gray height of the wall that does not disturb them in the cushioned horror of their living room. They are in their own home, one made familiar by the cat that has already jumped down from the windowsill, busying themselves before their glass cabinet with the colorfully kitschy porcelain. Soon they will eat, though they won't taste any danger on their tongues as they stick to their customary routine, they being blessed and able to unwind, they having been given what defines them. Meanwhile, it's different for me. If indeed I'm alive, it's due only to my reflection. Light and shadow overlap each other, an image emerges, breathed into and called forth: "Now exist!" I am that image; to the degree that it speaks to me, I respond, appearing before the wall, which functions as protection, because before it I can exist and rise to become a figure that is visible and casts a shadow, though within myself I remain an indeterminate entity.

The wall before me has never disappeared; I have known it for many years, not knowing when it first sprang up, though I didn't always see it. Only when I peer forward intently and want to believe that I exist do I see it. Otherwise it does not appear to exist; for hours, often days, even many weeks on end, I do not notice it. Nor does the wall stand always at the same spot, for suddenly it will loom up where I would never have expected it. Sometimes it shimmers with wetness, almost like the flowing crest of a wave, then at other times it rises up dogged and heavy, composed of piled-up, dense patches of fog, though always it's the same wall. Whenever I feel invigorated and brave, I stride toward the wall, farther and farther, and yet it always stands before me. It is never far from me, but I have never gotten all the way to it. Indeed, I rush toward it, wanting to reach it, storm it, and overtake it, yet no matter how much I tirelessly try, it always remains there across from me, securely fixed and implacable. Wall of my vicissitude that often from an insatiable distance lures me onward, until I collapse before it exhausted, abandoning my pursuit. Then I kneel before it once again, wanting to sacrifice myself before it, but it only scorns such a desire. It does not care about me; it merely appears, rises, towers, admonishes, warns, even threatens, though remaining furtive, fooling the eyes, retreating silently, slowly, and steadily, drawing me toward it or holding me back, sometimes offering resistance and yet wandering off. Tirelessly this game repeats itself. I don't own the wall, but it belongs to me alone, it having been created for no one else, meaning nothing to anyone else, neither good nor evil. Nor can I show it to anyone, prove it to anyone, or explain it, for it remains inexplicable to me as well, it being my wall, and only my wall, as it doesn't belong to those who simply are self-evident, who hardly ever come up against it.

It's thus that I realize that I don't belong to human society. I and the wall, we are alone, we belong together; there is nothing else that I belong to—what any academic would call an asocial existence. If I have been granted a consciousness, it doesn't allow me the possibility of sharing a basic understanding with others who sense they are conscious. I am not part of any continuum that allows those who are self-evident—so they maintain, at least—to discover something in common or at least assume it. But what makes others tick? They run along their way, driven by their senses, intentions, wishes, and duties, they remember, which in turn nourishes them along their journey's path. Does memory not lie at the root of all society? Yet I suspect that people each have their own wall. If this is so, then my belief is confirmed that the much lauded continuum of those who are self-evident actually doesn't exist, that it's only a dream, the conjuration of those who simply appear to be self-evident which vaults over the abyss of that which is not at all self-evident. Could not the continuum be evidence of a mighty past, the conscious symbol of a golden age, the myth of paradise, an exalted state of innocence or a dreamy fairy-tale existence that has been carried off but still stands separate before us, a looming, unreachable wall that, as an inscrutable archetype, perpetuates our descent from a society that once existed but has long since been lost?

I can talk about most anything with Johanna, but even this protector between the self-evident world and myself balked with tender consideration at following along whenever I wanted to implicate her in this mystery. She always firmly stood her ground when I began with it and she could no longer hold me off. "I grant you your wall, Arthur. I know that you need it. It's the protection granted you by nature." I pressed her, asking whether she believed that it's real. "That's not up to me. It's real for you, and therefore let's leave it at that." Only compassion persuaded Johanna to grant the existence of my wall for my sake; she was not convinced that I was talking about something real, about the true embodiment of my very being, which, after all, is nurtured and nourished by Johanna alone. Myself between Johanna and the wall—that is my plight, which the most fervent talk cannot reveal and betray to anyone. Only the wall listens calmly and without repercussions, but it answers none of my prayers; it is simply there, though it has never yet considered me worthy of contact. Johanna believes she has no wall; I don't dispute this, for I recognize that she is not in any way in touch with her own ungraspable mystery, although through me she has drawn close to it for good.

When years ago I spoke with Johanna about the wall for the last time, which I have kept myself from doing ever since, I insisted on inquiring whether she herself didn't recall something similar. She at first avoided the question, but when I protested she replied.

"I can't see far enough to see a wall—I mean, your wall. Believe me, for that you need to be farsighted."

"I'm nearsighted, dear."

"Because you see the wall. That makes you nearsighted, that's what gives you this feeling. But I'm nearsighted because I can't even see as far as your—forgive me, I mean a, or at least any, wall."

"But what indeed do you see in front of it?"

"In front of the wall? I already told you, I don't see any wall. What I see is simple, a narrow wall-less perimeter. That's why I feel my way forward.

You, however, have the gift of seeing something, a border; you don't have to feel your way."

"I can't feel my way at all. You know that. I depend on you, on the wall, on everyone and anyone. It's terrible. I'm dependent and yet I'm totally alone. Those who think they know me don't know me at all. Forgive me if these words hurt. It's a confession that simply slipped out."

"Arthur, I'm no match for you. I can only follow you, I'm here only for you—to watch over you, to listen to you, to be grateful for your riches."

"Riches? I don't have—"

"No, don't say a word! Oh, why are you laughing? Let me say something for once! I'm not good for anything except helping you. It's my great purpose in life, even more important than the children. Perhaps it's my only purpose. But I don't dare question you. What others wanted to take away from you—namely, freedom—that, you see, is what I want to give you."

"Freedom . . . ?"

"And that means that I can't get mixed up in your affairs when they are beyond me. You try so often to bring me before your wall, which doesn't want to reveal itself to me."

"Reveal itself? No, it doesn't reveal itself. If it did, I would know what to do. Everything, everything would be different. It is the impenetrable. It is fate."

"Yes, exactly that. Though I feel not just fate alone but also a disguise. And a disguise is protection. I honestly believe that the wall is your protection. It separates you from your past, from all the horror. The fate that has transpired, what has been overcome . . . I know, you don't like that word, but forgive me, I know no other way to say it. The most horrible things that you have survived and experienced are now beyond one's grasp—for you, for me, perhaps for all human beings. You can no longer get at it, a curtain hides it. That is perhaps a wall less severe. If you say it's fate, that holds a double meaning for me. It is also an enormous grace."

I was touched that Johanna tried so hard, always attempting to extract the uncanny from the storm of my agitation and bring it to lee, then to soothe it, and with a confidence that always hoped to make it dissolve for me into something blessed. For that I must be thankful, for it holds me together. A benevolent undertaking, and often a solace to me, when, especially in the early years of our marriage, it diverted my all too emotionally charged daily existence into tolerable channels for the first time. Nevertheless, this encouragement, this conciliatory manner of Johanna's, is never a cure but, rather, something that calms me and works for a limited time. Yet the way that Johanna manages again and again not to tire of this ultimately futile effort and to remain patiently supportive is astounding. No, the wall is not conquered or explained through such gentle tact, nor is it properly identified, although this interpretation is lovely and has often fascinated me. Certainly, if I have a past a wall stands between it and me, that I can't deny, but it's not my wall, not the entire wall before which there is no complete resolution and no real decision that is valid, much less valid for good.

The wall keeps everything at a distance from me and also coalesces everything for me, depending on the side from which I approach it or from which it regards me. A wall that defines nothing and yet defines me. A wall that changes me more than I want to be changed. A wall that advises me and is also my adversary. Johanna's ultimate explanation often made me wonder whether it could even convey or temper my beliefs. I tried to imagine if I could even think as far back as the first time the wall appeared. I never could. No matter how deeply I look inside, the wall has always been there, and when there's no going back any further there stands the wall. For as long as there has been something in me that says "I," so it has been, and for just as long there has always been for me this wall, that which separates, which is unique, that which does not seem as incurable in other people but which certainly threatens me with expulsion from the continuum. To go it alone, this desire, which so many people acknowledge, seems to me not worth remembering, for nothing is more certain to me than exactly that, since, even if I don't wish to call it my curse, it is still my greatest burden. Whoever has a wall is a loner; whoever doesn't have one would alone be able to take part in the continuum, able to know what is held in common. In all humility, I cannot say this is not a blessing, yet I don't want to assert my desire for what has been closed off to me as an ideal true for all. But is the continuum that I dream indeed simply there, unquestionable and self-evident? This I don't know. If one is not aware of the wall, is he then not a part of that which is self-evident and thus a part of the continuum? This I don't know, either. Perhaps others who don't worry about such things are just part of the herd, are not individuals at all, and are not part of any continuum. Then Johanna would be right and those people would have no wall; they would just be a part of nature, a creature of contingency tossed back and forth in its element without knowledge of its limits, nourished by unknown currents, susceptible to the beat that moves one to dance.

No such beat, however, stirs or moves me, for I dance to my own drummer, always on the margin, the odd one out, the recalcitrant crank, and yet I'm not at all sure of being that blessed. This doesn't make me despair but, instead, feel exposed, with no feeling of having been born of a woman. If I had just a single tiny picture of my mother, or perhaps just a picture of me as a child, then it would be easier for me to imagine myself a descendant with parents. I have no way of tracing the lineage of my features, for all those whose faces I have not seen for years exist only as a shadow without the help of a picture of them. Is that why I feel so distant from my mother? She has sunk away. I call out to her memory, but there is no answer, no echo resounds; as there was no mother for me, no one held me in her arms, rocking me and singing a lullaby. When I appeared, I was the same as I am today; what happened before remains unknown. No family home, no protected childhood, exists in my memory. Johanna was the first to teach me what that means—here are the parents, here the children, Michael and Eva dancing in a circle, then the mother enters. I look on. But where should I enter? When was it a part of my own upbringing? Can someone without a past of his own fulfill the present? The past, which helps Johanna and most people affirm their present, has left little within me and instead has left only instability, most of it being dead or, at a minimum, deaf and unreachable. Often, Johanna pleaded for me to describe my mother. To no avail, many words occurred to me, yet whatever I said turned out dry and empty, like a report from a file or an arid book. There is nothing comforting in such accounts, nothing that eases or fulfills me. I arrived, or so I say in horror at the paucity of my knowledge of my own birth; all I have is headlines, chains of letters linked together as part of an understanding that the heart cannot embrace. It's not fear that prevents me from bridging the gulf but shame that holds me back from pressing the investigation further.

It is similar to the shyness I feel whenever I see a mother and father on the street with their offspring, one perhaps carried, another pushed in a little stroller. Even then I wouldn't dare mention birth and procreation; the children are just there, not created but, rather, having only arrived, after which they grow up fast, their clothes getting too small, though a veil remains drawn over where they have come from. The grown-ups wander about everywhere in ready-made fashion, having no link to the beginning. No matter how far back memory bores, it must still cease, a rupture occurring, though the abyss of such monstrous ignorance is not released, even by all the accumulated heights of learning. What drives the grown-ups to procreate is also well hidden and has nothing to do with parents and children. The animalistic ties between the sexes involve a particularly libidinal and amply documented yet insufficient knowledge, for it says nothing, is unknown to me, even if it so keenly informs the lives of ever so many wise men. When human beings associate with one another in general and in doing so do not think about sex, they only point to the ancient ties between them in familial terms, though they are hardly any less separated from one another than I am. They have their families, feel themselves to be family members, but even if they live alone they still protect the family legacy, even if it amounts to no more than shabby goods. Beyond this they have another gift, which I lack: they can hold the familial inside them, talk like father and mother, citing similarities and dissimilarities to each and telling the children about them.

If my little ones ask me, I come up with stories for them as well, for I don't want to disappoint them, because the children's only burden should be that they are my offspring, and nothing more. In their presence, of course, I try not to betray good old customs, as Johanna keeps an eye on me and offers some clever inspiration, hoping that this will do not only them but also me much good. I don't want to disappoint Johanna, and so I play along as best I can. It's not even particularly hard for me to assume the role of the father of the family. As soon as Johanna is nearby, or when I guess what she has in mind and how things are supposed to happen, all in order, one thing following another—the beloved run of the day, the morning jokes at breakfast, the walk to school, playtime with the children, a merry romp outside in the fresh air, the settling of a fierce dispute, reward and punishment meted out through praise and reproof, the end-of-day gathering together while saying prayers at night—it's all easy for me to do and nimbly pull off, any impediments being easily overcome. I have a reserve built up that is there for the goings-on around me, and which the children can tap, Johanna thanking me when I spoil Michael and Eva a little each day. Nothing within me, however, has changed through these riches; I have not changed as a result but, instead, have gathered together something that enables me to have something for those I love most, who should not have to suffer because of my own sorry state.

For years I was unaware that, for the most part, I terrorized others. I was naïve and had no idea how I hurt them, and even when I learned to recognize that I did, I still had no idea what caused it. Even Johanna didn't at first recognize how odd I was, or misunderstood it. Later, it was she who with diligence and imperturbable patience helped me to see the offense I committed, until I learned to protect those around me, as well as myself, from my many outbursts. I had to consider the needs of my children, which helped to keep some things in good order, while Johanna arranged the rest. All of it helped me, since I worked hard to maintain a protective layer around me, which I called the storeroom of the indeterminate day. Never do I find myself entirely gathered up inside it; rarely am I even a guest, since I feel like a tenant who in exchange for his rent has won the right to put away the goods he's brought along in an orderly fashion, so that this anteroom of my being almost becomes a completely fitted-out room. I dare enter it only with care, so that I don't break anything or cause any damage, for none of it can be replaced. What has been stored there serves me with stubborn recalcitrance; it's not good for much, for with my own strength I can hardly protect it from either friend or foe. No, it really cannot be maintained. If someone were to take it away, I would not even have the right to complain, for what is there transforms itself without my doing anything, especially as others mess about in this room and shift things around without my knowing. If I put it all back in place, I still know that other hands have left their traces.

Once again Johanna comes to the rescue, helping me clean out this room and carefully leading all who ask for me into this room, the visitors, being fooled for their own good, imagining that they have been led to me. Pictures of me hang in the room, pictures that speak, and which turn slowly and sway, swirling together as soon as someone looks at them and asks something. This works rather well, and makes for a lovely impression, the people satisfied when they are received so. Yet, for me, relations with people are made easier through this, for while I remain hidden from them, silly goings-on full of empty babble and crumbly creases prevail in a rented room. Thus I find it bearable, even when I know that all of it together, what at least lets me think it is me myself, is nothing but an artificial agglomeration of leftovers and flotsam, patches and strange decorations, a bunch of smoke and mirrors for which I should be held accountable, or, at least, as far as I can answer for it.

Perhaps I'm only a vestige of myself, borrowed goods, hearsay; certainly that must be so. In a prehistory difficult to explore, there must have been something—or should I say someone?—which was me, a person, supposedly a person with an ordinary birth, with a childhood, sprouting up tall, as well as making a step-by-step exploration of his neighborhood, where everything became a part of himself and helped him discover his essential nature. Back then he felt connected, sensing within himself a free spirit that could bound across the lawn, propelling him forward, he blindly plunging into childhood's flood tide, learning, in fact, to forget for a moment, then awakening down below in the depths before emerging again with the densely probing urge of his accumulating thirst for action, experiences of sweet sins and sweeter virtues, wanting his own history, his . . . his! That would probably have been me, crammed together with others like me for whom my talk meant something and resounded, to whom I could talk, you and I cavorting like polliwogs in the large pickle jar in the schoolyard, followed by the teacher's magical whistle, the charming bustle of school-children swallowed up by the school's main gate, then into the classrooms, two by two in four rows, quickly folded into desks in order to be tamed, subordinate next to subordinate, surreptitious rebellion dared, then quickly brought to task through punishment, a heart subdued, the fundamentals— reading, writing, arithmetic, the famous dependable laws of nature—all of it developed and prepared for the curious mind. That was me, one among others, dressed properly, believing what I was taught, the examples given. How wonderful to compete at one's studies and participate, the hands going up, wide-open eyes shining, drinking in the alluring bits of wisdom while listening unabated, me taking it all in unquestioningly.

That was me, belonging to the others, not separate; through the bonds of community I was carried along and was allowed to feel and know myself. Family, friends, and country—the kinship of all creation before the Creator prepared me well, my delight in the joy of all creation incorporating me into the realm of the living and of all things, feeling fulfilled and able to join in without worry. How everything around me gleamed as I called out and felt affirmed by the echo. I suffered no damage, not even when a shadow crossed my brow and my hands covered my eyes in darkness, or when, suddenly, a sharp pain gripped me for a moment that seemed to stretch on forever and yanked me from the agreeable surround, though soon such suffering came to an end, and I was welcomed back into the fold.

The years of my first investigations passed, and doubts began to punch holes in the dense web of that pure realm. Yet I didn't grow weak, but instead applied myself and became stronger, powerfully engaged, uplifted, and humbled, as I suffered and rejoiced, all the doubts only enriching me. Those years helped me grow, childhood and youth stripped away, mistakes and achievements building my character, myself able to stroll through good and bad nights, to sink into loneliness, to formulate the murky question of justice, to recognize the difference between similar creatures, such that I laid claim to a measure of judgment as well as a view of a world created for my sake, in which with proud humility I confidently placed myself at the top. Always I remained on track; I was not destroyed, nothing able to force from me the confession that I did not exist.

How, then, after such a promising start did I come to my downfall? How did all certainty cease, such that I came to believe that I was only what others saw me as and I didn't know myself any longer? No particular set of developments, no specific harm, or any kind of sickness reduced me to such poverty—not poverty, for I would have been poor no matter what, but, rather, plunged into confusion and reduced to nothing! It didn't happen because of anything I did, nor did it suddenly mushroom, such that I couldn't help seeing that I was losing my moorings. No, I kept my wits; I believed in myself and did not notice for a long time that I had disappeared. Yet, indeed, that is what had happened.

What lies between the time when I was me and now, when this is no longer true? This cannot be completely forgotten, but it resists being articulated, for it digs in, puts up borders that cannot be crossed. I feel that one does not die within, that it comes from without, as one is suddenly or stealthily taken away. And then there are those who have power and, behind their wrinkles, will. They say, "Him there? No, he doesn't exist. We did away with him already." Pleading protests are raised against them, but no weapon in defense. You are simply hunted down, but you don't admit it. Instead, you hobble along, legless and missing your head, through suffocating and impassable neighborhoods. Laws are proclaimed which maintain that this is not possible. You are simply confused, because you are dead and present yourself as a dead mistake, a vestige of yourself amid the funeral march of the frozen ghosts in their dance of death. Yet, because the masters of this world are so concerned with their own power, they don't notice the whirring, and so they patiently choose to consider this rush of bodies nothing more than the day's residue. They know it will come to nothing; it's not worth the effort to deny those who have been expunged the last throes of their dance of death, as it will be finished by the break of day. I'm not saying this is what happened to me; it was probably quite different, this being only a depiction of my dissolution, perhaps a small part of the picture. It's an unfit allegory. The entrance into the loss of one's essence cannot be made visible, for memory digs its way into horrid trenches, downfall and downtrodden, the fallen remaining, not all dead, but the arisen are also extinguished, their being wiped out behind pale hungry eyes, each living in want, even when they are awake and appear everywhere, speaking words that cannot be heard. Done away with and hauled off, and yet composed, and yet still there. Thus they are, but am I among them? How so . . . me . . . ?

A clamoring bell, and I am dragged out from behind the curtain. Then came the blows. There was a war in which many fought and either perished or survived, others not fighting but likewise perishing or surviving, while still others could neither fight nor not fight, though all of them perished and none survived, even when you made it through until a certain day, when you suddenly let in the light, paused at the window, and some voices shouted, "Everyone out! The war is over!" I also count myself among those who heard this simply because they had made it through and yet had not survived. Someone stretched out his right hand and laid the middle finger of the left next to it. Six was what he was trying to indicate, having lost the words—six years of war. That's a long time, a lot can happen, and at some point during these long years I died. What befalls millions of creatures at the outbreak of peace, and how can that be realized without the roar of fierce battles? All die, both victors and vanquished. Yet I belong to neither, nor can I recall having been overtaken by the storm of battle. I was not sent into the fighting but instead stashed in the hinterlands, and the hinterlands were endless. Yet since the war was no longer limited to a single theater and it scoffed at all those hidden away, it's quite possible that I was part of those who fought.

How it really was I hardly know, and I cannot remember having ever felt the throbbing heat of battle or combat, only that a distant rumble reached my hideout. The voices around me knew very well what it meant when they called out, "Planes!," be they planes attacking or planes defending. But, then again, no one knew who was being attacked or who was being defended. Whether it had anything to do with us as we lay hidden, no one said, for nothing was shared with us. Later there were more thuds, not close by, but the earth shook. Bombardment, we were told, and pulsing cannons. Round us every day, murder raged on. Even today I don't know if that was part of the war, as the enemy never burst into our sheds. The narrow confines in which we were enclosed and stowed away were never disturbed. Those who murdered us were allies, friends. There was no one to stop them, certainly not the enemy. The murderers didn't say very much; their shrill screams were short, though they carried themselves, it seemed to me, as if they were just doing their job. Assiduously they went about their business, doing it with diligence, and if my heart were not consumed with the fear that at any moment these heroes might relieve me of my bodily existence, I would have marveled at their dauntless zeal. Out of cowardice I avoided them and stayed out of the front row if I wasn't able to crouch in a corner somewhere. I just didn't want to attract attention and only hoped through fate, through some invisible entity and sheer luck, to escape my own murder. Did I in fact succeed? Doubt still eats at me even today. Others around me died because they were killed; I died because no one noticed me. Is there any difference? During those six years, my memory was strained. Because I was hidden away, it was stretched to the limits, drunk down with the agreeable arrogance of my youth. That gave me strength to cling to life, wanting to remain true to it so that it would have mercy on me and stand by me. I continued to hope. It wasn't clear what I hoped for; I just remained within myself and waited for morning to come, just for it to be there, and then another morning, always another morning.

And so I went on. The days passed, though I never noticed that with each day I became weaker. The murder of my companions consumed me, yet I had no idea that each died for me, and that with each I died as well. Did I brood over my own fate? Time melted away inside me. Before I knew it, beneath the foamy froth of this roiling madness my very being had become pale and thin, shrunken to a fragile husk that resulted from my being fed nothing but a few meager morsels. I was given just enough food to keep me alive and alert enough to feel hungry and to crave more bites of food. I was denied them, and so I dreamed of them, which nourished me and granted me a steely strength. The deeper I sank, the more I distanced myself from myself, withdrawing from the reduced means of existence that maintained me and yet continued to weaken me as well. But still I defended myself against all the dangers that threatened me from without and from within, helped on by believing that protection and rescue were possible. Thus I prayed throughout, praying myself always away, really away, and into this intense engagement with the unknown I disappeared. The transitory wore me away. On the day they announced that the war was over, there was nothing left but a snakeskin, a dried, brittle skeleton that I could discern through tender self-regard, though I the living animal had slipped away, gone without a trace, no longer to be found. I tried to tell myself that the damage was not real but rather only a deep numbness: Patience, you will live again. In the meantime, I felt it best to live as if I were healthy and sound.

People back then were used to all types, therefore I didn't stand out. It was hard to distinguish between murderers and the murdered. Wherever I showed up and was soon asked something or was drawn into the everyday buzzing chatter, I was completely unknown. A cold disengagement was almost everywhere buried beneath the hectic pace of a destroyed world that fed upon itself through a kind of empty jubilation in which the walking dead were discussed in a matter-of-fact tone, as if they were standing right there. I joined in the cozy warmth, and it felt good. The day of the new powers seemed to have dawned, the fanfare of freedom boiling over into explosive noise. I was spared having to prove that my heart was still beating. You just spit out your name without anything to back it up—documents and witnesses were not called for—and before you knew it a civil servant was warmly extending his unwitting hand to you. That was all that was needed for the superficial passing of any given day; you just waved a piece of paper and everything was fine, a smile accompanying it, though no one bothered to actually look. Soon the scrap of paper was no longer any good, but I wasn't worried at all, for you were either forgotten or forgiven. I traveled through distant lands, not needing any money, and yet I always ate and drank well, a bed with warm blankets always waiting for me. The borders were passable; all I had to do was say, "It's me!," and immediately the guard would acknowledge me and let me through. Helping hands pointed the way. Whenever I asked to ride along in someone's car, he just invited me in with a wave and was happy to have the company.

Thus I arrived late one afternoon in my old city. It had changed very little during the war, the old stonework, massive and dignified, had survived the years well, only the paint and plaster having suffered here and there. The streets were also grayer than earlier, while, unexpectedly, in the public parks a network of graves spread out among the dug-up earth. The grass, which it used to be forbidden to walk on, was worn away, broad tents erected in which people camped beneath the tarps as if it had always been so, the people looking satisfied and at ease. I had left my knapsack at the train station, an unrelenting desire to look around pressing me up and down the streets, which didn't mind that I was there, though they no longer seemed to recognize me, since my steps in stiff boots struck the patterned cobbles in a half-confident, half-unfamiliar manner. Many people moved back and forth, both residents and newcomers, all of them caught up in their fates, whether large or small, yet each so certain, as if they knew just what was going to happen to them. Children romped around, grabbing one another's hands, chasing after balls, raising a real ruckus, though no one got into any trouble. Soon I was caught up in it, swept away by it all, as if death had never once had an eye on me.

With bated breath, a tired back, but my legs still strong and my eyes full of curiosity, I turned a corner where people moved about more energetically. Here no children dared to jump into the heaving noise of the rumbling traffic, as cars rushed by in earnest, a policeman directing traffic in a silent fashion. I looked around me with harmless pressing glances at the many faces. How clueless they all seemed whenever I tried to decipher my own obliterated memories within them. All were strangers. Also, when they noticed my curiosity they didn't stop, for they hadn't expected me. Whether they thought anything of it I couldn't tell, since it wasn't possible for me to turn around and look back at them, for fresh faces continued to flow toward me which I gazed at with ever more pressing questions. And yet these were strangers as well, nor did I learn anything more from them than I did from their predecessors, who had already been swallowed up in the flow of traffic. Once you were late and were no longer expected, your arrival in the past doesn't go well. That I had to realize.

But why despair as long as there is another corner to turn? Another one approached that was more familiar than most. Sleepily I walked along hunched over, slowing my steps warily, since I wanted to be ready in case I encountered my father. I was almost afraid to be surprised by him too suddenly. Indeed, I had no knowledge of what had happened to him other than that he had been murdered. That also happened in the war, but way off, as I wasn't there, murder having occurred in too many places. But that just couldn't be; perhaps I was only the victim of a frightful rumor, and therefore could still hope that my father had survived and, just like me, was gazing at the people streaming by, looking for those who recognized him and could help. But there was no father in this street where papers were hawked, cigarettes were sold, brash sweets were wrapped up in garish colors, and sausages reeked of garlic, the uncooked ones hanging in the open air on a rack, while the cooked ones looked much more appealing as they waited for customers on a wide griddle covered in grease. The vendors didn't wait on me at all; in fact, they didn't even notice that I was there, letting me pass by coldheartedly, I myself eagerly searching for some kind of response in their yellowish sullen eyes. My father was nowhere to be found; no one was there to greet him as they used to when he hurried by without a hat and coat. There was no father, nor any longer the vendors that once knew him and loved to chat with him. So I passed by the booths, dazed, my legs heavy, my feet hurting and schlepping along, the ground resisting more and more, until my feet were held fast in thick muck. Also, dense fumes, thick and creeping, surrounded my ears, such that I couldn't hear, while far-off calls gradually managed to penetrate the distance between, myself hardly perceiving that they were meant for me. But after they continued to pound into my head like hammer blows, I finally had to note that without a doubt someone was calling my name: "Herr Landau!"

I stood there frozen to the spot, not moving a single limb, waiting, the name repeated again and again, yet even stronger, it supposedly directed at me, or maybe not, for how could that be possible? It was my good father they meant, he having for decades occupied the Reitergasse, Haberdashery Albert Landau, or HAL for short, adored and known throughout the city as a solid brand, the brand name appliquéd on soft linen shirts and bright silk ties. Once again, the Reitergasse welcomed back old Herr Landau, who had disappeared. From all the booths and opened doors of the shops, from office and apartment windows, one could hear "Herr Landau!" being called. Although I couldn't move, such joy couldn't help but make me think that he was nearby. I also tried to press the words with a half-injured tongue through my lips and called out, barely audible, "Herr Landau!" It wasn't loud enough, but I hoped that my father would be able to distinguish the voice of his son amid the chaotic babble. I actually managed to turn my head in order to look around, searching here and there for the face of my father among the many faces around me. Yet in vain! I was struck blind and cursed the fact that his beloved features no longer existed in my memory. Wire-rimmed glasses, I told myself, glasses and a tall stance, though no doubt somewhat bent over by the years and the worries. But what good was it if I couldn't remember him any better than that? All I could do was believe that my father would notice me if I kept waving. I lifted my hand, then my entire arm, though I looked tentative and foolish. Yet nothing happened that I could perceive. Only his name continued to be called out in a continuously audible chain, hanging damp and heavy in the air, as I slumped out of sadness that no one paid any attention to me, the one returning home. With a weak voice, I said, "My name is also Landau, and I am his son." After which I feebly pointed a finger at myself.

That did it. Someone came up to me, shook my hand, said how happy he was to see me again, and slapped me on the shoulder. But I didn't recognize the man, nor did I want to ask who he was; it didn't matter to me. He had to be someone from the Reitergasse. I waited anxiously for the man to disclose something even more important to me, but he just stated again his joy, until I interrupted him and asked him for news of my father and for him to take me to him right away, since he must have just passed through here, though we had, unfortunately, missed each other. I only wanted to talk to him as soon as possible, since it had been so long, because of the war, since we had been able to talk.

"He must be in the shop. I need to hurry in order to get to him before it closes. For then he won't want to open up, because he'll have to tally the receipts and feed the cat. Then he runs out the back door and is no longer to be found. Please, take me there, I'm tired, I feel dizzy. Go on ahead of me and let him know that I am on my way. But be careful that he is not done in by the joy!"

"What. . . . What's that, Herr Landau, who do you want to see?"

"My father!"

"Your father. . . . Where might he be?"

"I don't know for certain. He must be in the shop. You know which one I mean. Quick, before it's too late!"

"In which shop . . . ?"

"Don't be that way! There! A couple of buildings farther! First you cross the Römerstrasse, then just two buildings on—"

"I don't understand. . . . You'll have to—"

"What don't you understand? Don't you see Herr Kutschera's fruit stand there, all those boxes and baskets taking up half the sidewalk? Just past that? It always bugged my father how sloppy Kutschera is and how his stuff stood in the way of customers wanting to get to our shop. Don't you see it? There's the shop, HAL—Haberdashery Albert Landau!"

The man looked at me appalled, his mouth open, he not knowing what to say. When I asked him once again to come with me, that there was little time left, he ever so lightly tapped me on the forehead, said something in-audible as apology, turned on his heel, and left without saying goodbye. "It's me! It's me! Why are you running off! I didn't mean to upset you." But the man didn't turn around and had already disappeared. Nor did I hear any-one calling out again the name of my father or my name; instead, strangers flowed on by me without a care, none of them concerned as I looked around helplessly in all directions, wondering if anyone else might indeed recognize me, though in vain.

There was nothing else for me to do but venture on and look for my father unannounced. Hopefully, he wasn't out front in the shop but out back in the office or in the workroom or the storeroom. Then from behind the counter a salesclerk would ask in a friendly voice if I needed any help, most likely not one of the old ones but someone new. I would then take the salesclerk aside and tell him that I was the younger Herr Landau—indeed, just take a look, it's me, though I've changed quite a bit, the long war, though I'm fit as a fiddle, but you don't have to worry about your job, for I'm just a meager scholar and no salesman, since I don't know anything about selling clothes. But, please, just go back and tell my father that I'm here. Prepare him for it carefully, for I don't want the shock to kill him! Just tell him that a gentleman wishes to speak with him, and make sure to tell him it's no stranger but someone he knows, so that he slowly comes to experience a wonderful surprise, rather than him thinking that the dead have risen from the grave, as used to happen in the old days, though if you think about it, such an event is not that pleasant to think about. Go to my father and carefully let him know that someone wants to see him! And, once he's listened to it all and is curious enough to push you to the side and walk out to the front, take him by the hand, making sure that he doesn't hurry, and then tell him very quietly so that he understands: Herr Landau, it's someone who knows you very well, a friend. It's Arthur, your son.

That's what I imagined would happen as, with eyes blinking, I quietly crept forward. I had already crossed the Römerstrasse on the old familiar way home to my parents' apartment, and I was already at the baskets of fruit and nuts eagerly displayed by the Kutscheras. I shoved my way past the crowd of customers and saw that today my father had closed early, the shutters all down, only the large display window still left uncovered. I didn't dare go any closer, because I was already terrified to see that the shelves were empty—no shirts, no beautifully appointed goods, nothing behind the pane coated with a thick layer of dust, only the empty depths of the showroom and its closed display cases, past which I could gaze into the pooling twilight of the shop's depths, all the way back to the counter and even as far as the very hazy shelves behind it full of boxes. I pressed against the neglected pane, closed my eyes for a little while to make sure that I simply wasn't seeing things, then opened them again to spy what was before me. But everything was real. Or was it? Was I standing there? Was this the old shop in the Reitergasse? Why had I let myself become confused, and why had I wandered here? Hadn't an inner voice warned against ever returning to this city, as it no longer held any trace of home or anything good, both of which would be easier to find elsewhere than in a place from a past that had disappeared?

There I stood in front of a wall, my gaze sinking into the tidy little realm that my father had run for so many years with diligent work, and now it stood empty, not even a stranger having moved in. The window was too dusty for me to see whether the counter and the shelves really were still in their old locations. I stood up on my toes, wiped the windowpane, but it was covered with dust on the inside. In order to have a better view, I jumped up and down a few times, but this also failed, me feeling ashamed in case the Kutscheras or anyone passing by had seen my foolishness and thought of me as a dog whining before his dead father's house. He was not there; there was nothing to be found here. A final glance confirmed that the shop's sign had disappeared. Only the empty frame, whose glass had broken, loomed. There was no sign to read.

I wanted to get away as fast as I could. Wherever everything was lost, every moment disappeared. If I wanted to find out where my father was, it would be better to check elsewhere, be it with relatives or friends, but perhaps best of all at home, not in the Reitergasse. My father was already an old man, which had not occurred to me. He was now way past seventy, and therefore he would have preferred to close the business rather than sell it to a stranger. That would have pained him to no end. Instead, he had decided to rest and enjoy what he had earned. He had always looked ahead to a comfortable old age and wanted to have a large garden on the edge of the city, where he could build a little hut to get away to on the weekends in order to be closer to his flowers on warm, lovely days, his greenhouse full of exotic plants and his beloved cacti. I needed to hurry home, where Father would be meeting Mother on such a lovely evening when the strawberries were ripening, though neither would be expecting me. If it so happened they were away, I could leave a message with the porter and ask him where I could find the garden, and then hurry on to it as fast as I could.

But that's not the way it worked out at all, for I couldn't convince myself that the hope of seeing my father again in front of the shop in the Reiter-gasse was entirely useless. I also couldn't help thinking that it was a long way home, and that Mother would have no clue that I'd be arriving. I had not shaved in days, and I had been gone for years. A father would understand that, for he would think of the war, but it wouldn't be right to show up in front of my mother old and haggard, tired and dirty, in a tattered uniform and clunky shoes. To call home with a voice composed would be the best, or to ask Frau Kutschera to help me out. Unfortunately, the Kutscheras were not very pleasant people, but as an unexpected arrival I could hope for a little courtesy. In any case, it made the most sense to ask at the fruit stand, for hanging about in front of Father's shop made no sense and was depress-ing. As always, the Kutscheras had a lot of customers who didn't at first step into the shop but instead lingered outside on the street. The couple and the two harried salesgirls had their hands full and no time to keep an eye on each individual customer. It all happened fast, but whoever wanted to be served did better to call out loud what he wanted, rather than wait outside and expect to be served. But how should I make my presence known? I stood among the group of shifting customers, all of whom were trying to be served next. Their number hardly shrank, for there were always new people arriving as soon as others withdrew. Nonetheless, I remained hopeful and stood there very patiently, believing that one of the Kutscheras would notice me, though it was a salesgirl who finally looked at me with concern, because it bothered her that I kept peering in at the Kutscheras. No, I said, I didn't need any help. I quickly shifted my glance, and the young girl turned on her heel to help someone else.

Something had to happen. After some dithering, I decided that it was better to approach Herr Kutschera rather than his shrewish wife, whom my father always hated to deal with whenever he had to again complain about the garbage that would end up in front of his door. And yet I also didn't want to ambush Herr Kutschera with a question out of the blue. If I bothered him with questions that he found disturbing, he wouldn't want anything to do with me. What I needed to do was make him curious and buy just a little something in order to get on his good side.

"Herr Kutschera, two kilos of your best apples!"

The vendor looked up quickly when I said his name, but he didn't recognize me and just pointed gruffly at a sign that said, "Only One Kilo Per Customer." Ashamed, I called out, "Oh, then one kilo!" Kutschera ripped off a bag from a bundle that hung down, slid his hand in, then blew into the bag, grabbed some apples, quickly threw them onto a scale with its trays clattering, and briskly switched apples in and out until the exact weight was achieved.

"Herr Kutschera, do you recognize me?"

He looked up again. His gaze didn't reveal that someone he knew stood before him. But he didn't worry any more about it and just busied himself again with the apples and the scale. What was I to him?

"No."

Sullenly he busied himself with the apples. The kilo refused to come to the exact weight. I needed to help Herr Kutschera out.

"It can be a bit more than a kilo, it doesn't matter."

"Didn't you read the sign? To hell with your stupid trick!"

"Oh dear, forgive me! Before the war I came here often."

"And so did many others!" he snapped, closing the paper bag and holding it out to me, waiting for the money in exchange. Frau Kutschera, who was busy with other customers, was already bothered by my talk and muttered angrily to herself as she shot me a dirty look, but that was all it took, for her curiosity won out as she scrutinized me more closely, then was suddenly so taken by surprise that a scoop full of hazelnuts fell from her hand, the tiny balls bouncing all over the ground.

"Jesus Mary, the young Herr Landau is alive!"

With this exclamation I was only partway there, as the woman stared at me a little while longer. Then she abandoned me for her customers and left me to her husband, who also thought he now recognized me. His bleary eyes looked me over with suspicion.

"Is it really you?"

I didn't care for this question, though I pulled myself together and laughed away the feeling of revulsion rising within me.

"Of course, Herr Kutschera. I've just arrived, and right away I wanted some of your apples."

"How flattering. Indeed, your father bought these same apples. The very same."

"Now he grows his own in the garden outside the city, right?"

"In his garden?"

Herr Kutschera said this so loud that his wife again pricked up her ears. But why didn't he say anything more? Confused, he just stared at me blankly. It looked to me as if he wanted to say something, or perhaps he was thinking hard what to say. Or was he just stunned and at a complete loss? His silence was painful to witness; all I wanted was for one of us to say something.

"Tell me, Herr Kutschera, did my father give you the address?"

"What address?"

"His, of course. I just got back from the war and want to head out to see Father."

"That's not possible, Herr Landau. The old man . . . went off . . . also to the war. . . ."

"At his age?"

"Even at his age. Terrible, don't you think?"

"And hasn't returned? Back to his garden? Not even now?"

Herr Kutschera picked a bad apple from a basket, turned it playfully in his hand, and looked at me as if I were mad. Quietly he shook his head, his low brow shrinking between his fat cheeks and his forehead. He was thinking something, but it was something sad, because his eyes grew damp, he finally wiping his nose on his shirtsleeve. Then he cleared his throat.

"I don't know what happened to your father. No one knows, no one here. I never saw him again. I can't help you. He was a good man."

"A good man!" Frau Kutschera called out as well, she now having twice as much to do as before, since her husband wasn't taking care of business.

There was nothing I was going to get from these people, and I didn't believe a word they said. How could they know anything? Since my father had retired from business, he was loath to cast an eye on the Reitergasse. There was nothing more for him to do here, and he certainly didn't want to look at the empty shop any longer, while Kutschera's was the last place he wanted to buy any fruit beyond that which he grew himself.

"Thank you. What do I owe you?"

"Nothing. Nothing." Herr Kutschera turned red and looked more stricken. "For old friends, it's my honor. Please do me the honor again!"

I thanked him, though I couldn't help feeling that it wasn't right. As I said goodbye, Frau Kutschera also called out to me.

"Be well, Herr Landau! Be well! Goodbye!"

She meant well, perhaps, but her screeching voice left my ears burning, thereby causing me to hurry off as if I knew where I was headed, the apples under my arm for which Herr Kutschera had not gotten anything. I didn't dare look at Father's shop again and stormed through the Reitergasse. I didn't want to see anyone or be recognized by anyone. It was clear to me that the people in this neighborhood couldn't tell me anything about my father. I had to first gather myself together and settle down before I made any more decisions about how to go about searching for my father. Then I reached the Karolinenweg, where there were loads of people walking along together in two cumbersome but swiftly moving streams by which one was relentlessly carried along unless one pressed tight against a store window or fled into one of the wide entryways. The cramped sidewalk threatened to burst with workers pouring from the offices into the streets. The workday was done, most of the businesses closing.

Thus I let myself be freely carried along until I came to the corner of the quiet Helfergasse. I extracted myself from the compact flow of impatient people moving along the Karolinenweg—it taking a while before I had freed myself—and finally was able to stop and catch my breath. The flood of people had not done me any good, it being all too much to take in, and I was hungry besides. How lucky, I said to myself, that I have Herr Kutschera's apples with me, for they'll taste good. Yet the moment I opened the skillfully folded bag I immediately felt that it would be better to just give them all away, for I had no right to be tasting forbidden fruit. Adam, Adam, don't take a bite, mind what you do, and do what's right! Danger is afoot, evil comes to no good. My father was always an honest man, his basic principles unshakable, and by which he conducted his business. There was nothing sleazier than a vendor who sold his goods under false pretenses. I was ashamed of the apples, which I could feel round and firm inside the bag that was painfully pressed between my chest and my upper arm. If only there were a beggar who could mercifully take them, a pale child whom I could give the apples to! But no one passed by to whom I could give the strange goods. If I wasn't going to leave them sitting on the next wall, I had to hold on to them. I tried to take comfort in the idea that my father, in order to keep good relations with Herr Kutschera and his wife, had many times given them little gifts, such as a bunch of handkerchiefs for Christ-

mas, now and then a tie, sometimes gloves or a colorful scarf. Certainly
Kutschera had thought of these gifts when seeing me after such a long time,
his conscience bothering him, and he was glad that he could do something
for the father via his son.

Yet what kind of son was I? What good was I? I had not saved my parents
from the war, had not sent them the smallest of gifts, not even the smallest memento that the dullest of soldiers brings home to his dearest ones in
order to assure them of his love, and that he had faithfully thought of them
while in the trenches, he having brought some crude little thing, a picture
frame for his mother, a cigarette holder for his father, which he had carved
himself with a pocket knife during the melancholy hours of those endless
days. Then the parents, who had believed that their own flesh and blood had
disappeared, would know that the love of a son never fades despite the years.
I had failed to do anything; dull and dejected, I hadn't brought the slightest
gift. But then I had an idea, for there I stood, Kutschera's apples in hand,
which I could lay on the grave of my dear parents.

"Take and give thanks, my dear dead! Blessed may you be with this food!
You will never be forgotten, you who took the trouble to feed and clothe
me. It is only a meager sacrifice that I carry over the threshold to you in
your holy silent realm, but please accept it with grace! One thing is certain:
this gift carries no guilt. I didn't shoot the enemy in his garden in order to
steal from his fruit trees. I was not a good soldier, nor did I become a good
murderer. Instead, I was cowardly. I stayed back in the hinterlands, though I
was not fed. No sweet apples were handed out; it was a meager time, neither
an easy nor a dangerous stage, though I don't wish to talk about that, for it
wasn't particularly difficult, because here I am. Indeed, it's really me. It's my
own skin and bones. Why don't you answer? Don't be so cold! You have to
hear me, I have to find you. Please, open the door! I know you're in there,
hidden deep inside, for I can hear Father in the bathroom drumming on the
large mirror, as he always did whenever he shaved. Then the clatter of the
dishes and silverware—only Mother could make that sound, nobody else.
Why can't I get to you? This wall, this awful wall; I can neither get through
nor over it. Oh, how impossible it all is."

With a quavering voice I said all this in a soft rhythm, determined to
move forward, and yet not taking a single step. I stood there frozen in the

Helfergasse, the seething rush of the Karolinenweg nearby. Pleadingly I held out my bag of apples, yet I couldn't help noting with a shudder how miserable it all was, a pathetic attempt at an unsuccessful return home. Then I wrenched myself away from the spot, passing continually back and forth as one does when one waits for someone on the street and can't stand still. Perhaps someone would come along, a relative or one of the old servants, Herr Nerad or Frau Holoubek, a person who is always tied to us, and even today is still a part of us, as such closeness never disappears. All I needed was a little patience, for by the time evening settled in someone would have to come along who could help me. I reproached myself sharply for not writing a single letter the entire war, not even sending a simple card home, myself the disloyal son. Why should he expect anything now in return? Indeed I remembered that we could not send any mail, for our guards would not allow it, as they hated to waste time with such things and simply said no when we asked permission to mail letters and cards. Yet that was no excuse. I had simply done nothing but remain silent, ever silent, as only the dead are allowed to remain! No doubt Mother would remain silently in the background, knitting away, stitch after stitch. Could a mother renounce even such a bad son? No, she was sweet and almost deaf, though Father was highly enraged, not letting her know that I was nearby, which she could not perceive, lost as she was in the melancholy of her lonely knitting. If only Father didn't stand in the way, I could have gone to Mother!

"You're not getting past me, Arthur! Can't you see that your mother is decorating the shroud of her dead son with stars? A noble piece of work done by ever-faithful hands."

"Father, I brought you apples, fragrant shining apples! Mother should peel them with the gilded fruit knife and cut them into pieces! She can sprinkle them with sugar and arrange them in the shiny crystal bowl for us all!"

"Too late. You should have come earlier. Others came home a good while ago. You made us wait so long."

"The war—"

"I know, the war. That's what one says when he perceives the long-neglected love of his parents as an inexpiable wrong. We couldn't wait any longer for you. Even if it's you, we don't recognize you. In the cemetery, when they erect a gravestone for children who have died far away, they will collect money for it, and we will have your name engraved so that you are remembered. Get out! What I'm telling you is the only comfort you're going to get from me."

"Do you really not recognize me? Do you really want to deny who I am?"

"I'm not denying you, and indeed I recognize you. Lift up your arms! Turn around! Once more! Slower! Yes, that's right, I'm sure of it. You look just like him, and must even have known him, for I'm sure he told you about us. Otherwise you couldn't have found us. Nonetheless, you are not our son."

Then I wanted to walk right up to my father and offer him my apples before kneeling down to embrace his legs with my arms. He threatened me, however, with a fist raised high, and I knew that I couldn't try to win his sympathy for my muddle-headed existence. Mother, meanwhile, kept knitting and knitting, sitting there beneath her light and working ever faster on the shroud, though I could hardly see the glow of the stars on it. All I could see was that she used red yarn. Then I called to her again. She might have heard me, for she paused, her hands now still and folded together, she looking down at the strands of yarn that now lay like a fountain of blood upon her dress. Then her head quietly swayed forward, her mouth closing softly, her forehead sinking solemnly and peacefully into a deep sleep. I waited for a while to see if she would sense that I was there, but she sank ever deeper into sleep. Father seemed to have forgotten my presence, for he walked over to Mother and observed with great interest her oblivion. He seemed quite used to it, for he didn't look at all concerned, though a deep, unfathomable melancholy took hold of his slightly bent figure. Thus he stood there, strong and rigid, his open mouth somewhat aghast as Mother slipped ever deeper into her slumber, and with a heavy nod let her head sink irrevocably low, such that her plain gray hair fell in fine strands over her face. It was almost impossible to see beyond the drooping hair, though her neck was visible, and there I discovered a nasty swollen scar that had indeed healed, but only recently. What had happened to the good woman—how much had she endured? The painful discoloring seemed to be fading, but not yet entirely. Father sensed what I observed, and he turned toward me with the full weight of his age, as if he wanted to see just what the pain I perceived in this wound might do to me. I could barely stand the sight of my mother anymore and was relieved, even if Father didn't at all approve, to have a reason not to lie down next to her. What Father expected of me wasn't clear to me at all, so I didn't say anything. Finally he spoke, and much more quietly than I would have expected.

"You still don't believe that we don't need you? You don't belong to us. You are wrong, you are dead wrong. That's not your mother, and I am not your father."

Whatever I might have said in reply simply didn't occur to me, and so I didn't say a word. I folded my arms across my chest and defended myself against the father who pressed against me, there being nothing in me that wanted to urge him toward a milder judgment. I simply had to accept that I would remain banished. Too much had passed during the years of separation that prevented our coming together again. Thus parents and son had to separate. So it was decided for good. I reconciled myself to it as easily as I had the moment before thought that it would be possible to be with them, though I faced facts and remained firm that I had to prepare myself to say goodbye for good. I also realized that this was the only chance I would have to say something in parting that might lend decency and dignity to the situation. I had to say something and looked deep inside myself for what my father would take away as my final and only legacy. But my intentions came to nothing. My father firmly raised his arm and waved it back and forth, such that I understood for sure that we were done with each other and that I had missed my last chance at any moment of grace. Indeed, all I could do was take a few respectful steps backward, though I continued to struggle to leave my implacable parents. I tried to gain a last glimpse of my mother, but it was impossible, as she was far removed inside a shadowy veil that her knitting had been transformed into and which was impenetrable. With his right hand, Father held me off, and with his left he covered his face as he coldly and mechanically and strangely spoke to me.

"Time's up! Now go! Off with you!"

Then I retreated quietly, softly, creeping on tiptoe. I didn't want Mother to hear that her former son was leaving her forever. I had to really make an effort to get away, for the air had become so thin that I could hardly breathe. As I left the ancient lost couple, the old man's voice called out once again.

"You should leave the apples! I could really use them!"

Whether that was the porter to the House of the Dead or my father speaking, I had no idea. It sounded too normal and pleasant to be my father. Yet I was relieved not to have to worry about the fruit any longer. I wanted to gently lay down the bag, but I was clumsy and it fell from my hands, the bag springing open and the apples tumbling across the ground. I was shocked and ashamed to have carried out the order in such a poor fashion, but I didn't want to pick up the apples, either, as they rolled around on the ground. Upset to no end, I simply fled.

It had gotten no cooler outside, but evening was approaching, the shadows stretching out long and deep over the pavement, the last rays of the sun now anxiously springing off the peering panes of the windows before they were extinguished. People hurried along, having been granted their evening as they reflected on the hours of celebration and their many pleasures. All the routes I had taken had been in vain, for I had achieved no clarity whatsoever. I had been disowned, the city didn't care about me at all, no one would look out for me, no one would offer me a roof if I wandered aimlessly around the streets. At best I would encounter a policeman, and after a suspicious look he'd order me to move along, dispatching me with a slight push in case his look wasn't enough to get me moving. No, I couldn't risk walking around the streets at night, but I had to, since the way to my parents was closed off. I had to keep a lookout for my own apartment, for it would provide me refuge, even though it had been seized at the start of the war.

I had little money on me, only the small amount I had taken along when I set out on my journey. When I arrived at the train station, I made sure to locate the collection point for homeless war refugees and asked for support. I had imagined that I was home, so I didn't think any other kind of help was necessary. You had only to walk and move a little farther along until you recognized the right building, stormed up the steps, knocked on a door that opened right up, the ruckus and roar of overwhelming welcome greeting you: "It's really you, yes, it's finally you! Just look, this is no prodigal son!" Cries of blessed thanks follow, questions and talk muttered in a sweet unconscious manner, for everything has turned out well. Between the kitchen and the living room, throughout the entire apartment the family members walk restlessly back and forth, glasses clink, plates rattle, anything available in the cupboard and pantry is hauled out and served up in order to regale the one long missed. Wasn't this how I pictured it all so beautifully? Not entirely, for I knew they were dead, all dead, yet there was one still alive, one of many, a representative, and so I deceived myself into thinking that someone would be there for me. Wasn't I born in this city? My childhood games still linger in certain corners; the familiar chatter has hardly faded. I can still hear it—it was just yesterday, it cannot all have gone silent! If that's so, why do I have to speak to some civil servant? I had left my pack at the station, someone having been happy to take it, myself unburdened and hoping for a fresh start. It smelled as of old when I walked out of the station, the wind wafting the dust of home onto my face, me hurrying next to the trolley stop across the way. I wanted to keep moving; anyone who is away for a long time doesn't let the dust gather. And so I bounded along impatiently, and as I saw the park before me I had no urge to wait. Weaned off the old place, I had to entrust myself to its walls as a convalescent; the slow allure of the remembered streets should ease the wounded heart and grant the right state of mind. Thus I had chosen—now I had to savor the error and was lost, not wanting to return to the station in order to submit myself to a horrible asylum, ticket in hand from a gruff fatherly warden, led off to a hall in a shelter full of bad air and dust: "So here's your bed. A blanket spotted with stains at the foot of it. Ten o'clock is lockdown. Seven o'clock, everyone up. Eight o'clock, coffee. Nine, everyone out."

Away, away! I had to get away. I was not in the city to which I thought I had traveled. Or if indeed it was that city, it was not me who was here and already lost within it, swallowed up by the evening. How could I begin? Away, away! Perhaps that was the wrong corner; nothing is to no avail so long as I keep walking. The wall yields and retreats the moment I really wish to go on; one step may be all that I need to take. I staggered on, I didn't know where to, yet I sensed that I was moving forward—no memory of where I was, the street names unfamiliar, the way unknown, everything shyly retreating from me. Once, I stumbled and fell down. It hurt a lot—my knee was badly done in. I staggered like a child, eventually falling hard, ashamed and weeping. All I could think to do was lie there and wait until Mother came, until she called, "Stand up! Stand up, my child! Off to bed, the bed is already made. I'll just blow a puff of air. Then the sandman will come, and Arthur will know of nothing more. Early in the morning, when you wake up, everything will be fine again." But I didn't do as she said and stand up; I was too afraid of falling again. Mother should grab hold and pick me up, for I was so light and thin, just like carrying a feather.

Yet no mother came, and no one picked me up. I didn't want to lie on the pavement until I died, so I had to help myself. Two men passed by undisturbed, one saying unkindly to the other, "That's a result of the war. The fools are not right in the head; they can't even stand on their feet. They get drunk as a skunk and roll in their own filth. Yet then they sleep well and completely at ease." The fools could have helped me, not insulted me. I wanted to yell at them, but it made no sense to get involved with strangers who showed only animosity. Already they had moved off and didn't turn to look back at me again. Awkwardly, I lifted myself up, yet I was so weak and annoyed that I couldn't stand but could only get on my knees, though one was bruised, me groaning loudly and lifting my hands in desperation, a begging little dog who couldn't help himself. A pathetic creature, I pleaded with desperate gestures. Someone should put a collar on me and attach a leash, give it a little slack, then say, "Arthur, come," with a sharp pull of the leash in order to yank me from this miserable spot. Yet no one looked after me, each person who passed by soon moving off in disgust.

Finally, a young man sauntered by who at first looked at me haltingly, then slowed his gait until he stood quietly before me and reached out his right hand. I grabbed hold of it hard, and he lifted me up. Embarrassed, I thanked him, for now I was sober again and no longer just a dog.

"Are those your apples?"

The man pointed to a ripped-open bag that lay on the ground. Two apples had fallen out and lay shamefully old, gray, and ugly in the dusty street. Were these apples mine? I should have answered no, for I had given my apples to my dead father. How could they again have ended up in my possession? I stared uncertainly at the ground, since they lay there plucked and ignored, helpless and tossed away. There was no doubt about it—Kutschera had picked them out for me. Yet hadn't many customers gotten them? No, they couldn't be mine. It would be too cumbersome to explain to the young man the long story, the visit to my father, and then the remarkable coincidence that, right at the very spot where I had fallen, there lay the same kind of apples, but which didn't belong to me. All I needed was to tell a white lie.

"I don't eat apples."

"Apples that cost a bundle these days? One can't just leave them lying here. If they don't belong to you, may I have them?"

"It's not up to me. Many thanks for helping me out in such a friendly way. I have to get going, it's late."

The man gathered up the apples and hurried back to my side, for I had taken a couple of blind steps on my own.

"Man, what a killing! You don't find apples on the street every day."

"Oh, I don't think it's that hard. There's Kutschera in the Reitergasse. He has the most beautiful apples!"

"In the Reitergasse? Kutschera? Oh, him! Is that the one next to the closed shop?"

"Yes, next to Haberdashery Albert Landau."

"Was that a clothing store?"

"Yes, of course. Men's clothes. Very nice clothes."

"Probably at the start of the war? One of the ones that were closed at the start of the war?"

"Was it closed at the start of the war?"

"I think so, for it's empty now."

"You're not sure?"

"No. I mean, not exactly. I wasn't yet in the city back then. I moved here later. But surely you know as well that many shops were closed back then. Simply taken away. Some were sold at a loss, some were taken over by others. Whether or not they will return to the same hands—who knows? I don't. Yet most of them are dead."

"Yes, Landau the clothier appears to be entirely dead. I stopped by there today. Kutschera is alive; Landau is dead."

"Landau dead. That could be. But many are still alive. Not all of them were killed. Some escaped to other countries or were liberated. Landau isn't one of them."

"How do you know?"

"It's what I think. He would be pretty old already. They were all killed, if they didn't leave beforehand."

"Yes, but how could you know him if you weren't in the city and never visited his shop?"

"I don't know him. But as you talked I remembered that a girlfriend of mine knew all about it. She once told me as we were walking through the Reitergasse that this family was sent away."

"So your girlfriend knew . . . ?"

"Yes. I suppose she did."

"Do you think your girlfriend knows more about Landau?"

"Certainly possible. But I can't guarantee it."

The young man thought to himself for a little while and then looked at me, as unsure as when he had helped me to my feet.

"Listen, I have an idea. Let me visit my friend Anna Meisenbach. If you have the time and inclination, you can come along."

I looked at him gratefully. Would I like to come along? Did I have time? Perhaps I had time; in any case, I was tempted to find the time. The lost years had stolen time from me, or it had unraveled, someone having yanked away at it too hard and it tearing into thin shreds. I couldn't go chasing after it, for I was held back, submerged, then everything was lost. Once I finally could walk away, I had to move as fast as I could in no time at all in order to save what I could.

"I might just have some time."

I said that for myself, really, and asked the man not to walk too fast. Although I had my fall as an excuse, it was not so much the leg that kept me from keeping up with his stride as the nagging fear of having met someone whom I didn't know but who could possibly produce evidence about my father, my mother, and even me. In addition, I didn't feel quite right about rudely detaining a man who was rushing to his girlfriend, for who knows how impatiently she might be waiting for him, no matter how generously he offered to help me. That's why I forced myself to walk along more quickly; it was indeed in my interest to figure out if I had come to the right city or if everything had to remain to no avail. I was tempted to ask the young man about his girlfriend, but I didn't think it right to meet his friendliness with curiosity. What did his love or his love story have to do with me? He was in love, and if he felt loved in return, how happy I was for him! Twenty-four or twenty-five years old, I guessed, but he could also have been only twenty, the war perhaps having sped up the maturing process. But then how old might the sweetheart be? No doubt some young thing, most likely younger than the boy. How could I have any idea about her if she had been no more than a child at the start of the war? What information could she give me about my parents?

She'd never met my parents and knew about them only from hearsay. She was the daughter of a customer who complimented the nice clothes and who came home grumpy one day and said, "You wouldn't believe what happened! I was walking through the Reitergasse and it suddenly occurred to me that it wouldn't be a bad idea to pick up some new handkerchiefs. How lucky to have Landau right here! But I looked and looked. Everything was shut. As if boarded up. The fruit vendor next door, with a fat, ruddy face like an apple that's been baked, he stopped me and said nonchalantly, 'You buy from him? Well, it's all gone now. Yesterday they closed the shop.' I asked, 'How is that possible?' Just imagine what he said! It all happened quickly, he told me. Two men in a car pulled up, went in, threw Landau and his employees out on the street, thrashed around inside the shop, hauled out some stuff, loaded it in the car, locked the door, sealed up the joint, and saying, 'All right, let's get out of here,' they sped away in their car. Just like in a gangster novel." The girl's father had told them about this between bites of his supper, for he could hardly believe what was happening these days, and yet he had to keep chewing, for he was very hungry, and his wife could only shake her head and say, "It's hard to believe what's happening. Those poor people." Then she dished out the pear compote she'd made, each getting a hearty portion. The father sighed quietly, the situation bothering him, for he couldn't swallow well at all, and then they talked about other things in order to lift their spirits.

The daughter had matured early and was striking. She took all this in stride, although the situation didn't mean anything to her, nor had she asked any questions. But, ever since that day, whenever she passed by the old shop in the Reitergasse she remembered the story, until eventually she shared it with the boyfriend. It wasn't right to be brought along to the girl; it was senseless, nothing more than pressing weakness on my part. What should I say to such a stranger, given how I looked? What kind of looks and talks would I have to endure? Why was I schlepping out of my house so tired at night? All of it just to satisfy a morbid curiosity that could only end up a useless, painful lump of knowledge? I no longer wanted to see the girl.

"Listen, I really don't want to bother you."

The boyfriend protested that I wasn't bothering him at all. There were perhaps other unknown men, I thought, but not such as I, instead people with purpose and intent, led by reason, people who lived there and would stay awhile, who were expected and would bring along flowers or lovely apples, but none like me. That's why I wanted to impress upon the boyfriend that my visit was pointless. Indeed, I actually had something I had to do this evening; perhaps I could look him up another time, so if I could just write down the address quickly and then send a card, though tonight there wasn't enough time for an unexpected guest. And yet I couldn't get out all of my objections, because the boyfriend began to chat away mindlessly. Then he looked at me again and asked whether I had been injured in my fall, since I seemed so tired as I got up. "You need a doctor" is what he said. I clearly heard it. Though he meant well, it sounded hard and threatening. I had no desire to see a doctor, and refused to do so.

"Is it taking too long, or do you see that I'm limping?"

That wasn't it. The young man smiled. I was walking fine, nor did we have too far to go, as it was close by in the Klemensgasse. It was already dusk when we arrived there. He pointed to a new building.

"Here she is."

"What a way to talk about a person. You mean your sweetheart, but then you point to an entire building!"

I had said it sharply, with painful fervor, and I was conscious for the first time of an embarrassing transgression as the young man stood before me and grabbed hold of my hand hard.

"I didn't mean to upset you," I said. "It was spoken to the wind—strangely, absurdly, no doubt awful and insulting to hear, but I swear to you, it wasn't directed at you."

"Well, then, at who?"

"At . . . at . . . excuse me, not at you, not at you and not at me, at no one at all. It just slipped out."

"Frau Meisenbach is not my sweetheart."

"I have to tell you, I had no idea. I meant no one at all, least of all you. It was just a dream. I also don't want to burden you any further. It's already late. The evening sky is red. I have to be moving on. Not to worry. I will write sometime and explain it all. I have your name and address. Goodbye."

The young man didn't let go of me. I didn't have the strength to pull away.

"You still want to—"

"Certainly. But another time. I promise. But not now. Please, let me go! Someone is expecting me—"

Then I was overcome by a horrible weakness, only his clinging grasp of my wrist holding me up. I dangled from this grip, a helpless puppet, having also lost the ability to speak.

"You must come with me now. There's an elevator. So you don't have to stay in the street."

The boyfriend realized that I couldn't move on my own. He took me under the arm and dragged me through the front door to the elevator. He then pushed the call button and, rumbling melodically, the car descended from a higher floor.

"I really can't do this as a stranger, and in this condition. . . . Please try to understand. . . . What will Frau Meisenbach think . . . ?"

So I stammered on about not wanting to be an intrusion, but that made no impression, and in fact I had to give in, for I would have collapsed on the spot if I hadn't entrusted myself to the care of my companion. Also, a glimmer of hope rose within me that I might find some kind of mercy, a haven, one that perhaps would manifest itself under the roof of a proper apartment building. Perhaps Frau Meisenbach would suggest that I stay for an hour or so and rest until they decided where I could spend the night.

With a rush of air the elevator arrived, and the boyfriend opened the door. I looked questioningly at him and hesitated once again, but it had been decided already. I was shoved forward, the outer door banged shut, the inner door was pulled close, it clanged, then it growled low and deep, the two of us rising continually upward. There was a mirror in the narrow car, but I closed my eyes. I think I slept on the way up, for I was aware of nothing. The door swung open wide as I opened my eyes with trepidation and gazed ahead, blinking into the milky light as if looking through dust.

"We're there, Herr Lan—"

"Long . . ." No, don't say the name! I was on my toes and quickly corrected him. "Long. No, it didn't take all that long!"

I didn't give myself away and got out of a pinch, though what my stupid sentence said was the opposite of what I felt, and that immediately helped. For the first time since I had gotten off the train, I was awake and clear-headed, my self-confidence rising. Things were now steady, the experiences lining themselves up in an observable pattern and displayed across from me, readable as a wall and clearly something that was independent of me, not tangled up with me, which even made clear that I was myself, without question a being in an allotted place amid certain surroundings. I braced myself in order to remain strong, my worries capable of being shoved away, but my legs betrayed me and I faltered. The elevator that rose through the stairwell was cold and only caused me to sense that a clammy heat oozed from my pores. I looked around, a shadow in front of me covering up the sight of the young man who had gotten me into the elevator or had wanted to do so without my knowing.

"You'll send the elevator back down now, right? I can't help thinking that it needs to be back down below soon."

This I said because I heard it moving and was pleased that the narrow chamber, with its dangerous mirror, was moving away. The strangeness of my talk no longer surprised the young man, for he had gotten used to my foolish demeanor. If he at all regretted having picked me up off the street, there was nothing to be done. Now he was indeed obliged to take me to Frau Meisenbach. He approached a door and I followed slowly, the light flickering before my eyes. The boyfriend pressed three times quickly on the doorbell, which gave off a shrill sound.

"Three times so that she knows that it's us. . . . I mean, you never know these days."

The young man intentionally ignored my words and said nothing, standing in front of the door with a broad chest and blocking it. I stood two steps to the side. As things began to stir in the apartment, I looked meekly in the direction of another door. "Peter!" my companion called out, and the door opened right up as I strained to decipher the letters on a nameplate, as if I weren't with my companion. Not wanting to surprise anyone, I waited patiently to see if I would be invited in.

"I brought someone along, Anna, who wants to speak with you."

There where I stood, half in darkness, I couldn't be seen at all well. Twisting around to look at Anna, who peered searchingly out the door, I recognized her immediately. It was Anna Seiler, now Frau Meisenbach, the younger sister of Arno Seiler, whom I went to school with. I stepped toward her and said hello.

"Perhaps you don't know who I am. I've changed a lot, and it's been a while, but once . . . How is your brother Arno? We went to school together."

Anna's gaze remained fixed; she gave no sign of recognition. Peter shook his head for reasons that remained unknown to me, perhaps out of anger, though I spoke to her again. The apartment appeared to consist of only one room, it being large, but also seeming narrow, because it was chock-full of furniture and bookshelves to the ceiling. I was offered a chair, which surprised me. Anna was dressed in black—in fact, all in black. Was she in mourning? It wasn't at all clear, for it could be that she chose the dark material to set off her pale cheeks. Anna waited to hear what I had to say, Peter pacing back and forth in the room, the narrowness of the room forcing the chair to be leaned up against the wall. I was tempted to say how much his restless wandering bothered me, yet I kept quiet, since it didn't appear to bother Anna. Discontented or embarrassed, I sat through this annoying back-and-forth through the narrow passage for a while, hoping futilely that Peter would finally come to a stop and say something. Yet there was no help coming from him, and I had nothing to say. How I had gotten here now seemed distant. I was only happy that I could rest, though I shuddered to think how I might save myself in the next hours. Anna made my situation no easier and seemed clueless. She stood there puzzled, looking concerned and becoming more and more serious, thoughts full of worry pressing at her countenance. Then I remembered that I hadn't introduced myself. She had not recognized me at all and was wrestling with the reason for my visit. I owed her an explanation, but I didn't want to divulge my name. Finally, I broke the silence.

"Sometimes one goes to other people and doesn't know what one wants. That's what I've done. A chance encounter in the street"—I nodded obligingly to Peter—"a fleeting incident, then a request—one is invited"—again I nodded—"and is too weak to say no. Then you are there, sitting down, bringing confusion in tow and remaining powerless to speak or admit your mistake. I thank you for your hospitality and ask your forgiveness."

With that I wanted to rise, bow deeply to the lady, wave to Peter, and get out of there. But I was detained.

"You can't just leave now. It's too late; I've prepared a meal. Peter is hungry, and you must eat with us."

I would have been happy to lie and say that I had already had dinner and that this evening I had an important appointment, but Anna could read the falseness of all possible protests in my eyes.

"It can only do you good to get some sustenance. If you want to leave, we can talk later. But I've prepared plenty of food."

Turning her attention away from me, she brought out everything needed. It all looked lovely, but not as one would expect in a regular household. Plates, little serving bowls, a little basket, and the silverware—all of it mismatched and well used. Clean as each object was, everything still had a strange glow, as if it were broken, or didn't belong to Anna, almost as if it were something accidentally or hastily passed along, and which the new owner had not gotten accustomed to yet. Peter had finally ended his restless wandering through the room and attentively helped Anna, yet somewhat clumsily and childlike. I would have been happy to help out, and offered to do so, but they refused, for it didn't take much and everything was soon done. Then I asked if I could wash my hands, as I had not yet been home today and wanted to freshen up a bit. Anna said she was sorry that the bathroom was so full of stuff, for she had too many things that she didn't know what to do with, nor would the hot water be on now. Peter showed me the way and then disappeared, but then soon knocked on the door again, Anna having sent a fresh towel.

I was happy to be able to collect myself alone and also give them the chance to talk about me, given the circumstances. I would have loved to figure out how I could finally conclude my visit, how I could reveal who I was and, after a credible explanation of why I had come, get out of there as fast as I could. Yet since I couldn't come up with any kind of clever plan I simply decided to take things as they came, such that in general anything I said would be as close to the truth as I could make it. Then I would ask Peter whether or not he could recommend a cheap place to bunk for the night. He'd be happy to do so and would give me some suggestions. If he didn't know of any, then I would just have to ruefully and quietly creep back to the train station, where they would have to send me to a homeless shelter or to a police station to sleep.

When I came back into the room, everything was nicely laid out. The two of them were already sitting, though they had waited for me to start eating. Anna looked much fresher than earlier; Peter's boyish resolute face remained open and curious. The food, good and simple, tasted wonderful. I was pampered, the two of them having given me the best portions. They had decided together to feed me properly before they let me go. It tasted good, for it had been many hours since I'd eaten, but I was no smarter. I not only had no idea what they intended to do with me; I didn't know whether Anna had actually been told by Peter the reason for my visit. During the meal there was only a bit of light talk, then Anna cleared the table and Peter made coffee. I wanted to start talking right away and say to Anna that I owed her an explanation, but she was the one who turned to me.

"You asked about Arno. So, then, what can you tell me about him?"

"About Arno. . . . It's been a long time. I've hardly seen him since we were in school."

"Hardly. . . . Okay, you say hardly. But maybe that's right. I mean, you know . . . something about his last days. Before it was over."

But there was nothing for me to know. Arno, that was long ago. I had nothing to do with him. Because of the war, I had not had anything to do with him for ages, and I had hardly seen him in the years before then. In the earliest school years, I had always liked him a lot. He was clever. Professor Prenzel praised some of his essays, he being always eager, always smart, too much for me, one of the brave who believe they have seized hold of life, rather than being led by life, a force of nature. But later I was not so fond of Arno, and his opinions hardened. Only when I happened to bump into him did I exchange a few fleeting words.

"I don't really remember."

"Don't go easy on me! I already know a lot. He is not the first one that I've lost."

"Arno is dead? How terrible! He shouldn't have died."

Those were careless words. I was shocked at my coldness. This Arno, a person, how dumb . . . What did that have to do with anything? The poor soul—I should be sympathetic, for he was dead. . . . Anna didn't draw back from what I said, so my tone had not sounded so cold after all.

"Don't you know? I thought, even if different people meet different fates and your questions at the start revealed that you didn't know anything about his end . . . Nonetheless, one tries. . . . Well, yes, you have come for completely different reasons. . . . Peter already told me."

"No. I don't know anything about Arno. I am really very sorry. I never saw him, never heard anything about him. Really. Which is why I can't help you. I can only express my regret. My sincere regret. Too many have been lost."

"I am always trying to learn something."

"To learn something, of course . . . Who isn't?"

Anna looked blank and hopeless, but not destroyed. The brother wasn't her only sorrow. Peter thought for a minute, needing to explain something.

"Arno was political."

"Political? Yes, so many were political. It's always the same story, whenever . . ."

I sought for words in vain and felt how much I looked the fool. I should have apologized for this nonsense, but to my surprise it was Anna who offered words of forgiveness.

"Now the survivors are coming home, and indeed they were away, for sure. . . . One can see it. Please understand, whenever I meet one of them, then I think that perhaps I can learn something more specific from him. . . . "

"Does one want to know?" I asked.

"Perhaps . . . perhaps one doesn't. But when it touches you personally, then you must. And you said you had been at school with him. We heard that he's dead. Someone wrote us. He supposedly was a cobbler there. People learned to do new things. Then he got sick . . . his heart . . . dead. It's what killed my father years ago."

I murmured something, nothing but empty blather, there being no real sympathy in my words.

"Don't worry. I understand. It was all too much, it all went wrong. I can imagine how there was no one there who knew him at the end. But you always think that something will happen, and someone who was there will show up and pass on a greeting, a last message, a little memory that you can hold before your eyes and really believe."

"No, I wasn't there. There were so many places where we were. It must have happened someplace else."

Anna said the last word she had from Arno had been more than three years ago. Everything fine, just as she had gotten used to hearing every month—he was healthy, confident, almost carefree—and then ten days later the official word: it was all over. Despite diligent care and good medications, or so it said. Nothing did any good. Anna's account, indeed, was full of regret and sadness, yet I remarked all the more keenly that my having been at school with him was simply not enough for the sister, for she was looking for certainty. That I could see for sure.

"Yes, I agree, one wants to know. When we don't witness the death of our parents or siblings, when we can never be taken to a cemetery and told that they are here under this mound, then they are gone and remain gone, but they are not dead. We have no peace and must look for them. Often, you are startled and believe, there they are. You hear voices, mistake others for them. There is no peace to be had—sleep and dreams and truth comingle and cannot be distinguished from one another. That's how it is for me. It confuses me, makes me afraid and overly sensitive. You look for a witness, someone who was there when it happened. The most unbearable truth is more bearable than the somewhat familiar fog of sweet uncertainty. With Arno it's not as bad as it could be, Frau Meisenbach. The authorities at least let you know that he is dead. Terrible that he's dead, and yet good that he's dead, something certain around which different ideas can form. Certainly he suffered a great deal, all of it inhuman, violence, abuse, murder, harrowing and beastly, especially if it went on for many days before the light was extinguished or he met a final coup de grâce. There was nothing graceful about it. But the end is certain, it is recorded, it can't be changed. You can, you must, believe it. But how when there is nothing, neither an end nor a continuance?"

Peter wanted to know what I meant by that, whether the lot of those missing is more terrible than the fate of those who have fallen and been killed. I didn't know how to answer him, saying that it remained to be seen if it was a fate at all, for it was without name, and I was not at all certain if the nameless could have a fate.

"Those are just words," he replied. "The missing and those known to be dead—there is no real difference between them. The cases where someone returns will, nonetheless, remain rare."

"Ah, it's not about whether it's rare or never or often. If one turns up and is there, then he will speak. But the condition of the missing who have gone away is that they are away, far away, not a word from them, even the place where they have been taken unknowable, whether they have been shot or poisoned and the bodies burned and the pulverized ashes scattered; no one wrote it down and preserved the names, because it is memory that has been murdered more and more thoroughly than a speaking life. That is not fate. That is worse than the missing in action. A marked departure into the unknown. A war memorial will have a name that one can think about. But the ones I mean are never even allowed to be called missing. They are the non-missing, of whom there is no account. Completely and utterly done away with. Unwanted and therefore not missed. Disappeared, the loss of their memory met with derisive laughter. Released from all fates, expelled from the worst of fates. People who existed until a certain yet unknown date, then no longer, no longer people, not even dead people but, rather, nothing at all. Do you understand that, Herr Peter?"

The young man turned red, snorted several times, and shrugged at what I said, but he didn't take it in at all.

"Just Peter, not Herr Peter, please! Oh, God, people! Of course that's awful, yet all are expendable. We mourn, but the world doesn't. And later we probably won't mourn, either, and our descendants certainly won't any longer. One doesn't weep for one's great-grandfather. But things of value that are lost are irreplaceable. Burned-out galleries, Gothic domes, Baroque palaces—these are the true losses. That's what I think."

What Peter thought was completely understandable, but I couldn't understand it then and was insulted, and it took a while before I could trust what I thought I had heard. I said with a weak voice: "A person, a single person who survives, is equal to all the destroyed treasures on earth!"

This was not at all what the young man had meant. He said that I was upset, the war having done in the nerves of many, yet I needed to think clearly and admit that people value themselves too much, the self-love of their hungry will to live, but works are worth infinitely more than their creators.

"So, then, you believe," asked Anna, "that the world is worth more than God?"

The young man fell silent and lifted his shoulders ambiguously. I didn't want to get tangled up in such deep matters, such heavy words, but there was one thing I wanted to know from Peter.

"Things went well for you in the war, yes?"

"Yes, I suppose you could say that. Indeed, they did. I was neither in battle nor locked up."

"And nothing happened to you?"

"No. Nothing at all, really."

"And no loved one died, nobody disappeared?"

These questions bothered Peter, as he fidgeted in his chair, grabbed the coffee pot, and poured me some. But he didn't give any answer. So I pressed harder.

"You said to me earlier on the street that you knew that many had died, especially older people. Do you remember? You weren't at all affected?"

"Not a single old person of mine. Please don't grill me! There was plenty of bad news in my family. My oldest brother was burned in a plane attack. I loved him very much. I will never forget him. But to always think about that? My God, what good does that do when one wants to live? I want to live. I don't want to perish."

"Ah, to perish—what that even means! But suffering, do you really know what suffering is?"

"I don't think about that. I know all I need to know. Without justice, there's also no life."

"Not only without justice. You are alive or you're not. Justice is something completely different and hardly has anything to do with life."

"You should know that Peter's wife is in prison. He's working to get her free. She didn't do anything. The way things are these days . . . I can't say anything more."

"I know little or nothing about the way things are these days. Just so that you know the truth, I arrived here today. Why, if I may ask, was your dear wife . . . ?"

"Why was she. . . ?" Peter repeated the question. "It's always the same. It happens. Injustice never ends."

"But she's alive? You know that? You also know where she is?"

"Yes, I know, and I damn well shall set her free as well!"

"Look, then, all is not lost! You have something to live for. You even think you'll succeed in the end. You just need to point out that an injustice has been done, that's what I think, a terrible injustice. But you don't have to worry about your wife being murdered. As bad as things are, she isn't going to just disappear into thin air."

"But the disgrace!"

"Oh, come on! There's no disgrace in prison, and injustice disgraces no one!"

"No, it's not prison or whatever you might think. Just pure disgrace. A pack of drunken victorious soldiers attacked women, even young girls. That doesn't seem to bother the noble liberators."

"And how do you know all this?"

"You're so naïve! You just know it if you want to."

"Really? Were you there and saw it all happen?"

"May I speak for Peter? Rape, hunger, abuse, and murder. Even children are not spared. Anyone knows who is at all interested."

"That can't be true!"

"Oh, it's true!" Anna made perfectly clear. "I'll tell you all about it, if you want to listen. The streets have indeed been cleared of trouble, but they're all locked up in the stadium. But, I agree, unhappiness is not always inescapable. One can help out and do something. Peter will manage it; he's smart. He's allowed to visit his wife. It costs a lot, but it happens, for the guards are corrupt. In addition, one can also learn from them what's gone on."

I was then informed more precisely. The deeds of the liberators were laid out, Anna and Peter allowing me to forget the reason for my visit. Messengers. Torches burning, skulls cracked open and bodies spewing blood. Old people shoved into toilets, where they drowned. Children starving in prisons, wasting away amid the vermin until they died of neglect. It was all so horrible. But I was a lucky man, for I could now be happy that I was free and no one abused me. I had survived; what did any of these new troubles have to do with me? The tales of the horrors returned past terrors to me as present once again, all of it plausible, I not doubting any of it, though it was hard for me to listen to such beastliness, for it was something I no longer had to see, no longer had to suffer.

Before this day everything had been an evil saga, I told myself, and yet I thought, because I had been set free, it was all over. Only as the dark blazing power of the past did this saga hang over me and dog all my future days. There stood the bent figure of my father. He was almost naked, and in his right hand he held a lovely new shirt, like a loaf of white bread, and offered it as a modest gift to a splendid man on a leash who had the head of a dog. Father wanted to save Mother, who, with closed eyes and lips, stuffed in a gray sack, stood behind him.

Father began, "Listen, my friend, behind me is Eva, the mother. She bore two children. A daughter who was taken from her at birth, and a son, who is alive somewhere. Spare this mother!"

The man with the head of a dog looked at the old couple, and the begging old man displeased him. The dog's head nodded a snide disrespectful reply. Why should he spare her? He had bashed the heads of children against walls and not learned to spare them. The father knew nothing of the dog head's bloody hands and proffered the shirt, stroking it with trembling hands to smooth it out, in order that it lay spread before him like a virgin snowfield, though the dog's head stared at his victim with fierce disdain before he stamped it into the ground, staining it with shit and blood, until it was no longer a shirt at all. Then the dog's head stared at his victim up and down. But the father had no other gifts, and pointed with his arms toward the ground, where the ripped-off sleeves of the shirt, two burst stems, lay stretched out and rigid, hardly recognizable.

"I can give you no more, but only serve you. If you give me flax, I will spin and weave and dye it. Then I'll cut you a new shirt and sew it for you."

The dog's head stood his ground: he didn't need any clothes. He was fitted out from head to toe, he was the armored power, ready to murder and gobble up anything in its path. Such power had no mother and therefore knew no mercy. It stepped forward, at first slowly and hesitantly, then suddenly stomping for real and pummeling the ragged sleeves of the disgraced shirt. The father still wouldn't yield, and stood like a solid wall, yet he was pushed aside; his limbs collapsing, he sank to the ground. The dog's head lashed out and pounced on the silent mother. "Eva, Eva!" he said. "Your old man can't protect you, Eva. Your children are murderers; your own blood betrayed you. There is no end to hate. Brothers and sisters are at each other's throats and, never satisfied, they gobble up father and mother." Then the dog's head killed the mother, such that she no longer was and was gone for good. The world had become motherless.

Then everything went dark, only the sharp eyes of the locomotive glaring as it raced through the grim night, the raging dog's head hissing through the deathly afraid, sleeping lands. I lay chained up on the open coal car behind the locomotive, which pulled the thundering unmanned train over clanking bridges and through echoing gorges and could do nothing to stop it. The power of the locomotive was massive, but I lay on the coal, half deaf and my back rubbing raw, and then it started to rain, hopeless streams of tears. I surrendered helplessly, there being no lever to reach for to stop the relentless forward motion. Then, hissing, it began to climb the mountain, where, way off, an immense gate inscribed with huge letters rose up. At first I couldn't read what it said, but soon enough I saw it shine brightly: "Welcome to Peace!" A wild roar rose up, voices mixed in, something unintelligible was sung, glowing tatters of lofty music, but also the abominable shriek of saws, drills, rattling motors, mechanical valves—all of it getting louder and louder. After we were finally through the gate, suddenly it all went silent, everything dark, nothing more to hear or see.

I didn't know whether I was meant to go on, nor did it seem up to me to decide. Yet, since peace was promised me, I also now had to win my freedom, and so I sought with my last strength to break my chains. I almost managed it, but the chains were too strong and wouldn't burst. Then I strained painfully to see whether I could vanquish the darkness—if, indeed, there was peace. My eyes darted about. I saw, I saw, it worked, and mine was the victory! Something pressed back at me, at which I wearily turned my head to the side, which made it easier, while on my hands I could still feel the clamps, though I quietly sensed that it almost allowed me to rest. The space around me was suffused with a mild light, amid which a question was posed.

"Are you feeling better?"

"What do you mean, better? Why am I lying here?"

It took a while before I came to and reluctantly learned that I had taken ill. I had been placed unconscious on the divan and treated with wet cloths and cologne.

"What trouble have I caused you?"

"None at all," said Anna. "Not if you're feeling better. What do you need? A cognac? Coffee? I have the real stuff. Scrambled eggs? A doctor?"

"No, no, I'm fine. I've taken up too much of your time. I have no idea how that could have happened, nor how you've had to put up with such difficulties."

"Please, let's have none of that!"

"Good, good. But I mustn't bother you any longer."

I stood up, feeling a bit chilly.

"It is certainly much too late. I really need to be getting home."

Peter offered to take me home, but Anna felt—and she was right—that I was still too weak, and maybe later would be better.

"Tell me, is it very far? Where, in fact, do you live?"

"I can't say," I whispered sadly, and then once more, "I can't say. Yet I'll find it, nonetheless. It can't be that far. Around the corner. Behind the wall. If I could just get going . . ."

"But only if I accompany you," said Peter.

"Why, because of what happened earlier? You're too kind. But, really, I'm all right. All that way, a gate, welcome . . . peace . . ."

"What's that? It seems to me you don't have an apartment. Come with me! I have a good couch free in my room. Shall we?"

I looked gratefully at Peter.

"If it's no bother. Naturally, just for tonight."

"As many nights as you wish, until you find something good for yourself."

It was late. Peter was ready to go, and I was just as ready myself, yet I still wasn't steady on my feet.

"Why don't you stay tonight. Tomorrow we can talk about it all."

"You couldn't take in a stranger," I replied.

"A schoolmate of Arno's."

"I really wasn't friends with him."

"That doesn't matter."

"And you just have this one room."

"That doesn't matter at all."

"But your husband. What will—"

"I'm a widow."

"A widow . . . ?"

"The war."

"I see. But what about the other tenants? If it got around—"

"Not to worry. You're being childish."

"You don't even know my name."

"You never introduced yourself."

"No, I didn't."

That's all I said, rather than set things straight.

"You seem to have had a rough time of it. Yet I don't need to know your name."

"You should."

"As you wish."

"It's difficult. The name is difficult for me to say. There's too much attached to it. Too much of the past on top of everything else. But I have to say it."

"Give it time!"

"You know there are people who forget their names, their addresses, everything."

"Yes, I've heard of them. That must be terrible."

"Terrible? Not at all, for it would be nothing but a boon. When you have had everything taken away, there's nothing to know. I could well imagine that one could begin over again. Such people are taken into a city, asked nothing about what used to be, and the authorities give them papers with fresh names."

"You could just change your old name."

"I could, that's right. But that doesn't help. You still know the old one, and that still troubles you. One has to begin completely anew. Nameless, in order to get a proper name. Neophilius Neander."

I had to laugh, but I didn't feel well when I did. I was tired, and yet I stood and looked around the room, only because I was confused. No one was tempted to extend this conversation, and Peter asked if he could help with anything. He wanted to leave, as it was almost midnight. No, Anna didn't need anything. Then it was agreed that Peter should come the next day, but not too early. My immediate future would be decided then—whether

I would move in with him, and my entire situation. Peter reached out his hand to me, his grip trusting, yet too strong. Confused, I thanked him, and he smiled boyishly, yet in a leathery manner. He left behind the apples from the street, for they indeed belonged to me, or at least that's how he felt. I protested. Yes, I had some apples earlier today, but they disappeared long before I fell. Peter didn't continue to insist that they belonged to me, but they also didn't belong to him. Lovely apples, he said. Anna should have them. Then he left, whistling low, and didn't say anything more. It occurred to me that Peter was one of those carefree people who suddenly and with no particular purpose show up in a streetcar or a train compartment when it's fairly crowded or completely overfull, such that you have no chance to flee when he begins whistling in your ear.

Anna walked her guest out the door, saying that I should make myself comfortable, it wouldn't take long. I thought that she would wait for the elevator with him, but as she quietly closed the apartment door behind her I knew that I would be alone for longer. At first I looked around a bit, the books attracting my attention. Upon closer inspection I noticed that only the spines were wiped clean, whereas the rest of the books were dusty and had not been read. I felt like reading, as I was no longer tired. I had already run my thumb along the spine of a brown volume and pressed my middle finger at the top of it. Then I changed my mind, I had lost all desire. How about a philosopher? No, I didn't want that. I pulled my hand back and saw the soft flecks of pale dust pressed into the length of my fingertip, the mark of a rummaging bookishness. It was strange. I had to rub awhile before the flecks were wiped away. Then I sat down in an armchair that filled a corner of the room.

Herr Meisenbach would normally come home at night, shake away the dust, and sit himself down, a book in hand, the assets of wisdom, he happy to read and read, the pages turning as his wife tends to him, and he reads aloud to her. And now she is unfaithful; it's as easy as that. All it took was for him not to come home just once, he having made a mistake, for he was dead . . . the war. A stranger, or almost a stranger, sits in the realm of the dead one and doesn't say his name. The books now represent neither assets nor wisdom, for the dust has gathered on them. I was ashamed, yet I was defenseless. What excuse did I have? There was no picture of the deceased anywhere in the room. Alas, Herr Meisenbach was gone without even a picture left behind, since he was no longer welcome, done away with, only one thing still tolerated, and that was the dust. Not a single sign that he had even lived. The books now ownerless goods, abandoned, strange, no longer even cleaned. Ordered out of his home, he left wife and apartment and all his possessions behind. He would return, a cheerful wave, turning the corner, around a wall and gone. He would come, an echo bouncing off the walls. He would come, he would come, it was true, promised at the last moment, there was no doubt of it. What kind of man was he? He had deceived the future widow and was gone. Frau Meisenbach had to put up with it all; she was trapped. We all have to die, and doubt did no good at all. But what was I doing? I roused myself awake in my armchair and looked up.

Here I sit and see what's around me on West Park Row, and I still don't recognize anything. I have let myself drift too far into the otherworldly, and that's the reason nothing is left of me. It's the cause of my difficulties. Others simply make up their minds or their minds are made up for them, and thus they find a place in the world that is their own, it becoming clear that others are pleased with them. They keep themselves neat and have a job. It makes little sense for me to compare myself with such people, especially in this country, which seems so secure. I learn nothing from such comparisons, for, without feeling envious, I can't help feeling that it wouldn't do me any good to be more like them. They go their way, and thereby I recognize an order that is surprising, and by which I am almost awestruck in my feeling of detachment from the frigid night of these surroundings. The rest of you, just go your own way! The world left me behind on my own, more and more from year to year, the postwar years only reinforcing this separation after some doubtful breakthroughs that took place and were done, it all having been put into effect during the war. Still, I had hoped to be able to get free of them when, with tentative hopes for a new beginning, I fled the place of my overwhelming past for the metropolis. But here I was, at a dead end on West Park Row. With a great deal of skill, Johanna had discovered the little house and brought me here, but with the acquisition of this hideout I was not so much snug as always hidden, and now here I was, once again setting forth into the rattling fan of days, fed and cared for, allowed to rest and sleep through the night so that I would have enough strength for the waking hours and keep myself busy, even as the day rattled on, thought following upon thought, the last one always falling away with the next churn of the fan.

Thus was I administered to, Johanna making it all happen, providing for my every wish, setting things down in dry terms, giving me something definite to do, something easy and yet meaningful, something certain and harmlessly predatory, such as the green market, with its fruit and vegetable stands, Johanna sending me there twice a week in the morning with two large sacks in order to choose and purchase something useful after I took Michael to school, he trembling with excitement and mischief as we crossed two dangerous intersections. Johanna embellished me, she the master, turning me into what she wished for, such that I would be a naïve, cheery man. She created him, she set him there, yet I am only a child sent outside and cannot go my own way. She fills the hours that I should know on my own with playful stuff in the little garden, letting me count the blossoms on the strawberries. Everything is lovely, she thinks, and she's happy when, uncertainly, I tell her the number of blossoms, it sounding like a dark echo of her own voice. Johanna portions out to me what's bearable, such as the rumbling sounds of the boy, the rummaging curiosity of our little daughter, Eva, it also often showing up in the sweetness of the mindful sounds with which Johanna fills the patient house while tending to things from morning to night. Johanna is happy to do so, because she loves me, and if I could feel thankful I would express it always in the morning and never at night. But Johanna is fast and goes about her business quickly, though she never looks for gratitude. Instead, I am always surprised anew that she is satisfied. I get worried about her when I see that her activities have no real point. How long will she stand my showing only empty hands each evening, it all threatening to go on indefinitely? I ask her, touched to the core, but without betraying what I feel, whether she is disappointed at not being able to change me, yet she dismisses it all. She says we have enough to get by, as I swallow down the last of it.

"A husband's support." I said that once, only as an attempt to seize hold of a fading wish, but Johanna shot back nothing more than merciful surprise. Sometimes I tried to figure out whether what she would have me believe was real, but I only sensed a suppressed pain in her that was not visible.

It's all the same to her: the worries themselves, the numerous shortcomings of our household; none of it bothers her. It serves only to inspire her to a higher art. The essence of this art is patience; that's all that's needed, and it provides a relaxed, ongoing play in the return of reassuring conditions for my difficult-to-reassure, always disturbed, painful existence. How well it suits me that this tattered house puts up with me as an inhabitant in this meager neighborhood of careworn people. One can think whatever of me, but people live their lives without having to know about my empty troubles, for the stranger doesn't bother the street at all.

Only Johanna knows, but what does she know? Almost nothing, and even that she covers up. Welcome to Peace. But will the children ever know it? No, Michael and Eva don't know anything, at least not yet; that way, they don't get confused. They have their time, and what is past should not bother them. When they finally learn, it will by then be lost, no way into it through memento, dream, or memory, at most a long-lost history, an account in a book one can read but which remains unknown. Michael and Eva, already members of the circle of street kids, the boy already at the school that harmlessly takes him away from his father, the father's speech only a distant resonant sound that will not find new voice in the next generation. Thus they look at their father with hardly any feeling of danger, nothing more than a playmate, his place in the scheme of things undoubted. I, however, don't disturb this fantasy, but rather protect it and feed it with jokes and games. Johanna also helps out, dismissing with a smile any groundless question, and wherever shadows creep or rustle she's there to set things right with her hands. Quickly I shy away, leave quietly, and am glad to be back in my study. The children are allowed to run free outside and return to the light of day, unaffected, no loss having touched them.

Then I pray to an unknown guardian, he perhaps able to protect the children such that they have no idea of what they have mercifully been shielded from. The father should remain within their love as only the familiar stranger who once appeared, was there, then went away; yes, a passing ship, already having landed on the island and found the mother. Yet earlier there was nothing, only waves, nothing ever having happened. So it is in the world. One suddenly arrives, a ship, and everyone must travel to this island for the first time, an island where one can be and forget. Now the foundation is laid, the arc of Being lifted, the bridge erect and no longer capable of being destroyed. Above lies the light of all the stars, sacred and undisturbed creation presiding, the earth illuminated in the hand of the Lord. Whatever has fought against this no longer exists and has damned itself to darkness and discord, never to be again. Sheltered prosperity, the joyful vicissitude of a good family passing from fathers to grandchildren to their children's children with all daily hardships taken care of, but also blessed in itself. The sanctuary of the sexes that do their work, and when one dies a noble grave awaits him; kept gratefully alive in memory, he lives on as an example, nothing having been in vain. His acts will inform his descendants; they are not unique, but in being true they reveal what is just. No doubt presses back, such that the sinister severs the chain and casts away and destroys its earlier roots. May this be true for the children!

What will happen when the children no longer believe this? They will retreat from me and take me to task. You were a vagrant, a vagabond and a layabout. You just crept your way into this city; you are not our father and don't belong to us. We don't owe you anything, and we will disown you in order not to suffer eternal shame. And what will I, on the other hand, say to you? You are clever and gifted; how many years will pass before already you're grown. Also, words will no longer comfort your mother. She would gladly stand sympathetically before the door of my room, but son and daughter will demand a royal entrance. Then I have to welcome them. They mess about in my drawers and demand the key to my desk. "What do you want to know?" I'll ask. They will answer, "You!"—"I don't exist," I'll assure them, but they will explain: "That is only half a memory. We want to find out about you. We want to know what is there when we see you— something horrible in your past, something disreputable which you keep secret."

Then I'll have to talk a lot. Trapped in a corner against the wall, I will tell them something I know nothing at all about, conjuring the semblance of it in order that the children tremble and shake; however, they won't be shaken by it, for they are well shielded against the language of sin. "I don't exist, I don't exist! You simply have to believe that, for both your sake and mine. I don't exist, and though you torment me with your penetrating curiosity, you'll still never find out, for it's impossible. All that is there is impenetrable strangeness, because I don't exist." Should I expect this day to come, one in which I am overshadowed by Michael and Eva, such that my memory also will likely come to an end? It won't change me at all, for I have decided that though the red seal of my guilt is long since reduced to dust, the future of these children will indeed be impugned. Can I protect them? Both the truth and not the truth will lead to the same doom. What, then, can I do? Why did I have children? O dull pointless lust! The belief in blind generation, for I madly wished not to be the last of my tribe, my precursors having been killed! To die childless felt like a sin. A world without children of the curse, and without memory of the fathers who suffered for them, so that there would be children of the curse. But Johanna? Her right to be a mother. The blessing of the womb, the transfiguration of birth, the soulfulness of a lullaby—all lovely, but it shouldn't have sprung from my loins. Johanna wanted me. I pursued, it's true, but she had consented, and that's her fault. Yet, at the time she was attracted to me I didn't know her; she had no idea what she had wreaked! Unhappy mother, who in conceiving children in her belly also bestowed on them an inextinguishable curse! Whatever staggeringly dumb vanity burned within me, away with it—go away, go home, go proliferate and fulfill your inchoate flesh and trembling spirit through children who are pure. Though you on your own can achieve no grace, see that the earth is inhabited with your blood and bones! Though you yourself have lived amid sin and error, you have indeed atoned for them, because you have tended to and hoped the best for your children. You have taken it upon yourself to make sure to balance your shortcomings with better intentions, such that they will be decreased, for benevolent is the Lord in the beginning, and he will forever forgive.

Dreaming before the wall, marking time. Slowly the earth gives way and sinks below you, the years elapsing before your doubled-over supplications. With your supplicating grasp, the net of confusion begins to loosen. You work hard, not wasting a single day. Task after task you have fulfilled; you haven't dwelled on your frailty. Therefore don't despair too much, and trust yourself to believe that a lost one will be comforted, for I am your rock and your redeemer. Voices that I hear, and which shimmer around me, immersing me in the inapproachable whenever the enemy's rattling surrounds me, such that I do not perish, even if I am unworthy of being held within the mesh of grace. Let it all pass, let everything pass! But I am carried through it. If I was too blessed at the wrong time, then this sinking into the ground is the sentence I must serve because I was too devout and not active enough. Now, however, you are there again. How can I resist you? Yet you still shimmer all about me, such that I am extinguished by the glow! Too much experience makes me empty, wisdom silencing any possible speech within me. Succor is my garb. That is what has happened to me; the rest is just extended sound. "You will be your own just reward." But whose just reward will be my just reward?

Impudent, I stand before my wall. Is it the Wailing Wall, where the sadness of all prayers is nurtured? Sadness? Prayers? No, it's not the Wailing Wall. Yet my state plunges me into the depths. A continually sunken resistance, which nonetheless hardens and does not budge. I remain silent within my abyss, completely guilty and always guilty, nor can I even once do something for myself. That I still exist cannot be reckoned with. How can I ever confidently exist even for a moment? You, however, say that I can find forgiveness, for your grace is endless. You ask that I not doubt so intensely and not doubt myself so. You send me forth upon the four winds, such that I gather myself in both the seas and the deserts, the open fields and the dense cities. You command trust because you have sounded out my weaknesses, and into the world's battles you drive my steps so that they can learn to transform themselves into peace. This I say aloud, drawing the belief in the truth of the unimaginable into the sensual poverty of my slack limbs. I turn away from the dreamy misery of the resentment and dissatisfaction that I had been carrying and apply myself to the future legacy of my children, who have no idea of my misery, but who need to heal in order to fill the chasm between which I have created with my scattered existence.

When I look at Johanna I am often happy, though sometimes also sad, yet always something is affirmed, and many fears are tamped down. What happens between us folds in upon itself and creates an understanding; we trust each other, there's no need to search for anything else. Thus we stoutly believe in each other. No matter how strange and distant we are, our hands are always entwined as one. Perhaps I am wrong about Johanna. It's easy for me to be near her, for then I am lost to the light. She is awake; she has unconscious control of me. She beams at me, she wants me, she makes me real, she sees me, she talks to me. This is the deepest effect she has on me. For she is never despondent; seemingly docile, she conquers my sudden, often startling disappearance with action conjured out of nowhere. When I don't exist, she doesn't break down; if anything, it entices her to provide all the more strongly what wouldn't exist without her confidence. All of my weaknesses are only inducements to her. It almost seems that she needs a weak man. For the fact that Johanna has chosen me remains as unfathomable as it does unrewarded. Did she consider the consequences of our relationship? What ingratitude lies in such a question! I am amazed, and it still upsets me when I recall how it all happened. My long journey, my hope coupled with a new country, the strange hazy city, so much fog, for weeks given the runaround for no apparent reason, then a glance exchanged at a gathering, and there was Johanna, once, then again. I didn't know why, but I spoke to her, and already the marriage was settled.

I had been referred to others along the way before I had taken flight, and my friend So-and-So provided me entrée in the metropolis and to what I told myself were influential personalities. They welcomed me politely and led me into their circle like an exotic mythical beast, and indeed I was met with nothing but wincing curiosity and a gaping desire to know more. Meanwhile, I just took it all as part of the urge to extend to me a friendly invitation to join their ranks. But no, I didn't mean anything to them, for they just stared at my mouth as it spewed out surprising news that they wanted to listen to, only to go on making light conversation, the stinging accounts about the horrors endured pleasing the spoiled ladies and gentlemen. But I myself disappeared, a passing folly who was persistently mistaken in thinking that he would be taken good care of, though I was nowhere present in any of the stories themselves, and was not at all even comprehensible, even when they listened to my own story. How foolish of me to feel satisfied with how others were astonished at me and fawned over me with cheap courtesies. The allure of the stranger soon dissipated, everyone having heard enough of my plans, all fondness for me dissolving. Awkwardly, I displayed my displeasure and could not regain the advantage; the beginning of my isolation had been fatally set in motion.

In the first days, I was invited by Herr Dr. Haarburger and his wife once or twice a week, they being wealthy refugees in a luxuriously furnished villa whose contents had all been purchased in their native country. During one of my first visits, the Haarburgers had arranged for me to come to dinner, after which friends and some guests of rank and renown were summoned to appear, handsome men and bejeweled ladies who drank their coffee and gawked at me from all sides while eating cake and smoking cigarettes, Frau Haarburger having urged me in a well-meaning way to make sure and show them my best side.

"Make contacts, that's all, my dear Herr Landau. Professor Kratzenstein is president of the International Society of Sociologists. He has fantastic connections, as well as with publishers, and he has access to loads of money and stipends. But you need to be in good form, Herr Landau!"

"He will indeed be. He's certainly clever, Hannah!" Dr. Haarburger reassured.

"And can he do something for me?"

"But of course, and a lot! Indeed, he can!"

Frau Haarburger then counted off those whom Kratzenstein had already helped.

"He's tremendous. But you have to make your move! You can't just be difficult. And Frau Singule is nearly as important as he is. You must know the name. No? I'm flabbergasted! What do you make of that, Jolan?"

"Nothing to worry about! Please, dear, he can't know everyone. Actually, Singule used to be a zoologist. But that didn't work out so well for him."

"Then he turned to medicine."

"He was great at that. But now he's general secretary of Europe for a rich, perhaps the richest, American foundation. His central interest is natural science, biology. But, nonetheless, the job suits him, for he's someone who is interested in everything. Indeed, his word is as good as gold. Too bad that he's not here himself. He has so terribly much to do and rarely can get away. Perhaps next time."

"For Herr Landau it's probably better that he doesn't come. Don't you think so, Jolan? Frau Singule can handle it all herself. Just a suggestion from her to her husband—that's all it takes to get his ear and have him on board with anything."

Frau Haarburger's hopes were fulfilled, for Singule didn't show, his wife apologizing on his behalf with great fanfare. Instead, others appeared. Kratzenstein was the star attraction—"What a head! Could anyone look more clever?" Then there was the bookseller Buxinger—"All I need do is say one word to him and he'll lend you any books you need!" As well as Herr and Frau Saubermann, a rich couple who owned factories and had humanitarian interests—"How much good they have done, and with such humility!" And Resi Knispel, a Zurich press agent—"Simply brilliant, well educated, and works for some kind of literary agent as well!" And, in addition, Fräulein Johanna Zinner, an official in a refugee organization—"Not so important, but a heart of gold. Jolan and I love her like our own child!" There were others as well, but none that I recall any longer. First, I was introduced to Frau Singule.

"Herr Landau—in fact, Herr Dr. Landau—just arrived, our new friend. You'll see how famous he is! He can tell you all about it!"

"My pleasure, my pleasure."

"The pleasure is mine, madam."

"All that happened to you doesn't at all show. Maybe what happened wasn't so bad, but bad enough, I understand. Or were you lucky?"

"Lucky, madam."

"Yes, that's what my husband says as well. Too bad he's not here. He never has any time. One of his family members died. How terrible! Too many. Most likely you would have known him if you were there. Dr. Berthold Singule, an attorney. He was such a good person."

"I'm sorry—"

"Really? But I find that amazing! You were there and didn't see him? Unbelievable! He was loved by so many! We've heard reports from survivors how well he carried himself. You mean to say—"

"You said it yourself, madam, there were too many! There was no way to know everyone. I'm often asked about relatives, and in almost every instance there's nothing I can report."

"One hopes for a chance encounter."

"Certainly, madam."

"That is really awful! One wants to know!"

"Of course."

"That's what I'm saying! And then he was sent away. He didn't deserve it. So kind. And not a trace more, nothing. Gone."

"That's how it was, madam. Everyone gone. In the end, it was left to chance who remains and who does not."

"That's what you say! But one really wants to know just what happened. When, where, under what conditions? And whether the poor dear suffered much or not?"

"Certainly, madam."

"Oh, it's horrible that you can say that so easily. But, understandably, one must be blunt."

"Not quite, madam. At least not me. I want to put it into a larger context."

"That must be terribly interesting and is certainly very important! Congratulations—no, I mean what courage, Herr Landau!"

"That's what I meant to say," Frau Haarburger said, interrupting. "Dr. Landau is the man for the job."

"I can only recommend my friend in the warmest way," said Dr. Haarburger. "That's a head that will impress your dear husband. Terrific, I say, the very best!"

"It's a shame that he always has so much to do. Overwhelmed. Looking over applications all day long. By the way, one might be of interest to you, Herr Landau—something about experiences with typhus and lice. Ugh, simply disgusting. But the poor fools who died of it! Terrible!"

"Herr Dr. Landau knows all about that, Frau Singule," Dr. Haarburger confirmed. "Your husband would be interested to hear all about it."

"Naturally, if only he could! It's horrible! Just imagine, tonight another meeting about the dispersal of grants for the next quarter. That can last all night."

"My dear Frau Singule," offered Frau Haarburger. "Take our young friend under your wing! Tell your husband about him!"

"But of course, with the greatest pleasure. I will see to it."

She nodded at me and smiled promisingly. Then I was presented to Professor Kratzenstein, who put to me the most clever questions in the world. Soon Fräulein Zinner joined us, yet she didn't say anything, but instead just took it all in with lowered gaze. The professor found my scholarly plans interesting, but he felt that a sociology of oppressed people would indeed be too great a challenge. I countered by saying that I was not proposing to advance a complete system, but that I wished to work out the underlying cause, to delineate the contours of the problem and stake out the borders. Kratzenstein explained that this sounded interesting, but he was just concerned that the closer I came to explaining it more precisely such a knowledgeable man as myself might allow my theme to get bogged down in ethical matters, thus getting all tangled up in such nonsense, whereas what was needed was simply to state the facts—this and that happened—just put it down, detail the sources, interview witnesses, compare statements, consider the psychology behind them, measure the evidence statistically, and then something useful would come of it all.

"However, whoever was actually there is rarely right for such a task. Anything subjective is dangerous, I warn you. How can that lead to any kind of precise research? Each of us thinks differently, even about morality. You really have no idea what one can imagine that involves, and scholarly integrity suffers when in the presence of half-truths, just as it must from the implementation of any prevailing value system."

"I don't wish to present it so simply."

"Not at all simply? It's very, very complicated! And indeed because of that it has to be simplified in order to provide the mind with the structure of reality, all of it able to be taken in. Facts—it all depends on the facts."

"Of course, the facts. But then from those to begin something, to grasp, to think, to conclude."

"Not the way you imagine it! To let go of empiricism? A fundamental mistake! Scholarship must present its material in a pure manner. Everything else is almost always a metaphysical joke or nonsense. I'm warning you. Consequences are not the purview of science, for it's up to society to work them out before the politicians do."

"But that's not what happens."

"Ho ho! Not so fast!"

We went at each other fast and furious. I spoke all the more frankly the more the Professor came at me. He maintained that the times had passed me by. It was understandable and regrettable. Whoever was unlucky enough to have been condemned to such isolation, such a one couldn't understand matters correctly, even if he was stuck in the middle of it. Because, as a result, not only had one lost contact with life; one had also lost the proper standards. In order to counter that, I had to first free myself of all judgments. That I had been a witness to the catastrophe was all well and good, but I had long since lost any inherent right to research such material, rather than only be a part of it.

"If I were you, I would just write a short, clear account about how you got through it all, what you experienced and observed. Just that. Reflections about it all should be left out. They will only muddle your account, making it too emotional, such that no one will take it seriously. All of that is worthless. I don't mean to sound so harsh, but that's how it is."

Frau Haarburger approached, took Resi Knispel by the arm, and was pleased to see Kratzenstein talking with me so animatedly. Good for Dr. Landau, said the housewife, such excitement is always productive. She then deftly assured the Professor that it would be well worthwhile to provide all the necessary concrete support for my highly ambitious plans. The famous sociologist nodded obligingly, saying one would certainly have to think about it, although right now the situation was especially complicated, for there were always higher and higher demands, and that, incidentally, he believed that Herr Dr. Haarburger would be the most fitting person to use his immense influence here to set up the proper circle of contacts that would best suit my purposes. Frau Haarburger felt flattered and agreed, but couldn't help underscoring that her Jolan was also heavily burdened and that, even without this, he was doing everything in his power that he could. To her regret, she had to admit it couldn't amount to much. She had tossed it around with her husband and they came to the conclusion that it would be best to help Dr. Landau give a lecture at the International Society of Sociologists.

"That's worth considering. Obviously, I will need ahead of time a more precise understanding of what Herr Dr. Landau is really proposing. The thesis must be narrowly focused and new as well. It has to be absolutely clear. Understand? Perhaps you could give me a call. But not this month. I have to go to a conference in Paris on statistical reconstruction, something very interesting, but I'm expected to give a paper, which is always demanding, and then I have to be in Amsterdam for a week at the invitation of the Dutch government. As I understand it, Herr Dr. Haarburger will be there at the same time. I'll certainly see him there, won't I?"

"Naturally, Jolan is looking forward to it immensely. Maybe I'll also tag along."

"That would be lovely, my dear."

"Wouldn't it?"

"But excuse me, Herr Professor, when should I get in touch with you? Next month?"

"Excellent! Somehow it will happen. You have plenty of time, don't you?"

"But of course."

"Fine. Then best would be to let me catch my breath a bit after I return. Let's say around the middle of the month."

"Well, then, just past the middle of next month, if I've got that right?"

"That would be fine with me. Just call Frau Fixler, my secretary, at the ISS."

"ISS? How's that?"

"Yes, it will be my pleasure. You can count on my secretary. But I should tell you now that at best, even if a lecture were to be announced, it couldn't happen this year. The schedule is too crowded already, nor do I even know what to do about it. But we'll nonetheless find an open date for next year."

During this explanation Herr Dr. Haarburger had approached us.

"My dear Professor, next year, isn't that a bit far off? Don't you think that there's some way you could indeed arrange something for our friend in the next few months?"

"Unfortunately, that will be quite difficult. But wait, I have an idea. Who's to say that it has to be a lecture only by him? That doesn't even work that well for someone who is not well known. Listen, Dr. Landau, perhaps you could work on a concise text, only the results of your research, that you could present as a lecture in the regular meeting of our small working group. But the lecture shouldn't be longer than ten, at the most fifteen minutes. By doing that, you'll get to meet a lot of people."

"Would that really be possible in the coming months?" I ventured to ask.

"I do believe it would. Though you will have to be patient and wait until late autumn. Beyond this, all I can do is make a recommendation. But we'll see. As soon as we've talked about it in greater detail and we've come to an agreement, I'll give it all my attention. You can count on that."

Professor Kratzenstein smiled at me indulgently. I looked into his face for reassurance or something, but to no avail. He had become almost invisible, the Zurich press agent having breathed into his ear, perhaps saying something to him, though nothing sociological, and then he disappeared. I sensed that I would not be able to find him again, for I simply didn't exist for him. "Get away, get away from here!" That's what I heard, and later heard ever more often, but something kept me there. The Haarburgers had gathered these guests for my sake; I couldn't just secretly disappear. Yet I was disappearing on my own, even though a hope rose within me: I exist. For I had also not given up. I had shown up; someone would take me in. This belief made the hope true. I stood, I went into the glittering salon— glasses swung toward me, sweets fell into my hand, I chewed and staggered onward. Then Professor Kratzenstein was there again. I looked at him; he was surrounded. "It only takes one word from him and you will be a made man!" Someone whispered that to me. The encouragement felt good, but for the moment I had forgotten the sociologist once again.

"Who do you mean, and how so am I a made man? Please, introduce me to him!"

"You've been talking to him for a good while. Don't you know whom you're talking to?"

Ah, I see. I had been talking to someone, to that gentleman there, tall and gaunt, such a man, a knowing, guilty face. The whispering voice continued on.

"You should pay more attention to Professor Kratzenstein! He's important. Flatter him!"

"You think? I tried to. He didn't like it."

"You have to take advantage of the opportunity!"

But there wasn't another opportunity. The gathering moved about and began to disperse. No, people didn't go home; rather, they pressed more closely together than before, and I was left out.

"That wall there?"

"It's not a wall."

"You could be right. It's easy to be confused. It shifts, it moves. It's frightening."

"The things you say! Why are you so nervous?"

"I don't believe that at all."

"Look here, don't be so serious! These days, what good does it do?"

There they sat together. Little tables laid out flat on crossed legs, set up on the carpet, thin and light little tables, all covered smartly with felt. Shiny new playing cards glowed and were dealt deftly, flying into hands to be sorted, a tidy quick juggling. Above them, long-nosed faces waggled; they smiled heartily and reflected success. "That's my trick!" King and queen battled together, and always four cards fell upon the green, biting the dust, quickly gathered up by greedy hands and turned into tidy little piles laid crosswise.

"It's a great game, Dr. Landau. Wouldn't you like to join in?"

"I really don't know how to play."

"But it's important to. One can endear oneself by being ready to serve as a fourth."

I couldn't do it. My hands were too clumsy, each trump failing, the walls snapping back and forth, my head spinning, already another trick.

"You have to learn how to play!"

"Of course, madam."

Off kilter, I crossed the room, taking huge steps that stitched through the walls, the cards disappearing. There, in the corner, some sat together, three in all, myself the fourth. Get away, get away from here! "You don't play, either?" Herr Buxinger the bookseller said that, for he found cards boring, better to read a book. Frau Saubermann, the factory owner's wife and benefactress, agreed.

"I always say, my husband is so cultivated, but, unfortunately, he plays as well."

Bookselling was important; it kept one serious, pages being better than cards. Frau Saubermann asked Fräulein Zinner what she thought of it. She didn't think anything about it, for it could be an innocent pastime, but she didn't have the knack for it and didn't play. "Herr Doctor, sit down with us!" said the bookseller. "Otherwise we'll just have to look through your legs, like a wide-open gate," he joked. The factory owner's wife laughed, such good humor, Fräulein Zinner moving over a little, the others as well, as I sat down comfortably in the corner. There we sat quietly together in order not to disturb the sacred quiet that surrounded the hurried players like a protective cloud. I really should have been on my way, for it was not right that as a potential fourth I only spent time with those who weren't playing, for here that felt a bit odd to do. The room probably was completely harmless, the light shining on just the familiar, but I was something else, a strange body, a closed-off lump of layers, legs crossed. I had been summoned here, but now here I was, weak and fragile. I couldn't just simply get up and leave; I had to at least explain myself, justify my rushed appearance, my getting up, though I couldn't, the armchair was too deep. Despairingly, I looked up from my corner, the books there, me rubbing a dusty finger.

Then I heard some commotion outside in the hall as steps approached. The door of the apartment closed tight, then the clatter of a key, the snap of a door bolt. As I pulled myself together and opened my eyes wide, Frau Meisenbach stood in the middle of the room. Not the actual middle, for the room was too densely furnished, but near the large round table that was near the middle.

"Forgive me for letting you wait so long. I still had to speak to Peter. He is so distressed. I can't help him, but I have to counsel him."

"You don't have to excuse yourself for me. In this apartment, I feel like a burglar."

"Oh, don't be ridiculous! You're tired, that's all."

"Yes, tired. That's right."

"I will make up the bed right away."

"In this room?"

"Yes. It's a small apartment. I only have to turn the cushions on the divan and the bed is finished."

"Here, where your husband—"

"I'm used to guests. Even in recent weeks. Often, someone has to be put up on short notice. Peter has also slept here."

"I see, Peter . . . and now I have booted him out."

"Oh, don't be ridiculous! Peter has a perfectly nice room and is in no danger."

"Am I in danger?"

"Of course. You're not yourself."

"Whoever is not himself—"

"That's right."

"You know, it's normal. If one arrives in a place that used to be home, or at least was thought and said to be . . . and then everything is gone. But why should I blab on to you who knows it all already. Your husband gone, Arno . . . Others stopped searching. But one can't help but continue searching. Even if it's pointless."

"You're tired. You'll think differently in a little while."

Out of drawers in the foyer, who knows out of how many corners, Anna fetched sheets and blankets, as she lowered the back of the divan, flipped three large cushions, and carefully set up the bed.

"I can't let you do all of this alone! Can I help?"

"No, it's nothing. It only takes a minute and it's done. Do you like your pillows piled up? Two of them, three?"

I had to laugh, but that was no way to respond.

"Forgive me, I'm so stupid! It doesn't matter to me."

"I only meant what was most comfortable for you."

"You know, I used to always have them piled up, way up. It was a bad habit. But now . . . if I can just lie down . . ."

"You're very tired, aren't you? You can lie down right away. Here, just take this! It will suit you well. And here is a dressing gown. If you want, you can change here and I will step outside. Or the other way round—I'll stay here and you go to the bathroom."

"Thank you, thank you. But I'm not so tired, it has passed. If you don't want to turn in yet . . . I mean, I really owe you an explanation."

"You don't owe me anything; don't make such a big deal! Here, take these! If you want to talk a little more afterward, I'm ready to."

Anna held out the things to me; the linens had a faint scent and were neatly ironed. I saw that they were monogrammed with "HM." A lovely bit of handiwork that had been sewn into the dead man's body, and now it was for me to wear such a symbol, but without the right to carry "HM" on my chest.

"Was he called Heinz?"

Not thinking, I asked this tactless question, realizing straight off that it was wrong, but a quick answer showed me that no recourse could make up for my callousness.

"No, Hermann. There's nothing else I can give you. Now go!"

Ashamed, I bowed, but not to Anna, as I wanted to, but rather to the wall or the door, which I ripped open, the strange pajamas and the dressing gown burning in my arms, me not looking behind me. My head hurt with intense shame; I stumbled into the bathroom and clumsily locked myself in. Here I let everything drop and sat myself down on the edge of the tub, then I forced my eyes to look around. The closeness made me uncomfortable; it pressed at me and stifled me, the window placed way too high on the wall and much too small, not suited to any kind of saving leap into the shaft of light. Sweet, sharp, and flat odors mixed together anxious and sad, damp little underthings on a stretched-out line hung together clumped and rippling, sad sites of self-attention, of the care of worn-out limbs and hair, of accumulated jars, little vials and tubes for the supple adornment of face and hands, patient and loaded bins, brooms, rags, tools for shoe work, all kinds of junk. All of it surrounded me, stark and pressing, overwhelming the tiny space, overwhelming me. What did any of it have to do with me? What was I looking for here? Hermann should have shown up to grab hold of the large broom and bash my curious nose with its handle and throw me out. But there was no longer any Hermann; a strange beast had slipped through the cracks and nested here. Anna put up with it, and maybe that's even what she wanted, she needing a pet, Peter once being that, the young restless one, then the unknown homeless one, whom the restless one had hauled in off the street.

Before me stood the toilet bowl, white and clean under its two lids, a cord with a tassel grip and a water tank, everything in order. A place of shame, rising out of courtyards and isolated corners almost in the middle of the primped satisfaction of sedentary people, the emptying out of the lazy voiding of our lowest nature spewed into the plunging tunnels of the subsurface canals of the city in order that we know nothing more of the disgusting necessities of our bodies. But they are heard through the walls, nonetheless, Father outside, Mother outside, condemned just like you. It can be heard from the neighbor's apartment as he closes his door and whistles a song, believing himself alone, yet eavesdropped upon unwittingly, and when he finally disappears the water stirs for a long time in the tank. It had been a long time since I had been locked in a bathroom with a toilet. It was like it was in childhood, when sinful forgetting consumed me. I shouldn't stay outside so long, my mother said firmly, it's vulgar and vile, but the dream of being alone was nowhere else to be found in the metropolis.

Only in the thick folds of the forest or in the loneliness of the toilet was I in charge of myself, because in the apartment, indeed in the entire city, there was not a single corner that was mine alone, all other places being either far too big or too easily entered, for anywhere you could be taken by surprise or watched much more easily than here. Material existence, where the toilet not only crouches in the bathroom but is alone with its surroundings, closed in only by the narrow walls and a door that didn't need to be opened at someone's calling if I didn't want it to. But in this apartment I was nothing but a guest; I couldn't stay here for any length of time. Anna was waiting and would grow uneasy if I dawdled.

I listened hard to see if anything was going on out in the room, but there was nothing to hear. Also, there was nothing to hear from the other bathrooms in the building or the neighboring apartments. And the elevator, whose creaking drone could be heard through all the walls, had long since gone quiet. Perhaps Anna had gone to sleep in the meantime, had given up waiting for me, thinking that I was ungrateful or rude. Oh, if only she were asleep; that's what I hoped. I had left nothing behind in the room, carrying all my possessions on me and hiding them in my pockets, and Hermann's things could just remain on the floor. But I could also pick them up and neatly lay them down if I were to just leave, wanting to get away from Hermann. It was only a few steps to the apartment door; even in the dark, I could rush down the stairs quickly, the only impediment being the locked door. Where might the button for the superintendent be? No, such an escape wasn't possible, it was forbidden, to even consider it was foolhardy pretension. There could be no dilly-dallying; I had to go back to the room, the night had to be gotten through.

I gathered myself together and slipped my fingers around the edges of the buttons on my clothes. I was free of my clothes before I knew it and took off my socks. My back hurt a bit when I stood up. I stretched, then I looked down at my poor nakedness, a strange body that I had to carry. The marks of deprivation were deep and gray, nothing familiar about these wasted limbs and nothing at all childlike, no boyish flesh. I was not at all lovely, for I had been denied too much and used for nothing good. Amid this sorrow there was certainly no longer the soul of a sanctified house, the behest of my parents having been debased to this wretched figure. I had not looked at my body for years; there had never been time to, nor the opportunity or even the wish to. Torso and limbs, a head on a neck that was much too thin—how strange I looked, the legs trembling slightly the longer I looked. I dreamed of the quiet pleasure that comes with feeling the health of one's own body, even if it was vain and a bit objectionable. Yet this didn't suit me at all, for it felt too naïvely cheerful to think that I could embrace such pagan nonsense. There was no more body, there being nothing left but a shrunken skeleton that hardly existed, unaware and afraid, consumed by deprivation, unhealthy and condemned. I shivered as I touched my belly, bloated and pasty, and yet scrawny and puckered, the haunches flabby, the long arms like twigs. What could one possibly do with it all? I unfolded the dressing gown, soft and cool in my hands, the monogram embossed upon it. That was good, for it provided a strength under which I could hide my anxious human figure. I already had the sleeves spread out and wanted to slip my arms into them. Then I stopped short, for sewn into the collar was the silken name of the firm: Haberdashery Albert Landau—HAL—Reitergasse 8.

That I didn't need. It was too much for this hour. I asked myself angrily, how can you wear this article of clothing with the monogram "HM"? How could you be so unjust! HM was an account, the good standing of a paying customer. Back in the workshop sat the hunched-up old Fräulein Michelup, tirelessly stitching monograms with her needle-thin fingers. She never came out into the front of the shop. One brought her the goods and instructed her briefly, at which she nodded, and that was all. "This needs an 'HM,' please—that pattern there, you know the one." It was ordered for Herr Meisenbach. Therefore Hermann had bought from my father or Anna had, most likely she, for she had known the shop since childhood. She wanted the best for Hermann, nothing cheap, for it wasn't good enough, and she wanted good value. Father himself had served her, standing next to her with a knowing smile, running his fingers over the fabric so that she could be sure of what she chose. The clothes were always better after they were washed, and they lasted a good while, much longer than Father in the Reitergasse, a memento of his superb good trade, his impeccable honesty. Unforgettably, his clothes were still worn throughout the city and far beyond the neighborhood and throughout the land. The clothes rested in the drawers and slept, a soft treasure bound with small paper bands, perfumed with lavender, reminding one of pleasurable, cool memories of celebrations at home. Gravely the father looked down, for he knew that he profited from clothing the nakedness of the citizens in the warmth of smooth fabric. But now there was no longer any father and no Hermann, I having come instead to assert my right. I kissed the precious label that was now familiar to me, sorrow withdrawing deep inside me and into my innermost parts, pride and joy suffusing me on the surface. What I possessed as clothes in my poverty were meager threads that didn't belong to me, yet they were mine, they were mine! Somehow they had found their way to me.

And there I stood in fine trousers and a handsome jacket. I turned toward the mirror and stood there in this outfit. I was myself again, happy to be so, for I had chosen my garments myself and shouldn't be ashamed of such splendid things. I no longer needed the dressing gown. The way I was dressed now, I could let myself be looked at by anyone. Therefore I took the dressing gown and lay it over my arm, wanting to go to Anna outside in the room. Then she would recognize who I was, and she would find me handsome and somewhat like my old self—a person, someone who would make her forget her husband and all her friends. No introduction at all would be required, for who but the son of Albert Landau could so unselfconsciously step out? After just a few steps, any tempting vanity would be satisfied. But something held me back, the dead man's monogram. Was it on fire? I couldn't cause Anna such a shock. Perhaps with my teeth or nails I could pull out the stitching. But no, the monogram was too firmly embedded in the fabric; only a couple of threads were plucked out, poor Fräulein Michelup bent over in the back and nimbly sewing. It just wasn't right. Maybe cover up the tag, as if it irritated my skin—that was an idea, its prickly fire needing to be subdued—but I couldn't really hide it. A hand covering a name, and the name placed over a stranger's heart, what unbearably close relations! And so I relinquished my disguise.

Whoever loses his home against his will, simply because he has been expelled by the powers that want to annihilate him, cannot return alone to the site of expulsion as one who happened to be saved from joining the fellowship of the murdered, no matter the reasons that move him. He can no longer go home, back to where he came from, for only a foreign land suits him, and he cannot get far enough away from the place that bore him. This

I had realized before I began my journey. Nonetheless, I had to at least risk such loss, seeing that I was this and not that, observing the traces, taking in what was left of the past, gathering it and burying it. But now I knew that it was futile, it was forbidden. I no longer wanted to be here. Yet how could I get away, myself too tired and my strength gone? And so I thought. How pathetic the nightshirt from the Reitergasse had been, how sinfully foolish my desires. Hermann's torso was the same size as mine, but my legs and arms were too long, a little bit of my hands and feet remaining uncovered. The father had in mind a stranger's measurements, mine having long since been crossed out. "The young Landau?" came a painfully hard voice. "He no longer shops with us."

How could I let Anna look at me, a joke at this hour, now too late, a dreary, sad man turning up in front of a strange woman? She would judge me harshly, and I had to inform her of who I was. Should I stay in the bathroom and sit on the edge of the tub or on the toilet? If I sat there, I'd fall asleep. Anna would also fall asleep in the room and forget about me. If she remembered me and knocked on the door—"Where are you, Hermann? It's late!"—I could say, "Don't be upset that it's taking so long! I'm here. I'm here for you." I threw the pajama top over my shoulders, it being an old piece softly worn through that fit me surprisingly well, striped fleece, the colors shimmering. The shirt didn't belong to Hermann, for he certainly wouldn't have liked striped clothes. Maybe I could find a monogram on it as well, but I had not paid attention and wanted to spare myself the effort. I could already tell that it belonged to my school friend and Anna's brother, Arno the politician. It smelled of him, a little sour, while on my tongue there was an aftertaste. Thus I was properly dressed. For Anna and for me it was best, the tension between us dissipating, her own man and the strange one forced out of the house. Quickly I got my clothes together, not wanting to bring them into the room, and hid them in a corner under a hand towel.

"I no longer exist! I no longer exist!" Softly I breathed that through my teeth as I emerged from the bathroom. I knocked tentatively on the door of the room and heard a dry sound that formed itself into no words. Anna lay awake and covered in her bed, her hands moving uncertainly about, her expression dreamy yet untroubled. I relaxed, cautiously ready, standing back in the right corner at the other end of the wall. The bedding was laid out such that our feet were pointed toward each other when I lay down, our heads resting at either extreme.

"I no longer exist! Anna, I no longer exist!"

She looked at me questioningly, as if she hadn't heard right, yet she said nothing. Then I spoke louder, and it sounded unmercifully loud.

"I am not Hermann!"

"What's the matter with you? What's that supposed to mean?"

"I wanted to ask you to forgive me for being so terrible."

"Forgive you . . . what do you mean?"

"Oh, nothing, it doesn't mean anything. A dumb thing to say. You don't know me; sometimes I say such stupid things."

"Is there something else you need?"

"It's too much."

"I mean to eat or drink."

"I'm a widower."

Anna sat up halfway, propped up her elbows, and rested her chin in her hand. She looked at me as if my last words were a heap of tangled, cut threads underneath Fräulein Michelup's worktable, meaning nothing more, me needing to at least explain.

"Not only Hermann, Anna. Myself as well. I am also dead. I mean, the woman whom I was married to."

"Dead?"

"Yes, completely gone. No longer here. Just the same as Hermann . . . Did you love him very much? Were you happy? And now you have to look for your Hermann in every person, in every man? Or has he sunk away, the surface closing smooth as a mirror over him?"

Anna lifted herself up higher and shoved the pillow behind her back.

"How can you ask me that? And what do you want me to answer?"

"I know it's unreasonable. It was too much. I don't want to impose—no, that's not what I want. Understand, it creeps up on me. I imagine everything in the extreme—that which once was, that which is lost. Until a certain, but unknown, moment, when it's still all there: anyone you wish, your Hermann, your brother Arno. Two years or more he sat on the same bench as me in class. Everything there. Also Franziska, my wife. Then gone."

"You loved her very much, very much."

"I still love her. But she is more gone, much more than my parents. I miss my parents and keep looking around for them, expecting always some sign. And I can confess to you that this dauntless pursuit is what brought me to you."

"Your parents?"

"Let's not talk about them now. Maybe later. But I don't miss Franziska. I can hardly remember her. She is nowhere, nothing. She also has no hold over me, but I love her. That's all."

"And what do you know about your Franziska today?"

"Nothing, nothing at all! I can, and should, try to find out about her."

"Is she dead for sure?"

"Is Hermann?"

"I don't know. The notice was clear. Of the entire platoon, not a single one was still alive. A direct hit to their bunker, everything gone up in flames."

"The same for me. But no notice. Just everything in flames."

"Even a woman?"

"Everyone!"

I stood exhausted in the room, where it was cool, the window hanging open. A view out. Nothing built across from it. The space was open; nearby I could see the slow-moving dark-brown river. Anna said nothing. I didn't look at her, and yet I could feel that in this short span of time she had grown distant. Perhaps she blinked shyly and also had a couple of tears in her eyes. My hands ran along the bare round edge of the table, everything feeling very far off. As a child, I had always enjoyed running my hands around the entire circumference, but now I only rubbed a short stretch to left and right, then I brought my fingers back to the starting point.

"You could catch cold if you stand in the night air. You should lie down, Herr . . ."

"Landau."

"Landau?"

"Landau, yes. Haberdashery HAL, Reitergasse 8."

"Clothing?"

"Not me. My father. Hermann's clothes. I don't have any more of my own."

"So Peter was right after all."

"Why Peter?"

"He thought so and said so to me."

"You knew him, my father?"

"Yes. I always shopped there. My father did as well. And I know you as well. Now I know. I simply couldn't remember. Back then you played with Arno in the park and, if I'm not mistaken, here in our apartment as well. Everything is so changed."

"Nothing has changed. Especially me. Nor you . . . still the same round face, also the hair, only back then it was neatly parted. But I, on the other hand—"

"Don't worry at all! Sure, it's upsetting when you aren't recognized, and the time, so much has passed! But don't let it cause you any pain."

"It doesn't hurt but, rather, amazes. I don't even think that I can stand it."

"What's that? Are you feeling ill? You've grown quite pale. I'll make some coffee, and you can lie down."

"No, then we won't be able to sleep. Please, stay! Don't get up! It will only cause trouble, and I really don't want anything. Perhaps it would be okay if I just lie down."

"But of course!"

"Should I turn out the light as well? We could still talk in the dark."

"The switch is there by the door. I'll turn the small light out here once you're in bed."

"Or a little later! We can still talk. The small light feels so good. It's much better than the dark of death."

"As you wish."

I had taken off the dressing gown and not looked around at Anna as I rushed to my bed. The sheets felt cool and fresh against my body as I nestled into them. The blanket rustled as I pulled it up almost to my neck and lolled about until I felt comfortable. I squinted, for I didn't want to see Anna, but that was a pointless worry. If I lay quiet on my pillow and didn't raise my head, the table blocked my view.

"What a wonderful bed!" I called out. "I can sleep here as good as at home. Did you know my father well? Perhaps also my mother?"

"No, Landau, unfortunately I didn't. Your mother I barely knew by sight, your father just in passing. A dear man, he always had a joke at the ready."

"When did you see him last?"

"Just before they closed his shop. He had an idea it was coming, probably knew already. He was very sad. I tried to comfort him. He had no confidence and said, 'It's all over. After slaving away for so many years.' I agreed with him. 'Everyone must see that,' I said. He replied, 'Nothing is seen, we're simply unwanted. Our assets are what they want, and our death.' 'Doomsayer,' I teased, and laughed. But he just smiled sadly back: 'You don't understand, my dear Frau Meisenbach. But it's better if you don't. I also don't understand it, and there's no one who can help me. Here, please take these three shirts. One can't find such goods anymore.' Meanwhile, I didn't want to take the shirts, for I had no money, and I was ashamed to run up a bill. 'No, you don't have to pay,' he said. 'Money is no longer worth anything.' Then he handed the shirts to me and went into the back—I believe at that time he had, at the most, one employee—and brought out three much nicer shirts, the kind Hermann had never owned before, showed them to me, let me touch the heavy silk, as if all of it were up to me, and then wrapped them up. 'Don't get caught,' he warned in a whisper, and bent toward me over the counter. 'Otherwise, you'll have a helluva lot of trouble, and I'll be up to my neck in it.' I was shocked and didn't want to take the packet at all, but he got really mad and scolded me like a schoolgirl, asking if I was a silly goose or a scaredy-cat, and so I had to do as he asked. Then he stepped quickly around the counter, as if I was used to him doing that, because he, as you know, was always so deliberate, even if he never moved slowly. He shook my hand, tears in his eyes, as he saw me out. I would have loved to stay in order to say something nice, nor had I even properly thanked him. He, however, pushed me firmly out the door, turned around at once, and disappeared inside his shop. I wanted to call after him, but my voice faltered, and then it felt better to get out of there, quickly across the street, the packet pressed close to me as if I were a thief, and quickly, quickly home. As I walked through the Reitergasse with Hermann a few days later—he had not yet been called up—wanting to pass on my thanks with him, it was too late. The shop was closed, the shelves empty. I never saw your father or your mother again. I should have gone to their apartment, but then there was trouble with Arno, and we already had the police in our apartment. Some months later, I heard a rumor that your parents had been taken away. That's what must have happened. Everyone was powerless. All we had was scandal and shame. I looked for those shirts for you today, for they've hardly been worn."

"You didn't accompany my father?"

"How's that? I mean, what are you saying?"

"Nothing at all. Accompanied is all I mean."

"Where to? Good Lord! What was I supposed to do?"

"Save him!"

"How so?"

"I don't know. I was just thinking. One could see them off, even if they couldn't be saved. Perhaps at the train station. To wave with a white handkerchief, or with a blue one signifying hope. As soon as the train starts moving. Until it no longer can be seen."

"Forgive me, but did you go to the train station?"

"No, I couldn't. I was no longer here but gone. Away, far away. I thought, Perhaps the old ones will be spared. What a foolish idea. Why should they be? It was because of my parents that I stayed in this country. Also my grandmother, who was almost ninety then."

"Was she transported as well?"

"No. On the day before she was supposed to be, she was prudent and died. All by herself. No one did anything to her, and it wasn't suicide."

"How fortunate! But of course such old people they didn't—"

"Yes, they did! Why wouldn't they? There was no one too old to go."

"How do you know about the grandmother if you were already gone?"

"Those who came after me told me so. I also learned about my parents from them, and about many, many others. And what happened then? Don't ask. I know, and I don't know. In any case, there's nothing to say about it."

"But Franziska?"

"Her parents poisoned themselves. They didn't want to suffer and just took some pills to go to sleep. That happened months earlier, after they had given up their apartment and moved with two other older couples into a dismal little room in a musty old folks home. They were discovered much too late—they couldn't be woken. When Franziska and I showed up after breakfast in order to start the move, they had already been taken away. Franziska ran to the hospital with me, but she didn't see her parents again, neither alive nor dead. It was not allowed, and she pleaded to no avail. Then came the burial. They should have a grave in the central cemetery, if everything is still the way it was."

"Nothing happened there."

"The dead, who are still among us! It's good that they're there! Simple graves, thank goodness they still exist!"

"And tomorrow? After tomorrow? The future? Will you just keep going?"

"Do you have the desire to? Not me. Time has stopped, or I have stopped. It doesn't matter what happens. Whatever happens tomorrow or in the future has nothing to do with me or with this day."

"You said that you still love."

"Yes, I did, and it's true. That's a time frozen still. That's Franziska, who is always there, for she doesn't exist."

Anna then turned off the night light. The sudden darkness blinded me, and from the window the cool air poured in. Anna didn't say another word, but only rustled her covers, perhaps curling up small beneath them. I didn't know why she had turned out the light so suddenly, whether out of fear or because of my talking, whether out of compassion or tenderness or only because she was tired. Anxiously I listened for some sign, but the thick darkness released no sound. I could have said something, or at least wished her good night, but I was too uncertain that my voice would be lost to the darkness, the risk of being cut off by it frightening me. All that Anna gave off was a quiet hesitancy, nothing else, she having drifted off, or she not wanting to give any explanation in her own apartment. Therefore my silence was warranted; no word could possibly be expected of me. Already my eyes had gotten used to the dark, and yet the surroundings were hardly recognizable, only the nearby table's edge recognizable in the light gray of the submerged room, the window soon appearing as if cut out of the darkness, behind it the drab and milky color of the night's lofty freedom and the tender starry lights in the distance that floated above the hill's slope on the other side of the river. I raised myself up a bit in order to better see the lights, but they didn't appeal, for they were cold and unmoving. No stars shone that way; they were too fixed and hard.

Soon I turned away, settled myself into bed, pressed my head into the pillow, turned slowly toward the wall, as quietly as possible, and beheld nothing more than a weak, washed-out glow. It was neither comforting nor hopeless, only near and nonetheless uncertain, but at ease, since I didn't disturb it. As I closed my eyes, the same indistinct wall remained, only thicker. It didn't bother me, but instead finally left me alone. I had raised the covers higher, pressing my chin in between my folded hands, because I didn't want to be anywhere else except by myself and with myself, no matter how strange the room that surrounded me, no matter how strange the acceptable covers and the strange web extending from my father's hands to my body. What belongs to me? I asked myself. What do I own? "Myself," I whispered. "Myself, and nothing but myself." But that is also only a fiefdom, a fleeting possession. The Father can always take it away, and then I am no more. I loved someone. Why had I confessed that to Anna? And whom did I love?

Franziska is no more, but outside the wind blows, and my love is there. Will she enter my lair and dally with me? Why would she do that? She has no room, and if she comes closer, all the way in, she won't find any. Is she not sitting there, or is she calling from a distance that cannot be measured? Then I let myself drift off to sleep and wandered away into the silent vanished joy where I once met her before we were husband and wife. Was Franziska in the fog or in sunshine? Franziska at my side as we walked, someone next to someone, or also no one. Now we were where one shouldn't be, hidden dreamers in a green forbidden landscape. The little train laughed and carried the wanderers with many resounding whistles slowly along the length of the river, a traveling home, for the lovers wanted it so, and everywhere back then was home, everywhere a place of love they chose to visit. Here I am, it said, Here I am, the echo, and every place became a destination, home reached via the shortest journey. Soon the train stopped, and love stepped out, the gravel under its feet crunching, tickets gathered at the exit by a heavy hand, then vendors offered things for sale, wares offered up on portable stands and waiting for loose change, also baskets on the ground in which seasonal fruit was piled up. Soon there followed an imploring array of vendors, there being a ramp across the rails. All the hopeful merchants hawked their goods on and on, the children barefoot, accompanied by chickens and a sullen black dog. There was no more time, or had it dissolved into the dense cover of forest that wound around the path that climbed toward the heights? The blessed escape into the many-layered heights from the open flats, where summer forgets that there it feels like autumn. Trust in the light of day, the limbs warm, and all at the ready. The path forks, softly moving on, and where shall we go today?

"Are you awake?"

"No, I'm asleep, Johanna. I've been asleep for a while."

"Then I'm sorry that I bothered you."

"Don't worry! I'll sleep some more. I always sleep."

"You can't anymore. The order has arrived."

"Please let me! There's still time till tomorrow."

"Unfortunately not. It's already tomorrow."

"You can't scare me. It's today."

"No, you're wrong! It's already tomorrow! Just read the date!"

"I don't want to. I can't read it."

"You have to, because it has to do with you. Later, you can sleep without end."

"So read it to me, if I have to know it so bad!"

"Oh, don't be so difficult! The men are already waiting outside!"

"What do they want?"

"They have brought your coffin, Arthur."

"I don't need any coffin."

"Propriety demands it. You have to."

"What, then?"

"One can only be cremated in a coffin."

"I don't want to be cremated. I just want to be buried in the coolest earth. Near a spring, out in the green forest, where there is plenty of shade."

"Perhaps your wish can be fulfilled, but it's not possible without a coffin. In any case, you have to get up, because they want to take you with them."

"I'm not dead. Just send them all away!"

"You know your job. Duty is duty. At eleven you are supposed to be cremated."

"I don't want to. I am not at all dead. It must be a mistake."

"It's no mistake. Here it is in black-and-white. Arthur Landau, the corpse, is to be picked up and brought to the crematorium. The cremation is arranged for eleven, the mourners are planning to show up on time, the flowers and wreaths are ready."

"That's nonsense, Johanna! I don't want any flames swallowing me up!"

"Save me your useless concerns and hurry up! I already have my mourning dress. It's lovely!"

"I don't want to be dead! Can't you hear? Chase away the men! No one burns anyone who is alive!"

"How can you be so stupid, such a clever man! Everyone will be burned when his hour has come. I'll weep for you. The children will honor your name and never forget."

"It all seems to me so stupid! I won't go!"

"So do you want them to yell at you and beat you until you lie in your coffin?"

Then I became sad, much sadder than I had ever been in the darkness of my life, and I hastily stood up, turned around, and beheld the order that Johanna held clearly before my face. I couldn't believe my eyes. Yet, as I read, my doubts were bitterly disappointed, because there it was, clearly written, that the pallbearers were supposed to pick me up in a black oaken coffin and seal me inside it in order to get me to the cremation punctually at eleven. I blinked at Johanna, who stood there calmly and offered me such an unforced and fresh smile that I doubted whether for her own sake she thought of me as valiant or whether she felt hardly concerned at all. Out on the street, it was darker yet. The men who stood quietly outside appeared to be in a hurry, but I took my stand before the door, determined to fight off any threat with my own bare fists if necessary. The order was indeed clear, which then recommended the greatest caution. To my great joy, Johanna was not in any mourning dress, although she had pretended earlier that she was. Instead, she had chosen her severe gray traveling outfit that she only rarely wore in order to protect it.

All of a sudden, I discovered that the children were also running around the room, but they had kept so still that I wasn't surprised that I had overlooked them until now. I pointed at Michael, who absentmindedly turned the wheel of a wooden car, and then at Eva, who crouched in a corner and shyly clung to the little arm of her stuffed doll, sawdust running out of its wounded hand. Johanna sensed that the presence of the children was somewhat painful for me, and, indeed, made it clear that I didn't have to worry about it, for she had already explained to them that today their father was to be taken away. Children absorb such things so easily, for they hardly know what it means, Eva having no clue, and Michael thinking it was a great honor that was being awarded to me. I was only happy that the real truth was lost on them. All well and good, I grumbled angrily, and accused Johanna of being callous in her handling of the children. She found my rebuke strange, and said that I shouldn't be so high-strung; the less fuss I made, the better it would be for the children. The longer it took, the harder it was to hide my disappearance from them, which is why it was better to let them in on it right away. This would also give me the chance to sweetly and tenderly say goodbye forever. I didn't think at all about that, but nonetheless it helped to play with the children. I drew close to them and snapped my fingers playfully. Johanna didn't interfere and seemed satisfied that I would bring the situation to a reasonable end. When at last she began to doubt whether I was at all intending to say goodbye but, rather, was just stalling for time, she grabbed me by the hand and looked at me disapprovingly.

"You are insufferable. If you keep stalling, I can't stop the men from coming in and making short work of you. What would all the philistines from this neighborhood think? How embarrassing, don't let that into your head! You're making things completely impossible for your widow, for the neighbors will cut me off and talk nasty behind my back. Nor will anyone play with the children! The landlord will give us notice, and that I will have to find another apartment is all the same to you. That's the way people are these days! But if you don't make a fuss and just lie down in the box, hats will bow to you and people will feel bad for the children. Then everything will be fine, and no one will know who you were."

"Do you not want me around anymore?"

"But, Arthur, who do you think I am? Don't you know me better than that? It's not that way at all. Feelings are better left out of it. There's no time for them."

I no longer recognized the Johanna I once knew, she had changed that much. All the care with which she had coddled me was gone. Everything was now only for Johanna, and I was forsaken! But then I tried a risky approach.

"Little Eva, my dear Michael, pay attention! Do you want your father to stay? Your dear good papa?"

Michael didn't let go of his car, the little one crouched down with her doll, yet I was satisfied, because both children looked up.

"It's true, then, you love your papa?"

The children looked at me curiously, making no sound and not moving an inch. I wanted to draw closer and gather them in my arms, but Johanna stepped in between to protect them.

"Do the children not recognize me?"

"No. They think you're dead."

That was too much for me. I turned away from Johanna and the children and walked outside, where the men who had set down the coffin lazily grabbed hold of it and with heavy boots stomped on the hard cobblestones with one foot after another.

"Can we finally have the body?" the one in command asked in a level tone.

"No, you can't! There is no dead man to have, or at least I'm the dead man."

The man who had asked—there was no doubt, he was the one in charge—scratched himself with his long fingernails, making an awful sound.

"We don't want anyone living. Only the dead! Where is he?"

"You'd better look elsewhere for your dead man! There's none here!"

The other man became uncertain and poked his companion in the side.

"Then we better get going, Brian."

"Don't butt in, Derek, and shut your mouth! The house number is right. Bring out the dead!"

"Try and find him!" I said tauntingly, and opened the front door.

On the street stood a handsome large hearse, the driver sitting bent over the steering wheel and seemingly asleep. He was not at all worried about anything and certainly wasn't in a hurry to haul away a dead man. That set me at ease, and calmly I turned toward the house, where the men were not satisfied with my arrival, and fervently dealt with Johanna. Perhaps she had abandoned the room for her own reason; maybe the men had locked her out. Without abandoning their toys, the children had crept out after her, yet they were shooed back into the room with hand gestures and shouted commands.

"Let the children be—they shouldn't have to lose their father!"

"Good that you're back, Arthur! What are you doing gallivanting out on the street? You're only causing me great embarrassment. The men are waiting for you and want to take you away."

Brian got angry.

"We don't want this guy at all. We want the dead man, or I'm calling the crematorium."

"That is the dead man!" Johanna yelled, wringing her hands despairingly. "You have him right under your noses!"

"What's his name, then?"

"Arthur Landau, if I may, my husband!"

The leader stepped closer to me and shoved me nearly as far as the street in order to get a better look at me in the light.

"Is she telling the truth?"

"The name is right, I can't argue with that."

"There, see?" Johanna interrupted. "I already told you so!"

"Yeah, if that's the case," Brian said, "then you have to get in the coffin. We have to catch a train."

"There, you see," Johanna said triumphantly. "And you didn't believe me."

"Keep still and worry about your own affairs. I'll settle this alone with the gentlemen."

Johanna made a pleading gesture toward the men, which remained a puzzle to me, and then retreated into the room, still shaken and giving me a contemptuous look, but also clearly saddened.

"You can see that there's something wrong here. I'm tired and somewhat sleepy, because I've worked too much. You know what that's like, right? But dead, just take a look at me. I'm really not dead. Don't you agree?"

Derek poked Brian in the side again. It was clear that he wanted to prod him to make a quick exit in order to avoid embarrassment, but Brian poked his colleague in return and didn't stir.

"Whether you're alive or not, I couldn't care less—"

"But you don't disagree, then?" I shot back quickly.

"I couldn't give a damn. But it's right here in black ink. At eleven you're supposed to burn. And then, I guarantee you, you'll be dead for sure."

"But until then . . . Look . . . try to be understanding!"

"Until then? Hmm . . . !"

Again Brian scratched away, as he had done earlier.

"Look, could you please not scratch while in my house? I think you should wake up your driver outside and disappear. Otherwise, I'll chase you off."

"Mister, I'm a civil servant, don't insult me!" He said it angrily and sadly at the same time. "You won't, I tell you, improve your situation that way. Just think about this!" Brian said as he waved his fist. "You certainly won't have a chance against that."

"What a joke," I wanted to reply, but I didn't, for both men looked so ready to have at me while blocking my way as I tried to slip between them and into the street that I thought it smarter to keep quiet for a while and wait for a moment that would be better. Meanwhile, the leader grabbed me by the shirt and tie and threatened me.

"Look, I just want to whisper something to you. If you want things to go well, then I'm advising you to just get in the coffin on your own. We'll just put the cover on loose and not nail it shut. That way, you'll have the chance to tell your story to the director of the crematorium yourself. Maybe he'll let you go. I'm only making this one exception for you, and because you want to live. But, once you lie down in the coffin, you'll see how all your desire to live will disappear."

I didn't agree with this suggestion, but by now I was well versed enough not to openly resist the man.

"I don't want to give you any trouble, but I'd like to make a different recommendation. Put the coffin in the hearse and let me remain outside. I give you my word that I will walk there on foot in order to straighten everything out." Quickly I added, in order to come to an immediate understanding, "How's that sound, gentlemen?"

Whether it was this last comment, by which I put myself on the same level as the pallbearers, or because of caution in the face of a situation never encountered before, the leader seemed willing to consider the suggestion and was no longer keenly focused on my ruin.

"Well, yes. But, as you have to understand, that can't happen. Orders are orders, but we're the ones who have to handle the situation. As for the coffin, that seems fine, if you don't want to ride along. We can tell Jock, and he can drive ahead with the empty coffin. But you'll have to get a move on, and we'll all go together."

That I wanted to avoid. I didn't want any escort on the way to the crematorium, for I wanted to speak privately with the director.

"Couldn't you just go in the car and say that I'm coming? I'll be right along."

"No chance. Man, do you have any idea what I'd be risking if I let you walk? So it's either into the box and off with you or to walk there, but only with us along!"

I had to agree, and breathed a sigh as the men shouldered the empty coffin, carried it out to the street, and stowed it in the glassed-in rear compartment of the hearse. I looked on and was amazed at how knowledgeably Brian and Derek went about their business. To my surprise, since I didn't know where they had got the stuff, they neatly arranged sprigs of flowers on the coffin lid and made every effort to make certain that everything looked just like a regular funeral. These bright decorations of gladiolas and tulips, mixed in with the deep, dark green of palm leaves, made me feel sure that someone really did want me dead, there being nothing wanting but my assent. I almost regretted missing out on such a dignified opportunity, for it would be merciful to suddenly counter my decision and quietly say, "Look, I've thought about it, and I'd like indeed to give the coffin a try." There was nothing left but to ready myself for the final passage, it only being a comfort that no one on the street will know how dead I am, for no one thinks of a pedestrian as being dead.

The men had finished decorating and looked over their work once more from all sides before carefully closing the back of the hearse. Unfortunately, their work sparked the interest of the neighborhood. From the nearby houses, grown-ups and children appeared who looked on and observed and whispered among themselves. From the large apartment building across the street, people looked out their windows, the two women and their cats among them, everyone looking on with interest, though without concern, at the fatality. Such detached interest was horrible to me; I drew back almost as far as the front door and would have loved to close it, though of course I couldn't commit such a breach of trust against the men, nor would they be very pleased by it. Nonetheless, I was curious how everything would unfold. Then I heard the squealing voice of Mrs. Byrdwhistle as she wished her neighbor Mrs. Stonewood good morning.

"Looks to me as if the stranger is a goner."

"He should have pulled through."

"It all happens so fast. I say it's a shame, a crying shame!"

"Yesterday I saw him still horsing around with his kids. You know, the stranger—he's just like a child."

"Yes, yes, just like a child. Indeed, he loved to play with them, always horsing around with the kids."

"He's all played out."

"Yes, played out."

"Yes. You know, Mrs. Stonewood, if he had stayed back there where he came from maybe he'd still be alive today."

"Perhaps, that could be. You think then that if . . ."

I didn't listen any longer to what Mrs. Stonewood said in reply. The men were done with their work, and Brian turned to the driver, who was still snoozing, and thumped him hard.

"Hey, Jock! Are you awake? Let's go!"

Jock rubbed his eyes, looked confused, and shook his head several times.

"Okay, then. Everything go all right?"

"You'll see soon enough. Get going and tell them that we'll be coming along later with the body."

Jock opened his mouth to say something more, but the leader lifted his hand and gave him the signal to drive off. Then the ignition turned, the gear shifted quietly, and the car began moving and was soon gone. The pallbearers stomped back into the house and laughed, saying they had done it. Johanna was also there, letting children back into the hallway who had not been able to see what was going on. The bright ringing of voices rose as they bounded around in their uncontained joy over the visitors, who looked around them, they not half so powerful without a coffin.

"Look, Johanna, I'll do whatever you want me to. I'll get my passport and papers and will be happy to go off to die."

I had not planned to say that; it just slipped out. Yet, before I could catch myself, Johanna took advantage.

"Look, that's exactly what I said. Wouldn't it have been easier the other way? Now you'll have to hoof it in order not to be late."

"Don't you worry, my dear! There's still plenty of time. I'm looking forward to the walk, it's so refreshing."

"Okay, whatever you wish. It doesn't matter to me what you batter away at with your thick skull."

I went to my study; it looked completely cleaned out and seemed much bigger. Yet I was also convinced that things had been left untouched, the furniture standing pressed up against the walls as always. I had no trouble finding my papers, which I gathered up along with my checkbook, calendar, and notebook. "It's important to know what day it is." This I said aloud. The men outside heard me and thought it was a question, because Derek then told me the date. I thanked him, for he was nice—indeed, pleasant for a pallbearer. Unfortunately, that was little consolation, for I recognized immediately, as I inspected my birth certificate, which I had been issued back there after the war, that he was right. It was curtains for me; I didn't have a chance. I thought of how I had come to this country with a visa that was good for only four weeks, which is why, after I left the ship and followed the curving path to the left, marked "Foreigners," two border officials put their heads together and discussed whether they could let me into the country. One of them felt that since I would be in the country for such a short time there was no cause for concern, for the stranger would then return home. But I didn't leave, for my stay had been extended, and I had been given extra time on a number of occasions. Now the deadline was passed. I could expect no more leniency, and would have to be sent across the border, whether on a ship, into the water, or into the fire. Brian and Derek were here to maintain the border in their own fashion. Whoever didn't leave these shores on his own was picked up by the officials of death, locked in a box, such that he died behind the border, done in at last, that day having come. That was also the reason that Johanna no longer stood by me. She knew this country much better, having lived here for some years already.

I looked at my books, I peeked into the cabinet where my writings were locked up: everything was in order. I could relax. It would be best to fill a suitcase with the best of it in order to stash it away. But that was nonsense. It would do no good, for publishers had turned up their noses at so much sadness and didn't want anything to do with it, no one having ever shown any interest in sinking himself into my thoughts. My melancholy work was of no use to me, since I was to be cremated. I should have asked the border officials whether anyone at the crematorium might be interested in my writings, but at best they would have laughed at me. Why confuse Brian and Derek, who didn't know anything? My works were best buried in the drawers in order that they not be burned up. Johanna believed in their worth and would hold on to them. Widows and orphans help, for someone would show up wanting my things, and Johanna would sell them to an archive. So I left behind my soul, the works and thoughts of my intellectual pursuits.

"I loved you all, because in you I have borne witness. You will remain when I am no longer deceived by my own vanity."

"It has indeed deceived you, Arthur."

"Why are you here, Franziska? You never liked funerals."

"I still don't like them. It's only because of you, my friend . . ."

"Well, then, what? Spit it out! Why so quiet?"

Franziska said nothing more, even though I asked her again. Then I looked at her blank face. She was elsewhere, transported, having disappeared into the unknown without a trace. I called after her.

"Are you lost to me for good? How can you leave me at this hour?"

I was given no answer. All I could hear was the border officials outside as they scratched and cleared their throats, and I knew that they would soon grow impatient.

"Are you still there?" I called out without opening the door.

But the men didn't answer. As I listened at the door, I could hear no sound. Ashamed, they had no doubt crept off. I dared to hope for such a miracle. There was nothing to fear from death; on its own, when it turns away and spares us, it's a blessing we are given, and we say a prayer of thanks for being saved. Franziska had sacrificed everything for me, and I rejoiced, for she had come in order to scare away death, she having at first removed the coffin from the ship of death of her own volition, and now the bearers of my heavy guilt as well. I turned to a wall and prayed, bowing my head, the blood rushing to my skull, me digging down and holding on in order that I not lose my grip if, indeed, I was finally alive again. "Just a little while, I know, but give me just a little while and teach me, so that I don't foolishly waste the days I have been granted but instead consider every hour sacred and invoke your name, your glory, and your will. For you, my Lord, are the Lord, and I am nothing when I do not exist but rather only a fleeting creature before your eternal presence. Thus, in this hour, answer my—"

There was a knock at the door. I was startled, such that I could no longer pray. Yet I had said all that I wanted to say and was satisfied. Johanna stood in the doorway, pale and full of reproach.

"Okay, Arthur, where do you think you're hiding! We're all waiting for you; the breakfast is cold."

Why should I eat anything? I asked myself, and stood there wavering.

"Come on, then!"

She motioned for me to follow, half angry and impatient, half friendly, and she couldn't understand why I stood there so obtuse, as if her words were a puzzle. Since I continued not to stir, she took me tenderly by the hand.

"Do you have to cause me such trouble on this day of death! The men are so nice, and are eating with us. But you stand there lost, as if you didn't have a heart. Don't you want to have your last meal with us?"

"No, I don't. Nor is it going to be my last meal. Things have completely changed. I'm staying home today. Please, just leave me alone!"

As far as I could see, Johanna was not backing down; instead, for the first time that day she showed understanding and lightly patted my shoulder.

"You dear, dear simple man. If life were only as easy as death, then you would have won. Have you forgotten why the men are here?"

"Franziska took them away."

"Franziska?"

"Yes, she came and gave me life. Now you can be a lot happier with me. My stay has been extended."

Johanna shook her head in quiet sadness, looking at me deeply and painfully as never before. It touched me and impressed me that she hesitated before me so helplessly.

"What's wrong, Johanna?"

"With me? Nothing. Only with you. Sit down. Come and eat your oatmeal."

She took me by the hand. I could have resisted, for I felt strong enough to hold my ground. But Johanna was overcome with sadness. She, who was otherwise so strong, was all of a sudden a compassionate fragile creature who had to be treated tenderly in order not to be wounded. Shyly, I ventured a final word.

"You know, dear, one shouldn't leave anything unfinished. They are just trying to do their job, I can tell."

"It's not unfinished, dear. You've done enough already."

"It's easy to think so, but it's not true."

It wasn't possible to protest any further, and so I quietly retreated down the unavoidable passage to the room off the garden in back, where the table was much too festively laid out. Spirits were high, the pallbearers pleased with the food, smacking their lips and joking with the children, which pleased them. Johanna had not scrimped and had prepared a huge breakfast. There was ham and eggs, lovely toast, butter, honey, and marmalade. The men slurped down tea with pleasure from our best cups. For me alone, there was oatmeal in a little bowl, Brian and Derek preferring their more ample helpings.

"Well, then, sit down, Arthur. It's about time!"

"We thought you were dead already!" the leader added rudely but meaning well. "Your wife—boy, can she cook! What she does with her bacon, soft as silk, simply *primissima!*"

Brian talked with his mouth full, bits of fat on his lips. I forced myself not to be rude in reply.

"If it tastes so good, you can come back again soon—both you and your friend!"

"Thanks very much, we'd be happy to! I'm a widower. To have a wife like yours would be easy to get used to!"

The leader was rude and had no idea that he should be ashamed, rather than looking straight at me with a big grin. He stuffed his mouth full, chewed, and called out with pleasure.

"Nothing shy about me! I'm a man!"

The children both trembled. Derek noticed and wanted to put them at ease.

"No need to be afraid, my little sparrows! Brian there is a good guy, and funny. He won't do us any harm."

"No, little bugs, no need to get all worked up!" yelled the leader even louder. "I won't be coming back."

"No? Really not?" Michael asked anxiously.

Eva began to cry. I saw how it was too much for her mother, for, in addition, Michael was not at all eased by Derek's words and also began to sob. I would have been happy to comfort Johanna and come to her aid, but I could sense her deep resistance like a cold wall, she fearing for the children more in regard to me than to the men, a dead father being no blessing but rather something that would harm the children. Therefore I looked at the pallbearers in seeming confidence, and turned to Brian.

"I think there's no more time left to lose. If you're full, we can head off."

"Right! You're no fool!" the leader confirmed.

"But you didn't eat any oatmeal and hardly drank your tea!" Johanna said with slight disapproval.

That was the last straw. I stood up and was firm with the unwelcome guests.

"There was only a little bowl of it, and it was for me. And besides, the gentlemen don't eat oatmeal and, what's more, I'm sick of this whole charade."

The men had not expected such decisiveness on my part. They were taken aback, stuffing their mouths with several bites more and shifting uneasily in their seats.

"No hurry, don't choke!" I joked. "Whoever eats last eats best."

Johanna had taken Eva, who wept bitterly, onto her lap, Michael meanwhile pressing his head hard into her.

"If you want me to go with you," I warned the men, "then behave as if you do. I'm done and will wait for you out front."

My sudden hurry annoyed the pallbearers, but they didn't dare risk showing their displeasure, instead devoting themselves with undiminished desire to eating more, drinking their tea in haste, and, finally, indicating that they were ready to follow me. Yet they continued to sit there. Johanna wavered as to whether she should be thankful that I had taken command of the situation so forcefully or if she should speak up and ask me not to leave the table without having eaten, since I had hardly touched a bite. Suddenly, she came to a decision and passed by me and down the hall with Eva and Michael in hand, painfully trying to hold the children away from me so that I couldn't touch them or nuzzle them. Once outside, she called back breathlessly that she would be right back, she just needed a moment, because she wanted to accompany me and the men to make sure everything went all right; she just had to leave the children with Mrs. Stonewood. That seemed unnecessary to me, but I said nothing. As I looked for my coat and hat in the hall, the men continued to sit at the breakfast table back in the room, me becoming worried that there was something wrong. Therefore I went back to make sure everything was all right. They were shamelessly stuffing into their pockets what was left of the meal, nor were they the least disturbed by my appearance.

"Do pallbearers always steal?"

The men didn't stop, and grabbed anything they could, not leaving behind so much as a slice of bread. As soon as they heard Johanna outside again, the thieves straightened up and pressed at their pockets to smooth them out, but with no sense of guilt.

"We gave you a break," said Derek. "Now give us one. And, besides, you won't be needing any of it any longer."

Johanna stepped into the room and saw with one glance what had happened, yet she didn't say a word. In a matter-of-fact manner, she spoke firmly.

"The children are fine. Gentlemen, we can leave."

I wanted to let the men lead the way, but they didn't trust me, and so I had to go first. Johanna followed last and locked the house. West Park Row seemed much busier than usual, for there were people everywhere, a striking scene. I was amazed. I had always loved the neighborhood precisely because, even at weddings and funerals, there were never many idle gawkers.

"Is it because of me . . . ?"

The men, who had donned white gloves, gave no reply. It was frightfully clear to me that I had to snake my way through this crowd. I'm sure the men would have helped me if I had asked them, but I dreaded doing so, for they were now solemn and even more disgusting, having put on their shiny black top hats, a showy bit of finery for such a throng of gallowsmongers. I would have been happy to have Johanna at my side, for I wanted to cling to her. I had so often depended on her steadiness amid the pressing crush of people whenever we had to go into the city, where I, weak-kneed from nausea and dizziness, allowed myself to be steered through the clogged and swarming clumps of anxiety. Yet Johanna, though not seeming upset, was not ready to take my arm. Not once did she reach out to me, as if she had agreed with the men not to do so. She appeared braced to avoid any commotion, not wanting to escalate it through any show of sympathy. Since I recognized many I knew among the crowd, I was shocked. I said hello to no one, nor did anyone greet me; instead, they regarded me with a peculiar mixture of mild contempt and indulging regard. I peered back at Johanna to see if she acknowledged anyone, but her demeanor remained unreadable. She seemed neither to care about the people nor to care about me, even when she cast a quick glance my way. I didn't know if it was because there was such a crowd or because of the gloomy weather, but the sweet numbing stench from the sewers was especially heavy. The vapors wafted over us, containing the sadness of an entire city, such that tears ran from my eyes. I held my handkerchief to my nose, but only for a little while, for it attracted attention and made me look like a weakling. Johanna also smelled the terrible odors, but no one else seemed to notice.

The pallbearers, who pressed close to me, were unconcerned and only annoyed that people stood in our way. Luckily, Brian and Derek were especially tall and stood well above the others, especially with their tall hats on. And so they were able to make their way through, the crowd giving way to them without their needing any assistance from the police. Meanwhile, I would have been happy to talk with someone, be it even a little chat with Derek, though less so with Brian, if only to remove the suspicion that I was someone to be shunned, and whose removal was the only point of an otherwise miserable day. But the people around me were too shy to acknowledge my welcoming glances, while Derek and Brian didn't even think of talking to me, either. They only kept a watchful eye on me, making sure that I made no sudden move, they not even speaking with each other except for the odd fleeting word here and there. As for striking up a conversation with Johanna, as was my right, I would have been glad to, but I somehow felt that might damage her reputation. I also didn't want to cause her difficulty. So there was nothing left for me to do except silently make my way forward on my difficult path, step by step. This wasn't that hard, for I felt alive. However, it was very clear that I was expected to die, the shyness with which I was greeted being stronger than any rampant curiosity that brazenly emerged from people's glances and demeanors. There was the rustle of fall in the awful air, a column of smoke also arching aslant and heavy across the cold sky. I couldn't tell if it came from the squat chimney near MacKenzie's or from the crematorium farther off. It was not at all still, nor could one expect that it would be, but no shouts or alarms of any kind were allowed, the onlookers only pale and tired, having slept badly the entire night; if I wasn't mistaken, mild disappointment could be seen on their faces. A woman whom I thought I knew, having seen her often at Simmonds's, accidentally bumped up against me, and it surprised me that she was carrying a full bag of groceries. Curious, I looked inside it and saw a lovely large head of cabbage.

"Good morning. What a lovely vegetable."

"Unfortunately, it's really just a balloon."

I turned away and was annoyed that the woman was making fun of me. I looked around to see whether anyone had observed our exchange. No one seemed to have, but it didn't matter, for I felt that everyone had turned against me. The crowd barely hid their joy over my disappearance. That was why it was good that we moved more easily ahead, step by step. Perhaps the police had given them a sign, but when I looked around I didn't see them anywhere. There were a lot of people still in our way, but there was not such a crowd, the curious having given way, the thick swarm behind us not following along, but instead beginning to break up. Now we could walk faster, which made my legs feel good, me quietly thinking about what I would say to the director of the crematorium in order to get him to understand my situation.

"Director, you have to see that my time is not yet up. You're too early, nor is it your job to read any weather map. I agree that it's difficult, which is why I don't resent the trouble you've gone to for me and my family. I don't expect any kind of compensation, Lord knows, for a day lost is no tragedy, but I want to get this all cleared up. You think that my name is Arthur. How wrong you are! Indeed, I agree that I am called that as well. Here, underneath my photo, is my signature, and it says that in fact I am Arthur. But in reality I am called many things more. I have all the names that you could possibly think of, because I am called Adam. Please, don't laugh, but I am the first man, the one who is still alive and who does not die. Once I was called, and I wanted to hide. But that was a long time ago. Now I will hide no longer. Therefore I stand before you. I have brought the ancient curse to the world. Yet that marks a great step forward, and you have me to thank for it. Just wait! Wait with me for the call! You will see that it's for your own good."

Thus I sketched out my speech and warmed to the clever ideas that occurred to me as a defense. Unfortunately, I couldn't develop them any further, for we had come to a halt again. Near MacKenzie's, the string of cars that rattled somewhat as they attempted to enter or leave would not yield. Vainly, Brian and Derek tried to get them to let us through. They waved their arms and shouted at the drivers, but there was no stopping them. Some even laughed openly at the pallbearers and honked their horns, letting loose a frightful din, my enraged escorts becoming angrier and shaking their fists. I couldn't blame them for getting angry. But, finally, the noise was too much for a watchman at MacKenzie's, for he produced a bright-red flag that he waved back and forth. That worked. The drivers braked, and we were able to cross the entrance. There was no longer anything standing in our way. The men walked quickly, for they wanted to make up the time lost. As an experienced walker, I could keep up with them, but for Johanna it was a challenge. She gasped for breath because she had to walk so fast, which was twice as hard for her, because she had put on shoes with higher heels than normal. Again, I would have been happy to take her by the arm in order to help her along. I think she would have accepted my offer, yet I hesitated, fearing that I would be rejected. Between us there was a wall, Johanna most likely going along with things in order to keep up appearances. It worried me that my wife no longer belonged to me, but since I had suffered such terrible separations many times over, I was patient. I looked at Johanna surreptitiously and remembered back. How might I have prevented all this from coming to pass?

I took out my watch. It was an old piece that steadily kept the time, its lovely second hand sweeping across the clock face. It was almost nine o'clock. Actually not that late, but who cared? Only to the pallbearers, the steadfast pair, did it matter, because they wanted to deliver me on time. I didn't care that the cremation was at eleven. Why do people love to schedule these events in such precise fashion? Death approaches; there cannot be much time left, but even the best doctors can be off by several hours or even days. Then one is cremated and buried, and right on time. Everything done to the minute. Things get in the way, but one overcomes them. Someone glances at a watch and decides that it's time. The guests and the personnel are happy the time has come, it having been kept, for it's never good to be late. Death must be allowed to roam free, surprising us in the middle of life, for that is its right. Only murders are often pedantically scheduled, they needing to be carried out at particular times, even when the right of the state takes on such a task and the poor victim is executed. But I was a mistake, for I was not meant to be scheduled for a sanctioned or an unlawful murder, the men having said nothing about it. Nor is one supposed to be killed in a crematorium, for there death is devoured, not life. And what did any of this damn nonsense have to do with me? There was no reason to be walking through the city with Brian and Derek, my dumb good nature alone having let me leave my apartment with them. I decided that as soon as possible I would turn around and take note of certain markers so that later I could find my way back home without Johanna's help. But it was a needless precaution, for we were passing through a long-familiar neighborhood. And I then recalled that there was in fact a crematorium not far from us.

We were already on Middleton Avenue and, past the railway bridge that we were now crossing, we had to turn left onto Temple Road. There stood the flower shops with their wreaths and even lush potted plants, all of it reminding me, as it captured my attention, that I should really buy something nice for my memorial. I plucked some coins from my pocket and pointed toward a flower shop. Johanna figured out what I wanted, but Brian and Derek both felt that there should be no interruption so close to the end, both of them indicating that the crematorium was just ahead.

"Couldn't my wife go?" I asked, deciding to break the long silence.

Brian indicated that she could do as she wished, but there was nothing for me in the shop, nor could we wait for my wife.

"Why such a hurry?" I protested.

Derek, who was much more understanding, reminded me that flowers and wreaths were already on full display for me in the hall, though perhaps I had forgotten. Brian, meanwhile, had had enough of this nonsense and looked at me with contempt.

"Bloody hell, the dead should never be allowed to wander around! I knew it. Just be nice and you end up paying a price!"

Johanna motioned to the men to cease; she was afraid that such talk would upset me. I had by now lost interest in the flowers and approached the spacious display of a stonemason with a vast selection of gravestones, magnificent crypts, and modest urns. Some of the memorials were carved with loving thoughts, others were smooth and cold, but otherwise they were finished, all of it so peacefully smooth and innocent, the sugar-white marble embossed with accursed grief, carrying the weight of mortality, the column broken, the garland and ribbon, Psyche mourning with her hair in disarray, her contorted body naked. How good it is that the inclement weather at the cemetery here doesn't wear away at her, for at the stonemason's she is protected along with the little angels that tenderly look up, their index finger at their lips. I stood before the little angels, probably angering the men, though there was nothing they could do to stop me.

"I like it here. I'd like to have a stone of my own."

The chief angrily tried to pull me away.

"If you touch me, I'll scream! Let me be! I just want a stone of my own. It's great to have such a big selection."

Johanna was happy to see me put up such strong resistance, but she still didn't venture to openly come to my aid. I had to urge her on.

"Just send the men away! They just keep waiting!"

"I can't do that. We've reached the border. You have to take the last steps."

I felt betrayed as never before and began to weep. It was easy for the men to drag me away from the stonemason's to the crematorium. The high wall stood there, stretching out endlessly, behind it tall thick trees, an open forest, me pining to be let loose in it. But I had to keep moving; between two false walls the wide somber portal opened. As I looked in, I could see groups of people I knew gathered together and sunk in silence. They didn't acknowledge me, though they nodded to my wife, several of them quietly raising a hand in greeting. Meanwhile, Brian and Derek remained always close by, either right next to me or just behind, thus devoting neither the watchfulness nor the attention befitting the dead. They only pointed emphatically toward the portal, which I answered with a mercurial smile. Then they stood up proudly, with heads lifted high in order to present a good example to me and the gathering, and walked toward the door without turning around to me. Thus, whether out of stupidity or ultimately from an awakened sense of judiciousness, they had freed me; I did not have to follow them. I actually hesitated for a moment and did not move from my spot, but then I lost myself again, the will that had manifested itself that morning suddenly retreating, for I no longer felt it to be real.

No matter how hard I looked and looked, it was no longer possible to see anyone; a weakness of the eyes or some fog hid everything from me. Thus I knew of no other way out except to follow Brian and Derek, meek as a lamb. Did I no longer have a wish to go it alone in the world? I wavered, but no, it was simply unbearable; loneliness was far worse than everything being ruined. I lurched forward, it being hard to move, my legs having fallen asleep. I could hardly lift them from the ground, and I pounded on my thighs in order to loosen them up. It did little good; I had to use my hands to move one foot in front of the other. It went awful slowly. In order to salvage something from my mishap, I decided in despair to ask the pall-bearers to help, even if I felt ashamed and was a little afraid of them making fun of me. As I turned around to look for them, the fog had grown so thick around me that I realized there was no battling it, nor did it make any sense to call out. And yet I did call, though without any words, for they just didn't come. I tried to be as loud as I could, to be heard amid such desolation, but my voice was weak, only a peep emerging, and soon just a hoarse scratching, a thin whimper that didn't even sound human. Nor was there a door to be found anywhere, for I could see nothing and had lost my sense of direction. I tried to control my fears, and told myself that I could still get where I had to go, even if I didn't know in which direction I was headed—all I had to do was go on. But I was wrong. No matter how I flailed about while drowning, I never found the portal.

Fortunately, it became easier to walk, and I even managed to reach the wall. But I didn't find the door. I tried a couple of steps to the right and then to the left, but always there was the wall and no entrance. Then I grew sad that there I was all alone, everything different from what I had planned at home. Johanna stood at the ready someplace else, estranged from me, perhaps even lost, and the children as well. I had no hope of finding her still on West Park Row, and Mrs. Stonewood would refuse to give any information, or maybe not know anything at all. And how was I even to find my way home? I had vainly convinced myself that I could take in everything along the way in order that it be stamped in my memory, thinking this way, then that, it all seeming like child's play. Now I believed that I felt the wall, it being wet and slippery, and I could grab hold of it, my fingers slipping away, though it hurt to bang into it. I decided to be patient until the weather grew brighter. It was a busy neighborhood; surely someone would soon come along who could tell me in which direction I should toddle off. I was mistaken, for I remained alone. It wasn't cold, so I sat down like a beggar and waited—for what I didn't know.

As I rested I began to feel better, even comfortable, though I was surprised at how gloomy the light had become, the sky hanging low and flat. Had the trees behind the wall suddenly grown, or had someone closed the curtains, not caring how much that bothered me? Maybe I had been resting long enough, such that I had forgotten that daylight had passed. I could glance at my watch—that would tell me something—but it was stuffed too deep in my pocket, such that I was unable to reach it, my hands digging around for it. Then I thought I heard someone opening the door quietly, though I could have been wrong. Nonetheless, it was a familiar sound that convinced me that there must be a way out, if not for me, at least for others.

"Shall we finally get a move on?" asked Anna. "Otherwise, we'll never make it there today."

I rubbed my eyes, jumped up, and called out quickly, which is what I do whenever I want to hide the fact that I had been almost completely out of it.

"Yes, of course. How nice that you came to get me."

"Why wouldn't I? You said after breakfast that you needed a bit of quiet, and then you kept me waiting downstairs."

I asked her forgiveness and pulled myself together, shifting the knapsack. She had already closed it. I was grateful to her for making the sacrifice and heading off to the lovely mountains just so that I could see them once again. How often I had told her about these mountains in the past months, for ages and ages. She felt that I should go, for it would change me and do me good, make me happier than anything else would, it being something I would have been happy to do even if it were not a question of my health. I could think of a thousand reasons to delay this journey, for the memory was too strong, my fear of the encounter overtaking me. How could I dare enter Franziska's realm, where everything was an expression of her soul, whereas I was nothing more than an unbidden intruder in a world that didn't belong to me? Forest, everywhere forest, the furtive feel that threatened to push me away or to engulf me. This was not permitted; I didn't dare risk it. For the journey threatened to do me in the moment the train traveled up through the valley of Angeltal. She saw that I was never going to decide, and said, "Any day now, I don't have forever," yet for almost a week she planned to travel with me in the mountains before I left this land forever. She had done it only for me. Now it was the third morning, and today we had to risk making the great trip that I had so wanted. She urged me on and grabbed another little scarf from her room. Then we stormed down the wooden steps, the innkeepers waving, wishing us well, and were on our way.

The day was clear, the grass shimmering with morning dew and the ample fields with flowers, soft mist rising from the ground, the cool air breathing in the warmth that arched above. I had never felt so good since I had come back. Soon we were climbing higher up toward the Girglhof. Then, however, came the forest, calling to us, inviting us freely to enter it, calm, dense, powerful, growing up from the hard ground, the earth black and green, often damp and marshy, then hard and stony, milky spots of gray, also covered in green and with dark roots, heavy and feeling like home. With solemn earnestness the spruce trees rose upward, their aureoles almost entwined with one another, soft light pouring down from above, making the ground and the shadows darker yet, all of it comforting and secure, there beneath the folds of a many-layered canopy, alive and continuously moving. The ground was varied, a soft carpet of moss covering the broad flats, skeins of lanky forest grasses gathering where the trees parted from one another, coppery brown needles covering the forest floor far and near, now and then knobs of roots pushing up out of them, tender long shoots of sallow plants here and there sprouting up, sorrel also lifting its glassy filaments above the ground. The path was lined with rows of blueberry bushes, which often trailed off into the forest, and similar, somewhat darker, but not as high, the healthy shoots of lingonberry bushes spread wide.

We climbed silently. I didn't look much at her who had made the hike possible. I only left it to her to lead the way, she having taken charge and seeming satisfied. More and more I wanted to disappear into the forest, to feel it all around me and everywhere, in each tree, memories and hopes at every point, a guest in a home that had survived so much and will survive so much more, that allowed me to enter and took me in and yet didn't even know me, untouched by all my suffering, yet also wrested away from forever, the close-knit fabric on the edge of the anguished country that was no longer my country, not at all here inside the mountain forest, where the hillside offers no one any refuge and soon the valleys must dream of being emptied of humans.

I was never at home in these mountains but always a stranger, yet more deeply enclosed than in any old city, or anywhere in the country or the world. Never had a landscape been so alive to me in its sounds, stimulated more tastes or more smells. I loved it when the long beams of sunlight poured down, when the branches were warmed and the underbrush crackled. I loved it in the rain, when the water dripped heavily from the raspberry bushes, when layers of fog rose and fell, or the wind blew cool in summer or nearly toppled the trees in autumn, when the powerful blasts of thunderstorms threw sultry fear into the tall rumpled crowns of the trees. I loved the mountain forest in any weather, hardly known paths having carried me into it for many hours, where an always renewed sense of fullness, whose blessing was secured by the view, left me alone with myself, a man in the world of trees, a man not among men, a man with a chosen and friendly companion, a man next to Franziska's loveliness, she who felt herself the guardian of a secret realm amid the protection of the surrounding area, myself a man in the hidden reaches of the dense covering that granted me more freedom than the open fields, because I remained unto myself, rather than one continually searching, and therefore unobserved, never locked out, never held back by fences, not warned to stay away and forbidden to enter. And if I chose to walk through my territory and relish it, it would stand strong and thick, me treading every loved piece of it with grateful feet. But when a stretch of meadow or a forest, an outcrop or an elevation briefly granted a view, sometimes from only small nooks and not for very far, often narrowly hemmed in by thickets, and only sometimes stretching off into the distance, or down into the valley, across to a wall of trees, upward to the cloud-covered peaks of Angeltal, across the river to the next string of alps, to Prenet, Brückel, and Panzer, or farther to the dells, from which Eisenbach and Regenbach get their water, and the swelling surge of forest behind it that doesn't end, with Kuppen just beyond, which was often barely visible, and the Hahnenriegel towering above all, then Pamperberg and Fallbaum, each higher than the other, Laksberg with its broad cliffs and Falkenberg thrusting steeply upward, a mountain world that suddenly was there when I wandered along this side of the ridge, it then becoming solemnly quiet, desire and longing falling away, turning in upon themselves. The joyous feel of solid ground.

All of this was granted with time, it only requiring the will to bring it on, the rest of it coming naturally as I wandered along, be it for a long while or a short time, a single step often being enough, a couple of leaps, and once again the forest was the lord. The culmination, which gave the soul pause through such calming experience, manifested itself suddenly and quietly. The view, which the distance provided, remained potently there and sunk within itself, entirely at rest, covered over and entangled, it being able to be invoked again, only a step, a quick jog to a certain spot being all that it took to reveal itself anew to the curious. Whoever lived in the nearby towns or worked in the valleys or pounded away in the forests, whoever went along with his daily chores here certainly could not discover it in the same way as the committed visitor. However, Franziska and I expected to find it here. We were never disappointed, because we brought our hardships to the mountain forests. The days linked together like shooting sprigs, or was that the placid treetops above us? There were no days as usual, for they rose above the usual cares. Yet within this lay danger, for they themselves grew desirous, wanting it not to end. Thus they almost gave us too much, because freedom is a dream but not a human property.

This became clear to me as I pressed deeper into the forest with my companion and indulged myself in happiness once more. Nature and human beings, was what I thought, but in between there was sin, or Adam cut off from the garden of blessedness. Yet I didn't let these thoughts flare up too much in my mind, for I felt threatened enough already. It had not diminished in these past few days. In the middle distance I had once taken comfort with Franziska, but no longer, for spikes pierced my being and tore through me, the piercing background boring through the forest, perhaps the next moment cutting into my face. So confident was I that the gentle mountain world would continue to convey the magic of its forests, I was transformed deep down—or, better yet, I was drained and left in a heap, and then filled with the dark fruit of decay, which didn't fall from my branch, nor could I get it out of me. Ripe within me I carried the legacy of a deep reluctance, which as a penitent had served to make me resistant, bowing my neck and, even under blows, refusing to accept my demise, since I had always ventured to uphold my being, which after my long patient journey I no longer possessed.

But now I was in the mountains that I never thought I would see again when I longed for them from so far away. Now I had communed with them, and everything in them was still the same, just as I had once known and sympathized with. Away from them, I had to somehow survive. But I had not in fact done so, for I was someone different, one in search of himself, now here again, and yet what was it I encountered? The other one who traced the same steps as a boy here in the forests, the woman at my side so strangely accommodating, an aid to healing and yet injured herself. Recently she had become engaged with her husband's cousin. The couple hoped to soon leave the country, and my own departure was set for even earlier. Now we walked along together. It was goodbye, for both of us, bound for elsewhere, wanted to partake of what was unforgettable about the countryside.

The Teufelsee lay before us, placid and without a wave disturbing its surface. I had forgotten it. I opened my hand and looked at it, then lifted it to eye level, then beyond it to the water, on which my hand floated like a ship. Where the lake creek took a cool drink from the still waters of the lake and flowed on, we stood motionless before the blank mirror, moved by the cliffs and the forest and the steep drop, a distant cold splendor still present when you stood on the edge and gazed down at the steely depths. The somber spruces were visible on the lake's surface and looked even more somber as they sank into its depths, the powerful lake knowing no boundary. Water is stone; everything that touches the lake is stone, be it the algae in the viscous damp, the gray roots that cling tangled and wounded to the cliffs, the blackened trunks that have fallen and, relentlessly tough, still loom above the surface stretching out, the path that winds along above, all of it stony, even the needles of the fern with its brown spores. The lake is the cool eye of the mountains, undisturbed, the lake's rim a craggy brow.

We didn't stand there long. The path soon left the lake, the trail growing wider, the forest no longer composed of trees weighted with time, the light forming itself in thick pools. Until we reached Rotgraben, the incline was gentle. There, however, we turned left, where the path became steep and led along a half-wild lane toward the lake rim. The slope was brightly lit with daylight, the air smelling wonderful as we entered a new patch of trees. Whatever hindrances lay in our path didn't hem in the desire to press on. I felt strong again and was happy that my weakness fell away the more firmly each step was met with resistance. My companion smiled at my urge to charge on and was pleased to see me looking like a boy who did not yet know about heavy limbs. She moved her lips to form a word, but then didn't say anything, only her gaze revealing her understanding. She was happy to help out when too big of a log blocked the path. The edges of it split into long strips, the naked pulp still fresh—clearly there were loggers in the area. One could hear their axes pounding against the branches, their rough calls also breaking through, though we couldn't see the men themselves as they worked away, hidden in the woods. We climbed higher and were soon rewarded, a new patch of forest rising with young trees, slim beeches, here and there a single spruce or fir tree. The path grew unexpectedly more gentle in its slope, then it disappeared. We had reached the top, an open, flat stretch of garden, but not too wide, as on either side it sank abruptly away, its edges rounded off and falling deep down, until it completely disappeared into the shimmering foliage that hinted more at the view beyond than being open in itself. A garden meant for us; we were astounded and happily took it all in. The ground was so soft and smooth, covered with fresh green grass and rustling leaves, not a single stone pressing through the gentle earth, the severity of the mountain turned into delicate reflection.

"A garden to remember, Anna. Don't you think?"

"I never would have expected it."

"No. Yet there are such gardens in the mountains. They are always highly lauded. It's not at all true, but it's easy to think that the vast depths of the forest are only there because of this. A magical garden of astonishing loveliness. And one can't help but speak of it."

"I feel that as well. Is that what you wanted?"

"Come, we need to rest."

We sat down, feeling warm from our efforts without being at all tired. It was pleasant, feeling the peacefulness of the grass under our limbs. I opened the knapsack and shoved it toward Anna. She nodded and prepared us a snack.

142 / H. G. ADLER

"Here you can't help but forget, or at least only remember the good."

I sat up and looked at her.

"What do you mean?"

"Oh, I'm sorry. Forgive me, it's so easy to forget. Were you here with her?"

"No, not here. We were farther south. The town is called Aussergefild. What do you think of the name? From there we pressed on, where it was more severe, more dense, more lonely. The forest thickens, and before you know it you are ensnarled by it. You can smell the high moor; it is acutely mysterious. There you can get lost forever. But there is another town, much closer, which I already pointed out to you from the train. You caught a glimpse of it yourself when we stood at Tomandlkreuz. Remember when yesterday we explored the area around the Panzerberg and came to that forest meadow? There we looked across. There she and I were together, and there we first got to know each other. That is now forbidden ground; I don't want to go there. It's also too far. But where we want to go today— namely, to the top, which you want to feel beneath your feet—there we were together. That's enough. I don't ever want to walk again on the ground that I covered with her back then."

"You know, it bothers me that I always end up talking about her, for it feels like a raw wound. Nonetheless, I always hope that it's of help to you. Since that night when you stayed with me after you came to me, I have always worried about you. You told me many things and upset me, but you've also remained silent. I don't like it, it's true, but since we're both a wreck, you above all, it's occurred to me that I understand you better than you think I do. My only wish was for you to get better. That's why we're here. In this garden, that can happen."

I looked at Anna thankfully, but in fact said little. What she shared with me were only the chatty ramblings of many conversations in which I told her something about myself. She meant well, but she came at me much too strongly. Yet it was my fault that it had come to that, for I had often and too intensely admitted my fears and anxieties to her. There were only a few people who even fleetingly knew of my former world, and Anna was one with whom I always shared it. Of everyone in the city, she alone treated me in a straightforward manner, without mercilessly dragging my heart through the fire of the years of extermination in order to continually revisit the trembling ghostly light of the past, but instead engaging me just as myself. When I was confused, when Peter's foolishness or encountering other people was insufferable and painful, I sought comfort and ease from her, or at least a distraction. She alone took what I said to be a delusion, and never at all madness, her sympathy being clear. Nor did she, like other women, seek brief comfort, for we demanded nothing of each other. Franziska was a part of me and remained locked within me. Therefore I was doubly happy that Helmut, the pale returnee with the big lit-up eyes of a child, who had so cleverly got hold of some harmless clothing, soon won over Anna to the extent that she entrusted herself to him. He was the right man for my friend; Helmut was a nice young man. We had little to say to each other, but he was captivated by me in a somewhat awkward way, always wanting to hear my thoughts and doing many nice things for me. The most touching was the fact that he was the most enthusiastic supporter of our farewell journey into the mountains, for he talked to me quite heatedly when Anna went silent over my protests, envy and jealousy being entirely foreign to him. And so we could travel together. A lovely understanding existed between Anna and me. The dead from our past granted it to us; the escape we prepared for strengthened it, even though our fates and our reasons were very different. Neither Anna nor I felt compelled to leave this land, yet, nonetheless, both of us had to: I, because of what had happened here, and nothing more being left for me; she because of what had happened now, which meant that she couldn't stay. Up in the mountains everything remained good, but in the valleys you had to prepare for departure. Up above, we tried to ignore it and pretended to have found a home that was loved and devoutly erected within us, though it was not a home at all.

"Who after us will enjoy this garden?"

My question came out of nowhere and wasn't very clever, yet she attempted no answer.

"We have said too much already," she suggested.

"Yes, too much indeed. Yet you can be pleased with me. I have experienced something here, something that, once again, has moved me more deeply than anything else, and yet has not shaken me. Mostly, it has been forgotten. Not really forgotten, for you know me well, but simply absent. It happened in my youth, and had such a powerful effect that it has outlasted the fate I was dealt. Thus there is something that doesn't tear me up. But in the towns, the valleys, and the far-off lowlands it has no place. Only here in the mountains does it exist, intangible, ourselves taken in by it, encompassed by the very heights themselves. We disappear when we entrust ourselves to the mountain forest. Only there do I experience what no other landscape does for me. Yet it doesn't last. The secret doesn't leave the mountains, and we cannot remain here. Or, certainly, I cannot. We are only taken in by it when we enter it. Indeed, that can be repeated every day, always heading for the forest, always sinking into its midst and being surprised the deeper we immerse ourselves in its density, or follow marked paths or logging trails that fork and finally lead to a grove, the tracks of a gamekeeper, or blindly on to an impassable pile of stones, the warmth of open spots of sun, and then once more into the damp surround of cool bushes. There is nothing else one needs to do, no need for an occupation, no worries and no money, or the daily cares that eat away at your being. Just live—it's that simple: live. Who can do that? Not I. Yet when you leave the mountain forest you no longer have any power over others. Only a yearning exists that reminds us of the forest, saying, 'Don't dally, come back, come to me so that finally and forever I can encompass you.' I no longer think about it, Anna, but I know that, as a young boy, for weeks with a friend—it was So-and-So. Sure, go ahead and laugh, Anna! Anyway, it was So-and-So with whom I hiked all around the forest for weeks. We had a tent with us. So we never once had to go into town at night, and, as we awoke early in the morning, we were surrounded by mystery. Only every second or third day, when our provisions ran low, did we look for a village in which to buy what we needed and could carry with us. Then off again. But, you know, that's no longer possible. The short reprieve we were allowed rested only within the existence we are forbidden to maintain."

I closed the knapsack and lifted it up as we left. All around us was birdsong, very soft and rhythmic, accompanying us through the garden flooded with light which ran the length of the narrowing and descending ridge. The birds were nesting there, a flock of finches, happy to break off their mounting clamor before their song attained the cadence of its short beats.

"We've startled them," said Anna.

"You're wrong. They're not startled. That's just what finches do sometimes. They're spoiled boys who, because of their somewhat elaborate ways,
don't take anything too much to heart."

From the west a light wind blew, rustling the beech trees and the more
tender birches that stood out brightly amid the rest of the garden. The
earth rose up soft beneath us, our heavy shoes making no noise upon it.
We floated along, hurrying. But as the tongue of ridge narrowed ever more
and finally fell away steeply, we had left the garden. A couple of steps farther stood a pole with many signs in the middle of an empty clearing that
pointed to a number of different directions. We had reached the country's
border. Two paths offered us a choice—one running along the border which
had followed the crest to here, another which fell away from the border and
ran a bit lower, and which was not as arduous and was better protected from
the wind, though it stretched out in almost the same direction as the one
that ran along the crest. I recommended to Anna that we take the easier one.
She thanked me for being so considerate, yet I should have been the one to
choose, not she, since the day belonged to me. I pointed ahead of me and
set out on the path that ran along the border. Anna followed in silence. After
a brief climb, we managed to scale the Zwercheck without halting. There
then followed an easy stretch along the narrow seam and down the hillside,
after a short while winding through the ample forest, first right, then left
along the border markers. White and new and carefully spaced out, these
marked one of the oldest borders on earth.

For this border has existed for a thousand years or more, no war large
or small having changed it, no one having called it into doubt or seriously
questioned it or needing it to be marked by anything other than the mighty
heights of the mountains. There had hardly been any battles on the border,
the dense and massive snowy outcrops of the ancient forest having defended
it from all the wars. Even the feuds that neighboring lands continued with
one another gave way to the inhospitable mountains and pushed on across
the passes, taking place in the surrounding lower hills or seeking out other
areas where there was more room to maneuver. The villages and isolated
farms on both sides of the border held peaceful people hidden by forest and
weather. Yet still a son, or even a stalwart warhorse, would have to go off to
war, for it wasn't possible to do so in this blessed district, and so they would

go, the army marching elsewhere. No battlefield was pointed out to the visitor, nor any destroyed fortress. Even Bayregg, the fallen castle that guarded the entrance to Angeltal, situated with its old streets built of salt which narrowed as they neared the mountains that had hardly been touched by war. The border kept it away. Over generations, the surveyors always happily came to the mountains and worked together on figuring out just where the border ran. They first did it in the 1760s and, as a memorial to their visit, dates and names were chiseled into stones. They lasted a long time, graying and becoming covered with spots and disappearing into the thickets only when people forgot about them. I saw them once myself, here and also farther south. I was fond of them, and they strengthened my faith in the peaceful survival of people in these neighboring countries. These stones faithfully did their duty for a hundred and seventy years, and served the needs of the forest people no less than those of the distant regents. But then, finally, someone recalled the advances that had been made in the world and sent the surveyors out again, and even they found themselves in agreement. They just knew everything much more precisely, which was the mark of progress. Nonetheless, even after such a long time the art of measuring had not advanced that much, because the men moved a stone only here and there, when they didn't end up leaving it in its old spot, moving it a step or two into one country, then elsewhere into the other. Rarely was it three steps or even four. None of it did any harm to the border and the countries, and it could be hoped that it would suffice for the next hundred years.

Yet this time things were different. After only a few years, the border fell. There was no battle over it—or at least it was one that took place far away from here in a magnificent hall, where, bent over maps, red pencils held in greedy hands, the supreme leaders had gathered. They didn't look at the mountain forest; they hardly knew anything about it, never having even seen the border. There they sat in the cold, bright splendor, envious, blasphemous, and afraid, pencils quivering in their fingers. Then they swept away the border, not considering the price to beloved peace, which the border had never destroyed. And as the border ceased to exist, so they pledged themselves to war, which those who were afraid wished to avert and those who were defiant wanted to unleash. The battle didn't happen in the mountain forest, for the murderers kept their distance, the fields of ruin lying far from here, they not having the heart to attack the forest, sparing, as well, the villages far and wide that also did not suffer as cities on either side were smashed to pieces. From each country people were rounded up and sent away, denied any sense of security. And anyone the leaders—who paid no heed to any old border—no longer wanted around, because they were not worthy of living in their borderless tortured empire, were shunted here and there until they were knocked over the head and were dead within the hour.

When the war was in its last days, there being nothing but moaning and spasms and decay to the east and to the west of the dark-green mountain forest, powerful formations of the fast-moving tanks of the victors pressed through the mountains, though not over the ragged peak, or through the dense forest or through the narrow thickets and the inextricable wood; instead, upon a few wide roads they moved through the passes here and there without paying any attention to the border. With just a glance at the map, they knew that they had crossed the conquered border, after which they leaped into the heartland, in order to finish off the beaten opponent, who hardly amounted to anything and was soon whisked away in dirty bunches to prison, every last one of them.

Now the old border meant something again. Undisturbed and secure, it cut off suffering from the newly separated countries that sensed it and wondered what to do. The border markers on this path do not look as if they have ever been ripped from the ground. Did the old ones just crumble away and disappear? It is astounding, yet they have survived and have just been freshly painted, given a new white coat of lime. I was surprised that the reestablished border was not guarded, no guards to be seen anywhere. Did the border mean so little? It was clearly not secured, as if the war had never happened, the mountain forest shared peacefully by the two countries as always. Yet whoever lived on this side, be it in the nearby valleys or farther off in large and small towns, he no longer had a homeland when raised to speak the language that was spoken beyond this border. The border here in the forest, besides providing smugglers with protection, no longer protected anything the way borders should but instead only threatened. He who yesterday had a home, who wanted to set down roots, had lost his rights. With feeble mothers, with old gray fathers, with babies and children the women could pack their things in a hurry and be off, everything they'd worked for taken away at a single command, the love of one's country ripped away from its home source, thrown together with others into a couple of prison camps and there sometimes mistreated, often no husbands with them. They had wanted indeed to leave home years ago and had listened either knowingly or unknowingly to the evil ones—and now they hang on somewhere in many different countries or waste away, shoveled into unmarked graves. Many women don't know what happened to their husbands, no known address, given over to fate and abandoned. But if there were still men among those who were displaced, or if they returned home, they were given orders straightaway and were taken, sometimes with their wives and children, while they who had been sinned against had to make amends for the sins of their neighbors through the torture and misery of forced labor.

But here the border rose up on its own and had no notion of the debacle afoot in the valleys; the living and their scars were not brought into the exalted silence of the forest but, instead, those stolen away were sent across the border in sealed trains with officials riding on them, armed and in uniform. Nothing of them remained here. The path along the border of lost dreamers that one can think of as having wandered off into the tall forest, it didn't get us into trouble. We saw no one who secretly slipped across the border to bring news or carry away goods. No one wanted to flee; none took the opportunity to do so. If it weren't so bad, fear would not have forced those threatened to steal away on secret paths. Sometimes I stopped and listened to hear if anyone might crawl out of the underbrush in order to block our way and demand to see our papers. I had a valid pass that stated that I had been released. Out of sheer faith, I had been granted it when I applied at the office for returnees on the second day. They looked at my face and gave me the red card, which said I was a part of them. Some returned home across the border under duress, penniless and pale, while others were forced out in twos. A border unable to be healed, superfluous amid the worlds of the harsh patriarchs—isolated, ignored, and undisputed. I sought nothing from the other country, and from this one I'd already been cut loose. "When at last we are gone, then it will be different. No longer will we belong, not us, not to the mountain forest with its border!" Anna didn't hear me. I looked at the path that fell away from the crest, promising, shady, and narrow, winding down to the valley of the other country, though from that country no one approached the border. Was it meant to be closed? Who needed this path? Who ever used it? Now we had reached another peak, its top a stony flat ledge covered with impenetrable sticky young trees, with a couple of taller ones rising above it. No view of the countryside offered itself.

"I can't see where we are," said Anna.

"Are you afraid? Soon we'll come to a place where one can run away."

"Without any bags?"

"If you don't want to stay, then you don't worry about the bags. It's best to escape inconspicuously. If you're stopped, you can say that you are just out for a hike, a carefree wanderer out for his own pleasure."

"Do you want to leave? Where to?"

"I don't know if I want to. And to which country? Where it all happened? There's a wall between me and it."

"Then why do you talk about moving on?"

"I just do. I'm toying with the idea. I'm searching for me. The feeling of being lost in a bottomless alienation. There's no home for me here anymore; it only leads to anchorless thoughts. Look, here's another little path. It looks quite pleasant."

"Will you try it, just for a bit? Not in earnest, just for fun. Just a couple of steps, so that you feel in your fingertips what it feels like to escape."

"Please, be serious!"

"I am, really. I only thought it could help you."

"It doesn't help me. It's also enough that I can imagine precisely what it means to enter the unknown. The forest is the same there as it is here. I know it, because I've wandered around over there a good bit myself. Down there lies Lohberg or Egersberg. I can show you on the map. First, you walk down. When you reach the first buildings, it will release such a shiver of joy inside your tensed-up soul, for you will be saved, your escape complete and a success, nothing more can happen to you. I will be recognized as a political refugee and will be able to begin a new life. I will speak to the first wary farm boy I encounter. No, he won't be afraid of me, for I mean him no harm and want nothing from him. He only needs to point the way ahead, the next best path toward Lam. There I will certainly be taken in, perhaps not happily, but I can talk with the people. In Lam there is also the last station of the little train that will take me out of the mountains."

"So you want to leave? Just tell me somewhere in the world where you'd like to stay!"

"Stay? Here! I don't mean exactly right here, not in sight of the border. But nearby. In a little forest cabin or a warden's hut, in a forester's house. There I'd like to stay, where I cannot be, where I cannot remain, where I do not belong. Can't you see that, since I know I don't belong, I can't stay? I have to leave, and I'll land somewhere—somewhere that hardly pleases me, or only a bit. There I'll stay, because I can. Where that will be, a country that awaits me, I can't say today, but that doesn't matter. It just can't be here—not here, not on either side of this border."

I said it all calmly, yet Anna stood there listening carefully. But I wanted to move on and give Anna the chance to see that she might learn the peace that the path grants to the wanderer when he follows a stretch of woods through the mountains and doesn't see a single soul on either side of him. Anna should see how the tree line grows ever shorter, how the soft lobes of the leaves shift ever lower, as before us in the distance a train crosses the valley flats and disappears, appearing again from its depths to climb abruptly, the spruces towering up around it, and the chug of the train gently swaying off to the left and up, seeming to disappear. There the forest wall rose up, mighty and tall, reaching for the dark-blue stretch of sky and touching it with its tall peaks. Carefully I urged Anna along, hardly saying a word. She needed to sense what enchanted me here, the green feel of an inevitable end that we could never escape, except to know that it is not an end but rather something soluble through which we could carefully stride without knowing what happened. This type of wandering suspended us in a silver rush, expectancy taking hold of us, it being good when the path is arduous, such that we have to pay attention to its peaks and valleys, the view of the endless open distances also requiring one to observe the near-at-hand, constantly thinking about the next step in order that it be made safely. In this way, we moved right along, neither too fast nor too slow, a wavelike, disjointed syncopation stepping into the glowing high afternoon.

I felt grateful, grateful was what I felt behind the woman striding ahead of me, who wanted to be united with a man again in order to seek a new life, though I was even more grateful for the undeserved moment of grace that this place had granted me in such pure fashion, such that in these enchanted hours I could rise above my plight. It was wonderful to be able to show Anna this forgiving secret place after such difficult days. For so long I had been denied the chance to share its freedom with another person, the border almost hidden and not traversable. It would have been good to say something, but speech seemed imponderable, and no one said anything, nor was I able to. Much as I was moved to say something from deep inside, nothing came out when I tried to put it into words. Everything remained clogged up inside, tightening upon itself, stagnating and unable to be shared with another. Yet here was a place that dissolved the source of comprehensible speech. The grave that first turned consciousness into something unsayable, confusing and burying it, had opened up before me again. I sensed that Anna followed suit and sensed something, herself blossoming in the distance of the mountains. Only children can speak correctly and be understood, I thought, and that's why one loved them and feared them. We, however, Anna and I, were forced into childhood through the benediction of the border, its echoes reverberating through it.

Now the path wound back and forth more often, our goal for the day near, the mountain path rising ever higher, always steeper, sharper, more sparsely overgrown. Not many crests were as craggy as this within the mountain forest, such that the trees that crowned it were not as dense as the others. The first thing the hiker encountered was the hard, naked cliffs with their jagged thrusts. From the path that we had chosen they were the first things we could see, a wall that rose up above the forest wall. The steep path grew smaller, embedded among the rocks, the border not following along and remaining behind. Above the Kegelberg, it bent like a horn and shot its bare crags high above the neighboring land. And, farther down, the hiking lodge stands across the way—indeed, closer to the border.

"The border is not entirely straight," joked Anna.

"The border is too old for that. Who knows who came up with it."

"That anyone could even think of agreeing on it. I can't imagine how they even decided to construct it."

"It's hard to imagine. They think too little about it. The lake, the river, the crest line, the way things are laid out here, or where languages divide people—that's all obvious. But to divide it up haphazardly across areas that are not at all different on either side, that's astounding."

"As a child, I was really afraid of it. I always thought behind the border everything must be different. Almost every summer our parents traveled with us children outside the country. I was always really nervous. The border station, that I understood, but then I was told that was not the border. I looked out the window in order to be sure not to miss it. My father had to point it out to me. Whether or not he knew where it was I don't know. He'd suddenly call out, 'There, look!' Then I was satisfied, no matter if it was there or not. I just imagined that the air was different here than there, a different smell, and that made me happy."

"It was the same for me. The crossing into a different country, which I believed could hardly be noticed, and yet there was something wonderful about it, just as you say, be it the air or the smell. Maybe the people would look different as well. But here in the mountain forest, even above on the crest, we noticed no difference. The land was the land, and the forest the forest. It could be that you had to seek out the people in the valleys in order to be convinced that the countries were at all different."

We had reached the hiking lodge, but we wanted to walk up to the peak before we turned back. The day belonged to us alone. The afternoon had already passed, nor were there any other hikers nearby. But earlier visitors had left traces, the ugly remains of bits of food and thoughts scratched into the placid rocks. The peak had already been conquered. Last came the flat top of the cliffs, with a stile marking the summit. We didn't say a word; only the west wind blew upon us. We could see a long way, but our gaze remained on the nearby forests, heavy and thoughtful, and then immediately around us. Then we looked back in the direction from which we had come, the blackish-green arched ceiling that stretched all the way to Zwercheck, where it fell away. Then we turned toward the south, where the mountain forest split and branched off far into the other country. That is Pfahl, a name meaning "pile" that was well chosen. I pointed out to Anna the peak whose name I knew to the south of the great Arber, the only mountain of the range whose round top towered so high that it would tolerate no trees. All that grew there were knee-high evergreens, while farther up there were only the muted colors of mountain meadows. Separated by a chasm, the ridge ran down to the smaller Arber. Then we were closer to the mountains, yet separated by a valley that widened, each peak a step lower—the Enzian, the Schwarzeck, the Ödriegel, the Mühlriegel—smaller mountains following, then many other high peaks that looked about the same, stretching out ever farther into the countryside. They could be distinguished by their greenish-brown or blue spots while sinking ever lower and more gently into the milky gray distance. Between us and Pfahl was the Valley of White Rain, which greeted us nearby with its bright fields and meadows. There its peaceful villages showed themselves so dainty and humble, the mountain on which we stood rising up from the valley so broad and powerful that it dominated it entirely. The Osser is a proud, majestic mountain, though it is not by far the highest of the mountains in the range, and yet it rests its case on being the last high northern bedrock of both countries.

"It's looking down at us."

I had to explain to Anna what I meant.

"At the roofs of the houses, at the people in the houses, into their very hearts. The otherworldly becomes intimately familiar."

This I had often felt, and loved it. A lookout, where whoever entrusted himself to the peak of such a mountain shared its power and might, and the allure of both. He becomes part of the mountain itself. He relinquishes his own human fears and cannot be harmed. If his duty becomes too much to bear, then he runs straight off into the protection of the forest, becoming small again and, once small, safe again. Anna didn't entirely understand. She found that I had changed and looked sideways at me. Indeed, I had changed, the mountain world having given itself over to me for the last time. Sadness had holed up inside my heart. Indeed, no wall was broken through, but I had exchanged my very being with it; no one could say now what was the wall and what was the person. The search for the wall and for the person, the separation of the conscious and the unconscious—this I could not acknowledge. A painless dissolution, the torment sifted out, and that which had no voice was now a part of me. Thus was I saved. Indeed, without any feeling of home, and yet a place to be. Adam within the world once again.

"Do you recognize me?"

"You are strange, Arthur. I never understood you, and I admit that if I thought that you'd feel better in the forest I was wrong."

"Everyone is wrong, everyone. That's just the way it is. Don't let it bother you. However, we won't forget this day. It's a gift to us both. I couldn't wish for anything more."

"No, nothing more. If you are satisfied, I certainly am as well."

"Satisfied . . . No, there is no word for it. Just let it be! Look at the central ridge here in front of us. After this foothill, it falls away completely. But it's beautiful country. The mountain behind that blocks our view is a mighty sentinel. It dominates the Choden countryside around Taus. And here, the outlying areas to the north with their forests, and the last peak to the right, do you see it? That's the Ratscher, a modest but much-loved mountain. That one I know well. I have often been there."

"With Franziska?"

"Yes. You always want to hear the name, even though you know it already. There we were. There, I believe, we promised ourselves to each other during indescribable hours."

"You believe? One indeed knows, no?"

"I no longer know for sure. Nor do I want to."

"Wouldn't you like to go back there sometime?"

"To Ratscher? No. Certainly not. I no longer know it. It's too much inside me."

"Oh, everything you say has a double meaning. You can't make up your mind."

"How could I? There's nothing that's at all certain. Don't think that I'm just being contrary and don't believe in the real, the sublime, or even the holy. They are simply indefinable. People were much too certain, and too many still are today. They fall into error, but, when they are consoled by it, it must be all right. You can't stand in their way. Yet, for me, it's not so. You have to be able to feel broken and yet not damn the world, to not become callous, not hate your neighbor, not the guilty, for they are your neighbors. You can't separate them from those who are not guilty. Doubt and lack of faith are two very different things. Beware the one who exchanges one for the other, or mixes them up! Avoid negation, and embrace the end, even praise it! For the end is also a gift and is part of the plan. At the end, you submit yourself and accept your fate."

"That's so bleak."

"Not bleak. Not me. It just involves surrendering yourself to oblivion. That may make you uncomfortable. But I think—and this I am very aware of—that you can't also negate the negative. Only then, I feel, really only then can you embrace the positive with all your heart, humbly and reverently. Whoever doesn't love the negative—I mean, who doesn't love it as a test, who doesn't accept his destruction and recognize his Creator because he sees nothing more than his own human misery, and who curses the Creator and all his creation, he only takes the miserable to be true and thinks and acts so."

"Is that true for all?"

"I wouldn't risk such a pronouncement. But I certainly would never maintain that it's only true for me or for such people who have experienced the same or something similar. It's indeed valid, but it's not so obvious to all. And you can't force someone out of his house, out of the house of his soul, out of solitude. Solitude, Franziska said, is the house of the soul. No one can be forced out of it, out of the house in which he indeed knows himself to be safe. But—and it's worth asking—who still has such a house? Who will have such a house tomorrow? Who has his own solitude? Those beaten down must provide the warning."

"Is that your mission?"

"It's not for me to decide."

"What do you think about, then?"

"Nothing. I just try my best, that's all. The rest has already been decided. I don't have to wait for it. It will come of itself. If I can just be, then I am also ready. Otherwise, I don't exist at all."

"What to make of you, Arthur? Especially when you say it all so fervently! I can't compare my experience with your suffering, and yet there's something—"

"Oh, you've been part of so much! Don't object to what I say or explain to me what I know!"

"Fine, I don't mean to say you are bitter. There's no comparison. Yet my life seems to me a dream, and so I walk through life as if through a dream."

"Are you then saying something different than I am?"

"Not really. Or perhaps only that everything seems much simpler to me. If I wanted more, I would lash out. Do you understand? Lash out, such that I would hurt someone and end up wounding myself. But you can't do that—or, more humbly, I can't do that."

I agreed with Anna, and had nothing to say in reply, and turned from her back to the view. I pointed out toward the Ratscher forest, where the landscape, often covered with trees, opened out ever more among fewer and lower hills into rolling fields and flats that faded into the thin silver of the haze above the ever-spreading landscape. "In this direction," I said, "lies the old city." I said its name in an almost imperceptible voice. Anna didn't know why I was whispering. There seemed nothing about this name that one had to keep quiet about. But when I informed her that it was so for me she understood, and for a moment took hold of my hand in sympathy. Above the far-off haze, which stretched out on the horizon like the dense edge of a veil, cumulus clouds floated almost still with their subdued glow. I couldn't stand this scene for long, for I sensed the coming darkness, and the stark waning of the day, so familiar to me, reminded me of having to leave. It was indeed time, the shadows lengthening, the smell of evening pressing its cool feel into the warmth of day. Even the easier path that I had planned required vigorous effort, and I wanted to avoid darkness.

Anna agreed, wanting only to take in the nearby softness once more, as well as the alluring green of the hills drifting off. That was a lovely moment, for our eyes flickered before the enchanting distance. We felt as one the pangs of a pressing pain, yet it came more from what we took in than from our wayward wandering. Once more I pointed down at the Angeltal; quietly, several settlements seemed almost to pass before our eyes. But the peace that the distance offered granted only brief satisfaction. I sensed how the buildings floated there lost, after which my eyes sought the comfort of the mountain train rising up the slope from the right. It displayed to us its sunny side, with its little bridge, as it headed farther up toward the narrow peak rising out of the time-drenched rocky contours of the land like a silent lasting message. However, I tore myself away from this enchanting scene in order not to be lost in the boundless distance.

We didn't need to exchange a single sign as we began to walk down more carefully than was needed. Our limbs felt heavy, ourselves almost done in. As I turned, because the next step required it, everything trembled before me on all sides; at once free of suffering and saturated with pain, it stood gathered before me. I still thought it real, but I could no longer grasp it as it spun around, the border shattered into tender pieces and separating in every direction; peak and valley, sky, the forest splendor, and the green fields mixing with one another, a dense, soughing song pressing into my ears. Was it the mountains? Was it me? Was it the impending departure? I didn't know. Yet it was good that I couldn't lose myself for too long in this alluring, all-encompassing feeling. Indeed, it was warming, but, amid its glow, a deadly chill also alarmed me, a bliss almost drunk with destruction that offered itself in an undignified manner. Pleased and relieved, I saw the hiking lodge before us, ridiculously austere and disclosing the riches of its empty plank tables and backless benches.

It looks abandoned, Anna thought, but I didn't believe it was. As I explored the building, she sat down at a table. The doors were ajar, but they resisted opening with a squeaking noise, as I pushed into the gloomy front hall. Before I pressed into the guest room, a young girl appeared. She didn't seem at all pleased by the visit and asked me sharply what I wanted, as if she wanted to get rid of the disturbance as quickly as possible. There was nothing to eat. However, we didn't want anything. But at least something to drink was offered. There was no milk available, nothing special that had been brought in from afar. Black coffee—chicory, obviously, for what else could one expect?—could be ordered. No, no thanks. Soon it was pointed out to us, even if we didn't want any, that beer was the only other thing available. Fine, then. I escaped outside to Anna and sat down. She had spread a little cloth over the table, and we ate what we had brought along ourselves. After a while, suspicious and grumbling, the girl showed up carrying two glasses of beer. Thin beer from the country that had been destroyed. But at least the drink was cool and pleasant. Anna hesitated, but I told her that this beer wouldn't make her sleepy. The girl just took a couple of steps back, placed her hand on her hip, and stared at us. She was mad at us. And so I called to her and asked to pay. Would she take money from the other side of the border?

"If I have to. At a rate of one to ten."

I gave her what she asked for. She didn't even say thanks for the tip.

"You shouldn't look at us that way. We've done nothing to you."

She lifted a hand and pointed over the border.

"Not me, I'm from over there. But there they . . ."

She didn't say what she was thinking. I had no desire to explain, but Anna nodded at her sympathetically.

"I know it's not right. But we don't feel at home there either."

The girl looked at us as if she would have liked to say something about not wanting anything to do with us. She placed her hand back on her hip. "It's fine by me."

Cold and hostile was how she had spoken. Then she walked back inside the building with a strident gait and closed the squeaking door behind her, though she wasn't happy about being stuck inside and leaped up to open the door a crack. The girl didn't look at us again. Soon we left. Anna had hardly emptied half her glass.

I thought of the slow-witted girl who on the first day at the tank station had offered us fresh eggs with pungent boletus mushrooms, a delicious meal. The woman belonged to another people. Perhaps she had regained control of her property from the regime that had stolen it, having had to forfeit it when the border fell, or perhaps she stole the inn from someone else once the border had been restored. The woman herself did not bring the food; instead, a local girl who worked for the proprietor was sent out in a little Cinderella dress, carrying a bowl, a small young girl of grace and mercy, who worked for the expiation of her unconscious acts, as long as she remained in that country. Meanwhile, Anna had been upset by the incident, and I didn't wish to remind her of it. I kept quiet, both of us quiet and concentrating on the path ahead of us.

The open peaks now lay behind us, the forest surrounding us again, the path leading steeply down, the border behind us. We sank into the King's Forest, huge, lovely, proud, and protected from sharp winds. Soon the craggy path downward was behind us, the way now more moderate along the length of the hillside. When we reached the forest road, we began to walk fast, a long stretch between us, as if we weren't walking together. I had seen enough for today, and knew only that forest followed forest, that I was one with the forest, a forest without end, a forest possessed of the goodness of its own loveliness, a forest that I would no longer be able to experience after leaving it, though there were still many wonders awaiting me along the way: famous tall trees, old beeches, ancient lindens, the wild Klammerloch waterfall, with its swift cold water, the lake black in the late light, as if spun from the evening itself. All of it was still there. I looked on at it, yet I needed nothing more, for it repeated itself with the same pulse and spoke to me, sucking me into its changeable permanence, wearing me down, mocking me, talking me out of who I am and tossing me as a little speck of shadow into the fullness of its unfathomable richness, such that I sank away into it, into its deeply secret and exalted night, into the mottled coolness that rises from the bell flowers, the burial song of the immortals, a humming knowledge, spreading its spirit in the dance of dying thoughts that, empty of desire and fleeting, quietly twine themselves ominously around that which stands tall, grasping the bark, sensing the strong taste of the hidden in the swaying height, carefree and undisturbed, yet always gathered in the splayed needles of the young shoots, cradled in the crackling sway and higher yet, where the squirrels skitter away in fright, where no bird nests any longer in the loneliest treetops.

Forest, forest, and the forgetting that cannot be conquered, yet, below, the sure step that trusts the ground without paying attention, without having to think about it at all. Forest, forest, in the evening, in the weariness branching through one's limbs, in the secret stroll of sleep that would find a home among society, in dwelling and the transformation of dwelling, forest of the dead, forest of the living, forest of those who return and those driven out, the same for all, since only the dreams differ, each possessed of a face and its grave expressions that we grasp with our eyes between the eyelids, calling out a name when we remember it or when a book or a list reminds us, witnesses to our past and to everyone's past, carried over into the sorrow and length of our hours, since everywhere we are met by a face looking at us, demanding and fixed upon us, having tossed away its unexamined questions so that we don't boldly decide to take on their most imposing demand, but such that we also have the heart to stand upon our feet and take hold with our hands, and that we force the lazy lips of our no-good oafishness to heartfelt avowal. Here we are, the children of the forest within every border, ourselves walking entities of the days denied us, and there you are, children of the same forest, all of us foreigners made brothers, ourselves entities, yourselves images as caught by the nimble artists, the confident pencil capturing your expressions, they then painting your faces, always a look followed by a brushstroke, careful, intent, as good as can be, flattering and yet fatuous, but it almost seeming as if done with love, a memorable work to be handed down to your children, who then gather up the likenesses and place them in frames, a sacred legacy, a drawn-out inheritance passed from tree to tree, carved and always kept in the same forest where the houses stand with their many dwellings.

On the walls hang the family trees, reverently dusted off, always branching out from the main trunk, Father and Mother, each of them looking alive and present with serious faces projecting from the past into the present, the sweet eyes meaning something to the grandchildren, the offspring in the forest comfortably gathering around and holding their breath before them. The first reverence paid by gazes that can barely understand, looking up questioningly toward the walls, their own strange future gazing down from the preserved faces, their own hearts full of wonder. A people born of a memory renewed in each new generation, as down through the parents, the grandparents, and the ancestors the first parents continued on, about which the Holy Book spoke, no longer as being in the forest but as sand from the ocean, each a grain created by the same law. Human beings have treasured that which has been; though it might have been in vain, it was also dear to them and, indeed, one often heard it said how important it was to remember. That's why such memories were cherished in those rooms and protected with touching diligence.

Then, however, the destroyer arrived, calling out to the living and leading them from rooms in which the last warmth glowed, the hunted taking with them only a little travel bag, no longer a settled people and also this not an exodus toward salvation but, rather, aimless wanderers, cool and matter-of-fact, almost athletic, hardly having taken one last look around the decrepit dwellings, drawers, and wardrobes standing open and ransacked, only the ancestors remaining undisturbed on the walls, always looking down, steady and true, their mien not in the least withdrawn, though not letting on whether they noticed the horrible changes and the sudden emptiness. No one carefully wiped the frames any longer; no one dabbed tenderly with a white cloth over the similarly colored canvases, with their spreading cracks, or over the faces behind glass. Since the ancestors were frail and old, they could not help themselves and relinquished all responsibility, such that they drowsily turned gray with dust. The faces became wizened, the eyes dull, the hair dry and thin, and the throat weak, their garments meager—a poor people, encased in several coats of grime and soon invisible. Even the frames suffered and broke, gold fading, flaking off in an ugly manner from the wood.

Thus the old time came to a sudden end, and it lasted a long while, until a couple of strangers noisily pressed their way into the dwelling. They stomped coldly and insensitively through all the rooms, their hands raw and wrapping their uniforms tight. They strode around confidently, and yet not at home, and wrote down things as being so long and so wide, so tall and so short, not paying any attention to things, counting, measuring, turning this way and that and knocking things over. Finally one of them looked at the pictures, shoved his way over, growled and whistled, a finger leaving a mark in the dust.

"Hey, look at this! Worthless, everyday stuff."

Then the bunch of them tramped off, having noted down everything that slept fitfully in the dwelling. Again, many months passed before another loose regiment showed up with a thrashing bluster. The men chalked letters and numbers on beds and tables, lifting the groaning pictures off rusting nails in the walls and marking them with the same fat red pencil and signature on the back of each. In crates, suitcases, boxes, sacks, and bundles they packed it all up, schlepping the weight with shuffling steps down the stairs and out to the street, loading the decaying goods into the back of an empty van. Things tossed in any which way, coming apart at the seams, breaking into pieces, dumped in all together, all of it worn and tattered. One wearing a cap looked intently in all the corners of the ravaged dwelling and clapped his hands as if he wanted with the echo to tease out anything concealed in all the hidden niches. Yet nothing appeared, and now the inspector reached up to grab a window's crossbar, rapped on the wood of the swaying doors, then closed up the emptied site, hurried to the truck, gave the driver a nod, and already the load was off to the warehouse. It was to the ceremonial hall of a cemetery outside the mountain town that they traveled. When they arrived it was raining; otherwise, it was still all around. The men jumped from the truck, the turnkey heard them from inside, scratched his head, and came out to have a look at the load. He nodded a greeting, complained about the weather, wrapped a broken dish, his bald head wrinkling with a smile. The inspector handed the turnkey his consignment book, everything written down in it, the names as well.

"Eugene Lebenhart and Emmi Lebenhart. Hey, that's the Lebenharts from Ufergasse! They must have had some nice things."

"Not really."

"A lot of it is broken. Sure. Yet they had money once."

"You always know everything, and everyone."

"Of course, I knew them. You don't believe me? Who, I ask you, didn't know them! Fancy goods, that was quite a shop! They did a tremendous business!"

"Buy something for yourself!"

"I can't buy anything. But they used to be rich, that I can tell you."

"No, what did they have left of it?"

"Left of it. . . . You got it all!"

The men said nothing more about how good things had once been for Eugene and Emmi Lebenhart, nor did they say anything much, for they had to hurry. The cargo had to be quickly unloaded and stuffed in the ceremonial hall. All the furniture was carried, carpets were piled up, mirrors, glass, and such stuff handled with some care, so that it all didn't rattle to pieces, books stacked on one another, kitchen stuff placed in the foyer, sewing stuff in the morgue, though for miscellaneous things there was no room. The turnkey complained that it was high time all this junk was cleared out, which the Department for House Clearings had to get through its head, what with every day more loads showing up and no room for all the plunder, which also needed to be sorted through. The inspector nodded, yes, there was no telling where to take it all. But the turnkey said that everything here was a mess, and he knew it. The workers pushed and shoved the load into the storehouse, the pictures also hauled in and placed in a corner where many others lay in the dark. Then the inspector left with his workers. Soon after the warehouse was so full that finally others listened to the turnkey and hauled most of the rest away.

The pictures went to the school, three classrooms filled with them. They were hauled upstairs, one after another, not very gently or orderly, only the big ones being watched out for. Thus all the things from the house were stacked up and banished, thirty and fifty of them at a time. With battens they cut from laths, the stacks were secured so that they didn't collapse, narrow passages between remaining free.

Herr Schnabelberger opened up and led me into the first room. The air was muggy and warm, a sweet gray mustiness rising up in the darkened room, into which daylight wearily spread its yellow through windows half blocked off by shades. My eyes would soon have gotten used to this darkness, which felt a bit odd, but Herr Schnabelberger snapped on the light, it flooding the room with a brownish-yellow glow that reminded me of mellow apples in bins from the previous year's harvest.

"You're not really an art historian, but that doesn't matter, Herr Dr. Landau. It's good work. And you are intelligent and know how to help yourself. Otherwise, I will help you out when necessary. Here and in both rooms that I still have to show you is our collection of family pictures. All in all, there are around five thousand pieces. Some excellent examples, in which one recognizes right away the hand of a good painter, were separated out right away. The loveliest one is already in the exhibition room and is museum quality. But, also, the paintings in my room and what you see in the staircase are worth hardly less. We hope that someday we can hang it all in a dignified manner, restore any damage, and make them available to the public in a gallery of our museum. What's here in this room and what otherwise might show up among the inventory of portraits is probably not worth very much, most of it weak, nothing more than trash, simply useless kitsch. People let themselves be painted by mawkish, fashionable painters, by ridiculous dilettantes, sometimes not even from life, but just from photos, flatteringly, and therefore clumsily flattered. There are even photos painted over with oil paint."

Herr Schnabelberger stopped. I didn't know whether he was expecting me to speak. In order just to say something, I quietly said, "So many, many terrible paintings of our dead."

"One can't say that without knowing more. Certainly there must still be something good to find. I'd say that, among over five thousand paintings that have hardly been touched, there must be something decent. That will indeed be your task, and perhaps, even most likely—I have no doubt about it—amid the entire crowd you'll uncover real treasures."

"A treasure hunter, then?"

I smiled in bemusement and moved to lean on a stack of paintings.

"For heaven's sake, be careful! The laths are just loosely inserted and can give way! All we have is paper dowels. That would be a fine mess! I have to ask you to always take care and, you know, this is a matter of trust that we are asking of you, even if I wouldn't exactly call it treasure hunting."

"What actually needs to be done with it all?"

"Inventory, Herr Dr. Landau."

"Who do they belong to? In order to give them back to whoever survived, or possible descendants?"

"That could maybe happen, but you yourself know—"

"Rarely."

"Very rarely. And then the problem of verification. We're not at all qualified. In any case, matters of restitution are long and drawn out. Luckily, we have a right to veto them when it comes to objects of special artistic, historic, or museum-quality value. Frau Dr. Kulka already has her own special plans for the museum and its future development. Therefore she's hard-nosed and ready to fight like a lioness when there are things that we want for ourselves. But we're pleased that so far not much has been asked about. People don't think about the museum; they want houses, businesses, and banknotes back, or jewelry. It's only natural."

"Of course."

"But through research we can help, that's clear, and I don't agree with Frau Dr. Kulka's view. She actually feels that no one can force us to share our results. I'm of the opposite opinion. But no matter how it is, until now we've hardly had to hand over anything. The number of ongoing claims is very small indeed."

"That's actually terrible."

"I think so as well. But what good does that do? We have to save what we can. And then there's the museum to consider. At first, I didn't share that. No wonder, for you should know that I was actually trained as an electrician. But you change with the times. The past is past, and soon you approach things anew. Once you've been here a couple of weeks, the same thing will happen to you. I guarantee it."

"If something is beautiful, really beautiful, I can imagine that if no one comes who claims to be the rightful owner, then I can see how one would want to save it, as you say. But when there are things that hold only private meaning but otherwise are of no interest—that is, no interest to a museum, and are therefore worthless—doesn't that present a monstrous burden?"

"What are you thinking? The only justification would be a lack of space, though the government has promised to give us all we need. But, above all, it's something Frau Dr. Kulka simply won't hear of. Nothing is worthless to a museum! Just think of the singular opportunity to bring together such a broad collection of portraits! Even with a limitless budget over decades, you couldn't bring it all together under one roof in such a way!"

"So then will the museum become a kind of memorial to our dead?"

"No, you don't understand! But I can't explain it to you as well as Frau Dr. Kulka can. Such a memorial is not at all what it's about. In fact, we have very special plans. You'll see by and by. No, we are not at all thinking of presenting this collection in its entirety, either from an art historical point of view or for the clueless viewer to whom it all looks the same, although we do want to display an extensive special collection. Yet the tasks that we have before us are quite different. The reason they have been directly set before you is because you are a sociologist. A general overview tells us nothing, nor would two or four paintings, for that's not enough. But now imagine hundreds, thousands, of such paintings! Everyone could then study them! Anthropologists, physiologists, family historians, local historians, general historians, even those interested in fashion; in short, what can I say, for you yourself can add up the number of perspectives on your own fingers. We possess a singular treasure trove of family portraits from citizens of the city from the past hundred and fifty years."

"I see. . . ."

"There, now you understand. And that's what you'll be cataloging. How big the painting is with and without a frame, whether it's painted on canvas or wood, in oil or pastels, a description of who is portrayed, be it an individual or a couple or a group, the head, from the chest up, the entire figure, straight on, in profile, the hair color, eyes, nose, mouth, chin, the approximate age; in short, the particulars you find in a passport, though you can record them more vividly and in greater detail, and then the clothing, as well as the jewelry, what's depicted in the background, and special attributes, the condition, commentary on the type and quality of the frame, when possible the confirmation of the name of the one portrayed—in any case, the consignment number and other details that make the identification easier, or a description of the painter, whether there is a signature or it is anonymous, what year it was done or the estimated time period. By doing this, you'll develop a catalog that will be of real use. We already have a model to follow. Frau Dr. Kulka did one up. It's easy, in fact, but also interesting, even a pleasure, I must say, and you'll be pleased to be able to be a part of the museum's staff."

"Shall I do it all right here?"

"Oh, no. You'll get a lovely small, well-lit room on the third floor, with an office. You can set it up however you please."

"And the paintings?"

"You will also have assistants to help you, as many as you wish. Perhaps Herr Woticky, he's very nice. Work with the material at your own pace. As soon as I can get you a secretary, you can dictate everything onto the typewriter. Frau Dr. Kulka will explain it all to you in even greater detail. You can always ask her for advice. And, of course, I'm always here to help."

"Many thanks! Where do the paintings go?"

"You mean after they're cataloged? We've already found a solution to that. Some rooms will be emptied out—in fact, this is one of them. Here we have heaps of prayer books, ten thousand of them, and they—"

"Prayer books?"

"Yes. From all the emptied-out houses throughout the country—single-volume, three- and nine-volume editions, unfortunately many of them missing pages, though many remain just the way they were found. What can still be used in some way needs to be bundled into groups of ten or twelve and for now will be stored in the cellar. Sometimes you'll have to supervise. We have some internees doing the work who are paid a pittance, collaborators, but seemingly harmless people who don't like to work. That's why you have to buck them up a little. A cigarette often works wonders."

"So they're also in the cellar."

"Unfortunately. That doesn't seem right to me, either, as the cellar is not completely dry. But the prayer books are just in the way. There's nothing else that can be done with them. They are of use to no one."

"No one."

"No, no one, it's a catastrophe. Yet we hope to mail a large shipment of them to America sometime soon, though, of course, for a trifle. That would be the best solution. We've already begun negotiations with members of the Committee on Reconstruction."

"And the paintings?"

"They will be placed in the empty rooms in proper storage. We have already completed the drawings for a three-story set of wooden bays in which the paintings can comfortably be accessed and arranged by catalog number. I recommend that while cataloging them you always do so in groups, such as similar sizes, which is easy to do. The ones that give us the most trouble are the large-format paintings. But for these beasts we will perhaps build special bays."

That reminded me. I asked if I could perhaps see one of the paintings.

"With pleasure. Just be careful, for the paintings are incredibly dusty. But you'll soon get used to that."

I lifted up the next average-sized painting, carefully but a bit clumsily, a coat of dust covering it that I blew away.

"There, right away you see the consignment number. That's a help. Unfortunately, during the war they were so sloppy and didn't always pay attention. Then we end up groping in the dark."

I looked more closely; perhaps it was a painting from the house of someone I knew. It trembled in my fingers, the frame slipping from my hand and falling with a soft crash back onto the pile from which it had come.

"I'm sorry, I'm a bit clumsy."

"That I see. Look, this is how you grab hold of a frame and don't get yourself dirty."

Herr Schnabelberger carefully lifted the painting high with hands spread out flat, yet the picture frame had loosened and the canvas fell out. I bent down to pick it up.

"That, unfortunately, happens fairly often. The paintings have not been handled right. It's a disgrace."

"A disgrace. Really. Sad."

"People were overwhelmed. Also, they had no interest, always in a hurry, and you can't expect any understanding of art from the Department of House Clearings."

"It's a kind of graveyard."

"Yes, but we awaken the dead to a new life."

"When it works."

"That's our task."

Herr Schnabelberger tried with some deftness to put the painting and the frame back together. Like someone experienced in selling paintings, he told me about the quality of the painting itself.

"A lovely old grandpa. The beard tells me it's from 1880 or so. Of course, it's a conventional piece, a bit of bourgeois finery. The frame, this typical black-and-gold, is not worth anything. Look, it's plaster that's crumbling. Carved frames were too expensive, but it had to look splendid."

The old man with his white beard bobbed before us and looked on serenely. His stiff demeanor did not ease, no matter how vigorously Herr Schnabelberger handled the painting. What happened to the old man remained distant and unknown, the eyes gazing dully and a little sleepily—so helpless, as if they wanted to be cleaned off. I took out my handkerchief in order to try to get a better look at him.

"If he were cleaned up, maybe one could recognize him."

"You shouldn't do that, Herr Dr. Landau. It doesn't help the painting at all and could ruin your handkerchief. Are you really that interested in the man?"

"No, not really. But one never knows. I've always got my eyes open."

"Sometimes the consignment holds the key."

I bent down and read the number on the back.

"There's also a name. But I can't read it very well."

"Here, I have a flashlight."

" 'Eugene Lebenhart, Ufergasse 17.' "

"Someone you know?"

"No. A stranger. But is that the man in the painting?"

"No. You can see that the name and the address are in the same handwriting as the consignment number. Therefore that's the name of the last owner of the place, who was shipped off."

"I see, so that's what happened!"

"Sometimes, as I told you already, not always. Usually the names and addresses weren't noted. It's unfortunate for us, for any clues are welcome."

"So you assume that the painting is of a member of the Lebenhart family?"

"That's not clear. Names are always only a hint. One can, of course, assume that it's an ancestor of the one deported—perhaps a grandfather, maybe even a Lebenhart, but only maybe. There are too many possibilities. But, if you want to pick up the next frame, that's no doubt the companion piece."

It was the companion, an old woman with a brooch at her throat, the face tired, yet cheerful and carefree. I looked at the consignment. There again was the same number and "Eugene Lebenhart, Ufergasse 17."

"That's it! We now have the name of the last owner."

"And who is now the owner?"

"What do you mean?"

"The owner of the painting."

Herr Schnabelberger put back the painting, crept through the stacks, and turned off the light, pushing me ahead of him and locking the door behind.

"Yes, you probably mean the legal owner? Not everything has been made clear. First and foremost, there is the museum. They are working on the statutes. Right now, we are effectively the custodian on behalf of the state. But there is no doubt that it all belongs to us. The people are dead or have disappeared, and therefore it would be very difficult for them to make a claim."

Herr Schnabelberger took me up to the third floor and opened the room that was to be mine.

"You can have the key. I recommend that you lock up whenever you leave the room. But when you leave the building, leave the key with Herr Geschlieder, the porter."

The air was extremely dry and much too warm. I asked if I could open a window.

"Yes, of course. Don't forget to close it if you leave the room for any length of time. It hasn't been used in months—not since the end of the war, and maybe even longer."

"Since the war?"

"Yes. Most of the ones who worked here back then were hauled off. You know, of course, that the workers were not here of their own choice but were forced labor. Only a few escaped being sent off or came back to the museum like us, who couldn't just let it be. Most of us were sent off in the last months of the war. Some came right back. . . . Yes, you know what I mean, I don't have to tell you. There were many commendable people who in the middle of the war set up the museum. An indescribable loss—we miss them day in and day out. You see, Herr Dr. Landau, that's why we need new blood, and we are especially pleased to have you with us."

Herr Schnabelberger said this in a wonderfully friendly manner, and I thanked him. Then he excused himself, saying he had to go to his office, but if I wanted to come to him in an hour that would be good, for then he could introduce me to all of my fellow workers, above all Frau Dr. Kulka, my immediate superior. In between, I should set up my office according to my wishes, for I could do whatever I wished with it. Herr Schnabelberger smiled encouragingly and took his leave.

His steps echoed down the hall, and I walked over to the window. I looked down into the schoolyard. It was still, no children to be seen, the last traces of their youthful spirits having disappeared. Only some empty boxes stood open and desolate, as well as some dented suitcases soaked by the rain. Was there no longer any school here, no teachers or children? It didn't look as if any teaching was going on, all the desks having been taken away. My room was long and narrow, a closet for school supplies, certainly not a classroom at all. Maps must have been stowed away here, fat round globes with the countries of the world and their mountains and rivers, as well as the blue of the long-dry seas. The circles and dots of cities, the pointer having followed the red lines where the trains traveled fast from place to place with many, many people carried past all borders. The teacher spoke softly amid the boyish wonder, but on the last benches dangling legs swayed and a forbidden pocketknife sharply carved into the green surface of the desktop. "What are you doing back there?" came the stern question, passing over all the rows. Quietly the knife snapped shut and disappeared into the depths. There the men lived through mining, tunnels were bored, and with luck the miners went down into the caverns to the prayer books and hauled the coal out of the seams. What could be wrong? They were protected from the bad weather and had their Davy lamps to see by, a blesséd invention. Then the bell rang, the students shifted in their seats more loudly, the teacher took a breath, the maps were rolled up, two leather straps encircling them and holding tight their narrow bulks. Then the class leader, Adam, lifted them up and wandered upstairs to the closet, the teacher hard on his heels. The teacher pointed to the proper place, the boy nodding and then excused, quickly disappearing into the bustle of recess.

I listened to see if I could hear anything, but everything was quiet; there was no recess. The children were sitting docilely on their benches and paying attention, their discipline good, Herr Schnabelberger a good teacher, the students making progress, he himself teaching them energetically. Frau Dr. Kulka, however, now gave instruction in art history, learning the frames by heart, dividing them across a hundred and fifty years, the bad ones designated as kitsch, the good ones exhibited, though no one was ever let go. The school of life was what it was called, and for it everything was taken up and described, and no descendants had the right to these students. What did it matter that all descendants had disappeared, or were dead, their limbs scattered to the four winds, if only the students of this antiquity were alive and within the dust of their desire were gathered for free. They appeared completely satisfied and patient; things would come along, quietly anticipated, the names faint or obliterated. Thus they revealed their age, and I was responsible for them, a teacher meant to be enveloped by their two-dimensional mind so that it did not wrinkle with grief. The new benches already existed, the fresh wood sawed and planed so that the students could sit in peace, and I, the son, received the new class book of my father and mother, having to record the noble lineage and its dates on white cards. It was good work that I had to get started on, for I could be the legacy of my students. "Don't forget the number! Below on the back of the frame it's written small."

Among the rank and file of ancestors who don't need names but only numbers, there was comforting parity, be they good paintings or bad, for they all had their numbers. It was only the prayer books that no one cared about; they could be bundled up and stowed in the cellar. There it's dark and damp, but the prayers can sleep, blessed be the Lord, and love the Lord your God with all your heart and all your soul, for then the prayers, if they are not ruined, can be sent to America for a paltry sum. Alas, no one wants them. Their prayers have been ended and must remain down in the mines where the Lord cannot hear them, a single silent cellar prayer where once the coal slumbered in the dark without the protection of the Davy lamp against bad weather, the prayer now sleeping down among the footings, rolled up and torn, the building threatened, though the walls remain essentially eternal, the Lord of the world, who was king before all was created. Below it repeats itself a thousand times and ten thousand times, the morning prayer of the grave with its holy blessings; we miss them at every turn, those that laud the rock of redemption, the eternal Creator. Above lies harm, for there the rooms are crammed full, the musty classrooms holding five thousand consigned pupils in broken frames, though for the most part it's unknown stock, the past not pressing through, even when the paper rots between the book covers that hold it. In this building it's all gathered, a hut, a tent—how lovely are your tents—and the bodies of the living as well as the dead are all scattered, their existence disgraced, the names sealed off and never available again. Yet the blessing remains and is tightly wound up in each, and whoever can no longer live is still transformed by it, the lament having its arches, its grave, its cellar, its walls.

I walked across my room and looked through the closets and shelves to see if there was anything that reminded me of old school prayers, but everything was empty, the prayers having long ago disappeared from here. Nor was there anything else there from the school, the wisdom of the teachers and the eagerness of the pupils having both vanished into thin air, leaving behind nothing more than thick piles of junk. Heaps of paper, organized and disorganized in disorderly piles, notebooks, scattered books, yet no prayers, empty boxes and others full of curling forms, many posed photos of sporting teams and gymnastics meets, discarded trash with souls eaten away, something quite distant from the pupils' eagerness or the teachers' command. The walls looked miserable, dark yellow and shabby, paintings scattered and broken, stacked up in the corner by the metal furnace and black with soot. In some spots the paint was scraped clean where paintings had once hung but which had long since migrated from this room. Only pictures of young girls and forgotten beautiful actresses cut from newspapers were hung on the walls with tacks and stared dryly into the emptiness. Also, a calendar from last year was out of date and illustrated the last autumn of the war. I looked at the first week and sighed deeply; it must have been a week of death. On a table there squatted a dented washbasin made of ugly, dirty zinc, dreaming of its stained and senseless end. I quickly put it into a chest where earlier I had found a blue pitcher with a rusted bottom, some used bars of soap in a little bowl, and some dirty hand towels. When I took away the washbasin, I noticed for the first time that the table was moldy and crusty from old soapy water. I took a brown sheet of packing paper, spread it out over the surface, and nailed it down tight.

On the desk could be found what my predecessor, who had disappeared, had left behind: a dried-up inkwell, rusted steel pens with gnawed caps, a decayed feather pen, pencils with broken-off points, and miserable stumps of broken-off erasers, two rust-flecked rulers, a broken blotter that fell apart in my hand, honey-yellow glue with a useless brush, a dirty typewriter, paper clips, stickers, piles of crumbs, and other useless things that I looked at uncomprehendingly, the detritus of a former office. But these ownerless goods had not entirely gone to waste, because as I went through them a spider withdrew that had settled undismayed among this clutter and was now getting as far away from me as it could. I followed its path of escape from the desk to the wall until, with haste, it disappeared behind a chest of drawers. Now I was ready to settle at the desk, but before I sat down I removed from the chair a worn-out cushion whose sawdust leaked from its flattened body. I began to rummage through the baskets that were on top of the desk. Nothing special turned up: old newspapers full of accounts of unbelievably old victories that weren't true, the ridiculous decrees of officials long gone. I took the useless stuff and threw it in the garbage can next to the furnace. Even the drawers were full of useless junk—old rags, a dark-blue apron made of thick paper, and from the very back two pieces of bread uneaten, rotten, and covered with green mold with traces of dried-up butter.

Was my predecessor not hungry when he had to leave this room? Or was he chased away so quickly that he had no time to take his things with him? I was really sick of rummaging and pushed the drawer shut, for it horrified me. Whatever else there was to find could wait. I felt that the smartest thing to do would be to put things in order little by little. So I cleared off the desk in a superficial manner, pulling it away from the walls, which bothered me the most, and decided to go look for Herr Schnabelberger, for perhaps he would allow me to choose some paintings to decorate the walls. Among the paintings, I expected to encounter someone I knew, for there were too many for me to be spared. The brisk men from the Department for House Clearings walked around in a hurry and emptied out the stores of booty, one after another. They trotted swiftly down the Römerstrasse toward where my parents lived, there being no one there any longer, and so they made their way in, my father's thick key ring clanging, though the clock did not chime anymore, as there was no electricity, Herr Schnabelberger having turned it off and unplugged it so that it could slip into the museum proud and solid. Then my parents' house was shut, many empty pages strewn about, the unspoken prayers having fallen out or flattened under the heavy weight, yet I was afraid I would find their traces in the school. Or not. The parents I prayed to did not grieve on any of the walls; they had never been painted, nor their ancestors, there being only photos of them that were not collected in the museum. I squirmed around in my chair and was nervous, sawdust leaking out again that gathered softly upon the faces, but I didn't pay much attention to what was going on around me in the room.

"Look, what's happened is that I don't have a single little picture of my father, while of my mother I only have one of her dressed up for a masked ball; the only other—and it upsets me to say it—is a pointed caricature by an amateurish hand, for I hate caricatures, even when they are well done. I find them completely humiliating, inhumane. Forgive me for ranting, but for me there's something obscene about caricatures."

"How can you judge them so harshly?" said Frau Saubermann. "Often they involve just an exaggeration, sometimes a humorous or biting disclosure of the entire character."

"That's what I think," said Herr Buxinger. "I'm happy to be caricatured when it's only for fun. I wish I had good caricatures of my parents and not just those stiff photos that they took back then."

"No the photos are much better," Frau Saubermann assured him. "Even my husband takes excellent ones, and also collects them. I'd be happy to show you some. You should come over sometime soon."

"With pleasure, madam."

"Most of all I'm amazed, Herr Dr. Landau, if I can be frank, that you came here at all, but even more that you don't want to return. It's indeed a good job, such a museum, especially if one can help to build it oneself. All the modern approaches at your service. There my husband felt as if on virgin soil; he had revolutionary ideas. You should have heard him, Herr Dr. Landau. So much to profit from. You could return with great zeal and set up your museum. I think that would be wonderful. Wouldn't you agree, Herr Buxinger? From the viewpoint of a bookseller and a friend of the arts, wouldn't you say the same and immediately seize hold of the opportunity to create something?"

"Yes, there's something to that, Frau Saubermann. But we who left before the war, who now exist here, we no longer belong there."

"Nor here!" exclaimed Fräulein Zinner.

"No, my dear Johanna," advised the wife of the manufacturer. "You mustn't say such a thing, you of all people! You can't only halfheartedly decide to live here."

"Decide, decide!" the bookkeeper admonished her. "And there we find the heart of the question—one must decide to stay here. Homelessness is a horror. One must indeed decide—here or elsewhere, but decide. That's my view."

"That's a view, Herr Buxinger, that I happen to share. We indeed have a foothold here. One knows where one is and where one lives. One can't keep relearning things forever, but for Herr Dr. Landau the situation is quite different. He remained there, taken by surprise. Fine, that's not pleasant at all. In fact, it's terrible. I'm sorry, that's the way I see it. But if one survives, then one has responsibilities, even when one is the freed citizen of an emerging free country. Thus a museum, just think, the building of it, what a future there is for it! And, besides, you are quite young, Herr Doctor. One can see just by looking at you."

"Not all that young."

"Well, can I guess? Thirty! What do you say?"

"Almost forty."

"You don't look it. And so much behind you. But nonetheless young, for forty is not old. Especially today, when life begins at forty."

"Not for me, madam."

"Go on, you're a pessimist or entirely at loose ends. In two, three years you'll see matters entirely different."

"I've never been pessimistic, as you say, for otherwise I would have stayed back there. That I left shows that I had hope."

"What lovely hope!" said Herr Buxinger. "But how can you say that? Our country is now poor after the war and offers a foreign-minded worker a tough existence."

"But there's my work. I'd like to have a research position. Perhaps at a university, a library, an institute. Proper affiliation. Dr. Haarburger is so kind, as well as Professor Kratzenstein. . . . Frau Singule is going to speak to her husband."

Frau Saubermann lightly applauded.

"My dear friend, you are an optimist! All good spirits should credit you with that! Therefore I don't wish to say anything against this or that splendid person who has done so many excellent things. Each of them is wonderful! Don't misunderstand me. But think of the situation! I know them through and through, and Herr Buxinger will back me up, and certainly Fräulein Zinner as well. It's incredibly difficult. One needs sharp elbows and luck and who knows what else in order to assert oneself. You should know what it's like to be down and out! It's horrible! My husband and I provide many poor wretches with enough to get by on, but not everyone can work for us at home. Then the charitableness of this country, for which it is so renowned, would disappear. We must help, and we're happy to do so, my husband and I. We do what we can afford to. It costs a fortune, for one cannot just let people go hungry. We feel sympathetic, Herr Doctor. But, really, it's simply become too much to handle."

"You really think, madam, that I came to this country in order to put people out because of a local sense of charity?"

"I would never think that! I don't mean you, and I wouldn't hurt a fly. I'm only talking in general. But, I swear, what would you do if you didn't have something to nibble on?"

"Madam!" whispered Fräulein Zinner.

"I don't mean any harm. I've already said I would never hurt a fly. And perhaps Herr Dr. Landau can show us that he is, in fact, one of the few intellectuals who can do something. All the better. Then I'm right. What do you think, Herr Buxinger?"

"It's not easy. But don't let it get you down too much, Herr Dr. Landau. There are still possibilities, and relationships sometimes change overnight."

"That's right. I see it particularly from the vantage point of charitableness. I can indeed say a little something about that. In any case, Herr Doctor, the situation is completely bedeviled. If I were in your shoes, I would certainly have stayed where you were. Where so many had been murdered, brrr, it would have been horrible, but new able-bodied blood is certainly needed there."

"It's a graveyard."

"You're exaggerating, Herr Doctor. You're being too emotional. Of course, you're always happy to see the dark side, but a graveyard is alive and blossoms and requires a horde of gardeners to tend to it. Yes, it's true. Surely you cannot hold my decency against me, and new life blossoms from ruins. A German poet said that. And life brings us joy, so said another."

"Madam, I beg you . . ."

Then I stopped, though they kept talking. But why? My hands began to tremble. The talk went on, cards floating from mouth to mouth, little packets that fell into four stacks. Why did I listen? Mere vanity, all my limbs hurting because of it. Uncomfortable sensations crept across the chair, sawdust everywhere, filling up my mouth, me unable to swallow another mouthful. My stomach was bursting as Frau Haarburger came over to me proffering a little bowl of fresh, sweet chatter. No, thank you. I only gestured my thanks by pointing at my stomach. It was all so disturbing, the way they opened their mouths so that the bounty of sweet chatter continued to flow. I was getting more and more tired, my hands dangling at my sides, as I yawned continually. On tiptoe, coffee was brought in. Shh, so that he doesn't wake up! When will the card game finally be done? I wiped my face doubtfully with my handkerchief. I often looked askance at Herr Dr. Haarburger to see if he would take pity on my pressing situation, but he was far too wrapped up in his own thoughts and only rarely cast an encouraging glance at my group. As soon as he did that, I smiled at him beseechingly, but he mistook this sign of my desire to be rescued and thought it only a sign of hopefulness or an expression of my feeling fine. He took in my state with a fleeting glance and turned away, satisfied. I fell apart inside and fought against my feeling of powerlessness. Luckily, my speaking partners were finally done with trying to discuss the right or wrong way for me to proceed from afar, and instead asked me to speak in greater detail about my previous experience. Thus a request ignited me. I instantly felt more sure of myself and in my element.

I loved most to share my views about the discontinuity of human consciousness in society and the resulting social ills. I based this on the impossibility of attaining a mutual shared feeling among a large number of people and explained this inability as a main cause of the general lovelessness that did not shrink from barbaric forms of oppression and contempt for others and, at a minimum, forwarded a hard-hearted sense, never mind the sensibility such ills led to. Quickly I found many connections to my own experience and observations, which I had really pulled together after the war. Full of the urge to share, but without satisfactory explanations, I needed to get my thoughts across. But I was hardly capable of recognizing how much my listeners could stand to hear. Today, I know that this was a last attempt to exist, to unfold a personality that, as I wished to be, was a tower of arrogant pride amid despair.

That's an illusion. But how long before one reaches one's own limits! And now even I, who had no more limits, was consumed by the points of reality that continually flared up here and there, and which I quickly and yet clumsily lurched along, never reaching the end of them, since they dissolved in between. Thus, for me, life is like non-life, being and time having become invalid. All that remained was this: to be completely at the mercy of others, a figure, even the vestige of someone different which I played, the expression of one who has endured, not because that is what I needed but because it is what they saw reflected in a lowly mirror, which one could look into with pleasure or pain, perhaps becoming wiser through me and no longer needing me at all. At such moments, when I was in some way conjured, permitted to exist, viewed, and taken in, I could either feel happy or fall into the deepest despair. But if it is one or the other, even if it is despair, then it's almost fine with me; it's a comfort, because I am perceived and I perceive. But that's no way to live.

How does one live? The street hawkers press threateningly along West Park Row. No, they don't threaten, they only want to sell their wares, and that's why they're so loud, the poor fellows hungering after money. That's an existence, and they can't call out enough, whether it be to offer mussels or little crabs, yellow ice cream in cubes stuck between waffles or piled up on pointed cones. It's the same for the hawkers as it is for me. Only they are not as down as I am, as they cry out more heatedly in their work, indeed begging and cajoling, unrelentingly appealing to the children, who are already running, Michael and Eva as well, holding their coins, trembling with throbbing desire as the men effervesce over their excess of wares and ever more wildly hawk them with mounting lust that chases the children into their homes with demands: we want, want to buy, give us the money! There's no use calling out to the dead, and my life is too uncertain for me to make much of a fuss. Who would buy me to have in his hands and throat? That's foolish. I have no wagon overflowing with goods, my hands are empty, my heart lies hidden, a constant pain runs throughout my limbs; I cannot offer myself in the same way as the hawkers. But back then, when I arrived in the metropolis, at the Haarburgers' I called out just like such a salesman, offering myself, though I had no goods, for my complaints and forthright advertisements were unsellable goods. That was no way to live.

Nonetheless, I spoke. Fräulein Zinner listened to me. My onslaught appeared to frighten her, but she patiently held herself together. Whether she felt my talk was poignant or clumsy didn't matter to me. I looked at her. She didn't seem curious, which was almost always the case when new acquaintances in the metropolis listened to me talk, seeming shy and somewhat nervous, which always struck me. It always felt good that someone in such circles devoted such attention. Thus I worried less about the bookseller Buxinger and the benefactress Saubermann, though they egged me to talk on. Soon my words were directed only at the silent one. I hoped she would say something, and I secretly wooed her, though without any success, for she preferred to listen, me holding forth on awkward and clumsy matters not all that cleverly. Finally I could see that, every now and then, with a breaking voice she would pose a pertinent and impersonal question. The more I wanted to capture Fräulein Zinner's attention, the more embarrassed I was to look at her. Suddenly, I interjected and asked my listeners if they could imagine that a healthy young girl who as yet had remained seemingly untouched by a dark fate could ever marry a man with my gloomy past. I was shocked to find myself having made a pass in such a completely unreasonable and also foolish and almost completely obvious manner. I could only expect an awful reply. Fräulein Zinner didn't think long, and responded quietly but firmly before the others knew what to say, such that it hit me almost cold when she did.

"It's as clear as day. One marries such men—I mean, it's almost your duty!"

Herr Buxinger was simply surprised, but Frau Saubermann didn't know what to think. She sat there with both hands clutching the back of her chair.

"Duty. . . . Duty. . . . That I find indeed a bit much, my child."

I was not at all happy to see how quickly and matter-of-factly Fräulein

Zinner looked back at me. As I considered how to go on with my talk and was searching for the right words, Herr Buxinger came up to me. He nodded meaningfully.

"How surprising. But how lovely of you, Fräulein Zinner."

Frau Saubermann let go of the back of the chair, having gathered herself once more.

"Lovely or not lovely, it was said impulsively, my dear child. You simply can't make such general statements about questions of marriage. It's a duty when feelings compel you, though I'm splitting hairs! Such a marriage cannot be simply theorized. There is only one theoretical duty, my dear child, and that you will simply have to believe from someone who is very experienced in social matters, and this duty has validity because it can be fulfilled in practical terms. That is the duty to be freed of moral duties."

"Do you always feel that way, madam?" Fräulein Zinner asked politely but sharply.

"I beg of you, who have known me since childhood, how can you ask me that? I am morally free."

Frau Saubermann turned the conversation to herself and began to share her views on love, marriage, duty, and freedom, not sparing any practical examples. I cursed myself for having unleashed this unpleasant wave that only showed me that I was nothing but a bungler in the company of others. Soon the most holy things were talked to death; a cold onslaught that I could not interrupt spread outward from Frau Saubermann. If the humanitarian factory owner's wife meant at all well, it was lost on me, helplessly overwhelmed as I was by the wave of talk! Useless intellect devoid of any reasonableness or worth, not even woven from one's own views and spreading heady interests across every realm—this always left me cold and made me sad, but now I was especially miserable. Frau Saubermann's lecture made me feel sick, like someone wasting away and suffering from her dry, bloodless knowledge. The others listened in wonder or, at least, listened patiently. "That doesn't interest me at all!" Why didn't I say it? But no, I didn't utter a peep and, luckily, kept myself in check, but my head was throbbing. I bit my lip and kept my mouth shut in order not to embarrass the relentless woman. I looked off at nothing and tried to imagine that I was socially backward and therefore not capable of agilely and easily tending the splashing rudder in order to safely navigate through such thinking.

If you sit down with others, you cannot be so squeamish, dear Arthur. If you provoke others, then you cannot complain about what they throw at you from head to toe. Swallow it down, as if it were a sweet biscuit, and take a drink as well. Thus I put on a polite face and nodded now and then as if granting approval, not agreement. So it went, until suddenly I heard: "Things are a lot different now." That I agreed with wholeheartedly—yes, very much so. One can hardly believe it, but it is indeed so. I had certainly changed and developed. Alas, "developed"—that's a stupid word, it's not right. "Experienced," that's really more like it. I had experienced change. Little ship, little ship upon the wall, traveling forth and on and on, hold yourself together, don't fall into the flames. Away, away, I should get away. Far beyond Dr. Haarburger's lovely house, where the father lives with his beloved among the cooing leaves at night, the beloved handing him a biscuit that she ripped from her body, and he takes it, biting into it with the sharp points of his teeth, the sawdust pouring out of the heart drop by drop, me biting a biscuit as well. Two and then another—the next one, please, that's swimming in blood; myself, however, in a little ship on the other wall, a little sheep in a little ship. Marriage is fundamental. One must cement it with noble-mindedness, a little lamb that my father bought, though the marriage was the better. That's worth something, two guilders the cost. . . .

No, I can't lose my way. I must recognize that the people who watched the maelstrom from another coast are different from those who sailed forth without house or land. They stood and watched, forgetting themselves in the midst of today, sleeping in bed as the past burned on. Thus they survived, without the least bit of their inner natures living. This, I told myself, and held my right hand in my left in order to better restrain myself. But as Frau Saubermann's cautionary tales continued on, I became angry and could keep my patience no longer. Having imagined a sign of sympathy from Fräulein Zinner, I took my opportunity when the triumphant factory owner's wife paused for a breath.

"Madam, that's all well and good, indeed also informative, but it has nothing to do with my case!"

"It's about every case!" Frau Saubermann tried to interject.

But I left her no chance to say any more and talked over her so loudly that my words reached across to the cohort of card players, disturbing some of them, who, with quiet reluctance, looked over at our group. Frau Haarburger wanted harmony in her house and lifted a threatening finger toward me. Yet she didn't get the chance to devote more time to us, as Professor Kratzenstein politely sidetracked her.

"My dear lady, it's your turn!"

"Yes, I'll play!"

"Hannah, let our young friend have his way," Dr. Haarburger cajoled. "Such fire—it suits him well, and his temperment!"

I quietly continued on.

"It has nothing to do with my case. That would be true if you were speaking about the years Jacob spent working in order to win Rachel. . . . I was speaking about me, completely personally, not just a theory. I meant it practically."

"I see, practically. How interesting!"

"Yes. I mean in terms of my marrying."

"Are you engaged?"

"No."

"How, then, is it practical? It's indeed only a theory! Look, you think too much about yourself, and that's wrong. You are not the center of the universe just because you suffered. That can only lead to trouble! Suffering should be heard, Herr Doctor, don't get me wrong. But there's no doubt that a man such as yourself . . . naturally, understandably . . . under the circumstances . . . I regret to say. Then one must also appreciate that one can't properly mature after having lost so many years, as if having slept through them. You do understand, don't you?"

"Just like Sleeping Beauty!" I snapped.

I couldn't go on. I hadn't noticed that Resi Knispel, the journalist, had sidled up to us. Now she intervened.

"Sleeping Beauty as a story of our times! How original! That would, of course, be a brilliant idea for an article. Don't you think, Buxi?"

"You think?" the bookseller called out. "I thought we'd had enough of all that."

"That's right, Herr Buxinger," I agreed, and whispered further, "The poetic methods of these vultures . . . blood and tears of the murdered, so that the journalist-novelists and film directors are fattened up . . ."

No one heard me. I didn't want to let myself get in trouble for nothing, and so I was pleased when Herr Buxinger and Fräulein Zinner helped out by taking the conversation in another direction. A lot of conversations crossed over one another in the salon, the more so as the card players slowly finished their game. Frau Haarburger then busied herself as hostess and brought around little bowls of goodies, the party beginning to crank up and get louder. I slipped away from Frau Saubermann and got hold of myself, no longer hearing everything she said, nor what was happening amid the spots of light and shadow all around me. Frequently I looked over at Fräulein Zinner. She didn't avoid me, but I couldn't tell if she was keeping an eye on me, either. Yet, as my eyes swept over the room, she caught my gaze with a soft pallor and stood there calmly without saying anything. The conversations got louder, becoming ever more distant from me—slivers of opinions, the chaff of tiny concerns from washed-out mouths that reeked of sweets and schnapps. It seemed to me that my plight was buried in a grave full of frayed murmurings, as they harmlessly talked on about such strange things and assuaged it with fuzzy words and concealed gestures. Any company is crowded when one who is lost stands in its midst. Therefore I became all the more quiet and just shuffled in a disconnected manner through the waves of good cheer. I became superfluous, and that's an awkward condition, but it saves your strength and you feel more free. It helped, for I felt better. I could easily have excused myself from my hosts with a pleasant word of goodbye and gotten away. But then Fräulein Zinner unexpectedly came up to me.

"I feel like one can talk to you. Will you listen to me?"

"But of course."

"Then come along!"

She pulled me over to an empty card table and shoved it somewhat to the side, causing some cards to fall to the floor. I shyly picked them up and held them in my hand, but Fräulein Zinner smiled and took them from me and laid them down. We sat there and were not disturbed. She started to talk about herself, hesitantly and carefully at first, always checking to see how I reacted. Yet, because I encouraged her as she talked, she lost her inhibition and spoke more freely. Ten years younger than me, she came from over there, yet from the south. She had wanted to be a violinist, had had a wonderful teacher who shaped the whole person, not just the playing. But nothing came of it. On her nineteenth birthday, she left with her two younger brothers. Her parents stood at the train station, smiling with a shared knowledge between them. The father was already old and yet spry; the mother much younger, but sick and fragile. The hands holding white hankies waved their long goodbyes. Thus the parents had sent off the children and did not follow them, did not want to follow, could not follow, the parents just having to bear it, nothing else to do. They had lived their lives; the children had to leave. The weapons on the border glinted, the violin too valuable, not allowed, thus taken away. And the train traveled on, thundering across the bridge, the border giving way. Mistrustful glances welcomed them, but then they were let through, the train's thundering echo advancing until the salvation of the coast.

"They wanted to save us, but it didn't completely work."

Fräulein Zinner stopped talking. She thought and nodded quietly, setting a strand of hair in place, which wasn't at all necessary.

"But why am I telling you all this? It's so irrelevant."

I disagreed and asked, because it seemed the safest subject, about her violin playing.

"I was given one. It made me happy, for I could write home about it. I also practiced, for the sake of my parents, as long as I could, until the war began. Then, of course, not at all after that. I never touched it again."

"A shame!"

"No. I still have it. It's sleeping in its black coffin. Do you want the violin?"

"I don't play."

"I would love to give it to you. It's just wasted on me."

"Couldn't you start playing again? You shouldn't give up something like that. You should start again."

"You think so?"

I talked to her some more, but she refused. "That's over—the hands are no good anymore, too many dishes, yard work, grinding work in a factory."

"And your siblings?"

"No, it's just me. The brothers weren't saved."

Fräulein Zinner said this with sudden, strong bitterness. I looked at her, surprised, because until then she talked on easily. As I tried to distract her, she waved at me almost angrily. Why shouldn't I know everything? The brothers didn't survive the war. One had joined the army way too young after he had been imprisoned for a year. Then he sailed on a troopship that was torpedoed. The younger brother went to school on a scholarship and had done well. During the holidays, he wanted to come to the city to be with his sister. She should have prevented it, but he begged and pleaded. Then an air raid; he was only twelve years old. She had to bury him, as the older brother was in prison then, and couldn't come. Which was why he ended up in the army, as the prisoners were conscripted.

"And your parents?"

They knew nothing about it, which is good. When the bombs fell, the daughter didn't write to tell them that they did; when the ship sank, there was nothing more to write. No, they hadn't been deported. The parents were spared that. Fräulein Zinner was happy about that, and smiled. They just died of old age, one shortly after the other, within a week. First the father, then the mother; yes, from reliable sources she heard in a roundabout way, and it was confirmed after the war. "Nothing is more dignified when it comes to death than to have the inner decency to pop off at the right moment." To my complete surprise, Fräulein Zinner served up this raw sentiment. I winced in response.

"A whiner!" she whispered. "A whiner is all I am! Tell me, how did you manage it . . . I mean, all those years?"

"I don't know. There's nothing that can be done about it, or—"

"Or what?"

"Or because of it is what I would say, if you really have to know."

"I see. I understand already. I've read a lot of reports that tell you all about it. But you shouldn't at all think that my parents . . . Naturally, I would have . . . But as to what happened . . . I can't help thinking. And sometimes that helps. You also lost people?"

"Yes, I did."

"Of course you did. I shouldn't ask such a dumb question."

"It doesn't bother me."

"So you're not a whiner. Look, I hardly ever talk about it. But when someone was involved so directly . . ."

"That I don't know."

"What do you mean?"

"I don't know if I was all that directly involved. I didn't in fact die, and therefore I don't know."

"I don't entirely understand."

"There's not much to understand. Only the dead were there, because they alone remained. The rest of us only passed through. That's just the way it seems to me, something entirely different. I can't really remember."

"So you escaped? You didn't want to be there? Is that why you ended up here? Is that so?"

"There was a lot back there that I didn't want to hang around for. That's one reason, but not the only one as to why I came here and prefer to be here. If you want to call that an escape, then you're right. But only then. There's no other escape. There's no such thing, nor can there be a successful one. I wouldn't therefore speak of any kind of running away, for I know that I can't get away from the persecution. The monstrous is always at my neck. But this experience and my memory are not one and the same."

"Explain!"

"I don't mean forgetting. That I can't do. Such things are still present to me as experiences and images, and I want to investigate them, since I cannot do anything else. Until everything is thought through and made clear, I cannot rest, let alone find peace. Thus there can be no escape. But memory is something else altogether. It's the identification with the deportation and all its consequences, therefore with those who suffered extermination. That I can't do. At best I was broken, perhaps shattered, but, because I indeed stand before you, I was not exterminated."

"At best? Isn't that bad enough?"

"Yes, bad enough. But to be exterminated would be better."

"So you don't want to live any longer?"

"Oh, no. I very much want to live, perhaps even too much so, but only my own extermination could amount to a true memory of what happened."

"What is it you want, really?"

"Nothing. Only to be."

"That's comforting."

"That's entirely unsure. Listen to what I say: One has in no way the right to call his behavior good."

"Why be so hard?"

"Excuse me, but I've gotten off track. It's so tiring to have to hold your-self together, to think of yourself as an individual entity. I repeat again, nothing is for sure. The extermination was not successful, therefore there is no complete memory. In short, memory is unattainable. A person on the edge of things remains in abeyance."

"That's what you mean by nothing being for sure."

"Correct. The decision has been set aside. One is neither alive nor not alive; one simply goes on. Probably that's not true for most people, and for others it's unacceptable. But for me it is certainly so."

"So you are at odds with yourself."

"Set aside for later, not for good. With that comes a sense of guilt."

"For you as well?"

"How so me?"

"I always thought that our guilt was that we simply left, that we left our loved ones, that we left all of you to fend for yourselves."

"Meaning that you should all have been ruined like us? No, that's not true. It's indeed good that so many left."

"Your saying that is perhaps not yet a comfort, but it does make it easier. I've never again had a peaceful night, simply because I left. Those left be-hind stand right before my eyes. Having failed to help, whether it be even the most minimal support or reaching out, such chances were neglected. That's a pressing guilt that I can't forgive myself. And now you talk of guilt, and also perhaps accepting that we left our loved ones to fend for them-selves."

"That's one of the hardest questions, but, indeed, I do accept it, in most cases. You know, sometimes I felt deeply sorry for all of you out there."

"There was no feeling sorry for us."

"Oh, yes! Even a great deal. That's how it seemed to me. I often imag-ined how those on the outside pined away, powerless and not knowing how others were managing, while some of us attained a spiritual freedom that didn't exist here, one that otherwise in life you attain with great difficulty and certainly only rarely."

"That completely surprises me. Compassion for us and spiritual free-dom, in the abyss, amid ruin."

"Near-ruin, on its outskirts. We were not the ones to feel sorry for; we only needed help. Meaning rescue. As far as I see it now, that was the essence of the situation, which couldn't be solved by a few but was ignored by everyone. There was too much sorrow for us, and too little help. Sorrow, compassion, and, above all, the help that never came through. That was our plight—compassion combined with the powerlessness and the coerced idleness. In addition, it seems to me that those who survived also need to be felt sorry for a little bit, and when it comes to actual help, not much has changed."

Frau Singule had heard the last part of my talk and was upset.

"Well, that's one helluva thing to say! I myself led an effort in which, during the last weeks of the war, we gathered ten thousand pairs of socks, two thousand pairs of slippers, and at least the same number of shoes, four thousand sweaters, countless shirts, underwear, and handkerchiefs. As soon as it was possible, the things were sent on to be divided up among the deserving."

"Yes, and the entire lot was never cleaned or mended! It was a scandal!" said Fräulein Zinner quietly but sharply.

"How can you say that for sure?"

"Because I saw the things myself."

"But you have to agree there were also brand-new things mixed in! I donated some myself. On top of that, you can't expect that people in short supply of textiles and who literally donated the clothes off their backs would sacrifice their best things."

"I'm of a different view," said Fräulein Zinner simply.

"No one can expect that!" Frau Singule replied with barely concealed anger. "One cannot expect anything at all. It's best to be grateful that you are still alive and don't have to run around naked. Indeed, too many survived. It would be so much simpler if all were killed and cremated, every last one, for then it would be easier to speak of the crimes and all the victims could be mourned together, a sea of tears in sorrow, fantastic, all done in solidarity, public demonstrations, the outrage of the entire world, the heart-rending speeches of famous friends to mankind, lavish contributions from all over the world, as well as a competition to erect a monument to the poor innocent victims. Wreaths and sonorous speeches at the dedication: 'Never again, we swear to you, the dead . . .' Then, after a fanfare of trumpets, all will head home deeply satisfied. That's how the hyenas of international sorrow will bring it off! That some dare to mourn the end of the war—ah, such a blunder. I mean, to have survived, it's unforgivable! Each living witness is each day a nasty flaw in the workings of organized humanity!"

Frau Singule looked at me, speechless, before she continued.

"I have nothing to say, Herr Landau. For heaven's sake, don't get so excited! People are not as bad as you believe."

"Ah, but I don't think they're terrible at all."

Against my inclinations, I was once again the center of attention. Fräulein Zinner was nowhere to be found as I looked around for her in vain. But after a little while she came back.

"For the most part, I never talk about such things," she said quietly, and went on with what I didn't entirely understand. "Tender feelings exposed in the wrong places I don't like at all. It's better not to reveal what one thinks. I have to go, my bus is coming. It was a pleasure, Herr Landau. Exceptionally informative."

"Could I sometime . . . ?"

"Yes. Give me a call. Goodbye."

Fräulein Zinner left without even reaching out her hand to me. I was struck by how short and brusque she was, appearing no longer interested, turning sharply away, there and then saying goodbye, accompanied by Dr. Haarburger, leaving the party. It hurt. I was sad that in my excitement I went too far. No one expected me to have friendly feelings toward Frau Singule, and yet I still had no right to inflict my indignant outburst upon her, no matter if it was a thousand times true. If I had gotten into such a touchy discussion with Fräulein Zinner, I would have shut up the moment someone else entered in. I would have liked to explain as much, but her hasty departure had prevented that. I couldn't think too long about my clumsiness, because soon I found myself lost to the senseless chatter droning on, which had no depth at all. Many thousands of people stood around me, turning into me. Even Professor Kratzenstein sidled up to me, but then quickly drew back when he recognized what I was about to say, as Resi Knispel compassionately approached me and almost went too far in inviting me to visit her. She gave me her card and wrote down the nearest tram stop to her apartment. I should certainly come visit sometime soon. It would be an honor for her to help me—your experiences, my dear friend, what an inexhaustible treasure it would be for me. Fräulein Knispel thought of a novel; it should be titled "The Miserable One," for though she knew the risk of such a title, it was still so juicy, for it spoke to both the persecutor and the persecuted, though I might not find it very clever. I should write it as fast as possible and bring it to her. The party began to break up, at which point I made an effort, having been encouraged by my hosts, to gain whatever it was humanly possible to do for me but which I had failed to accomplish as yet. So I shoved my way back and forth, casting myself in the full glare so that I might be taken seriously. Unfortunately, I dismissed the fact that I just looked like a fool, a passing wave of foam coughed up far and wide by a spring flood, the fleeting brilliance soon ebbing away, the sensation at an end and none to replace it the next day, myself already forgotten. Then there I was, sitting in my study just like today, though even more tormented and no longer so patient, and I waited.

I sat with my work, which I had pressed at as if I were being hunted down, working quickly as never before and as I never would again, and waiting. I waited for the telephone call, having been promised that it would come at this hour on this day, for sure—"It's of the utmost importance to me, Herr Landau, of the highest interest." The call did not come at the appointed hour, nor did it come later, for it never came. I rushed to the telephone, wanting to call myself, but no one was there and there was no one to speak to. I should try again, tomorrow, then in a week, later yet, never. . . . I tried relentlessly: "You said indeed today—you promised me, you said . . ."Again, all in vain and, again, an impediment, an unforeseen occurrence, a sudden journey, an illness, a conference, a pressing matter, an unexpected visit, the approaching holidays, just back from vacation, patience, patience. Johanna despaired because it weighed on me so and got me down. She tried behind my back to arrange matters to my benefit, but she had no success and had to finally inform me how she had failed. The sickness of these unsuccessful attempts to meet ate at my heart. I was again saddled with my plight, unable to let go, as I collected new excuses, remembered this one and that, which I should have taken as an attempt to be friendly. But all to no avail, for I wasn't just being put off; I was being neutralized. That's what I had to learn, that you did not exist if you did not exist: nothing but a bothersome occurrence that got in the way of things, something that was a bother for a little while but then which could be run over, and then forgotten. The order of the day was such that I did not exist within it.

"If you don't exist, write letters, so that you exist." I read that once. How often it occurred to me during these years, during which I especially wrote a lot of letters. For millennia people have written letters for many reasons; people humbly write letters for the very same reasons today. To share something with others, to ask about them, to reach out to someone and ask for an answer. Indeed, many are lost, are not paid attention to, not valued enough or misunderstood and are doomed instead of blessed. Countless letters have been sent that never receive the desired response, or they arrive too late and pass each other in the mails. Any of this can happen. Over the course of time, certain rules and customs developed that threatened to restrain the richness of exchange; whether it be language that is mangled or the expression shrunk, many letters lose hold of their original purpose and end up repeating a million worn-out and tattered tropes. But letters they were, letters that still conveyed a message, and when you received one it was an event; you took it in hand and read it and knew. That's no longer so, but I have sampled such pleasures; the many exceptions that still exist have little effect on the general perception.

I threw myself into writing, thinking that the least I could do was write. They were long or short bits of news that I formulated, often in a hurry, though later more slowly and more carefully, because I became suspicious when I noted that my letters strayed into nothingness and didn't seem to reach any point. I actually thought, Consider the words line by line, myself going over what had been written, making sure that it really contained some content, a mind that could be experienced and shared. It was and had to be comprehensible, and so I would read it once again the next morning. Then, when I was satisfied, I'd seal the letter and send it off. I sent letters to friends or strangers with familiar and unfamiliar names. I said what I had to say, explained myself, offered myself, reported on people and events, and often carried the letters to the post office myself.

Three times a day the mailman delivered the mail on West Park Row. I recognized the sound of his steps already from the window, and knew exactly what time he came around. I sat at my desk and looked out at the street in anticipation whenever I heard the gate of the neighboring house click shut. Then he was there, passing by our house, and if he saw me sitting there he waved, indicating that I shouldn't expect anything. Yet sometimes our gate also clicked, then he came with quickly measured steps to our door, but I was faster and threw open the door in order to receive his gifts in my hands. He brought brochures and newspapers, bills and reminders, he brought something else as well, he even brought letters that were certainly meant for me, but they were not the letters that I was expecting. And then, finally, a letter of this kind arrived, which I opened hastily, yet there was nothing in it, the words empty, barely hanging together, written in a rush and without any attention. I strained my eyes in looking at it and studied it for a good while, asking Johanna to help me with it, but she couldn't extract anything from it, either. "It says nothing at all!" I bent over the sheet and turned it every which way. Unfortunately it was true, nothing but a disappointment. The letter was empty and was not a letter at all. This was worse than ever, for some words stood out, such as "unfortunately" or "noncommittal" or "perhaps," the address overly formal ("My Dear Sir") all of it clear, each letter in place, the signature also recognizable ("Entirely yours" or "Respectfully yours"), and between the address and the signature the empty sentences stretched out over many lines. The only thing that helped was that a letter had at last arrived; this I told myself with satisfaction and plucked out individual words. I did so again and kept doing so, thinking about what they meant. My head grew heavy; I couldn't think straight. "Did he say no?" said Johanna as she entered in expectation and wanted to hear what he had written me. Then I read it aloud slowly, but she couldn't understand what it was really saying. An answer to my letter it was not, all of it strange and dark, perhaps meant for me but not just for me. Johanna had already left the room several times and come back. Finally she looked at me directly, and I had to say something. After a long look at the piece of paper, I made my decision. "I think he is saying no." I didn't let on how I felt, but kept it inside as if nothing had happened, as if I didn't care—a simple no, something one might choke on easily discharged. "Can nobody be gotten through to? What's the point of your having survived?" Thus she sighed as I spread out all the copies of my letters before me and looked through them as if through an illusion, hoping to discover who had written them if only I tried hard enough. I had written the lines with my own hands. My handwriting is strong, so nothing could be mistaken about what I read, because it wished to be spoken aloud, and was not just meant for the eyes. Since I had made copies of the letters, they could be compared, and I asked of them and myself, almost with the pressing need of a prayer, whether they could be deciphered. I just needed to know how they had been read. Secrets that one had to be privy to, the clues hidden to me, no advice given. As I was trying to get a real answer, I wrote new letters, each word chosen carefully, perfectly understandable. I put myself into the letters, me, in order that they be comprehensible. I read them aloud to Johanna and gave them to her to read; I listened to her advice, did another draft, culling everything that she had suggested be taken out. I also made a carbon copy and kept it, so that there would be no doubt when the answer should come. But this effort, though it sharpened my mind and made me more alert with self-awareness, did nothing for my pursuit. It kept repeating itself, leaving me empty or making me more destitute. I thought about it for a long time, because there had to be someone in the world to whom it was worth writing. I felt too weak to do this on my own; I couldn't write any more letters. It was vile to advertise oneself and to keep appealing to no one, having to wait when I had already been waiting for too long.

No one could know that I was alive, therefore I had to write. At that, I would hear something inside my head. It said, "Why should anyone expect that you survived?" I imagined that others must be looking for me, other returnees having also been found in the first days. To search was to me the first responsibility that anyone in the world had. What did they want from me? For so many years writing was forbidden, and now it felt too difficult, the hand out of shape and unable to say what I wished it to. News headlines blazed from impenetrable walls. If one risked pushing through, he could not hope for any leniency if he was caught. Now this was no longer true, letters being allowed once more, but the situation was not clear to me. To whom should I write? I didn't know anyone. To whom, then, to whom? Peter listened to me attentively.

"You have to decide. The borders have been open since yesterday; one can send letters to other countries. You should write straightaway."

This was easy for Peter to say, for everything seemed so simple to him. I didn't want to, but he was hard-nosed.

"You have friends and relatives out there. My friend, how can you be so dumb! Give them a sign that you're alive; they'll be happy to hear from you. You once said that you've kept hold of a couple of addresses all these years. Try one! A letter will spread like wildfire out there. Someone will finally help you and you'll be able to leave."

But where to? I didn't know. I wanted to leave. But where to? There was no knowing. To slip through, get out, and then be off; it was ridiculous to even think of. No letter could help make that happen. Some kind of international center for refugees had set up a search service, therefore it was up to them out there to take care of us. Me, the lost foundling. Peter laughed, irritating me as he asked about the people I knew on the outside. An old uncle, who really wasn't an actual uncle but rather a cousin of my mother's. What was his name? Karl Strauss. The address? No, I only knew the city, which was not very big. Peter thought that was fantastic. Just the city—the post office knew what to do. I said that I had never been that close to the old man. What do you mean by not that close . . . that was ridiculous, said Peter. But I said that I would not be writing to such a city if Uncle Strauss were at all inclined to look for me. Peter assuaged my anger. He was so helpful in such matters, and pointed out ways forward for me that I didn't care for or shied away from.

"One only looks for next of kin. The son of a cousin, that's asking a bit much. But don't let that hold you back. In such a situation, write and they will answer. They'll even be grateful to you for writing."

I found that ridiculous, but Peter talked me down and argued stubbornly that I accept his point and get hold of myself. Fine, if I didn't want to hear anything of Uncle Strauss, then I should write someone else. Friends were great, even better than relatives. Finally, I agreed. Letters to friends and relatives. I wrote and wrote. But I didn't mail what I had written, because I disapproved and was inept at pressing myself onto the world. I got into a routine, and soon the writing came easier, but when I read through it I found it weak and the sense too meager. Finally, I decided to write a letter to one of my best friends, perhaps the best that I had before the war, which was So-and-So, as I called him. To him I wanted to write in detail before I sent any other letters. I threw out all the drafts that I had already written to different recipients, and thought about what I wanted to share with So-and-So. A portrait of my sufferings poured out of me. I suddenly said, after many long sentences, "Death." That was too heavy and cumbersome. Yet the best place to end, in a fragmentary manner, when I thought about it, for I had to admit that I had not gone too far. To cover it all in a single letter, that was impossible; namely, to state my case and to convince the recipient that the letter really was from me and nothing in it was exaggerated that might seem suspect to the recipient or would be tossed away in anger. How do you speak to someone when in fact you are not dead? Which words can convey the truth, such that the person believes you?

"You write about what you experienced."

What had I experienced? There was no beginning, and thus I had not experienced anything. I had to find something, a story. Once, there was a person. He was born in a house that was in a city. His parents lived there— definitely, they did. You could visit them, there was a way to get there: from the Reitergasse you turned onto the Römerstrasse, then came the Karo-linenweg, until finally you were there. The parents were happy to see you, and you congratulated them, asking what the little one's name was. The parents then responded, Yes, we have named him, he's called Arthur. What did you say? Me? Buttons fiddled with, counting off one, two, three, seven, does she love me or love me not? For real? Or not? Arthur and Franziska. What happened to them? Didn't people come and again offer their congrat-ulations? The two celebrated their luck at having found each other. They decided to live. Why did Peter keep standing here, why these nagging ques-tions in his face full of such blind faith? Would it be better if I were talking about Adam? Listen! Then he left and searched, but he could find nothing. The bloodthirsty fields were all dried up. Or had his eyes simply become cloudy? They saw nothing good and blinked sadly while looking into blank space where the wall still stood. What was behind the wall? Forlorn Adam, whose story had befallen him. One had to tell it, just how it happened, first one day, then another, then. Yes, then . . . What happened then? Something wrapped around a branch with fruit, then a letting go. Gazing at your hands, feeling your own skin, somewhat too dry, the skin peeling. Peter, the apple has become wormy through and through; it's no longer edible. The guests have not touched it and have turned away. The parents are now alone, happy to be with their little Arthur, who whimpers unaware in his crib. He will have a future, says the father, and takes the mother by the hand. Then they tiptoed out the gate. Could you write that to a friend? No matter how hard I tried, conjuring up a useful fable was not my forte.

"No fables! Say that you were there, that you survived, and you need their help!"

Nor was it a topic for conversation. You didn't say that you were there. Either it wasn't true, and therefore had no point, or it was true, and therefore pointless to talk about. You didn't point a finger at yourself. Nor did you talk about having survived; if you were writing, then you had survived and it didn't feel right to say, My dear So-and-So, I am still here and have survived. Survived what? you ask. Yes, you're right. Well, let's see, what has been survived is time—years, war, myself—and that is why I am here. I don't know if you remember me, but I should hope so, because earlier we were friends, and on top of that you always had an excellent memory. Isn't that true? Do you still recall why we called you So-and-So? You gave yourself that name and would nonetheless always be furious when we teased you with it. Finally you got used to it, my dear So-and-So. We shared the same interests, talked a great deal with each other, did a lot of things together, for we were, so to say, friends and thought it likely that we would maintain a close friendship as life went on. I certainly can't remember all the particulars. The reason being that they are not pertinent ... meaning they are pertinent (the idea that I don't need to explain anything to you because you're probably familiar with it all already—that's circuitous, disingenuous, skips over too much), for certain reasons that are not easy to express, in part because they hardly lead to a proper understanding, and in part because it is hard to understand the reason our hopes and plans never came to fruition, such that our relationship, unfortunately, was interrupted.

Why should I write that? It might shock the recipient, for So-and-So was always hypersensitive. There was also no reason to think that he would welcome such a letter. Nonetheless, I had to write something if I was going to write. But the reference to reasons that could not be revealed, never mind be valid—there was no reason to go into that. (Our relations, which I considered close, they having always been especially sweet and easy, suffered an unforeseeable interruption, which you, I am assuming, also noticed.) That was a risky assumption, but Peter and Anna were always inclined to encourage such presumptuous expectations. Sometimes they succeeded in convincing me that I was entirely right, but when I began to write it down I couldn't maintain a proud self-confidence. I had to change the point I was trying to make, for it could be expressed differently, or at least more humbly.

The ties we maintained have nothing to do with the fate I have suffered of late, even when looked at in the most favorable light, which is why I ask that you not think of me as out of line when, in good conscience, I have also imagined that, from your completely different perspective, it is possible to feel sympathy for me. If I am wrong, then blame the circumstances, and please forgive me! You don't have to answer, but instead just throw the letter away. . . . After such reductiveness and emotional presumption in a first letter after many years, strong objections cannot help but be raised. I showed so little confidence in the constancy of my friend's attitudes that I ended up, first, presenting myself as a poor witness and, second, suggesting that I didn't at all expect to be esteemed as a true friend who has remained loyal. I had to be determined to move ahead more boldly and, in the process, be more reserved as well. I gathered together all my powers and wrote this letter:

Dear So-and-So!

No doubt you will be surprised to receive a letter from me after so long and somewhat unexpectedly. Perhaps it will also make sense to you just why I ask you to think of the first sentence as not having been written. Forget it, take it in stride, and quickly read on. All I ask is that you choose one or the other possibility and don't be angry with me!

Look, I have indeed reappeared before you—in written fashion, yes, and yet almost directly. It's my handwriting. It hasn't improved with the years but, rather, the other way round, yet you will certainly recognize it and think, indeed, it's the same old me. I haven't grown any older, for the war years simply don't count.

And, in mentioning this, I have thus informed you why you haven't heard from me in so long, for certainly you will think, What, you mean throughout the entire war he never thought it necessary to send me a little card to tell me what happened to him, all the while I was worried about him, and now that the whole affair is barely over and everything is back on track, then he steps to the fore and pretends that nothing happened in between?

I can't deny any of that. When I think back, this is exactly how it seems: damn little has happened, my friend, but you can believe me when I say that during this war the mails functioned miserably. How often I inquired with the appropriate authority whether it was possible to write to you, but my request was only scoffed at, while I had to keep quiet so that they would think me harmless and not suspect me of being a spy. That's why I couldn't follow through on my intentions, and therefore it resulted in an awkward disruption in our correspondence.

As you well recall, you quickly took off right before the war began and hardly had time to properly say goodbye to me. But I was not upset about that, I really wasn't, but rather concerned, for I was worried that, in between, too many things could happen that could take you away from me. Those are reactions that you have to forgive! They would have been quickly dispensed with if it had been at all possible for you to visit here even once or invited me to visit you. Everything would then have been cleared up, and I am convinced that we could have continued our conversations just where they left off before the war.

I am deeply interested in how you are. The news that reached me made it seem that things were not at all easy for you all on the outside, and I can imagine that it would be hard to overestimate the difficulties endured by the citizens. Hopefully, you gained a foothold somewhere and lived with others you could trust. It would only set me at ease and please me no end to hear from you that everything went as you hoped it would.

That's also the central reason I am writing. I can only imagine that you and other old friends feel a horrible hesitancy in trying to tie together the frayed threads of the past. Please believe me that such thoughts, at least on my part, are not necessary, for there is no reason that you have to worry about me. The weather is as lovely as ever—a lovely summer and an even more glorious fall have come to the old city. The streets and parks, in which I spend so many exhilarating hours thinking of you and so many other dear people, are full of joyful hustle and bustle, and whoever can ignore the fact that a familiar face rarely shows itself hardly notices that any kind of unusual years have occurred in this country.

Which is why I have to readily declare that one should not be too sentimental about such things, because otherwise weak nerves could cause one to feel gloomy. People have even been overcome by such feelings. Only with steady calm can one tread upon reality. Then you can bear life in a cheerful state of mind and reassure yourself that you are no exception.

If there is anything I can do for you here, be it privately or through the authorities, please just let me know!

That your dear mother perished, you no doubt have heard from others, as well as your father, Walter, whom I was often with (we became very close; he was a real character). Also, our mutual friend Hans Georg is no longer alive. Do you remember Arno Seiler? He was very political and paid for it with his life. I still see his sister Anna often, whom you also no doubt knew. Yes, it was especially tragic with Hans Georg. He appeared to have survived up until a few days before the end, when, during a march, he was shot by the troop escort because he was so weak.

Those are very tragic events, which one experiences here at every turn. They cannot be ignored, and so I mention them, even when I assume that you have already heard more about them than you care to. However, I will spare you the details. It's always the same story again and again, and that's why I think . . .

No, I can't expect So-and-So to understand such painful matters. It was smarter not to mention anything that could upset my friend. I erased the last two sentences and wrote something else.

You'll certainly be pleased to hear that the situation here has generally gotten much better, signs of progress visible almost every day. People are moving on with fresh courage and dignified cheerfulness toward a better future. . . .

Peter came into the room and looked over my shoulder. "You are completely mad," he said, not wanting anything to do with this approach, which he disapproved of as dishonest. As I began to defend it, because it seemed to me practical, he got upset because of my indifference to the fate of so many who suffered such misery. Even if his bride were to finally be released from prison, there were still ten thousand others locked up, and another hundred thousand hunted. This made me feel ashamed that I had written such optimistic claptrap. As an excuse, I quietly suggested that I couldn't report on the new injustices being done, for the mails were censored. Peter laughed at me for being so stupid. No one was asking to hear from me about such expulsions, and indeed there had never been any need for me to go into such drivel. My task was first and foremost to just share the most important things. Should I wish to suppress anything uncomfortable about myself, that was no reason to conjure misleading nonsense. Thus I had to erase again and write something anew.

There's little to say about the situation here. I could imagine that to you our circumstances here seem somewhat otherworldly. Even if that were not true, the newspapers, in which everything worth knowing is printed, would be enough to give you that sense. That's why I'm limiting myself to telling only about me personally. Hopefully, I won't bore you too much with it.

Certainly you will be happy when I say to you: I'm well, in fact surprisingly good. I live comfortably with a friend in a quiet suburb that is near the forest, with easy connections to the city and, since a couple of weeks ago, a really good job that suits me quite well. Don't laugh, but I am working in a museum! In fact with paintings, exceptionally interesting ones. I'll perhaps tell you more about them another time, for my skills will hardly allow me to describe them properly in a few words.

The life that I lead is thoroughly orderly and stimulating, as well as simple and humble. It suits me quite well. However, I have to think about where I want to be later on. I have to look for my own apartment, which, unfortunately, is not so easy, and there are many other questions that are pressing which under constantly changing conditions anyone here has to face, more or less.

What So-and-So might imagine lay behind such obscure sentences was anyone's guess. But I let them stand, though Peter didn't like them at all.

How keenly and inwardly free I felt in approaching these and other problems, and without any fear of insurmountable difficulties, and thus I thought at times that it would probably be more reasonable, given my talents and my research plans, to try to spend a longer time in a foreign country without decamping there too quickly. This was why I had not taken on too much, mainly because of a dearth of possibilities. To explain myself more precisely:

You must know that I am a bit isolated. I say that without any squeamish self-pity, but it's true and carries with it advantages with which I would think you could empathize. There are still people outside who know me, or should know me. Unfortunately, I have had no success in coming into contact with them so far.

You are the first one I have written. That explains why I am going at it in such a circuitous manner. Can you understand that? You know, it's hard to keep your sense of balance when you have been alone for so long. I don't want to overwhelm you, and certainly I don't want to ask of you something that is not possible, but perhaps you indeed still have time for me, even if in today's world, after such a hard battle to get a sustainable situation, you cannot help me. Please understand that I certainly don't need that at all, and you should certainly not misunderstand me; I am only asking for friendly advice in order that I can form an idea of how things are on the outside— what I should aim for if I wish to get ahead without expecting too much, such as perhaps giving a lecture in my field, and to build contacts who could be useful to my further studies.

I am still interested in the same things as always (having learned too much already, my friend!). I have prepared reams of notes for a long work, and already a first draft of some of it. I have done all of this in the years . . .

What years? What have I done? He will not understand what I'm trying to get at. I crossed out the sentences.

You must know that I have not sat idle. The old ideas that mean most to me in regard to the sociology of oppressed people, which always met with your approval, have naturally deepened over the course of time. They have ripened through some of my own experiences and intensive consideration. If, as one heard expressed everywhere in the first excitement over the new peace, they are serious about founding a new and more just order on earth, which many voices support in the postwar years, then one should recognize that my far-reaching plans at this moment are not at all inappropriate.

Please, say what you wish! Point me toward where most people's interests lie today on the outside, how I might get started, how to rise up out of the depths, and, most of all, how to begin to be seen again. Perhaps you grasp what I mean. I don't want to go on and on about it, and I trust your capacity to empathize. I trust that you won't keep me waiting too long once this letter has reached you?

And here's another request: Tell me as much about yourself as possible—I really need to know. All of it interests me. I even feel a bit lonely here and am hungry for news from old friends. Unfortunately, I also can't keep from sharing with you, as I had wished, that things in this country right now seem a bit forlorn, if not hopeless. Too much is missing that one used to love—meaning some are no longer among us. But you shouldn't be concerned about that. I can say to you with a bit of pleasure something that you'll recall from when we used to translate the Latin authors: "Unhappiness and misery are the natural run of things when a country is consumed by war." That's the way it is. Old men of our circle who stayed behind here are, for the most part, no longer alive, some young men also having parted from us. Also, Franziska is gone. But, really, no more of such sad matters.

I'm taking good care of myself; I don't let myself go and have not given up on life. And so it goes on. If you could see how I'm sitting here by an open window in the almost-summer-like foliage that still looks out unchanged at the wonderful vineyard, you would smile and shake your head and say, "That's Arthur, just like I always knew him."

Oh, there's so much I could tell you, but it's probably better if I close now. Not only concern for you demands it; one shouldn't make the censor put so many holes through a letter.

Be well, my dear So-and-So, and write back soon! I will wait impatiently, but I know as well that the mails here don't always run on time and things can be delayed.

Always yours,

Arthur

So, roughly, if I have rightly recalled the first draft, that's how I wrote my first letter to someone outside the country after the war. That took me many days, because I kept discovering problems in my crimped, prim sentences, and I kept polishing them, though none seemed to improve. I only wanted something to come from my hand that at least could be answered, that was not too disturbing, while I also couldn't stand for it to be stilted, and it had to at least be softened. I tried as best I could to patch back together what had been torn apart. When I was satisfied with the letter (meaning I wasn't satisfied at all, but I could at least live with it), I wrote it out at Peter's urging on several pieces of paper, though not trusting myself to send the letter off on its own, for I could not at all determine whether I had said the right things.

I suffered from a stifling uncertainty, even fear, that something harmful or otherwise inappropriate had slipped into my words. My condition was bad on many different levels, and denied me awareness of any understandable relation between my feelings and my words. I especially felt that in my lines there was nothing that really spoke to my situation. I wanted to avoid that, because I was afraid—so I thought—to shamefully expose myself and to evoke unwelcome impressions of myself in So-and-So.

Consumed by such doubts I turned to Peter and subjected myself, more indulgently than I should have, to his judgment, he being someone who was often afflicted with cleverness. He was indeed good-natured, sincere, agreeable, but also a small, even narrow-minded soul. He also led a life that often bothered me. He was inclined to random lies and little dishonesties, though these things were probably also harmless and even forgivable. Sometimes it had nothing to do with anything bad but was, rather, just a meaningless fib shared while bragging, for which one couldn't get at all mad at Peter. And yet if he was really annoying, Anna—who through Hermann was distantly related to him—had to talk to him and straighten him out, not holding back any reproaches, eventually getting to his more forgiving nature and engaging it. I granted him no real power over me, for I guarded myself against it, but I still surrendered too much of myself to him. His certainty, which felt good to me, must have replaced or stood in for mine, as he had a hold on me, causing my strength and will to fail, he fighting with the authorities on my behalf, helping me to find my way, clearing away anything uncomfortable, and I can attest that it would have been hard to survive the postwar years even halfway well without him. Peter was stateless, which at that time was a rare piece of luck for him, just as his family background served him as well after the war as before the years of occupation, because through his father he is still a part of the people persecuted and oppressed in the name of victory, while through his mother, on the other side, he is part of another people in whose name many similar, yet more intense, nasty things were done earlier. Thus Peter has escaped many dangers, having successfully held his own during all the confusion of the war, but now having to free his bride from prison and to find the most convenient means of getting her across the border and home. His luck or his cleverness often helped the much less endangered Anna and also was of use to me.

Sometimes it feels wrong to have relied and counted on Peter so much, although I condemned his shenanigans. They were outrageous, but I couldn't do without him. What Anna did for me, what I let her do, was worth so much more to me, though I didn't tell her about many of the woes that I suffered, for I didn't want to overburden her. But Peter always took care of things, I have to admit, for he was tireless. Nothing that I asked of him was too much. Very often it was me who lacked the ego, the kind of versatile, practical approach necessary for all situations, and a stand-in for the man I was not. Peter also served as a stand-in rooster among the hens he strutted about with, and which he even occasionally offered to me, though when he told his stories about his girls I found it disgusting. Since I shared a room with him, it was sometimes hard not to know, but Peter, who spared me with a quiet smile, always had a solution. Once he went out with his most recent choice, letting me know the time that I should stay clear of the room, sometimes putting me up with friends of his for the night. I went along with it all and was ashamed, the more so as his bride, whom he several times visited on the sly during lucrative ventures, had asked me, when she said goodbye before crossing the border and returning home, to keep an eye on Peter and make sure that he "didn't stray," as she described his hardly loyal ways. That's why I spoke to him in good conscience and pretended to be his guardian in carrying out the most pitiable role I'd ever taken on. If he was in a good mood, he listened to me and acted as if he agreed with everything I said, but when I finished talking he shook my hand trustingly and too strongly and presented me with a broad smile spreading across his entire face. Thereby I became helpless, without anything with which to respond. He undermined my ethos and forced me, without ever verbally agreeing, to look on at his activities with patient good will and leave him alone for at least a week.

That was the guy, sixteen years younger than me, who controlled me and turned me into a willing witness to his strange way of life. It was as if I didn't exist. What Johanna experienced later and had to endure, since there was nothing else left for her to do if she didn't want to leave me, this I had given over to Peter consciously. I handed over to him what I was not, in order that I could be, and therefore my gratitude to him remains intact, even if I never wish to see his face again. Most likely, I will be spared that. It points, however, to a great difference between my relationship with him back then and the way I am with Johanna. Johanna makes it possible for me to exist, if only through her. Because she takes on my weight, carries me along, and lends me at least the shadow of an existence. It was different with Peter, who really lived for me. He didn't at all worry if I could be something but, rather, he was simply me. It was all for me, and this resulted in an abysmal dependency, because everything he did for me was more than just done in my stead; it was I in the midst of his being. I couldn't answer for it, because there was no answering for it, especially as I had no chance to determine it, except in very limited ways, even though he used me as justification for his behavior.

I don't know how a relationship such as that between me and Peter could otherwise occur. A friendship, if that means a high measure of affection and trust, never existed between us. Back then, my desperate state on the first evening set everything in motion, which then evolved within a few days to almost the closest of relations that I had ever had with another person. I still see Peter approaching as I lay on the pavement in my misery, until he stood there before me and reached out his hand. He pulled me up, he being strong enough to do so, me at his mercy, entrusting myself to the guidance of a stranger who had charge of me and my things as long as I was in his country. He occupied me, but he didn't control me. Do I still know how it was? It was indeed so: he held me with a strength inside of which I was weak, where everything quivered away incapacitated, but my frailty, this state I had come to feel at home in, this Peter hadn't seized at all. That was what separated me from him and prevented his helpful grasp from becoming too unbearable. That's how Peter could do a great deal for me, and yet not everything. That also explains how my relationship with him could so quickly and easily dissolve, as if it never existed. All it took was for me to leave the country. If Peter had not helped me so much, I would still be stuck there today, provided I was still alive, wasting away among my senseless days in the museum.

Three years after my departure, which involved almost insurmountable difficulties in order to get away from there, Peter also left the city and country as part of an adventurous escape. Certainly it all went much more peacefully than my well-regulated departure. Because of what had happened to me in the war, I had forfeited all my papers, most of which could be replaced only through a lot of running around and even some clever bribery. Peter took care of it all. Passes were filled out and granted, with random stipulations that prevented me from entering any civilized country simply because of my mother tongue. Peter knew how to get around anything, for he wheedled, swindled, and juggled questionable documents until at last I had a passport, without which I never would have been issued a visa to the country I wished to travel to. Also, Peter was the one who taught me what to do in order to get hold of the coveted visa. Without him I would have had to keep hiking, just as on the mountain trip with Anna, hiking over the border, at peril because of my frailty, from one non-country to another, leaving almost everything behind—my writing and the squalid memories on which my heart hung. How easy it would have been to remain stuck there and fall into the hands of the border patrol. Alas, that anxious dream that still haunts me today, caught in the border's meshes until squeezed of breath . . . Always the desire to escape and the anxiety before the escape, the pressure to escape and the impossibility of escape! Then the need to shoo away doubt that you existed, that you were alive and could make something of yourself . . .

Peter had spared me the hardest decision. Can it be that he only delayed it and burdened me with it forever? I will never decide, for it's long been decided. It could also be that Peter simply made it easier for me by rendering me stateless, handling it all selflessly. Or not? Did he not want me to stay? No, such ideas meant nothing to him. So I really believe he did it out of selflessness, for he got nothing out of it by acting for me. It must have been clear to him that with my departure he relinquished me and all rights to me. He did it. He wanted to use me, not to annihilate me. It was his most touching act, to sacrifice me; it was a genuine surrender. That's why it would be unjust of me to lay out his shortcomings. When amid Johanna's protection I maintain his memory, I wish only to be grateful to him, no matter how difficult things are. It would be deplorable to point to his weakness in order to avenge myself for having abased myself before him. Peter, can you hear? Would you like a letter from me so that you can better recall?

Dear Peter, I have long held off writing you a letter and am only now doing so because Johanna also agrees that I have to overcome such hesitancy. But now it's a moot point, because I will not write to you in the way I should have then, except for a few stupid lines after my arrival here, which you never answered, followed by the printed notice, which I went ahead with against the wishes of Johanna, in order to announce my marriage to all the world. You acknowledged such news somewhat frivolously with witty good wishes. I was angry with you. No, I won't write to you, although I am in fact doing so, for you are no longer alive for me and have no effect upon me. I'm pleased to learn, as Anna shared with me, that you have married a girl, even if it's not the former bride whom you left behind at home, and that you are living a prosperous life in New Zealand, while, hopefully, in between you have also become more mature. Publicity people with thousands of lurid ideas, such as yourself, are certainly in demand over there. If that isn't at all the case, I still know that it's no doubt easy for you to sell your talents as advantageous to others, such that they are proud to take advice from you. And so things are excellent for you.

You no longer have me, that's true, but be comforted—oh, you are already comforted—because that's no loss. With Johanna, who best helps me to see what I can expect, I have found great good fortune, even if she is not blessed with those qualities which will bring our union certain supreme material success. Johanna has two children, to whom she is the best of mothers. She does only what she can, though she would be the first to admit that she cannot do all the things you could do. Some months before our boy was born she had to give up her job, and since then she has mainly busied herself with taking care of the house, while I am always with her. Two do-nothings—that's not your style. Your wife no doubt makes a tidy sum, true? I would hardly recognize you! With us, it's different. I can't speak about such matters with Johanna, for she's very sensitive; and she has every right to feel hurt. Nor is it exactly true that we're do-nothings, certainly not Johanna, for she never quits. Children are work, and a husband like me doubles the load. So I remain a do-nothing who sits and looks on as time passes, watching it go by.

I love most to sit at my desk and pretend to seem very busy, the walls protecting me as I look furtively out the window. It's a broad window, with five panes, that looks quite posh, it almost seeming a treasure. From there nothing in the street escapes me. I see many people, children who frivolously don't pay attention to the cars racing by, kicking their balls from one sidewalk across to another and then suddenly jumping into the roadway without thinking. I also look across at the windows opposite, where birdcages hang, the yellow companions flitting around inside the bars and belting out their song with powerful throats. I look into the windows and at the street full of faces that have long since become familiar, such that I could tell you at any time just what kind of mood each one is in. This lingering and gazing is my main occupation, nothing very productive, but it suits me well. The people who know me have a keen sense of how deplorably and dissolutely I pass the time, and they judge me and feel sorry for poor Johanna, who is touched by such sympathy. She is mainly of the view that my observations are valuable. She praises my efforts and the days well spent and protests when I'm criticized. May her sincere belief in me always remain! She maintains that it's not my fault that I've been denied the proper attention and support, and she's angry about it, for hardly anyone notices. My knowledge and capability lie fallow, and I am unjustly denied the kind of engagement I deserve. Clearly, Johanna cannot come to terms with it all.

If you were here you would, I'm guessing, soon make fundamental changes. The snooty ladies and gentlemen, who represent everything counter to what I already stand for, you'd set straight in no time by making them see what asses they are, while I am a genius. You would make something of me; I have no doubt of that. Nevertheless, I'm glad that you're not here and that, as a result, I am—you love strong words—a complete wreck. That's always preferable to me than being at the vineyard, spoiled by you. I realize things should be much different for the children, but they hardly go without. They are growing and are healthy; they have what they need.

Dear Peter, but how can you exist without me? You must miss me; we talked so well. But no, there's no need for such worry, because certainly you don't need me. Whoever exists doesn't need someone else. Like a dachshund, you certainly follow the trail. Don't you remember? You didn't need me there either but, rather, it was always the other way around. Do you recall how you used to shake with laughter, as finally, after many weeks of tense waiting for a response from So-and-So, a letter arrived? You handed it to me as I came home late one night. You hadn't opened it, although I allowed you to open any mail addressed to me. I told you that it didn't bother me at all. As I pounced with curiosity on the letter—a long epistle typed on a terrible machine with a miserable colored ribbon—you went into the kitchenette and brewed some coffee. You could deal with any unpleasantry and always worked to hold yourself in check whenever you wanted to oblige me. "Call me when you need something," you said, and shuffled off to the foyer and the bathroom. Then you were right there, with a jaunty step, the moment I called you. The coffee was done, you filled two cups, I should drink some right away. I must have been quite confused, which amused you. You were a rascal, yet you also displayed your funny sympathy, slapping me on the back as if to reassure me that it couldn't be that bad, as I reread the letter—which I had rushed through in my excitement—one more time, slowly, from beginning to end.

My dear, dear Arthur!

What unspeakable joy, what a monstrous relief did I feel after so many years of pressing worry that darkened my days like a black curtain, when I held your brave letter in my hands, nearly the first sign of a world that I had continued to think was completely gone. Each of my friends who, albeit more happily than I, was able to hold up a weapon during the liberation had been given your name and a precise description of you in order to seek you out and connect with you. It was all in vain. Also, the list of names of the survivors that was posted here by the Office of Refugees never let me breathe easy. Arthur, to see your handwriting after six years! I was so happy that people on the street looked at me as if I were crazy. So much has happened, so many terrible things having overwhelmed us all, such that with any piece of news that one receives you can't help but ask, Is it true? What you read and hear is, unfortunately, always much worse than what one thinks in the worst of hours, for reality is always worse than fantasy, which indeed leads one to the brink, but also, and that is its blessing, it allows the nasty shadows to disappear, such that even the worst calamity appears more bearable and is not just romanticized through false comfort but rather revealed for what it is.

I wish your letter (which I've read a hundred times already, often out loud, and which I've given to others to read) had arrived earlier. But imagine what kind of mix-up caused your letter to take nearly five weeks to get here, and, as you can imagine, there was little point in answering you right away, because I at least wanted to provide some of the information you asked for. That's why I didn't wire you, for I didn't want to alarm you. And so I had to let you wait, for everything takes time, nor are people these days as fast or reliable as one would want them to be, despite one's justified impatience. But I didn't hesitate for a moment, that you have to believe, and I wrote as soon as I could.

What most captivates me in reading your letter is the incredible will to live and the courage evident in each word. When I read how you depict it all, I can hardly breathe, for now I know from a serious person that certainly much was not so very horrible, as many in these parts believe and who in understandable rage are shaken by such horrors. Certainly, I don't wish to diminish anything. It must have been terrible, and the wounds ripped open could not have healed so fast. Thus I read with greatest sympathy about Franziska. I'm so saddened, and that's hardly saying anything—such a lovely person. She, above all, had to have survived; that's what I always hoped, and even now I ask how it can at all be possible. In spirit, I reach out to grasp your hand. You must realize that I want to know more about this misfortune, if it won't upset you too much, my poor Arthur.

I have also since married—which only shows how one betrays one's own principles—and Karin, my wife, whom I've told much about you and others, was just as pleased with your having written and sends her warmest greetings.

I find it very touching that you are at all concerned about how things are for me. It shames me. Nonetheless, if I tell the truth, and you would expect nothing less from me, I have to admit that everything here is extraordinarily difficult—the strange new language, life in an unfamiliar and unwelcoming neighborhood, and the overall feeling that the scholarly occupations are no bed of roses. In the first years, I suffered great privation. Over the course of time, things indeed got a bit better, but still my situation doesn't allow my earnings to cover even the most elementary of needs. If one is not rooted somewhere and wishes to lead a transitory existence, this is the place. And yet I am alive, and that's the main thing.

Certainly I will make no bones about the fact that it would be easier to build a life over there than it is here once the postwar developments quiet down a bit. The sums made available by such a small country for cultural renovation are very inviting and almost make me envious. I've also seriously thought about the question of whether or not I should consider going back, even if one simply doesn't wish to give up his hard-won little success in the new country, which my wife is against, she also fearing the problems with the language she would have among you (German is indeed not liked and has little future there!), while also out of her work comes a relatively large part of our humble family budget. Just to inform you, Karin was originally a sculptor and has made some charming small pieces—animals done in clay, the best being goats and gazelles, which were then fired, though here she, like so many, has entirely changed course and now makes dentures in a dental laboratory.

So I'm hardly likely to decide to return, although I would be glad to cross over and at least am hoping to visit and indeed see you again soon and talk about everything that can't be put into a letter. In between, however, we must write each other a great deal, especially about things that cannot bear to be put off. My dear mother has, unfortunately, indeed died (did you know that?), yet an old aunt who is almost deaf miraculously survived the war. It would be nice if you could visit her sometime soon: Frau Sophie Basch, Gerstengasse 44. You will likely have to ask the concierge, for she sublets there. In addition, it would be so helpful if you could personally pick up the things that my mother left behind with friends for safekeeping when she had to leave. Aunt Sophie wrote me about them and will know the address. Also, a conversation with my lawyer about the return of the house confiscated from my mother is very important, as well as other questions concerning, for example, the inheritance and further compensation. My practical advice is as follows: Look up my lawyer, Dr. Blecha. The office is at Kronenstrasse 63. Please tell him that I have sent you, and I will, of course, inform him as well. Ask him about the state of my affairs, and let him know that someone is looking out for me. I have heard that otherwise no lawyer will do anything. I have no use for anyone full of empty promises, who is lax about everything and only has his hand held out. Hopefully, my fears are unnecessary, for Dr. Blecha began in my father's office as an apprentice lawyer. But one never knows. I prefer to trust no one, and certainly things will move along faster if you apply yourself energetically.

You won't have to do too much on behalf of my case, whose execution I, of course, don't want you to take on free of charge. Nor will I have it any other way. I feel it's my responsibility to stand by you and support you a little bit. You need funds. As soon as a good, round sum becomes available—which, perhaps as a result of your direct intervention, can occur within a few months—I'll give you five percent of whatever I net. Are we agreed, Arthur? If through your efforts you mount up expenses, just let me know and I will instruct Dr. Blecha to reimburse you for everything immediately. As soon as my assets are solvent and available, I'll take my first vacation with Karin or come over myself, especially since the money, unfortunately, will not be allowed out.

Perhaps you can recommend to me where I should travel. Certainly you should come along if you have the time. I would especially love a winter vacation. All of my winter sports equipment should still be there—unless by some rotten chance it got sold! Just imagine, snow, genuine powder! Do you still know what that is? It's unheard of in these parts. I would most love to eat at the Fuchsberg mountain lodge, though the Schwarzschlag is nothing to sneeze at, either. Do you remember, the whipped cream, the egg cakes, and the brandy they had there was the best. You can't help but bask in the memories, my old friend, when you think of the Christmas celebrations, the fun New Year's parties in the mountains, such fun, and then strapped to the sled for a night journey into the new year!

You can see that I'm serious about returning. Just be patient, it will certainly happen. Before then, we can converse in writing. I have always loved correspondence and find that you have to apply yourself in order to avoid limitations inherent in letter writing.

You mention that you would like to visit us sometime. In and of itself, that's a good idea that I would heartily embrace. But just ask yourself how this could be done if you don't have the means. Here everything is too expensive. I've asked around and must, unfortunately, tell you that the prospects don't look good. You couldn't stay with me, because we only have two rooms and have nothing for you to sleep on. If it were only for a few days, I think I could find someplace for you to hole up in at night with friends. During the day I would be happy to put my apartment at your service. We only eat lunch at home on the weekends, but most evenings you could spend with us and also eat with us, as long as we don't have anything else we must do.

I wonder what you'd really want to do here if your visit were to be more than just a trip to pick up things. For I have to admit that it's as if I stood before a wall. I don't want to rob you of all hope, but prospects look dim when I at all consider what you could begin here. For your sake I have spoken with a lawyer, Dr. Haarburger, who has established himself here brilliantly. He's very educated, interested in many things, is influential, and a pleasant fellow with a wife who is the same. Above all, he is easy to inspire, for he feels solidarity, whereby you have to forgive the both of them a certain loquaciousness, without which one hardly warms to others or connects with them. Professor Kratzenstein is a member of his circle. Perhaps you've read something of his at some time. As a sociologist he's not entirely to my taste, but what does that matter, as he is highly respected. Well, Dr. Haarburger wants to thoroughly consider whether there might be a possibility to arrange a lecture for you through Kratzenstein or other colleagues at the Society of Sociologists—the theme has to be accessible to the public and also on a very high level. I am very much for this and will again press the matter. You would have the advantage of meeting an array of personalities while also receiving what, unfortunately, can only be termed a modest honorarium, since it's considered an honor to speak there. Only famous guests are honored. But perhaps through some finagling, which Dr. Haarburger has hinted at, a small per diem could be arranged for you. Unless we are really lucky, that is likely about the only thing that can be done for the moment.

I think about your sociological ideas with undiminished interest, even if through the local and the American schools I am headed in a different direction, and, to be honest, I can't help doubting that you and your methods, as one says here, are up to date. In general, one pokes fun here at continental sociology, and not without reason. Now, I can hear you say that your work has little in common with the approach recognized over there. That may well be, but nonetheless (or precisely because), your thinking leads in an almost completely diametrical direction to that which is in favor here. You have to unlearn it from the ground up, just as I and everyone had to, and even then it's unlikely that for the foreseeable future you will be able to catch up. Yes, if you had made a name for yourself before the war and brought out books or important essays in journals, then the prospects would be a bit better, but still not that good. Indeed, none of us had the opportunity to publish in the years before the war, and when our chance did come we were hardly done with our studies. Which is why I'm being crystal clear about the reasons there is no chance of a career for you at a local university. I haven't even dared to inquire with my own professor, even on the quiet. I could only do that if you had finished something, which also, of course, would have to be translated. Then I would have to have you take an exhaustive exam in order for everything not to be a waste from the outset, and my scholarly reputation harmed. One is always under suspicion here when you step out of line. Meanwhile, I am assuming that you didn't finish anything. How could you have—it would be a miracle!

Finally, I cannot end without explaining to you clearly, bitter as it may sound, that a sociology of oppressed people, no matter how much you might revise your old first drafts, which certainly could be built upon the foundations I well know, will nonetheless meet with no success here, as far as I can see for the moment and even in the future. What you are pursuing, my dear Arthur, would be called here a ponderous, romantic-idealistic philosophy of culture. I immediately hear your objections to such hated buzzwords, but that's the way it is, unfortunately, and let it be said. A social science whose kernel is an ethical conception, once cherished, yet it does not comply with the accepted currents of thought, and what you have called moral science or moral sociology belongs, indeed, to the realm of romantic-idealist speculation, for which nobody cares one jot.

You will have to work on a clear, limited theme that you can follow precisely—let's say a psychological-sociological investigation, such as of a certain group, for example a number of selected subjects who have suffered clearly defined duress while detained or in being detained (i.e., prisoners of war, enslaved as a result of the disintegration of certain civil rights), effects that can be subjectively and objectively certifiable, etc., etc. That would be something. But if I can give you some good advice, then give up on the sociology of oppressed people, for it won't go down well here. It is notorious for being unserious, and the danger of emotional bias, even with someone with your recent past, will only do you harm almost everywhere. I do indeed agree that the horror was in fashion for a moment, but already in serious circles interest has essentially waned. Before you could even get permission to visit, it will have completely disappeared. There are indeed some specialists who exploit such misery, Kratzenstein among them, yet they won't allow any newcomer or outsider in. It's best that you get any ideas about oppression out of your head. Popular sympathies won't help you, for they only depend on a dog-eat-dog approach and on journalistic skills, and the rest I've already explained to you. That's why I'm arguing that *under no circumstances* should you plan on making an extended visit under the premises you describe, or even think about immigration.

I'm sorry not to be able to give you better advice. I have written at such length in order to show you that there's no lack of good will on my part. I only wish for you to understand it all well. I swear to you, if I had enough influence you would be here tomorrow, and the day after you would have a professorship. See to it that over there you find a position that is bearable, which can't be that hard to do. You have no difficulties with the language there, and you'll make connections in no time at all. People over there will still be interested in oppression. If I can be of any use to you through word or deed (e.g., with finding books, materials, recommendations, etc.), it will bring me great joy. I am also thinking of how else I might support you, but nothing has occurred to me. Write me when you need something. My means are, unfortunately, reduced, but they are enough to humbly serve you, be it cash (don't forget to mention me to Dr. Blecha!) or anything else that you both might need. Though there's also less here than you might think.

A friend who is planning to fly over today will be bringing along a can of aspic with black-currant jam. It's exceptionally strong and rich in vitamin C. Take a spoon of it each day. As this friend has shared with me that he reckons that no proper shaving brushes can be had over there, I've also given him one for you. Let me know that it all arrives safely! If the rumor is true that our old teacher Herr Prenzel is still alive, please pass on my greetings. And keep your chin up, as always.

Always yours,

So-and-So

You looked at me patiently, Peter, seeming a bit derisive in a good-natured way. Then I held the letter out to you, or you took it—I don't recall exactly—and you began to read, at first seriously, soon mumbling something, then individual words aloud, here and there like a psalm, and, as I recall, "principles"—"prince-eeee-pills," you piped—and grimaced as you spoke. Other parts that moved you to immense scorn you also bastardized.

Such as: "Finally I degenerate to such stupidity, no matter how bitter it might sound, to sincerely con you into realizing that such an idiotology of the bent and stooped . . . certainly can't be dumped here, no matter how I rattle on and keep rattling." Not exactly brilliant, but you managed to succeed in brightening my grim, dismayed mood. After reading, you were really in fine spirits and took shots at example after example, full of droll and biting expressions used to nearly blast poor So-and-So to bits. Do you remember his letter?

"Tell me again, Arthur, why is the guy called So-and-So?"

"I'll tell you. He couldn't stand it when he had to say his name during ho-hum introductions. It was pointless, he thought, nor did anyone remember a name. Therefore he mumbled something incoherent: So and So. Soon many people called him that. Then he got upset about that, but then started to use it himself and was in the end proud of it."

"A lovely friend, the fool, your So-and-So. Are you taking this drivel seriously? Come on, don't be stupid. A kick in the rear, but gently, so that you don't waste your time with him! It takes all kinds. Just wait, we'll keep a spot warm in hell for him."

"How can you say that? The letter doesn't contain a single attack. On the surface, it's all nice and smooth. He handles himself well."

"Who says that we want to go after your dear friend? That's not at all what I'm thinking. We'll just latch onto him, you see, so that he cannot escape."

"He should be the one to latch onto me!"

"He can do that as well. But afterward. It's more important that we latch onto him first and for sure!"

"I won't write him again. Such noble support he offers! Shaving brush with black-currant jelly. No, I won't have anything to do with it."

"Just let me take care of it."

"This time you won't change my mind. I won't write to him again!"

"The question is *how* you will indeed write to him, your dear So-and-So! We'll let a couple of days go by, and then you can write to him. He won't get away from us!"

"He's already gotten away from me, more than I have from him. I need funds . . . as soon as a nice round sum becomes available . . . if I just keep after Dr. Blecha . . . No, I can't just sell my dignity in order that So-and-So can sleep more easily with his renowned conscience."

"Arthur, don't be stupid! He has to vouch for you in order for you to get a visa! That's the main thing, and we'll certainly engineer it to happen! Everything done just right, so that you don't have to pay a thing. As far as the oily nonsense in his letter, we won't worry ourselves one bit."

Thus Peter reassured me until my anger subsided. He understood so well. He had helped me with so many other such letters. No matter how many of them arrived, and no matter how different they all were, they almost always said the same thing! I also wrote many of them myself, more and more letters to those who once knew me, people that I was looking to contact, for now I was the one who wished to find them in the hope of recognizing myself through them, of living through them. Always the same worry, wanting to grope for and hunt down apparitions. Never was I too humble to ask. And then the answers came, letter writers from far off, creepy little worms from out there in the world, in a city that had been saved. I could read their joy, hopping little worms with very tiny hearts, unfortunate hearts, for that's what it always said: "unfortunately," each letter overflowing with it, all of them poor, consumed with worries and to be felt sorry for. They fished for my approval. I needed to understand, not resent them but grasp their need, advise them, share information, run errands for them, while, most of all, the worms yearned for my solace. Peter cursed like a fishwife whenever he thought I played the servant. Then I no longer wrote at home but, rather, at the museum, where no one bothered me when I was alone in my office.

The office had become my main headquarters, where I ruled over my riches. I was laden with things that wanted to be with me, things without mind or being, the fate of sifted possessions, I now the proprietor. My ears were struck with lashing blows, legal property. I was entitled to them and they were mine, my hands schlepping a suitcase, my pockets stuffed such that my sides hurt, until I could toss away the coffins along with the dead and bury them here in the dingy cupboards. Yet why? My memory called out to me, Listen, the names, they are people you know. You need to go. They are waiting, and they are waiting for you there; you will recognize them. The comfort of your days lies in things that fulfill you, that you possess once again. Only one who possesses things can be. Then my heart pounded, I grew warm, I propelled my feet forward, this raging stumble through erstwhile streets that had returned, the old row house washed pale by weather and tired, hoary plaster, often already flaking and crumbly, falling down when I knocked. Then through a gate, shadows closing in as soon as the latch clicked shut, then the smell, cinnamon dissolved in a watery solution and the mustiness of dirty clothes, the breath held, the steps climbed, as quietly as possible, yet weakness in the legs, sweat on the brow and down the neck, already the knuckle of the index finger scrunched up and the knock. Who would hear it? Better to ring the bell. Another past sound again reawakened, which draws shuffling steps from inside, the lock snapped with foreboding, mistrust soon eased by names. Hands extended, my heart no longer pounding but storming reluctantly into the dungeon, where Franziska and I hid our humble treasures. Bent over in my chair, matters pressing, there I am, there you are, a cloud of rambling laments, waves of sympathy. Where are the others? Silence amid the extended floors. Lost. Most of the things lost. No longer there. My parents' collection. Little made it through, not even the clothes from the shop in the Reitergasse.

I didn't complain about losses anymore. They were indeed a blessing, for as soon as from the wilderness in the first weeks I managed a return that was more survival than triumph, that which was familiar appeared now too familiar, accusing me because I had not recognized it, though it wasn't me but someone different from me, the me that was bound to the familiar, dissolved in fear, the me that disappeared suddenly there with naked objects that drew the soul from the body, object and soul delivered, there on the transformed table, eyes falling out of the head, small shining tears, eyes clinging to thin strands that are tangled with one another and choke the eyes, then the head eyeless with two empty chasms out of which blood flows, slowly, yet unstoppably, gangrenous with age, an insurmountable separation of soul and heart, in between an impeding wall, the murky dead light.

Soul and entity having escaped and the heart lying down with the body, condemned to live—or soul and entity in the night and the heart with its body hounded like a shadowy fate through the ruins of the jagged city in headlong flight, where the heart jolts and is not pitied but, rather, catapulted back, damned to oblivion and, despite the strength of the heavings, still caught among the jagged ruins, drowning in the smirking consequences of the temporal and a shiftless life that doesn't exist, incapable of any avowal or sign, and yet forced inescapably to feel. If I don't want what I want, I can sense it, and yet I can exist in a broken fashion, this indeed being a blessed yield, a shadow of Being amid its denial, the echo of a judgment that cannot be heard and which is broken off from the start, which in the silence of its desire does not wish to consummate itself, yet nevertheless is something gained, because the heart and Being of the alienated person do not have to split from each other, and because the eyes, even if they are hopeless and in the dull-witted clutches of a certain end, do not fall from their sockets and provide the inverted images that have emerged from the given world.

"Oh please, you must believe me, you are mistaken. Who could know better than I? That belongs to someone else; it always did. Don't disagree! Her eyes never saw that, her hands never held it. Everything that she had looked entirely different. Recall for yourself, try to remember what she wore for necklaces. It had large amber stones, dark-blond drops of honey that smelled of the forest and the mountains. Not pearls! Certainly not! Please, not pearls! She didn't like their watery sheen. Too damp, too strange and painful, she said. You have to believe it! She always spoke the truth. She couldn't stand the feel of pearls, nor could she stand the sound when they slid through her fingers."

The pearls lay there pathetic and only in their closed box; they were ashamed of themselves amid the lush brown velvet, which, quiet and forgotten, smelled sweet. The box didn't know what to say and turned this way and that, the top quietly snapping open and shut. The string of pearls wound itself in ever-tighter circles, shivering. Someone would surely want them, but, distressed, I refused to help. I hardly looked at them and held up a hand to guard against jewelry and little boxes. Across from me, the other head hanging there nodded. A small chin and gray hair.

"That's right. She loved to wear amber. But there's no amber here. Unfortunately. No amber came through. There are pearls, a property ready to go. Lovely large pearls, real pearls. Much more expensive than amber. Whoever has pearls can exchange them and get a lot of amber for them."

The old man's tender hands laid them out, shoved them forward on the hand towel, fingered the pearls, closed the lid of the box, and snapped shut the lock fastened to it. The figure got up almost soundlessly, looked for something in a drawer, something crackling with an acute, sharp sound. The white satin sheet unfolded, covering the table like a hanging flag, light and shadow bathing its pure surface, four fingers bent over the trembling sheet, the second hand lifting the little box, the sheet spreading out under it, watchful eyes following the ark that quietly floated upon the combing waves of light, thumb and middle finger steering it roughly toward the middle, which at last was reached, a delighted look, not at me but at the almost finished display, both hands then working powerfully, twice folding the fabric, the ark drowning in ample snow, more folding, two wings lifting up tautly and sinking down once again, the pale bird now flying aloft, though the hands grasp it and hold it, one palm extended flat, holding it, though it did not struggle, it being patient or asleep, a dark-red thread creeping, long and lugubrious, the free hand already having seized hold of it and laying it down upon the white surface, then both hands turn quickly and twirl the small weight until it was wrapped and tied, the trimmer only saying a brief word as he cut the thread, the bundle finally exhausted. It lay there finished and could rest, the eyes still above it, though soon they withdrew cautiously. Behind the table they rested. Desire slept and knew nothing of the darkness.

I indeed no longer looked on and also bowed out, trembling with blue fear, for it went on, the process not over, the other head suddenly rising up, steps heard, determined, if also quiet, no, not a stagger, a long retreat, yet shortened and turning away, a searching that rustled. I knew nothing and wanted nothing. My heart stood still, though I couldn't remain so. I had to look, intently, and the old hand then back again, trembling, poor Father, weeping bitterly, yet why Father? It's not his time, no, no time at all, but the watch, the watch, and gold, nothing but gold on all sides, the heart of it still always still, not a beat, the watch having no language, not Father's speech, me not believing the strange workings, a monogram that I didn't recognize. Nevertheless, I had to listen, for the watch was mine.

"There was also a chain with it. Unfortunately, I don't have that. The watch and chain came together, lying here with me for months, both of them at risk. It was all supposed to be given away. Two days earlier, your father, as you already know, was still here. He said, 'I didn't do anything.' Like a child. I said, 'No, you didn't do anything. Only what was good.' He said,

'That's of no help to me. I have to go away.' I didn't believe it. However, he showed me a note. There it was, written out. The place, the day, the hour, and an immense threat. Your father also said, 'It's forbidden for me to show it to anyone. Nonetheless, I've shown it to you, so that you won't forget me.' I said, 'They'll ship you back, because it's a mistake. You'll see soon enough. You're also too old.' He said, 'No, I'm being sent away. Me and my wife. No one is too old.' And so I had to believe it, though I didn't believe it at all. Which is why I said, 'It's terrible, but soon things will be good again.' Your father said, 'No.' To which I answered, 'In three months it will all be over, then you'll be back again, you and your wife. Then we'll celebrate.' Again he said, 'No.' I could say whatever I wished and all he would say would be No and No and No. Then he wanted to look at the watch. I brought it out. He took off the chain, a heavy, thick chain. I don't know what he did with it. The watch he left here. He said, 'Someone once gave it to me as collateral and never redeemed it. I've hardly worn it.' Thus the watch remained with me. There it is."

I was happy, because I could protest that I didn't want anything that had been pawned—well yes, the pearl necklace, if I had to take it, but not the watch. I protested that my father had never worn one. It was no good to me. The watch, which gave off no sound and with its enclosed clock face had hocked time for a bunch of gold, had to come with me without a chain. Two hands took hold of mine, a voice praised my father, the good man. I listened and then was gone, the steps slipping away under my feet, my steps plunging into the chasm, while I would have fallen if two eyes had not landed on the balustrade of the stairwell. The door stood open, allowing me to leave, horrified streets pulling me into their weaving strands. It was raining; the wind bore hard around the corners. I panted as I fled into the damp evening, and was afraid. Yet I wasn't being targeted. I was no longer followed; that was long over. But I felt uneasy. I felt that I was being followed. If, indeed, there was someone behind me, I was ready to stop the tormentor and curse him outright. Even amid hopeless escape, I knew who I was, the victim seized, but not the ghostly figure that is chased from behind, called names and peppered with addresses, strange faces before me, gaping faces with slit mouths that in large numbers, and recklessly, rumbled through the famed enduring history of the city, always pursuing a deadly desire that answered to no one. Then I found that I was knocking on a door again. Old Frau Holoubek, once my grandmother's servant, had tears in her eyes as she embraced me. Soon I was sitting in a chair.

"That's a beautiful coffee service. Don't you remember, dear boy?"

"Excuse me, Frau Holoubek, but I've never seen this service."

"My dear boy, the blessed dear lady, your grandmamma, always used it whenever she had guests."

"Really?"

"If I could only tell you! I can't believe you don't remember! She always put it away herself, underneath in the credenza, where she locked it up. No one was allowed in there."

"I see, I see, Frau Holoubek. That could indeed be."

"If I were to tell you . . . but that one could forget something like that, no, my boy!"

"Yes, I've forgotten."

"How the dear lady would get upset! The service with the gold trim! Ten cups there are. There were always two missing."

"So it isn't complete."

"That doesn't matter, my boy. The dear lady always said they could be replaced by the factory. Perhaps they can."

"That would be expensive."

"Yes, they are indeed expensive cups. But ten is fine, ten cups! When the dear lady died, you know, Fräulein Greger was supposed to get them."

"I see, Aunt Olga Gröger."

"Yes, the aunt. And then the trouble started, and she was already terribly afraid. They wanted to send her away, she said, and so she took the service and said, Look, Frau Holoubek, here is the service, which my mother—God rest her—got in her dowry. It would be a shame, she said, if it got lost. Take it from me, Frau Holoubek. . . ."

"Don't upset yourself too much!"

"It was a disgrace, my boy! And yet I said, Fräulein Greger, no, something like that, that's too much for me to handle. But take it, said the fräulein, take it with you, it doesn't matter. Then I said, Yes, I'll take good care of it, Fräulein Greger, and then my husband went to her. She packed it up, and some other things as well, and my husband took it, and now it's here."

"Frau Holoubek, don't you want to keep it? I'd really be pleased if you did so!"

"But, my boy, what do you think I am? I'm not like that. How could I? No, that I can't do. It belongs to you, if no one else from the family is there."

"You know, I am alone. . . . I have no use for it. Oh, please, do keep it!"

"No way, my boy. Don't tell that to Frau Holoubek. You'll need it again sometime, for sure. One day soon you'll again have a lovely apartment, then everything will be good again. Guests will come, and you'll have the lovely service on a table at home, and then you'll be happy that you have it again."

"I don't believe so, Frau Holoubek."

"You don't have to take it today. I'll take care of it if it doesn't suit you now. But you must have it eventually. I can't keep it, my boy!"

So I agreed. I couldn't expect Frau Holoubek to again painstakingly stow away in cupboards and drawers the crystal bowls, vases, egg cups, and other things she had stacked up in front of me on the table. She was pleased as she marked my change of mind and hurried to help me with the packing. She had a lot of paper and wood shavings at the ready. Thus everything was carefully guarded against breaking, piled into large unwieldy cartons, tied up with string through and through, and fitted out with handles so that I could take away the burden. I was already gone, the unsaved ownerless goods led away with my weak strength. How was I to handle it all? With it I had a new assignment, which Frau Holoubek told me about at length, asking if I didn't remember the old washerwoman, Frau Krumbholc, who had done laundry for my grandmother.

Soon I had found my way in a confused manner to Frau Krumbholc's, a terrible apartment, though it was clean, the fringes and tassels of the green tablecloth neatly combed, the kitchen door open, dirty white steam discoloring the room, the smell of sauerkraut, slices of apple cut into it. Frau Krumbholc was sad, she said, for she had long been widowed, and pointed to a picture behind glass on the wall. I couldn't see much. The widow couldn't hold back her tears as well as Frau Holoubek and asked me ten times, with whimpering amazement, whether it really was me. Several times she shook my hand, squeezed gently, and let it go again. Then she circled about me some more, but suddenly she was off and dragged in a misshapen suitcase that supposedly belonged to me. The lid popped open with a rasp, the densely packed contents pressed painfully against one another—old bed linens ready to be used, lightly yellowed at the corners, though they were good wares that could no longer be had and would be useful today. The suitcase wouldn't shut, the washerwoman's knee pressing hard against the lid, it bursting open, the lock clicking on the right, but the left not wanting to snap shut, so I had to help, my powers waning, rubbed raw by the strange deep sleep that did not refresh me. Meanwhile, I still had a name to look up along the way and needed to make sure not to forget Herr Nerad.

Breathing heavily, I made it to the museum with the suitcase, Herr Geschlieder helping me up the steps with it. Then I was alone and glanced despairingly at the weight that calmly crouched before me. The suitcase yawned open before me, my arms buried in dead bed linens, coldly and roughly grabbing hold of them, then other treasures sprang out of its depths all rolled up and rising toward me—wool jackets and vests, ripe red, milky yellow, sharp green—trembling plunder in my fingers, all of it clean but reeking of mothballs, the smell almost stinging my eyes, though nonetheless a lot of it eaten away by moths, cord meshing springing back, all of it rustling. When I lifted out the thin goods, from the bottom there stared at me in surprise and barely shining an almost completely dulled-out mirror. It was incredibly heavy. Now I knew why I had to struggle so with the suitcase.

Then I was there with the dried-up small Herr Nerad, once the factotum in the shop of an uncle who had died more than twenty years ago. Herr Nerad had always been devoted to Aunt Rosi. Now he unpacked three old purses, carefully wrapped in several layers of paper, that belonged to my aunt. I took Herr Nerad by the hand, looked innocently into his wrinkled countenance, which understood nothing, and said as tenderly as possible what beautiful purses but that I couldn't use any of them. If he didn't want to keep them, would it be possible for him to do me the pleasure of giving them away. Then Herr Nerad withdrew his hand convulsively and was nearly insulted: What, the purses were still quite nice; one couldn't buy any like those today. I had to take them, at least as a memento. There were still little mirrors buried within them, the pale-pink powder in the powder box and the pad that went with it, all of it crumbly with extended sleep, used tickets for the tram from many years past, a scuffed-up little leather book with well-thumbed addresses, recipes, lists of things to buy, such as eggs, butter, flour, rice, dried prunes, and apples, receipts for bills from the coal handler Burda, also a worn-out change purse that would no longer stay shut, its clasp squished flat, two nickel coins slipping from its folds, yellow with endless neglect and almost no longer worth anything. I staggered heavily in the face of it. Herr Nerad also loaded me up with more names that I didn't recognize, but that's the way it was, me sent from one keeper to the next, and new people turning up whom I had to see for sure. Did I know indeed where else Aunt Olga had stashed a bundle? Secretly it was whispered to me as if it were still forbidden, and there was something from Uncle Alfred as well. Reluctantly but irresistibly drawn, I shuttled between well-meaning little people who raised a hand to their foreheads with half-open mouths when they sized up my appearance, their hoary astonishment melting into thin joy. They nodded at me, saying My, my, followed by regret, a memory, a sigh, a handkerchief, and tears. Then they put on splayed cloth gloves, stuffed handbags, clutching a dust cloth under the arm, creeping off to a trunk or to a storeroom, already back with something and pleased to be getting rid of a burden, since I should give it to my heirs, it was valuable. Doomed, I tried to fend it off, but I was ignored, or they didn't believe me and felt it only right, which is why it all was quickly shoved at me, along with the lesson that mislaid goods never gained value, for what was I thinking, a memento, yes, that they wished to have, but only something small, nothing more.

If such a visit was unfruitful, then I was thought mean, yet worse was what I had to put up with from such figures from the past. Their thanks, which I gathered from every corner, rubbed me the wrong way, the long talks, the wearying reports, the questions from dull philistines, the forced counterquestions, the litany of spoken sorrow amid sighs of futility. In the chilly brightness of living rooms or the biting smoke of kitchens, I whittled away empty hours. The living rooms smelled of being cramped and sweet, and forced me to play the part of the guest by sipping fruity drinks, or fresh bread that trembled before the knife, a homemade recipe of crumbly rich cake. The plate wasn't taken away, the cup was filled again to the brim, followed by the threadbare request for me to stay longer. There's so much time. Already evening approached, thirst sparing me the sight. When I finally felt I'd almost gained release, chairs and tables got in the way, I couldn't get past them or through them, the watch that I pulled out was berated as being unacceptably bad and had to quickly crawl back inside my pocket. Then I felt ill, my limbs shaking. Others noticed it and showered me with concern, pushing me toward the most comfortable chair, into which I had to sink myself and cower, just to recover a bit, already feeling better, right, as the schnapps glass twinkled, but stiff and clammy, biting my lower lip, my teeth clenched, my tongue almost bloody, me burning deep within the maw of a dark torrent.

Patient and lurking about, they stared at me expectantly. I should have said something to thank them for their help, yet my throat was constricted; I stuttered my embarrassment. Regret was swallowed inside an empty collar, my tongue clinging fast to the gums. I babbled through long breaths— the air, the good air!—and wanted to get out of my chair, to just run away quickly without suffocating. Yet no one understood what I wanted, but only tore open the window, the evening pressing in its chilly grime and slamming against my forehead. Something rumbled from down below, an immense noise rising up from the courtyards and hitting the walls of the room and dripping down them. I felt bad and had no strength, something speaking for me, standing there in hot and searing fragility, asking could I go, could I, only that would help, could I, if it was all right, could I, please, let me, fast, before it's too late, don't waste any time, already late, late, late, the watch, now please, no help, no, only open the door, hurry, gone. The door, room, door, kitchen, door, apartment, many doors, please, thank you, you're welcome, thank you, please, the door shutting. As I fled down the stairwell, the murder of the past nearly buried me from all sides.

Then I couldn't see anything, though I had finally slipped out. Weakly I stumbled away, the street sweepers' stirred-up chaff stuck in my eyes, causing them to sting, nothing but black fire, choking voices blazing high, hurting my ears: "That belongs to you now!" Yet it didn't belong to me, a brittle exploded nest from which everything near turned away, remains, even if they weren't unspoiled, rubbish, the formless husks of original forms, yet nothing but husks, emptied out and blank in their naked transience and the hard, frozen past, which lasted and promised to last beyond any future. Thus the goods were allotted me and yet were never mine, thorns and splinters in my hands painful with wounds that had been commanded. From some neighborhoods I groaned with the weight, always like a thief who had been condemned to recognize the uselessness of all possessions and to carry his booty until the end of days, forced harshly to take in the scope of all the plundered homesteads for the museum and make sure that its owners never find it. I saw people in the street who hungered for possessions and eyed my load covetously. How happy I would have been to give the poor things my embarrassing goods: Please take them; I'm grateful that your sensibility aspires to wrongfully acquired goods. So take it away and enjoy your possessions. I, however, could not and retrieved the meager riches; they were entrusted to me, I being their guardian.

How uncomfortable it was to get them through the streets without harm! Sometimes I had the notion of inconspicuously abandoning a package in a corner or in a doorway. The museum didn't need the treasure, and I could hope that someone would take mercy on the possessions left behind and would bless the unknown donator. But this unburdening was denied me. I couldn't relinquish anything; that would have broken a trust with honorable guardians, whom I never could have faced again. Only once did I have the damnable courage to let a heavy bundle of pots, pans, cooking spoons, and sieves slip inconspicuously to the ground. Straight off I felt I'd succeeded, no one seeming to have noticed. I breathed a sigh and pushed on without a care. But, after only a few steps, a houselady called after me, upset, saying I should please pack up my stuff, otherwise there would be trouble. I didn't want to stay there at all, but the voice called out much more sharply from behind me. I stopped, turned around with a slight bow, and played dumb: "There must be some mistake; they are not my things." I'm sorry, the woman humbly said, while leaning on a broom, but if she wasn't afraid of starting something, she would take the bundle to the office for lost property: "They'll then just yell at me! Don't fool with me. I saw it with my own eyes, how you let that lump of stuff fall, just like a criminal. If it doesn't belong to you, then take it yourself to the office for lost property. It ain't staying here, and now off with you!" I didn't trust myself to run away, I was so weak; so I had to return and pick up the burden. When I bent down, the woman looked me in the eye suspiciously, threatening me with her broom, and shrilly showering me with words of anger and shame, as I miserably schlepped on.

Sometimes I relieved myself of my load in little bars, asking the barkeep behind the counter for a beer even when I wasn't thirsty. I only wanted to see if he would notice me and fulfill my request. "Nice weather today!" I'd say in an attempt to relax. I awaited an answer and hardly got a glance in return. "What I have to carry is so heavy!" Nor did that work, either. Had I said nothing? But the barkeep brought me a full glass. I blew away the foam, tasted the beer, and thanked him for his interest. The man sucked his lips, indifferent and bored as he wiped the brass top of the bar; he didn't understand at all what I wanted. When with both hands I shifted my goods, he slowly shook his head. Yet the barkeep looked at the money that I tossed to him and let it disappear straight off into the till. He spent no more time with me, nor did I enjoy the drink. Soon I placed the half-full glass on the platter that was spotted and wet, the barkeep still wiping down the bar, though to no end. My goodbye was left unanswered; a customer smiled and gave me a funny wave. I had to steal off through the forlorn labyrinthine streets.

Then I hoped to be attended to in little shops where the dealers and salesmen, when they weren't too busy, would get lost in curious chatter. The worn-out bell willingly helped me enter without disturbance. A welcoming voice greeted me. I asked for shoelaces, buttons, pocket combs, picture postcards. The selection was narrow, the wares cranked out of factories without care, scrimpy and expensive. I rummaged slowly among the dusty inventory and praised the goods as if I were a shopkeeper. I kept roaming around, such that I was attended to as a customer, while my suitcase lay on the dirt-encrusted floorboards. Occasionally came a good word, I leaned forward, and since there followed a pointed joke, I could laugh. But then everything was over, all harmony quickly dissolving, and I had to pay at some expense. Quickly I was turned away, the rusty tin handle heavy in my hand—the load, the sore arm, it quivered painfully all the way to my shoulder.

I looked around another shop; I couldn't risk going back into the same one twice. My activities were too conspicuous; it would be hard for anyone to have a good impression of me. Again I stood before a small shop, mopping my brow uncomfortably with my handkerchief. Then I felt very exhausted, as if I had endured a test of my heart and kidneys. Too conspicuously near me was the dispensed load that had been parked, swollen like a sponge under leering glances. I leaned down easily against the scratched counter and promised urgently that I wished to become a regular customer, but, rather than endearing me, that made me seem stranger. Also, what I wished to buy was too shabby. Hastily, I assured them that I was serious, but my talk was met with obliging reflective grins. Was I deluded? Arrogantly, no one strained at all to pay attention to the flood of my words and took it for blarney when, in as friendly a way as I could, I asked for better service. I looked directly at the salesmen in order to show that my intentions were honest, but they turned away bored or mischievous, hiding with one hand the sharp wedge of muffled laughter and hurrying to end our business in order to get me quickly out of the shop. I then tried to turn to them as quickly as possible, as if I had just thought of something else that I urgently needed to buy, and asked in a neutral pleasant voice for an ashtray. Sighing, they assented and hastily brought what I had asked for. They were horrible things, one with an owl on it that blinked sleepily, and a little bowl with angels and butterflies. I didn't need an ashtray, yet since dilly-dallying was no longer possible my valid choice was honored, and because I dared to waste more time with talking, a foot kicked my load and I had to gather it up, at which I was met by a frightful shrug of the shoulders as I was led step by step backward and to the clearly opened door, they bowing low in a measured fashion and the door closing behind me decisively. Once again, I looked around and debated returning to the shop in order to innocently ask whether I had forgotten my handkerchief, I was so distraught, please forgive me. But by then I was too disheartened to shamelessly lie. Indignant, they would have clapped their hands together—"Off with you, get out of here, otherwise . . ." That was a terrible thing to hear; I couldn't even bear to think it. So I crept off and busied myself with my bags.

Often, people on the street watched what I did, such that I felt uneasy. Some people wanted to know what kinds of stuff I was carrying. Good food was scarce, clothes were in short supply, as well as shoes and other wares. Therefore the black market blossomed and spread through the streets; it was difficult to fend off nasty suspicion. I would have to admit that it was not my property, I having neither attained it in a shady manner nor wanting to hawk it, carrying it along with me only because I was moving. I gave other reasons for my load, necessity rousing right away my resourcefulness. Only I couldn't tell the truth; a terrible price to pay in having always to remain silent. I couldn't risk even once resorting to saying that it had to do with salvaged goods that I had held for Aunt Olga and Uncle Alfred and now wished to give back. No one would have believed a word and would only have scolded me harshly. Then I would have had to report to the police who I was, where I lived, my rights in the face of eternity. With knowing smirks, the armed law would not even have heard out my explanations to the end but, rather, ordered me to follow them to the station, where only after many hours of painful interrogation, searches, and probing inquiries among all the people I had betrayed, my story would be accepted. No, I had to keep still, be humble, and serve the ownerless goods as best I could.

I then staggered to the next tram stop and stumbled up the steps of the tram, which was rarely empty. To the anger of the conductor, I dumped everything in a corner of the wagon's platform. I was only met with constant grumbling, the doubled fare, as well as the mulish annoyance on the part of the riders when I tried to protect the cargo with my arms and legs. If I hadn't in fact had too much with me, I would have been happy to navigate my way to the inside of the car, where I could have shoved some of it under the seat and held the rest on my lap. If the tram had filled up, my situation would have been much worse. Since I didn't want to miss my stop, I had to disturb my neighbors and the standing riders in order to pull my things forward. I asked politely and entreatingly for their patience and indulgence, but what good did it do? The space was narrow, the disgruntled people betrayed loudly their unwillingness to help, and lectured me that when you transported such junk it would be best to arrange for a moving truck or to take a taxi, the tram not being built for such things. I agreed, and humbly reassured them, explaining that, unfortunately, I didn't have enough money; otherwise, I would have been happy to follow their advice. Meanwhile, I squirmed about the floor of the wagon in order to grab hold of my burden and wrench it through legs and other impediments until I had hold of everything and, with many requests and excuses and thank-yous, forced my way to the next exit. Behind me there was loud cursing, the conductor was cross, the driver stomped with his foot on the bell switch such that it rang, he being ready to drive on.

I shuffled around the corner and on through the familiar streets, where the school stood closed, as well as the museum. I could barely stand as I knocked, having set down my load. Someone finally came, and the heavy key turned. Herr Geschlieder, the porter, was a friendly soul and didn't mind at all once he saw how weighed down I was by the accumulation of all these riches as the meager protection of the door shut behind me, although he betrayed pity toward my goods, his well-meaning gaze drying up when I extended to him the flood of gifts. Geschlieder declined, deeply embarrassed, though he indeed helped me with the load when I slowly dragged it up the three steps. I owed it to the dead to present at least a glimmer of joy to Geschlieder: Saved, Herr Geschlieder, saved! What a wonder, despite the dead prayers in the cellar, or before the gazing portraits of our ancestors who have disappeared for eternity, saved. God bless us, there are still good people, such that all of these wonders found their way to me over the endless duration of the earthly time out of joint. The porter nodded, how lovely that must be: Yes, there are still good people in the world.

What was mine was not mine: such poverty knew no end. I lifted up my hands, draped, burdened, buried, gripping it all. Peter couldn't use that much, and Anna only a little. Protesting, she would take it, and only out of sympathy, as her apartment was already overfull. I had long known how many strange goods were stowed there that no one came to pick up. Anna and Peter recommended that I sell some of it, but I couldn't bring myself to do so. If I couldn't give it to friends because they couldn't take any, nor to strangers because it was forbidden, how could I sell it to fools! Peter offered to do it for me, but I couldn't allow it. If I wanted to avoid increasing my misery even more, there was only one way to do so: I couldn't take on any more. I didn't look for any more people who might want to give me something, and so I avoided Frau Holoubek, Frau Krumbholc, and Herr Nerad.

No more wandering into the past. Yet that was easy to say. The past had long exceeded all of the future with a decisive resolve. The wall before me, which I sought to get past or to pardon, was not so completely impenetrable as I thought: only my wishes were prevented from passing through, no matter how much I pleaded. The wall was behind me and pressed at me from behind. If I had let up, it would already have overtaken me from behind, the future lost along with me. I stood amid the chill of the past, my hand holding the handle in vain. The lost shop in the Reitergasse was closed; a command had been sent me from the garden, such that behind the wall I had to seek out the works which I had set on earth to do. Thus was I driven out and imprisoned before the wall of the lost shop. I had gained nothing when I hid myself, for I had been found out and had to rise up.

"You must return to your beginnings, Adam!"

I stood naked before the voice, which brooked no objection.

"Who are you?"

I pointed disdainfully toward the shut-up garments of the shop, at the dismantled counter, the smashed cartons.

"Who told you that you are naked?"

I hid my face in my hands in order to see less of my nakedness.

"Do you see something?"

No, I saw nothing. Only the wall, the wall of my hands. The command was yelled loudly and shattered, pointed splinters of it reaching me.

"Look! There it is. Do not deny it."

I did not deny it and submitted myself entirely to the command, but what I saw was that there was nothing to see. Taken by the shoulder and shaken, I was supposed to recognize my face, the one that saw. I reached for my head in vain. The headless one could not see. I whispered my dismay.

"No head!"

Laughter hopped about behind the bars of all the cages. The entire shop shook, the weeds shot up, the foliage and all the trees. Also, many animals and worms gathered about. Then a voice came forth that was strong and was intended just for me.

"No head, that's well said. No head for these times. Back to your times, Adam, you old good-for-nothing."

My knees rubbed against the sand.

"I want, want, want . . . !"

My throat flushed, whereupon the old night had mercy, but not the unleashed time that disdainfully whistled away pell-mell. The lost shop collapsed and disappeared in yawning despair. The doors were swallowed up within it and the soft breeze cut across my face.

"The children would love to go for a walk with you."

"Really? Which children, Johanna?"

"Michael and Eva."

"Why do you say the names so solemnly?"

"Because you asked which children? Right, then. Don't give me that look, Arthur. Go with them! I have to clean."

"The window is open, Johanna. Fresh air. Do you have to really?"

"At some point. The fresh air alone won't sweep away the dust. At some point, I have to do some serious cleaning. To clean out for real. You've made such a mess of things."

"Not intentionally!"

"I don't mean anything by it. What's happened has happened."

"It's about time I cleaned it up myself."

"You always say that. Then you don't. It's not your fault, fine. I believe you. But that's why I have to do it for you."

"Johanna, please, listen. Is it today?"

"Always, dear. It's today."

"And yesterday? Tomorrow?"

"That's something different."

"How, then, can it always be today?"

"You know, that's exactly what you don't understand. Yesterday, today, tomorrow—a string that presents itself every day."

"How, then, every day? Today. You said it is today."

"Today, I say: today. And on every day, indeed in your own time, I say again: today."

"And the past?"

"Indeed, every day of your time was today. You get that mixed up, not me."

"Can you explain it to me?"

"I can try, but it won't do any good. You'll never get it. Your understanding of time has been destroyed."

"The clock, the clock—I can read it! Look, the calendar. I can rattle off the seven days of the week, the days and months add up together—seven twelve and seven twelve. And each year is made up of them, this I know. It's true that the reckoning of time has changed many times over the years, but always the day has consisted of the evening and the morning. When that no longer works, there is leap year, and everything is good again. See, Johanna, my awareness of time is not destroyed, it's intact."

"Not at all. You deceive yourself. It all runs together, it seems to me, every tick and tock. Clock and calendar mean nothing to you. In fact, leap year doesn't even make up time for those who have no grasp of it."

"I have a grasp of time and don't need to change. There's nothing wrong with me, Johanna! I have it."

"You take it away, even from me—a time thief. Indeed, you have no time. Thus you have to take it."

"But I do indeed have time. Can't you see?"

"No. You have no grasp of it whatsoever. What was and is no longer, that's because of time. What is and never will be, that is also because of time."

"The same time?"

"Ah, the same . . . You talk such nonsense. Time is not forever, but time is always the same, though not the same time."

"But you say, Johanna, that I have no time."

"You have none at all. I feel sorry for you because of it. You have fought against it, brought yourself in opposition to it. You believe you can play with it, even control it. But it plays, instead, with you. Now, please go off with the children!"

"I have no time. You already said so."

"Ugh, such sophistry! I mean now. You should go now! For that, you need no time. All you need is the clock. Make sure and keep an eye on it so that you're home in time for tea. That's all you have to do."

Johanna kissed me softly and slowly pushed me out of the room. Then I awoke completely for the first time and laughed.

"Was I dreaming?"

"You're a good man. Just go, it will do you good."

Now it's time. I felt it more clearly: it is time. When I stepped over the threshold, the children romped into the hallway and cheered.

"Father is coming! Daddy has time!"

Johanna had dressed up the children, as she always did when she sent me out with them. Michael romped along and jumped about me; Eva took me dutifully by the hand as we shuffled through the door. Johanna yelled to the children to "Be good!," waved goodbye to us, and disappeared. She remained behind in her time. Michael called out our destination, Eva agreeing completely.

"We're going to the rides!"

"To ride on the donkey," piped Eva. "Yes?"

Three or four times a year the rides and the concession stands are there, yesterday today tomorrow, and then they move on again. Michael already knew everything his father would do better than did Eva, who just needed to go along with her brother's wishes. Down West Park Row the children cheered, knowing the way to the rides exactly. But you didn't have to know at all, for it was impossible to miss them. You could even hear them, the sound carried on the wind—the sound of loud thumping music rolling closer in waves. It wasn't far to Shepherd's Field, only the railway embankment crossing the end of West Park Row blocking its view. Then that was behind us and we crossed Halstead Way, which bordered Shepherd's Field. Toward the left side of it, the pointed peaks of tents and concession stands had been erected. Droves of children streamed about, dragging along compliant adults with them. They moved along fast, for Michael didn't want to miss a thing. We approached the funfair from the side, motors snorting and dogs snarling on their chains. Eva grabbed my hand tighter, but Michael had no fear and had to be warned by his father. Already we were surrounded by the hubbub, the noise swarming around me, the children cheering and bursting with demands.

"Father, did you always go with your father when your mother said that you should go with your father?"

"Yes, he always went with me."

"And did he always let you do as much as you let us do?"

"He let me do a lot."

"Did he also say that he got dizzy when he spun around too much?"

"He could stand it better than I could."

"And your mother, could she stand it better than our mother?"

"No, she never could handle it all that well. She always had to look on, and even that made her dizzy. She had to look away, or she closed her eyes."

"You don't have to look away, Father, do you? You can look at us and keep your eyes open? You always have them open."

"You can see for yourself, Michael; you know so already. Why are you asking?"

"Father, look! Father! Can I toss at the coconuts? Please, please!"

"When you're bigger."

"I'm already big. Only Eva isn't big yet."

"I'm also big! Mommy says that I am."

"You're both big. But not big enough."

"Oh my, Father, please, please! Let me toss at them! Just one try! Maybe I'll get a coconut."

"No, my child, you're not getting one. You have to have a lot of strength for that, and also be very clever."

"Aren't I clever?"

"Not yet enough."

"But, Father, you're clever! Go and buy some balls and knock down a coconut!"

"No, Michael. I'm not at all good enough."

After I finally dragged the children away from the coconuts, my lack of cleverness was still bemoaned for some time. At first, some cotton candy that amassed from a churning cylinder worked to placate them. Eva loved this swirly foam on a wooden stick, her mouth and tongue battling happily with the brittle sweetness. Michael liked it as well, but he wanted licorice— long, black, thin strings of it. Then Eva rode on the carousel for the smallest children, and Michael, who seemed too grown-up for this ride, thought bet- ter and decided to accompany his sister in order to make sure that she didn't scream or fall down from her swan chair. And so her brother rode along with her. Next came the large swing seats. Eva was too small for them and wandered on farther without fear on a path she already knew, allowing her brother to ride the swings without envy. No one could deny her the chance to ride the donkey. The animals strode along quite slowly, a short way back and forth, it hardly being worth the price. The time was too short, and the children complained loudly. The tall tower of the slide was the right size for the boy. Eva pressed her little fist into my back when she looked on, amazed at his steep slide down through the narrow winding chute to a straw mat. She asked, "Daddy, why don't you slide?" Meanwhile, the mouse circus lured us on with its pretty pictures. The entry fee was modest, and when we paid we were told, "Stay inside as long as you wish!" Inside the tent, there was nothing but a glass house on a low pedestal in the middle. The white mice, at least a hundred of them, ran through grottos, over stretched and swaying lines, tumbled over teetering bridges, crouched on swings, and had to climb steep steps to the tower of a knight's castle, wanting to nibble on white bread that was strewn on the balcony.

"What cute bunnies! Such long tails!"

"They're not bunnies!" Michael informed her. "They're real white mice. Like the kind the bird store sells on Truro Street. They're very cheap, and Mommy says they make a lot of mess."

"They don't make any mess!" protested Eva. "They're so white and clean. But they stink a little, and the tails are ugly. Little white bunnies! Could we have one?"

"I don't think so, sweetheart."

"No!" Michael asserted. "Mommy doesn't want one."

Michael was ready to leave the mice, but Eva was so entranced by the scurrying around that there was no pulling her away. Michael nudged her and pulled at her sleeve.

"Cowboys, there are cowboys! Eva, have you seen them?"

"Lovely little white bunnies!"

The brother didn't let up, and scolded her. But when I pointed to the colorful signs for the cowboys Eva finally turned away from gazing at the little bunnies. Michael hopped to it, knowing already where to find his favorites.

"I know, I know the way!"

There was no stopping the boy. Along the way we came upon a colorfully painted wagon, its doors standing open. Inside was Fortunata, the resplendent and celebrated original fortune-teller and real Gypsy, a niece of the most famous fortune-teller of all time and all countries, looking proud and glistening before the noisy surge of people around her. Fortunata advertised nothing; she just waited. I would have been glad to wait for her in order to see who would be her next customer, whose times she would reveal: yesterday today tomorrow. But Michael was too impatient and pulled at my coat.

"They're over there! We shouldn't be standing here! Oh, c'mon, Father, c'mon!"

He pulled me away and squinted angrily at the Gypsy, because she'd stolen my attention. I couldn't resist Michael any longer, as a new performance by the cowboys was being touted with a wild clamor. A loudspeaker played a recording of loud fanfare; two bells, a thudding kettledrum, and a snare drum announced the pressing news. On a high stage, show people stood splendidly and presented themselves to the honorable public below in the dust, where there wriggled about, romping feverishly, wild and outlandish children, with docile or mistrustful men and women looking on. Through the brightly colored megaphone, the announcer's cascade of hawking phrases powerfully rolled. Michael had quickly pressed forward. Eva pressed tight against me, though she wasn't afraid, but simply drew my hand to her as protection as I gently stroked her head.

Standing tall and proud, Roy Rogers rose up, king of the cowboys, all decked out in full splendor in a costume of rugged brown, his hat dashing with its wide brim, a flashy scarf worn loose at the throat, two mighty pistols stuck in the holsters of his decorated belt, his legs thrust into high boots. Two girls in tightly gathered dresses with white blouses looked at the crowd, serious and demanding, one of them holding three flashing knives with long blades, the other holding her head between two shimmering bare halberds. A blond-haired boy in a brown jacket could only be the master cowboy's apprentice. In the glassed-in booth out in front of the tent stood the cashier, dressed exactly like the other girls. In a black suit with gold braiding strode the announcer, microphone to his mouth, walking back and forth across the stage in a commanding manner. He appealed to the honored guests below him with fiery tributes to the wonders of the performance nearby, yet the rising storm of the ragged music and the flapping roar was too strong to allow one to make sense of anything he said.

Soon it got better; the distant fanfare quieted down, and now his appeals could be understood. Fun and instruction for everyone. Satisfaction guaranteed, no tricks, just the real thing. You had to see it for yourself. Unforgettable, unique, exciting, full of danger, and yet harmless. Suitable for the smallest of children. This man, Roy Rogers of Texas, is a wonder. Whoever is not satisfied will get his money back. Satisfaction guaranteed. A shilling for grown-ups, half price for soldiers and children. Members of the royal family had graced a performance with their presence. It's written here on this placard. The announcer lifted it up high, solemnly panning the holy object to the left and to the right before the astonished gathering, while whoever was able to read it had to be convinced. No one should wait; it's only three steps up and the show will begin. Parents, bring along your children! Children, bring along your parents!

Some had already decided to do so and climbed up to the ticket booth, disappearing behind the curtain. Yet it was just a few, too many of those looking on agape proving fickle as they remained standing there patiently and waited for what might come next. They weren't disappointed, for already the announcer was at it again, saying fine, since there were so many who couldn't decide, they'd give them a free performance. He brought out all the members of the troupe, each offering a polite and charming bow as the names were called out to the crowd. Roy Rogers looked on in all his splendor, but I caught his gaze, which indeed seemed a bit bored by the foolishness of the crowd. But the cowboy in him took charge, didn't let his boredom show, drew his guns, holding out one of them and spinning the other on his stretched-out index finger. When the announcer had finished presenting the artists, Roy's apprentice rushed forward, tossed a spinning knife high, grabbed it, and tossed it up again. Then he showed how his master had taught him to handle a lasso. It wasn't a complete performance, yet I was impressed. It had to be difficult to make a rope move in modest leaps up and down in such a sublime, solitary dance. Yet this demonstration of the art served only to make the mastery of it seem all the more marvelous. Then the boy took three steps back with obedient charm, bowing to his master as was his due, brief applause erupting as he did.

Then Roy Rogers stepped to the middle; the others onstage moved to the right and left, looking on in astonishment in order to set the right example for everyone. Only the announcer hardly moved; like a herald, he divided his attention between the hero and the audience. Four blades flashed as they spun in a whirring fashion up and down, turning in flight, which was marvelous. Then a long lasso danced sinuously in seesawing circles and sharp spirals. Suddenly, Roy Rogers jumped inside the circling rope and rose up within it, standing on his tiptoes as if making a pirouette, sinking down on one knee, then both, spinning around as well, the wild twirling continuing until finally the rope collapsed, coming to rest in large rings that looped from the right arm to the shoulder. I would have been happy to stand there awhile and extend my appreciation to the master, but neither was allowed, because everyone up on the stage, the announcer included, even the tireless Roy Rogers, released a huge cry of "You saw it with your own eyes, it's unbelievable, it's all the proof you need, but there isn't a moment to lose, today's the day, now, it won't last forever, come on, come on, come on, all of you have to come, the artists are inside waiting, the show will begin, don't wait any longer, for what you have seen is only a taste of the wonders that await you."

By then most of the crowd was moved, unable to resist any longer, coins leaping from their pockets as they besieged the cashier, who dealt with the onslaught. Michael's legs jerked, and I let him run. Happily he stormed ahead, already having disappeared into the tent as I stayed behind with Eva. In order to make it up to her, I allowed her to have two more rides on the carousel. Again, she rode on the white swan, not wanting any other, and she wrapped her arms tight around its neck worn smooth. The outside of the stage was now empty, only the cashier stuck in her booth, smoking and shooing away small boys who kept trying to jokingly do handstands and somersaults.

I peered over at the Gypsy, who was still sitting in the door of her wagon. After a little while, a female customer arrived and disappeared through the door, which closed behind her. The Gypsy Fortunata had business and needed to look into the future. Placards announced how well she could tell the truth; she was a wise woman who understood everything—the stars above, the lines in the hand, and the loops of one's handwriting. Since the truth was revealed and confirmed in three different ways, there could be no doubt. The mix of fortune and misfortune, an unchangeable destiny, was revealed through wisdom's insight. But why do people wish to learn their fate from other people? Was it not already fixed, whether heavy or easy, and always inescapable? Did they have to hear it said in order to be eased by a fate well fashioned? Did foreknowledge ease its power? Or could one's fate be eased? Not eased, perhaps, but slowly dispersed, at least held fast and patient by the distant future if a wise woman conveyed it.

To seek one's fate, what a desperate wish for certainty! But fate is a wall that does not allow our questions to pass through, no matter how much they may seek answers. The Gypsy Fortunata actually knew many answers to the questions. All that was uncertain was whether the answers were moot because the one seeking the advice either didn't understand it or had heard it already or because the answers amounted to no more than a pointless echo, thus providing no news, nothing new but, rather, just the danger that could be announced from afar, thus sounding perhaps more bearable and yet much more terrible, because now it seemed all the more uncanny and kept the listener all the more behind the wall, which pressed down upon one all the more. But it couldn't remain so. The Gypsy Fortunata wished to and had to inspire awe, but she could not frighten her customers; she had to comfort them, or at least ease them, if she wanted to at all make a profit in handing out further advice. She had to raise up the despondent and calm the excited. Good fortune, no misfortune, was what was valued. And when there was misfortune it couldn't be in the future; in the past, yes, misfortune was in the past. It had been conquered and should remain forever invoked. People were often unhappy when they came to Fortunata to complain about their plight, but here everything changed, the run of misfortune appearing to dissolve. As soon as the door opened, wonders occurred, the threat simply dried up.

Always misfortune was only in the past, and had power enough to last only to the present, until today, there no longer being any tomorrow for it, because from this hour onward the clear future emerged, its blessing arrived. Speaking the truth meant to invoke blessing. One only needed to decide to step beyond his past, for then the transformation occurred, the door shut upon worries left behind. How strange that so few of the afflicted never allowed themselves this way out. And, because they were cowardly or foolish and did not risk climbing the few steps, didn't so much misfortune prevail among them? And so they wandered about outside of what was certain happiness. The path to happiness appeared free; yet it's not given that you know that this path exists, short and safe as it is. Fear stands before it, and doubt, base and common; skepticism, the obstacle to the weak will. We cannot do it. We've also been told that it is forbidden. The Witch of Endor was cursed and, along with her, any reading of signs. Therefore we cannot be happy.

Yet what holds me back from happiness? I could bring the children home and say to Johanna, "I have time, now I have time, and so I have to head out again." And so I did. The children happily jumped around in the living room, Michael glowing with excitement and love for Roy Rogers, and his partner, Eva, continued to chatter on about the little white bunny. Tea was prepared for the chatterboxes, the two of them pouncing on their slices of bread, but I said thank you and excused myself. Johanna was completely taken aback, yet she said nothing; she never stood in my way. I ran back to Shepherd's Field, this certainly being the last hour of unhappiness. When I saw Fortunata's wagon, the door was closed. Someone must have been finding happiness inside. I could wait. The goings-on around me pressed on, rumbling with loud merriment; it didn't bother me. The final day of tribulation could not last much longer, an early evening setting in with its gloom. That didn't bother me, because my needs were ready to be filled by Fortunata. She had to know that I was there. There was no time left; if there was, it couldn't last, it couldn't remain, it was forbidden. The doors opened, yet no, there was something stopping them, for they only twitched, a problem with the lock, the latch preventing them, but Fortunata knew what to do—a sharp pull, and already the sky ripped open, a bundle of happiness quickly scuttled down the little steps and sank into the dusky crowd, having been saved. Above, Fortunata looked on calmly, proud and satisfied. She had mastered misfortune; she was sure of herself.

"Now, how about the gentleman?"

Whether Fortunata appealed to me with these words or other words, I cannot be certain. She might even have remained silent, knowing already that I would come to her; she had to know, as it was her job to. She betrayed no sense of doubt when I stood before her, the proximity of happiness already having marked my forehead, for whoever knows his goal recognizes what streams toward him. Fortunata said absolutely nothing, not pleading with words the way the artists on the stage did, the announcer right then, for absolutely the last time, urging an audience that hung back without being convinced not to miss the last chance, as Roy Rogers and his assistants were already inside the tent and had to begin their performance without worrying about no-shows. Through such clamor the low or the high arts can be recommended, but not fortune-telling. In order to maintain her secrets, she had no desire to urge the unwilling or to plead with the stubborn. She was not at the fair for the sake of big crowds. Yet why had she lowered herself to the pitched tents and wandered along with them throughout the country?

Salvation should be available to the people; thus grace was nearer for those who thirsted for it. Fortunata just smiled, this being the grace with which she greeted the fear of the one who approached and quailed before her grandeur.

I lightly skipped up the steps that lifted me like a feather toward Fortunata, laughing as I did. At ease, she welcomed me and thanked me when I closed the door in order to save her the effort. Then she led me to the chair at her table and sat me down across from her. "Shall we look at handwriting, your hand, or the stars?" she asked matter-of-factly. Before I could even answer, she pointed toward some cards that lay in a bunch on the table, then toward a crystal ball, tipping it up with the long nail of her middle finger, because in the crystal ball she could read anything that one tried to hide. I thanked her and said that I trusted her to choose what would be best for me, whatever might bring me salvation, as I sought only pure happiness. Which is why I am here to seek your advice. My confidence in her pleased Fortunata; I looked straight at her, earnest. Then she mildly asked about the fee, it being best to get that over with at the start. Unfortunately, I didn't have much money, though I didn't wish to be stingy when it came to happiness. She nodded in satisfaction and assured me that she would do the best she could, whether the hand or handwriting or the crystal ball was best suited to me, and that ten shillings was the special price that I could count on. I agreed to it happily, for it seemed little for the task. I shoved the money across the table to her and felt ashamed, for her wisdom deserved a much larger sum. She, however, was moved to smile at me encouragingly, as if she were being richly rewarded, the note disappearing quickly. Again, she asked me to choose—the palm or the crystal ball? When I didn't respond, she opted for the left hand and the crystal ball; she would try both. Silently, I consented and offered her my left hand. Fortunata grasped it with practiced tenderness and picked up a large magnifying glass to help her as she bent over it.

"Tell me, Miss Fortunata, do I exist?"

She briefly looked me in the eye and then looked me over, more serious than surprised. Then she looked again at the hand and simply said, "First I'll look everything over. It's better that you ask me questions when I look into the crystal ball."

Fortunata knew a lot about my character, much more than I knew myself, but she said nothing that seemed to me improbable. A good man and father, she said, two children, a boy seven years old, a girl, who is almost four.—A good man and father . . . She no doubt wanted to be nice, but also bold. How precise she was when it came to the children! Had Fortunata perhaps seen me earlier with them? I didn't ask. The questions had to wait until the crystal ball.—But a dreamer, too much of a dreamer. The world is different than the gentleman thinks.—What did I think? Often, I had doubts.—Yes, that can be bad. Which is why caution is advisable, always caution. There are also worries, the line of fate. There wasn't quite enough income, a weakness in Mercury. Work with the head, that was clear.—Was my hand too limp? I curled it in a bit, but Fortunata reminded me that the hand has to remain open, please relax. I obeyed.—So an intellectual occupation, it's often hard to be happy in that. You think and think and think, which causes worries.—I agreed.—It's not good to think so much. Good-natured, and not at all ruthless, yet entrepreneurial. That's clear. The gentleman has traveled far and is not from this country.—How did Fortunata know that? Of course, she must know everything, I forgot. From which country? I dared to ask. I didn't at all expect an answer; it was just self-doubt rising up inside me. Fortunata rejected the question. I should know that myself, and what you know you shouldn't ask about.

"If I knew that, then I would feel a lot better."

From Europe, replied the wise woman immediately, and didn't want to spend any more time on ascertaining where I had come from. Pensively she pressed at the lines on my hand with a fingernail.—There's so much to see, also something sad.—I agreed. Yes, sad. But that is the past, I protested firmly, no longer now, it cannot happen again, it's over now.—One would think so, Fortunata confirmed, much having happened, the war. Ah, that was awful, to be taken away unwillingly from your home, hard times, but you got through it and survived it all.—My parents, I called out, my parents and Franziska.—Yes, they are long dead, the poor parents.—Why didn't she also mention Franziska?—The parents suffered a great deal, she said with a sigh.—That can clearly be seen in the hand, I was assured. With such a line of fate, anything is, unfortunately, possible. But the gentleman should feel hopeful, because he can.—Can I really?—Oh, certainly! Everything comes with time. I just had to make sure not to be too weak.—That I am not, I replied tentatively.—He who dreams so much is weak. Trust in yourself, have a bit of courage, then life will go easier. Just keep your head high and don't lose hope!—There's not much hope, I admitted.—Fortunata couldn't let that go.—Hope is warranted, she said firmly. You don't have to make it so hard; it depends on your heart. One can be too sad and cannot decide anything at the right moment. Fortunata also believed that I spent much too much time alone, shunning society and its pleasures, making it easy to become too serious. It's no surprise with me, as I am often so disappointed in others.—I agreed with Fortunata; I always expect too much.—I must have been gullible. As a child and as a young boy, my view of the world was too rosy, an optimist, and then, unfortunately, most everything turned out quite differently. It had all happened with a vengeance, for now I was often unhappy and despairing. Fortunata looked up and gazed at me with sorrow.

"You are a good woman. You certainly help many people, your heart is in the right place."

Fortunata was pleased that I recognized her goodness, and I praised her even more. Then she grasped my hand more tenderly than before and said so many lovely things about me that I was ashamed. Her praise wafted over me and sounded so good that I didn't trust myself to consider whether or not it was right; she didn't allow me to deliberate, as I almost drowned in the frothy comfort of her adulation. Fortunata continued to touch me so deftly with an even-keeled, thin, subdued voice that I didn't notice how quickly she came to the end of it. It suddenly occurred to me that the sweet perfume of hope had rapidly blown away, which hurt, leaving me cold, a bit miserable. However, I didn't want to lose control and pulled myself together. My hand still lay there, distant and tenderly spent, the guilty hand of Adam and his branching fate. The hand had grown from the earth, through the table, a five-pointed flower, and didn't belong to me.

"May I?" I asked. "Is that my hand?"

Fortunata had pulled her crystal ball toward her and looked somewhat confused.

"What do you mean, your hand? It doesn't bother me if it remains lying on the table."

"Always? For always?"

"What do you mean? It's your hand, you have to take it with you."

"But not right away?"

"No. When you leave."

"So I have to leave? I like it here with you so much."

"Why don't you want to go home? Be reasonable! Your wife is waiting for you. The children."

"Yes, that's right. But do you really believe that?"

"Yes, of course!"

"How terrible! I don't ever want to leave you. I feel so good with you."

"You can't stay here, that's out of the question."

"And if I could be of help to you? A servant? To shop, cook, clean, help you do whatever is needed?"

"No! What are you thinking? My dear sir, we have to hurry! If we still want to do the crystal ball, we don't have much time. Other people also want to visit me."

"Of course, I would hope so. I don't want all the happiness for myself. But let me stay! Please, give it a try. I can hide in the back, if it bothers you, or wait behind the wagon until everything is finished. Then you can send me into town; I can find out where to go, or show you where. I can also look for people whom I can tell about you and bring them back with me. You'll then make them all happy."

Fortunata angrily shoved the crystal ball to the side, stood up forcefully, and didn't look at me at all kindly. She didn't want to hear any of my ideas and was ready to show me the door.

"So you don't want me and I have to leave? Oh, you don't have to be afraid of me! I mean you no harm!"

"If you will be reasonable and promise me that you'll stop talking nonsense and afterward disappear straight off, then I'll still do the crystal ball. But only if you promise that for sure!"

I promised, and felt deeply depressed.

"You are very harsh with me. I'm also afraid that you've misunderstood. I don't want anything that's not illegal; I am completely incapable of harming anyone. I have never done anything to anybody. I came to you because I had to, and with the best of intentions. You indeed see everything and know that I have nothing but doubt. How can I bear it? Only with you does it feel easier. That's why it feels better to be with you than anywhere else in the world, which is why I want your protection forever. But I don't want to burden you."

My talk made Fortunata uncomfortable. She ignored it, and probably didn't even listen to me, but she wanted to take pity on me and appeared to actually do so, for she lifted the crystal ball with a flourish, placed it gravely in front of her, and stared broodingly into the glass. From then on, I was not to disturb her with my pressing talk. Fortunata's eyes shimmered as she looked at me.

"You must be very careful; otherwise something could happen to you! You should never go to fortune-tellers, because they are dangerous for you! As a result, you could lose your mind!"

"I can't lose it. In that, you're wrong. I cannot lose anything, nothing at all. Do you understand? I have nothing. I am nothing, nothing whatsoever. Has anyone ever come to you who was already nothing?"

"No, but you are indeed something. You are a husband and a father."

"No."

"I saw you earlier today with your children!"

"They are not my children. I don't have any."

"Your hand showed me clearly, nor did you say no when I said that you did."

"I am often too weak to say no."

"Why did you come here if you don't exist? Nobody before has come who doesn't exist. There's no such thing."

"Nobody at all?"

"Nobody."

"Then I am the first Nobody."

Fortunata bristled at this, thinking that I was stubborn, crazy. She no longer tended to her crystal ball but instead squinted at the door. Maybe she wanted to call for help. I had to reassure her, and so I lowered my gaze and spoke urgently and quietly while barely moving my lips.

"Please, don't be afraid. I am not mad, and I certainly won't do anything to you. Someone who is nothing can do nothing. I will also disappear, as you wish. You don't have to call anyone for help, for you will see that I am obedient; a lamb couldn't be more docile. Please believe me, I only came to you because I felt that I could be here, here with you. I always need to be with someone in order to know that I exist. That's not crazy. Please remember, Fräulein Fortunata, that right after I arrived I asked whether or not I existed, and you said that I should put that off until you turned to the crystal ball."

Rather than explaining anything, my talk confused the Gypsy woman all the more, yet she was no longer anxious or hostile.

"I say to you, as the all-seeing and faultless famous Gypsy fortune-teller Fortunata, that you exist, and that you can go forth from me without worry and at peace for all time, because nothing will happen to you. You will also exist if you are no longer in my wagon. You will exist for a long time, because you are healthy. You will remain protected, and almost all of your wishes will be fulfilled soon and in the future, most of your worries and the evil past fading away forever. Then you will be happy and forget all the terrible things, because everything will be as good as I say."

Fortunata said all this with a singing tone, like someone telling a fairy tale. But she hardly turned her gaze from me, and certainly not toward the crystal ball, so I didn't put much stock in what she said.

"Did you see all that in the crystal ball? Aren't you saying all of it because that's what you think I want to hear?"

She lifted the glass up and lightly played with it in order to examine its secret. I felt that I could expect nothing more and stood up. Fortunata followed me.

"Just one more thing! Then I won't bother you again. Would you let me look into your crystal ball just once?"

Fortunata pressed it to herself and covered it up with both hands.

"There's no point, sir. You wouldn't understand. You wouldn't see anything. Only I am told the truth."

I staggered to the door and was so upset that I didn't even thank her or say goodbye. I plunged down the steps, without turning to look back at Fortunata, and disappeared into the tumult. I didn't leave anything with the Gypsy woman. I took myself along with me; even my hand, which hurt a little, remained attached to my arm, but was weaker than usual, and I was also weaker than I had ever been before. Only naked shame careened through the surging mass, garish floodlights and chains of shining lightbulbs blending together. The dark night sky was even blacker, dust and overly sweet charred odors rising toward it, and I didn't know where the tears that streamed down my cheeks had come from, the cheeks of the excluded and the lonely one driven away from the clang of the horrid music, the empty air of the barren evening, the crowd of distasteful people rushing back and forth, the buzz of their voices of immeasurable misery rattling from them and echoing back unintelligibly in a roiling damp mixture seen through the prism of my tears. Already I had freed myself some from the crush and crossed the street, but then it surrounded me again, only the fair having sunk behind me, the old city there as ever, it existing, while I did not, though because of the anxious gleam of its streetlights I could no longer see it. I pressed ahead, feeling lost, because the streets, with their spotty lighting, took no notice of me and were, what I had not yet realized, occupied only with the trickle of rain that flowed along the sidewalks in dirty rivulets or here and there gathered in murky reflecting puddles.

So I walked along querulous and anxious, not noticing that we were already at the train station; Anna with her groom Helmut, Peter and the faithful Herr Geschlieder from the museum were with me. They were escorting me and had not allowed me to carry my own suitcase and bags. I must not be burdened at all was what they wished, unburdened by the weight of goodbye, a free man who should have no worries. Such care didn't feel right to me, because without any luggage in my hand I couldn't be certain that I was departing; I felt like a lazy onlooker who wasn't responsible for anything, afraid that at the gate, or later on the platform, I would not be allowed on. A man with no luggage, which is what someone could take me for, shouldn't be trusted, no matter how eagerly he brandishes his ticket. I would have been happy to discuss the matter quietly, but the continual chain of our stomping feet prevented it; the old city sucked me in and forbade any talk. Nor did I manage to say a word. So I stayed quiet and walked on, though I kept to the side in order not to block anyone's way. I was not certain of my escort; they could all suddenly disappear, as the crowd was thick, but they didn't let me out of their sight. Peter, especially, stayed close and laughed at me jokingly as best he could with his wide, distorted mouth. Anna didn't offer any encouragement and yet was my only hope of a successful escape. Then the crowd began to thicken ahead of us; we had reached the great hall and now stood at a standstill, pressed among many people, hardly able to move.

"We've come too soon. Much too soon."

Someone said that; muttered and barely audible, these words must have come from Peter. Then they flowed in heavy waves slowly ahead and hung themselves wearily between the inert hands of the great clock that guarded the entrance to the trains and performed its time-saving duties only in fitful jerks. Helmut insisted that we had at least half an hour before we would be allowed through the gate and remembered that we still had to buy platform tickets. He recommended going to the station restaurant for a cup of coffee and they could get the tickets on the way. I was not willing to take a single step that would draw me away from the trains.

"I agree that it's not very pleasant here, but I'm not leaving. Go on, if you want, I'll wait here."

"They'll announce the trains," Peter reassured me.

"That might be. But that's no good to me. I have to stay here, for I'm not going anywhere."

"Come on," said Peter, "don't spoil our fun!"

"You can all go on. It won't bother me at all. You can stay there or come back, it's all the same to me. We could even say goodbye now."

"Yes, Herr Doctor," offered Herr Geschlieder, "I'm afraid I have to excuse myself. Your friends are here, and I really have to get home."

"Could I buy you a coffee?" asked Peter.

"Many thanks, but I'm afraid there's no way. I have to get going. And so, my dear Herr Doctor, be well and don't forget us! I hope all goes well over there, and safe journey back!"

"Thank you, Herr Geschlieder, and goodbye! Please pass on my best wishes to Herr Schnabelberger, Frau Dr. Kulka, Herr Woticky, and everyone at the museum. And to your dear wife as well! Thank you so much for accompanying me and for having been so nice to me!"

Herr Geschlieder reached out and squeezed my hand so hard that I almost cried out, and then weaved his way through the crowd, tipping his hat several times as he did until I lost sight of the hat and of him. Peter was angry that I had driven him away and insisted again that all of us, myself included, should go for a coffee before it was too late. This stubbornness made me mad, but Anna saved me the need to respond.

"It's not really that important. If Arthur doesn't want to, we can also wait here awhile without coffee."

Peter looked at me half disdainfully and half sympathetically, but left me in peace.

"Everyone in the museum thinks that you'll be back! Why didn't you tell them the truth, even right up to the end?"

"I couldn't. Perhaps they would not have let me go. Frau Dr. Kulka was against the journey right up until the last minute and could not understand what I expected to gain from being abroad. You stay in your country and earn an honest living, that's her view. Whoever wants to leave these days is certainly a coward and also a terrible patriot. My fears for the future here and for myself she found ridiculous. Nor could she see any way that my being abroad and reporting back could be of any use to the museum. In her opinion, that can all be done on paper. It would be better to have visitors come from abroad. That would be better press for us than to have our people visiting other countries. She didn't trust me. She even resented the couple of photos that Schnabelberger gave me. She never liked me. What I had worked on was never right to her. Everything that I had done I had done diligently, but to her it was all highly superfluous shenanigans. To save artworks, protect them, describe them beautifully, and install them tastefully that was all that was possible, according to her. But to be a human witness to the past and to sacrifice oneself for the most recent tragedy, that was a secondary task best left to the archivists and the historians. A museum must serve the living, not the dead—that was her mantra, and she was right about that. She just thought of it in a different way than I did. In any case, she had watched the preparations for my journey with suspicion and nearly blocked the necessary recommendation from the museum to the consulate for a visa. 'I know you only want to rush it all through,' she said. 'But I am warning you, either let me in on your plans or I will get involved, and that will be the end of it all.' So I had to pretend, though no doubt most everyone in the museum knew what I was up to. Herr Schnabelberger openly supported my plans. Whether or not he did so completely selflessly I have my doubts, but he nonetheless was happy to be rid of me. I didn't resent him, though, because I owed him a lot."

I had begun to babble and could have kept going if I hadn't been afraid that someone could overhear me. Then my plans could quickly have been thwarted. Secret emigration was frowned upon. I quietly closed my mouth and lowered my gaze, my cheeks glowing. Helmut had pressed his way through the crowd and returned with platform tickets, which he handed out.

"Is there one for me?" I asked meekly.

"How so?"

"I'm also accompanying me, and you only brought three."

"Are you kidding?"

"What do you mean, kidding? I want to accompany me. Is that so strange?"

Anna nudged Helmut in order to prevent him from answering. Then she spoke quietly to me, such that no one else could hear.

"We've done everything we can to make sure that you don't remain stuck here. There's not much time. Don't worry! Another ten or fifteen minutes and they will let us through. Then you go on ahead, with nothing to be afraid of. Show the man your ticket; he won't have to examine it any further but only punch it, and not even look at you. It will be easy. Then you'll already be at the train. We'll find the right car. You already have the ticket for your seat; it's in the top right pocket of your vest. Don't be so nervous! Promise me that! Promise yourself as well! Then you'll sit in your seat. We'll take care of your luggage in order to make sure it's nicely stowed. We'll wait on the platform until the train leaves. We'll wave to you and wish you luck. Then you'll travel on, traveling, traveling on into life, into the future. Soon tomorrow will be here. Yesterday is past; even today will be behind you! You can do it. Stay calm when you get to the border. Nothing will happen to you there, either. Your passport is real, all the visas are good. You just show the passport and everything that they want, but everything will be fine, for it's all in order. There everyone will be friendly toward you. Then the train will travel on and you will be beyond the border. Then you can celebrate, the last worries falling away. You are free. Then you will feel tired, completely tired, but happy. You will have to sleep in order that, when you arrive, you are wide awake."

Anna said all this and more to appease me. I was grateful to her and loved her at this moment, which made me anxious about leaving her, for she had been so good to me. The first night after my return came back to me, the days in the mountains just a few months ago. But I also knew that I had done the right thing in not appealing to Anna and not allowing her into my unease, which she protected but couldn't fight off. I was happy that in Helmut she would have a loving husband, which is what she needed— someone strong and simple, always there and never to be doubted, someone who didn't just chase after his dreams but steadily moved toward them. Anna needed a resting place, not my abyss and my unresolvable past. In addition, Hermann's and Franziska's shadows stood between us and the dark fate of the native city that she would have to bear without me, but which would not have allowed us to be together freely in the world.

"It will soon all work out for you, Anna, for you and Helmut. It's good to know that there are steadfast souls and not just the lost."

"You are not lost, my dear. You will soon come to see that."

Often, Anna had spoken to me comfortingly and tenderly, but never had her voice shown such affection for me. Was I letting go of the only person who, though she hardly understood me, nonetheless knew nearly everything of my plight? There would likely be a warning about the need to leave the platform, one that signified a last, irrecoverable moment. I didn't have to travel on into the uncertain future yet; I could still risk saying to Anna that I was better for her than the handsome jolly Helmut, who good naturedly stood smiling next to us and in his heart was probably glad that I was clearing off. I was envious. Helmut was healthy, his eyes hardly having been touched by suffering. But I trembled, my eyes had no strength, everything around me grew blurry, aswim in a drizzling mist. Was Anna still next to me? I didn't trust myself to glance at her in order to conceal my disappointment that she was already with Helmut and probably leaning on his shoulder. Between Anna and me there was a wall, only razor-thin, even transparent, yet impenetrable and final. I had lost Anna because I was stupid and cowardly. What good was it that I could still hear her voice so close by?

"Everything will be okay. Don't worry. The two of us are good friends, but we don't belong together. You must know that."

I murmured thank you to Anna and felt ashamed.

"Peter, at last you'll be rid of me."

"In a little while, unless there's a delay."

"But soon, even with a delay. Such a heap of nothing must at last be off. . . . What a weight will be lifted from you! Or will you be sorry?"

"I know how to take care of myself."

"I hope so. It will also be nice to have the room to yourself. You will have to clean up after me a good deal, I'm afraid! Nothing, and yet I leave so much behind."

"But that's good. That way, I will laugh and cry at the same time that you are gone and have finally left me in peace."

Anna turned to Helmut and played with his right hand. This pleased him, but when he noticed that I was watching he stepped away. He was a simpleton.

"She's a beauty, your Anna!" I said rudely and almost too loud.

"I agree!" he said proudly in return.

He wanted to add something, but Anna put a finger to her lips in order to silence him.

A railway man lifted a departure sign high and shoved it into the display board; the express train to beyond the border was arriving as they called out its name. I burrowed in my coat pocket and pulled out my ticket and wanted to grab my two suitcases, but my friends wouldn't allow this. Peter was faster than me and already held the suitcases, although there was still plenty of time, for the passengers were only slowly beginning to gather for the rush. Nor was I able to grab hold of my little suitcase and my bag, Anna and Helmut having got to them before me.

"Both suitcases—I can't have that, Peter! You must give me one!"

He just laughed. At that moment, I felt him capable only of scorn and bad will.

"You must, you must!" I begged, but in vain.

"You will have enough to schlep, dear Arthur. For now, you must allow me the pleasure."

I could have asked Anna or Helmut to hand over the goods they carried, but I didn't want to upset them; if Peter carried my things, they had to do the same. Now, haltingly, we moved along with the thick stream of people. I looked up at the clock; the minute hand quivered and jumped with a jerk to the next minute. Not a patient clock, for it stutters, I thought. My escort moved on ahead of me. That was fine with me, as I didn't want them behind me, and it would have been awkward otherwise, though there was no clear reason why I should be bringing up the rear. I should have been in the middle. Peter took the front spot, which I thought good; his carefree frivolity didn't restrain him, making him the best suited for the situation. Deftly he wound his way toward the gate and was already through without even glancing at the ticket puncher. Anna scurried along and laughed at the railway man, as if owing him endless thanks for the enormity of his good will. Meanwhile, Helmut followed along like an innocent child.

Suddenly, I felt uncomfortable in being the last; it would have been better to have someone behind me, because now I was afraid to lose sight of my friends and to have to hold on to my ticket book longer than I wished to. But I couldn't get ahead of Helmut without falling painfully; I'd have to tug at his sleeve or even shove him. I couldn't do that, so I had to patiently remain in the rear. Helmut had already slipped through the gate without a problem. Now I only needed to take another step in order to present myself to the ticket puncher, who was already eyeing me seriously and coolly as the next one in line, but I felt it almost impossible to move. I wanted to peek again at the clock in the hall, my gaze shooting almost straight up, but was no longer able to see the clock face. Still, I hesitated, there being the tiniest bit of time allowed me to have a last moment in this city. The dark sense of the word "destination" suddenly came to me. Beyond the gate was the train station, but no other destination, no longer the city. Though I was leaving it of my own free will and wanted nothing else but to do so—this was the moment that I had sought since the day I returned, and for which I had longed with hardly any anxieties holding me back—I was nevertheless anxious, feeling abject and cast off, because, with the goal having been reached, I was also expelled and without a destination, no longer having rights to a burial in my native city, not even of any kind of remembrance, everything having slipped away: childhood, my parents' house, happiness, and plenty of unhappiness. Yet no, the unhappiness is there, but now it will be different. It will transform itself into the pursuing tumult, an unhappiness that will plunge forward behind me through the gate, it already weighing upon me and holding me by the neck; I wanted to shake it off, but it wasn't a piece of baggage that could just be taken from me. That's why it was a blessed stroke of good fortune when my friends took charge of my things, as I still had my hands free and could let them to sway back and forth, not having to suffer checking the clock, time indeed not being recorded anywhere as it frittered away somewhere far off in the lonely, twisted corners of this city. By then, I needed to stretch my gaze in order to detect those hiding spots.

Really, I should have tried to look back; it was still possible and not forbidden, but nevertheless I didn't risk being a coward again. I was afraid to think of the protest that would flare up behind me. I held my ticket high, it being the only weapon that could save me, yet I clutched it too tight, such that it wasn't suited to battle, and there I stood, still paralyzed, my escort already having moved ahead, no longer an escort but, rather, deserters who had left their comrade behind and betrayed him, such that he had to face his demise alone. The lips of the gatekeeper yawned open, fleshy full lips, revealing a powerful set of teeth brown with pipe tobacco, a hefty tongue rising from the maw, wagging back and forth and glistening in his mouth. The beast's nose gathered into a thick knob, the nostrils flaring, sticky hairs standing within. A voice issued from the throat, the right hand swung the barrier, a black thumb pressed back and forth on the lever, such that the single tooth bit into the empty air. But I heard nothing and was confused. To move ahead was not allowed, and though my hesitation was probably much shorter than my anxiety made it seem, it still lasted too long for me to please the gatekeeper.

People pressed behind me, but I didn't wish to block traffic; at the gate some passengers had already begun to go around me. "I'm going, I'm going," I whispered as apology, yet I did so inaudibly as the monitor waited atop his high chair so impartially, confidently looking on at my supposedly lawful actions, myself able to go about my business and he gracious enough to smile at me and my ticket in an approving manner, as if he was happy for the long journey that awaited me. I was now in the middle of the gate, still brandishing my unsuitable weapon. Then it was the ticket puncher who gently pulled it away, though I did not willingly give it to him. After that, I meant nothing to him; by surrendering this pass I had forfeited everything, that which until now had preserved the last semblance of meager credibility. Reverent and with eyes lowered, I followed every gesture and movement of my master as he, with touching patience, tended to the little ticket book—

the red cover, which he gravely stroked, opened with a flourish—and bent over to thumb through the many tickets as if wanting to count them. But he didn't do that, nor did he examine it at all but, rather, seemed satisfied with the handsome bundle and with two fingers grasped the first ticket, which was more stubborn to get hold of than the cover, though my attendant knew how to help and moistened his index finger with his tongue. This did the trick, and the ticket was punched. Now the master was satisfied and folded up the ticket book, everything in order. It was mine to keep. The man looked up and shoved the book into the happy hand, and said, "Thank you!"

"Platform Three, Track One! Have a good journey!"

How nicely he had called out his little rhyme! I had already slipped through the gate, but I turned around once more, and, as thanks for such courtesy and for the well wishes, I bowed slightly. The ticket puncher didn't look at me, nor, unfortunately, did he take in my polite goodbye. He had other things to do and looked over the next person's ticket, or who knows how many more. I stuck my ticket book in my pocket and looked back for the last time into the large hall, tears almost welling up in me. Yet I was very relieved and also had no time to sink into melancholy thoughts of return. My friends had long left the platform and were hurrying off, myself unable to make them out in the murk of the long passage. It would have been ungrateful to let them wait any longer, nor was it at all necessary for them to send someone back to ascertain the reason for my miserable dawdling. I waved blindly ahead in order to ask for patience, because I was unable to keep moving forward. As always, my suit coat was open, a habit I had taken from my father, though now I felt the need to button the coat properly, wanting to look prepared, really ready to travel. Unfortunately, the coat was a bit tight, it being something Peter had got hold of somewhere and right away thought good for me, since only the fingertips of his hands were visible from the sleeves when he put it on. Since the coat was now too tight, I had to press to button it, the freshly altered buttonholes of the thick fabric straining against the large buttons. It was uncomfortable, took a long while, I having to fuss with it too much, which frustrated me. Yet there was nothing I could do; that's just the way it was, even if the buttoned coat, which I would take off as soon as I got on the train, was pointless. Then I calmed down, and as I finally climbed down the step, almost with bravado, my shield lent me a bit of security, though I also had to laugh at my foolish-ness. Below, my steps quickened in order to catch up to my friends, whose indulgence I sought out with a look. Peter shook his head, half annoyed, and laughed at me.

"First you can't get moving fast enough, and then you keep us waiting for an eternity. It seems to me you really don't want to go."

I stammered something foolish about having been kept waiting at the gate for so long. Peter didn't believe a word, which I noticed, but I didn't say anything more. My friends took my luggage, and again I put up a fuss about it, demanding to carry at least one item. We reached the third platform, the long train standing ready, a conductor pointing the way to my seat, a corner seat in the direction the train was headed. We all climbed into the rail car; Peter stowed my luggage without asking me, though I couldn't have arranged it more comfortably myself. He was proud of himself and said, "Now you're all set." There was nothing to say in response to this. There was nothing to say at all. Laboriously, I unbuttoned the coat, hung it on the hook, and placed my hat over it. I was subdued, feeling empty and miserable and also so naked that I took the coat back down from the hook and slipped it on again. I even put on my hat and would have preferred to put on gloves, which I never used. No other traveler had yet entered my compartment, no other seat but my own having been reserved. Having put everything in order for me, my friends sat down and relaxed as if they were at home. I was the only one who stood, feeling like a stranger and belonging to no one, while my escort behaved as if they were about to set out on the journey. Normally I would have indulged them, especially on that day, but, because it was not their train, this casual behavior bothered me. Peter hardly took notice, yet it bothered him a great deal that I would not sit down.

"Why are you so nervous and uncomfortable? I can hardly stand it! Are you getting cold feet?"

"I think it would be best to walk back and forth outside. There's still plenty of time."

"Okay, okay," said Peter. "Just as you wish."

He immediately stood up from his seat, Helmut following more slowly, the decision to head off causing Anna some duress. Perhaps she was tired, perhaps sad. I should have watched out for her more; in fact, I was sorry that because of my impatient jealousy I had destroyed the peace of goodbye. It would have been best if I had ruefully said that it would be fine by me to sit comfortably there with everyone in the compartment, but Peter had jumped up so quickly that I figured he would misunderstand my change of heart as mere fickleness. That I didn't want. And so I remained firm, being the first to leave the compartment as I hurried along the corridor with powerful steps, if only to rob my escort of any claim to a further rest stop in the compartment. Already I stood on the platform and glanced peevishly at my friends, who, with noticeable difficulty, neared the exit and, so it appeared to me, angrily and almost clumsily stumbled down the steps, each of their hands on the railing, which looked silly, but which I found amusing. Anna, who was the last, was nonetheless upset and—I could now clearly see—very tired. I didn't know any longer what was the case, whether it pained me or I felt sorry for her, as she looked much older and more helpless than she had ever appeared to me before. Helmut, usually so attentive, forgot to attend to his bride. So I jumped and nearly lifted her down.

There were not many people on the platform; after the press in the great hall, this surprised me. The travelers had indeed parsed themselves out onto the train or were on other trains, there being few who had business beyond the border or they simply could not leave. We walked back and forth, and soon it happened that we walked in pairs, Peter and Helmut ahead, Anna and I behind. The two men chatted casually and pleasantly, me not taking part, as they had already distanced themselves when we said our last goodbye. Helmut swelled with wan friendliness; I no longer felt any envy toward him and was ashamed more for him than for me, not wanting anything more to do with him. Even Peter, who was so faithful in tirelessly caring for my daily existence, slipped away, for he was no longer a part of me. Even if I no longer felt close to him and only resented him somewhat, which certainly was not very pleasant, I was nonetheless incapable of revealing my ingratitude. Peter, in general, was a handsome young man, and Anna thought the same, his shoulders raised pompously and his whole manner funny. I avoided his gaze as much as possible; this allowed me to discover further shortcomings in his figure and appearance. Was it wrong of me, since he was a part of my past, a disagreeable witness to my humiliation? I would have liked to ask Anna that in order to ease my conscience. Yet what would that have gotten me but misunderstanding? It would cast me in a bad light, both of us feeling oppressed, myself meanwhile wishing to avoid nothing more than these last awkward minutes, which were superfluous and belonged to no one.

It was difficult to start a conversation; not because of the sanctity of this farewell but because of the pressure that surrounded us. It was the most senseless, horrible delay I have ever experienced, an artificially restrained separation that had already manifested itself and yet had not been fully acknowledged, if only because the train schedule had by chance afforded us some time. Thus every word seemed insipid, even if one tried to say something deeply meaningful, full of disgusting lukewarm sentimentality; the appeal of a joke, which could take care of everything by destroying such a feeling, remained beyond my grasp. At the same time, it occurred to me that I was too pathetic to take seriously such a farewell, because it would have meant once again bringing on the sorrow I'd already felt, or really for the first time be caught in a sharp upsurge of it, such that Anna and I would be trapped in the midst of it and be granted the feeling that the moment was blessed and free. But no such possibility lay within the slightest corner of the realm of my powers.

Like me, Anna felt, without saying so, what this train station had meant in terms of the departure and arrival of so many of our dead, along with us, exit and entry existing in the same unbroken existence and not in the guise of ghostly horrors dispensing destruction and doom. There was nothing to do but be silent. It was also not possible to remember that we had traveled to the mountain forest amid the last echoes of our imaginable past, and, after the crowning week, had found ourselves returning crestfallen and mouthing mindless chatter here among the bleak days in which we were immersed, more gloomy than ever before. Did I dare still to think? To already be gone, that was no kind of thought! Which was why I wanted only to be sitting on a train already under way, because I couldn't expect the separation to occur any sooner. I listened for the conductor's whistle to finally announce the departure.

Anna, with her soundless gait, which always surprised me anew, moved along with quiet steps next to me—indeed, more quietly than ever. I watched how gently she set her feet on the hard concrete and wanted to imitate her, yet no matter how carefully I tried to take my steps I could still hear my heels striking the platform. I looked at Anna's feet and mine, not allowing myself to look any higher or at the face of my friend.

"You can walk so quietly, Anna. That's always amazed me."

"Really? Then perhaps you won't forget it."

"What do you mean, forget?"

"Well, you won't. Something is always remembered. Often something unimportant, something minor."

"Others then latch onto that."

"Yes. I think especially men. At least for me, Arthur, it's different. There are only many minor matters."

"But what, then, are essential ones?"

"That's too big a word. I don't like it. It's easy to get tripped up by it."

"You're right, Anna. But there are essential things. Yes. There must be some. I can imagine them. They haunt me. But I have nothing essential. That means I don't know them. And that's why I think they haunt me."

"You have to stop that, this torment! That's my main wish for you. In the mountains, you felt better. The essential things were clear, and you also saw the minor things. Then you were much more satisfied."

"That's not entirely true. But, even if it were, the minor things are indeed only ornaments, certainly quite lovely, and it's important not to ignore them. Nonetheless, I'm telling you, Anna, the essential things remain, somewhere they exist. If I could find them, even just one, the wall would be penetrated or, even better, it would be behind me. Just like crossing the border."

"That's right! Your journey, Arthur. There!"

"Yes, there. I'm not there yet, and there can be here, everywhere and nowhere at once."

"Why are you going?"

"I have to. You know that. Don't ask me about it."

"Okay, then, there."

"Yes, there. It will at least mean a change. But the essential thing, I know as well, will not be won as a result."

"You say that, but you don't know. You don't actually know that right now, do you?"

"I wish I did. But I can't speculate that much. It's beyond me."

"There's talk of peace."

"Anna, peace, yes . . . there's talk of it. Nevertheless, it has to be different, something completely different, a submission to Nothing, in order that one is returned to Being. I'll say it quick as a phrase, and so it goes: Through Nothing to Being. That's the secret out of which the world is created. And as for people. . . . That will be the charge, you see, the essential thing. We must repeat that again. Alas, what am I telling you? The wall, the wall . . . the essential thing behind it . . ."

Anna wanted to reply and started to, but she stopped short of saying the sentence and said nothing in reply, either because she felt that I couldn't stand it or she thought that there was no answer that worked. Probably she wanted to reply, my brash slogan and all my talk seeming too pretentious to her. We stood before my train car. After a little while the men joined us, their good mood planted pertly in their faces. Peter and Helmut had already climbed aboard and reported that there were many free seats, there had been no need for me to reserve one. Peter had also surveyed the locomotive as it coupled with the train and marked down its number.

"Do you want to write it down?"

He said it slowly, and added with the certainty of an expert, "A first-class machine. She will be sure to get you across the border in good shape."

This was said with such a deliberately strange tone that we all laughed.

"I hope you all soon get the chance to have the same locomotive!" I called out happily.

"If I ever get the chance to leave, I'll fly! The train is too slow for me."

"Better today with the train," remarked Helmut, "than tomorrow with the railway!"

"Better today with an airplane," said Peter in a feather-brained manner, "than tomorrow with the train!"

No one laughed anymore about it, but this had all set me at ease; I could regard all of them and even Anna less self-consciously. Essential things or minor things, I didn't have to bother about them anymore. I was pleased to see the three of them standing across from me, Anna between the men but closer to Helmut, almost leaning on him; he didn't really grasp these subtle emotions, yet with humble pride let himself be pleased, while Anna's manner toward me was comforting, and therefore also decisive and more distant. It felt good to think about this group a little while longer, because it prepared me. Which was why I didn't realize, as did Helmut, that the train was a bit late. I would not have noticed at all, given how unconcerned I was at that moment about the journey. Peter couldn't understand why I didn't respond to Helmut's announcement, and when I felt challenged not to lose patience Peter began to prod me with sniping comments that I was just too heavy and that was why the train couldn't move at all. Since I continued to remain silent and only grinned politely at the idiot, he then got snarky.

"Your heart is always sinking to the ground, fearing that something will happen. Now that seems indeed to be the case. Do you see the policemen over there with the railway worker? They are noticeably whispering to one another. Maybe they're going to haul you off the train."

"That could well be," I answered in all seriousness. "But this time I don't believe you. You no longer have any power over me. And, besides," I lied, "it and whatever you are up to at the moment don't matter to me at all."

Anna had pressed herself closer to Helmut. She appeared upset about this stupid hostile chatter, and because of that I cast a sideways glance at her, smiling and wanting to say, "Minor matters!" The corners of Anna's mouth betrayed displeasure. Then I very quietly turned my full gaze toward her to show that she need not worry anymore on my account. Did my friend understand how warmly I approved of her alliance with Helmut? Her face was blank and too colorless, but grateful; I believed she understood me. Turning more toward Anna than to Peter, I spoke to him more pointedly.

"You want to make it easier that we will forget each other soon. That is very nice of you. I was always a minor thing, dear friend. Which means only one thing: out of sight, out of mind."

Peter looked at me, shocked, not knowing how to respond to my words and certainly not wanting to part from me in strife. He made me feel bad, so I stretched out my hand.

"No offense, Peter. Here's to our friendship!"

He shook my hand, but there was no warmth in our handshake; there was no bridging the gulf that had opened up, even if we continued to vigorously press our hands together several times. The hands withdrew, knowing that they could no longer maintain a tie between us. Peter had forsaken me; I had fled from him. That was the only thing certain about this farewell.

The conductors' pipes blew. Once more, I stretched a hand toward Peter in as conciliatory a manner as I could, then to Helmut, who had stepped away from Anna for the moment, as if it were too much for him to stand together with her to wish me well, while finally Anna's and my hands touched, and only just touched, a shyness holding us back and not allowing a strong grip, though we were so moved that our left hands found each other. With a sudden upsurge of emotion, I bent forward and lightly and fleetingly kissed the back of her right hand, which stretched out cool under my lips. It was fine with her, but I was taken aback and quickly stood up straight, only our hands perpetuating our bond, they still belonging to each other, otherwise we would already have separated. Perhaps it lasted longer than it should have, especially for Helmut, but finally we had to let go of each other, as the conductor approached with a door key, our arms lowering, limp and yet resolute, slapping at the sides of our legs, a strange awkward sound, but freeing us as Anna took a breath, she having been swept up by this unconscious clasping of our hands as much as I was.

I had already hopped up onto the steps, the door crashing behind me. I hurried to my compartment, yanked open the window, and leaned out as my friends drew closer somewhat more slowly. Inwardly disengaged, yet friendly, Helmut and Peter stood before me like off-duty soldiers, calling out all kinds of funny things. I didn't pay attention and didn't respond, but just nodded along with them. Peter churned his arms the way children do in imitating the motion of train wheels; I played along and waved at him as if the train were, in fact, leaving. Anna didn't approve of these antics but, instead, looked at me steady and calm; we knew everything and had nothing more to say to each other. I noticed how the signal post had lifted the sign for departure, which didn't prevent Peter from notifying me as well. I stretched out my right hand, which everyone shook, and then the train began slowly to move; I hardly felt it, so softly did the train pull away. As if on command, my friends stepped back, unfolding white hankies and walking in the direction in which the train was headed. That wasn't enough for Peter; he ran fast and caught up with me, boasting that he was much faster than the train. It should have got on my nerves by then, but I didn't want to spoil his fun and was amazed at his childish ways. "Marvelous, marvelous!" I called, and that was my last word. Anna and Helmut had remained standing far back, and now Peter also drew up, standing there pompously as he began to wave. I waved back as long as there was a last flashing glimmer of the swaying hankies to be seen. Then I stopped looking back at the station.

I was alone in my compartment and thought of settling in for the many hours of the journey. But I remained standing at the window, knowing I had to close it soon, since we would soon be crossing over the long viaduct. Then the lights of the station area went out as the panes of the window were covered with impenetrable smoke. I could have then sat down and comfortably prepared everything for the night, because the trip through the viaduct took more than ten minutes, even on the fastest trains, as witnessed previously on many long and short trips. Yet I couldn't settle down, I couldn't bring myself to sit, deciding instead to pocket my handkerchief, take off my coat, hang it up neatly, and remove a cinder from my hat before I tossed it on the seat. I stuck my hands into my pockets and, alternatively, into the cracks between the seats several times as I listened to the joyful clatter of the turning wheels. This music pleased me quite well, its rhythm full of promise, and out of all expectation I began to whistle, searching out the tune for "Oh, You Dear Augustin."

Soon the compartment started to feel too cramped, so I slid back the door and walked up and down the corridor, most of the compartments were barely occupied. Whoever wasn't traveling on his own was locked in excited conversation, the lone travelers reading the evening edition of the morning paper or sitting there with bored, indifferent faces, there being no telling why they were there, or they simply were in total self-control. They hardly paid attention to me. I also sought to appear indifferent, for nothing was so obvious in the world as the fact that I was using this train, each being the secret master of his own journey. If I had specific intentions linked to my journey, no one had any idea, but if I were forced to disclose them, then I was the special envoy of my museum. I stopped whistling "Augustin," the little song being much too inappropriate. Soon I again walked back, swaying somewhat, to my compartment, where the motion of the train caused the sliding door to move back and forth.

Energetically I rallied myself; it was wonderful that now, at least, I was a free man, able to think what I thought was best, much more intense and threatening than I usually was. Who was as independent as I was? I said out loud, "The money for the trip is arranged. I have the right to leave. I'm traveling because it pleases me to do so. I am, at minimum, a passenger, a pa-pa-ass-ass-enger. No one can deny me that. I am traveling from now to there and thereafter then." That was the message I wanted to convey if someone were to ask me with the politest expression for an obligatory explanation. Anyone traveling the same route was free to inquire, and if it didn't please them, well, they could just toddle off.

"Who are you, then?"

"I'm me."

"Are you Herr Adam, the Adam who was expelled?"

"Not that I know of! You're mistaking me for someone else."

"But you look so familiar to me."

"That's right. You as well. Haven't we seen each other somewhere else before?"

"I'm so pleased. You're right. I'm also called the same."

"Naturally, now I remember. That's what you're called."

"You doubt it?"

"Actually, quite the contrary. I am, there is no doubt of that."

"Does doubt begin in earnest when one doesn't exist?"

"Certainly. Just as you say."

"You're exceedingly friendly."

"I'm always friendly. I'm even friendly when I travel."

"Very nice. It's certainly worthwhile to do so. I also like to travel that way."

"You, too?"

"Me, too."

"You exist."

Thus I presented myself in turn and made an entirely good impression. No one disagreed, for which I was grateful. Then I stepped to the window, satisfied, and drummed on the pane alternately with my knuckles and my fingernails. I stopped and pressed my nose against the glass, for I expected that we would exit the viaduct at any moment, and I didn't want to miss that. No bright light announced that we were outside, but instead there was deep night, impenetrable smoke pressing against the window, though the change in sound was a sure sign. I quickly pulled down the window, because I hoped for a moment, before the train turned at the bend, to catch a glimpse of the neighborhood where for sixteen months I had been Peter's roommate. But I could only make out in which direction it lay, the garden hill with its lit crown rising above where the vineyard must be. Otherwise, there was nothing to see, the darkness weighed too heavily—no moon in the sky, hardly any stars visible, it most likely being cloudy. Then everything was already behind, the train traveling too fast and it feeling good to me; I would not have to stop. There was only one stop ahead that mattered, and it took hold of me and was carrying me away into the surrounding night.

Far below me a street ran alongside which I knew well, knowing, as I did, almost every corner of this city, right down to the last exits to the fields and forests of the empty suburbs that stretched endlessly through valleys and lowlands, growing every year and rising up the hillsides and far off along the chain of hills. There below we passed a tram, and I believed I could pick out its grinding from the surrounding noise. Slowly the moving car pursued its way along its humble path and was fully occupied, many people having to stand, an apricot glow pressing from inside it, and from this leisurely, sleepy light many little violet sparks sprang from the wheel of the power rod above. Then it was gone, the bridge shuddering above the river. I tried to look between its passing pillars while, over the flashing play of the river mirroring lights of the old royal castle with its towering dome, there rose an arresting picture from a childhood erased long ago. Now it stood before me in a dreamlike faded glow, but the image I knew didn't really appear, only the illusion towering above me, me laughing in response, feeling stronger and healthier than it, even enduring and less fleeting; so vain and presumptuous did I feel on the railway bridge. Yet soon it was past, its rumbling silenced, and with it was drowned the distant view of the wonderful illusion. Now we were crossing a suburb, shattered streets and factories, again a curve, the train slowing down, the brakes gripping hard and squealing; the dusty suburban station, through which not even the fastest trains had been granted free passage, demanded that we stop.

Should I get out? If I hurried, I could just make it, no matter how heavy my bags were. The platform lay on the other side, and I had to see it, to see the chance it offered. Then I was in the corridor, where I also shoved down the window and looked out, thinking that perhaps I could hail a porter. But there weren't any, not even a single passenger waiting for our train, only some people sitting heavily bundled on the open benches, waiting for a slow commuter train that would carry them off to stops nearby. Otherwise the only other one visible was the stationmaster, whose steps resonated on the checkered tile surface. The man stepped slowly toward the train and appeared in no hurry, not knowing anything about where we were headed. Two conductors had left the train, though it was hard to know if they were really getting off or if each was just hanging on to a stair railing with stiff, outstretched arms, swaying his lantern back and forth such that he looked to be impatient and in a hurry. I leaned out fairly far, but no one paid any attention to me, no matter how conspicuously I turned in every direction, trying too eagerly to catch someone's eye with an upraised finger, there being no chance to do so. A devilish game with the danger of misfortune occurring—so I puckered my lips, though I didn't whistle "Augustin," but instead turned serious and felt in my pockets for the book of tickets, passport. Everything was there; the journey could continue.

I wasn't paying attention at all, having let myself get too wrapped up in my own thoughts, when we started off again. A strong burst of air hit me, spraying moisture with it, though it wasn't rain but condensed steam from the locomotive, and so I pulled in my head, which much too carelessly leaned out the window. The tightly woven outer districts of the city gave way, then we meandered slowly toward the river and sped along right next to it for a ways, though it was too dark to see its water. When the last suburbs on the other shore, with their lights swaying on the water—more remembered than recognized—were behind me, I switched from my perch to my compartment, shoved the door quietly closed, freed the straps holding back the curtains and closed them, such that the embroidered coat of arms, with its two winged railway wheels, stretched out properly.

Now I was alone in my room and safe, except that it was too cold, even though the heater spewed out heat, and so I raised the window, leaving it open a crack. I remained standing as before. In your room you can gather what is dear to you, everything here being mine, belonging to me, the riches of the world. I had paid the rent and taken care of my bills, and thus I could rule the roost. And yet what feeble pride there was amid this doubtful joy! What had I won and what had I fulfilled, such that I seemed so certain, when in fact I remained adrift and could determine nothing but, rather, had to wait for what would be allowed me and what not? The trip was pleasant, but what was the point of the destination awaiting me at the end? I slid into the corner of the compartment and hunkered down there, it being the only thing I was owed, for the ticket still hung there on a thin cord saying that the seat had been reserved. But I was under way; what was and what will be did not exist here, they were excluded, and between the cities that were exchanging me I was still indeed something, which I could assert, since here there was a protective code with which no one could argue. As long as I followed its rules, I would be carried along, the code having taken me in and encompassing me with its order.

Once again the door rattled open with a rush, the curtain swept to the side, an official cap, ticket puncher, and lantern appearing before me as someone said good evening and asked for my ticket. Quickly I handed over the booklet, the eyes sinking down, a pen marking a cross, the ticket puncher snapping, then the booklet was handed back and was quickly shoved into my pocket. "Stretch out on the seat," I heard, "but put newspaper under your feet. The train is empty. It will be a long journey. Good night." Then the back turned to me, passing through the door, the door rattling shut, once again the lantern lighting up and passing on. Only the curtain wasn't properly closed, and flapped miserably. The conductor was right; I was tired, if not sleepy. The curtain straightened out, the window entirely shut, only the vent opened, my coat hung up on the hook, my shoes off and placed under the seat, I stretched out on my back, my eyes half closed, blinking at the light and waiting and traveling on.

The night had plenty of time, far more than I did; it took me into its core and I dwelled there. It stretched from the dark quadrants of sleep to the rush of endless forgetting and was not at all concerned with me. For me there was still the light in the compartment, not as a means of protection but as affirmation that I could look at the night's pure darkness through the existence I had been granted. Thus could I speak to it and tell it that a life existed. It listened patiently. I assured it that, really, a life existed, and the borders of this life flowed into it. Shadows spread, stretching across the traveling room and orientated to no particular stop, but there and allowing the soft darkness to slip through fine cracks, back and forth, quieter than the dormant wind that hardly stirs. Franziska moves about, admirably dead and not afraid of the night, since she no longer suffers the borders that hold on to life with fingers that gently grasp it. But, indeed, there is life, though not much of it, and what is there is on loan from the sacred night, and yet it exists, sensing itself there in the midst of it all and remaining there, calling silently to silent death.

"Was it bitter?"

"Was. Yes. It was bitter."

"Is it no longer bitter?"

"Was, was, my friend, was."

Life could be heard above the roar outside, slinking away from the lights as the past dared to rumble along. Yet Death also dared to come closer, its dry scent uncurling sweetly from the light toward Life and extending still further into the unknown future. Are we alone? it asked silently, repeating this noiselessly in waves: we alone, alone, -one . . . Can Life travel on? was the question hesitantly asked by Life in return, to which came the answer, It travels, but it does not escape, finding itself come to a stop in the realm of slumber. And again Life asks, Does it have a right or a point? Oh, it has a right to exist, and that, and nothing but that, is the point. But when Life wishes to assert itself and step beyond the fear of its limitations, what right does it have to that? Oh, it has a right, and its point is indeed encompassed by that right. You say encompassed, but is it free? No, something other than free, because it is indeed encompassed. Which is it, then, dear Death— encompassed or free? Free of encompassment and freely encompassed.

Then Life drew itself up into a tight bundle in order not to deny any part to Death's deeper grasp, in order that he could find a way to it, and not upset him with any kind of stubborn resistance, which indeed pleased him. Life also diminished its own questions, submitting its questions quite humbly in order not to disturb the inaudible with the lisps of the audible. But Death was patient and kind, sending out imperceptible rays of feeling that still reached beyond the borders to Life and commanded it to be. Should Life then ask, Do I exist? Should it do anything except just exist. But a voice spoke, and it sounded loud and clear.

"Life wishes to know: Where am I?"

Then, in one mighty gulp, the stillness drank down time, and one could hear it, there being no answer forthcoming, because Life is endless, endless right up until the green depths of Death. Thus everywhere Life stumbled on. Indeed, everywhere, but that is the wall and not a different place. Then a last question rose up from the depths of memory.

"Will you release me?"

Then there rose to the crest of the deeply stirred night the unmistakable voice of Franziska.

"Whether you exist or don't exist, I release you."

Then the night opened up and collapsed in upon itself. In thinly folded layers it wound itself around my lit-up, sealed room, but the voice faded away, swallowed up by the other half that was heavier, quietly sinking back into the closed-off past; the second half quietly dissolved into the future, quotidian night nestling down in confusion, clinging and small. Then I felt again inside: I am free. The journey also pressed on, layer after layer, and did not want to end. Indeed, it was time to begin something. Though I had not promised anything for sure, I knew that I would be held to my word, and therefore I lifted myself up and brushed off my pants and jacket. The instant I stood at the door, I had a moment of weakness in which I wondered if I should fulfill my promise; it could also be put off. It might not happen in a day, or even a week.

Though I hesitated, I nonetheless cautiously turned the handle, looked back once more to see if everything was in order in my little room, turning off the light so that only a little light from outside shown murkily into my room before I left it and closed the door behind me. I crossed the short hallway, with its soft carpet, then I turned and climbed down the few creaky steps to the phone booth, where I lifted the receiver, tossed in two coins, and turned the dial, having memorized the number. The number rang, and soon a voice answered, "International Bureau for Refugees, Search Office." I asked if Fräulein Zinner was there. "One moment," I was told, then I heard her voice. I said my name. I probably did so too haltingly and not loud and clear enough, for she couldn't understand me and I should give my name again and say what I wanted.

"Landau. Arthur Landau. Dr. Arthur Landau."

I said nothing about what I wanted, though because saying nothing wasn't going to help me at all, I quickly added, "Fräulein Zinner, you must remember me. We met briefly at Dr. Haarburger's."

Luckily she remembered, that was clear, but perhaps my call came as an embarrassment, and so I asked her to forgive me if I was bothering her; I could call back in a couple of days. Then the voice changed, as if it recognized mine for the first time, and Fräulein Zinner said warmly that of course she remembered me quite well, it had been an interesting evening, and was there anything she could do for me? Do for me? No, what could there be? Her excessive politeness made me feel uncomfortable.

"I just thought that we had talked about seeing each other again, no? And I even thought, That would be rather nice, don't you think so? So, to get to the point, Fräulein Zinner, could we sometime soon . . ."

She didn't think long before agreeing. But when? I thought to myself, She should decide that, as I don't know when she is free.

"You know what, Herr Landau, are you perhaps free now? That would likely work best for me."

"Yes, if you're not already busy . . ."

"If I were, I wouldn't be suggesting it."

She asked where I was at the moment, and when I shared the name and address of my guesthouse she explained, which I knew already, since I had looked at the city map, that we were in luck, for I was only five minutes away from the Search Office. She wanted to tell me the way there, but I interrupted her, as I knew already which way to go. Then she asked if I could come right away, and I answered that I could be there in ten minutes. That was fine with Fräulein Zinner; she knew of a cheap restaurant that served good food. There you could linger after finishing your meal, which was rare for this country. If it was all right with me, she would like to invite me to dinner there. She had no patience for affectation, and so it was agreed.

I ran up to my room and got myself ready, trying to straighten out my reluctant hair as best I could. In front of the mirror, I realized that I had again neglected to get my hair cut. But there was nothing to be done about it now; perhaps I could improve this mess by wearing a nice tie.

I owned three splendid ties from before the war which bore the label "HAL—Haberdashery Albert Landau." In a package that my father's old salesman had given me, I found these ties. "Herr Landau," the man had said, "I've heard nothing from your father. He was afraid that they would come and search my house. But your dear wife gave me this package. She said I should take care of it as best I could, for there were things inside it that her husband had written which were irreplaceable." Indeed, Franziska had saved my work, for I found everything, including my almost completed doctoral thesis, by which I hoped to become a lecturer, and in the middle of all those papers there suddenly appeared three ties, carefully wrapped, like new, myself having hardly even worn them or able to remember them. They were the only things still left of my old clothes, and they were also from the Reitergasse. When I was given them, several months had passed since my return, and I was no longer so sensitive about things almost long gone, yet I could hardly bear the sight of these ties. I felt them, pressed their heavy silk between my fingers, though they didn't wrinkle as I gazed at them in earnest and worried that I was handling them too roughly. Then I wrapped the ties awkwardly in tissue paper and that night brought them home from the museum. I offered them to Peter, because they didn't suit me.

Peter laughed at me, calling me an ass, since at first I had pined after lost things, but when chance placed them in my hand I behaved like an impudent child and wanted to give away the ties. I said that I knew I would never touch them. My words didn't sway Peter, for he maintained that it would be much worse if he wore them, for then I would have to see them on him, to which I replied that it wouldn't bother me all that much, for after a while I would get used to it. I fended off Peter's suggestions and brought the stupid matter to a close. I firmly rejected all advice, but secretly I felt a pang of envy, feeling ever more unsure of my own position and having to keep from growing angry if I were to sway Peter with my lame talk. Despite his ribald, even coarse response to such imponderably fine matters of tact, he suddenly had an idea and most decidedly turned away the goods that had been offered him. "You have a box. Put them in it and then into the closet. Don't look at them, and stow them away! Someday you'll be glad." I actually played agonizingly with the idea of giving the ties to someone else (Geschlieder would have been happy to have them), but instead I talked on in order to annoy Peter, who no longer listened to me but instead just yanked the ties away from me and put them in the box, which he carefully closed and tossed into my drawer. There it remained until shortly before my departure. While cleaning out my desk, I found the ties, which pleased me, and so I carefully packed them.

The wardrobe that I managed to put together after the war was meager and a mixed bag. Decent new things were not to be found, while, in accordance with what was due me as a survivor, I rarely received anything useful in the shops, sometimes nothing at all or badly made versions of discontinued goods that wouldn't hold a crease. Some things I had to take from Anna in order not to upset her, mostly clothing, though it was painful for me to walk around in Hermann's clothes, my skin on fire with them, it being almost impossible for me to wear them. I also got some things from those who had disappeared, though in most of them I looked like an ill-fit beggar whose poor Uncle Alfred was too rotund, it being a shame what I had to put up with. Then I had a few things that were better which were given to me here and there, whether handed out through charity organizations or sent from abroad. Uncle Karl Strauss from America—I never wrote to him, but Peter had dictated a letter to me—wanted to ease his conscience by sending a package that contained many things that didn't fit, nor were even good for trading with others.

Thus I arrived in the metropolis poorly outfitted, where luckily I didn't stick out, or at least I so imagined, because not much depended on my appearance. In addition, most of the people here seem dressed shabbily enough. But now I cared about how I was dressed, as I wanted to look dapper, more meticulous than I was at Haarburger's. I looked for what best suited me, for I would be with Fräulein Zinner and didn't want to appear pitiable or too poor. I needed different shoes, So-and-So having sent me a good pair when he was once in a good mood, then the lovely ripped sweater that Anna had knitted for me out of reserves of fine old wool, though the most important was what tie I would choose. It was then that my three new ones stood me in good stead, I having not yet worn any of them. I lay them on the bed in order to have a good look at them. They lay there almost untouchable, humble and patient, seductive and repellent at the same time, while I felt gratitude welling up, my fingertips stroking the silk, their history no longer mattering to me, as I was lost in the inane idea that in the paltry male garb of the century only the tie was used to display any flare and convey one's personality. Smugly I said to myself, "They're just the trick for your shaken self-confidence."

Finally I selected a tie that seemed to me the most sumptuous and stoked my vanity the most, a dark-red one, made of heavy silk with a touch of yellow in it. Carefully I tied the knot; it didn't sit right. Then I did it again in front of the mirror, which is not my habit. The knot swelled up like a big piece of fruit. An Adam's apple, it occurred to me, and I laughed, though I quickly looked away from the mirror in order not to see my contorted mouth. I was ashamed of my vanity; but what good did it do, for I couldn't just do things halfway. I shook off with annoyance the faint disgust with myself that rose up with my having so shamelessly primped myself. I almost jumped with crude pleasure, it seeming as if the inert wall of my feelings was pleasantly taken by surprise, or, better yet, that I had tricked it, for already I new that such an onslaught could not last very long without being punished and avenged. If I can just get through today, I thought, then I'll be pleased and will face the consequences later, for I had committed treason by trying to overstep my own poverty, my position in the world having been given up in order that I could strut like a peacock in borrowed finery for a few hours—indeed, innocuous finery whose glow burned within me. The red fabric that I had wound around myself was so tight around my throat that it could strangle me. Was that Adam's second fall, the fall caused by the consciousness of his sins? I pressed a hand between my collar and neck; it was an unusual grip that reminded me of my mother when she reached into her high-buttoned blouse in order to straighten out her necklace. I pulled at the collar in order to reassure myself that there was enough space to breathe freely, even if I suddenly swelled up. Then, struck by it all, I told myself how childish and pathetic this game was, and debated whether to choose a more modest tie made of artificial silk or wear this one; but indeed I would stick with the sumptuous one, it was decided.

I finally turned from the mirror and saw my father before me, a depressing old man with tears in his eyes for the lost son and a hand lifted as blessing. I couldn't bear such despair any longer, either my father's despair or my own, and so I closed my eyes in order to free myself from this vision. It worked. I saw nothing else before me. Then I grabbed my hat and coat and quickly left the room. When I closed the door, it slipped from my hand

and shut with a thud, something my father would never have done. He was gone. I no longer stood within his power, though I was also no longer under his protection. As I passed through the hall below, my glance fell upon my watch, and I was shocked to realize that I had wasted at least ten minutes with the tie and other stupid things in my room. I should have been at Fräulein Zinner's a while ago, and I was worried whether she would be upset by my lack of punctuality, since nothing is worse than to have to wait for an appointed visitor. Impatient and brusque, as I thought she was, she had perhaps given up on waiting and had already gone home.

I walked along the streets and was happy that they were not crowded, but what didn't help was the darkness of the strange metropolis, which only increased my already deep uncertainty and nervousness. In this country of coal, no lights burned in the side streets because of a shortage of coal. I was worried that I would get lost and was only reluctantly willing to ask someone for directions, since I often found that the advice I got was not all that good. How different it had been back there, where, no matter where you were, you could ask someone and he would be eager to help and send you on your way, whereas here it had usually been my experience that, because of my terribly heavy accent, I either couldn't be understood or I didn't understand the answer, or people reassured me that they themselves were not from around here, having just arrived and not being familiar with the area or something similar—it was a city full of strangers, there seeming not to be any natives—or it happened thus, which was the most painful for me, that I was shown the way, but such that even intersections and corners that I should watch out for were listed, though they would prove not to be there. Then I would end up lost in some neighborhood that hardly anyone walked through, not a soul to be found anywhere to take pity on me, making sure not to let go of my flashlight as I fervently pointed it at houses, garden fences, and street corners, never finding addresses or house numbers, wandering around for hours before someone finally helped me find my way out of my quandary.

Back there one can no longer live, I thought, and here I'm forbidden to live or am simply not wanted, a hopeless life of confusion in which the best city map, here known as an atlas, is of no use, since the almost endless flatlands were broken up into individual fields across one hundred and twenty pages on which I found it hard to locate myself, and the tiny printed names of the streets, especially in the dark, could hardly be deciphered. It was cold, a bad winter having settled in, but I wandered about in my confusion feeling hot and sweaty, miserable and hopeless. Yet today it wasn't quite as bad, for I had learned my way so well in the past days that it was hard for me to lose my way. At every intersection and turn I stopped, considered, and reckoned where I was in order that no mistake got me into trouble. Thus I succeeded at reaching my destination without any trouble after a while, which to me felt like too long a time, though it couldn't have lasted more than eight minutes. It was Ivanhoe House, a somewhat neglected magnificent building; the massive portal stood open, behind it the hall laid out with heavy marble tiles and lit up.

I stood before the gate for a moment because I had gotten hot. I didn't want Fräulein Zinner seeing me so breathless, with a knocking heart and weak knees. Yet it was late; I couldn't wait any longer, even if my condition was hardly any better. I walked on. An old porter looked out from his booth and tried to stop me before I even told him what I wanted, saying I should come back tomorrow, as office hours were already over. I was so shocked that I immediately stopped. I wanted to say something, but I couldn't find the words to make myself convincingly understood in the foreign tongue. The man waited, disinterested, for a little while and then, as if I hadn't heard right, repeated his shocking announcement.

"You must be wrong, I'm expected!" I said out loud and yet meekly.

"That's different," he said, nodding. "You should have said that from the start."

The man was an old codger; how was I supposed to say anything to him, since right away he had overwhelmed me with his surly speech? He looked me over carefully, yet in a friendly manner, and seemed to be waiting for me to say something further. I, however, was also waiting, for I didn't want to get myself into more trouble. So I forced him to ask a question himself.

"Who are you here to see?"

"Fräulein Zinner, International Bureau for Refugees, Search Office, Section . . ."

"She's certainly already gone. Try again tomorrow, but before five!"

I doubted it was my fault that I had missed my appointment.

"That can't be possible! I am expected! I just spoke to her on the telephone twenty minutes ago!"

"That's different. You should have said that in the first place."

Again the porter nodded approvingly and wanted to know my name. He turned to a telephone and dialed carefully. It took a while before he reached Fräulein Zinner, but then he announced that everything was okay, he being as happy as I was, for he was pleased at his accomplishment and that I was the beneficiary.

"On the fifth floor!" the porter said, calling out the room number. "The entry to the right. You'll find it. Normally you could take the elevator, but after five it doesn't work. It's turned off."

"Many thanks! I can manage without the elevator."

That was, of course, not at all true, for the stairs were very hard for me. The stairwell was poorly lit, as everywhere people cut back on anything they could, so why would it be any different at the Search Office, where people did research on the lost! The stately building, although some years ago it had been elegant and well cared for, had lost its splendor and was now crusted over with dirt and sadness. If you took a breath, it smelled sour and damp, and it irritated my nose, causing me to sneeze, which then echoed resoundingly in the stairwell. My knees began to quiver, so I stopped on a landing and had to interrupt my climb several times. When I got to the fourth floor, I felt so miserable that I stopped for even longer. I didn't want to press on any farther, but rather the opposite, yet to hang about between the porter and the fourth floor wouldn't work at all. Which was why I did nothing and just waited. Inside, I hoped for a sign of rescue in order to conquer my inability to move.

I hadn't felt so bad since the war. Sweat poured from me, my forehead and neck wet, and I was dizzy. Back there during the first weeks, I often thought that my health had been broken, but it didn't matter to me; I didn't want any help from doctors. It is what it is, I stubbornly said whenever Anna reproached me for my recklessness, though finally I gave in to her nagging and a doctor poked around me, tapped on my breast and back, took my weight, stood me up before the fluoroscopic screen, and asked me a couple of questions. The doctor nodded in satisfaction: "Nothing organically wrong with you." He could see that I was very weak, a bundle of nerves, he said, so it was no surprise that I felt so bad, but otherwise he was satisfied and said, as he prescribed a restorative and wrote out instructions for extra monthly rations of butter, milk, and eggs, that I was surprisingly healthy and in good shape, and that I should see the poor devils that came to him. Above all, this stiffened my will, which always fought against sickness, and I told myself, "You survived, now it's your responsibility to be healthy." That's how I thought, for I didn't think of myself as war wounded. No matter how much I deceived myself about my condition and overestimated my staying power, I recognized first that I was in the metropolis, in unfamiliar though fervently sought-after surroundings that had more to offer me than I could handle. I felt stress that I'd never felt before, nor through any measures or any amount of rest was I able to assuage it. Even though my condition had previously been in question, now it was destroyed. This I saw clearly, sensing it and yet not daring to admit it, nor allowing others to take notice of it. I was afraid that my frailty would harm me in the eyes of others and ruin my prospects. If one was going to be amazed, it made more sense to consider how well I had come through it, and to such talk I simply smiled and felt flattered. I didn't like the weather, I found the food terrible, I could never get enough sleep or sleep well, the way of life bothered me, which is why I constantly felt under a stress that threatened to do me in. Now I was lost in the middle of a sad building, in a strange stairwell, where I had not come in search of anything, office hours now over as well, while in the stairwell there slumbered an uncomfortable and awful stillness that caused my inner unease to hammer on all the more.

I couldn't stay here forever, so I had to decide something. If nothing better occurred to me, then I had to sit on a step and wait until someone came along and helped me. Eventually Fräulein Zinner would have to lose patience and leave the building, which gave me hope that she would find me, unless she used another stairwell that I didn't know about. What would happen to me then I didn't dare think about. She was prepared to welcome a difficult guest (though who knew what had moved her to do so, perhaps a moment of compassion), though she wasn't at all prepared for a patient who would have to be tended to and who could not go to dinner. She would stand before me, tall and strange, her head lifted up high and above the protective scarf, though from my perspective, bent down and somewhat bewildered, perhaps even repulsed, myself indeed small and meek before her, a cowering puppy on the stairs. I couldn't allow myself to sit there. I gathered myself together and had already decided for sure to mount the last floor, no matter the cost, but the steps rose higher than my feet and wouldn't bow to my weakness. I had to querulously acknowledge my powerlessness and rest awhile longer to gather my strength and attack the devilish ascent.

I leaned against the window, but I was immediately shocked to find that the paint did not stick to it but instead came off in washed-out flecks that stuck to my jacket. Thus I could no longer lean against it and had to try to wipe the nasty traces from my jacket, but neither rubbing nor swatting at them seemed to work. Like spongy flour, they attached themselves to the fibers of the fabric. While saying a quick prayer, I sought release from my plight, but it hardly eased me, my pleas crumbling to nothing, unfortunately useless. Then I sought refuge again on the landing and clung to it with both hands, my gaze wandering cockeyed over the wall, following its surface halfway up to the next floor. Graffiti, scrawled in pencil or scratched out with knives or nails, waited for the absolving hand of whoever might paint the room, the names and monograms obliterated and painted over which sat here unused and pointless, probably inscribed by those in search of something, having seen their day, a beginning without end, even in the double strangeness of an international bureau for refugees and its search office, perhaps posting a silent request—as I had once been told back there in the Office for Returnees—passing searchers who wanted to know that not everything was lost, there were some who had been saved and were found again, the harvest of gentle patience, just once, after many years, indeed.

I decided to try to find this stairwell during daylight in the next few days, once I again felt better, in order to carefully explore the graffiti from the ground floor to the top. It certainly made no sense to do so, but such never-resting desire could be just the thing to provide an enticing sustenance. There were so many people once known and yet forgotten, the mention of their names enough to bring them back, and that could indeed be good. They exist, they exist, even strangers exist, and it's comforting to know they exist; one should know them and gather them and humbly commemorate the signs they left behind, this being perhaps a first step toward self-awareness. Names written down—oh, the courage of avowal, where all the others have already fled—then to bow before the wall of life and in hasty humility offer up that they exist, when indeed they no longer exist, stumbling up and down the stairs in further flight, now indeed more prepared for their own passing, since with bold recklessness they have inscribed their names. Trembling, I pulled a pencil from my pocket, a worn-down stub from who knows where. Wait, now I remember that, absentmindedly, I had taken it from the phone booth of my guesthouse, a stubby thing that was useless, though here it was, me staggering to the wall, bending over and getting down on my knees, for I wanted to be way down, down where it hadn't even occurred to the others to search for a spot, where the wall was only marked by thoughtless feet, that being where I scribbled it ever so slowly, nothing but an "A," a big clumsy "A." Then I let the stub fall, it being no longer of any use to me or to anyone else, rolling away, at first slowly, then a bit faster, nearing the landing where I expected there would be some resistance, but the gap between the flooring and the iron bars of the landing that ran below was large enough to let it pass through, soon rolling on and disappearing, floating on air, though I couldn't see it but instead felt it, a soundless flight down through the stairwell of the Search Office, a message descending from the dreaming Adam, me listening and finally hearing it hit, two times, one right after the other, it likely having hit and bounced up, the horror of such a fall wishing to occur twice in one life. But then it was over—stillness, nothing moving and the porter in his cell hadn't heard a thing, or it simply didn't worry him. He had seen too much in his job already to ever be frightened by a mere thought.

I pulled myself up and felt a pang in my hips, but I staggered over to the landing, though I didn't look down; I hadn't lost anything, my head feeling heavy. Then something rattled; it could have been the wind or something rustling in my ears, perhaps someone opening a door. I can hardly describe the alarm it set off inside me. All I could do was smile about my flight of fancy, for it was only an illusion and not an incident, or an incident in the most hopelessly serious sense, myself again aware that everything had collapsed, the stairwell empty and fallen. I had done nothing, yet all of it was burned out, no flooring and no roof, only an empty shell, a flourishing space amid nightmarish growth extending to the wounded ends of the universe, and something there within it, unfathomably small and lost, almost nothing, only the shiftless tiniest trace of a past without a home anywhere in the world. Then I no longer looked at the markings and names that I had not read, nor did I even look at my own "A," which could have been just three scratches, a chance rune, nothing in particular and nothing worth bothering about, no "A," it already having been sucked into the filthy cloud of dust and covered over, gone. No, I had done nothing. It rose high above me, the steps finally carrying me up, always very steep, though they held my step, and as the first two lifted me upward, they did so more easily than I expected. Above, steps could be heard, me feeling premature joy as I was still far below, for it was just an echo, those not being my steps. Then I looked up and heard her voice, not at all impatient but instead full of calm assurance, but friendly, and tinged with only a touch of concern.

"What took you so long? I called down again and then came out to look for you."

"I'm coming!" I called with a breaking voice.

It sounded more uncertain than I wanted it to, so I tried to make up for this bad impression by quickly bounding up the stairs two at a time. Fräulein Zinner stood there in her hat and coat, her purse under her arm.

"You don't have to hurry anymore!"

Her response disappointed me, for why had I exerted myself so? I didn't want to say anything in return, yet when she started to come down the steps toward me her heels sounded loud and I was bitterly affected. I was also scared by the thought that I would immediately have to go through the adventure of the stairwell again. Although this time I would be headed down the stairs and accompanied by someone, at the moment it felt like too much.

"No, no! Please, no! Wait there! I'll come up!"

I said that with such pressing and beseeching urgency that she stopped and could do nothing but stop and do as I asked.

"Well, as you wish. We can sit for a while in my office."

"Yes, please! That's the reason I asked."

I don't know how I managed to stumble upward—perhaps through some kind of magic, for certainly not through my own strength—myself almost stumbling head over heels, my legs having dragged themselves along and barely lifting one after the other over the steps. Reeling and exhausted, I felt that I knew what it was like to be left for dead. I couldn't stand on my feet, and as a distraction I extended my hand, though in truth I really did it in order to seek support, which she returned too slowly for my needs and gripped too softly.

"Good evening!" I rasped, and saw that she didn't understand me. "Please, do forgive me for being so shamefully late!"

"It wasn't so bad," she replied, somewhat distracted.

She wanted to let go of my hand, but I grabbed her more tightly in order that she see that, at the moment, I couldn't yet relinquish her help.

"It wasn't so bad that you have to excuse yourself that much. In these parts, we don't make such a big deal about such things."

"I haven't gotten used to that yet. I'm totally inexperienced. Totally! Where, indeed, might your office be?"

"Do you feel all right, Herr Landau? Your hands are cold and damp."

"No, I'm fine. Forgive me! I'll be all right in a minute. A bit faint. Please, your office. Maybe sit for a while. Very, very weak."

Fräulein Zinner took me under the arm and carried me more than I walked along myself to her office door. Here she had to let go of me in order to get the key from her pocket, but I held on to her shoulder, my only wish being to sit down. She unlocked the door, turned on the light, after which I sat or nearly lay down on a chair. It was uncomfortable and pressed at me. She looked at me seriously and with such extreme pity that it shook me and made me tremble inside. I turned to her sharply and yet beseechingly.

"Don't worry so, and just give me a minute! Everything will soon be all right!"

She turned on a space heater and pushed it closer to me.

"Many thanks! But I don't need it. I feel warm, much too warm."

"Do you have a fever? What's wrong with you?"

"Nothing, nothing at all! Just give me five minutes! You'll see, everything will be better! It was just the stairs, believe me. Really!"

From my hand Fräulein Zinner took the hat that I had absentmindedly played with, and then I managed to free myself from the oppressive jacket without standing up. She then took the jacket as well. I quietly let her do so. My hostess said nothing. The quiet pleased me, and slowly the whizzing inside my head calmed down, the cold sweat ending, my heart not beating as fast as earlier. I stroked my hair to straighten it out, as it had again fallen into disarray, and blinked feebly at the garish globes that suffused the room with an almost consistently strong light, but which didn't bother me. Fräulein Zinner moved to sit down in a corner, which I observed without interest, though even if I didn't care what she was doing, I did nonetheless note that she moved around with some glasses, pouring something into them, busying herself with a tin cup, then with a plate or a little dish on which she laid something, most likely a dry roll. When she came over to me, I forced myself to look in another direction and heard a second chair being shoved around and a tray placed upon it.

"Can I offer you something?" she whispered. "It will help you feel better."

Then I turned toward her, though I didn't look at what she was offering.

"You really are making too much of a fuss. I'm feeling better already."

"You may be better, but you haven't been well for some time."

"You know that?"

"Of course."

She lifted up a glass, indicating that I was to take it. It was full of red wine, sweet, but too much so, and strong. I drank it all down slowly, without setting the glass down.

"That will warm you up. That's it."

She took the glass from me and filled it again. I waved my hand and she understood, setting the glass down. Then she handed me a little plate with some glistening sugary cookies. I took one, broke it in two, and chewed slowly.

"Now I'm healthy as a horse!"

In order to prove it, I tried to stand; I certainly could have done so, but it wasn't allowed.

"We're in no rush. You'll feel better in half an hour."

Then I made myself more comfortable, smoothing out the pleats of my pants as best I could, as well as my shirt, and ran my hands to the right and left of my collar. Then it occurred to me to feel whether the knot of the poor tie had held or loosened. I poked at it and everything seemed to be fine. It only bothered me that my behavior was so unsuitable, as my outfit could hardly go unnoticed. Therefore I had to say something as a distraction.

"The tie is old, but hardly ever worn. A tie that pleases me. It's from before the war, just imagine!"

"Here most people only have old things, often many years old. Even the natives. It's not easy to buy things; people have to economize."

"You don't understand."

"I'm sorry!"

"No matter. Whatever one owns here and is old, at least you've always had it. Nothing is interrupted, all your own things, a consistent string of time wonderfully split up into days, even if it were a thousand. Now do you understand?"

Yes, she understood and, with lips barely moving, she asked my forgiveness.

"No, that's not necessary. You couldn't know all that. Back there and here, everything is so different."

"I know that, and yet I don't know it well enough, for I have never known and have never known enough. That's the main reason I wanted to get to know you. You see, I've talked to a lot of people and have read a lot, but the picture I have gotten from it all isn't enough. I've heard about how many horrible things happened, but it's not enough to simply describe the horrible; it doesn't say enough, it's dishonest, perhaps even unintentionally distorted. The truth must have been different. Not the horrible, but rather the human amid the horrible, is what's important. Isn't that so? I had hoped that you would know a lot about these things, and I hope you can share them with me."

I looked at her doubtfully.

"I know you can share some of it to some extent, certainly you can. Everything that I know is not enough. I'm sure of that."

Since I said nothing, Fräulein Zinner talked on.

"I have the feeling that you've been through a lot because of how you've been shaken to the core. And you seem to me to be truthful and talkative."

"Talkative . . . well, yes. Perhaps too much so. But truthful? That I can't judge. Though I do try my best."

"That's what I mean. My urge to tend to misfortune—you understand how I mean that, don't you?—is what pushes me to take on this hopeless and thankless job. It's all so lifeless. And it's good that they will soon dissolve the

Bureau for Refugees, which our Search Office is a part of. The lease is up next summer, and it won't be renewed."

"What will happen to this big building?"

"It was once a hotel. Hotel Ivanhoe. Maybe someone will open it up as a hotel again."

"As a hotel . . ." I said absentmindedly.

"Maybe not, but they say so. It doesn't matter to us."

"But what do you do here besides close down the place, if I may ask?"

"I work on the card file of refugees with two other girls and a man who oversees us. The card file is supposed to be cleared up and closed down. Then it will be taken to another institution, where it will be stored."

"What is this card file? I can hardly imagine."

"Names, names. Anyone who has ever come to the Bureau for Refugees for advice, help, support, placement, or made an inquiry has to give his personal information—not to me here but rather at the other offices—and then this material comes up to us, is checked over, edited for all its statistical information, and then filed. I can tell you, it's somewhat dismal work, but perhaps still the best to be had here."

"Yet a lot gets done?"

"Illusions. Paper. Almost all just paper. Big words. Lots of activity. Names with hardly any people attached to them. The people were sent away, and all that's left is the names. But I can see that saddens you, and perhaps I've put it too bitterly. When there's too much hate for one's neighbor rather than love, then such a bureau as ours is needed, and in the end something good does appear to come from all the waste of paper."

"Tell me more!"

"There's no lack of good will, but paper is stronger. It only uses names and dates, gulping them down insatiably, like a gristmill, and life, as a result, ends up too short, indeed ground to bits. That's why we have the Search Office, which is why I'm there. There the names are consulted, and sometimes a miracle happens that rewards all our efforts. A brother finds a sister, even entire families come back together. I'm egotistical enough that I have made this my main job, while my colleagues sink themselves much more into the paperwork than I do. I can only think that they just don't feel as much pressure as I do. They're happy when everything on the page is in order and the Search Office has its role in making it so. Thus the paper finally does, in fact, come to life. We also have open office hours, where we give out information on names and addresses. Fates hang upon them. How empty our card file seems when people come to me to ask and to beg for information about their next of kin, and the cards are blanks and cannot help or advise. Eyes empty out before me, behind them nothing but raw despair or simply disbelief that erects itself against disappointing news, and then the request to look through the cards themselves. If there's enough time, I let them, if only to assuage their mistrust, although it's always pointless, because, first of all, our cards are not in such great order, and second, they are of no help to the person roaming around in search of someone with no peace to be had. Disappointment only rises in ever greater amounts when this senseless search produces no results, when similar names confuse people, until finally they grow bitter and either break down or consume themselves with blustering complaints about what a hopeless system we have, or something worse. I patiently let it roll over me, because I hope that it will ease the misfortunate a bit, but my colleagues do nothing of the sort, choosing instead to complain that their lovely card file is now a mess, mauled and marked up by dirty fingers. Indeed, visitors are not allowed to peek into the card file, so my boss officially doesn't know anything about it. He puts up with it, but silently so, and only because I have often pressed hard at his conscience."

"And what do you do with people when everything looks hopeless and pointless?"

"I send them to our researchers. There they tie them up with long forms that are filled out in detail. Or I tell them to try the Red Cross and other organizations. Then the people head off. Some of them leave without even saying goodbye, though I don't blame them."

I then asked to see the card file. Fräulein Zinner wanted to pull out one of the heaviest drawers from the iron cabinet, but I couldn't let her do that and got up in spite of her protests and walked over to her.

"Do you really feel better?" she asked with anxious doubt.

"But of course. How many times must I tell you that it really was nothing at all. I should have put off my visit to another day. It wasn't right for me not to consider my weariness, forgive me, and then on top of that the many steps as well."

"Oh, what do you mean 'put off'! We've already put off too much, and that alone is half the reason for our unhappiness!"

Fräulein Zinner didn't want to hear any apologies from me, but instead just wanted to figure out whether I really was better and didn't need further assistance. She doubted my claims, but I stood up firmly, stretching my back and lifting my head in order to reassure her strongly inquisitive gaze.

"Well, you do seem better. But I'm not entirely pleased, for you are pale to the bones."

"I'm always that way. Even as a child. My mother—"

"You looked better at the Haarburgers'."

"I hate to disappoint you; it was only the light."

Fräulein Zinner could see that she couldn't say anything more without upsetting and embarrassing me. She let me have a look in the open drawers, where the cards were arranged according to some kind of system that she indeed explained to me, but which I nevertheless didn't understand, all of them neatly mounted and movable on metal rails. They could also be lifted halfway out without being removed from the drawer, though with a bit of manipulation they were easily taken out. The cards were numbered, and on each of them there were last names, first names, names of wives or husbands, names of parents and children, addresses, changes of address, old addresses, occupations former and current, dates and data from different countries, many coded symbols I didn't understand, though Fräulein Zinner explained them readily, and then more numbers, crosses, stars, and notes, many of them written down in red ink, a bare graveyard with names and, invisibly behind it, a life and its twin life of worry, sorrow, hope, madness, glowing passion, pale disenchantment, and, yes, also illness, odors such as Lysol or chloroform, befogged, full of anxiety, and then death: a startling coldness in each card, unreal, belonging to no one, not of the present, but not of the past in any troubling way. In addition, everything was much too ethereal and mute, a finger running over them as well as uncertain and questioning glances, all of it set down cold in metallic type, the black letters of the machine pressing into the white flesh.

"How can you stand it here?" I asked impolitely. As if wanting to take back these rude words, I added in a great huff, "Of course, it's your job."

Fräulein Zinner deliberately ignored this platitude, having already not paid any attention at all to my previous lack of tact.

"Now you can see for yourself," she said simply.

I turned away from the cards and looked around at Fräulein Zinner's desk. Behind glass and simple frames were five pictures: the father, serious and slim, the eyes coolly observing, yet full of good will and sympathy, the look of a doctor, while the mother was slightly hunched, somewhat rotund, diligent, homely and plain, though also lively and keen. Fräulein Zinner looked much more like her father. Comparing them, I nodded to her.

"Was he a doctor?"

"Yes, heart and lungs. Very much loved. They're the last pictures of both of them that were sent on."

Parents sent on? I was startled and grabbed hold of the desk hard.

"Always right here as you work. Except when you have to turn to the card file, and, of course, when you deal with visitors, not then as well."

What I said made no sense. It was the shock alone, the anxiety that rose at the thought that there were dead parents in the photos.

"The resemblance is strong. And they died in their own due time."

Why had I said that? Fräulein Zinner's disclosures at the Haarburgers' had been clear. That I had now spoken of the resemblance was not at all reflected in the look Fräulein Zinner gave me, even though just the resemblance of the photos was what I meant, the belief pressing through doubt that photos can at all be similar to those depicted, that one can at all recognize or acknowledge someone in a picture: that, in fact, that is who they are or were. Names like to be remembered—they exist in memory or are preserved in letters, but what resemblance do they bear to people? Names can attest, but as symbols they lack the power to stand up to the figure they are supposed to fulfill. Pictures, on the contrary, are at the very least vicarious symbols of living figures.

"More like the father," said Fräulein Zinner somewhat admonishingly.

"Yes, indeed the father. But also the mother. In short, similar. One can have similar features."

"Are you surprised by that?"

"Yes, it's surprising. For what is similar is also familiar, the 'familiar' being something handed down through the family, and thus what leads to what is similar in the familiar. But that's another matter. I'm only talking about the pictures and you. The link between you is the similarity in your looks, and that is almost overpowering, for I can hardly believe it. Yet I don't mean to talk about that, either, just about the pictures. You said the pictures are similar to how they looked?"

"Yes, very much so."

"That's lovely and remarkable. It must give you a great deal of peace."

"How so? What do you mean?"

"I mean, you have your parents. Over there in the card file, no one has anyone. There are statements there, perhaps correct statements, but nothing more. What one can get from them you explained so yourself. But 'pictures talk' when they bear a similar resemblance. We had pictures at the museum, and so I know. There it was exactly the same, and in most cases we didn't know the names at all. An unknown man, an unknown woman, an unknown child. Clearly unknown, and that's painful enough in itself. But still there, and better to be unknown rather than to have disappeared with nothing but names cut loose. That's the way it is—do you understand? And now these pictures rest here on your desk. Memories assure you. What luck! Hence you still have your parents and don't have any doubts about ever having had parents."

"My friend, they could still be alive!"

"That's exactly right. The parents at one time could have been alive, but they can no longer. That is for sure. Oh, the ones who still have them! The difference is threadbare, but important. Nearly a comfort. You yourself said it crassly just a while ago: obliterated!"

Fräulein Zinner began to cry.

"Forgive me, sometimes I'm too harsh. But not coldhearted, certainly not coldhearted."

"Who said you were? Please don't get upset. I won't say anything more."

"Say something! You must."

"Really, you think so? That's very kind of you."

"Don't you feel the same?"

"Of course."

"Yes, that's exactly how it is. Only through language can we fend off danger. Though that's not quite right, for that which is overpowering cannot be fended off, only secured, ascertained, so that it is defined, thereby allowing life to be a bit more furtive amid the unknown. Only through language can we conjure, can we try to save something. We want a house, a home, a life between four walls where we are protected and can hide, such that we will not—and here's the main point—be called upon by the unknown, which takes us off guard by asking, Where are you? The desire to escape speaks to what I call, not entirely to my satisfaction, the fending off of danger or the unknown. It would be more correct to say to 'avert the overpowering.' We must therefore speak in order not to be continually asked, to be continually threatened. And thus I have explained to you, indeed, why language interests me."

"What does that all have to do with dead parents?"

"At least your parents are dead."

"That's bad enough for me."

"But dead for sure! Do you know what that means, Fräulein Zinner? Most likely they are buried somewhere!"

"Yes, in the cemetery. There's not much solace in that."

"Solace . . . Who would dare to use such a big word? Certainly no solace, and that's for sure. But a place. One that you can go to."

"I don't want to."

"That's different. No one is asking you to. But you can. This lack of solace, which I don't want to make more comforting, because it remains lamentable, doesn't deny all solace, for it is indeed a certainty. First the parents died—you have reliable information; you know the date of death or you can find out and then the dead were buried, in a cemetery, where you can find the spot. Thus there is a place where the dead clearly are, where they have come to rest, their grave, having found their last resting place, or whatever you wish to call it. It's not at all strange. You should be very grateful for it!"

"Consequently, when I think about what you're saying, consequently you're right. But only consequently."

"Fine, consequently. And that's again something key. That is, also consequently, already the start of some kind of solace."

"It's so hard!"

"A whiner! You said you were a whiner."

"Do you notice everything anyone says?"

"Actually not, only very, very little. I have a bad memory."

"That doesn't seem to be so."

"Indeed, it is. Make no mistake about it, Fräulein Zinner. There are only a few things that I can recall precisely. Not really things but rather their scope, a kind of network. A memory for structures is what I call it. Hard to fathom, no? Let me explain. I mean, a memory for the relationship between things, for the dense interweaving of experience. I cannot forget any of that at all. But no memory for the phenomenal, for the eventful, the singular, the precise. Or only for single moments of clarity among the incalculable number of single incidents out of which I preserve the spirit of the relationship between them, really the structure. That grants me a certain continuance from day to day, which at least makes it bearable but also turns all of life into a burden, an agony. If I dispense with all the experiences that are comprehensible, and with whose help I can find my bearings amid the flurry of time, then it's awful, and lost with it are those moments of clarity. Then I don't know whether something is or is not. There can indeed be a means to replace the moments of clarity or even to fabricate them, and if I have that, then all the better, because then I can convince myself that they are not false, that they really exist. Again a small comfort, or at least the start of one, when one has something like this. Do I—well, I've already said so. The means is, namely, possessions, as possessions serve and support memory; also, the strongest of memories is supported by possessions and is in fact built upon them. A strong memory, however, is the true cornerstone on which human life is built. For then it is built solid as a wall. Without it everything collapses into rubble and is not even questionable, like the most miserable of lives, but, rather, worth nothing."

"That's right, but you are alive. What do you really need to own?"

"You think we disagree?"

"I mean, all you need is life."

"We disagree, it seems to me. You have something when you possess something. I didn't at all say that I do not possess anything. If that were true, then I wouldn't be alive. Yet besides life—one might even say, more precisely, naked life—well, besides that I have shockingly little to feed and clothe this life. More precise would be to say 'to support this life.' Hence it's a meager life, one of privation. Do you have any idea how hard that is?"

"You're not complaining about how poor you are, if I understand you right. But I don't understand much more than that. You're thinking of what's irrecoverable."

"Right. Irrecoverable possessions. Ineffable things. The indications that there is something, or was, which either doesn't exist or only in memory, and that is uncertain, for even the best memory is unreliable and can hardly make up for what has been lost. Something that you possess, even when you do really own nothing. Fräulein Zinner, think of the very value that one possesses. 'Value'—just, consider for a moment what this word means. It lies at the center of the sociology of oppressed people that I have formulated."

"Wouldn't you like to tell me more about it?"

"Really? May I?"

"But of course!"

"Human dignity involves the material and immaterial sanctioning of value, as proscribed by society, and guaranteed by it. The complete fulfillment of this dignity rises from the optimal freedom from oppression. An oppressed man is one whose external or internal value is denied or withdrawn. The starker and more immediate this withdrawal, the less free the person. Disenfranchisement and exploitation, bondage and slavery are made manifest through the clear withdrawal of value, though the slave need not be robbed of all dignity or value, which are the same. On the other hand, someone who was once enslaved or in some other way oppressed cannot, through the easing or abandonment of his social conditions, ever again replace the value denied with one that is in part completely fabricated, for it is in essence irretrievable; it can never thus be found again. That is the tragedy of oppression; entirely irrespective of one's psychology, its marks are in all cases indelible when in the course of one's life it is significantly intensified. This happens especially through the withdrawal of attention or other measures that socially uproot the oppressed. If one is born into oppression and attains during the course of his life more dignity and value, as well as possessions, such that he is granted more rights, then that's different. Thus only alone does one achieve a greater freedom from oppression. Society is a system of value; the social order is an ordering of value. Freedom in a society depends on how it is achieved, what kind of awarding of value its own members experience, whether it's maintained equally or unequally, whether groups are different or roughly the same. A fundamentally equal and unified awarding of value for all members of a society would indeed need to be declared programmatically and in a constitution, though that has never happened. However, history has often shown the willingness to withdraw value from individuals or, much more frequently, from entire groups, and indeed in the many different kinds of societies that have been formulated. But I feel as if I am now delivering a lecture, and that's not right."

"Oh, I'm very grateful to you for explaining it to me so fundamentally. I'm afraid I'm just not the best audience for it. I feel I just don't deserve it."

"Now you're mocking me."

"No. I use words quite simply, in an everyday manner. I don't know very much about sociology or other disciplines. But, please, you look so sad again. . . . Please don't be. At least believe me when I say that I have the greatest respect for what you're sharing with me."

"And these are . . . were they your brothers?"

"Yes. That's Richard, and that is Eli. His proper name was Elias, like his grandfather. But he was called Eli. Father thought Elias sounded too heavy."

Fräulein Zinner picked up the picture of Eli as a boy and blew away a speck from the frame; it was probably a tiny bread crumb that had fallen there as a lost victim. Eli, the little one, upon whom the house had collapsed at the end of the school vacation, didn't need anything to eat. His sister was right to run a cloth over the glass in order to make it shine. Lost crumbs of bread pained one too much. Wipe it all away. It had been rude of me to so carelessly lecture, useless arrogance, but my abrupt shift to the dead siblings was a hideous way out. How could I be so unkind! I couldn't get rid of this wretched feeling as I clawed at my hair in an ugly fashion. That was embarrassing, for it must have looked awful, not to mention the sound of scratching, just like an ape. It occurred to me that my hair must look badly rumpled; that was the price for my sins. And then the vanity! With both hands I smoothed out my hair, while it would have been best to pull out my pocket comb, but I left it, feeling that I had already done enough damage. Fräulein Zinner took it all in stride, feeling that I didn't deserve all this and speaking out of forgiveness.

"You get so dirty in the city. Here you can mention that you have a spot of soot on you, for no one gets upset. It's not at all ill-mannered."

"Yes, so much soot, and yet so little coal."

She had placed the picture of the boy Eli next to his brother, Richard, again and shifted it around for a bit, as if it was particularly hard to set it down in precisely the same spot. She wasn't being at all pedantic, but it felt like that to me; I pulled myself together in order to hide my disapproval, because Fräulein Zinner was suffering, her cheeks tired and lank, and then there was the dead brother, who deserved some small act of care. I could not transgress by showing any disapproval or discomfort, for commemorating the dead was to be honored, as was the memory of the dead. Just be, it occurred to me, just stand here, for I feared that I would seem too mawkish. Such senseless thoughts weighed me down. I pulled myself together in order to get hold of myself.

"That's also a family picture."

What I said was so shamefully dumb that I really did have to shift my demeanor and make it seem as if I meant it in an uninhibited manner. I reached out my hand, grabbed hold of the group portrait, and held it up in front of me. But even up close there was not much to see, all of it blurry, nothing at all to see, memory failing the contemplated picture, and therefore it no longer revealed anything, just a gray shadow, perhaps twilight, with light and dark flecks. I blinked in order to awaken my dreaming eyes, which worked, for there stood the picture again in its place, nor had I even picked it up. Why hadn't I? All I had to do was handle it in a concerned fashion in order to be nice, Fräulein Zinner expecting me to do so, which she had a right to, though I didn't give the slightest indication of doing so. Instead, I looked sharply at it, but without picking up the picture. The children were still small—Richard eight and Eli two, the sister around eleven— all of them frozen in their childhood, standing unchangeable outside of time, as if freedom were seized hold of in an eternal moment, though it was no freedom at all. An altogether different Zinner family, the daughter transformed, but still there, the others dead, buried memories that didn't belong to me; how terrible to be surrounded by the dead! Eli fidgeting and irritable in his mother's lap, she who only wanted a keepsake for her children. Richard leaning against his father, young and alert and conscious of the photographer, the father having the same expression as the later picture, just fresher and not so serious. In the middle stood a bashful smile full of hopeful expectation, playing the violin, the young girl standing between the parents, curls hanging on each side with little bows at the end.

"So it can sit here before you each day for you to look at. It doesn't bother you, and it's pleasant for you."

Fräulein Zinner looked at me as if she didn't know whether she should feel sorry for me or for herself.

"Usually I don't bother to explain what I say," I quickly explained. "Yet I need to make myself more clear. I mean, it must be hard to look at, your loved ones, but it doesn't bother you because you have to and want to. Indeed, that's also a rudimentary kind of solace."

"I never am free of it. There's nothing else. The past and serving others. Isn't there a prayer that begins with 'Consider . . .'? I don't know much, but I always say something that begins with 'Consider. . . .' Then I receive a reply, quite simply: 'Serve!' And that's how it goes: Consider that you serve others, and serve others so that you consider what it means. No, I can't ignore the past. I need to serve."

"You shouldn't ignore anything, Fräulein Zinner, if it doesn't go away naturally. You're right to follow that. You're also right if you believe that it won't go away, for that's the reason we reflect. I don't have any pictures of my parents."

I paused. She looked at me searchingly, moved her lips, but said nothing.

"No picture of my parents, nor of any of my relatives. I was given so many things, most of which I had no idea about; no picture was among them. That's the way it is. Which is why I earlier said so much about your pictures. There's so much to be observed and discovered among everyday things. I don't have such rudimentary kinds of comfort. I don't know the place or the day of my parents' death. Somewhere in the east. No need to try to look it up, I was told, there's no point in trying. Thus I don't know whether they are alive or not, even though I am certain that they were killed, that they are gone. But it's all so unknown. That's what I meant."

Fräulein Zinner turned over the pictures such that they lay on their backs on the desktop. I couldn't allow that, so I carefully stood them up again.

"You really shouldn't do that. Thank the eternal ones that you have these pictures; it's a blessing. If you actually think I am capable of envying you in the slightest because of them, then please throw me out!"

I went over to the coat rack where Fräulein Zinner had hung up my things, took down my coat, and slipped into it. She was pale as a ghost, didn't pay any more attention to the pictures, and stared at me intensely as she leaned against the desk, an arm arched behind her for support.

"Herr Landau, you're right, if you'll allow me to say so. I deserved that. I'm being egotistical and thinking only of myself. But you're welcome to go of your own free will, not because I shoved something onto you."

"And you want to stay here?" I asked sadly with my hat in my hand. "Come along with me!"

"May I really?"

"You should! You invited me."

She seemed relieved, her demeanor relaxed, but she still didn't stir from the desk, and looked at me uncertainly.

"Shall we go?" I asked encouragingly.

"Are you really feeling all right now?"

I had to smile, and wanted to say, "You are a dear, sweet child." But I held back.

"I feel just fine. If you were to look a bit more happy, it would make me feel even stronger."

Then at last she smiled, stepped closer to me, and held her purse in her hand. Then she remembered something and cleared away the tray with all its things, at which I had to empty a half-full glass of wine. After that, the chair and anything that would remind one of my visit had to be straightened out. The only thing Fräulein Zinner had missed was the card file. I walked over to the drawers and was about to close them, but my effort failed miserably. I laughed while motioning apologetically, and Fräulein Zinner laughed even louder as she rushed to help. One shove and the drawers were effortlessly shut. There then seemed nothing left to prevent our leaving, though at the last moment she discovered that my coat was dirty.

"You must have rubbed up against something somewhere. I can brush that away in a snap."

"Yes, the wall. There are traces left there. I leaned against it."

She walked over to a cabinet, returned with a fabric brush, and scrubbed hard at me, but the spots were stubborn and impossible to get out.

"The wall must have been wet. I'm afraid I'm not having much luck at getting them out. The coat will dry out overnight, as long as it doesn't rain. Then with a dry brush you can easily sweep away all the dust granules. Do you have a brush, Herr Landau? You can take this one."

I had to laugh again, and assure her that I owned a brush, but that I could be a bad boy who didn't take good care of his things. Then I was made to promise to make sure not to forget to clean my coat first thing the next morning. Then, finally, we left. We quickly descended the stairs; our steps echoed, but that didn't bother me, and I was happy to leave the Ivanhoe building and its Search Office. We also didn't stop to greet the porter, as was normally done when leaving work; I was afraid that Fräulein Zinner would get caught up in conversation with him again.

The darkness in the streets seemed to have grown more dense, and it was colder as well. Soon we had walked in so many different directions that I no longer knew where we were. I felt uncertain and extended my good will and faith to my companion. I would have to do anything she asked me to, for I was too defenseless to resist the slightest attack. Yet why did I think anything bad would happen? I could just run away from her and immediately disappear into the dark, after which I would be able to find my way and ask someone for directions. After all, I had an address, a room in a guesthouse for which I had paid, and so because of that there was no reason to be anxious. No one lets those who pay in this world perish; no one leaves them alone, and they are taken care of much sooner than those who are miserable, who have to beg for what they need, but who have no shelter and therefore remain lost.

What idle anxiety I allowed to overcome me instead of patiently trusting someone who meant well! Fräulein Zinner really did mean well, and she knew where she was going and had a restaurant in mind, so it was up to her to get us there without any digressions. She was headed the right way, and there was no need to worry, not now, for everything was out of my hands. The endlessly confusing city had, under the protection of a savvy guide, lost its power over me; thus I could let myself be led, clandestine and clueless, through any area. I would have liked to talk, but since my companion remained silent I didn't say a word as I walked through the strange streets. It was better to know that she was near, right next to me, than to just pay attention to what she was saying, which would hardly have put me at ease in the accumulating darkness but instead made me anxious. She was me. Because this was so, I had to take care, nor could I endanger this subtle dependency with any kind of provocation that would suddenly break it. Once, I stumbled so clumsily at an intersection while stepping down from the sidewalk onto the street that my ankle cracked and I felt a stabbing pain rise up my leg that was not awful but irritating. I didn't say anything to Fräulein Zinner, yet she drew closer and took my arm, very gently yet firmly, just like a nurse helping a convalescent with his first steps.

And so we moved on. I don't know how long we walked. It could be that it was not long, but it seemed endless to me, the way my feet unswervingly pressed on ahead while my body remained behind or slowly followed, much heavier and more inept than my eager feet, though my head was the heaviest as it glowed in the cold, unable to keep up with the reduced speed of the torso, such that the unfortunate skull almost fell all the way back, an unwitting stranger who was being dragged along unwillingly. Poor head, which was hardly made for such strain and which would have been grateful just to be left alone, it being better to have a carefree rest than to have to suffer such wanderlust. Finally it succeeded, the head remaining alone as the body and limbs plowed on through the storm of haphazard streets without stopping and finally—who knows where?—sank into the far distance. The head, however, leisurely followed its own path. It didn't need to figure out where it was amid the dense streets, neither here nor in a different city, it needing such a small little spot that it always found one, able to hide itself in the narrowest of corners in order to wait for what doesn't come, and then, contrary to expectations, it does; or, at least, not exactly what is expected is there but nonetheless something that could be expected and indeed was at least as good as what was expected. The head indeed didn't have to expect anything, not once, and therefore could do many things, such as forget or be forgotten. Who worries about a head that only marginally and harmlessly lives and has no body? No one bothers with such a thing, for even an attentive street sweeper would, at the most, smile, though it wouldn't occur to him to toss a lonely strange head into the rubbish.

I was a self-sufficient head that needed nothing, only a feeling of weakness overtaking me, although I stayed quiet and rested on a soft spot. It was too soft, I soon noticed without alarm, because I sank into it, and because of this descent I couldn't hang on with either my mouth or my eyelids, as at first they could hardly move and soon not at all, nor could I shove my tongue between my lips, the wall of teeth closing before it, the tongue growing ever more dry and sticking hard to the gums. It was then that I felt all was lost. Such a head could not live for long, too quickly having been cocksure to be able to live without a body. It was all over; it had been too stubborn and too gullible, and as a price it had to die. Yet in a last moment of despair it braced itself against perdition, the memory of the head of the executed anatomist Jessenius causing a ray of hope to flare up, since it is said that his friend the executioner immediately placed the head on the severed body and then the mouth opened, though it didn't release another word. But in following this particular example the head ripped open its mouth and managed to call out, loud and clear, the ears hearing, "Franziska!"

Then the eyelids managed to open. I could see, I lay there, and I could feel my body again nearby, including the limbs, still severed, yet near, almost attached, everything healed, only far off and deep a pain that stabbed in the foot or the knee, the memory of a fall surfacing—yesterday, I must have fallen, sometime yesterday, on a street in a city. Yet if it was all collected together, healed or unhealed, that bothered me less, if only it was so. I still didn't dare believe it to be true, for it had all dissipated to such a degree, and I could feel so little and so dully. I still needed to wait it out until everything awoke together. But I could see around me and even turn my head, the room appearing to me at once strange and familiar. Franziska was nowhere to be found. I could have called out for her again, but I grasped that she wasn't there. Instead of her there moved an unknown woman about the room who appeared not to be surprised that I was lying in bed. Occasionally she looked over at me, just quickly and then away, inconspicuously kind, then carrying on with her tasks unconcerned, as if it was all the most natural situation in the world. I no longer dared do anything; I simply wasn't capable of anything decisive. By and by, I felt better and more alive; the window was open wide, and brilliant sunshine spilled into the room, bringing with it muffled sounds from outside. It all felt warm and wonderful as it pressed against my bed.

"How did I get here?"

The woman, dressed in a light summer dress, remained where she was, laughed, and looked straight at me, and knowingly.

"Already awake? Or do you need to sleep a bit more? You can have breakfast in bed. It's all ready."

Breakfast? That sounded very nice. But in the house of a stranger? How could I eat it and, above all, in bed? I didn't say anything, hardly moved, and just looked at the woman gratefully and beseechingly.

"Do you want something else? Is there anything I can do for you?"

Why was someone being so kind to me, while I had neglected Franziska so, as well as who knows who else? I brought out a hand from beneath the blanket and rubbed my cheeks and forehead. The woman had turned away; she was full of concern, or she had simply given up bothering with me since I had remained stone silent. I propped myself up a bit in order to be able to better look around the room, and then I knew where I was.

"Good morning, Anna. Is it so late already?"

"Not too late for someone who came home just last night. It's nine o'clock."

I jumped up from the couch and hurried to the bathroom. Again, or as always, my leg hurt, but after a while the pain went away, only the kneecap burning. I felt awake, or at least much more awake than on the day before, nor was it hard to get my bearings here. I was so at ease and satisfied, as one can feel only in friendly surroundings. The long evening before, with its conversation running deep into the night, was still very memorable, the bathroom and the entire apartment feeling comfortable to me in particular ways, such that I was myself again. Everything seemed to be set up to serve me, to help me get my bearings, yet without belonging to me. Only Anna's little household meant something to me, it feeling like when you are in a hotel and everything is laid out for your pleasure. How well everything is set up, I realized, and pushed away the thought of ever having to give up this comfortable setting. But then the notion arose again and made me anxious, thinking that I couldn't stay here, not this soon, though I would have been happy to let myself be taken care of. What else was I supposed to do? It bothered me as I recalled that I had left my bag at the train station and had to pick it up today. Indeed, to have to walk along the street and stare at the two colors of the patterned granite tiles of the sidewalk seemed a heavy imposition. A walk through the streets could in no way lead to good memories but, rather, only hopeless memories of childhood that still simmered inside my gutted soul.

It wasn't right of Anna. I should never have come back here; it was no homecoming. It was nothing but a nightmarish mistake, the kind of thing you foolishly do at the end of a war. You travel somewhere and expect something, hoping for a hand that will open up, inviting you and showing you what to do, until at last you're at peace, though your rights will have been long lost. If I had already reached my goal in coming to this city, then I wanted to stay in this building, in this apartment, this being the only reasonable place to stop. It was astonishing that there was an apartment in which I was allowed to be a guest. The fact that Peter had encountered me on the street and brought me along was a hint that I wouldn't be sent on. What calmed me here was the situation that no one could have prepared for me ahead of time; namely, Hermann Meisenbach and Anna, the two of them living here the whole time and wanting to be happy together, and then someone brought me along. That was something; it was a sign that people shouldn't disappear. In the distance a cuckoo called, nowhere to be seen, as carefully his wings beat among the branches, myself at home in my tended nest. Now I could stretch, but it was also good not to stir but rather to wait, always to wait. In between, something could happen, maybe come out of nowhere, late-breaking developments, nothing anyone could see, and then all of a sudden a welcome result. I listened inside my cave; it was completely quiet if I didn't move, only an image arising that was very old and exalted: Adam at the expulsion. Adam and Anna, I heard someone say, clearly, Adam and Anna, the dreaming Adam without the apple, Anna having crept off on tiptoe. She didn't want to disturb his summer with a cuckoo's call, so that he wouldn't feel any pain in his poor knee. I listened closely and asked, "How shall I begin, so that today I don't have to give up my refuge and then have to live alone in this city in perpetual misery. How shall I slog across its pavement after the fall with my wounded knee?" In the bathroom I felt good; I would have been happy to be locked in there, and yet how brief even the longest stay had to be. Suddenly, the next moment a future arrived with painful power. To have a plan, that was indeed pointless. I couldn't dally anymore; it was rude and could bring suspicion down upon me, something that, as far as I knew, should now have been in the past, because I indeed wanted to settle down, wanted to be able to say that it was my apartment, it's always been mine, I had only been threatened, but now the time is here when everything will be good and right again. I am the master of the house here and will tolerate no one who denies my wishes. Everything here is mine; I recognize it all once again. Then, obviously, I will have to live here alone, yet that would mean giving up Anna, for no one would then take care of me. I would be openly hanged from some floor, and then the regained property would mean nothing at all.

Once my mind was clear—everything was over, everything was thrown out—I trifled between the breaks of a shattered order and formulated ridiculous plans to form a mosaic that did not want to come together right and also immediately fell apart again. Should I try the old trodden cobblestones? Crawl again into buildings that lingered after everything had been destroyed, no matter how bad they were, and thus behave as if misery were the only permissible realm for the soul? To not tread on the trodden, even those from yesterday, as you hole up in your pain from today? To give up on time, no matter how bad it had been for you, to grant that your youth has disappeared and your old age will be curtailed? Questions, muddled pressing questions that heat up the mind but find no cool answers. Dazed, I stumbled the two steps to the door and tried the lock, but it wouldn't budge, until finally I was able to hammer at it with the handle of Hermann's razor, thus allowing me to get out of the bathroom. How awful! Otherwise I had hardly touched his things, or any of his clothes, still clean and fresh, which Anna, as if it were her task to do, had sweetly laid out on a chair for me, they sitting there undisturbed, as if it were my own private plunder all divvied up. I didn't look all that good, but at least every thread was mine and didn't come from this city.

In the room the breakfast table was set, all of it looking just like at home. Whether Anna noticed right away that I had turned up my nose at all her gifts I couldn't decide; her look was calm and gentle, making me feel good. She served me silently, and I let her do so. "I'm being coddled," I said to myself with a mixture of concern and satisfaction. "I'm not used to this." Perplexed, I broke the silence.

"Is this what happens every morning? Always breakfast on a tablecloth?"

"Yes, isn't that . . . ?"

Anna cleared her throat and didn't know what to say. She looked at me, injured and concerned.

"I . . . I only meant," I said, embarrassed.

"Do you not like it?"

"No, no. It's all fine. Wonderful! I'm just not used to it. A beggar picked up on the street who is then tenderly fed."

"What do you mean?"

"Then the beggar leaves, or at least that's what one would expect. Otherwise, the beggar is chased off. But he's indeed fresh and won't let himself be handled like a dog, as, having found refuge, he feels better, as if at home, in fact totally at ease, but then someone gives him a kick and the door slams behind him with a crash."

Anna listened, feeling strange, not knowing what was going on. She almost had tears in her eyes.

"It's terrible, what I've done! Forgive me! I'll leave."

"What do you mean?"

"Oh, nothing! I'm impossible! Everything is impossible!"

"You need to take it easy! Wait, just wait! Take your time!"

"Thank you. You are so patient. Forget all that about a beggar, please! It's just not so. Don't take it literally. If you take a look at me, the way I stand here, then you get what I'm saying, right? What I said is all so ungrateful and obnoxious. But I'll do better and make sure to stifle any such talk."

"I've already forgotten it. See? Simply gone!"

"I wish I'd never said any of it."

"You have to get hold of yourself, Arthur! Maybe what I say sounds dumb, but, nonetheless, please don't be so bitter! No one is going to chase you off. You're always welcome here, and often, always, whenever you wish! You can also stay here for a few days, until you settle down. Time heals."

"Heals who? Not me! One can say the exact opposite: Time kills."

"Yes, it does that, too, you're right. But it also heals. You'll see, it heals. Be patient!"

"Should I move in with Peter? Won't that be too much of a burden for him?"

"Not at all! It would be good for you. Even for him. He'll help you, and vise versa. He's pleasing and practical, as one says, but somewhat immature. He needs a strong hand. Hermann always provided that, for he was a distant cousin of his. But he's a nice young man. You can take him under your wing and show him the way."

I had to laugh.

"You've come to the right man! A strong hand, me? You've got to be kidding."

"I do indeed know something about people."

"You've got me wrong, believe me! I can be nothing but trouble. And that I can do splendidly. You know, outside of here I stood among a heap of people, and with cranes they yanked away the good souls. I was too heavy, having been lucky or whatever, and so I was spared. Since then I've been rejected. Just look—nothing but bad thoughts, small-minded and cruel."

"Your despair doesn't bother me at all. Why would you feel anything different? I believe in you a great deal."

"Too much, Anna!"

"You are a strong, an incredibly strong, person. You'll land with your feet on the ground, or you'll create the space in which to do so, and then everything will be good."

Anna said this quietly and with a conviction that would not stand for any back talk, no matter how strong the urge rose within me.

"You know what, Anna? You're giving me immense credit and are at peace with how I'll waste it."

"Yes, credit, if that's what you want to call it. That seems unbelievable to you today. But someday you'll recall my words. When you are yourself again. Yourself, entirely yourself."

"Do you really believe that?"

"I know it."

Anna's words hit me like a hot, dry wind, causing me—as best I can put it—to utterly despair. They didn't change my situation at all, but they were a result of her belief in me, which then and long afterward, whenever I recalled this encouragement, granted me strength and confidence. In such manner, Anna had helped me; I'm still grateful to her and will never forget it. What she said was a blessing, which always wrested the morning free of its confusion and set the day, no matter how much it seemed headed toward a dark mess, on the right track.

Next we talked reasonably about what could be done for me, and what I myself should undertake. I suggested not waiting for Peter to pick me up, but instead that I go alone to the Office for Returnees to register. Anna had said this was an essential task, after which I could pick up my bag at the train station and come back. Anna was pleased that I wanted to get off to a good start, but she thought I should indeed wait for Peter, because the Office for Returnees, like the train station, could be reached almost directly if you walked up to the vineyard where Peter lived. At the Office for Returnees they were, in fact, very nice, but one would have to wait in line, and it would be much nicer to pass the time with Peter. Anna thought that as soon as I had the ID in my hands everything would go better for me. After the Office for Returnees, I should go down to the station with Peter, and from there it would be easy to go to his house. Anna assured me that I would like living at Peter's; the neighborhood was very quiet, the room nice, the view pleasant and peaceful. Anna was happy that the area around the hilltop vineyard was not a problem for me, as she called it. What she meant was that relatives or friends of mine had never lived there. Anna suggested a plan as to how I could then move my things into Peter's, he bringing me food, while Anna promised to visit every evening during the next few days. That way, I would slowly settle in and wouldn't need to leave the house at all. Just rest was what I needed—to sleep a lot, not think, read a little, look out the window, until I regained my strength. Once I was recovered, I should gradually make my way around the neighborhood, reflect on matters, and begin to think about the future.

"Just take it slow. Eventually you'll conquer the city."

"Don't talk about conquering. That's not the way it is; I refuse to think so."

"You'll come around, Arthur. You are standing on a growing and thriving island. You need to press on. Keep looking around you. Until you know that you are at home."

"No, not at home. Not that. That doesn't exist. It's senseless for me to have come here."

"You so wanted to."

"Yes, I wanted to. Nothing forced me to do so. Yet it was imperative. I dreamed of finding something. A cat that was taken from the boy up to the hayloft and killed, but which he doesn't know about and comes and looks for it, expecting a miracle in vain."

"You don't know that at all. You haven't looked around at all."

"No survivors."

"You don't know that, either."

"It's so."

"Are you so certain?"

"Yes, I know all too much. And what I don't know, I feel."

"Really, no one?"

"No one who was really close to me. Hardly any. Yet I'll have a look around. I'll start somewhere. Oh, the fruit vendors, just like the greedy Kutschera. You know that guy, don't you? Concierges here and there. I see how they scowl at me, as if they want to jump on me, their stifling greed sunk in a bath full of diluted sorrows. Oh, these lies! The whining faces of these thieves who will pour out their hearts. But, nonetheless, I realize I have to do it. To inch forward. From one address to another and then ask around. 'Good day, here I am. Yes, just look! Could you please tell me . . . ?' Anna, it's so shameful!"

"Shall I help you?"

"No, you can't. I have to do it alone. Such draining, dried-up memories can do you in if you don't stomp them down or flee them as fast as you can."

"But you're not a coward."

"I don't know that. But it has nothing to do with cowardice. The city is dead to me. I became convinced of it yesterday. And that will not change. Only lingering thoughts, an unrelenting sense of obligation, also fear, curiosity, desire are what lured me here. Then a stupid sense of hope crept in. Some days ago, while on the journey, when I needed to sleep, I stayed at a hostel. There I spoke with a young man about the same age as Peter, a nice guy who told me he had listened to the radio as they read out names from lists of survivors. 'Franziska Landau' was what he said. He swore he'd heard it, since I said I knew the truth for sure, but 'Franziska Landau,' he said, and then again, in order to make sure there was no mistake, 'Franziska Landau.' I said it as well, 'Franziska Landau.' It was crazy. And then I hugged the pale young man, kissed him, and jumped around the hut and then outside, saying 'Franziska Landau!' "

"They have the lists at the Office for Returnees! I'll go get them right now and call you!"

"But, Anna, Anna! Didn't you hear? I know."

"What do you know?"

"I know everything! There's a Franziska Landau! Why can't there be? But not my Franziska Landau! I let myself get carried away. Such a name as this, and I was baffled and pleased to hear it. I ran out of the hostel into the night, somewhere among the nearby fields, until I stumbled. Then I stood there and grabbed hold of my head."

"And . . . then . . ."

"That was it. Over. Burned out. Ashes. Finished. Nothing. And then I pulled myself together. I didn't want to get caught up in it all again; I didn't want my mind to be pierced by disappointment. Which is why I decided not to dawdle anywhere for a single day but to move on as fast as possible. To be free of dreams and instead to sink into truth, no matter how merciless. It will be hard for me, Anna, but there's no other way. I want to know the truth, to submit to it, and if I am still able to fulfill my duty I will submit testimony as merciless as what it will reveal in itself."

"And that's why you came back."

"That's why. No, that's not quite right. I came here because it's a stopping point. You have to understand: on my own, without this city, there would be no way to begin. The city means little to me, almost nothing. But as soon as I arrived here I felt a certain sense of equilibrium. That was a starting point, as I said. It could grow, perhaps, and I thought it possible. I have to live somewhere in order to exist, and here has suddenly made the most sense. Do you understand, Anna?"

"I can indeed imagine what you mean, but go on!"

"You see, a starting point, the hope for a starting point where I can find myself. Lists of returnees that we hear read out loud, about which one asks, one reads. Arthur Landau, born on and in, returned. Maybe someone will remember and want me. Do you think that someone over the border . . . ?"

"But of course! People there are concerned. All of them are looking. They are waiting for lists. There's just no way to make the connection. There's no mail—letters are out of the question, telegrams arrive only with great difficulty. But individuals travel back and forth—soldiers, couriers who carry news. Do you have anyone over there . . . ?"

"I don't know. Hopefully. We can at least think so for now! A starting point where one can perhaps recognize . . . but, indeed, recognize what? It's confusing. But you're right. We shouldn't delay trying to contact someone over there. Let's see, people outside the country, to link up with them, be recognized, me in particular, lists of returnees. It's all quite clear, isn't it?"

"Yes."

"People who want to look for Arthur Landau."

"So you have people over . . . ?"

"No way to know. I can only hope. Some relatives, not many, most of them scattered, hardly any remaining close by. Ah, I didn't even think of them."

"Who, for instance?"

"Friends, once really good friends."

"They won't abandon you."

"They would certainly come at once."

"I think so, too, Arthur. We have to find them!"

"They should just come here. They should take me away."

"What do you mean?"

"Away from here. I don't want to stay. I just want to go."

"You mean somewhere over there?"

"As soon as possible."

"But do you really know what it's like here? Yesterday you heard too much about the bad from Peter."

"I know little, but I can well imagine. Much too much."

"It probably wouldn't be so bad for you here. You'll even get your returnee's identity card today, which is important and will give you many advantages. Then you can go to the authorities, who will receive you anywhere, as they will recognize your ID. You'll have rights, remunerations for the Reitergasse shop. . . ."

"You think so? Reitergasse. What would that be? If they can just let me be in peace. I don't want anything more from them. They should take me in over there. I mean, the friends. If they really are there, if they're still friends."

"You should go to the Office for Returnees and the aid center. Tell them all about it there. They'll have you fill out a form, as well as approve extra rations for you, take care of your health, support you, advance you some money—"

"No need to go on."

"Good. The aid center is where to go, because of the international connections, inquiries, and so on. Some are there the whole day for such, but I don't think you'll stand for that."

"No, certainly not."

"Yet you'll register and let them know who you're looking for."

"Who I'm looking for, okay ... Who am I looking for? Let's see. There's no point in my continually bothering you with my problems. I can apply for something there."

"Do you have their addresses?"

"Only the names and perhaps the towns. I no longer know the addresses. They most likely are no longer any good."

"Many have in fact found them through the aid center."

"You want to make me hope something will happen, Anna?"

"They will certainly help you, Arthur. If you want, they will even help you leave the country. They arrange collective transports, and you can sign up even for a one-way trip. It won't take long. Yet it will be difficult, for you need papers, guarantees, visas, sponsors, and so on. Your friends—"

"Have to find me first."

"And as soon as you are out you can arrange for me to follow."

"Do you also want to leave, Anna?"

"Who among us do you think wants to stay? But I won't fill your head with our worries."

"I see. The so-called revenge against the intruders! But isn't it only the culprits, the really bad ones? And, in addition, a couple of violators, who will straighten out over the course of a few days or weeks, such as Peter's bride and the like?"

"Guilty or innocent, that's a difficult question, but here there is no distinction. It has nothing at all to do with guilt. When an entire people have to believe as one, then everything is different. That means no more incursions will be allowed."

"Is that so bad?"

"I'm not exaggerating."

"Is it bad for you as well?"

"Not so much, but that's not what I'm talking about. I can indeed make my way through. And I even have some special income, as they call it—for instance, the inheritance from my mother, something from my own past that I can be very proud of, and Arno for everything else. The money comes from him. Oh, it's so sickening! But he had really good friends who know me and continue to take care of me. Today it's tough for you, they say, and tomorrow it will be our turn. It's a chain that has no end. What can I say to them!"

"Before the war we lived well here, all of us in this country. Aren't you being a bit dour?"

"That's what you think? You know, I really don't want to burden you with it all, but perhaps it will help you if I tell you something about us. About us, not me, for I have nothing to complain about; everything is fine for me. It's very bad, Arthur. I'll spare you the details! But they just take people away, just like how they took you all away a few years ago."

"Really, is it that bad?"

"No, forgive me! You make me feel ashamed. It's of course different, and no comparison should be made, but it's easy to feel wronged when you suffer and are persecuted. True pity seems harder even than love. A lot more happened to all of you, something more systematic and precisely carried out, bureaucratic and requiring loads of paper. It was written out in long-hand with cold calculation. What's happening to us now is for the most part not as bad; not as many are dying as back then. One can hope for more for the better part of us."

"Don't you see? It's all because of those culprits."

"It's not that simple. It's true for most, if not all. The horror we face has a limit. There was no limit to what was done to you, as long as there was still someone left breathing."

"It will be all right, Anna. We didn't suffer so that injustice would prevail."

"It will be all right? Unfortunately, it doesn't look that way. People are hauled off. Even friends, papers, and bribes are of doubtful help and do not last. A bad example was set, and everyone got the picture."

"Are you in danger?"

"I already told you, I'm fine. Right at the moment, I'm almost certain. I don't expect anything bad to suddenly happen. The people in the building are seemingly decent, the porter is on the straight and narrow, and that's the most important. He managed to fend off the mob that came inquiring from house to house right after the war. Then he spoke so well of me to the police, the national security, during the investigation of war criminals, to the governing authority for the identification of state enemies and traitors, and who knows who else? Yes, my dear, that all surprises you! 'Frau Meisenbach is one of us,' he said. 'She behaved better than many of our own people, and her brother was a hero who died on our behalf.' I don't make too much of it, but until now it has kept me safe. As have Arno's political friends. Then, after a few days, I received a declaration of harmlessness from the police, a red card. That's the best that one can get. It's signed and is stamped in several places. But whether that will last forever? Even though I don't have to leave, I don't want to stay here."

It was soothing for me to learn of so much unfamiliar sorrow and of Anna's personal troubles. I was wrenched from the loneliness of my own pain, yet it affected me almost more than I could bear. Expulsion and flight, the urge to steal, hatred of others, bitter people, the sword of injustice; I knew what it meant to feel powerless, and the despair of those who feel worthless. Such ruin had not ceased, and it claimed victim after victim.

From outside, military music thumped along closer, tin horns and drums, pressing at me and hurting my ears, although the noise was muffled, since it came from somewhat far off.

"We have to hear that every day, and sometimes more than once a day. At Peter's, up near the vineyard, you'll hardly hear it at all."

"Military music in any country is unbearable."

"I don't like it, either. They celebrate so much right now, and they need it for that."

I closed the double windows in the face of the lovely June day without even asking Anna, but it seemed the right thing to do. The warlike flood of noise could hardly be heard. Smiling, Anna said that the closed windows had the disadvantage that it would be hard to tell when the band was finally far enough away.

"Should I open them up?"

"We can try it in ten minutes. By then the festivities will certainly be over."

Then Anna said that she had to go out to do some shopping, and that she'd be gone around fifteen minutes. If I wanted, I could come along, but she would understand if I preferred to stay in the apartment, which is what I decided after mulling it over for a bit.

With a large bag in tow, she headed out. I wanted to accompany her to the elevator, but I only stood up and closed the door behind her. I had agreed with Anna that I would not open it, even if someone rang the door-bell. Peter would certainly not be coming in the meantime, and, besides, I know his signal: three quick rings.

Left alone, I inspected Hermann's books more closely than I did yes-terday, but, once again, I didn't pull out any of them. I was too deeply shy, the books themselves causing me to feel this even more than the thought that they belonged to a dead man and were left behind to no end, beautiful books calmly standing one next to the other, arranged according to height, though perhaps also color, rather than content, the works of most older writers in several languages, many philosophical works, history, memoirs, and letters. In some ways, all books were letters to the world—envoys, com-plaints, bearers of joy, intimations, endless information, and public news. But who is meant to read them? For whom were all of these thoughts really put together? All had proclaimed themselves, had expressed something to the formative memory of those living in the present and to future genera-tions. But who had the many continuous letters actually reached, and did they all really wish to stand there exposed so obviously as a pack of lies, such shameless lies? Each book a corpse, describing something that once was but is no longer; in fact, it never was, my dear girl. If one blocks one's ears against the silent chorus of so many dried-up voices, then there's nothing to hear, not even time. It had all been said, love and hate, but all of that had been said already and didn't mean a thing. No, the books seemed like inept messengers who had failed in their duties and didn't mean anything to me. With my thumbnail I flicked across a row of them from right to left, rais-ing a soft whistle like a long, drawn-out note. That was strange—the letters were effaced and were worth nothing anymore. I did it again and again, then I had had enough. The spines of books are sensitive; my fingernail could leave marks, and that would not have been right.

I had hardly read any books in years, wisdom having escaped me and no longer found within books, the withered remains persevering on their own, though they were indeed hard to keep together. Anna was right not to worry too much about the treasures lost among their pages, as it only meant caring for the dead, guarding plunder that only took up space in the small apartment. The fact that I had once written and thought about writing books that could have been printed, bound, and sold now seemed to me implausible, though indeed such ideas had often buoyed me during the war years. In the same spirit, I collected so much experience and carried it along with me, so much pressing deep into my memories, held there as I told myself I would need it, and now it appeared to me it was indeed lost, myself unable to find it any longer, Franziska's death and my survival having shredded the volume that gave the contents some kind of sense, all my stowed-away knowledge now covered in dust and ground down to a pulp. What had prodded me to say later that I would write it all down, feeling that I had finally experienced for real what I had learned about only in my lifeless studies? A book? I thought of the Inca tribesman who was handed a book and told that it was the truth, and so he took the book, shook it, listened, and responded contemptuously that it hadn't said a thing, and threw the book to the ground. How vainly I had sought to gain solace with all my plans! In cleverly developed sections I had conceived long works, written by Arthur Landau, news straight from the source, no mucking around in libraries, where one just writes what another has written, no cheap history, no beating about the bush or simply compiling other people's stories; no, here is the real thing that had been tested and come through, and so your thirst for knowledge will be quenched! Foolish interweavings and entanglements, the powerlessness of words that won't hold their place! I dreamed of all my plans, and I dared to think that, having survived all the horror, I did not survive for nothing, for I could say that I had been there, my life, love, and sorrows not only having been consumed by it all, but now, with a sharp mind and the keenness of an observant witness, I could go to my desk and set it down. Thus would my story fulfill a purpose, and everything wouldn't be simply unappeased laments but, rather, such fortunes would be shared with my neighbors and the world, myself even coming to value my fate, it being unfortunate that I had been granted it, but good that I had not failed it.

Then I sat powerless in my first days at Peter's near the vineyard and could not write a book at all. At night, ceaseless thoughts plagued me, shrill voices and interjections crossing one another, though all I wanted to set down was one word, and yet it all remained bottled up inside me and I was unable to draw it out. What I also thought made no sense, as it was full of holes and seemed the height of hubris. Everything that I had remarked on earlier seemed to have dissipated, especially when the war was first getting under way, as I buried myself in my research, sunk in the misery of my fellow brothers who had already died, searching for something like a doctor searching for a disease while taking his own pulse, calling out to colleagues puzzled at his condition, "Have you never seen anyone about to die?" And so I figured these writings were lost and didn't mind that they were; should they ever surface, they would be obsolete and faded, truth's lye having already eaten through them.

Then one day I held my works in my hands again. Franziska had lovingly packed them away, first in tissue paper, then covered with a thick piece of paper to protect them from water and any kind of decay, then bound together through and through, just the way she had wrapped all her gifts, such that one took great joy in opening them. Now I read through them, disturbed and ashamed, almost in tears, but my hostile feelings against my failed attempts soon dissipated. It felt as if I were looking through a murky transparent wall at a frozen life from ancient times, not my own life but a monument to a history that had disappeared and yet was still credible. In a rush, I put it all together—namely, what could be garnered from the retrieved writings and my memory. I hadn't worked that long at the museum, but I began with what I'd learned there while trying to improve this or that text and to start to work on new books. When I arrived in the metropolis, the sociology of oppressed people was just in its early stages, most of the chapters, or at least the most important ones, having been drafted, while other studies were finished and new ones begun. What I didn't think I could accomplish with all this activity and from these new projects! Whoever I spoke with, be it So-and-So, Dr. Haarburger, and whomever I came in touch with, I would always try to explain the basis of my work, setting forth my most important ideas, making the case for my deeply probing learned views and asking people if they would read a bit of it. If someone listened to me with attentive, careful respect, I was indeed happy, for then I would feel certain that whatever help they could give me was assured. Yet how foolish it was to hope for something, especially when someone would casually say, "Very interesting, Herr Doctor, but of course everything really depends on the finished product. One would have to see that first, then maybe something can be done." I threw myself into my work and regularly spent nearly half the night at my desk, egged on by skeptical comments from So-and-So, who in the early days brought me books and articles to study, while I had taken too literally to heart the old saying that ninety percent of inspiration is perspiration. Indeed, that was not altogether untrue, but it had nothing to do with the actual workings; namely, the approval, funding, and completion of a successful project. Perspiration has nothing to do with genius; it only accounts for the discipline that one needs to complete something, and no one becomes a genius through perspiration alone.

I got smarter and no longer thought myself a genius, and I'm still just as hard a worker to this day. All that perspiration means is that I can persevere in order to hope to get something out of my otherwise wasted days. But back then, during the first two years of my landing in the metropolis, when I felt overwhelmed by even myself, overambitious, driven, and restless, I suddenly found a brilliant voice and capability inside me that allowed me to overcome all barriers in the world. The cynical irony with which I was greeted by people I knew and met I approached with naïveté or deliberately ignored, because I didn't wish to give it credence and, with the overarching drive to achieve success as well as a meager living that I hoped to make from my chosen profession, I continued always to patiently sound out support that was vital to my future amid all the empty promises and even open refusals. I have never really known if I was treated any better or any worse by those who didn't expect to be confronted in a social situation, as they kept their own willfulness in check and never let it show. For many years I didn't understand it, but nonetheless played along. Even Johanna put up with it, she who had such faith in me, who did everything for me, and tapped her countless professional connections without knowing that she was not at all suited to the new way of things that had never been seen before. How could she know when even I, as a sociologist, had no idea that the social network had organized itself as a community, even though within it the rules were always changing, such that for certain functions in both private and institutional settings there were always correlating ways to say and do things that one had to employ in order to attain any success. Such understanding eluded us, and soon Johanna learned that people were just smiling emptily when they spoke with her, or avoided her altogether or simply sent her on through a chain of one person after another, each of whom, with a shrug of the shoulders, would turn down all the unsuccessful requests for help and still innocently ask, "Well, my dear Frau Landau, what is it you really want? The best thing to do would be to send your husband around to an employment agency, and if he doesn't get anything, then you should have a look for yourself!" In the end, Johanna no longer knew what she had even been asking for, and those who had been approached offered only the backhanded compliment that she certainly was a brave woman.

If I look back evenhandedly at my career path, as it is called, in the first three or four years since I arrived in the metropolis (and it's important for me to do so, since I'm working on a study that I plan to call "The Position of the Creative Artist in the Age of the Large-Scale Social Organization That Threatens Culture"), then I haven't a clue, since the intertwinings of my efforts are confused. The particular reasons for my failure are much less clear to me than the general rule that describes such failure. That rule says: Social institutions run or maintain culture or sustain themselves in a neutral manner when serving the clear purpose of supporting the well-being of the community and nothing that undermines its individual members. Out of this comes the corollary: Should social institutions no longer serve such clear purposes, then they will be utilized for other purposes than those for which they were meant, as these institutions only serve themselves, whereby the well-being of the community is threatened and the development of its individual members is inhibited or even harmed. If things should go this far, then it's bad for culture, as it is then directed by institutions that are themselves marginalized, depleted, and finally replaced by ideologically run, industrial-sized disasters, the result being that any possible freedom for people to attain their own intellectual feats and works is continually shrunk until it disappears. Unique achievements of value become rare, while sound achievements that link to tradition are devalued and the realization of both is threatened, if not entirely forbidden. That which is produced independently is constrained if it does not come under the yoke of a totalitarian tyranny, having to forsake distribution unless it takes on a plethora of economic and social burdens. This rule tells us of the collapse of art and scholarship which is caught unawares or is no longer desired at all, since everything has attached itself to guiding principles that have been set in place by the powerful and totalitarian realms of overarching institutions. Only that which follows these declarations will be deemed worthy, while only that which is produced through the aid of institutional powers—which today in the West means through the press, the media, or the control of advertising—will be supported or even allowed.

This is the situation in which I ended up. The social ineptness of a person such as myself, who has been kept out of almost all social organizations, rather than just declassed, makes it impossible to gain a foothold. Any foothold is taken away the moment you contact someone, prepare to make the proper approach, and set off but never arrive, nor does your work ever arrive, you being like a letter writer who writes letters to unknown or unauthenticated addresses. This tragedy, of which I'm a part, describes the position of the creative artist of this epoch. I can see, then, how it all connects together and prevents my taking part in society in any possible way, for it is all confirmed in me, which I also observe is what has happened to me in detail, this daily and weekly collapse, while these pinched attempts to escape this entrenched, but also this perpetual and not entirely perceivable, loneliness, I have not yet explained. The less of a person I am because I am not allowed to exist, the more the world is closed to me and cuts itself off behind a wall. If that didn't exist, if it only had a door and could be walked through, then I myself would be this wall, but the world would also be the wall; put another way, the world and I would be bound together through the wall, and we would come together as a single seamless wall.

As I first appreciated this insolvable conflict, I did something I never thought of doing before in my life. I wrote a story. The shallowness and meaninglessness of most of the letters we write had always pained me, for I think of the letter as a primary symbol of the person who has been excluded from something. And every person is excluded, every person reaches a border, no matter how many different ones may be drawn, some closer for some, for others farther away, or as visible as the Great Wall of China or spreading out into the distance in endless glittering flatlands, often not known or recognized, and yet the root of all human misery, sensed as eternity, the depths, as the source of our behavior and the driving force behind our vices and virtues, the source of all despair and hope. To be human is to have a border, and to want to cross it through letters that will reach beyond to their goal. I worked hard on this story for a long while, polishing it, copying it over, and changing it, though it always remained unfinished and did not please me, as I am not a writer. Nonetheless, though it is also a failed piece, it still means a good deal to me, because it says more about me and my thinking than I have ever managed to express in my scholarly work. Which is why today I have picked it up again and revised it thoroughly once more. Here it is. It's called:

THE LETTER WRITERS

Letters, for those who do not know, are an ancient invention. You write them, feel unburdened, and write some more. So it was millennia ago, so it remains to this day, no one finding it surprising, all thinking it good. People sit at home, look out the window for a bit, and think of their friends, then look up addresses that are often hidden away, take out envelopes and write down the names, towns, and streets with solemn letters. Then they reach for writing paper and spin away their thoughts.

Meanwhile, outside it has grown colder. Whoever does not have pressing business does not move along the streets, where at this time of year misery most likely awaits. If the letters are finished and sealed, one often strokes them tenderly, protecting them with religious or superstitious measures from the evil eye—from all harm—and from the danger of loss, carrying them out quickly at midday when the cold eases up for a little while. Many people, especially women, carefully wrap the letters in a scarf in order to protect them from the frost. Whoever does not want to pay to send them as registered mail, or does not trust only the large boxes at the post office, walks to the next mailbox, into which the anxiously guarded cargo is carefully slipped. Then the writers turn back home, anxious or relieved, though with an inscrutable mien, to write new letters to the same or other addresses.

Once your own addresses have been exhausted, you call up someone and say that you have some free time and would like to write the friends of their relatives and friends. This way, you get new addresses and are also asked to give freely of your own stock of them. This way you can build a treasure trove of addresses, and a good number of people are known for possessing loads of addresses. No one would admit this openly, for in contrast to the vanity that attaches itself to anyone with money who accumulates valuable things, in this case each is silent about his riches, at best alluding to it only by saying, "I'm busy, I still have many friends to write."

The advantage of having many addresses is obvious. You do not lose hold of those that you must write to, and it pleases you the more that your collection of addresses grows, providing you with the revitalized prospect of increasing the number of your friends. This explains the popularity of the saying that one finds in many family albums: "The friends of my neighbors are also friends of mine."

You feel good about your contacts, but no letter writer has ever received an answer back. If you abruptly ask one of them, he will behave like someone resting quietly in a church, but who has been disturbed by the suddenly loud babbling of a child, causing him to whisper excitedly with glazed eyes, "No, I haven't gotten any answer yet. But that doesn't matter, as long as there's still hope. One must be patient and can always wait." Perhaps he will then add, "It might be that I'll get a number of letters at once and from a number of friends."

Who came up with the convention of writing letters is unknown. The custom is very old. Some who think they know say that it goes back no further than the monks in Irish cloisters or in St. Gallen, but that is not correct. Others look back to ancient Greece, but whoever looks back more knowledgeably follows clues that lead to ancient Egypt and Ur. Lovers of the East also point to China and Tibet. The truth does not support their views. Though not as authentic as legends normally are, still attractive is the ancient legend of Adam as the inventor of the letter, and no history of the letter can ignore this possible source.

As the first person who heard the Lord's edict not to eat from the Tree of the Knowledge of Good and Evil, and yet who in foolish arrogance did so anyway, Adam heard a voice that said, "Where are you?" Adam, who before eating the apple was innocent and knew neither fear nor cunning, was now afraid and tried to hide. Never before did the Lord have to ask where he was, and it was also known that eating the fruit was a light offense in comparison with hiding from the Lord, who strolled in the Garden, it being the first unforgivable sin handed down from generation to generation, and thus the original sin. Harsh was the penalty for the awareness that brought death to Adam, but such awareness was given to human beings, they knowing good and evil to this very day, but harder yet was the penalty for hiding, because for that he was expelled from Paradise.

When Adam cultivated the earth from which he had been formed, he was sad, and Eve, full of sympathy, tried to take care of him. Adam said, "Do you see the cherubim with their flat hewn swords defending the path to the Tree of Life from us? Know that I love and desire life, but the Lord has said that I am dust and must return to dust." Eve knew what to tell him: "Go and make a sign to the Lord, so that he may know our wish and hear it." Then Adam broke off a stone from a cliff and struck it and chiseled a sign of his wish into it. Through the sweat of his brow he earned from above the gift of writing, which in the midst of his need he thought to have invented himself. Adam showed Eve the stone, she praised him, and Adam tossed it in the direction of where the cherubim stood. Adam was blinded by the brilliance of their eyes and the points of their swords, such that he could not see where the stone fell upon the ground. There was also such a whirring in the air that he did not hear when the stone reached its target.

Adam was again sad, and again Eve spoke to him: "You do not know what happened to the stone. Fear not, chisel a new stone, write down on it a sign of our wish and throw it again." Adam did as Eve asked of him. He did it more and more, and he continued to do it whenever his sorrow consumed him upon the field. Thus did Adam, according to the legend, invent the letter, and the first letter was a wish tossed toward the Paradise that had been lost.

Not everyone believes the ancient stories, which are taken as late attempts to grant the most important inventions of the human race handed down from antiquity a mythic aspect, rather than to content onself with more prosaic, alleged explanations that are nonetheless much closer to the truth. In any case, what is certain is only that the custom of writing letters is handed down from parents to children. In many families, the offspring are introduced to it at a very tender age; hardly have the children learned to write than the parents insist that the youngsters write a little letter every day. At first, mother dictates it; later, they suggest what one can write, while the father corrects errors and worries about the address, until, after a few years, the children take letter writing to be a necessity.

As people grow, at some point they experience a severe crisis, most usually between twenty and twenty-five. Rarely does this lead to a renunciation of writing, though sometimes it lasts for some time, and is then quietly taken up again. More often it occurs that young people assume that an address is too old or, sadly, they think that a friend has died long ago. Then they mark the address with a cross and lay it to the side. If their conscience bothers them later, they erase the crosses with a good deal of effort and write to such addresses in an especially heartfelt and tender manner. Whoever overcomes such temptations or never succumbs to them will have nothing to do with such matters and says, "You shouldn't do that. Who wants to see his friend in the grave?" This corresponded to the widespread belief that your friends have not died, have gained power and influence with age, or have produced able-bodied progeny who are full of joy over the devotion to one's ancestors which letters manifest. There are also cranks, most of them ancient, who are known as collectors of old addresses. They usually direct their letters only to addresses that are more, or at least somewhat more, authentic.

It is assumed that an original response will be received; otherwise, this practice would not have survived or spread significantly. One cannot know today for certain, yet we know a great deal, often from very old legends that provide impressive evidence of replies having been received. One can foresee from these stories the wisdom that our forefathers spoke, thus providing reports of responses found here and there, though always only as rumors. If you looked at them more closely, you'd be shocked by the degree of stupidity and irresponsible nonsense that is generally dispersed, not as a swindle that people grant credibility but as exaggerated gossip that quickly rings hollow the moment you scrutinize it. At best, you find traces of a family tradition that says a grandfather once received a response, but which he showed to no one, though from that moment on he was supposedly happy. Sometimes such news surges through city and country in wild eddies and sets everything to reeling such that it hardly abates, for it's fed with fresh material full of fantasies that frequently causes gullible people to turn such matters into fabrications.

From whom should the responses come? In serious circles, it is surmised that among the trove of still current addresses the overwhelming majority of the names are made up or invented; even where the names may, in fact, be actual, the town, street, and house numbers are in large part false. Some people are not afraid to admit such shortcomings, but they don't put too much stock in them, and explain that those addressed in any case live way beyond the border in a foreign land, a reliable map of which no one owns, though it's not necessary as long as the post forwards the letters. The main thing is that they reach those countries in which great care is taken to make proper deliveries, and the recipient is found or inquires himself. It's hard to battle against this belief; whoever doubts the truth stays silent and guards against the enmity of the streets. In addition, most keep quiet about their doubts when they begin to think about the worth of their own addresses. Hardly anyone gives up on his own, but almost everyone keeps using them, despite any ideas to the contrary, saying, "We humans, what can we know? We can't just give up."

Commonly, the telephone is used to gather addresses, even though it is hardly ever used for personal matters, whether in business or socially. This is somewhat surprising, since it was not so long ago that the telephone didn't exist. How such exchanges occurred then is unknown. Letter writing is indeed very old, and yet so little is known about its most recent history! The most likely version says that letter writers used to secretly seek one another out, whereby you would take a guest into an adjoining room and relay addresses back and forth through the closed door. Outwardly, this approach was supported by the letter writer's penchant for stowing away secrets, while a much more esoteric lesson can be seen in this secret exchange. It's said that the use of two separate rooms, between which a wall runs as a result of the closed doors, is modeled on an ancient ritual that invokes the desired exchange of letters across borders. However that may be, we cannot know for sure; one can investigate only those customs that are common practice today.

If you share your addresses on the telephone, a stream of fervent thank-yous follows. You are assured that you have done someone a great service, while it's also strenuously emphasized what pleasure is accorded the one who gives out such information, since now you will have helped get more news to your friends. This is according to the custom of announcing the intermediary when writing to a new address in order to praise the one who helped and thereby enhance his reputation with the recipient. Whoever is always eager to accumulate new addresses—and that goes for the majority of letter writers—is called a street writer by those who are against this practice. With this insult, the unappeasable address hunters are branded, and are thought of as fickle people, lacking in conviction and reliability.

Different are the noble writers, who claim that only a few people, and at best only one, should write to his personal friends, in order not to confuse them and not to seem insistent. Some of them argue that one should write only rarely, for only then is the recipient overjoyed to receive a letter, and that, indeed, one should share meager though solid news, if only to awaken someone's curiosity, and yet not bother those who are very busy. The adherents of this conviction attempt to make themselves into beloved ones who, as a result, hope to receive a response.

The belief in a best friend, or what many consider to be the same, a best address, is shared by a group that proudly calls itself single-letter writers. They excitedly advocate that there is only one address of any real worth, while the rest are, if not in fact unused, only meaningless. Unfortunately, among the single-letter writers there is no agreement as to what the right address is. Each individual adherent thinks he knows, yet not one can substantiate the truth of his claim. That turns this group, valued as it nonetheless may be, into agitators and cranks who rarely agree on anything and most often fall prey to suspicion. Only a certain shyness holds back the single-letter writers from breaking out into open battle, but with other letter writers they share the tendency to talk about the virtues of this or that address over the phone. One invokes the beauty of a name or different unusual aspects, such as the sound, the number of letters, wanting to constantly discern or discover from its sequence or shape a rhythmic charm. Endlessly the question is posed, "So, then, do I have the best address?," until someone complains about how much valuable time, which would be better used for writing, is idly being wasted through such talk. At which the other most often agrees, happy not to have to defend his hard-to-support rationale. Others avoid completely such pointless exchanges, though their own thoughts are occupied a great deal by this question.

Rarely will someone admit that he does not give out his best address, for this risks the possibility that he would not get any help from others. It can also happen, though rarely, that he turns down all inquiries. If he will respond only when someone visits in person, he is then called, with good-natured kidding, a whisperer, though it quickly gets around that there is nothing at all to learn from him, he being considered with a mixture of astonished shyness and indignation and called a lone writer.

Infrequent are those old fogies who spring up here and there like a weed and quickly explain in short order that they don't care about addresses, they are not at all interested in this scribbling, and want only not to be bothered with any of this. In this case there is no point in trying, for these heretics say nothing. What remains unknown is whether they still write letters secretly and, out of shame, arrogance, or eccentricity, don't say anything about it. Some questions are posed to the heretics: Do you not take part because you don't want any friends? Do you think writing is pointless because you don't get any response and can never expect to get one? Do you think there's a better way to keep in touch with your friends? But the answer remains unknown.

Some heretics are quiet and go their own way without bothering about the letter writers. Among them are nice people who don't want any enemies. Others are those—it's not easy to discover them, but nonetheless one senses their presence—who laugh at the letter writers, declaring with mockery that it is superstition and saying that foolish people should make themselves useful, and at least concern themselves with more everyday things than such a pack of received notions that only advance the ridiculous from generation to generation, all of it a barrier to any reasonable explanation. They maintain that a courageous government would ban such nonsense and penalize it. The letter writers feud with and hate these troublemakers, knowing that they enjoy the complete and full protection of the state, though they also fear the evildoers, for the hooligans among them threaten that one day they will raid a mailbox in order to search for the letters and expose this outrageous scam and shameful madness in a pamphlet in order to shine the hard light of day upon it. Yet none had risked doing so, for they were afraid of the law, which threatens the violation of the privacy of letters with harsh penalties. They also want to guard for certain against any such future action, and so all such mockery remains nothing more than a lot of hot wind that reveals its own powerlessness and only scares itself.

One would be pleased to know what happens with the countless letters through which the state pulls in millions each day owing to the high postal rates. What is not known is where the letters end up; only the postal administration could solve this puzzle, but not even the boldest of heretics is willing to question that, and the trust in the honest work of the post office is boundless. The fact is that the number of mailbox pickups has continually increased in recent years; writing is increasing at all social levels, and the colder it gets. Only in the summers, which grow shorter each year, does this passion decrease a bit, but hardly does autumn arrive than it increases with multiplied fervor. Statistics about the number of letters mailed are not published. Conservative estimates indicate astronomical figures, and reliable experts on the economy assure us that a significant part of people's means is dedicated to writing supplies and stamps, which for the welfare of the lower classes is critical. Even letter writers on the highest of levels who understand such things fear bad consequences as a result.

Through polls conducted to find out the general opinion of society, it recently and surprisingly came to light that today there are many letter writers who never use the telephone to help search for addresses, and that their number is increasing. Some people don't have a telephone and yet still want to write letters. It indeed has not escaped anyone's attention that there could be many reasons that people decline being connected to such a network, but it is assumed that these people are satisfied with their own addresses or they use a stranger's telephone. But not everyone wishes to disturb his neighbor or to hurry across the street to an unpleasant phone booth. Others don't like the phone itself, and find it to be soulless, or worry that the operator can overhear them, or avoid the loss of irretrievable time through long phone conversations. Others more mature with years decide, even when they have their own telephone, that they have now collected enough addresses, enough is enough, and thereby they write one letter after another with deeper devotion to those friends they already have. Often, they admonish the young, "Why do you keep writing letters to new recipients and thereby continually increase your troubles? Fewer is wiser. Too much writing results in a flighty and superficial nature. I'm telling you that to be frugal in the number of letters you write is a virtue. Only then can you really succeed in best serving the work itself and compose letters that contain in-depth accounts."

As one can imagine, the letters differ in appearance in both content and form. From very short ones composed of halting words written in the style of telegrams—often barely the length of a line—to endless sentences that resemble serial novels in their length, you find all levels in between. Many writers reflect their innate or acquired artfulness, many dissemble and write in a consciously different manner than their nature dictates, turning grandiose phrases while sharing everyday events, or formulate tracts marching out in paragraphs like laws or mathematical or chemical formulas, while still others compose tiresome poems with heavy measures that resemble the language of sacred texts, or employ a philosophical diction that demonstrates their learning, their inherent sophistication, their righteousness, their pious nature, though, on the other hand, some formulate a strange and dead language, especially when they supplement this style through dictionaries and grammar, inventing their own language and constructing a secret code whose key is hard to find, also adding drawings and marvelous little pictures, attaching notes or enclosing them separately. They choose small and large formats, they use different inks and pens, having their own letter cases and small hand presses at home, as well as embossing machines for normal print and for Braille. They don't use just paper but also bast, vellum, birch bark, silk, thin sheets of metal, and many other materials. Some use a stamped envelope with a return address and even include an empty sheet of paper for the convenience of the recipient, on which there is often a prepared response that the friend would have only to sign and return. What the content of the letters is can never be told. Both the general and the personal in lively exchange, sketches of nature or worries about love, homespun accounts and troubling questions, reprimands and confessions, requests and recommendations, familiar gossip and memory-laden reminiscences, essays on the everyday, trusted secrets, weather reports, business worries, announcements of happy or sad events, memories, nonsense, recipes, jokes, warm conversation, deep-seated fantasies—all of it makes up a vast and varied assortment.

So it goes, year in and year out. The urgency rises, matters get more pressing. Nonetheless, to this day not the least change has been made in this immense activity and its emotional costs, the marvel of which is difficult to express. Whoever considers it realizes that very little has changed, perhaps even nothing. Letters are written, but perhaps too few are written, or maybe too many, and it could be that one should never have begun writing them at all. You continually await a response, whether annoyed or undaunted, and sometimes you say aloud, "If only a single writer could get a single response, even if it was just a word, an empty page!" But, as experience tells us, you cannot expect that a response will ever come; the countries get larger, the borders are farther, the urgency rises tremendously, the desire for news persists bitterly into nothingness, while, at the same time, loneliness gets ever deeper and larger. It's pointless, today more so than yesterday, and tomorrow likely more so than today, but this doesn't keep cold humanity from waiting with determination and concentrated patience for the great miracle to occur.

Winter gets colder and longer each year. Now the assertion is casually made that the desire for a response increases with the cold, because it is believed that by attaining the longed-for relationship with one's friends the ice age will pass. The letter writers are mistaken, but they cannot admit it to themselves or to one another, for they wish to live and affirm themselves, they want to survive and achieve something, they having persevered from generation to generation, which has encouraged them to think that eventually they will be saved. They sit at home in their lairs and wait to be called, dreaming of the day when they can leave behind the awareness of good and evil, and at last be able to say to the unknown familiar recipient of their letters, "Lord, where are you?" But, as long as the Lord does not answer, each person affirms each day the truth of the ancient legends—namely, that each letter is like that first attempted toss of a stone at a lost Paradise.

When I first wrote down this story it was not as clear, least of all to me. I had conceived it as an allegory of a general fate that certainly said something about my own disposition but was not particularly attached to it. Meanwhile, my relationship to this story had evolved. It had conveyed something about me, I had grown fond of it, and I'd learned something from it. There was a lot that was still missing from it, and that I had to accept without totally giving in to such judgment, for it was important not to let my efforts go to waste. To give in but not to give up—that's what was needed. To slam into the wall as if it were not there, to flatter and play about with it, as if it would let itself be conquered, yet to acknowledge it and not doubt such knowledge of it, accepting that it's pointless to do so and will probably always be pointless. To exit the most secret depths with great vigor, as if victory were assured, and let myself be battered and defeated, pushed back, back into the hidden recesses! To hope for nothing and then to invoke the wondrous as if what I had never dared hope were already guaranteed. To write letters but not to expect an answer, though not to waste one's desires by the hour writing to false idols but, rather, only to make a plea out of a continually obsessed conscience, a plea directed at someone beyond all borders.

This I did not grasp when I first arrived in the metropolis. I had left the country of my home and my parents, and it was right to do so, for I didn't belong there anymore, as everything there had been destroyed, everything that I loved and needed, it all giving nothing back to me but, on the contrary, taking much more away by shutting me out, and because I knew that it faced a coming perdition that I believed I did not have to partake in, or could prevent, since it was no longer my perdition, nor should it rob me of my success, dignity, and existence, myself craving the chance to gain these very items in order to live again. This alone was a mistake. I also didn't want to search for anything in the areas bordered by the mountain woods but, rather, far away from the shadows cast by extermination, in order to find a way to break free, to live, to accomplish something. This I failed to do. Whether that was good or bad I had no idea back then. Only Johanna could see from the beginning how it was with me, but she hid it from me, for she wanted to spare me. She also did not share her views with others, as she was afraid to hurt me through such insinuations.

Besides, because of my aggressive behavior and my outwardly healthy look (one saw this in many who had survived the same conditions that I had experienced in the war), people believed in my vigor. However, because of this belief people found it easy not to be concerned with me at all. All one had to do was be nice to this Landau character, and that was all it took, for he didn't really need any help. Those who first called themselves my friends, such as So-and-So and others in the country, pulled away from me more and more with each passing month. Some avoided me; others beat about the bush, put me off, or informed me that I really needed to learn the ropes, that I would first have to learn how things worked here, and that it would have been better if I had come over before the war or at least immediately after it. But if I was now in the country and wanted to stay there, then there was no way that I should stay in the metropolis, where it was too expensive and hectic, since people with even more talent and skills than myself could not make a go of it. Academics had to live in shameful conditions, or they carried on doing undignified jobs, so who was I to think that as a nonresident I could simply get a post as a sociologist?

If I listened patiently to all of this and tried to appease the one giving such advice, then the allegations doubled, whether it be about what made me think to come here in the first place or that perhaps America was an option, but here, no way. As if I hadn't explained it all a hundred times before, I would then carefully lay it out so that they could finally understand. They would nod, say yes, now they understood, but it was too bad that I didn't go back where they needed me in the museum. Then they would pretend to sympathize with my view that, because of the chilly relations that had descended after the recent revolution, one lived as if in jail over there. Nonetheless, they would suggest that I saw things too bleakly, as there were certainly thousands of people there who were not at all unhappy. There must be millions of people who stayed behind, so it couldn't be all that bad, and I shouldn't take it all so seriously and needed to keep from getting caught up in so much talk about politics, nor should I totally rule out returning. Well, then, one really shouldn't talk about it if it's so upsetting. What I should really do is see to it that I regroup, as they called it, to quickly move to a little town where it was cheap and I could support myself and Johanna by teaching German or by entering some other useful profession, while, by the way, it would have been a lot smarter for her not to have given up her job months earlier than she really had to. Recalling Johanna's condition—namely, when she was pregnant with Michael—they felt that I was irresponsible and were angry with me. To have a child as a have-not, that was criminal and crazy. I should just make sure to push on soon overseas to America, for there the rich Uncle Karl could help us.

After many months of pointless pleas and begging, I finally succeeded in getting Professor Kratzenstein to meet with me. However, he didn't invite me to his apartment but instead met me at the offices of the International Society of Sociologists. I appeared punctually with several of my works in hand, as had been arranged. The building is situated in a quiet, genteel street. An attendant greeted me from his desk at the foot of the stairs and said to himself when I told him whom I was there to see, "Professor Kratzenstein? That's too bad." Today he apparently had no time at all, one meeting after another, in addition to which he had an unexpected visitor from Rome. The attendant would have been happy to set me out on the street, but I insisted so forcefully and continuously about having an appointment today and at this time that he finally gave in and called the Professor's secretary. After a long discussion, I was to go up. As another attendant led me up the white-carpeted steps to the second floor and along a long hallway to the room, I shouldn't have felt any sense of triumph, for the woman acknowledged that I did indeed have an appointment, but, unless I was willing to make one for a different day, I would have to, as she said emphatically, wait a good while, as the Professor was really overwhelmed today, and was in an important meeting and was not to be disturbed. How long I'd have to wait she couldn't tell—perhaps an hour, maybe less, but it could also take longer. Afterward, there was also a meeting that could not be moved, but the beginning of it could be pushed back a bit, and before it started the secretary, wishing to answer my pressing request, promised to see if the Professor could give me a quarter of an hour. The secretary offered me a chair, and so I sat there lost in the middle of the room and could only look on as she worked away at her typewriter.

After a while, I pulled a newspaper from my pocket. Whether the rustling of the paper disturbed the secretary I didn't know; in any case, she said to me that it would likely be better for me to wait in the next room, where I could read and sit comfortably at a table. I agreed, and was satisfied when she assured me for the third time that she would certainly not forget me and would remind the Professor that I was there. Thus I waited. The time went by quickly, the many lovely books a joy to peruse. Then, suddenly, Professor Kratzenstein sprang into the room, though he entered through a different door than I had, nor had he yet learned from the secretary that I was there. He slapped his forehead in surprise as he looked right at me.

"My dear . . . dear . . . please forgive me. Remind me of your name again?"

"Landau. Arthur Landau."

"Right. Herr Dr. Landau! Are you here to see me?"

"Yes, Professor. I have an appointment with you today."

"So . . . you have an appointment. It's lovely that you've come. We've met before, if I recall, at—"

"At Dr. Haarburger's. That was already seven months ago."

"Right, at Haarburger's. A wonderful evening. Yes, I remember. We talked then about . . . it was very interesting . . . about a work of yours on "

"On the sociology of oppressed people, Professor."

"That was it, right. My goodness, you yourself have been through such an experience. How did you manage it! The fact that you're not bitter and have maintained your love of scholarship, I congratulate you! Just wonderful, I say, wonderful! And we, of course, must do something for you, right?"

"Yes, that's very nice of you, Professor. You might recall that we have spoken on the phone a number of times, and that I then—"

"Yes, yes, with my secretary and also with me. It was about—"

"I sent you, as you kindly recommended, one of my finished papers on the central aspects of my research. You kindly said on the telephone that you wished to see whether it could be delivered as a talk at a meeting of the small working group—"

"Right, right—I read it, I and my secretary as well. Interesting. And we wanted to consider—"

The other door opened, and the secretary appeared.

"I've been looking for you in the conference room and everywhere, Professor. There's an urgent phone call!"

"I'll be right back, Herr Doctor! It'll just take a moment! Where is the phone, Frau Fixler?"

"In my office."

The Professor stormed toward the secretary's office, Frau Fixler following after him. I waited maybe ten minutes before the door opened again, though it wasn't the Professor but the secretary who stepped in and explained to me that the Professor had only accidentally run into me, that the meeting was not at all over but the Professor had only happened to come out from it for a moment, and could I please remain patient. Perhaps another fifteen minutes. Frau Fixler went over to a bookshelf but didn't find what she was looking for; most likely, it was the book I had taken down and leafed through on the table before me. I handed the book to the secretary, and she took it with a bittersweet smile. Then I was alone again and stood browsing before the shelves of books, for I didn't want to sit at the table any longer.

Finally, my wait ended as Frau Fixler came to me and led me into the office of the Professor, who seemed less distracted now than earlier, though he was still plenty inattentive. At least he still seemed to know what my visit was about. On his desk he recognized the text of my talk, which lay open, so I could at least hope for the best. He asked me to sit down, while Frau Fixler brought us some tea and a tray with cookies. Then we were left undisturbed, not counting the many telephone calls for Kratzenstein that interrupted our conversation.

"As I already told you, I've read your text, Herr Doctor. It is certainly not bad, but you'll allow me some honest criticism. For a presentation, it's not lively enough. You won't be surprised to hear that for publication it's hardly ready as it currently stands. For a scholarly article, it's written in too literary of a style, while for a literary review it's first of all too long and secondly too dry."

"I can change it any way that you like. I mean—"

"Yes, you certainly should change it, but I doubt that anything can really be done with it."

"I should then—"

"I've informed Frau Fixler of the basic situation, as well as the scheduling arm of the working group, as well as others. I've tried as hard as I could. Despite all the errors, I am well aware of the virtues of your work—I mean, above all, your own personal experience, although one should not overvalue that. Despite my efforts, I was not successful in convincing the scheduling arm of the group to invite you to give a presentation or to attend any other meeting for the time being."

"If I—"

"Don't be too sad about it! Quite frankly, it's no real big loss for you. With this subject matter, especially the way you address it, you would surely cause an uproar. I already told you that at Haarburger's."

"But it would be a great opportunity if—"

The telephone rang; the Professor could not respond. I soon figured out that it was Frau Saubermann, the beneficent wife of the factory owner, who was inviting Kratzenstein to a get-together. He said "very flattering" and other niceties and chatted longer than it seemed to me appropriate for a man with so much to do.

"Yes, if we . . . Where were we?"

"I had very much hoped to give a presentation, Professor, but you thought—"

"No, just get that out of your head! But I have something good for you. I have convinced the working group that it would be good for everyone if you were invited to the regular meetings. Frau Fixler has already noted it and sent you the invitation."

"Many thanks!"

"There your experiences could sometimes be of use, but above all, and this is much more important, you'll benefit from it, as you will learn how it's done. The proper method and all that. That makes much more sense than a presentation, which will only make you look bad. Everything depends on a first impression, but that's the way it is."

I didn't let on that I was beaten, for I wanted to defend my text and know more precisely what I should do in order to have it accepted. But that got me no further than my other pleas to consider my suggestions about doing a different presentation. In two or three years, the Professor reassured me, once I'd learned more and knew how to clear my throat and spit, perhaps we could consider the possibility once again, but no earlier. After this pronouncement it would have been a good time for me to leave, that I could sense, but it wasn't so easy for me to let go of such a crucial opportunity to get Kratzenstein to hear more about my central work. Even if I no longer believed that he was the right man to talk to, every conversation I'd had with Haarburger, So-and-So, and other people indicated that one had to get to Kratzenstein. One word from him and a fellowship would be assured, for his influence decided it all.

The Professor consented, so good, I talked away, straight from the gut, he listening attentively, though also asking that I make it short, as time was pressing. I hardly said two sentences before he interrupted me. This kept happening more and more often, the Professor distracting me with side issues, such that I lost confidence in the central argument and began to stutter. Kratzenstein then took the opportunity to give me a lecture about well-known matters that were already familiar to me and that were easily found in the literature. He couldn't emphasize enough that all suffering, insofar as it was not based in human nature, was the result of economic conditions. The concentration camp, which resulted from a specific kind of exploitation, as well as everything else that made it so abominable, needed to be explained through social-psychological methods. Above all, collective aversion, which resulted from deep feelings of inferiority that are then compensated for through aggression, must be carefully analyzed. Kratzenstein's platitudes, propped up with big words, soon had little to do with my thesis and wafted dully about my ears, completely dead, dogmatic declarations that did nothing but elicit the connections between multiple aspects and elucidate them. I said nothing, or just politely nodded. When at the end I asked what kind of support I could expect to have for my work, the Professor said, everything you need, he could certainly do something, even if not at the moment. Plans that had not yet been fully worked out needed to come to fruition, the next thing being for me to get going and to familiarize myself with the literature; one couldn't cut one's teeth on nothing.

"Yes, but how long—"

"Don't be in such a hurry, my dear friend! After your initial studies, you'll need six months for the first draft, then two more years to revise it. But you'll gain such respect, because you are so preoccupied with your thesis. That will give you the strength to convince me and the entire world. When your work is finished and is what I imagine it will be, then you can come to me. Right?"

"Yes, Professor."

"Look, that's what needs to happen! We can then discuss what we can do with your work."

"Yes, Professor. But could I perhaps ask you, Herr Professor, whether or not you see any opportunity as to how I might secure some kind of foundation whereby financially—"

"Oh, I see! Of course . . . That I need to think about. Just wait—"

"I mean, if you—"

"I understand already what you want. Unfortunately, my dear Herr Doctor, unfortunately . . . The International Society of Sociologists has no—"

There was a knock at the door, and Frau Fixler appeared with a soft nod, asking to be excused.

"Forgive me, Professor," the secretary said while constantly looking at her wristwatch. "Forgive me, but the gentlemen have been waiting for almost a quarter of an hour for you to be at the meeting."

"Look, Herr Doctor, that's the way it is. I'm really very sorry. It was such a pleasure to be of help to you, even if not to the extent that—"

"Many thanks! But could you please tell me quickly what I might still—"

"Dr. Singule, I think, or Dr. Haarburger and his wife they are such good people. You're already in their good graces."

"Professor!" Frau Fixler called out nervously.

"I'm coming! Goodbye, Herr Dr. Landau, and I wish you all good luck! You'll certainly stay in touch?"

"If that would be all right."

"But of course! It would be such a pleasure! Frau Fixler, you have his address?"

"Yes, Professor."

"And you made a note to invite him to the regular meetings of the working group?"

"Yes."

The Professor didn't extend his hand to me but waved quickly, said something else, and was gone. I picked up my presentation from his desk—he had forgotten to give it to me—and put it in the folder of other writings that I had wanted to show to him and leave with him in part, but which I had never had the chance to bring out. Frau Fixler wanted to call the attendant, but I said I could see myself out, and with that I said goodbye. I never got any invitation to the meeting of the working group. I called a couple of times, not too often, reaching no one but the secretary, who became ever less friendly. Then I finally gave up.

It seemed a reasonable idea to turn to other people. Sometime later, after I got to know Frau Singule at the Haarburgers', she took ill and spent half a year at a spa hotel in Switzerland, where Fräulein Knispel's brother was the house doctor. For the most part, Dr. Singule was not in the country but traveled from conference to conference and spent a number of months in America, but as his wife recovered and he was finally home again, Frau Haarburger insisted that I follow through on this very important contact. That was shortly after the disappointment with Professor Kratzenstein. Since he had just mentioned the name Singule, I wasn't too inclined to seek out an audience with this man. If a famous sociologist had shown so little understanding of me, what could I at all expect from a man who, because of his own preoccupations, had little interest in my work, and who, sadly enough, was known not to have any time for people asking for his help. My sense of mistrust was also seconded by So-and-So, who was dismissive of Singule. It's true that my friend usually had nothing nice to say about anyone he knew—about Kratzenstein he offered praise that was laced with numerous reservations—but he simply had nothing good to say about Singule and made fun of him with bitter mockery as of no other. Some years before, Singule had commissioned So-and-So with a specific project that had to do with the composition of social motivations in nineteenth-century Russian literature, but when, after some months, he submitted the work to Singule, the latter had no memory of the request, saying that for him and the American foundation it was worthless, he was no fool, and that he had never ordered any such thing. Vainly So-and-So tried to refresh the man's memory and had to take away his work without having any recourse against Singule, as he had nothing in writing. I related this story to Frau Haarburger in order to convince her that I really didn't want anything to do with Singule. She said, yes, she had already heard that from her husband, but first, you shouldn't take it as gospel truth, and second, even the best of men do such things, that was her opinion, and you shouldn't see it so tragically but, rather, I should visit Singule and I would see how splendid he is, how well I would get along with him. As I hesitated, Frau Haarburger went to the phone and called the Singules. Both happened to be home and, to my surprise, I was invited to tea on the following Sunday.

I rang the doorbell of the villa; a sweet servant girl opened the door and led me, as I told her my name, immediately to the salon. The couple arrived soon after, greeted me, and asked me to have a seat. Frau Singule didn't waste any time, and seemed very pleased to see me again. She was only disappointed that I had not brought along Johanna, and was taken aback when I said that my wife had not been invited, so I couldn't after all bring her along. Invitations, I was told, are always meant for both members of a married couple, especially in the case of such a delightful woman.

"A charming little person, your wife. From the best of families—one notices it immediately upon meeting her. I've known her for some years. One can only wish her all happiness. Tell me, Herr Landau, she does indeed make you happy, right?"

"One never really knows such things, madam."

"Oh, of course you know. You should know it, especially as a newly married man. And isn't it true that the children are not much of a burden to you, either?"

"Madam, I only regret that I didn't bring her with me."

"You should regret it. Every moment is lost in which such a treasure is forsaken. Her refinement is written all over her face."

"Yes."

"Well, it's good that you agree, and that's why you should not say anything wrong about such an angel. I know what she did for work. She gave it her all, but was always friendly, always pleasant. When the war was over, I went to her on behalf of my husband. How she put herself out to find any trace of my brother-in-law! Did she never tell you?"

"No, madam."

"What, she never told you how desperately we wished to find out what had happened to my brother-in-law, Dr. Berthold Singule, the lawyer? I find that strange!"

"No, she really didn't."

"She didn't say a word, but how hard she tried! Nothing but humility, especially if she didn't say anything! She went down a hundred different paths for us, calling every Tom, Dick, and Harry she could think of, as one says, and lots more. She did nothing less than move heaven and earth. And she never told you that?"

"No, madam."

"Well, then! But that's so dignified of her, one sees that—such discretion, and then, because she doesn't wish to bother anyone, not even her own husband!"

"I only know what she did in general."

"Yes, that's what I said! She's so refined! She spares her husband such things! And that's why one shouldn't burden her. She's had enough trouble already. Perhaps you don't know, but not only did her parents die over there; she also lost a brother here. Such misfortune—both brothers!"

"I know, madam."

"Good that you at least know that. But to have to carry such responsibility, how terrible! You must be thinking about it all the time. You should create a paradise on earth for her!"

"That's hard to do, very hard."

"Of course it's hard. Why shouldn't it be? Nothing comes from nothing. Which is why you have to work for it. What you want is what you get."

"Do you think so?"

"And do I! But you just have to work for it."

"That's true, but one also needs help."

"We're here for that—myself and, above all, my husband. If he only had time. He never has time. He's already left again just now. It's terrible!"

"So I won't have a chance to meet him?"

"Just because you don't know him, don't worry! He'll stand by what he promised. He's only gone off a short ways. Just a couple houses down. He knows that you're coming. He'll receive you. Certainly. I have promised Frau Haarburger that it would happen. How lucky to have such a friend! She adores you! And Dr. Haarburger as well. The talent you have. You're indeed a self-made man. You would agree. And then there's my husband. He's so mellow and ready for anything. Only one can't do it all. Which is why I always advise, you should arrange something practical."

"But you believe—"

"Of course, if only he can. Just imagine what is asked of him. He simply can't do everything."

"But you see possibilities?"

"Certainly, Herr Landau. There are possibilities. One only has to find them. But normally it's hard to, and then everything is in vain. I tell you— It looks like my husband is here. Indeed he is, or would seem to be. E-du-ard. E-du-ard! Are you there?"

"Yes, I'm here, Klara."

I was greeted courteously.

"How happy I am to make your acquaintance, Dr. Singule."

"Singule, just Singule, Herr Landau. I am indeed a doctor, but it's not customary to use it here. Just the last name."

"I've been told that's the way to address doctors. And you are indeed a doctor of medicine?"

"Correct, but I don't practice it. I'm a biologist—particularly bugs, vermin. Unfortunately, I have too little time for it. I have too many other responsibilities."

"But it's your main interest?"

"Actually, yes. I'm really fascinated by mites. Do you know anything about them?"

"Only from what I've heard, Doctor."

"Please, Singule! Make a note of it! There are as many doctors as there is sand at the beach, but we are the only Singules in the city. The name was never that common, and today it has almost disappeared."

"You two need to talk shop. Wouldn't it be best, Eduard, if you took Herr Landau across the way. You both have a lot to talk about, and I'll arrange for some tea for you."

Herr Singule agreed, and I followed him to his study. For some minutes, the conversation ranged through different subjects; I didn't have the nerve or the drive to turn the talk to my concerns. So the talk flowed on until the biologist surprised me with an unexpected question.

"Tell me, are you from Latvia, perhaps Riga?"

"No."

"Too bad. You should be from Latvia."

"Is it because of my accent?"

"It has nothing to do with your accent. I need someone from Latvia."

"To my great sadness, I have never been there."

"And your wife?"

"She's from Vienna."

"That's too bad. That doesn't help us at all."

"Why does it have to be Latvia, Herr Singule?"

"I need someone from Latvia. Your parents, your ancestors, anyone in the family?"

"None from Latvia."

"I had hoped for that especially for you, Herr Landau. It would have done well by you. I have something to give to someone from Latvia. A terrific assignment that will last at least a year, and with the possibility of an extension."

"Really?"

"Yes. You don't even need to know the language. Just Latvia."

"How nice of you to think of me."

"One tries, my friend, one tries the best one can."

"But hopefully you might find something else for me. I'm working, as perhaps you've already heard, primarily on a sociology of—"

"My wife already told me everything, as well as Haarburger. I'm well informed."

"Good. And therefore I wondered if there might not be a way to consider a proposal—"

"You can make a proposal anytime. You're completely free to do so. You don't even have to come to my office; I can give you the form right now."

"Thank you. And might I expect, if you recommend it, that I—"

"You didn't let me finish talking. The form and the proposal don't do anything for you. Nor can I recommend anything, even if I have the chance. And yet it must be approved, and there's the rub."

"Don't you decide?"

"Oh, I decide a great deal. Without me, no one in Europe gets anything. But I have to be able to answer for it, and I cannot decide everything. My dear friend, what are you thinking? I'm a poor man; the money doesn't come from my pockets. Yes, if you were from Latvia that would be fine, for then I have something, then I can do something. But alas!"

"Anything in my line of work?"

"Not immediately. But do you think I can really support a line of work? Not at all!"

"Then you have nothing to recommend to me?"

"For sociologists I have nothing. Certainly not at the moment. You can certainly apply, that I already told you. And I will see what can be done, though it's not up to me. Most of what we give is to natural science. Physics, chemistry, biology, geology and the rest. Otherwise, only when we get special assignments. They are very popular, and everyone goes after them, and then we choose someone."

"Will you think of me if something comes up?"

"With great pleasure. It would be an honor."

"And in between?"

"Take the forms with you! Have a look at them! Don't skip any questions, fill out everything scrupulously! It will all be reviewed. A lot depends on the accompanying documents. You need six copies of everything; photocopies of documents are allowed."

"I'm missing many papers. The war. I lost so much."

"How terrible! You have to have the proper documents! Couldn't you order copies from over there?"

"That would be very difficult—in fact, I fear, impossible."

"Well, my dear friend, how you take care of that is your business. I really can't be of any help to you! Somehow you'll have to pull a rabbit out of your hat. You'll need them everywhere, and not just for our foundation. Just imagine, if no one had any papers, how much crime could happen! Without documents, I'm telling you, you don't even exist."

"I don't exist, Herr Singule. With that, you've touched on the truth."

"Go on, enough of this romantic nonsense! What you need to do, if I may, is simply sit on your behind and write. That's not so hard, is it?"

"I write a great deal! But it's all in vain."

"In vain. . . . Do you need me to say something crass! What talk! Do what you have to do and write every Tom, Dick, and Harry, if need be, until you get those documents! If there's no other way, make a quick trip and take care of matters in person. They'll give you those documents or a proper copy—it's child's play. When you have everything together, then concentrate on a curriculum vitae."

"A résumé?"

"Yes, a vitae. Don't you know Latin?"

"Of course."

"Then do it!"

"What I don't know is what to say. Everything escapes me. The entire past . . ."

"Toss such sentimentality to the devil! What you experienced is of interest to no one at all. Just what you've done, a real résumé—education, dates, important events and achievements. That's all. And when you have that, then work on a thorough synopsis of your planned project. That's easy, right?"

"I hope so."

"Enough with such resistance! And submit a sample chapter as well."

"Happy to."

"It doesn't need to be long. In fact, it's better if it's short, for you don't have much time. They will only look at it and nothing else."

"I understand, Doctor."

"And get rid of the title! Are you so scatterbrained that you can't remember that? And then the most important part—you need three, better yet, four or five references. Why do you look at me like that? Is there something else wrong?"

"No, no! But what kind of references?"

"Recommendations from internationally recognized figures, if possible from your special area, if possible from this country or America, if possible with attestations of your previous achievements and the likely scholarly worth of the planned project."

"In all honesty, I doubt I can manage all that."

"My dear friend, I've never met an applicant as difficult as you! If I didn't like you so much, such talk by now would have forced me to throw you out."

"Shall I leave?"

"Don't be silly! And don't be so sensitive! You can surely find a couple of sociologists to befriend, can't you?"

"I should be so lucky!"

"Think for a minute. Do you know Professor Kratzenstein?"

"Yes."

"Excellent! Then it's done. He's as good as having two or three!"

"If he will write something for me."

"Oh, you're such a pessimist! Just get on the bus tomorrow and go see him. Or, better yet, call him. Do you know his secretary?"

"Frau Fixler?"

"Well, then, excellent! You know everything you need to already! Put together a text tonight, go to Frau Fixler, explain the situation to her and that the Professor should sign it, and then next day just swing by and pick it up! That's how it's done. Quite simple. And who else do you know?"

"Not many. Dr. So-and-So."

"Who?"

"Forgive me, Dr. Leonard Kauders."

"What does he do?"

"He's a docent in the history of economics, and the author of the book *Work and Climate*."

"Never heard of it. It must be recent."

"You know Kauders, don't you?"

"I know thousands of people, my dear friend!"

"He did some work for you once."

"There are hundreds who have! I can't remember them all."

"A consideration of the social themes in Russian literature—"

"Is he from Latvia?"

"No."

"Too bad. Then nothing can be done."

"I could get a recommendation from Kauders."

"Better to let that go! You need names, names! But if you know Kratzenstein so well, then I wonder why you don't simply go to him—"

Frau Singule interrupted this sentence with her entrance, laughing at us, pleased with how lively we talked with each other, and led us in to tea. The time dragged on, growing ever more unedifying. Dr. Singule complained about the shortage of good insect specialists, for whom he would pave the streets with gold, he being an external consultant to the firm Insecta, the biggest special concern in the area in the entire country, and Insecta had advertised to no avail for a good biologist. Things kept on like this until I excused myself for a moment. Afterward, the lady of the house was much cooler toward me. She set about to inform me that, unfortunately, her husband's hands were tied, the American foundation had very firm guidelines, one could not support proposals that fell outside the parameters that would be granted a stipend, no matter how much one might wish to do so. That was really too bad, especially in my case, since I have such a delightful wife, whom one can only wish the best for, but in the end the foundation is not the only place in the world that should appeal to me; on the contrary, elsewhere there might be much better prospects, such as through Professor Kratzenstein, it being good that I had access to him, while Frau Singule would make sure to put in a good word with him in the name of her husband the next chance she got. I prepared to leave, for Singule was out of time and had a pressing engagement, and Frau Singule wanted to accompany him. And yet I couldn't just run off, for the lady of the house surprised me with a gift that she pulled out of a table drawer. It was a bar of milk chocolate; Frau Singule didn't have anything more suitable in the house, but Johanna was so slight and needed to eat something restorative, and a little bit of chocolate would no doubt please her. Then the biologist asked me if he could give me a lift in his car, but I declined, and thanked him for the lovely afternoon as I left with the request from Singule to ask around to see if I could find anyone from Latvia, as well as effusive good wishes for my well-being.

Who knew whether I was either so stupid or so clever not to let myself be thrown off by such terrible disappointments, applying myself doubly to my work with the firm belief that sheer effort and accomplishment would carry the day. I was too blind, and Johanna too inexperienced, to know that such an approach could never lead to a livelihood. After numerous requests and appeals, Uncle Karl Strauss finally sent a small sum that my parents had managed to spirit away to America just in time, though for me it was almost a fortune. He controlled the money, which I only learned about after asking around a great deal after the war, and offered a thousand reasons that he couldn't just turn it over. The more I pressed him, the more stubbornly he insisted that I and my wife should emigrate to America, where we could both have jobs in his upscale clothing store. If one couldn't get any money out of Europe because the countries there were broke, then certainly one should not send any money over from America but instead thank your lucky stars that you had a couple of dollars tucked away there. I still didn't have the sum in hand when news reached me that Karl Strauss had suddenly died of a heart attack. We then used this amount to get ourselves through, although Johanna also had to sacrifice her limited savings and—with the exception of a small break when Michael was born—take in work at home, as she does to this day.

Herr Larry Saubermann had a factory that made artificial beads and other jewelry that was dipped in pearl essence or sprayed with it. During the war and after, there were not many good wares available. That was fortunate for Herr Larry Saubermann, who earlier had merely been wealthy but who now actually made money. He was a rich man, and he was capable and also posh. He didn't think only of himself and his wife; he also helped others survive who needed to—poor girls from the country and women who had fled from other countries and were in desperate need. He handed them money and asked nothing more than that they thread beads. Many beads. The more the better, for then he paid more. Frau Ida Saubermann was just as capable as her husband and knew her duties, for she helped him and had good ideas. On top of this she also took on other tasks, sitting on several committees, one of which she founded and headed herself, helping to organize medical relief where possible, attacking problems constructively as well, for she was practical and attracted so many good workers to the business of stringing beads and other useful work that could be done at home. Whoever had agile hands could do quite well at it. Both Saubermanns were good-natured, as well as being cultivated and beloved within social circles.

I didn't know the owners of the factory, though I had met Frau Saubermann once in passing at a party the Haarburgers held to introduce me to their friends. I didn't have a pleasant memory of her, because I had somewhat of a sharp exchange with her, though Johanna felt that I had been in the wrong, as our conversation had gotten off on totally the wrong foot, for, really, she was a nice woman who had helped a number of people. Johanna had a soft spot for her and earlier had enjoyed her company a number of times, and, moreover, Herr Saubermann was not at all bad and indeed was fond of Johanna, since he had been a patient of her father's and had much to thank him for, which he never forgot. Because of this I abandoned any feeling of resentment when Johanna said she wanted to ask Herr and Frau Saubermann if they could give her any work to do at home. Johanna called them and, to her joy, not only was she invited round for an evening at their apartment; I was as well. I didn't want to go along, but Johanna thought it essential that I accompany her, because that would make a much better impression. We arrived, as had been arranged, after dinner. It was a lovely home, full of many exquisite treasures; many wonderful things called out to be marveled at, only to have their splendor taken away somewhat by whatever stood next to them. The walls everywhere were filled with paintings, several of them good older ones, a few good newer ones, and too many horrible paintings with expensive frames, in addition to a number of caricatures, all of them of the husband and none of his wife, some with him wearing his beads and other jewelry, others without any such pearl essence. There were also photographs hanging on the walls and standing around, among them special-effects photos, portraits, landscapes, and still-lifes, all of which seemed to me more awful than the caricatures. Most of the photos were by Larry Saubermann himself.

As in a museum, we wandered from room to room, but the women soon retreated, as Johanna already knew the layout and her feet were somewhat swollen, the baby being due in only a couple of months. It didn't entirely sit well with the factory owner's wife that Johanna passed, with hardly any objection, on forging ahead with the tour, because the wife was of the view that you could not take in such wonders often enough, some of them having had their positions or presentations altered in order that you could take them in anew, or there was some new acquisition that merited attention, or, above all, it would have seemed right to Frau Saubermann for Johanna to see the effect of these treasures upon me, though now, of course, she had to deny herself this treat, which was too bad. "You can't have everything," Johanna assured her. Therefore the factory owner marched through the rooms with me alone, pointing out and commenting on everything, and when I missed something or didn't say much about it, I was taken by the arm and had to return until he was satisfied that he had gotten me to take it all in completely. Herr Saubermann maintained that his collection was at least as great as any to be found in a real museum, and not just because of the value and rarity of the objects but also because it was a collection that you would not find in a real museum, there being nothing but dust and stuffiness to pain the eyes, for all of it was personal, all of it lively, imbued with the spirit and love of the married couple in a way that you never saw in any museum. All art treasures in the world were presented at a distance in soulless public exhibitions, while high-minded and understanding friends of the museum, who, in the interests of preservation and social duty, offered up such goods and handed over the responsibility for them by loaning them out so that the public had access to such treasures. Then one could see who was really interested in art. Didn't I agree? I didn't disagree but instead expressed mild doubt.

"It's clear, Doctor, that you yourself have spent too much time in the museum. That leads to trouble. You and all the conservators and custodians of the world who are not complete fossils should be forced to live in houses that contain collections, just as I do, and the government should pay for the costs. Then you'd learn something! I've had plenty of museum people visit here. Most of them don't like it at all. What's your general opinion of my collection, Herr Doctor?"

"I'm not an expert."

"Really? Most so far would have formulated some kind of opinion, and, unfortunately, most have a bias, but no one has ever said that he was not an expert."

"Really, Herr Saubermann, I'm not competent in this area."

"But you indeed worked in a museum, you helped build a collection! Was my wife wrong?"

"And I got out of there as soon as I could."

"I see! Then I can talk reasonably with you, which makes you a pleasure to know. Do you also have trouble with the whole business of museums?"

"I can't say that, in general."

Herr Saubermann continued to beat around the bush for a while, but my views didn't entirely satisfy him. I was too tired when I tried to explain to him what my position had been in the museum. He understood me and our museum much less well, and as something that was entirely different from what most museums did. He finally gave up and led me back to the ladies, who were sitting in a little salon with something sweet.

"It's good that you're back, Larry. Was he pleased?"

"Why not ask the doctor?"

"Wonderful, madam, an extraordinary collection."

"Just imagine, Ida, he seems not to have a real connection to art history."

"I've thought the same myself for a long time. He indeed left his museum over there in the lurch."

"No, that was not wrong of him, Ida."

"Oh, yes it was. Certainly in his case. He could have helped build the collection. He seems to me to be a deserter."

"That's not necessarily bad, Ida. One only needs to know what one is deserting to."

"Look here, my dear man, there you have it. My husband is using almost the same words as I am."

"Ah, are you talking about me?"

"Yes, Herr Doctor," said Frau Saubermann. "Just so that you know it as well."

"Johanna, are you not feeling well?" I asked. "You look so pale."

"It's nothing, Arthur."

"Now don't you worry. The time to worry was earlier. Forgive me, Larry, but we are standing in the middle of a social situation. An object lesson, in so many words, a classic. I already told you something about the gentleman. Gifted, intellectual, imaginative, yet a total mess, having come here as a survivor like a gold digger to Alaska, but naturally without the same drive, thus a broken man—and I mean that well, I'm not trying to say anything bad by that—who expects that the golden apple will simply fall from the tree and bump him on the nose. Then he woos Johanna, who is too young for him, with sweet woozy talk, the sympathetic, dear woman then marrying him for nothing and starting off on a lovely perilous existence, whereupon Johanna is expecting a baby in no time and the misfortune is complete—no money, in ruins, miserable, everything."

"Madam!"

"Be quiet, Herr Doctor! I remember exactly what I told you at the Haarburgers'. And you know as well that's what I make of you. And now you're looking for a handout, and that is what I predicted."

"You cannot speak to me like that."

"Be quiet! Here I am in my own house!"

"Yes, in your museum, madam, with the responsibility that comes to one who is morally free! You are indeed morally free, but, unfortunately, much too free of morals! I recall every part of your lovely speech, to the letter!"

"Arthur, for God's sake be quiet!"

"Don't get so excited, Doctor!" said the factory owner. "You're as red as a lobster! You're getting much too excited!"

"Unfortunately, it's too late, Larry, too late for him to get upset. He wants to capitalize upon his misfortune. Just as I predicted! Irresponsible narcissism, egocentrism instead of refinement. It's all about me! And everyone else should just circle around in adoration!"

"And not a trace of refinement!" I hissed in anger.

"I'm begging you, Arthur, don't make a scene. The dear lady doesn't mean anything terrible by it."

"Whether terrible or not, we're not beggars. No one has a right to insult us."

"I can do what I wish in my house."

"You certainly can, madam, and that's why we're leaving."

"Arthur, wait! Everything can be explained!"

"Yes, please, my good man. Ida, what's the meaning of this?"

"Let me explain, Larry. One needs to keep one's dignity. The pure spirit of humanity that exists between these walls cannot be upset. That's why the Herr Doctor has to be taken to task."

"You're too kind, madam."

"Please, please, Arthur, don't say a thing."

"Larry, we have to do something! Decency demands it. And we cannot say, like the poet, 'Grave companions, to the gallows!' Especially when there is a child involved. Frau Johanna wants to string beads. Is there a spot for her?"

"It's good work, Frau Johanna, and one can feed one's husband—"

"What do you mean by 'one's husband,' Herr Saubermann?"

"I only meant it in general terms. Don't be so touchy! That's fine, Frau Johanna, but it's not really for your little fingers, such finicky work, and especially given your upbringing and background as a violinist!"

"That doesn't matter to me, as long as I can earn something in my free time."

"My dear child—I can call you that, for I did in fact know you when you were a golden girl—my dear child, what are you thinking! That's not any kind of proper work for you. If I had to stand before your dear father and say to him, 'Herr Doctor, your Johanna is threading artificial beads!,' he would turn over in his grave, and I would sink into the ground from shame!"

"Larry, I thought all of that as well and said the same to you already. But she needs it, everything depends on it! We have to!"

"Johanna doesn't know what she's in for, Ida, she doesn't know what she's asking for. Look here, child, it's not what you think—namely, to just earn something in your free time. You have to work from morning till night. Otherwise, it's not worth it."

"She's only looking for pocket money!"

"Ida, that's not the kind of pocket money that's right for her father's only daughter! That's ridiculous!"

"She can work some hours every day, Larry. I already explained it to her. In any case, do you have a free spot?"

"Nothing for at home, just whole days at the factory."

"That I'm afraid I cannot do!"

"You see so for yourself, Frau Johanna. I'm terribly sorry, but I knew it."

"Larry, do you really have nothing for her at home? I'm disappointed to hear it."

"No, I swear there isn't anything at all! We're overstaffed. I can hardly justify holding on to the worst workers. The business just isn't the same. Nice goods are becoming available again. I've told you so for months, Ida. We have to concentrate on better quality."

Johanna was very pale. She whispered something, knowing what she wanted to say, but then she couldn't speak. I looked at Frau Saubermann in anger, but she hardly stirred. I had remained standing the whole time and was waiting for the right moment when I could safely whisk Johanna away. She hadn't touched the cup of black coffee in front of her, and I knew how much she loved coffee. So I motioned to her as subtly as possible, and she grabbed the cup and emptied it in one gulp. I could feel her keeping an eye on me, trying to smile, which helped appease my anger and gave me strength. I certainly didn't want a new scene to occur, and even managed to pull myself together in order to thank both of the factory owners for a lovely evening as I drew closer to Johanna, first grabbing hold of her hand, then her arm, as she leaned on me and pulled herself up.

"I think it's time for us to be going," she said.

"As you wish, my dear child," chirped the factory owner's wife. "You saw how I did everything I could. You always know who you can turn to. Make sure to call me! Larry and I will not let you down, if things get even worse!"

"Hopefully, that won't happen, Frau Saubermann."

"Hopefully!" said the factory owner. "Hopefully! You really shouldn't be disappointed. Maybe later you'll thank me for seeming, only seeming, to be hard-hearted. And certainly make sure to call my wife, for she was speaking to me from the bottom of her heart. Come back soon, my dear little Johanna!"

The couple accompanied us to the foyer, me holding Johanna tight. We shook hands, and I hoped that we were free to go, but Frau Saubermann had other ideas.

"Larry, be so good as to talk to our dear friend Johanna for a quick moment! It won't take long. I still have something quick to say to the Herr Doctor."

I didn't know how it happened, because I was in no way willing to leave Johanna for a second, but suddenly Frau Saubermann had spirited me away and pulled me into a corner. Here a bright traffic light blazed, one that I can still clearly see before me, a framed photograph of the factory owner's wife bathed in honey yellow, the image the same forever and featuring a tense, toothy smile that neither a good nor a bad painter would ever have depicted but which, instead, had been captured by his lordship the camera bug.

"As an experienced, educated woman, it's not much that I have to say. You have behaved like a scoundrel to Johanna. You are nothing but a common seducer, do you hear? I swear, if it weren't for the child I would have no qualms about urging Johanna to leave you. You are not the man for her. You can expect nothing from us until you can show that you are willing to take care of your wife and child through honest work! The husband must support the wife if he wants to earn the right for her to also slave away. Are you a man? Say something! Can you swear to do what you must?"

I was silent and dully saw before me the wan, glowing face of the factory owner. I wanted to get past him, but he stood in my way in a lordly manner, whispering something to me that I couldn't understand, after which I thrust a fist at the factory owner, not too hard, just enough to rock him a bit so that I could get past him and head for the exit. I didn't bother casting a single glance at the man, who was talking sweetly to Johanna, but instead I grabbed hold of her and before we knew it we were both free of the place. We never again spoke of the factory owners. Johanna found other work to take in and could never forgive me for this disgraceful performance.

What Johanna took upon herself in order to make things easier for us she did because of her belief in my work and in my future success. I carelessly encouraged her. Indeed, some well-meaning people with a lot more love than suitable means supported us, but for one thing they had no power, or they didn't understand what we were trying to do, or they misjudged, however well-intentioned, where it was all meant to lead. Hardly anyone really knew how to help, and hardly anyone was of real beneficial help, as no one was devoted enough or was only capable of keeping a friendly eye focused on me, the result being that my plans and projects were, in my own sense, failures. When it came to advice, criticism, or rebukes, no one held back, but instead lacked the ability to take me by the hand with tact. I was cheered on insincerely, and my talent was unfairly thwarted. My efforts went the way of the world and came to nothing. The further along I got in the writing of my main work, the more often I gained entrance to a new acquaintance who encouraged me anew. Plaudits would follow, new hopes then slipping in, such that the lack of practical help for Johanna and me seemed about to ease. I actually don't know how I would have been able to maintain my outer composure if I had known, ahead of time, the continual failure I would experience in my first years in the metropolis; undoubtedly, I would have abandoned my studies, and my work would have remained no more than mere notes. Perhaps I should have hidden out in some office, as so many urged me to do, but that would have been difficult and would have been hard for me to take, or I could have given language lessons in private or applied for a post at a night school, or I could, as So-and-So and others urged, have begun a study that would have brought in money, or for which I was vaguely promised a stipend, or I should have taken some kind of job for which I was minimally suited, in order to keep myself afloat. But I refused to do any of this.

My ceaseless work proved too much for my health, as I found that it was so unsavory that I couldn't expect too much of myself. At night I was usually exhausted, such that I couldn't do anything else but rest, though I was never able to. Defeated, I sank into bed and immediately fell asleep, then woke much too soon and rose early without feeling refreshed. Later on in the fourth year of my arrival in these parts, when finished works still lay idle in my desk drawer or were sent back to me by experts or publishers, and then only after my having to write to inquire about them, my scholarly career—how strange that sounds!—not having ended, some acquaintances, who didn't wish to say anything about my misery, did something behind my back. Somehow they pulled together the funds, which they made clear in conversation were guaranteed, that, if I would be willing to study languages or history at a university, could be used to help me get a position at a high school. The suggestion to develop such a plan, although I never found out for sure, seemed to have come from So-and-So. Perhaps I'm only imagining that out of mistrust, but I can't help thinking that the point was to keep me from my scholarly work and thus eliminate me from the competition, while at the same time discharging any moral responsibility they might feel for me. The offer wasn't made directly to me but fell upon Johanna—who had just been sick with the flu—they no doubt thinking that she would bring me around. She had to inform me that a circle of unnamed well-intentioned people were ready to supply me and my family with a small sum until the end of my studies, provided I would be ready to fulfill the binding conditions of the plan. Johanna presented me with this ultimatum shaken and with a sad face, while continuously saying she was sorry, though she didn't expect me to capitulate, which it didn't occur to me to do, either. "We have to stick together and hang on!" were her words. I thought about it, indeed, but after a night spent talking about it we knew that I couldn't do it. I couldn't do anything more, for things had gone too far; I was simply too weak, overwhelmed and overwrought. Johanna volunteered to convey my decision.

Only in the first weeks, when I was promised the heavens, would I have agreed to such a proposal. Back then, I discussed a similar plan with the Haarburgers in order to allow me to get an extension on my visa and a material foothold in the country, but the two of them laughed at me. If I only worried about the future, I would soon be easily distracted, for how could a man of my talents sell himself for chicken feed, that was just out of the question. I should not lose a single hair over it, the Haarburgers would always take care of me, even if I needed something to get me through. Dr. Haarburger pulled his checkbook from his pocket. I was touched by so much kindness and yet declined it with my thanks, since I still had some means at my disposal. Johanna, whom I asked if I'd done the right thing, agreed that one shouldn't take any money unless he absolutely needed it. More than half a year later, after my disappointment with Kratzenstein and Singule, and yet before my horrible visit with the Saubermanns, I lightly raised the issue of my money worries with Dr. Haarburger, who responded as ever in a friendly and welcoming manner, but essentially the appeal fell on deaf ears. My suggestions were considered thoughtfully and just as much interest was shown for the advancement of my work. Haarburger thought my troubling conversation with Kratzenstein a real boon, his interest having been won for good, while an invitation to the regular meetings of the working group was no everyday honor, for the Professor would no doubt warm to me more and more, and he, after all, is the president of the society, all of it something that my friend Kauders would congratulate himself for if he were ever to make it that far. My doubt and anxiety were swept away. Haarburger was delighted that I now knew Frau Fixler, for she was a good soul, and Hannah should call her, no, better so Jolan. Anyway, Frau Fixler would take care of the Professor. Haarburger had already heard about the disappointment with Singule, which was certainly unfortunate but not disastrous, as support from the foundation just wasn't that easy to get, especially given how his hands were tied, the matter of Latvia, sociology, so little time, and everything else. What didn't work out today might well work out tomorrow. Had I sent in my application to Singule yet? I had not done so at all. Such a blunder, he complained, such a mistake. Hannah was beside herself: Do it immediately. What's that, impediments? They don't matter and, as for documents, pah, they're nothing, it all can't be done in one shot, but the main thing was that the application was there, and Jolan would be happy to write a professional opinion. Then I was fed splendidly and entertained by the couple, patted on the shoulder, and told not to be dismayed, for if I really didn't know what to do, at least then I knew something. And so I left with empty hands and warm greetings for Johanna, though I didn't feel at all disappointed.

Some weeks later, just after we had survived the terrible evening with the factory owners, I called the Haarburgers again. Frau Haarburger, with whom I spoke on the telephone, invited me over after some hesitation. When I arrived, she greeted me politely, yet was somewhat more reserved and cooler than before. Her husband was still busy; I had to make do with her in the meantime. We talked about this and that, the conversation moving forward in a wearisome manner, while Frau Haarburger kept talking about all the recent unexpected demands upon her husband, for I had no idea how many burdensome requests he was buried in, and that, in the end, one didn't live on milk and honey and one's wallet wasn't bottomless. Now and then I had to thoughtfully agree, but, above all, I had decided to be relentlessly open about my situation. I didn't want to be given anything; I was ready to exchange valuable goods as collateral against a loan. Finally, I seized the opportunity to put forward my request, but the words wouldn't come out. Meanwhile, did I know that Herr Buxinger, the bookseller, was having problems with cash flow? No, I didn't know that. Yes, indeed, Jolan had to put up a guarantee—one couldn't leave an old friend to flounder— and he will pay back everything, for sure. Those are the kinds of difficulties that any businessman has to face, and Buxinger is capable and will soon work himself out of it, but as a result Jolan's resources were somewhat reduced for a while. Again, I had to agree, and was about to lower the flag of my cause, but then Frau Haarburger gave me a sad and reproachful look.

"Tell me, I wasn't happy to hear about the Saubermanns. What happened? Dear Ida Saubermann is beside herself. What kind of person are you? Such a good person, so ethical to the core! It makes me despair to think of her suffering it all!"

"Madam, there's nothing I can do about it!"

"Oh, yes there is! There most certainly is!"

"I believe that in this case it's not my fault. The lady attacked Johanna and me. I'll spare you the details!"

"I wasn't spared anything. She told me everything, everything. No pleasure in that at all. You were completely brutal, she said. Aren't you ashamed?"

"No. Frau Saubermann was insulting."

"Insulting! Do you know what she's done for others? She's torn herself apart on behalf of others. As true as I sit here before you. And this accusation from you! No, that can't be! I won't let anything be said against Ida Saubermann."

"Madam, I'm not saying anything, either. It doesn't really matter to me. But when you begin to talk about it, then I have to defend myself."

"Don't defend yourself. I know that you've taken advantage of the fact that we like you, my husband and I, but the Saubermanns are not to be done ill by. Not by anyone. They have become ever more wealthy, and they do a great deal. People fed through honest work. Who does that? Show me!"

You've seen where they live, a museum to be envied. And how many artists have benefited, both living and dead."

"Especially the dead, I'm afraid."

"No, that's not for you to say! So unfeeling! How can you? And then you sing quite a different tune when you want someone's charity."

"We don't want any charity; nothing could be further from the truth."

"Charity or not, it's not about that. You wouldn't go there to ask for work at home if you thought anything of yourself. Like a beggar! Like a bum and, what's more, to make your wife do the asking. Jolan just shook his head when he heard."

"I'm sorry."

"I don't know how one can help you when you mess things up so with everyone. We presented you like a bonbon on a silver plate. That can't last forever. You have to understand. Nor can we take care of you forever, not at all. Friendship, yes, but then friendship. One hand washes the other."

"Madam, don't be angry with me! Look, things are not good for me, and I know that there is no one here who has done as much for us as you and the Herr Doctor. Where would I have been in the first weeks if I hadn't met you? Your home was my refuge. For once, let me please make a practical suggestion. I have no interest whatsoever in depleting your resources, I don't wish to be given anything. I own a few valuables, gold and such, things from my family, which I'd like to offer as security against a loan. My means are modest—Johanna also has only a couple of pennies saved—but there must be a way that we can be relieved of our misery and live for half a year somewhat free of worry so that I can finish my sociology of oppressed people. In a word, we are broke, and I need a certain amount of money to go on."

Frau Haarburger let me finish and expressed her concern, saying how sorry she was that I was caught in such difficulties. But I should have thought things through better right from the start. Back then, there was probably something that could have been done, it even perhaps having been possible to take up a collection among the Haarburgers' circle. But since then the situation had grown much worse, and now here I was, expressing my wishes much too late. Also, the idea of posting collateral against a loan—that was hardly done and wasn't quite proper. You either helped someone or you let it be. Slender hopes, only sorrow, sorrow, so much misery in the world—it's a crying shame, and if only one could do what one wished to. Life is just so hard. Frau Haarburger offered me a cognac, a good brand, and excused herself, leaving me there alone. After a little while, I heard her in the next room, she having taken a detour through the foyer, though I didn't know whether she had done so by chance or on purpose. She spoke with her husband; I couldn't understand what he said, just her, and even then not every word. Sadly her voice rose in indignation: "Jolan, he needs money, he has nothing to live on!" Then it was quiet for a moment, then I heard, even more piteously: "I'm telling you, he said he has nothing to live on! You need to help him out! It's all exactly as Ida said. I'm telling you, it's true!" Then I heard the doctor call out, "Impossible!" And then the answer: "It is so if I say so."

Not long afterward, Haarburger appeared with his wife behind him. He greeted me as jovially as ever and didn't let on about anything, but instead joked and was pleasant. Frau Haarburger hardly spoke and went to make a snack. When the doctor asked me in a good-natured way, "Well, then, how are things? What can I do for you?" I didn't hold back at all and said I needed money, and was there anyone the doctor knew who would give me an interest-free loan against collateral so that I could have a year free from money concerns in order to complete my book. Dr. Haarburger immediately began to praise my work, about which he knew only from my stories and understood only a little, but as to what I was asking he preferred to remain deaf. Yet I wouldn't let him do that, turning insistently back to the question. Finally, he said in a roundabout way that, unfortunately, he knew of no one, he'd have to think on it a bit. I repeated that I was offering security for such a loan. Yes, yes, that does indeed mean something, and he'd have to take that into consideration. What kind of security might it be? I had thought about that a long time and told him: the treasures that Herr Narad, Frau Holoubek, and other good people had handed over, my father's gold watch, itself a piece of collateral with a strange monogram, along with other watches and some jewelry from aunts and other relatives, Franziska's pearls—no, not those, Johanna had to keep those. Hesitantly I counted off everything. "Saubermann also collects jewelry," Jolan said with a harmless glance to the side, but, indeed, that didn't matter. "What's more, unfortunately, what I could give you would hardly be enough." Gold prices were down, and watches and ancient cheap jewelry had only sentimental value and were better stowed away as keepsakes than given away. Yes, large jewels, that would be something, such as triple chains of unblemished pearls, as well as emeralds, but not everyday third-rate gold confections.

I had nothing better to offer, and thus no security. The greatest of sorrows. I just had to keep my courage. Hard times. But time. Someone would help. Security would come. As well as better times, soon, just keep working, capably, successfully, Kratzenstein, gifted, we'll see, Singule, patience. The same for Buxinger. Books. I did have my books. Sell them. But no one bought books. Buxinger would buy mine, sell them. Oppressed people, a sociological tome. Whoever writes last writes best. Just write. No one will care. And yet there's care. Carat. A large diamond. Silver luster in the fanciest setting. A brilliant idea. Did you hear? Yes, yes, yes, yes. Accessories. Schmessories. Let's talk about something else. Do you know? No! She's important to know. Resi Knispel. Have you met her already. . . . She's planning something. Why haven't you visited her? She's looking. She's always looking. She's looking for you. You'll find. Very nice. No? I would strongly recommend that you . . . She wants to start a journal. Or something like that. And Fräulein Zinner, pardon me, your wife is expecting a child? How nice! How lovely! A little Knispel. A little tot. Maybe a boy, rather than a girl? Enough of that! You'll know soon enough! Progeny! A father's pride and joy. Haarburger's daughter already had a tot herself. But in Mexico. Lexico. Already talking, a bit of a lisp, babbling on, the little tot, teething already. Everything ready for the baby, it's important. That's right. Hannah asks, Mittens? Shoes? Diapers? Hannah can mend, Jolan will send. Wool, nice woolly wool. If I need advice, they'll be there, just say the word. To help, to pitch in. But I don't have any more time, I say. The Haarburgers sad, so sorry, but they understand, they're sorry. How it runs. Always at the ready. I'm really so sorry. No collateral, so I bowed. Already at the door the empty bow. Go on, off with you, down the three steps. A last bow. Hannah waves, waves, Jolan as well. So polite. Hope you're not disappointed. Quite the contrary. Advice and collateral and time, come see us again. Go see Knispel, don't forget, Resi Knispel, it's important. Greetings to your lovely young wife, she's wonderful, good luck with the little one, my wife, of course, is happy. Voices still echoing from the open door, take care, and waving. Zinner duped. And me in flight until the voice of collateral fades, and the fog lifts, and Johanna, who is waiting, embraces me with a lovely look.

I didn't see Dr. Haarburger and his wife again. Nor did Johanna go there, though right after Michael's birth she did receive a pair of little wool mittens for him in the mail.

Thus, over the course of time my sponsors disappeared, though others appeared, admittedly less and less, and I tried in vain to please them in a joking and clever manner. Yet nothing is harder than to please a sponsor who wants to do nothing but nourish his ideas of what he thinks is best for the one he cares for. Then it finally came to me. Unfortunately, I was too late. The time for refugees was past; they had all attached themselves to something or someone, and there was nothing left for foreigners, as the country had to take care of its own people. They fought for us, spilled their own blood, and suffered the pain of imprisonment. Chased from one place to another, I soon appreciated that there was one too many people in the world, and that was me. I simply couldn't be allowed to exist. Then, and only then, was this complex question answered. But how could I not exist! Indeed, I had not believed it myself, yet Johanna and others had tried patiently and had strenuously pointed out to me: You exist, don't deny it! You're suffering, so you must be alive, and it is you yourself that suffers. I repeated dutifully: The only thing that remains is that I exist, which is not some transcendental phenomena but, rather, something real, for one does not have to think it in order to realize it, even though the self rummages around in one's thoughts and cannot find itself, though indeed it exists. Here amid the search for existence, that's where I exist, having shown up and breathed and eaten, wanting only to be taken in completely, head and body and limbs, all of which are tired but are holding themselves together, one after another, not collapsing, forging on, all parts following the head. Yes, that is my central task. The culmination of this bothersome deliberation: Someone says it is so, therefore I exist. In addition: Existence can be experienced through dialogue. Put in a more mystical way: Existence arises out of dialogue. But that is indeed temptation and an inversion of the creation that has the Creator waiting when Adam in cowardly fashion doesn't respond to the call, "Where are you?" When he was asked, it was already too late for dialogue to occur, and therefore his existence was brought into question, and thus all impartial thinking on human existence leads back to the fall of Adam. I exist, thus I have fallen, and do not exist.

As soon as I, prodded on by others, began to believe again that I existed, I also found all such belief to be unpardonable, thus causing it to fade away and not remain. Neither existing nor not existing but falling somewhere in between. That's how I remained. But where did I remain? The question came to me before the wall. I did not answer. Or was it the wall that asked it? Walls don't speak. Perhaps the space between me and the wall. What was the space between? That was time, which I no longer have. In this form, I existed or I didn't exist, as the case may be, in much the same way that something decided to embrace existence or withdraw from it, such as when through a friend of Johanna's always obliging, capacious relative Betty, I was taken under the wing of the humanitarian, pedagogue, and manufacturer of wallpaper, Siegfried Konirsch-Lenz, who apparently was interested in me and my work, both of which he had heard good things about. By then I had been in the country four years, and Michael was a little boy of almost three. Konirsch-Lenz, who had a lovely house with its own garden, asked me to visit him and welcomed me with genuine good will—in fact, with praise that I had otherwise hardly experienced before.

"You've had a tough time of it here thus far, haven't you?"

"I'm seen as a troublemaker. I'm not supposed to exist."

"Splendidly put. The central allegation against you is that you were not killed."

"Right. And yet if I am indeed alive, I'm valued only as a curiosity. One can stand that for a little while. Then it's enough, and the curiosity needs to disappear."

"We all know what you mean. Whoever has escaped something horrible is guilty, is suspect, is intolerable. Whatever he sets in motion through others is hard to bring to completion. So much for brotherly love. It's hard to do, but ignore such beastliness. I don't make many promises, for that's not my style, but I mean it wholeheartedly when I say that I will help you. But please, one person to another: you have to tell me everything, completely and sincerely, man to man. Only then can I do something for you. And that I want to do."

Herr Konirsch-Lenz let me tell my story, calling my confession a beam of light cast in the dark chamber of life. Completely different from all the others before him, he listened to me with great patience, letting me finish and then asking questions only when I fell silent. He even helped me find the words when I felt inhibited or just couldn't find the right expression, and immersed himself in the details that seemed to him especially important. Most of the time he looked at me encouragingly, often nodding and noting things down in a little booklet. Then he asked me about my work. I was indeed afraid that it might be a bit beyond him, but he asked for more details, because, as he assured me, he already had some experience with social welfare; namely, with raising morally defective youths and other similarly difficult cases, even though he didn't know very much about sociology or even my special area, he never having had enough time and being always a man interested more in practice than in book learning. He didn't say this with any arrogance but in a matter-of-fact manner, while throughout it appeared that he wished to give my views his utmost attention. He questioned me extensively about all of my lost supporters, wanting to learn more, in particular, about Kratzenstein. I spoke bitterly of him, but carefully. But Herr Konirsch-Lenz laughed, saying there was no need to spare the clever stuck-up twit, for whatever I might say about the esteemed president of the International Society of Sociologists was nothing to him, as he knew all about him already. He, Konirsch-Lenz, had once been invited to speak about how to handle the rise in juvenile crime and, despite being short of time, he had worked very hard to prepare a text, then sent it in, only to get an acknowledgment of receipt and nothing more, despite repeated inquiries. When finally he demanded that the text be returned, it could not be found, and when Konirsch-Lenz threatened to get a lawyer the lecture came back covered in markings and accompanied by a letter, not at all from the noble Herr President but signed, in his absence, by Fixler, which said they could not use it, as it was more suited to a popular presentation for laypeople than to a scholarly investigation directed at an academic audience. That, then, was the the famous Kratzenstein.

As I told him about it all, I was nicely attended to and also learned about the new life of my friend. Before I left, I was quickly introduced to his family amid high praise. Two girls danced around me, and Frau Konirsch-Lenz was very kind to me. "Finally, bright people with a heart," I said to myself. I had to promise to make sure to bring my wife and child with me next time. Then I asked Konirsch-Lenz when I should come again.

"It makes no sense to set a time now. I need to ask around. I want to look for something concrete for you. I have an idea. I know a splendid lady, a press agent from Zurich—"

"Fräulein Resi Knispel?"

"Right. Do you know her?"

"In passing."

"I don't know her that well, either. But that's just an idea. Really, I'd rather not say anything at this point. You've been led on with vague promises enough already. It has to be something real, or it's better to do nothing at all. You'll hear from me soon. Perhaps in a week. I'll give you a call or drive by."

I had to take along some flowers for Johanna and some candy for Michael before I was seen off with good wishes.

Not a week had passed before Herr Konirsch-Lenz contacted me. Johanna spoke with him on the phone and found him charming. All three of us were invited to tea on Sunday; his wife would be happy to welcome us. He would happily pick us up in his car, but, unfortunately, it had to be worked on over the weekend. Johanna asked if he had any news to pass on to me. At that he laughed and answered, "Rest assured, it will be good." So we dressed up Michael, Johanna also spiffing herself up, and headed out while looking forward to a few lovely hours, as it was a bright warm summer's day. We were welcomed warmly, like old friends, Herr Konirsch-Lenz playing delightfully with Michael, who was then handed over to his daughters, Patricia and Petula, the boy ecstatic. Soon both women were chatting away pleasantly with each other in a shaded part of the garden, while my host led me to a table in the middle of the lawn that was bathed in the bright July sun.

"I love the sun, Dr. Landau. I love most to sit in the blazing sun. I can't get enough of it on my skin. Sit down and make yourself comfortable!"

Herr Konirsch-Lenz took off his shiny jacket and also his shirt, recommending that I do the same. But since I did not do well in the sun after those horrible years, I only took off my jacket and looked around to see if I could at least situate my chair in order to avoid the unrelenting glare. Herr Konirsch-Lenz laughed at me.

"I can see that you don't care for the sun at all. It would do you good. That comes from living like a recluse."

"It is an aftereffect," I said, hoping that I would be understood. But he didn't get what I was saying.

"Self-awareness is the first step toward betterment. Physical work would do you good. To dig around in the garden and such."

"I love my little garden. I already dabble around in it. Though I'm no expert, that I can say."

"Such a puny little garden, and you not an expert. One needs to really do it right, with hoes, spades, and shovels. But, as I can see, you shy away from physical work."

"Not at all."

"Show me your hands! There, I can see that you don't do a thing! Anyone with such smooth hands has never picked up anything."

"I've done a lot of physical work—a bit too much, in fact."

"That cannot have been very much. I do it because I want to. How does it go in Latin? *Mens sana in corpore sano*. Not just the garden alone, and it's certainly proper work that I do. Do you think I can afford a gardener? That certainly can be expensive, even if it was a laborer! I do it all myself. Everything right here at home. And I save a heap of money by doing so."

I acknowledged that. Meanwhile, the sun was hurting me, so I asked if I might sit in the shade.

"Well, if you must, you shadow dweller. Grab hold of the table and let's move it over there! No, not like that! Let me show you! Don't you even know how to move a table? This is how you grab hold! The way you're doing it, however, is damn clumsy. This way! There, finally! No, a little to the right and back. Not so far! Can't you see which direction the sun is shining? I want to stay in the sun!"

Because I was not at all doing it right, in a huff Herr Konirsch-Lenz shoved me aside and pushed the table around himself, while I stood by feeling hot and my heart pounding. That I stood there in need did not occur to him, for I was told not to just stand there gawking but to please go get the chairs. That I did, but I only received more scorn, for I had no idea how to properly place a chair in a garden. Finally, we managed to arrange things such that my patron sat in the sun and I in the shade. Herr Konirsch-Lenz's demeanor changed, and he looked at me with a different, albeit composed, expression of disapproval and began to lecture me.

"As you know, or should know, over twenty-five years ago I founded and headed the Lenz School, a boarding school for mildly criminal, at-risk, or otherwise difficult boys in Mecklenburg. I had some measure of success; my accomplishments were recognized. I devoted body and soul to it. I did that for almost ten years. Then came along the wretched developments that messed things up, which you well know, be it cultural Bolshevism, the pampering of criminals, etc. I can honestly say, without exaggeration, that I was an expert in this field and did an enormous amount of worthwhile social work. I also wrote something you should read sometime, and not just the lecture for that fool Kratzenstein. You will soon see that I know my way around such matters. It was indeed hard when all that cursed business came along and in one fell swoop, as you know, destroyed everything. I had to flee, stumbling away illegally over the border. What can I tell you? Particularly hard was the fact that through such work I had not managed to save anything. Whenever I had any money, it was sunk straight into the Lenz School. As an idealist, you can appreciate that. So I came here and had nothing, nor could I speak the language. I was completely finished. A school, social work, welfare for criminals? People just laughed at me."

I learned how Herr Konirsch-Lenz, after several unfortunate attempts and miserably paid jobs as a laborer, had the idea to manufacture wallpaper. At the Lenz School the pupils were trained in various tasks, almost all of which Konirsch-Lenz could do himself. Then, out of grace and mercy, he was given a rundown hovel that was no longer being used, and there he began to manufacture wallpaper out of modest materials, all of it designed by him and produced on a hand press in modest amounts. He had only one helper, who was also a refugee, then a very smart salesman joined in, and again another refugee. They worked eighteen hours a day, though one couldn't say they worked but, rather, slaved like animals, there hardly even being a Sunday free. Slowly they made progress, but there were also setbacks—a design didn't sell at all and wasn't to everyone's taste, or the paper was terrible, the press acted up, while, especially in the first years of the war, it was tough, the colors nothing but smeared rubbish, though it got better and better, and out of the little hole a workshop emerged, and now it's a lovely little factory with forty employees. The situation keeps on improving, as Kolex wallpaper has made a name for itself. You can ask for it in almost any appropriate shop. Soon the firm will be expanded by partnering with another such employer—a great idea—and new methods for doing multicolored prints will be developed.

Herr Konirsch-Lenz told it all in a lively manner; I could see very much how everything had thrived under his hands, causing me almost to feel amazed. It was obvious with what enthusiasm he wished to cover the walls of the metropolis with Kolex wallpaper, it being easy as pie, as it doesn't wrinkle and is long-lasting and washable. I was happy for the success of Herr Konirsch-Lenz. Then he clapped me on the arm and said, "Don't you see, I made it!" Then he shifted to say how the wealth he acquired gave him time to dedicate himself to pedagogical and sociological tasks, he being a consultant to some schools for difficult children, a visitor to a prison for youths, and many other things.

"When you work with youths who have lost their way, before they find it again, all those hoodlums and petty thieves who need as much love as they do strict rearing, then you also judge your situation. What are you but a man derailed, even if you are forty years old? You've never learned to conquer yourself and never had a real job. I've thought about that a lot. I'm offering that you can begin tomorrow as an apprentice in my factory in order to learn how to print wallpaper. I'll pay you something, and we can talk about that. It will in any case be enough, and no doubt much less than what I'll lose through the goods that will be ruined. That's a radical offer, but I'm a radical person. Are we agreed?"

Herr Konirsch-Lenz stuck his hand out to me, but I didn't grasp it.

"I'm afraid I can't agree to that right away."

"Why not?"

"I need to talk it over with my wife in peace."

"You don't talk about something like this with your wife. That just post-pones matters. You have to be a man. Your wife—just look at that delicate little thing—will just be impressed once you finally get into something rea-sonable."

"I don't know if it is so reasonable. I don't do anything without my wife."

"Nonsense! You're a wimp. But if you really want to, we can ask her right now."

He stood up and wanted to walk over to the women. I was defeated and felt worthless, but in no way did I want Johanna and Frau Konirsch-Lenz to be dragged into this exchange.

"Don't bother, I'm declining your offer. I'm very grateful, but I can't do it."

"You're throwing away an opportunity. It has to do with sweat and cleverness and self-discipline. You really have to learn those, for that's the weakness of your character. If you put yourself to it, in a year you can make a decent wage. For your scholarship, if that remains a burning necessity, you have the whole night through."

"I can't do that."

"Think of your family!"

"I am."

"It doesn't seem you are, you egoist."

"The last time we spoke, you talked much differently. You promised to think about how you might be able to help me. In this way you are of no help to me, and I'm sorry that I put you to any trouble."

"Don't be so impetuous, Dr. Landau. I've thought of everything. Frau Knispel is on vacation right now, and the summer is a bad time. Practical support is needed immediately—on that we are agreed, yes? I meant it for the best, and at my factory you'll be under my oversight and counsel. Not something to simply toss away. But, of course, there are other possibilities. Yet I have to tell you openly that you have no chance at any kind of existence by relying only upon your talent. We are all talented, but only a very few can make something out of it. Moreover, I'd like to read something of yours. But not the thick tome in which you have penned what you think about the oppressed. You don't seem to know enough about that and are a bit one-sided. If I want to read something about oppression, then I want it to be objective and not just personal experiences."

"My sociology of oppressed people has very little to do with my private experiences. Moreover, I doubt that I'll be laying before you this work or any of my work."

"No false modesty, for only arrogance hides behind it! Bring something along with you next time, and let me be the judge. But we don't need to talk about that now. No one can demand that someone else watch out for himself, which is why I told you my own story. You must remember that everyone had to suffer who came to this country before the war. Don't think that you know what they went through! We all went through it. There is no paradise. Do you know how many here were detained even though they were completely innocent! I myself was lucky; I got out after just two weeks. I had only my wallpaper to thank for that. That's how it is. But others were deported—to Canada, Australia—and they had to live there a year, two years behind barbed wire. That wasn't any bed of roses, either, and many died in the process. Torpedoed ships, and drowning miserably! What do you know of the victims of the *Arandora Star*? That, in fact, happened here in a free country. What can you say about it from over there? Don't tell me anything about the sociology of the oppressed. Everyone is oppressed, and everyone has to struggle on. Here, look at these hands; that's how one stands up against one's century! I know the misery of these times much better than you, because I saw it with open eyes and with the gaze of a pedagogue, not a dreamer like you."

"In other words, you're expecting it to go badly for me here because for a long time it did not go well for you."

"You sound impertinent, but there's something to that. It's the same for all. One has to earn his spurs. It never occurs to anyone here to offer us work suited to our tastes. What men with great names have had to put up with here! They had to be happy that their wives could work as servants. They had to stoop and bend, and they were always suspect, shoved around from here to there and badgered. Lawyers and doctors sitting lined up on the streets, the lucky ones being those who could find a dry spot for their behinds."

"I think it would be best if I left now."

Herr Konirsch-Lenz seemed very surprised. Go now? That would be cowardly. In a little while there will be tea. I shouldn't be so fussy. If I had another idea, he was willing to listen; I should just lay it out so that we could know where the shoe pinches. I told my host that it didn't seem right to me to deny me help that he had promised me because many who had fled here before the war were not welcomed with open arms. For this objection, I was sneered at derisively and told that no one can compare the fate of the refugees to those who remained behind, what I was saying was just rude, and, furthermore, I also needed to learn what it means to keep a promise. Someone as young as me should have disappeared before the war or hidden out, rather than just being hauled off to the slaughterhouse like a piece of cattle, and that only pointed to the weakness and incapability that Konirsch-Lenz wanted to cure me of. What I needed to understand was that no one had the responsibility to lift a finger for me, especially the moment that someone saw my healthy bones, which suffered only from laziness.

"You just have to dive in. Then no help is needed. And only then will help be found."

Frau Konirsch-Lenz and Johanna had arranged everything for tea. We were called, and so I was absolved of the need to defend myself further. My host busied himself with Michael and his daughters, joking with them and making more noise than the children themselves. He was polite to Johanna, complimenting her and the boy, saying how lovely he was. He even said very nice things about me, only pointing out how worn down I seemed, the worst case he had seen in some time, but that made the task of trying to help me work it all out seem all the more appealing.

"You can be assured, Frau Landau, I won't give up. Whatever gets into my head, I always make happen. 'Failure' is a word that just doesn't apply to Siegfried Konirsch-Lenz."

Johanna nodded gratefully.

"That is very good of you, Herr Konirsch-Lenz. We both value your friendship. My husband was so inspired when he got home after meeting you last time. He felt he had been so well understood."

Frau Konirsch-Lenz beamed on hearing this praise.

"My Siegfried understands people so well. You can rely on him, Frau Johanna. He's always had the greatest success just when things look hopeless, and your husband is lucky that he finds him so sympathetic."

"Mommy, what's 'pathetic'?" asked the older daughter.

"First of all, you got the word wrong," the teacherly father answered. "And, second, how many times have I told you not to get mixed up in grown-up conversations?"

The girl, ashamed, fell quiet and was close to tears. The mother wasn't comfortable with such a rebuke.

"Not 'pathetic,' my child, 'sym-pathetic,' and that means lovely. We find Frau Landau and the Herr Doctor to be lovely, just as you and Petula find little Michael lovely. But you are indeed done with your meal. Then it's best that you go off and play with Michael. You haven't yet shown him the swing. You love to swing, don't you, Michael?"

"Up and down, up and down—yes, I like it!"

"How sweet, my boy. But don't swing too wild with him; he's still quite little!"

"Yes, Mommy."

Patricia dragged off Michael, who was happy to go, and Petula jumped up and danced about the other children.

"Michael, we find you so sympathetic!" Patricia called out.

Then the children were gone. I was disconcertingly ill at ease, not having touched a bite and feeling awful. Frau Konirsch-Lenz noticed with displeasure how little I'd eaten, saying I should try the cake. I lied, saying that I hardly ate anything in the afternoon; Johanna looked at me uncertainly.

"Tell me, Frau Landau," said Siegfried, "isn't he rather spoiled? It seems that he doesn't find the cake good enough."

"What gives you that idea, Herr Konirsch-Lenz? Arthur is not at all fussy."

"You think so? It doesn't seem so to me."

"Well, what can I say?" asked Johanna uncertainly.

"Nothing, Frau Landau. I'm just advising you not to spoil your husband."

"Siegfried, shouldn't we be leaving that to Frau Landau? It's difficult for her, but she is so happy with him."

"I see. And how do you know that, Minna?"

"We talked with each other."

"Woman talk! You don't think Frau Landau would say the direct opposite? Just have a look at her!"

"What's the matter, Arthur?" Johanna said as she turned to me with concern.

I couldn't answer, but, despite all the heat, I was cold. Only my head was burning, and my hands trembled. Herr Konirsch-Lenz looked me up and down, somewhat suspiciously.

"There you see it! She spoils him too much. If I can give you a piece of advice, don't be so worried about his condition. It all has to do with his not being able to come to terms with reality, nothing but crazy ideas floating around his head. He needs a proper cure."

"Did you and Arthur have a disagreement!" Johanna whispered almost tonelessly.

"One can't come to an understanding with him. He is not real. He lives in a fantasy world. He has to get his feet on the ground first."

"I feel like I've been kicked in the head," said Johanna sadly.

Minna took her hand.

"Take it easy, my dear child! Don't take what my Siegfried says so hard. He is the kindest man on God's earth and only wants to help. He just has a rough exterior. He has to have that, and it comes from things not being easy for him. But you will see for sure how well he means it all for you both."

"That's right, Minna. You just need to talk to the sweet little wife. She needs it. Her nerves are about finished. Drink a lot of milk, Frau Landau, and don't worry! Let me do the worrying! I'll take it from here."

Johanna looked uncertain; I had rarely seen her so confused. Herr Konirsch-Lenz tried to raise her spirits.

"Everything is all right, my child, just keep your head up! If you really love your husband—and one can see that you do, and what a lovely wife you are—then everything will work out. Come along, Doctor! There, take the tray! We need to wash the dishes and clean everything up."

Thus was I left with no choice and, with a slap on the arm, driven from my seat. I was handed a tray, which Herr and Frau Konirsch-Lenz loaded up, my host placing the rest of the things on two trays and heading into the house with me toward the kitchen. I walked along as if on a forbidden path, but I was helpless before the will of the master of the house. He could now do with me as he wished. But he had conquered me only superficially. Listlessly I told myself that I had to cower but I didn't have to let myself be defeated. Then I stumbled over the threshold of the kitchen and the dishes on my tray smashed into one another, though, fortunately, only a pair of sugar tongs fell to the floor.

"Now set it down, you clod! It's sad to watch you go about any work! You must only help your wife at home by looking on, no?"

"Everything is peaceful and joyful for us at home. We don't fight at all."

"That I believe, but that's not because of you. Your wife jumps when you tell her to, right? That's the whole reason you're so satisfied."

I didn't say anything. Herr Konirsch-Lenz tied his apron but didn't offer me one. Capably and quickly he washed in the basin what was dirty, while I dried and had to clear everything away that was handed to me. I did it all as if asleep. Plates, cups, bowls, and silverware passed through my fingers and were soon gone. I was only happy that I was spared any aggravation and further talk about work. But, unfortunately, this buzzing activity was soon over and there was nothing left to do, and Herr Konirsch-Lenz came at me again with fresh vigor. I would have been happy to run off through the front door, but I couldn't do that to Johanna and Michael.

"You took in very little sun and have caused me to fritter away the afternoon. But sit yourself down here in this room! We can return to our debate here undisturbed. I'll just get my shirt from outside."

In the room there was a soft sofa and two comfortable armchairs. I would have loved most to find a place there to sleep, but because I could hardly keep my eyes open any longer and knew that I certainly would cause more trouble if I looked like a deadbeat settling down to a cozy nap, I sat down on a hard chair with a high back at the table, which was covered with writings and a bunch of stuff. There was also a cat on it that blinked up at me and curled up between the chair legs, stretched out its hind body, and snaked around its tail. Then came a purring sound from it as it sprang into my lap. I didn't know if it would be all right with the master of the house if I petted the animal, but the cat was pleased, curled itself up, and continued to purr. I didn't want to chase it off, and so I playfully stroked its fur. My host left me alone for a bit, though I wished it could have been for much longer. He returned with remarkable quiet, but there was nothing special to see. Perhaps I was only a bit dazed and imagined that his step was quieter than earlier.

"Do you like our cat Jim?"

"Yes."

"You'd better let him go. He sheds."

Jim, whom I gently stroked, didn't want to go, so Herr Konirsch-Lenz gave him a little nudge. Then he sat down across from me. Jim now circled him, but his master shooed him away and the cat ran off quickly and silently.

"Your wife would go along with your giving it a try with me and the wallpaper for a week."

"That's out of the question."

374 / H. G. ADLER

"Too bad. But, please, there are other possibilities. Unless you're willing to make adjustments, though, it's out of the question, and I would have been so pleased to welcome you into my firm with open arms."

"Why do you want to change me? Why must there be adjustments?"

"You talk like a child, completely immature. I already told your wife that."

"I see, you have—"

"Now listen! I'm not a brute, but I think like a realist. When you were last here, you opened up to me your financial situation with full access and in thorough detail. I have calculated here on this page the kind of measures you can take to realize savings that I can recommend to you, and if you spend the bare minimum on food you, along with your wife and child, can survive five, maybe seven months. If you were to manage to switch apartments—and that should be your first concern—leaving behind your much too expensive apartment, which, by the way is damp and unhealthy, in order to move to a cheaper neighborhood, let's say two rooms, which would be good to find farther away from the center of town, then I reckon you could stretch out your means to last nine or ten months. If you wish, I can manage your money. You would then have a better understanding of it and not be tempted to take out too much. Six to seven months should be enough to study a profession rich in opportunity. Such as auto mechanic, window decorator, watchmaker, or whatever else. You need to keep your ears open, think about it hard, and act quickly."

I held my head in a bowed position and was quiet. Konirsch-Lenz was so completely convinced that he had made the right impression on me that he interpreted my posture to mean that I had agreed to it all.

"It's good that you're reconsidering. I know you're sad. But that's the way it is. Soon you'll be thanking me, and feeling much differently—better, as happy as me."

My patron looked kindly at me, almost candidly. I remained completely quiet, feeling weak with anger and suffering. By now I felt that all strength had drained from me, but, nonetheless, I suddenly felt pity for this man who had secured my trust and had now abused it so. I was ashamed for him, because he was so dumb, blind, and hard-nosed without realizing it.

"I know you intend all this in a friendly and sincere manner, but—"

"No buts, my dear Doctor, there can be no buts. I really do mean it in a friendly and sincere manner; there's no lurking trapdoor. I know that you are clever. You can be convinced. You will indeed see, everything will work out. I ask you, then, do you want to come by tomorrow?"

"To your factory?"

"Yes."

"Not at all!"

"Good. Let's not waste another word on it! I've offered three times. Well, then, what else? You know that because of your lovely wife I want the best for you. I have a terrific idea. I have a good acquaintance at Self-Help who owes me, a Herr Scher. Is it Berthold Scher? You must have heard of him. No? Well, then, I will see to it, and you will soon hear from him. That's a terrific idea!"

Herr Konirsch-Lenz was so taken with his terrific idea that he left me in peace and began to chat lightheartedly. There was no further opportunity to protest, because soon Frau Minna walked in to fetch us. Johanna wanted to head home. A stone fell away from my heart, and I breathed deeply and laughed out loud. This appeared to please my patron, for he praised my good humor and proceeded to inform his wife of the plan involving Self-Help and Herr Scher, which she found to be a "brilliant idea." Then Johanna walked in with the three children behind her. Michael was cleaned up and ready to go home. I didn't miss a chance to speed up our departure, and Johanna watched me fearfully from the side, concerned about my hurrying so. Frau Konirsch-Lenz loaded me up with a huge bouquet of flowers and a little packet she had done up for Johanna, Michael getting yet another toy at the end and whooping loudly, though I could see that he was tired. At last we shuffled toward the door, our hosts following us. Patricia and Petula yelled so loud that my ears hurt, but it didn't bother me, for soon we would be free. The noise had the advantage that Herr Konirsch-Lenz didn't worry about me but, rather, about his daughters. The door was already open; I thrust myself quickly through it as the first out and bowed again outside as goodbye. Johanna shook Frau Minna's hand.

"Thank you so very much, Frau Minna, and you as well, Herr Konirsch-Lenz. It was a very lovely afternoon."

Then, unfortunately, my patron had another terrific idea. He proposed—

this, in fact, was a command—that his family accompany us to the bus stop. Although I politely declined, that was not even noted, for his wife and children had immediately agreed and were already out on the street. Patricia and Petula scuffled about who should have the honor of taking Michael by the hand and ran on ahead. I hurried after them under the pretense of keeping an eye on them. At least Herr Konirsch-Lenz left me in peace. The couple placed Johanna between them, both of them talking to her, lively, inspired, he especially leading the conversation. I heard the sharpness of his voice, which rose ever higher. But I could no longer make sense of it, all the talk blurring together, such that not even once was a single word intelligible. With the children just ahead of me, I felt like a schoolboy sent ahead by his parents and the teacher, who behind him moved solemnly, feeling sad about a misbehaving offspring, complaining, yelling, doling out admonitions until slowly and subtly, yet inescapably, they balled up together into a storm that made one's conscience anxious but which could not be escaped.

Then we began to climb a hill, the girls hurrying, dragging and lifting Michael along with them, me behind them, such that we were quickly beyond earshot of the grown-ups. Might they call out, "Arthur, not so fast. Be careful, you could stumble and break a leg"? No one called at all. I looked back timidly, but they were busy with one another and probably glad that I had gone on so far ahead. The separation would, indeed, have seemed fine to me if the two of them had not taken Johanna away. They would have to give her back; they could not ruin me. They had already tried hard to turn her against me, to alienate her from me, even to take her away, and none of it had succeeded. But this time it was different; I sensed danger. This Siegfried, whom I, like an ass, had tangled with in front of Johanna—I had to watch out for him. I didn't feel jealous, for this Siegfried with his Kolex wallpaper couldn't come between Johanna and me, but he could make enough trouble such that she would suffer and feel doubtful. Excitedly, I had described Konirsch-Lenz as a friend; now I had to work at shaking the impression that I had given rise to. Treated wrong, robbed of all means of strength, feeling entirely uncertain, I felt anxious in the midst of a difficult situation. I needed to pull myself together and get to Johanna, as well as break up her exchange with these people.

The children had reached the bus stop, and I took Michael from the girls. They were lovely and harmless children, but I felt enmity toward them, as they were Siegfried and Minna's children; I had to restrain myself to keep from being mean to them. Petula whined and begged to know when she could see sweet Michael again, and I said that we lived very far away, so it would likely be a long time.

"Papa has a car. It wouldn't take very long at all."

"I'm sorry!" I said, and sighed.

But that was too cowardly; seeing the children look wounded, I felt ashamed. I wanted to quickly get rid of such terrible feelings, and so I answered in a pedantic, dumb manner.

"Cars can be very dangerous. One needs to drive slowly and not too often."

I couldn't think of anything better. Patricia handled it straight off.

"Papa drives fast and is an excellent driver. He's never had an accident. That's how well he drives. And Mommy drives as well."

"Mommy drives slow," added Petula.

"It's much better if Mommy drives slow," I observed. "Then it's harder for something bad to happen."

I didn't say anything more, and let the girls talk about their parents' driving as Johanna, meanwhile, came closer. She was pale, for she had been pressed hard. When the three of them reached us, they fell silent; Johanna shot me a thin smile. Only the children kept on chatting; the grown-ups waited for the bus with hardly a word. It could be that Herr Konirsch-Lenz wanted to give me some more advice, but I stood next to Michael while holding the little packet and the bouquet of flowers, such that my patron had to curb all his good advice. When the bus finally arrived, having taken quite a long time, I turned around and dutifully stammered my thanks for all their kindness while managing to avoid shaking hands because of all I had to carry. Johanna rushed to lift up our boy, who had begun to dance about. Then we were on the steps of the bus, our supposed benefactors calling loudly to us, the children even louder, though I didn't pay attention and didn't look around. We drove straight off, Johanna with the child in her lap and me beside her.

"Dearest, didn't you find them delightful? So well-meaning and helpful!"

"I don't want to spoil your mood."

"You don't agree?"

Johanna was taken aback, while I had to restrain myself because of Michael, who looked at me with big sleepy eyes, even if he didn't know what was going on.

"In their own way they probably mean well. But they don't understand."

"The factory must be wonderful. Frau Minna told me about it, a nice atmosphere. Konirsch-Lenz is like a father to his workers. The factory is almost an excuse to take care of them, to give him the chance to raise them like his own children. Many lost souls work there who find their way again through his strong and good hands. A unique social experiment. He invited me to come see it. Isn't that wonderful?"

"I don't know, I'm not at all curious. Why are you nagging me, Johanna?"

"What's the matter, dear?"

"Look, the child is asleep."

"Michael had a lovely day. They spoiled him so."

"At least one of us did. That's good."

"It wasn't so bad for me, either."

"You can't fool me. They worked you over, didn't they, with all that about the factory?"

"You always know everything."

"It's not hard to figure out. And I should print wallpaper? Lovely Kolex wallpaper?"

"No, certainly not, if you don't want to. I'm not forcing you to do anything, nor should you. I only considered the possibility, dear, and you know it has nothing to do with wallpaper. It's—"

"The money?"

"Not even the money. Only the change. The possibility. Just listen! Not the actual work there; that's just an excuse. In reality you would be an assistant—a student, a prop for Herr Konirsch-Lenz. You would, of course, have to understand the business, the whole production process. Not as a worker but, instead, to take on a sociological commission. He even said that you could write, which I know will upset you—something like 'Kolex, a social experiment in which oppression has practically been done away with, because the foundation is built upon both love and trust.' He is not at all a believer in Frank Buchman and his moral rearmament, but he finds within the highest moral claims that are absolute, such as love, a useful fundamental idea that he has crystallized. Everything practical and neither socialistic nor capitalistic. If you wrote that and it pleased him, he would see that it was printed, and you could make a name for yourself. He believes that you are unhappy because you are unfulfilled, and unfulfilled because you've had no success."

"Come on, Johanna, what you're saying is nothing but nonsense."

"Yes, forgive me! They confused me so."

"I would agree. Please, just think what you're saying! I need to be improved, morally armed, of all things, in the human-wallpaper factory of Herr Siegfried Konirsch-Lenz. He'll have to find another fool for that."

"They think that you can do the scholarly work you love so in your spare time. But he would prefer to see something of scholarly rigor on his past and, above all, his current activities. That's what he most wants to help you with. If I understood him right, that really was his only plan."

"It was made without me."

"He was afraid of that and was sad about it. But look, don't be angry if I say that, after all, you have to forgive him. He really can't be all that bad a person. Because he senses your resistance, he wants to try to find something else. You already heard that there's supposedly, and surprisingly, an organization called Self-Help, which I'm not familiar with. He has a friend there. Through him he wants to do something for you, indeed so that you will know that he doesn't wish to exploit you."

"That would be nice!"

"Please don't talk that way! Can I ask you to do that? Just wait and see!"

"But only that! Nothing more! I won't be insulted."

"You don't have to worry about that if that's what you're afraid of."

"He can make an offer to me once. And then it's done!"

I said it as firmly as I could, then we said nothing more about it. We had to get off the bus, and we were both busy with our own thoughts. When we got off at our stop on Truro Street, I took Michael—who was almost fast asleep—from Johanna, and she carried the packet and the flowers. When we got home, I set the boy down and he began to cry. I kissed Johanna lightly on the forehead, asked her to forget about the afternoon, and said that I wanted to walk through the streets for a while in order to take my mind off things and I wouldn't be long. She said that was fine, and I hurried off.

In the streets beyond Truro Street where I wandered, a little cozy neighborhood with little houses all the same shape and gardens in front, I slowly regained full consciousness. I could sense everywhere the feel and sound of Sunday, laced with bored, sour, and bittersweet respectability, all of it tantalizingly foreign to me, though tolerable, even as I sauntered through in an easygoing fashion or now and then stopped. The people who hung about the houses, working in the gardens, walking along the sidewalks or standing upon them, whether alone or talking in small groups, were much more charitable than my friends, because they let me be. They didn't get all worked up about me, and therefore left me to myself out of common decency. Most of them just cared about their tended gardens and were only happy when I admired their work. The shrubs were trimmed, most of them cut square and rarely rounded, but there were also unusual shapes that depicted urns with handles, little baskets, and magnificent chalices, while even more spectacular were animals carved out of evergreen leaves, be it hens, roosters with arched tails, peacocks in full spread, and the high point of this plastic art, a group of five dogs with their heads and ears clearly visible, their four legs running, the tails upright. I was sorry that people couldn't be portrayed as well; who knew what timidity prevented it. In the front yards, the usual kinds of plants grew, many of them in bloom. Sometimes the plants were not kept in good order but were reined in, subdued, and restrained. The worst was when bad garden sculpture was employed. Figures of spiritless stone and horribly painted plaster squatted errantly or crouched shamelessly between blossoms and the grass—angels with sugary wings, gnomes, squirrels, rabbits, and other creatures—but also spiked castles were erected, covered with shiny glass, with snail and mussel shells, often painted with whitewash, as well as blue and green opalescent urns, with columns and roofs on them that functioned as feeders for birds nervously flitting around. In one garden, there were two worn-out tires carefully painted white, looking like lost life preservers that happened to have landed in the grass and now encircled fast-growing geraniums.

All of these adornments, even if they seemed awful, were better than my friends, for they offered themselves openly and knew no shameful lies, everything being what it was, and whoever was not blindly addicted could not be injured by such harmless nonsense. He who doesn't want anything can exist however he would like; that was obvious. Yet woe to he who wanted something! It wasn't enough that I had given up on existing, nor did any acknowledge my own will; I simply had to give it up. Nor could that be laid to self-deception, for there was no self to be deceived. That was why I had such strong desire, for my will, in being dammed up and then rearing up, had taken off, but people resented that. Only the humble and obedient will is permitted; any resistance was forbidden and resulted in one's existence being condemned. Thus, I did not exist in two ways—not as a self and not as a will. I moved through life without wanting anything, simply appearing among so much that is finite, such as fences, gardens, and walls, among the lanes, in the faces of others who do exist and perhaps are allowed to want something, myself an expression of something otherwise improbable, of the powers lent to me. Thus, indeed, there was still hope; it must indeed exist, for in the obedient house of the one who had been lent powers something existed which over time offered something—namely, a second existence; with all else annihilated, the self and the will were put to sleep, but a new creation replaced the previous existence. This was a razor-thin existence, extremely fragile and completely inviolable, needing to be marginalized in order to exist. It was entitled to hardly anything, but it was nonetheless there and could not be ignored. It revealed itself and yet had its own protective shell, and for every condemnation it had a response at the ready.

Only thus was I able to grasp that I had outlasted it all, that every past venture would be repeated, as well as the talk of it. This was a much more dependent existence than the earlier one that had disappeared, but I could exist and want something, perhaps even act. It was difficult and required a long journey, but it was possible. It also lay much further off than where I had already gotten to, for, in fact, so far it was not entirely there but rather summoned one, presenting itself as that which had not yet been experienced, rolling forward on the wheels of hope, also requiring the denial of memory. In drawing me toward it, it succeeded in my relinquishing myself, such that memory was allowed only as an aid along the way and not valid in itself; nor was the way itself valid, for the way was through memory.

But, because the goal itself does not exist, everything is the way toward it, though there is no real way, because it itself is already composed of past and future memory, the thin and yet so thick link between origin and destination, both no more than dreams imprisoned within consciousness, and not, in truth, known. At the start, everything is allowed, and, once you arrive at the destination, nothing else is needed, and in between is the murky choice. This choice is not free, though it appears to be free when it detaches itself from time and place. Small and retreating, harried and exposed, there I found myself, a tiny cell around me, the circumscribed choice, fourfold, a wall between origin and destination, a little person in between with the face of Adam, his confused, reawakened gaze staring at the wall, the walls, four walls that I had completely decorated and covered with memory and assorted items, as well as by day and by night, the wondrous blossoming outside the window.

My office was the only place where I could be certain that, for a few hours, I would be left alone. If Herr Schnabelberger, Frau Dr. Kulka, and my other colleagues had left the building, and only Herr Geschlieder guarded our treasures downstairs in what had once served as the janitor's apartment, it was hard for someone to surprise me here up above, and so on long evenings and over entire weekends I was happy to be there on my own. Indeed, I sat there amid the dangers of memory, an imprudent move, but it was peaceful, though without warning it could suddenly become threatening, nor did it ever provide a moment of certainty. Instead, it scurried forth from the painted faces and approached, perverting a possible order to the world and deriding any unseemly wish for it. But it tolerated me and my works, which were both commanded and voluntary, the careful touch of my tentative hands that sometimes caused misfortune. Paintings fell from frames, frames fell to pieces, flakes of paint fell off, thick mildew and heaps of dust wanted to consume the painfully extinguished with their gentle force, yet the faces had not given up and still looked out with the quiet patience of the ruined, still able to hope for help because we were there. The fresh varnish applied by the attendant employed by Frau Dr. Kulka in our hospital was administered tenderly, like a balm on a cool back, functioning as healing care. They brought to me the neediest patients, who were therefore the most deserving of loving kindness, which was a burdensome task for my conscience, which I had sought to sort through scrupulously so that those who had suffered could not accuse me of favoritism. Alas, all of the sick had a right to be saved, all pain deserved to be relieved; yet how poor was our hospital, how painful the choice was for me! How could I be just?

Then a consulting group met. Herr Schnabelberger was a good-natured hospital director, his responsibility as administrator being to worry about the costs. Frau Dr. Kulka, on the other hand, acted with beastly aggression, shoving away anyone who might be badly ill because she found them detestable and worthless, pulling out, instead, the somewhat fresh and hardly worn face of a boy, for whom a sudden love within her burned, because he had such a lovely smile, which was why the boy should be saved first, for he was young, and he could be granted a promising future. Frau Dr. Kulka, however, did not only favor the boy, for she was not so unjust; an unassuming little mother, older and with a very tattered silk scarf, could also captivate her. Quickly the beloved creature was pulled out, turned around for consideration and inspection, and showered with many a warm gaze. It was an honor and a courtesy if Frau Dr. Kulka nodded in sympathy to such a helpless creature. Finally we agreed, Schnabelberger and myself most often agreeing, the choice made; the sick one presented to us would be taken care of, while the rest had to be patient, for none would be allowed to perish. I had already written down a lot about the past of each of the invalids as they were presented for the catalog, for all our records on the sick had to be precise and detailed. This was good for the patients, for this allowed them, as far as our capabilities would permit, to last well into the future. Someday someone would thank us—that was what Frau Dr. Kulka thought—all of these treasures made available to the public once again, the entire past revealed. Frau Dr. Kulka fought hard with the authorities for approval of a bigger and more dignified space for a gallery as a permanent resting ground in honor of our patients. Yet I couldn't call them patients or the sick, for the doctor found that disagreeable. Angrily she said that she found such expressions perverse on my part, and yet I was right. Herr Schnabelberger sought to appease her.

"Dr. Landau has a deep relation with our paintings. Each painting is for him a living person. Therefore he treats them almost like a house doctor. We should be pleased. Let him have his fun when he talks about our patients!"

"That's a morbid view. I also find it tasteless. He talks as if they are guests here, patients and sick people, and that's not right. It makes us look ridiculous."

Herr Schnabelberger defended me again.

"He is high-strung. He cannot deem the pictures dead, and he stops short of saying they are alive. Instead, he thinks of them as something in between, therefore he calls them patients."

Frau Dr. Kulka was not convinced. She approved of my work, my diligence, even my ideas, but my behavior she had to condemn.

"No museum would allow this. We cannot tolerate any such exception."

I had to promise her that I would not refer to the paintings as patients or as students; for us there was only an inventory with many objects. This and nothing else was the proper approach of a museum that wished to concern itself with history. I could see what she meant and didn't want to cause any difficulties, but what one meant by history was to me unclear.

"How can you say that, Frau Doctor? History, and yet we are standing right in the middle of it."

"I don't see what your problem is."

"Not my problem but, rather, the problem of history."

"Do you need a definition?"

"Not really. I'm not interested in abstractions, for I don't trust pure philosophy. What really riles me is the difference between 'what was' and 'what is.' Where the past ends and where the present starts. In between is something that is unsolvable and unexplainable."

"Am I too dumb to understand?"

"But Frau Doctor," said Herr Schnabelberger, "we're all that dumb! I don't understand, either."

"Then we're in agreement. I say, yes, one can't explain it. There must be a bridge to the present, and that disturbs me and gives me no rest. Just think, yesterday something happened which the whole world talks about because of how many people it still touches today and will touch for a long time. When is it something that happens and when is it history?"

They listened to me, Frau Dr. Kulka thinking before she answered.

"When it occurs but has already happened and is already over, then it is history. But, of course, it has to be designated as such at some point in order to be known."

"And you have to bring it into a museum when it is adequate and can still be transported, when you can call it historical evidence, right, Frau Doctor?"

"Yes."

"But often it's still alive and is not gone by. As an object it presents itself, is there, or, I would say, is manifestly there, not as a piece of evidence but as a witness in itself, and yet it's supposed to be an object! Please don't think it mad or a paranoid obsession when I also find it haunting and horrible! I disagree completely. All of us, all of us here together, are history."

"Then a museum is a good place for us," joked Herr Schnabelberger.

"You are totally right. We are remnant survivors, who are there for all who are not. That's true in general; the living are there for the dead, for their predecessors, and thus we also represent the history of the dead. How difficult it is, then, to exist as oneself when we are also history, so much history! But we are particularly there for all those dragged away by force and annihilated. You know what I mean, those of whom not a trace . . . We are the history of the exterminated, the history of the shadow that consumed them. And we collect what was stolen from them, what we can store up of their remains. But that is indeed alive and really not history. It amounts to neither memory nor keepsakes; it is commemoration. It really hangs somewhere between history and an event, a fragile condition, yes? And, with that, hopefully I have explained well enough why it occurs to me to speak of the portraits as patients. I take that to be my charge, and so I see those who have been painted as living and possessed of a fate, indeed as persons, not at all as objects, and it pains me to think of how badly they live here among us, badly locked up in cages and castigated, covered in layers of dust, while the blood of those murdered can hardly be washed away. Anyone who finds themselves in this situation—"

"Listen," Frau Dr. Kulka interrupted intensely, but sympathetically, "you're dealing with horrendous problems. But these problems don't exist, they're chimeras. You have to recognize the illness that you are projecting onto the world around you. You are very wounded, it's no wonder. If I were in your shoes, I'd look for medical help in order to conquer these horrible visions. I'd also try to get out more when you're done with work. What you've accomplished is extraordinary. Herr Schnabelberger and I both appreciate that, as do the curators. You are managing a huge workload; it's almost too much. But I have to warn you, the way you are going about it is no longer healthy. Although I don't want to upset you, I'm afraid there's no way that you can continue at the museum in your present circumstances."

"If you don't want me here, then I can leave."

"Please, Herr Doctor, don't be so sensitive! Frau Dr. Kulka wasn't saying anything bad about you. On the contrary. Her concerns are quite justifiable. Anyone would have them, including me."

"I sense that both of you are not happy with me, especially Frau Doctor. I can feel it in every word."

"Don't talk such nonsense! I only want—and I know that Herr Schnabelberger agrees—that you have a healthy relation to life and especially to the museum. We mean well and want you to stay at the museum, not leave it."

"You know, you've just said what frightens me so: life in the museum. That's exactly it. We are a hospital, or not even that, a center for anatomical pathology. We deal with what is wounded and deteriorating. We take away the remaining life from things. Numerous specimens. In the process, we run the danger of wounding or killing ourselves. We don't realize that we are doing away with the connection between us and the paintings, artifacts, and writings. Thus we divest ourselves of these things, and that could one day come back to haunt us. But by then it will be too late."

Frau Dr. Kulka was impatient, but Herr Schnabelberger spoke to her and tried to calm me down as well.

"Each person has a particular relationship to our museum and to history, and, of course, to his own life. Our tasks here are unusual. We have to take care of the legacy of a catastrophe, and we do not know how the will reads. The three of us have our own views about it, but we also have to serve the trustees, the museum field in general, the ministry, and, not least, the government. Therefore there is no point in our fighting. Most likely, no one has ever had to fulfill a similar function before. Dr. Landau and I accidentally got tangled up in this. As an electrical engineer and a sociologist, neither of us is an expert in museums. We are, however, trying to accomplish something here. I was sent here during the war, but I confess, I still have the same fire, the work still interests me, I cannot pull myself away from it, and I remain just as inspired by it as when I first returned. What do I care about alternating current, continuous current, phases, rheostats, and all that? I would no longer feel as comfortable in an electronics factory as I do here. When it comes to an induction of energy, my friends, I have devoted body and soul to the museum. For Dr. Landau, the situation is different, as he came here voluntarily. Because he felt the need to and thought he could be of help to us. And that he has done splendidly. In terms of building the museum collection, you are the only art historian, Frau Doctor. So that's the way things stand, and that's why we have to stick together and not be too sensitive. The museum needs us, and we know our duty. So we need to get along!"

Frau Dr. Kulka and I agreed.

"I can see," she said, "that it's not easy for Dr. Landau. But, nonetheless, he has to try to appreciate my viewpoint and the objects themselves that our museum is meant to serve. Feelings are all well and good, we all have them, but we have to be practical. The catastrophe has happened, we cannot change it. Now it is over. Therefore one must also free oneself internally from it and make the best of what is left for us to save. That can only happen if you don't torment yourself and others as well. There are still many beautiful things, and we want to protect them and preserve them for the future. We are all agreed on that. But without optimism that won't happen. That's why I ask for a bit of courage! We want to ensure that everything is not pointless and lost. Of course, I have no trouble with how Dr. Landau thinks, as long as the museum doesn't suffer as a result of it. But I wish you could find a way to extricate yourself from your past, from all those horrible things that happened to you. It happened to others as well, to some just as bad, to many not as bad, to others even worse, and they nonetheless courageously, and even with a sense of humor, go on with their postwar lives. You cannot simply turn away from all pleasures as you do. You never go to the movies, you turn down invitations, you don't go on outings—my dear friend, no wonder you're so gloomy! Go out and have a laugh for once! It's unbearable to watch you sit there with your eyes swelling like sad flowers, a complete loner who sits stock-still in a hole, staring at a wall and not noticing how to the right and the left paths are completely free. You simply have to decide for yourself, and soon everything will work out."

"Madam—"

"Oh, please don't call me madam! You know how I can't stand that."

"Frau Doctor, what you say is completely right for you. When it comes to such questions, one can only decide for oneself. For me, things are different. I certainly would like, as Herr Schnabelberger put it so well, to work with you and everyone at the museum in a pleasant manner, without calling too much attention to my idiosyncrasies. I also don't want anything more to do with the old prayer books that are moldering away in the cellar. I've had enough to do with them already. Perhaps my manner is heavy-handed, for I have the feeling that I often bring up matters that you don't agree with. Please forgive me—I don't mean anything bad by it!"

"You don't have to apologize!" Frau Dr. Kulka and Herr Schnabelberger called out simultaneously.

"Oh, yes, I do. I also promise you that I will do everything I can to help things run smoothly. But for me nothing is simple. It's not possible for me to be optimistic without being thoughtless. I couldn't bear that. The confusion between history and the present is all I have; it lies at the core of my being. It goes best for me if I don't separate the two. Then they run parallel to each other and finally merge as one. No doubt there still must be borders between them, and I can't think of borders being impenetrable. Crossings over and through must remain open, as the case may be and according to how one sees it, or at least be maintained as possible. It's at these borders that I find myself, having experienced my own history. Only when I can imagine that do I grasp that I have survived, and by that I mean to have survived myself and my history. That causes me a great deal of distress and difficulties, but not despair. No. I fight against despair, but I plunge into distress and stand, I must say paradoxically, faced with the task of trying to find a task. I actually do not have a task but, rather, I know only that I must have one. That is what I'm looking for. I must therefore seek something. Only through this effort, it seems to me, can I rise a bit above history, and that's why I cannot abandon my gloomy torments. It is the only means by which to attain my future liberation. Please believe me, it is not a psychological problem, nor can any doctor treat it, nor should one."

Frau Dr. Kulka wanted to respond, but Herr Schnabelberger seemed to feel that this would only prolong a fruitless conversation, being afraid as well, although he didn't completely agree with me and didn't understand it all, that any misunderstandings on the part of the Frau Doctor could lead to something derogatory being said. He wanted to spare me from being upset. Therefore he spoke in a conciliatory manner and explained that it was now clear how I thought about matters; for that, I deserved consideration and all due respect, but the position of Frau Dr. Kulka must be valued just as much, without which the museum would have to close, something that I, Landau, certainly must know and acknowledge. Therefore it would certainly be best to break off our rich and clarifying talk, which had granted all three of us useful things to think about.

"That helps to clear the air, doesn't it, and now we need to get to work."

Frau Dr. Kulka extended her hand in reconciliation. I wanted to discuss with her some technical matters having to do with work, but she wanted to speak with Herr Schnabelberger about a shipment of another load of prayer books to America, telling me that anytime today, if possible, I could stop in at her office at my convenience. So I left the room, after which Herr Schnabelberger gave my hand a friendly shake and patted me on the back in a comforting manner. Humming, I climbed the steps to my office, not at all a good student, though I had indeed been praised, the teachers having been tolerant and conscientious in cheering on the afflicted one and not scaring him off. The portraits in the stairwell looked at me more studiously than ever, their curiosity about their fellow student being too much to contain. They asked, How did it go? I nodded at them, but I had nothing to report and continued humming until I reached my office. There I arranged some lists that I needed for a report. I had been asked to give a general overview of the condition, worth, quality, and special meaning of my schoolmates.

I didn't remain undisturbed with my work for long. Someone sent someone from the central office up to me, saying that I should come, as there was a visitor from abroad who wanted information and a tour. I put on my black work jacket and ran down to greet the guests. Herr Schnabelberger was chatting with them in the main office, the former conference room of the school. I could see that he had no time and really wanted me to take over for him. He introduced Herr Dr. Landau, who can help you with everything, to Herr and Frau Lever from Johannesburg. After bows and quick handshakes accompanied by smiles, Herr Schnabelberger excused himself and left the room in a hurry. I invited the guests to view our assembled, though not yet publicly available, collection. For that we need to go down the street, for no, there was hardly anything to see here in the old school, just storage and administrative offices, but around the corner in the temple, in the hermitage, there the exhibition is already flourishing, and that's where we wanted to go. Herr Geschlieder gave me the key, and so I accompanied the guests along the street. It hasn't changed at all, said Herr Lever from Johannesburg. His wife shook her head uncertainly. I couldn't tell if she was agreeing or disagreeing, but it seemed as if the lady had not had much prior experience of our city. Therefore she didn't know for sure whether it had changed much or not. I was very polite and didn't say whether things had changed, but Herr Lever wasn't comfortable with me holding back, as he certainly wanted to hear my opinion. He said that after having been away for eight years, that being how long it had been for him, the time having flown by, it was curious how one came back and looked and looked at all the houses that were the same as they once had been, the streets having the same names, as well as the shops and cafés, the castle with its dome, the incomparable feel and the air and the food—in short, all of it as glorious as it had been in childhood.

These observations proceeded until we encountered an old man, who looked at me inquisitively and appeared to recognize me. I was unsure and didn't remember him at all, though I greeted him warmly as if I knew him. Landau, the man said happily, it's Landau; then I recognized the voice. It was Professor Hilarius Prenzel, my old high-school teacher. He was happy to see me, thinking that he would not see me alive again, for he thought that before the war I had fled abroad. Manners dictated that I introduce the Levers to Prenzel. I wanted to quickly ask for my teacher's address, and I promised him I would visit him soon. No, no, insisted my professor, for he would not accept that I was unavailable right now. In order to do something with the man and woman, I assured him I would and tried to say goodbye. But Prenzel wasn't willing to give me any consideration and wouldn't let me go. I turned toward Herr Lever while making silent gestures explaining that I was meeting someone after many years, and he finally assured me that a few minutes didn't matter. Prenzel could not believe how I had changed, but a good teacher recognizes his students even after decades. Everything had changed, he said sadly, the entire city, only the empty shells of buildings still there, which soon no one would recognize, a fading history that was hardly perceivable any longer. Only a few of his students were supposedly there, some having emigrated, others having been hauled off or gone off to war, whether killed or captured, hardly any more left, and whoever was there had to or wanted to leave. And did I know anything about my classmates? No, nothing, no more contact, nor did I know what had happened to them, only Arno Seiler. Yes, Arno Seiler, he remembered him. Whatever happened to him? Unfortunately, not much. He became political, then was killed. And the students from other classes? Recently, a letter from So-and-So—that's Leonard Kauders. He had sent along greetings to Prenzel. Oh him, that's nice, for he was the best in his class at history, though he wasn't always that good with dates. Thank him for the greetings, and return my warmest. Everything has changed, Landau, everything, really everything. And Prenzel himself, did he have to leave? No, he could stay because of his wife, and there was also a nice nephew who had influence.

That was comforting news that I took as a chance for me to leave. Yes, I would be in touch, I promised for sure, but now I had to hurry off. During this conversation, which had at first made them uncomfortable, Herr and Frau Lever had slowly gone on ahead, then stopped and looked back expectantly at me. I tore myself away from Prenzel, who called after me, "Landau, you yourself are a piece of a past that no longer exists. Be well!" Ah, that old saying of his, which I hadn't heard in a long time, long gone, and yet still there—a passage that still resounded in my ears! Exhausted, I suppressed a sense of disorientation as I reached my museum guests. Herr Lever waved away my apology and began to go on again about how little had changed. If you looked around here, who could say that it wasn't just yesterday that you had been here, and that's why everything seemed the same as ever. He was quiet a moment, before he went on reflectively, saying, Yes, if you were here the entire time—the old man being someone who looked like someone who was here when the foreigners came and later left—then it probably felt completely different, which is why you needed to hear such opinions. After the encounter with Prenzel, I was even less prepared to share my own views—which were never at all fixed—with the couple from Johannesburg, and so I just talked in vague general terms, saying how it seemed changed, or not changed, one could take it any which way, which made it hard to say what it was really like; it depended on how you looked at it.

Herr Lever wasn't satisfied; my evasions bothered him. I should not be so reserved, here, have a cigarette, and would I say that I could feel as comfortable in the city as I used to? I let on that you really couldn't say, in general, and then, of course, there were the people. Certainly, the people, he said pensively, that seems the essential question, for they have been scattered across the world. The world used to be so large when people lived in a city and hardly ever left it, but now the world is indeed small, because people travel all over, home now being on the road, the good fortune of the airplane and the fast pace of news, but then you see the city, and once again everything is there, the question being whether one was ever away. I thoughtlessly agreed. I had heard similar talk so often, all of it riddled with helpless surprise, and that it was hard to see that something had collapsed, if only because the empty shells of buildings, as Prenzel knew, were not just carted away as rubble but, rather, the stones were still cemented together with strong mortar. And so out of the distance there arrived the weary, needy look of the former inhabitants, who wanted to see the old school, where there were neither old teachers nor the old students—alas, Prenzel brought this truth home to me even more sharply—while the visitors, with their clumsy halting steps, but otherwise not unafraid, were happy, not looking at all embarrassed and carrying themselves as if they knew everything, and wanting me to take note of that. I just needed to confirm that their overbearing confidence was justified. It was all quite correct, and, as for any doubts—no, I only had to reassure them.

"The main thing, Herr Lever, is that you're happy here. It really doesn't matter whether it changed or not." Frau Lever said this in a cheery manner, as if she wanted to intercede between me and her husband. "In the end, it's all just a matter of opinion."

While talking thus, we reached the hermitage. I unlocked it, turned on the light, and the couple stumbled a bit, as most strangers did, on the steps into the foyer, where they were greeted by old copper pots and washbasins with outstretched arms and open splayed hands ready to receive alms. Like everyone else I had brought here, the guests stood there looking somewhat lost. The result was an unease that was slowly lifted only when I began to talk and explain. But this time I didn't hurry to do that; instead, I drew out that feeling at a slow pace in order to present their lighthearted curiosity with something quieter and more modest. That happened of itself as soon as I struggled to lock the door from the inside, as otherwise it was not easy to do, which then helped me to feel better about displaying my power over all visitors in the process. Herr and Frau Lever soon felt this as well, stepping uncomfortably across the stone floor one foot at a time, whispering softly in order not to disturb me, and looking curiously at basins and boxes that returned their gaze in a particularly dead manner. Sometimes more venturous guests wanted to part the heavy red curtain in the main hall, but then didn't feel quite right in doing so, choosing instead to risk a few steps to the right and down the narrow passage that led to the old cemetery.

Once I had let enough time pass, I called out cheerfully to the chastened guests that, well, now we can begin. With a sweeping gesture, I pushed back the curtain and the visitors stepped forward with pointed, awkward steps. Usually this was when people would begin to sneeze, cough, or blow their noses because of the dry air, resulting in a look of mild admonishment from me. Then they would hold a handkerchief over their mouths and swab it around. However, if entering the hall didn't affect their breathing, then they hardly ever cleared their throats. At the ready, as there was no point in dawdling, they kept their eyes on me as if waiting for a sign that they were free to move about and not feel anxious anymore. I then proceeded to casually tell them something about the history and the style of the hermitage, during which I pointed with an outstretched hand at the arched ceiling, painted a light blue, and the fine white stucco. I managed to do this in such a compelling fashion as to cause the hard-nosed guests to bend their heads back and dutifully look up. Then I would talk on, now with an ever-stronger emphasis and also somewhat faster, pointing out the windows installed above on the right, then the balcony way up on the left, the heads turning as I did. Herr and Frau Lever did this as well.

Devilishly, I added, "As for the building itself, you can see that nothing at all has changed. It's been well taken care of, and during the war it was even cleaned and repainted."

Herr Lever lowered his head and looked at me. dumbfounded.

"That's unbelievable."

"You can see so yourself," I responded firmly. "In a certain sense, you're right. Nothing has changed. Some things have even been improved for the better."

"How is that even possible?"

"Quite simple. The conquerors not only made history; they also loved the old history and tried to conserve it."

"The conquerors did that? The same who—"

"Precisely the same, my friends. Does that surprise you? Here the conquerors have provided an indisputable service. The living were killed, and their past in stones, images, books, and objects, as set down by their ancestors, was collected, taken care of, and brought to life."

This well and truly surprised Herr Lever, who stopped and grabbed hold of his wife's purse.

"Just think, Mitzi, isn't that marvelous? Isn't that amazing?"

Frau Lever clasped her chin with her thumb and forefinger.

"Marvelous!" she chirped enthusiastically. "Really, I think so, too."

"Herr Doctor," her husband said in a factual manner, "the human soul is unfathomable. It's the same for us in Africa, where there are whites, blacks, and others."

I just nodded humbly and didn't allow myself to get distracted by such words of wisdom, but instead led the guests from exhibit to exhibit, explaining what was in the display cases. The manners and customs, beliefs and conceptions of an extinct people saved at the last hour for posterity by its surviving members, who had already been handed a death sentence. Their destruction had been suspended in order to preserve these wonderful and lovely objects for the sake of scholarship, for the sake of history, the mother of all scholarship. But the extinction of the people, no matter how much effort had been devoted to it, was not as completely successful as had been wished for; as with every human endeavor—much as with the Tower of Babel or even the original couple desirous of knowledge—this one was not met with complete success. All such actions are in vain. That's what the proudly ambitious men of history must recognize, and thus had the annihilated survived their own destruction, surviving history itself as well, their own history, the murderers disappearing, unable to haul off or destroy the collections of objects, which served as history's revenge, the treasures remaining behind, thrown together in heaps. The still-living members of the people overcome by history who were employed to work in the storage holds of their history could not, once they were free, fulfill the death sentence handed down and let themselves be lost amid the general vortex of the victory over the conquerors, letting history be history, laughing into their sleeves, though some returned to the oaths they had taken to preserve such things as memorials, their work as scholars having provided them with a living, they being ready to do it again, themselves feeling it was right, though, at the time, their souls were too numb to shudder while reflecting on the madness that lurked behind each item. They knew only that it meant money, a paid job. And so they squatted and scurried about again in the stored materials of their surviving history, although their eyes were as empty of history as their hands and speech. Thus they bored their way through history or trampled upon it, for they hardly knew anything.

Herr Schnabelberger and Frau Dr. Kulka belonged to this lost group that had nonetheless survived and found themselves here again, though they were different from the rest. They had grown accustomed to their charge without being too horrified by it, though they had tasted the blood of history in their mouths and felt a sense of revenge. These two, along with the other guardians who, in service to the conquerors swallowed the paltry morsels of servitude and had now gathered together again to serve the commemoration of the celebration of the near-successful destruction that had recently occurred, were not interested in the administration and public display of history; instead, a board of trustees was established that made clear what the job was, this singular opportunity needing to be maintained and developed in the kind of professional manner that was required. Which was why they employed some returnees, such as me. The hermitage, an old house of prayer, had already been turned into exhibition spaces during the war, and that's where the lives of the extinct people were now preserved in images. Yet neither the collected objects nor the labels explaining them nor the informative plaques were enough to do this, nor even a completely fitted-out kitchen and a dining room, such that every visitor could exclaim what a wonderful achievement it was, a terrific success, this being how these people had really lived. Now that I understand them and can imagine it all, one can't help being grateful for such effort and cost, how splendidly it rises above such destruction and thereby conquers it, thus allowing us to be rid of it. No, that had never been enough, for you couldn't just gawk at the dead and imagine them; they had to be seen as alive, and that was how one had to have them. To this day, art and ingenuity remain essential traits of human beings; that was also true for the well-informed conquerors and last trained members of those who would become extinct. Then they and the conquerors pulled together a collection that they advised upon, and then one of the heads gave a speech:

"You've done a beautiful job so far. We are very pleased. But it's not enough. Nor is it right to let you show us how you live, what you do, and what you know of your ancestors. For soon that will be of no interest to us, nor to the future. Your time is limited, and afterward we will be sad and will no longer have you. That's unbearable. You must exist, even when you don't exist, but it must not cost too much, which you will agree, nor can it take too long, as we're in a hurry and you have no time. We have read in your ancient book that your Lord created humans from a lump of clay. Go forth, do as instructed. Do not, I advise you, breathe life into its nose! You are clever, so think it over. You must not disappoint us! Not at all."

When the dying folk heard the last word, they felt energized, for it was a powerful speech, and it meant more to them at this hour than the voice of their blasphemed Lord. Their most courageous speaker replied:

"That's the way it has to be, which is why we are here. We will take your advice. Give us a little time and we will make mannequins that will look just like us, though they won't know what is good or evil. They'll be life-size and look entirely natural, not made of earth, as if resting in fields and caverns but instead made of an artificial material that is used for the kinds of mannequins one sees in the display windows of clothing stores, except much finer and more expressive, so deceptively the same that the only thing preventing them from being living souls is the lack of any breath. You'll be startled by how alive our people can appear, even when they are extinct. Then you can experience again the fear of us that has so possessed you. Cold terror will grip your spine and run deliciously throughout your very core and bones. But spare yourself any fear, for even stronger within you is the feeling of unconquerable power, for you are protected and saved; the mannequins, with their painted faces and hands and glued on hair, will perhaps not be innocent, yet innocuous and harmless. You can take comfort from them, as the mannequins are dead and will not persecute you, for a blow can break them. They will be alive only in your past fears, otherwise not at all."

The speaker had arranged it such that his speech ended with the very same words with which the conqueror ended his. The recommendation about the mannequins was approved, followed by a lengthy discussion of how the figures should be presented and dressed. Wax was decided against, as it was hard to handle and too expensive, nor did earth, stone, or cast stone recommend themselves, as they were too stiff. Something simpler was needed, and indeed the dying were inventive: a frame made of poles and staves covered with rags, flax, and coarse fabric to make up the raw forms, and over that a layer of plaster, on top of which there would be a pliant paste made of wood fibers and a binding material that would allow one to finely work the surface before they were set in their final form.

It was supposed to consist of a family: a grandfather, a father, and a mother, a daughter and a son. First, little mannequins were commissioned. Quickly, cute little dolls were made that were played with, smiled at, fitted out with flapping limbs, with characteristic alterations made such that they more closely resembled the distorted image of this ancient people as they were made in larger sizes. Then a wave of activity was set in motion; sculptors, painters, decorators, many hand workers and other skilled people worked with a minimum of rest in a hastily assembled workshop. They were driven and encouraged, even receiving more to eat, but they always had to be prepared to be interrupted by high-placed visitors, to demonstrate their progress under careful inspection. Proud, the men stormed in without knocking, their hands placed pertly on their hips. Sometimes a hand would free itself from tight-fitting silk in order to underscore a desire or command with a pointing finger. Humorless rebukes could be heard, but also encouraging praise. Monitored continually in this manner, the work moved quickly toward the sought-after result. Each face was a masterpiece, the glass eyes piercing, the brows wrinkled in concern and the eyelashes individually applied with tweezers, heads and lush beards appointed with real hair that had been cut from the heads of the dying and collected, the expressions of the faces and their mien true to the way the extinct folk had expressed themselves. It all looked magnificent, especially the grandfather with his venerable long beard.

Then the clothing of the family of mannequins was made. Tailors did this who chattered a lot when their gags were taken off, but soon the conquerors didn't want to hear any more of their childish suggestions. Garments from the somber times of extinction were distasteful to the conquerors, for that was no longer the time of this people, so instead the costumes of a hundred years before were requested, the fine clothes of the Biedermeier period, the good old days of this people, in which they flourished rather than were destroyed. And so it was done. Everything was prepared in accordance with old pictures, then heads nodded approval, the fabric rustled, the scissors cutting brightly through, the needles flying, the sewing machines singing; soon the most beautiful tailoring possible was done.

Yet how were the mannequins to eke out a living? They were not up to the long workday, so it would be better to present them on a holiday. Not a holiday of penance and sorrow, however, but one about freedom and joy. They should think of their forefathers, who were once slaves of the king in that land. But the eternal one, their Lord, led them from there with a strong hand and outstretched arms. If the eternal one had not led them, whose name must be praised, had not led the forefathers from that land, then their children and their children's children would have remained in servitude in that land forever. He had parted the sea for them, and they safely passed through it. Then the eternal one had required them to memorialize the story of the exodus as Passover and to tell of it, while those who told of it were praiseworthy. It must not be forgotten; if the people indeed were extinct, then the mannequins had to commemorate it, and not on just one day but every day, year after year, so that the liberation of the extinct folk would be commemorated for all time. Thus it was right, for the commemoration was not necessary only for the days of Passover but on all days. Also included were the nights of those days. Yet what was named was not only "all days" but "all the days of life," for the "days of your life" referred only to the length of their temporal lives, whereas "all the days of life" meant the time of consummation, when the Messiah would appear. Therefore it was right that this people no longer existed, but instead the mannequins awaited His coming.

Once the garments were finished, and shoes and buttons were prepared, the mannequins were wonderfully fitted out, mothers and daughters decorated with jewelry made of artificial gold and silver and appointed with artificial gems, necklaces and brooches, bracelets and rings, and everything that a rich family should have while celebrating the High Holy Days, while the men wore silk shawls and yarmulkes made of velvet. An initial display of the family in the workshop charmed the conquerors, as they felt no shyness in touching the faces and gently fiddled with the garments. An apartment was then set up in the hermitage, where the mannequins were given a dignified setting. On the street side, the hermitage had three spacious alcoves with windows beneath the women's balcony, which had already been divided into display chambers, one a kitchen and the other a room decorated for the High Holidays. These served to provide all the needs of home for the family of mannequins, the conquerors giving the command, there being no need to speak with the housing office. The move from the workshop was followed in haste. So that the High Holy Room display was not damaged, the mannequins' clothing was removed. The finely made things were sprinkled with white moth powder and placed in suitcases as the mannequins were laid in chests full of soft cotton and carried to the hermitage. Everything was placed in a corner, with cloth sheets draping over it, the mannequins initially assured of their rest.

What was necessary for the kitchen of a religious household was brought in, everything precise and exact according to ancient law. The living room was painted with soft pastel colors. Precious old shrines, chests, and commodes displayed the wealth of the mannequins; a Persian rug was rolled out, a sofa with a sweeping, stately back and silk covering invited one to sit, the wide circular table encircled by five comfortable chairs. A sideboard next to the window was covered with heavy old folios. A forged bronze lamp hung discreetly above the table, and four silver candleholders were attached to the walls, where some pictures were also hung in order to display the forefathers of the mannequins in quiet gravity, followed by a religious saying embroidered in silk and framed, and a delicately cut mirror. Homey doilies were spread out on top of the chests, as well as precious and useful items carefully set out, such as bowls, pitchers, cups, vases, plates made of tin or hammered silver, dull stoneware and bright-flowered porcelain, a sewing box made of rosewood, a heavy box decorated with ivory letters, another mirror that could move in a frame and be attached to a wash table, a soft pillow with gold-brocaded fringes and borders laid out on the sofa. The only thing that was denied this devout collection was a clock, for it was meant to continue forever; therefore, it needed no time and no means to indicate the time.

Otherwise, the mannequins lacked nothing. There was no reason to think that their live spitting images were expelled from the commemorative table of the Passover celebration and led to their death and extinction. Protected and enclosed, the mannequins had only to just be. In order that they not worry when there was no one living to spend time with them, nor any visitor to share their celebration, they were mercifully provided with lush plants in cobalt-blue majolica pots on forget-me-not blue bases. They were placed before the window in the middle, where the softly gathered curtains let the daylight stream through the delicately cut panes. Then the table was set for the model family, the cloth a brilliant white, two tasteful candleholders with ivory-colored candles (these having been burned a bit, so that the wicks were black), a splendid jug with its sides bulging and a crown cover for the holiday wine that had yet to be poured out. As good as it all looked, neither could the mannequins, who were given five cups, be relied on to pour out four servings of drink, nor did anyone believe the prophet would appear, whose goblet was also placed on the table. However, they did make sure that the mannequins had a meal that was set out on a tray, three flat loaves of unleavened bread made of white cardboard, with brown flecks that looked amazingly real, the other food made up just as artfully, be it the boiled eggs, the lamb shanks, the bitter and green herbs, or the two little bowls next to them, in which to dip one's fingers like someone arriving out of the desert thirsty for water.

Once the room and the table were fitted out after continual fussing here and there, the mannequins were carried in carefully, in order to make sure not to harm them, which the curators managed not to do, the move going as planned. As fast as caution would allow, they were dressed and attended to. The grandfather was set up first and a pair of glasses put upon his nose, since they worried that his eyes looked tired. He didn't say anything, but it was remarked how the glasses made him look all the more dignified. Next, the parents and the children were just as carefully placed on their chairs. Before the conquerors arrived to inspect the completed work, five precious little books were brought in that contained the story of the exodus, just as would be read aloud during the evenings of the Passover celebration.

They were different editions, but each was opened to the page that read, "Thereby we are gathered to give thanks, to laud, to praise, to extol, to exalt, to glorify, to bless, to give respect and to worship to He who gave us our ancestors and all of these wonders."

Jagged medals glistened on the doublets of the conquerors who showed up to greet the dead group encircling the table, three sagging men with bent knees. Reserved faces examined things closely, yet excitedly, but the conquerors could not hide their delight for long, for they were so moved, praising the installation as informative and useful. One of them, who was moved to speak first, carefully touched the grandfather's velvet yarmulke as he began to speak.

"Unbelievably lifelike! We will live and die, but our children will live. Then they will come and look and know. With gratitude the future will recognize our achievement. They were something! But we need more of them. You are gifted and clever. Get together and create a big group of elderly standing before the ark!"

The speaker for the extinct was shocked. He was not a religious man, but he trembled before this assignment and also didn't know what the purpose of the mannequins really was. He wanted to raise a concern and opened his mouth to do so. But the men were not at all willing to allow any objections. Then his courage died before such sharp threats, there being nothing else to do but fulfill the new order down to its last particulars. What was asked for was the face of a wise old man, or, at least, what the extinct folk thought looked like a wise old man wrapped in a long prayer shawl with his face turned toward the ark, his long arms raised up high, in his hands two wooden spools with the holy scroll upon them. The extinct listened with softly bowed heads and nodded in understanding. They were ready for anything. No matter what. And their fear of the conquerors was greater than their fear of the Lord. Thus this sacrilege was completed, going off without a hitch. A huge group of the elderly were created, their hands embracing the handles of the scroll and unable to lower the sacred text, which would be praised on high for all eternity.

The conquerors filed in again, their jackboots marching quickly and heavily across the floor before they saw what overwhelming strength had been granted the mannequins, for their arms would never lower again. They stared on, for no living person had ever held the sacred scroll high without faltering. Then the men erupted in resounding applause. They slithered up to the mannequins that rose up high above them. The conquerors, however, disapproved of the open installation, for it needed to be closed off, so before the shrine a sumptuous curtain was hung, an ancient cloth augustly embroidered with strong threads of gold and many other colors, depicting two powerful columns standing to the left and to the right, covered with grape leaves and grapes, while between the columns the areas were filled in with flowers, and above in the middle a large shining eight-sided rosette, above which was an ornate inscription in an intricate framework, to the side of which two lambent lions stood on their hind legs, double-tailed, on their heads a small lit crown, the lions holding in their paws a powerful crown glittering with jewels. This, the conquerors decided, was what was fitting.

The extinct ones bowed deeply with lowered eyes and thought, Now the wishes of the masters are fulfilled. The obedient were ready to turn back in order to take care of some minor tasks, but they were once again confronted with the will of their rulers, whose speaker clapped his hands loudly, such that the fainthearted stood transfixed as the horrible voice sounded.

"Listen here! Well done! But not so fast, we're not yet finished! There's plenty here from life, but now we need something from death. Life doesn't last forever. That's why we also need to know how you buried your dead."

Then the most courageous one took a breath and dared to direct the conqueror's gaze toward the cemetery.

"No, not those graves over there with their stones! That can stay just the way it is. We need that here in the hermitage; we have another arch free. Turn it into a crypt! In the middle of it a pedestal long enough to hold a coffin, with a crate on top of it covered by a burial cloth. Take out the window, drape the room in black cloth with only recessed lighting from above. The coffin can remain empty; that way, you save yourself having to make another model. But everything else has to be real, just the way the burial contingent carried out its burial customs."

The laughter of the high ruler burst forth as he finished this speech, and so death entered the hermitage. Everything was brought together, whatever was used to take care of the dead and to bury them according to ancient custom. On the wall, explanatory pictures were installed that had been enlarged from old engravings. Now separated by the walls of the hermitage were the festive room of the family of mannequins during their holy meal and the crypt with its coffin.

Once again the masters pressed into the room, this time tipsy from having had drinks, eager to see the artificial overhead light that was to be turned on for the first time at their command when they had assembled before the entrance to the darkened chamber. They could see nothing and waited, thick blackness pooling before their eyes, until finally the order was given—"Lights!"—and the room flooded with light. How their eyes lit up with joy over the timeless lost mourners, the overlord proudly rapping the bedecked coffin with the knuckles of his left hand such that it echoed loudly.

"You've done well. On top of that, you did it fast. We don't need anything more from you, and at some point we have to call it quits. But we recognize what you've done and as a reward we are sending you to a place where you'll be treated well. You can now disappear. We will still need a few of you. We will let you know in an hour who will be traveling. The journey is all set for tomorrow."

The courageous speaker from earlier, who had best understood the most secret wishes of the conquerors and with ingenious obedience had fulfilled all their commands, on the next day had to leave with most of his deserving fellow extinct workers. The shadows of those who had been thanked, little suitcases and knapsacks, as well as two armed guards who had a list of names, and then they were off. Not a single human soul ever heard of the travelers again. The high lords, however, continued to enjoy the splendor on exhibition and often visited the hermitage until their own hour came at the end of the war. Then they disappeared and left behind all the mannequins, with their treasures, in the hermitage. After that, not a thing was heard of the conquerors.

Which was why my guests from Johannesburg trudged around and did not see everything that I saw, and listened to my words without really understanding what I was choosing to tell them in keeping silent about some things, while Herr Lever, overcome with childish surprise, also had questions. Much had changed in the hermitage with the end of the war. Indeed, most of the objects had been left where they had been in the days of the conquerors; only a few things had been relocated, some being sent far away and others added, but the mannequins were quietly taken from the hermitage. They were not intentionally mishandled, and they were spared any punishment for their blasphemous behavior, but they were also spared any kind of tenderness, as they were carried off ingloriously to an unpleasant storeroom full of junk and decaying stuff. Here the family squatted on everyday chairs in a corner. Not even the holiday tray, with its food and empty goblets, was brought along as sustenance for the journey, instead remaining back on the covered table. Soon the mannequins were tired and covered with dust, their garments faded, the grandfather's beard unkempt, the glasses having fallen from his nose, moths having chewed at the mother's scarf. Yet the family's condition—which could be improved if someone had a mind to do so—was incomparably better than that of the decrepit old man who had to stand before the closed ark with his arms uplifted, looking wretched. Miserably he lay upon the floor, the long shawl having been taken off him, such that, with his paltry skeleton composed of wood and cardboard, the back appearing broken, he was stretched out painfully on the dirty floor, as neither the least bit of protection nor even newspaper had been prepared for him in the storeroom. Nonetheless—he was a pigheaded old man—he still kept his arms continually raised, and still the cramped fingers wished to grasp the sacred scroll, but it was gone. Thus the old man's existence had become senseless; the shabby model wasted away amid the mildew and displayed nothing more of the extinct people.

Patiently I had led Herr and Frau Lever through every nook and cranny of the hermitage. Now we had climbed up to the balcony.

"Mitzi, it's hard to believe that everything made it through. Such a war, and it hasn't changed at all. On the contrary, things have been taken care of and added to. The temple is somehow—how can I say it?—immediate, much more intimate. Only the congregation is no longer there; it was scattered across the world."

"We have many prayer books on hand."

Mitzi nodded at me and again worked at her chin.

"If they managed to save most of them, dear Guido, then it's good."

I didn't say another word; I had explained everything and leaned against a wall, somewhat dizzy. The couple traipsed about the glass display cases satisfied. Both of them bent over to admire weathered documents from which they tried laboriously to read excerpts to each other.

"A great era has passed," said Herr Lever. "But, as one can see, it is not lost. Saved, saved! Do you know what that means, Mitzi? Our entire history is set down here, like in an album between wonderful covers. One only has to open it and leaf through. Through it history comes alive!"

I let this talk go on for a while. Then I informed them that we had to move along, time was short. If the couple still wanted to make a visit to the cemetery, we couldn't linger any longer. Thus I lured them down from the balcony and led them toward the cemetery, though without commenting on anything else, offering up only a couple of bromides and then letting the couple ramble around the densely packed gravestones dating back more than six hundred years. No one had been buried here in more than a hundred and fifty years. Everything had been left standing, or had fallen over and was left where it was. The sadness of fathers and mothers had long ago withdrawn from here, for the children sank within it, followed by the grandchildren, even the great-grandchildren, and those who wished to mourn at the graves of loved ones sought out other cemeteries. Sadness yielded to the preservation of memorials, this land of the dead dedicated to that function. Many people came from all over the world to offer up small tokens, only to be amazed at the tightly packed silver-gray and weathered graves long having gone to seed, one after another covered with mysterious emblems, ornaments, and inscriptions. Visitors had to surrender their cameras at the entrance, but they could buy postcards, both colored and black-and-white, as well as guidebooks printed in several languages, some more expensive if they had pictures and the cheaper ones without, though they were also worthwhile. At certain times, for a modest fee, small groups were led through the entire thing and had everything explained to them. Thus time was quietly painted over, for they looked back at one past, as the history of the cemetery was sealed off, the extended decay of the site making it all the more impossible to access. Stones were propped up and expertly cleaned, and the weeds were pulled on the paths, but only enough to make them passable and to make sure not to disturb their charm.

Only the seasons changed. In winter snow covered the crypts and paths, which were shoveled free. In spring the leaves on trees and bushes turned green, grass sprouted, and moss and lichen were fended off in order that they not consume everything, while birds hopped along the paths or shyly retreated to branches. In summer the stones glowed, the vegetation sprouting high and densely wild. Most visitors came during this time of year, but the stillness was hardly disturbed. In the fall, the cemetery was at its most beautiful when the leaves changed color and slowly drifted to the ground, until it was covered in thick layers.

Because of the war, this transformation came about in a leisurely way, as, most likely, hardly anyone came here and no one paid attention to what was happening to it. First the visitors from afar stayed away, then tours and the sale of postcards disappeared, and finally it was forbidden to visit the cemetery, the iron gate at the main entrance remaining closed, and from which one couldn't see very far inside, while care of the site was reduced and soon almost entirely forsaken, until the cemetery lay asleep as if under a spell. Only the urge to preserve memorials remained faithful to it once the conquerors no longer cared for the offspring of the dead. As soon as the hermitage was set up by those men, they announced that the cemetery belonged to it, all of it together a common grave of life and death. The fine yet important distinction one might wish to make between the two was no longer recognized. Thus life and death were slung together into one shared dying, the things gathering together as thickly inside the hermitage as the stones outside, the past heaping up, there only for the curious, arriving soulless in a future meant to be reached or anticipated. Reached, because it was not there, and one had to fight through any dispute; anticipated, because one could say today is still yesterday, so yesterday has a future, which is why it will still exist after today, if one hangs on and doesn't lose patience.

Now I was there once again, hermitage and cemetery having taken me in. There had only been time, time in between, a ridge of time on the border between life and death. Time perpetuated me in order that I could perpetuate, always there upon its lonely height, life and death falling away below it. Perhaps my life and death also fell away in the process, but I remained always above, blinded and yet not entirely unconscious, the days propelling me forward, even at night, because the nights were part of the days. Thus it went on, and at the end, if it was an end, it was something reached and anticipated, or at least I was something reached and anticipated, or perhaps not I but the perpetuity that drew near and replaced me, a sustained trans-formation between the graves of the ancestors long overtaken by time, but neither father nor mother there, they having slipped away from the ridge running its razor-thin border through time, and thus they had no grave and no house, they were no longer alive and not yet dead, having died within time. However, I remained above time, all of us encountering one another within time but, nonetheless, never having met one another.

Time meant the curse that I had been and was, and above time life went on, or I went on, I having left, the places having fallen away and separated from time, cut off houses and graves; only time continued to ensue, time itself pursuing. Meanwhile, there was the desire for a future. Was it time's desire or my own? It was the desire of my own temporality amid the lost places that had now passed. That's why the places had ceased to exist in one place that could simply exist henceforth and for certain, reachable and anticipated. I looked out to where everything moved, a pane of glass before me, translucent and smooth, such that I could lean against it, toward the outside, since I could not wait until it was reached. To the right and left, nothing but the hermitage and the cemetery, while in between there were many walls, though no borders. Everything passing over so quickly that it was no longer clear what it was, nothing stopping it. Was that a sign that there was a future? But where was it, where? There and gone, and every border was just a notion, not something that existed—none of it was real. Soft mist covered the countryside, the sky was gray, houses passed by again, and again a cemetery.

Was there nothing but hermitages and cemeteries here in this land? It was almost winter, and yet the fields were still green amid the undulating countryside. Gradually it grew brighter, yet the sun didn't break through the pale mist that extended far off into the distance. They didn't look like open meadows, much more like gardens, all of them enclosed by hedges, even the pastures. However, there were hardly any words, only trees in a small patch or single ones in the middle of a lawn with limbs branching out wide and thick from the trunk below. Cattle grazed leisurely between far-off barriers— here there were sheep as well, or a single horse, no one appearing to guard the animals. It surprised me that the animals were not gathered into stalls for the onset of winter. Villages drifted by, some of them spreading out, but they were not really towns, nor were they even what I'd call villages, because all the houses that I could see had tiled roofs and looked mostly like villas.

Everything was strange and distant. Thus none of it belonged to me; it was home to others but not to me, though nonetheless it was dear to me; there was comfort alone in the strangeness of it all. What surrounded me seemed to me solemn; I was still nowhere, my destination unknown and undecided. "Let's hope," I said to myself, but what I heard back wasn't comforting: "Lost, lost, everything gone. Don't expect anything!" And was there anyone waiting expectantly for me? If only I'd reached where I was headed! Indeed, So-and-So had written, saying he would be at the station, I could count on that, it would be an honor, an old friendship would be renewed, he would also bring others along, Oswald Bergmann and his striking sister, Inge. Yes, Bergmann had since changed his name to Birch; only Inge was still called Bergmann. He had done what many others had done here, and now he was a recognized man who was greatly esteemed as an archaeologist and art historian, his books being famous and well respected. He could introduce me to influential circles as thanks for my having done some things for him years ago when he came to us in the old city over there, living with me and my parents at home in order to familiarize himself with my theories, which he found very fruitful for his own field of research and wanted to make use of.

The thought of seeing Bergmann—now Birch—again was pleasing to me; even today I will admit that there are few people whom I have felt closer to. He was always the essence of life itself. Franziska beamed whenever she saw him, for he was dazzling, a tireless source of energy, full of good humor that ranged from light kidding to exuberant jokes. Oswald's life force seemed inexhaustible and hardly allowed for sleep, he seeming always fresh and infecting Franziska and me with his beaming alertness. If you spent an entire day and half the night talking with him, you didn't feel tired afterward, but instead always pleased and stimulated. Once we spent a summer with him in the south, Inge also joining us, a spirited, dazzling creature, delicate and beautiful. She liked us and we liked her, and we could all talk with one another endlessly. She wrote short poems about the landscape, acerbic and sometimes brash formulations that she thought very good, more so than her nearly fantastic stories in which the relentless unfolding of the plot was forwarded through surprisingly witty occurrences, all of it expressed in tautly rendered sentences. Also pleasantly exciting were her children's books, from which she earned enough to allow her to live modestly and give small amounts to Oswald when he needed money. However, that summer trip two years before the war began unfortunately ended not only our relationship with Inge but also with Oswald. They rarely wrote to us anymore, and then we heard that they had happily gone abroad. Soon I lost all trace of them. Then, a few months after the war ended, when I, prodded by Peter, tried to reconnect with any former contact I could remember, I also reached out to Oswald after So-and-So sent greetings from him in his second letter. I was still reluctant to do so, because Inge had never responded to Franziska's letter years ago, but when I later told Anna about Bergmann her face lit up immediately with joy as I had never seen it before; it was the charm of his personality, which affected anyone who ever met him. Anna informed me that she had once happened to hear him give a lecture on a subject far outside her field. She had been dragged along to it, Bergmann having spoken about Neolithic marbled ceramics, but how interesting and terrific it was, much of it still memorable to this day, particularly the technique of scoring the surface, stringing bands of clay, and incised adornments. Bergmann had explained it so clearly that one could never forget it, an unusual occurrence. Anna was so full of this person that she felt compelled to see him again, and, through a fleeting acquaintance with a woman, she was able to gain entrance to a gathering to which Bergmann had been invited. Thus Anna spent an evening in his company and was even able to speak with him. "He is the sun itself; you have to write to him for sure!" That was at least what Anna felt.

So I wrote Oswald a long letter while Anna's story was still fresh in my mind. It was a confession of all that had happened in the past years; I had never opened up to another person so candidly and in a manner so heartfelt. I didn't just inform him about what had happened but, rather, explained it to him, presenting matters to him in such a way that it would be clear to anyone, despite our having experienced different fates. I also wrote him a lot about Franziska, something which today I doubly regret, for it not only lies closest to my inner being but also amounted to a transparent depiction of the unforgettable, which I never succeeded in doing again. When

I, soon after arriving in the metropolis, asked to borrow the letter, Oswald promised to give it to me, but then couldn't find it. At the end of the letter I had let my friend know, which unfortunately back then I did not shun, my present situation through oblique hints so that he might understand what I needed—namely, help through a bit of attentiveness, a path into the future. But I never got an answer, neither from him nor from Inge, while inquiries in letters to So-and-So were ignored or fleetingly addressed. Only once did I receive a passing greeting from a traveler, who could tell me little about Oswald, since he never really knew him. My friend had merely told him to look me up and had told him about knowing me just in case it might be of use to him.

Anna found Bergmann's silence off-putting, and she could hardly understand, for such an adorable person surely had to be loyal as well, and everything she knew about him said that he was simple and humble. Now she regretted that she had turned down an invitation to see him again because Hermann had been jealous, she being foolish and young, and in fact she never did see Bergmann again, though he had never escaped her thoughts. I should just be patient, or write again, my letter simply must have been lost. Should I try again? Everything inside me resisted doing so. I just told myself at first that Oswald had always been a terrible correspondent. What had to be shared with others he passed on through acquaintances, while anything intimate or important he had Inge deliver whenever possible. Indeed, he had hardly ever written to me before the war, preferring instead to send a telegram or, better yet, to call me out of the blue, while whatever I should have received in black-and-white was always written by Inge. I reproached him for this once and remember how he, as charmingly as always, roguishly smiled as he replied, "That you dare to complain, that takes the cake! I've raised a writer in my family who is fabulous, and you don't even appreciate it."

But I also remember Oswald talking more seriously about this matter. He loved to receive letters, he explained, but because of the wall that existed between people who communicated through writing he could never bring himself to reply. Correspondence had become an ever more all-consuming black hole. Something written should be taken as valid, and that he believed in very much, but with this validity came a continual danger, for then every-

thing was set in stone and there might never be the chance to retract something, this being an ordeal that easily led to persecution. Words followed
one, and therefore, he had to admit, even if it was honorable to keep up a
correspondence, he could not do it and would rather remain dishonorable
in this respect. In general, he said then, the age of letter writing was over for
good. Modern communications (and the means for it, such as the telegraph,
the telephone, and the radio) made the possibility of human interaction
much easier, though, seemingly, in reality they distance us from one another
much more and create chasms that open in quick-fire fashion, whereby the
old bridges that spanned them are destroyed without being replaced, the
near becomes the far, and all human beings are separated from one another.
As soon as Oswald gave up writing letters, he felt a sense of loss that personally caused him also to feel a new loneliness that within a few decades would
be felt in general.

In those days I declined to accept this, nor did I even entirely grasp
what he was saying; only later did I come to appreciate that there was a grain
of truth in such a renouncement. Already, back then, I was worried by the
notion, which beclouded my own hopes, that technical means, rather than
easing the communication between people, actually increased the distance
between them. I was never a fan of civilizing wizardry in society, but my
faith in the basic goodness of human nature had not yet dimmed. I wasn't
ready to demonize an invention that had practical applications, but, above
all, I didn't see that such inventions would inevitably threaten certain aspects in human history that had always been considered assured, if not exactly destroying them, such that traditional values would be threatened or
forsaken, whereby moral behavior would be hard to delineate and often in-
soluble problems would arise, and that finally—as I would express it today—
each great discovery, or at least its useful application, would be ripped from
the tree of knowledge and therefore mercilessly drive human beings even
further away from Paradise and ever further away from the original Paradise. Oswald's talk prompted me to disagree, and I dared to raise my strong
doubts about his views, for which I was dismissed with a wave of the hand
and an oblique smile.

It must be lovely, he declared firmly, to relive the centuries gone by with
such hope and sincerity, and it's one of your more touching characteristics.

Oswald hoped that I would always maintain what he called, to my annoyance, such idealism. But, unfortunately, he didn't believe in it; anything that shook one to the core, or a devastating disaster, could finish off such a noble creature. I didn't agree with this disconcerting praise and asked him pointedly whether he would indeed not answer me personally if it ever involved a really important letter that was about a matter of life and death. Indeed, I had chosen some passionate words. Immediately, his wry smile disappeared and he became quite serious. No, there was no need to worry about that, for if he didn't write any other person in the world he would in fact write to me in such an emergency, for such need on my part had to be honored, and therefore he would certainly answer me. He asked only that I not become impatient when it took some time, for it required a great effort for him to gather his thoughts. He explained all this much more at length and with long repetitions, which was not his usual manner, thus resulting in a firm and clear, even sinuous speech. Nonetheless, his word didn't feel sound to me; I was not certain of his promise. He could sense that, and so looked at me and assured me, "Arthur, I know that an unanswered letter can result in a murder. I'm not a murderer, and you are my friend."

Oswald was not a murderer, that was clear to me, but his neglecting to answer my letter felt as if he were. So-and-So's empty responses annoyed me, while the same traveler that Oswald had bedecked with his greetings to me blabbed on like a know-it-all when he had me show him the museum, which annoyed me. Though I couldn't hold it against Oswald for long, it becoming ever more clear to me with time what I loved about him; from him I expected a completely different understanding and courtesy than from the rest of the foreigners abroad, whose image had faded for me or whose behavior I was hurt by. I had to make contact with him; it was the utmost test of whether I was good for anything. After some time, I felt it would be right to compose a second letter to him. It needed to be something special and began, "You are not a murderer," and at the end I wanted to write, "If you don't answer, then you're a murderer!" But I decided against that, not knowing if my words would resonate within his excellent memory. Instead, I got Inge's address from So-and-So and sent her a letter asking if she had any news for me, as I didn't wish to bother Oswald, but perhaps she could write to me in his or even her own name, as I really needed to hear that things were well with her and Oswald—all I needed was a few lines—and if perhaps the two of them had any advice for me if I happened to be successful in making it over to the metropolis. Meanwhile, the weeks stretched on and I waited for Inge's answer in vain.

Alas, such waiting wore me down and almost broke me! The days crept by. Three times daily the mailman commenced his fateful journey through the neighborhood, it being unclear to me what filled his bag when he had nothing but gas and electric bills, coal bills, official notices, useless flyers, circulars, publisher's catalogs, subscription offers, or needy appeals from charity organizations, or generally decrepit and useless mail that I had no idea what to do with. Meanwhile, important news that arrived and spoke to one's humanity, saying you, I mean you, out of which something announced itself and from flat paper a figure rose that you knew, whereby you existed, such seemed hardly to be had any longer. Or at least it wasn't so for me, nor has it changed for me much to this day.

No, Inge had done nothing to give me even the satisfaction of a few lines. Perverse defiance rose within me, causing me to pine for news from Oswald. I was shameless enough to ask the beleaguered So-and-So whether he could help me out with Oswald or Inge, but So-and-So just ignored my question. Letters cut into emptiness; also, whoever picks them up and reads them is lost in them, shaking off those silent expressions, unwilling to take pity on the matters raised within them. Then you write something, the sentences going on in a nauseating manner with their bleak accounts and painful demands, divided up neatly into questions and answers, though there is nothing within them, as you hold the paper up to the light in the hope of something jumping out, or waft the sheet in the air in vain, there being only a rustling sound but not a single living word. Even someone such as myself, who has learned the art of reading between the lines, will not be satisfied as he anxiously reads on with choking thirst. Such a game of silence seemed to me so dumb, and so I confronted So-and-So:

"Please write to me about what's going on with Oswald, or, if you prefer, how Dr. Birch and Fräulein Bergmann are, what they are doing, whether or not they received my letters??? Why haven't they answered at all? Do I not exist? Or am I nothing but thin air to them both? Do they think I've kicked the bucket? And why don't you tell me anything when I've asked you to? Are you only reading a part of my letters? Do I have to always read your lengthy missives telling me what I'm supposed to do for you with the horrid Dr. Blecha, that slimy little attorney, and others? If I want something, why is it that you must deliberately ignore it? Oh, please don't be angry that I am so upset, but it's gradually become too much for me to experience nothing but despair! If you only knew, my friend, how the situation with Oswald Bergmann upsets me and makes me unhappy, you would do something about it today! I know your good will toward me. So tell the two of them that I feel I've been forgotten by them when they don't answer me. A letter left unanswered can be tantamount to a murder! Take care of this!"

So-and-So would have to feel compelled to do something, but all he gave in return was small nuggets of information:

"Above all, I would ask you not to be so high-handed. The matter of Dr. Blecha (I'm enclosing a note with some instructions for him) should really be a boon for you. It's as much in your interest as it is in mine. I believe it would be better for me not to acknowledge your misgivings about him—no hard feelings. Now, to your being so wildly keyed up. Here people have a different temperament; they are measured and reserved. We, too, have had to get used to that. If you press a matter, which is exactly what you're doing, you don't get anywhere, especially when it comes to friendship. You write, 'A letter left unanswered can be tantamount to a murder!' Ridiculous! Have you gone mad? If I were to share such—forgive me—balderdash with Birch, of all people, I would certainly get an earful. For letters he has neither sight nor inclination, and such heavy-handed blackmail will only hurt you with him. Nonetheless, because of your pressing lines I have gone to Birch and made your wishes clear to him, but in softer terms. After all these years, he still likes you, and he's your friend. You don't have to doubt his approval. He has spoken of you with such warmth, which he is amply capable of toward you. A letter to him and one to his sister have arrived safely. You shouldn't have any worries about that. Both are healthy. Birch is working on his atlas of cave drawings throughout the world and is more and more busy. It should be a great work. He and his sister seem fairly happy, send their greetings to you, and will be happy for you to come here. Birch says that he cannot write to you because it would upset him too much to do so. When I suggested that perhaps his sister could write on his behalf, he promised to arrange that, but she, too, has much to do. She's working on a new children's book that Karin will illustrate in order to try to make ends meet and perhaps one day be able to leave dentistry behind. But that is just a plan. Please, don't mention any of this in your response, for it will only upset Karin, for it's still highly speculative, and she is also superstitious. Birch also let me know that I shouldn't promise that you'll get any letter from his sister, either. Then he expressed his surprise (this I'm sharing with you in confidence) that you were still alive. What he pretty much said was "I would not have wagered one red cent that such a tender type as Arthur would have pulled through!" My reply was "You have seriously underestimated him!" He then said, and he was quite serious, "Of course, I know that!"

After that, I gave up asking So-and-So or others about Oswald, and Anna avoided bringing up his name. How moved I was when in his last letter to me So-and-So referred to Oswald and Inge again—moreover, that the two of them would certainly meet me at the train station! I didn't know whether I should be overjoyed or afraid, and it almost unsettled me how I was left to feel my way through the dark, as it was unclear why I was suddenly again worthy of the sympathies of the siblings. To certainly expect . . . what does it mean to be certain? The train flew past the switching point of a station stop, releasing a terrific noise, but it sounded to me like music, the certain speed of it, heading for our destination, both the rails and the journey directed at an endpoint, no falling away from it, as long as nothing bad happened, for nothing bad must happen. The train was still the safest form of travel—the roar of the machine, its thunderous snorting, the ring and rhythm of the wheels, rolling along the echoing rails, the certainty of the powerlessness of the detained who sits in his compartment, nonchalantly allowing himself to trust in the harrowing strangeness, like a letter traveling, sent from one person to another, sent off, delivered, received, opened, the journey there occurring between, cautiously, but irresistibly leaning through the curves, onward, onward, then always the drowsy, yet never weary gaze out at the passing terrain that remains stationary despite one's moving through it, the ticket bought, the border falling behind you, a traveling being upon a fixed line.

But where was freedom? Once you commit to the journey, then it's over, and no one knows if it means escape, or the choice to begin anew, or expectation. Oh, it was expectation; to be expected, no longer foreign, once one is expected. Yet you remained confused, not believing in yourself or in others, having gathered together your bags and looking out to wonder who will be there, who will recognize you, or greet you once the destination was reached? I could not imagine, as everything swirled around. The conductor approached; a well-meaning healthy face looked at me as I handed him my ticket, it already being worn out from having been checked many times. All that was left was a receipt in the ticket book. A long trip, I explained apologetically and wearily in the foreign language. The man nodded and muttered something. I didn't really understand what he said, though I also felt that the conductor hadn't understood me, and then I saw to my horror how he let the ticket disappear into his pocket. How was I to account for my journey at the gate? Too weak to stand up, I fidgeted mightily on the seat, as I had neither enough cash to bail myself out nor the right words at the ready to explain to the attendants at the station the misfortune of my ticket's having been confiscated. I had to have the little ticket book back!

"I need the ticket! The journey is far from over. There's no metropolis for far and wide. No slowing of the journey. No protective station."

The conductor looked at me as if I had lost my mind, as I spit out this flood of half-senseless words, but nonetheless he got what I was trying to say, laughed, and gave me a reassuring sign.

"You don't need a ticket. The train doesn't stop again."

"Doesn't stop again . . . ?"

"No. Just at the end."

"At the end . . . But at the station?"

"You don't need a ticket."

Then the conductor waved at me as if I were an unruly child, indeed saying, "Shh-shh," and then he was gone. However, how could he maintain that the train would not stop again and there was no need for a ticket? I rubbed my eyes, pressed my forehead with four fingertips, at first lightly and then more strongly, shook myself, stood up wearily and then sat down again, closed my eyes for a little while and then opened them as wide as I could, though there was no doubting that the journey continued on. Indeed, the dizziness let up a bit, but that happened because, to my surprise, the stretch we were traveling climbed gradually up a chain of hills that I had not been expecting to encounter in this area of the countryside. But I didn't dream, nor was I even sleepy, the presence of the day harsh before me, and, except for the damned ticket book, I had all my possessions together, each of them taken down from above. That was the way I was when we left, and that was how I remained.

Outside, lovely towns appeared and disappeared, artfully laid out gardens, all of it tended to, the winter having hardly settled in, the misty weather even providing a lovelier light, the haze lifting, the view easier to make out, the clouds rising higher and forming soft contours, though they didn't open to blue sky, ragged streams of the hidden sun trying to press through the thin silver layers here and there, such that it almost fell in tightly packed shimmering bundles, where it nestled deep in the embankment of an extensive delicate marsh that ran along the rolling ridge of a sparsely covered set of hills. Soon the train thundered into a tunnel, but the compartment was lit, a yellow tent, a safe haven amid the rumbling storms, the cushioned benches green as wild moss. The thick smoke at the window was like blowing snow and caused me to feel a loneliness in which I thought I would not sense anything again, that's how painful it felt. From the sounds it made, I could tell the train was descending again, the journey winding on until finally we were free of the tunnel, though the pressing smoke still prevented an open view; only slowly did the clouds part, a different country flowing by before my eyes, where the rail line, carving through cliffs in a lonely fashion, revealed the surrounding countryside only in little descending snippets, and soon finally rushed along over the flats.

If there was a destination, it couldn't be too far off, for the kinds of suburbs that like to spread out from large cities were beginning to pop up. Yet the train did not at all slow down, it seeming doubtful and yet at the same time uplifting. There was a snarl of tracks that broke off from our line and stretched out in different directions, others that ran into ours, melding into us, running alongside, and still others that we passed over or that passed under us, numerous outposts of the metropolis, I told myself, while the wide cast of its life, no matter how confusing and unfathomable it seemed to me, nonetheless lent me a certain sense of sureness that a mighty heart beat at its center, causing the one who sat here snug to feel at ease. Trains rattled along on other tracks, shooting back and forth, some coming from the other way, others moving in the same direction as us, though more slowly, such that we traveled alongside them for a short time until we overtook their strange little engines that puffed away in rapid bursts.

More and more station stops, which we rushed through without slowing down, passed by. Trains rested at the platforms; many people were gathered, swarming around the wide-open doors or patiently waiting in clusters. Soon came the suburbs, with their narrow houses with gardens pressed up against one another, and expansive park lawns in the thick of settled flatlands, though the train rushed on as if none of it was there. It occurred to me how colorless the city was, but that could have been because the light had grown cloudy again, falling heavy and murky out of the closed sky onto the roofs, or because of so much soot and smoke that covered everything in pale strands and dull flakes. Nor did the city present its most attractive neighborhoods to anyone entering it, and its monotony felt oppressive. I didn't want to let myself be disturbed by such first impressions, knowing, as well, that the journey would soon end, and so I gathered together my things, feeling anxious, my hands trembling, so that my suitcase fell clumsily to the floor, opened, and smashed one of my toes. An apple, the last of the ones that Anna had given me on the way to the station, rolled out and as a result was covered in an ugly layer of dirt. I let it lie there, but then I sadly shoved it to the side, not wanting it anymore. My foot hurt, but it was bearable. I couldn't let anything distract me now, in order to make sure that I pulled myself together and braced myself for the new experiences to come. The sudden opening of the suitcase caused me some concern, because my luggage was full to bursting, and now, since I was in a hurry, the suitcase didn't want to close. There was no one to help me, no skillful Peter, who would complain but also would know what to do. I had to press down on the case with my knee; it was harder than at all the borders I'd crossed where I had to show my possessions in order to lift any suspicions about my carrying something banned. But finally I managed to close the suitcase.

It was just in time, because as I took my coat and hat I saw that the train was traveling slowly over a bridge. The river was milky, the pride of the land, but I hardly paid attention. There was a sharp screech, the brakes having been applied. I shoved my things into the narrow passageway, confused, weary, and yet so tense that I felt I would explode. The few travelers in the car had all gone on ahead of me and were already gathered on the platform when I clumsily made my way through the long passageway and bumped into them. The train stood in the open hall of the station with its doors wide open. I looked out in search of a familiar face, but because of the poor position of the railcar and the pressing rush of people on the platform it was impossible to make out anyone. Suddenly I was worried that no one had bothered to show up to meet me and started to think how I was going to find my way on my own. To leave my luggage in storage was an easy solution passed on to me at the information desk (I felt ashamed of my stupidity, given how easy it was to solve my problems with this simple solution), after which I needed to buy a map, whereby I wouldn't need anyone else's help.

But then—well, what then? I would have to pull myself together. Then I would have to look for the quickest and best way to get to So-and-So's apartment. That I could do. If I were to meet someone there, it could even be Karin, it probably would be better than receiving a mildly annoying welcome at the train station, where I could be picked up like someone who is lost and really doesn't know what is supposed to happen. The clueless stranger would then be led off as if on a leash and would have to let a churning flood of questions shower over him, during which he feels weak and fragile, his gaze naked and astounded, unprepared for the hail of impressions crashing in upon him, the poor, unhappy man dragged off and not told where he is going, what he should say first and ask first, and thus unable to finish even a sentence because he is continually distracted, his words and thoughts interrupted, then quickly urged to pay attention to something else, then to listen for something, to look at something, then suddenly yanked from his restless state into yet more annoying uncertainty. No doubt a stranger is also quite helpless if he arrives alone, but at least then he can get used to all the confusion at his own pace, taking in and making sense of all the chaos, gradually gathering himself until he can reliably trust his own senses, his friends surprised and convinced by his safe arrival that perhaps he's not such a fool as they might want to make him out to be.

All the travelers ahead of me had gotten out and had engaged porters or had swiftly hurried off, only a few greeted by loved ones and triumphantly whisked away. It was nice that the platform next to the track was smooth and flat, such that leaving the train with my four bags was not too strenuous. A porter offered his services, but I had no desire, much less courage, to pay him to help, my means having shrunk, nor did I know the currency very well and I could so easily be taken advantage of. If my friends were nearby, I wouldn't need anyone, and, besides, the left luggage couldn't be that far off. The porter shrugged and looked at me suspiciously, as if he wanted to say, "Foolish, chintzy stranger, to the devil with you!" Before I readied myself to move on, I once again looked around carefully. It could in fact be that So-and-So had changed a lot, and I strained to imagine what his face might look like. Yet how easy would it be for him to recognize me if he also didn't have a good memory of how I looked? To recognize someone in a train station after many years is indeed difficult. You stare at many faces, observing people's gait, too many of them hoping to find one another and already shaking hands and kissing before the vague delirium of seeing one another sets in and, after losing themselves in rapid chatter, again separating from one another. The air is tense with the tangled threads of expectation; you are separated and wander off, having indeed missed someone, and, with a creeping feeling in your stomach, you stand mistakenly in the weather along with everyone else, abandoned at the dirty exit of the train station.

Yet I was fairly certain that So-and-So was nowhere in the vicinity, nor was I standing within the circle of Oswald's gaze, and other friends were certainly not on the platform. I lifted my luggage, taking a few steps with two suitcases, and then returning for the others, it thus going very slowly as I shuffled on, while most of the travelers were already far ahead of me, the latecomers having also overtaken me. Soon the platform was almost completely empty of people. Only the little automatic trolley laden with huge pieces of luggage hummed past me as I continued to trudge on and I was shocked to realize that the exit was a lot farther away than I had expected. After pausing several times to rest I had made it as far as the engine, and yet I still had not discovered anyone I knew. There was no real checkpoint, which explained my ticket's having been taken on the train, but instead a wide outlet, behind which a teeming mass of people moved about. Among them were hardly any who were waiting for a traveler from abroad. When I first reached this throng, I felt that I had arrived. I set down my things and wanted to rest before launching into my strange new venture. As I did this I looked in every direction, not wanting it to be my fault if I missed

So-and-So. Soon I felt better, and more ready to risk the adventure, only my hurt foot feeling painful and burning, it being an annoying obstacle to feel at all restrained while taking one's first steps in a new land. But I only squatted on my suitcase for a little while, lifting myself up and looking for a trustworthy face to ask the way to the left luggage, a man soon obliging me. I worked my way through the crowd, resigned to the fact that my friends had other things in mind than to pick up a lost one. As I went to place my things in left luggage, an uncertain greeting reached me from close by.

"Arthur!"

I turned around. It was Oswald, who stared at my face.

"There he is!"

He yelled it, much too loudly it seemed to me, and so I looked away, not wanting to cause a commotion. The attendant behind the counter looked at me questioningly.

"I don't know what it's about!" I stammered to the man unsteadily. He turned away indifferently, pulled back from the counter, and didn't concern himself with me anymore.

"We were afraid that we'd missed you, Arthur. Or, worse yet, that something had happened, perhaps difficulties at the border—you know all too well what I mean. But here you are, that's what matters. We were worried that they wouldn't let you into the country. Inge thought that, and Kauders was worried as well."

"Where are they all?"

"Wait now, Arthur, just wait! I'll get them all; they went to have a cup of tea."

"And the luggage?"

"What do you mean, 'the luggage'? What are you saying, Arthur? I mean, what are you proposing?"

I wasn't proposing anything, but I wanted for something to happen.

"I'd just like to know what's going to happen."

"Of course, of course, naturally, that makes sense. I mean, whatever you wish, Arthur. You can of course leave it here. Nothing will go missing, neither big suitcases nor little ones. You can insure it. Whatever you like."

"But what will happen with me?"

"Naturally, of course. You won't be staying here. Just give me a moment to get the others. Or, if you want, I'll stay here and you can go look for them yourself."

"I don't know where to go."

"That's right, naturally. You're completely right. I'd recommend, Arthur, maybe it would be best to wait here. I promise that it won't take long. Not even five minutes. Or you can leave the luggage and we can both go. Does that sound all right?"

I found it hard to decide; Oswald's talk didn't make my situation any easier. It bothered him how indecisive I was. I noticed how he was straining to find an exit. He looked at me, concerned and confused.

"Everything must, of course, be according to your wishes, Arthur. We are here entirely for you. I mean, your situation, since it is so understandable. But perhaps you have a suggestion, particular plans. Perhaps you'd like a cup of tea."

Oswald spit it all out in a harried fashion; it bothered me how hard he tried to please me. And yet it wasn't up to me to solve the problem at hand. I spoke to him as sympathetically as I could, almost abjectly.

"I have to ask you to make a suggestion, Oswald. I'll follow it—I just want to reach a destination somewhere."

I added the last sentence when I sensed that Oswald was again ready to say something that would hardly clear up the situation.

"Well, well. A suggestion. Of course, if that's what you want. But will you like it?"

"Just make one!"

"Okay, then I suggest that you stay put for now. I'll get the others. Is that all right? I'll be right back with all of them. Just wait patiently, it won't take long. Shall I get you a newspaper so that you won't be bored?"

"No, no!"

"Okay, then. Perhaps you can meanwhile think about what you'd like to do, or you can just rest. And then we'll all be with one another and together at last. Does that sound good?"

Indeed, everything was fine by me. I nodded my approval and wanted only for Oswald to leave for a good long time, for I had not yet got used to his indecisive but overbearing onslaught.

"Wouldn't you like a cigarette?"

Oswald held out an open pack to me. I reached mechanically to take one, but I couldn't get it out, whether it was because I was so unsettled or because they were crammed so into the pack. Then Oswald handed me the entire pack and pressed some matches into my hand before he left.

I had to laugh a tormented laugh, and I felt more lost than ever, having surrendered myself with abandon to some people—who knew how many?—who were supposed to be my friends and yet knew nothing of me. It was not the same Oswald that I had known, or was it vice versa? I was not the same person that he had known, a wall having been erected between us—here the lost one, improbable and still doubtful in his reappearance, there Oswald Bergmann transformed into the famous archaeologist Mr. Birch. Perhaps he had anticipated me as I was, yet I had not yet reached him. Standing around me was my luggage; I recognized each piece, having brought them along with me, and I knew roughly how I had divided up the contents within them. Only Anna's last apple had remained behind on the train and most likely was being scooped up by an attendant with a shovel and tossed into a rubbish bin. But otherwise everything was there, stacked and pressed together by a stiff outer shell, feeling sad for me and the senseless rush at our stop at an untimely place; and yet, even though all of it was mine, nevertheless nothing belonged to me, all those embarrassing remains abandoned by me, wasted relics, none of which I wanted. And yet I was responsible for them and had to claim them, because there were people coming who wanted to either pick up or get rid of their things and needed the space where my things stood awkwardly in the way. I reluctantly shoved my luggage to the side and sat down on a suitcase and lit one of Oswald's cigarettes. It was strong tobacco, which I was not used to, yet the smoke was pleasing.

The time during which I waited went too quickly, for already Oswald was leading his companions toward me. There was Inge, stolid and much fatter than I recalled. A corner of her mouth was turned down inadvertently or mockingly, something that I had never seen in her before. And then came So-and-So, with his swinging arms and fidgety legs, much more nervous than before the war. My friend seemed older, dour or unhappy, his hair now thin, his skin slack and with deep wrinkles that were more pronounced around the mouth than around the temples and forehead. He had not brought along Karin, while there was a third person I recognized, whom I had long forgotten—namely, Otto Schallinger, a classmate of mine in middle school, with whom I had lost almost total contact before the war. Hadn't he become a pharmacist? I thought I recalled that he had moved from this profession to work as a chemist. I had never been close to Otto; in his character there was something of the lasting loyalty of old tailors, an always pleasant, though to me somewhat boring, companion whom I never quite knew what to make of. That he had been asked to welcome me here in the metropolis, where I never expected him, was a complete surprise that I obviously couldn't take the time to mull over amid everything that was coming at me and making me feel yet more defenseless. My friends also had another strange man in their midst who blithely accompanied them and looked at me keenly. Was this perhaps one of the important connections that So-and-So wanted to bestow upon me? Already, from afar I could see how all of them devoured me with their gazes, sucking me up, myself complying almost unconsciously, which seemed the best thing to do.

I jumped up from the suitcase and took heart in order to greet the group in a manner as dignified and unforced as possible. All of them walked along at almost the same pace, a strange sad march, their gazes never shifting from me and seizing hold of me such that I had to make an effort to endure such an onslaught and not look at the ground as if being punished. No doubt it had to be a surprise to see someone whom you thought was dead suddenly appear, not trusting your own eyes or knowing if perhaps you were wrong. I would have been glad to take a step toward the group in order show them: It's me, come closer, and don't be afraid. But I let things be. I also felt that it wasn't up to me to say the first word, and so I only felt compelled to laugh at the little band, whose strange hurry was remarkably slow and approached me like a moving wall. Then Otto the pharmacist jumped out from the group, a camera around his neck that bounced along pleasantly in its leather case on his stomach. "There you are, you old fellow!" he called out with sincere joy, stretching his right hand out to me, whereby our thumbs quickly folded over each other's. But he held my hand for only a few seconds and then drew back. I didn't know what was going on, as Otto waved to the others not to come any closer to me, at which, like a street photographer who suddenly snaps your picture and offers you a card that says, "You've had your picture taken!," he readied his camera, lifted it high, pointed it at me, and snapped.

"We have a picture!" he yelled. "It's a triumph! A real event!"

"Hopefully, you're not a press photographer," I replied timidly.

"No, no, what do you think I am!" Otto reassured me, and then he snapped another photo.

Then, for the first time, the others could approach. One after another shook my hand, also the stranger, who introduced himself as Dr. Jolan Haarburger from Budapest, even Oswald shaking my hand as well, since he had failed to do so earlier. The last was Fräulein Bergmann, who, if I'm not mistaken, had to be prodded by her brother. Only a few words were exchanged, more abrupt calls of sharp surprise than anything specific. I didn't have anything to say in return and kept quiet until the others had nothing more to say but instead stood around me in a half circle and stared at me. I lit another of Oswald's cigarettes. Then I wanted to give him back the pack, but he wouldn't take it. As I held it out to him, he took hold of my hand and the pack and guided them into my coat pocket, and I had to just go along. Then I turned back and forth inside the half circle; I was curious what would happen next, but no matter what I did, nothing happened, only this half-astounded, half-shameless gazing at me kept going on, to which I responded by blowing smoke into their eyes, not even sparing Dr. Haarburger. At last he was the one to say how pleased he was to have met me. He thought it wonderful that I was now here, for I would no doubt be pleased. "The city of cities!" he whispered almost secretively, and winked as he said it. Then he pulled out his card and hoped that I would soon make use of his telephone number, for he and his wife would be especially pleased if sometime in the next few days I would contact them and pay them the honor of arranging a visit to them. I thanked him with a deep bow and promised that I would call soon. Then Dr. Haarburger explained that he didn't want to take me away from my friends any longer—he had bothered me enough already and had to be going.

"It was truly a pleasure. It's a wonder that you made it here, looking as good as ever after all that you've been through, and not even worn out by the journey. We are all here to help you. Think of me as a brother."

I was embarrassed and shrugged. So-and-So turned away, Oswald stroked his forehead, Otto grinned as Inge cleared her throat. None of it seemed to affect Dr. Haarburger.

"I literally stole away a bit of time from my day because I simply had to see you. I'm especially indebted to Dr. Kauders for having told me so much about you and letting me know what time you were arriving. So let me, in the name of all of my friends, say how happy we are to have you here among us. We need you. It's a difficult country, but, for you, certainly promising, very promising."

Dr. Haarburger underscored the last phrase emphatically, Oswald agreed with him approvingly, So-and-So smiled enigmatically, and I bowed once again. The friendly man was in a hurry to get away, but he hadn't reckoned with Otto.

"Just a moment, Herr Doctor. We need to get a photo of this! The whole group, please!"

As Haarburger hesitated and the others remained standing where they were, Otto said resolutely that we needed to draw closer. Otto took at least eight shots. Inge didn't like it, becoming ever more nervous and longing for it to end.

"That's enough now, Herr Schallinger!"

Inge gave the photographer a nasty look, such that he lowered his weapon dejectedly.

Sadly he played with his camera, but didn't put it away in its case, and when Dr. Haarburger was finally gone Otto turned mercilessly toward me and shoved me a bit to the side of the group.

"I need some more of you! I was stupid and only took two shots of you at the beginning!"

Then he took a number of shots until he had used up the roll. Only then did he seem satisfied, but not entirely, for he then took out the roll and put in a new one. I'd had enough of this, and the others came to my rescue.

"Now, let the beast give poor Landau a bit of rest!" said Inge. "Otherwise he will get a big head. Isn't that true, Landau—aren't you as conceited as ever? It's no wonder, given what you've survived!"

I couldn't believe my ears, but it was just as embarrassing for the others, especially Oswald, who didn't want to see either me or Otto upset.

"Inge is so high-spirited. Inge, you shouldn't talk so! Inge loves to joke, and, of course, she doesn't mean anything by it."

Otto only found it all a bit odd and wasn't upset, nor was I. He seemed satisfied with his yield of photos, while to me it was all the same. I only wanted to leave the cloakroom and the station, but, unfortunately, my friends did nothing to get me out of there. Had they come to no decision? They stood there as morose as before, awkwardly moving their arms and hands and looking at me almost ravenously. What did they expect of me? It was up to them to do something; they couldn't turn over to me what was supposed to happen in the next minutes and hours. They murmured something, but didn't seem to agree on anything, as I had hoped, because they went quiet again and kept shifting their weight back and forth on their legs as if they had worked out a pantomime with which to welcome me. I tried to encourage them by smiling, but they couldn't free themselves from their torpid demeanor. Perhaps my attempt failed because I had not smiled enough in a natural way. They had become more serious and confused, only Inge seeming somewhat less timid and looking on more derisively, but it was also possible that this was only because of her own uncertainty. There-fore I resigned myself to break up their torpor with more smiles and looked sideways over at my luggage, which sat pitifully on the floor. Perhaps it would be better for them to grab hold of it and at least help me with that. But all of these attempts came to nothing.

"Now tell me, how are you all?"

"We're fine, thank you!" Oswald assured me. "Of course good, very good!"

"Yes, I'm doing well!" Otto also announced. "I've completely settled in here. I have a little pharmaceutical lab that produces a couple of special con-coctions of my own, while I also analyze blood and urine samples, whatever comes along. Stool and sputum samples, should you need something. I do it gratis for old friends, cosmetics as well, though there's too much competi-tion in that, but I have a modest apartment with a native wife who is called Sylvia. We are happily married and have a child, who is called Sidney Keith. Sylvia passes on her regrets that she didn't come along. She doesn't speak any German, though she understands a bit and is a good cook, because she comes from the north. They cook better there than in the south. You will have to meet her, for she will be wildly pleased. She is musical and gives a few piano lessons. Otherwise she helps me a bit in the lab when Sidney is in kindergarten. I bet you're still as musical as you used to be in school. Do you remember? You both have something in common."

"That's wonderful," I said, feeling quite happy that I could carry on a conversation, no matter how little Otto's family history interested me. "And all of you are friends?"

"Not really! I just met Mr. Birch and Miss Bergmann here today for the first time. It was just a lucky coincidence that I had heard something about your arrival and could be here. Just imagine, only a couple of days ago I met So-and-So on the street, and he told me you were coming. What a surprise! I didn't know anything more about you. It's been such a long time. Someone claimed that you had emigrated to Peru or Brazil. I don't even know who it was, nor did I believe it, for someone also said, more authoritatively, that you had remained behind, and therefore I couldn't help but think that you were dead. My God, how many are dead! My brother, for one, and his wife and two little children. I believe you knew him. He was two classes behind us at the gymnasium. Do you remember? And many in my family are dead."

"Herr Schallinger is right!" Inge said with intense anger. "Dead, dead, dead—there's no end to it, so much that I prefer not to ask after anyone I knew. And there are too many who are still alive, all of them having no right to be!"

"Inge, you can't say that! No one has the right to wish anyone dead!"

"Really? And the murderers? Perverse. Oswald, you are perverse!"

"Let it go, Inge! You know my views. You must know, Arthur, that I've considered this subject. You can judge the murderer, but you must not wish him dead. He is a human being, certainly a horrid human being, but his life is also sacred, unique, and irreplaceable!"

"Nothing but the disengaged morals of an archaeologist!"

"Inge, now stop!"

"You and your squeamishness!" she said, dismissing her brother. "You have your sympathy for them, fine, but also with the murderers. Mine is for those murdered, only with the murdered, and even then not with all of them. You should just know, Landau, three of our aunts were killed—my and Oswald's aunts! I loved one of them as if she were my own mother, and I loved my mother very much, that you can believe. But this aunt did everything for us, and really helped to raise us."

Oswald was uncomfortable with Inge's outburst.

"Why do you have to say the same thing to everyone? It's not at all interesting, especially for Arthur. He's experienced enough horrible things already."

"Experienced, experienced—that's a big difference. He experienced what he did, but our aunts and all the dead experienced much more, for they're all dead. So he should be happy that he experienced only what he did. He's lucky to be in the world and to be able to laugh about it."

"Inge, enough already! That's so offensive! You'll have to forgive her, Arthur! Inge is sometimes so harsh. It's her nerves, which really are bad. In actuality, she doesn't mean it so."

"I do indeed mean what I say. He should just know it."

"Now cease this instant, Inge, or I'm leaving!"

Inge shook with laughter. Her brother looked at her angrily and then said something to her quietly, such that she finally reined in her extravagantly hysterical behavior and appeared a bit more measured. So-and-So, who until now had hardly said a word, smiled with annoyance at the controversy between the Bergmann siblings and turned to me.

"Did you see Dr. Blecha? Will something finally come of it?"

"He is a crook, and the government is even worse."

"But my parents' assets must be restored. The state can't simply gobble them up!"

"The state can do anything it wants, and Blecha can do nothing but accept his honorarium."

"Unbelievable! Am I entitled to nothing?"

"The question is too hard for me to answer."

"What. . . . Well, let's talk about something else. You look amazingly well, Arthur."

"You, too!" I replied.

"Sharp as ever. The years haven't changed you at all."

"That's much too flattering."

"Don't worry, I don't flatter anyone. I just didn't expect it. But, to switch topics yet again, you can't stay with us. Karin is sorry."

"Really? I had been so looking forward to it!"

"Me as well. But it just won't work. You can come over often. We have all pitched in—Birch, myself, Haarburger, and a few others—and have arranged for a nice room in a cheap guesthouse. We've already paid for four-teen days—"

"Yes, but the expense?"

"No worries. That's all taken care of."

"I mean, how will I pay you back?"

"It's all taken care of. I told you, we all pitched in together."

"Many thanks!"

"You don't have to thank us. It's the obvious thing to do. But you can't move in right away. The room is still occupied."

"That's too bad."

"For sure. But it doesn't matter. You can move in the day after tomor-row. Maybe even tomorrow. We'll check by calling them."

"And in the meantime?"

"You're not letting me finish. Everything has been taken care of. You can stay with Birch."

"As well as with Inge?"

"No, not with Fräulein Bergmann. Just with Birch."

"Naturally, Arthur, only if it's all right with you. It would be my plea-sure."

"If it's not a bother."

"No, no, no bother at all. Naturally, but really, when it's all right with you, Arthur. Otherwise, you could stay in the hotel. A room is already re-served. But it would be a real delight if you'd like to stay with me, for we could talk a great deal."

"I'd be delighted if it's not too much of a burden for you for one or two nights."

"Of course, you're welcome. Otherwise I wouldn't have said anything. Three nights, a week—you can stay as long as you wish."

"Shall I accept the offer, Fräulein Bergmann?"

"When my brother invites someone, then he must be fond of him, which is a distinction one must accept. It's a great honor for you, a great honor. That's what I say. For days Oswald has almost lost his head over you. Nothing but Landau. He's totally smitten."

"Inge, please!"

"Well, it's only true!"

"I'm very touched, Oswald. I'm so pleased."

"Not another word about it. But I have to to tell you, my place is extremely modest."

"It's lovely at Birch's!" said So-and-So emphatically. "You could not possibly feel better or more comfortable."

"Don't believe a word Kauders says," warned Inge. "But in this case he's actually telling the truth."

Thus I at last knew my next destination. Now what I really wanted more than anything was to leave the station. That's what I wanted to ask to do next, but then Otto suddenly seized control of the conversation with another offer.

"I'm thinking you could also stay a couple of nights with me. I just have to ask Sylvia, but I know she'll agree. I have a little room, which is really a bit small, for I use it mostly as a darkroom, but I can set up a chaise longue for you there. Many others have slept there already. I think that it even might be best for you, amid all this hustle and bustle, to stay with an old classmate, where you can almost feel at home while you get used to things. I can tell you everything about the city, what you need, and so on."

This suggestion was not to my taste. I looked searchingly at Oswald.

"Naturally," he said, "only what feels right to you. It will, however, mess up all the plans I've put in place."

"Just let Landau decide," interrupted Inge. "He's old enough to decide for himself. One shouldn't speak for him."

"No one is speaking for him," said So-and-So angrily. "The darkroom, Herr Schallinger, is a lousy idea. Nowhere can he be as comfortable as at Birch's. It's close by, and it means a lot to Arthur. That's been the plan all along. Now, enough!"

Thus I was saved from having to make a choice and didn't need to turn down Otto's intrusive offer. But now I had really had enough of the station and was growing impatient.

"Can we finally go?"

"That's not up to me," explained So-and-So.

"Me, neither!" I responded indignantly. "That's up to you, and you all finally need to decide. I cannot and don't want to decide anything, and I'm happy to leave it to you all, but I'm begging you to come to a decision quickly! Get me out of here before I collapse!"

"Are you tired, Arthur? Did you have a bad trip? A bit overwhelmed? Do you want to sleep? You can sleep at my place."

"I don't want to sleep, just to get away from here! I'm starting to feel irritable."

"He's irritable!" exclaimed Inge excitedly. "Irritable because his friends are only thinking of how to best take care of him! We should be irritable and not you!"

Oswald stamped his foot and threw his sister an angry look. Then he turned to me.

"Naturally, we want to leave. Not a minute more. The station is very stifling. Just say what you want to do. Or maybe Kauders has an idea."

"I have no idea!"

So-and-So was frustrated. He had never liked taking on the least responsibility, and perhaps more so now than ever.

"Arthur should decide!" he suggested.

"You know what I want—to get away from here! How to do that is up to you. Certainly, you've made a plan."

"We have," Oswald agreed. "Only if it's all right with you, Arthur. I don't tell anyone what to do. You are a free man. You, of course, know that."

"Oh, anything that gets me out of this station is fine with me. Just tell me finally what the plan is!"

"Well, there are several possibilities," offered Oswald, "any of which you can choose from. We could leave the luggage here, then head to a restaurant, for you are naturally hungry and thirsty, and it's time for lunch. Then we can look at my place so that you see where you will be sleeping. Afterward, we can pick up the luggage and then decide what to do next. Or—and this is perhaps the best idea—we can pick up the luggage first and then head over to my place. It's not very far away. Or we could also go to my place next, with or without the luggage, so that you can rest a bit and sleep, or not—naturally, whatever you wish—and then afterward we can go to the restaurant. We can decide, as the case may be, what to do with the luggage."

"Those are pretty simple possibilities."

So-and-So said that, and I didn't know if he was being ironic or not.

"May I decide?" I asked.

"Naturally, with pleasure!"

"If it wouldn't be too much trouble, I suggest that we take the luggage to Oswald's and then do what you would like. Perhaps we could do so without taking a taxi. I'm not so spoiled that I can't schlepp the luggage myself."

"Then my place it is. Excellent, but with a taxi. It's really the simplest and the quickest way. And, as for the luggage, we will—"

"That's out of the question!" said Otto, chiming in. "We can carry it ourselves. I'll, I'll carry most of it myself."

I didn't argue when Otto and the others took hold of my luggage. Even Inge lifted up my satchel, and I let her do it. Then I glanced back at the attendants in left luggage, in order to ask their forgiveness and to wave goodbye, but the men were unconcerned with me. I walked behind the others, who marched along like ducks in a row, weaving through the crowd and hardly noticing whether I followed behind or not. There seemed to be no end to the station's main hall, but finally we did indeed exit it. Oswald engaged a taxi driver, who took care of the suitcases, and before I knew it all five of us were sitting in the car. I sat in the middle, between So-and-So and Inge; Oswald and Otto sat across from us. We didn't drive fast, but I couldn't even get a glimpse of the city, for there was no way to look out with all of us crammed in so. It also didn't help that Oswald kept nattering on at me, pointing excitedly this way and that in order to explain the layout of the streets and squares and the significance of the buildings, about which I was not able to understand anything, since everything looked the same to me and this senseless talk only beleaguered me the whole way. Yet I said yes, yes to it all, for I didn't want to undermine Oswald's enthusiasm, my gaze appearing to follow everything that he pointed out, though the eyes didn't register anything at all. We traveled only for a little while, but it felt like a long time to me. The car finally braked sharply, causing it to lurch, Oswald and Otto jumping out quickly and busying themselves with the driver and the suitcases, while So-and-So, derided by Inge, worked to extricate himself with slow awkwardness. I wanted to follow quickly, and not to be mocked as well, yet Inge was actually nice to me for once.

"Let the fools be; they'll do it the way they need to do it. They're taking care of it all for you today, so just get out."

That was an unexpectedly comforting bit of advice, and that was the Inge I remembered, rather than the one who had shown up at the station. It was good advice, for my limbs were half numb, and I had hardly any control of my body, really wanting my friends to leave, for their welcome had over-whelmed me so. How easy it was to compare it with the send-off given me by Anna, Peter, and Helmut! I just wanted to be alone, and not see anything, hear anything, or feel anything! I almost said that to Inge, but I preferred to avoid any kind of intimate exchange.

"I'm not tired, I—"

"Not tired?"

"Believe me, it's true—no, not at all! But I feel a bit shaky. That's why I'm grateful to you for sympathizing with me."

"Grateful, ungrateful—I'm not here to argue with you about that. You are a poor soul. I know, Franziska. Don't tell me anything about her, I don't want to know! And now just get out and let what happens happen, so I can get out, too."

Thus, as quickly as possible, I got out of the car. My foot hurt more than it had earlier, as if something had bitten it, but I carried on, deter-mined. I leaned back in the car in order to be a gentleman, but Inge didn't want any help.

"Go on, go on! The others are waiting."

Which was true. Schallinger and Birch had disappeared into the house with the luggage; So-and-So stood waiting in the entrance and led me on ahead without worrying about Inge, who remained behind us. Oswald lived on the third floor and was there to greet me above, where he gave me an elaborate welcome, as if he had not already seen me. He wanted to lead me right away to a room where Otto was already, but since there was no sign of Inge, nor even the sound of her climbing the steps, he hesitated.

"What's taking her so long?" he asked, turning to So-and-So.

"I don't know. Should I go look, Birch?"

"No, no, you should, of course, take Arthur in to Schallinger. I'll look down below myself. In the meantime, make yourself comfortable, Arthur. We'll be right back."

With that, he disappeared. So-and-So led me into a large, sparkling-clean room with little furniture in it but many books, all of them organized in standard fashion, but feeling cold. Otto stood before the shelves and perused them, curious and dumbstruck.

"Look, Arthur, just look!" he exclaimed. "I also have a few books and even some lovely ones. But look at this! It's wonderful that anyone can afford such a library. Classics, philosophy, the moderns, and so much art. It's magnificent! Birch must be a fine fellow! Sylvia should see this. I wonder if I could maybe bring her along sometime? Such good taste. I wonder if he'd lend any of them?"

"You can give it a try!" said So-and-So.

"You don't think he would?"

"Don't be ridiculous!"

I didn't look at any of the books and sat down as fast as possible. My stupid foot; now it felt better. So-and-So was surprised that I ignored the books, but he didn't dwell upon it, whereas Otto behaved like a giddy schoolboy and could not stop being astounded at my limited interest.

"You've changed, after all! Books used to—"

"That I don't know. I don't exist anymore."

"Kauders, listen to what he's saying! If someone else said that to me, I'd say he was crazy."

"You're probably right, Otto, and I am crazy."

"Always the same old ironic Arthur Landau! Just like in school. Kauders, you knew him better. No one knew just what was up with him."

Otto looked wounded. I had to reassure him.

"It was really nice of you to come today."

"But now I should disappear! That's what you're thinking, right?"

"It has nothing to do with you. Please don't misunderstand me. I just need a bit more time to recover, and I'm asking you to be patient."

"Forgive me, it's so easy to forget! It must have been horrible and awful. We heard so many things and read about it in the newspapers, but it's still hard to imagine it all. You know, it would be best if sometime you told us about it all. In an appropriate way, but like it really was. It will do you good, and we will learn a lot. Then you can write a book about it. People have to know, so that nothing like it happens again. Then you'll be free of it and be your old self again."

"Yes, I'll tell you about it all. As much as you'd like."

"But not today!" So-and-So countered.

"Certainly not today," I said, reassuring him.

"No, not today," Otto agreed. "Today is for celebrating. We only want to remember something lovely. Do you remember our old school days? Kauders, you were also with us at school. All three of us in the same school, how remarkable! Do we know if our old teachers are still alive?"

"Prenzel is. He sends his greetings, So-and-So."

So-and-So didn't respond, and laughed to himself in satisfaction.

"Prenzel!" yelled Otto with glee.

"Not so loud!" So-and-So said.

"Professor Hilarius Prenzel, what a name. Man, was he odd, but not terrible! Whenever he would say, 'Cicero says, and Catiline says, whereas *I* say!'"

We all laughed, but Otto whinnied such that it put So-and-So's teeth on edge. I saw the immensely aged, yet still strapping old man before me when I said goodbye to him a week earlier. Despite his baroque manner of speech, both So-and-So and I had him to thank for a good part of our education, and an appreciation of history that, far from being just a bunch of strung-together facts, was really based on living people and the construction of society. I had had enough of the poor imitation of the man and turned to So-and-So.

"What's taking Oswald so long with Inge?"

"He's not with Inge," So-and-So said. "He is certainly alone. I'll bet that Bergmann has left, most likely in the same taxi."

"She would do that?" asked Otto, curious. "Miss Inge Bergmann must be a really interesting personality. In fact, she's a poet. I found her to be quite special."

"She makes life especially difficult for her brother," observed So-and-So dryly. "Nothing came of the illustration contract for Karin. She made so many sketches, yet Inge messed up everything with the publisher. Nothing but stubbornness."

"People are very strange," Otto acknowledged. "Wouldn't you agree, Arthur?"

"Yes, very much."

I closed my eyes, but Otto didn't want to acknowledge my tired effort to turn away as he pressed a cigarette on me. I had to take one, although I didn't want to smoke, So-and-So also helping himself. I could clearly sense that my friend found the pharmacist's presence more bothersome than I did, for at each stupid thing said he cringed. Fortunately, it wasn't long before Oswald reappeared, though Inge—So-and-So had been right—wasn't with him. He looked a bit confused, but soon all uncertainty was cleared up and he had control of the situation.

"Inge sends her warmest greetings and is very sorry that she can't handle company right now. She didn't want to spoil the party. She is so considerate, but she had a pressing matter. It will interest you, Kauders. An appointment with a publisher, this one very promising. Hopefully, for Karin as well."

"Really?"

"Naturally. She hasn't forgotten about that. And she hopes to see us again today."

"Is your sister always so busy, Mr. Birch?" asked Otto tactlessly.

"Yes, naturally, she has a lot to do," countered Oswald.

Then my host insisted that I should see my room, as well as the rest of the apartment and the side rooms. My luggage was placed in my room, and Oswald expressed his concern whether in fact everything that had been prepared for me was completely to my liking and suited me, while I had to go to some effort to reassure him that it did. When he was finally convinced of this, it was formally agreed what would happen in the next few hours. We decided that I would first wash up and then have a rest in my room. As soon as I was ready to go out, I should come to the library. I had to get Oswald to promise that he would come and get me if I should happen to tarry too long.

"You have to promise me, Arthur, that you will in all honesty feel completely at home here. While you are here, imagine that you are master of the house and that I, as you desire, of course, am your friend, servant, and guest."

Oswald Bergmann was at this moment his old self, speaking to me with such warmth, and accompanying me to the bathroom before walking off with quiet steps. For the first time I felt better; this renewed friendship, which had finally broken through the difficulty of such formalities, pleased me and helped me to hope for the best. I could see that the arrival had not only been difficult for me, for the anticipation had to have been just as difficult for Oswald.

Slowly I passed the time in the bathroom, dawdling there as I used to as a child, much to my mother's annoyance. I thought back on the evening of the first day that I spent in Anna's bathroom; this time it was very different. The fact that this room was lit so well was an essential difference. Since it was an older house, clearly the bathroom had been installed later in this space, which had originally served different purposes. There were some chests and hutches arranged, though there was enough room to make up a comfortable and workable space. Surprising was the toilet bowl, which wasn't on the same level as the tank, for you had to climb up two steps to it as if to a podium. It felt strange and sad to sit so high and awkward, which immediately brought up disagreeable memories of childhood and how my Aunt Olga always referred to using the toilet as sitting on the throne or visiting the throne room. I began to cry as I crouched down there up above; how happy I would have been to avoid it. I hurried as fast as possible until I noticed, to my horror, that people at nearby windows of other apartments could look in, I having neglected to draw the curtains. Hopefully, no one had observed me.

I would have been happy to dawdle in the bathroom, and would have loved to have a bath in order to wash off the grime from the journey, but because of the misery of such horrible memories I felt terrible. It didn't get any better when I closed the curtains, their iron rings rattling upon the curtain pole. But I had to shave, for the stubble on my face was two days old. Unfortunately, I had forgotten to unpack my razor. I wanted to get it, and so I hurried up a small set of stairs, for the apartment was half a floor higher than the bathroom. The steps creaked loudly, which disturbed me, and I was also so confused that I no longer knew which door led to my room. I listened at one door, not hearing anything. Carefully I opened it, but it was the wrong room. It had to be Oswald's study, for it had a huge desk with mountains of writing on it, though luckily no one was there, only a sweet odor, perhaps Indian incense mixed with old cigarettes. I quietly closed the door, listened at another, behind which my friends seemed to be gathered, though I couldn't be certain, or yes, Otto's laugh trumpeted giddily, while I moved to a third door, this one the right one, for I recognized my room.

Quickly I looked for my shaving bag and hurried back to the bathroom with it. In front of the mirror, I was shocked to see how stubbled my chin and cheeks were. I looked much older, but everyone had said that I hadn't changed! And Otto had photographed me in this condition, which upset me. What impression could Dr. Haarburger have had of me? Perhaps my looks had upset Inge and got her going. I thought it possible this was the reason she had been so aggressive toward me, then sympathetic and so ashamed at the end that she couldn't bring herself to say goodbye before leaving. What could the friends have thought when they said I hadn't changed at all? Were they sincere or not, were they mean-spirited, or had they expected to find a broken-down old man hobbling with a stick? Had they, after having escaped, written me off in their hearts and now felt their peace had been violated because I had been allowed to survive the war? Did they want me among the living, and did they want me here? Why was the friendliness of all of So-and-So's letters so forced? And why had the Birch-Bergmann siblings never even once gone to the trouble of writing me a single line? What kind of welcome had been prepared for me? A choreographed comedy! My arrival had not even inspired applause on the part of my friends; the more I thought about it, the clearer it became to me that leaving the station and the consequent fuss was nothing but an embarrassment. I felt as if I'd been led into something disagreeable and I was unable to go along with it openly, or even to disavow it, such that I was set upon by an inept posse and had to play the most pitiable role. So-and-So could extricate himself from it all in the most awkward of ways, which I was even grateful to him for. When it came to Oswald, there seemed to be true feeling for me mixed in, but it became apparent only when there was no one there to witness his kindness. How could I trust him until I had really had a chance to test him? But to test someone, how miserable was that, and what right did I have to do so? Then I remembered the question that So-and-So had harmlessly put to me at the station: Am I not entitled to something? And my answer was: The question is for me too cryptic. No, I had no right and I was not entitled to one! Just wait and see, wait and see how everything develops, watch and see what Oswald and the others really intended to do with me. Oh, what a shameful situation, to have to wait and not be free in the way that had been desired for so long. Why had I come here, why had I fled, what had I fled to, and had I escaped at all? Having escaped myself only to find myself again at my destination? Only an exchange of one misery for another? Or were my friends simply just as stunned as I, or even more so? I had to pull myself together and let them know that I knew what I was doing, even if they had their doubts.

Once I was shaved clean, I looked a lot better. I should now hope to emerge with some confidence. But no, this Otto Schallinger! It was so strange that it had occurred to him to come to the station and not at least say goodbye quickly, as did Haarburger. Otto's behavior, his empty chatter, cast a bit of a shadow. But eventually he would have to head off, then the field would be clear and everything would be better. We would then be among ourselves, and my friends would recognize how I really was. Confidently I left the bathroom, wanting to go back to my room without being heard, but I wasn't successful. Despite my stepping carefully, the stairs creaked and groaned; Oswald must have practiced a long while until he managed to soundlessly negotiate those stairs. This time around, I recognized my door and closed it quietly behind me.

I could then have risked making an appearance before my friends, as the time seemed right to me. It would probably have been a good time, since I had messed about for at least half an hour, if not longer, and it was now time for lunch, yet I couldn't decide what to do. My weariness had almost completely abated, and I only felt a bit dazed. After some hemming and hawing, which carried me twice to the door of the library and caused me to feel for the handle, I turned back with the intention of stretching out on the couch for a little while, ten minutes at most, if only to relax and lie quiet, though certainly not to sleep. It was a comfortable couch—wide, well stuffed, covered with nice blankets, a table next to it. There were also—I didn't know if they were for me—soft dark-blue and purple anemones, sweets in a bowl, cigarettes and matches, and even a glass of water set out. This last item was good, as I had not drunk anything since having tea that morning. I emptied it in one gulp.

Then I lay flat on my back, feeling comfortable, happy to spend the next hour that way. But I could not at all do that, and therefore had my watch in my hand in order to keep track of the time. I wanted only to have ten minutes, not a second longer. I blocked out all thoughts and succeeded in doing so immediately, despite all expectations, not letting the watch fade from sight and seeing that there were still nine minutes, the time passing wonderfully slowly, as if not passing at all, for there were still more than eight minutes, eight minutes, then almost eight minutes, the seconds stretching out, there still being a while until it was seven minutes. Thus could I rest and not doubt that I would regain my composure during the course of the time elapsed. I even risked closing my eyes a little, though not really, just a little, glancing continuously at my watch: six minutes. The only thing I noticed was how dark it had gotten, perhaps because of the fog that had spread over the city. I was even curious how you found your way outside in this weather.

I don't know what was wrong with me when I went to look at the watch face again in order to see if the ten minutes were up. I strained to look, but, no matter how hard I tried, I couldn't see where the hands were. Perhaps my eyelids had somehow stuck together, though I didn't see at all better when I forced my eyes open. I sat up and looked all around me, though there was nothing to see but darkness. I was frightened—was I blind? Like a horrible wall, the impenetrable darkness had settled around me. I wanted to scream for help, but I controlled myself, because as I strained to see, I discovered a bit of light that could have come only from the window. I was saved. Then, in another spot through a small crack in the floor, I found another sliver of light. There was no longer any doubt that I had fallen asleep, but I couldn't understand how that had happened. I still had in my hand the watch that I had so carefully kept an eye on, and felt ashamed and upset that I had rudely kept three men waiting for me. What a guest, they must have thought, making fun of me to boot. I had not looked around the room enough earlier in order to get my bearings here in the dark. I was afraid to knock something over the moment I began feeling my way about. Where might there be a light switch? I stood there for a little while without moving. Should I yell to let the others know that I needed help? No, I would just look ridiculous, a frightened child having just awakened from a bad dream whom they would rush to help in order to comfort. Then my intentions of emerging as the confident Arthur Landau would be somewhat damaged. I had to find my way myself, suddenly appear before my friends, and behave as if my being late was the most natural thing in the world. I felt around the table next to the divan and stretched toward the crack, whose glimmer showed me the way. Soon I was fishing about with my hand, trying to find the handle to the library door. It turned easily, I entered, and was blinded by three lights such that I had to squint, though I quickly got my bearings and was surprised by the dense smoke that filled the room.

Oswald and So-and-So appeared to be reading, each of them sitting there with a book in hand. Otto was nowhere to be seen. I greeted them as nonchalantly as possible and said that I well knew how improper my long rest had been, though I also said, in cheery fashion, that we would be able to talk at greater length because I felt so refreshed. They were nice enough to take this in stride, and informed me only about how sad Otto had been to leave, and that he wanted to call the next day. Oswald recommended that we head to a restaurant, though lunch would no longer be possible, since it was time for dinner. I agreed, and asked after Inge. My question annoyed Oswald, as he shifted around, upset, and finally said briskly that, unfortunately, Inge's nerves were bad, I had to be patient with her, but I should have no doubt of how deeply fond she was of me, for she was at her most aggressive only with those she loved most. She wouldn't be coming to dinner, maybe afterward, later that night, but most likely not at all, for she was weighed down with work and, in addition, had a headache today. I was surprised at how thoroughly my friend sought to make excuses for his sister and finally cut him off. Then he asked to have a couple of minutes, as he had to quickly take care of something, and then we could go. He had hardly left the room when So-and-So spoke up.

"You haven't lost anything in Inge."

"I'm very fond of her."

"That makes no sense. Hopeless love. You should worry about other people. Oswald Birch, yes, he's worth it. She is a spider, a nasty little beast."

"Don't talk so!"

"Oh, as high-minded as ever! I thought you had changed."

"It has nothing to do with being high-minded. Inge is a wonderful person. I sense only a tragic waste. She is filled with bitterness and sharpness."

"Forget that! You should listen to Karin. Dear child this and dear child that is how Inge flatters her and then leaves her in the lurch. Watch yourself!"

"I'm fond of her. Don't you understand?"

"You're being an ass, Arthur. Why didn't she come, and why won't she come? I'm not going to tell you. You'll soon find out for yourself."

"What you're saying is shameful!"

"Please. Save such emotions! Stick with Birch."

"You know how much he means to me."

"To hell with your pathos! Whether he means something to you or not doesn't matter. He's now an important man. The atlas of cave painting is done; one hears Oswald Birch's name throughout the country. It's called publicity here, and it has influence."

"You mean that for me he could—"

"Anything, if he wants to. Kratzenstein lets him have his way with him. And you need Kratzenstein."

"And will Oswald—?"

So-and-So shrugged his shoulders, took a cigarette, and offered me one as well.

"You should never drop Birch's name, never make any reference to him. He hates that. If he were to find that you did, you'd be finished with him."

"How, then, should I—?"

"You have to wait until he does something for you himself, or tells you what you should do."

"Please, be honest with me. Is Oswald very difficult to deal with?"

So-and-So stuck two fingers in the corners of his mouth and whistled softly, the way he used to as a boy.

"You've remained arrested in your intellectual development," So-and-So said earnestly.

I had no idea what he meant by this. I didn't say a thing.

"You have to watch out for yourself. To count on a future here would not be smart. My advice is, stick close to Birch. But be careful; handle him with kid gloves. He's very sensitive. Your long sleep—"

"Was not right. Was that what you wanted to say?"

"At least not very smart. He has scheduled his time quite precisely. He wanted to go straight to the restaurant. You upset his plans."

"I'll apologize."

"In no way! That will just make things worse. You can't let him know in any way what I've said to you."

"To be handled with care."

"Yes. You've been warned. You should have handled Dr. Haarburger differently as well."

"How so? I didn't do anything at all!"

"That's right. That was the mistake. I wrote to you about how important he is. One approaches such a man and says a couple of flattering things when he has made a special trip to the station."

"Was I impolite?"

"Who said that? I'm only saying you should start off differently. Call him soon. Maybe not tomorrow, but the day after tomorrow. He has heaps of money, and his is a meeting place of dilapidated intellectuals who call the shots here. Professor Kratzenstein, whom Birch spits on, is in and out there, along with Singule—that pig—and his wife, and many others."

"Who are they all?"

"Keep an eye out. You'll find out. Be grateful that you have gained entrée. Contacts, Arthur, contacts."

"Will you help me?"

"Me? What would make you think that? What I can do I've strung together already. I've gotten Birch and Haarburger interested in you. Now seize the moment. If you let it go, it's your fault."

"Oswald? That was not necessary. I've known him longer than you, haven't I? Didn't you meet him through me?"

"You are so naïve! To meet Birch once is easy. But then to engage him . . . Just try it! He wouldn't have cared a bit about you if I hadn't prodded him. . . . Now you have to take it further. But delicately. There's nothing more I can do for you. I won't go to Haarburger on your account again."

"But you'll come along with me?"

"I don't hang around there. No one from my circle. Kratzenstein and Singule? No way. Tend to your contacts, and remember that friends here are precious."

"You're scaring me."

So-and-So had his fingers in his mouth and commenced his whispering whistle once again. I recalled how amazed I was by it as a child and how I hated it later on, Franziska particularly not being able to stand it, for she found it vulgar. He whistled further, as if he had overheard my distress, and whistled me a tune. Then he stood right in front of me, rocking back and forth. Then he blew a puff of smoke into my face, causing me to cough.

"You smoke too much!"

"Yes. Does it bother you? But, to change the subject, can't you tell me more precisely where things stand with Dr. Blecha?"

"Happy to. You know already that I—"

I had to break off my account, as Oswald came for us, wearing his hat and coat, and we had to get our things and leave. Oswald wanted to call a taxi, but then he decided to go to a restaurant nearby that served Belgian food, which he especially liked. So we walked through the streets, which were almost as dark as during the war. Oswald and So-and-So started to talk about something I could hardly understand; I thought that it was about an exhibit of Peruvian antiquities that they had recently visited. As it didn't concern me, I remained silent. Soon I let the two men go ahead of me a half step, for my foot still bothered me, even if not as much as earlier, their talk reaching me like a distant whisper. I didn't feel as if I belonged with either of them. What So-and-So had said in his cryptic and yet pointed remarks about Oswald's difficult personality took me aback; my confidence in his goodness was not shaken so much as my own self-confidence. I felt more and more limited. Was it heartless, or was it true what So-and-So had said about my intellectual development? Perhaps I had become provincial as a result of my fate over there and my long imprisonment, even sour, clumsy, slow, and no longer flexible; I needed to be even more polished here and not plow my way through but, rather, delicately glide through. I had to first get my bearings and catch up on a lot in order to fill in substantial holes in my education and be able to move comfortably in these cultivated circles. I had been so happy earlier that day, and now everything was spoiled and tarnished, placing any possible sense of self-worth in question.

The way to the restaurant, which was supposed to be short, stretched on endlessly. I began to doubt if I would ever reach the Belgian meal. If I weren't so helpless among the dark sea of blurred buildings, I would have forsaken the meal, my friends, and everything else in order to make my own way or, better yet, to crawl into a corner like a weary bundle that someone passing would find and hand over to trusted hands in a lost-and-found. But what should one do with such a foundling? They would ask me questions about who I was, where I lived, what I was doing, why I was wandering around such a strange city. However, I wouldn't be able to respond. Adam in flight after the expulsion, that was all I could think of. The title of a painting that didn't exist. Please understand, I'm the title of a painting that has not been painted; when dug up in Peru, there I was fine, I lived fine, what I did was fine, for there I remained in the hands of the scholars—a rare find, they whispered, for they did not want to frighten me. They didn't do that out of brotherly love, though, but only not to lose me. Yet they were unlucky; they were careful, though not enough so. I fell to pieces, disappearing into the dust, nothing left, only the title remaining, for that they wrote down on a lovely note. Then there followed an illustration in a book, a cave painting: Adam lost and driven out in flight from his title in the darkness of a cave while resting. Found there, I couldn't defend myself. I was too important to scholarship and needed to quickly be placed on exhibit—"The Peruvian Adam" the title, entirely naked, though nonexistent, entirely so, the visitors coming and talking a long time about me, though I didn't understand a word, since it was Belgian and I spoke Peruvian, an extinct dialect whose name is unknown.

Then there was nothing but intense suspicion, intense before the long ordeal, and after the long ordeal and expulsion, the expulsion with my loved ones. I could have said, Oswald, please, Oswald Bergmann, he probably dug inside the cave before I fell to pieces, he was the one who came up with the title, no not Bergmann, no, Mister Birch, that's what he's called now, but I didn't note his address, only the title, and that no one understood, for I could only say it in Belgian, a restaurant, yes, that's right, we are there already or are on our way there, and my foot hurts, which is from falling from my resting spot while in flight, and because I have not yet eaten anything today, having only drunk the water next to the title of the painting on the little table next to the divan. I didn't want to mention that, for I had fled the exhibit, there being nothing wrong with this, for I could read about it in the catalog, yes, just look, you can easily afford this, it costs almost nothing, only one Hungarian pengö, in order to save yourself the trouble, not you, naturally, but the pengö, I mean the title, a hundred titles for a pengö, it's that simple, and if I say anything now everyone will be upset, that's not right, Inge Bergmann, Otto Schalinger, Sylvia and her northern cooking, not Belgian, but good, photographs, and then So-and-So, Kauders as well, Karin drawing me for the publisher in the Peruvian style, but I can't call out to any of them, for then they would only have more against me, then there's the station which one cannot get away from at all, I don't want to go there, the exhibition is not over because there's such a pressing crowd, many contacts to be made, but also whom one cannot speak to in order to save So-and-So the trouble, that would not be very smart, since Dr. Blecha entitled him to nothing, only clicked the camera, another shot, a snapshot, nothing for Adam in it, for it would be difficult to recognize him, it would not seem very smart, since I had remained intellectually stunted.

There was no point in my standing up to them, nor did I have Dr. Haarburger's telephone number, which was my last hope. In the face of such suspicion about who I was, the attendants at the lost-and-found had no idea where to begin, so I had to be taken to the police. It didn't help that I screamed, for they needed someone who existed and wasn't just a lost title. No, they said, the police wouldn't take too much of my time. "Your name, please!" Yes, the names. Let's see, I should have said loudly, "Here I am, here I am! As far as I can tell, here I am!" They wanted to bring me to consciousness and once again demanded my name. All I knew to tell them was Arthur Kutschera, whose father and mother sell nuts and apples at 8 Reitergasse, and next door there is a clothing store, clothing by Landau. Kutschera, that sounds good. The inspector would nod. And what do the apples cost? Sold out, I'm afraid, the train got the last one. Arthur Kutschera, the inspector would repeat, that can't be right. Really, it can't be right, a mistake of clear self-deception, for it's Landau, Arthur Landau. That's really much better, a nicer name. The inspector would say it again with a cloying tongue, the name turning in his mouth like honey. Arthur Landau, that tastes good. It's foreign, one can clearly see. Naturally lives nowhere, no place of residence. A large sheet of paper in front of him, the inspector would begin to write, finally, the title, a factual report. I had been lost and someone found me and brought me here. "Disposed of you" was his answer, saying it hard and sharp, "Disposed of you," like an apple, rotten goods, disposed of quickly over the border, across the sea, just the way you came here, or into the sea.

What can be done against this? Perhaps I had something. If an honest person had picked me up and turned me in, there was also the possibility that another honest person would turn up looking for me tomorrow, when it was light again, since the honest seekers come from across the sea and out of every hole. The inspector didn't put any stock in that, saying that they sought no one who was honest, as only criminals were sought, and they were quickly found and picked up. Filled with despair, I began to talk about my father, saying that he was an honest father whom they had killed because he was so honest. But that only raised more suspicion. Who had killed my father? My mother as well, both parents killed. Everyone lost. And even others on top of them. Had not an honest finder turned her in? I would be happy to claim her. The inspector slowly leafed through a thick register, it probably containing all the lost names and titles. Suddenly, he stopped and asked what allowed me to claim her? My honest name, I told him. He smiled in disbelief. "Those may be stories that work elsewhere, but not here on our honest island," he said. "Your papers, please!" I rummaged through all my pockets and handed him the documents and papers I had on me. The inspector put on white gloves before he reluctantly began to inspect my official documentation. "It's all worthless," he said coolly, "coming from a second-rate country. The paper even smells!," after which I quickened my pace, as I couldn't stand this torment for long. It was better to keep up with my hurrying friends and head toward the Belgian pub than to chatter away the last threads of my sanity with pointless questioning.

So I said in a softly pleading voice, "Not so fast, please! I can't breathe! How much farther is it?"

Confidently, a hand thrust itself under my arm and gave me much needed support.

"We're almost there."

The hand was so close, but the voice, comforting as it was, pressed at me from far away. It took a good while to ascertain whose it was. In order to hear it again, I spoke so that it might reply.

"Not long. Can you say that again?"

"Why, of course. It certainly won't be long at all. Hardly a minute. Why are you so anxious? Or are you just tired?"

This time the voice sounded much more triumphant as it reinvigorated me and made me feel warm inside. Nor did I have to remain a half step behind any longer, but could walk right alongside, supported by the hand, even able to perhaps slip ahead a bit, since I knew where we were headed. I believe I even said something to this effect, which was met with a joyful laugh. It sounded reassuring, but also a bit foreboding. I soon saw why. We came around a corner, and the voice spoke again.

"There, where you see the light, we're here already."

I should have gone on ahead, since that was the custom here, but as I was the stranger here I offered not to take the lead.

"You are certainly a shy one."

The door opened. We stepped into a pleasant, not too large dining room with niches to the side.

"I've never seen anything so pleasant here. Much more lovely than the Belgian restaurant."

"I'm so pleased. Do you want to pick a quiet corner?"

I looked at the face of the voice, as if I would find the answer there as to what would be the best table to take.

"Well, looking at me won't help you find a spot."

"Maybe it will," I replied in a carefree manner.

My companion only laughed, no longer worried about my foolishness, and moved decidedly toward a niche at the farthest corner of the back of the room. There was nothing for me to do but march along behind her. Then I helped Fräulein Zinner out of her coat, took mine off as well, and stood there holding them without a clue. She laughed as I stood there not knowing what to do with the coats.

"Either set them on a couple of chairs or there are hangers over there."

So I withdrew and playfully hung up the coats. When I turned back to the table, I could see that Fräulein Zinner was already speaking warmly to a waiter whom she seemed to know. She had already ordered for herself, and when I said that anything was fine with me, and that I'd be happy to have what the fräulein was having, she wouldn't hear of it, even though the waiter said that I couldn't go wrong with that. But that didn't do me any good, so I had to pore over the menu as I bent over it, meticulously reading it from beginning to end. Meanwhile, the two of them chatted softly, though I didn't listen to what they said. Once I had read through it all, I looked up in confusion, for I wasn't at all clear about what I should order.

"Forgive me, Fräulein! I'm so hopeless. There's too much to choose from. I'm not used to so much. The simplest would be to have them just bring me whatever. I'm sure it's all good."

She laughed even more heartily than earlier. However, the waiter remained serious and recited from memory the most important items on the menu, carefully pronouncing the name of each dish, sometimes offering an extra bit of panegyric, though, unfortunately, it was all too fast to help me in choosing a single dish for myself. I only continued to look in confusion back and forth between the waiter and my companion.

"It's all so much trouble. Just bring me the cheapest one!"

Fräulein Zinner was clearly amused at my incompetence, yet she was not happy with my choice, but finally came to my rescue and responded to my pressing plea about what she had ordered. Since I assured her that that was exactly what I would have ordered, she finally agreed and dispensed with the waiter's consideration by simply requesting what she had ordered. I only had to decide for myself what I wished to drink, for Fräulein Zinner insisted on it and wouldn't hear anything about my just having tap water like her. Finally the waiter withdrew with an amused smirk. I breathed freely and was relieved that I had survived the endless negotiation in good shape.

"You are a wonderful guest, my dear. How would you do it without me?"

"I wouldn't be able to at all. I can't help but admit it."

"And yet you did it!"

"Are you making fun of me? You have every right to."

"No."

"You are very kind. No one here has been so kind."

"I don't believe you."

"It's true. Believe me! It's all taken so much effort to boost my confidence and succeed. People are often nice to me, sometimes very nice, but there's no human warmth, or hardly any goodness, or it's so twisted and screwed up that it ends up crumpled and knotted. The friends I used to have here . . . I'd rather not say anything about them. It's horrible that it's all broken down. I feel like I'm deluded. I want a regular life, and sometimes it feels like I'm on the right track, but in reality it's all so uncertain. No one takes me seriously. There must be something about my manner that captures people for a moment, but then it's suddenly over, things get shaky, and they are put off. They feel my character to be a mixture of arrogance and inferiority. Something is knotted up inside me that prevents me from slipping into the social order. I often ask myself whether it's my fault, whether it is my fault alone. What do you think?"

"You're deeming me worthy of such extraordinary confessions, though alone I cannot decide for you. Are you not what you wish to be?"

"I would just like to be, period. You know, I don't even know if I am alive. But there is something inside me or perhaps outside me, I can't say for sure, but there is something, and for that I continue to live, or at least try to. Perhaps I only exist in as much and so long as I am able—I can't describe it—to live for that alone. I have often thought so. And not only when I find myself questionable, which happens quite often. For I feel questionable most of the time. I think of myself as something that is split into pieces, but not something pathological, because the pieces also are linked to one another, though this is questionable. The split-apart pieces know of one another; they just aren't joined up. Can you understand when I say that I am not my own master, and therefore am split, but without being sick? Look, this was particularly true when everything seemed questionable, not just me alone—for that would easily have been pathological—but instead the questionable became dominant in an environment where, for many, the questionable was transformed into that which could not be questioned, because doing so cast them down and ate them up. Perhaps I have simply ensconced myself within nothingness and cannot exist in any other way."

"But that must take incredible strength!"

"That's what you say, but I'm not so certain. I'm not at all so certain. I am uncertainty embodied. That's why it's hard to be friends with me, although I think of myself as someone who's good at being friends. But I exist only by clinging. Where others are independent, or at least appear to be, I'm lost. Then everything dissolves. Isn't that ridiculous?"

Fräulein Zinner smiled, not because she found my explanation ridiculous but because I had talked with a fervor that was pointless and only struggled along without any real grounding. Such talk had not at all helped me attain any kind of serious depth, nor was such foolishness suited to pleasant dinner conversation. There was also no justifiable reason to highlight my nullity in such a manner, and I thought that this could cause people too eas-

ily to see me as just a crank. To please Fräulein Zinner—this vain effort was
at the root of my foolishness in wanting to show myself as more likable. I
was lucky that the waiter soon brought the soup and the bread, for that way
I couldn't finish up what I had been talking about, and therefore couldn't
talk as much, and therefore could observe Fräulein Zinner more intently.
Neither my disastrous talk nor the unedifying episodes in the office seemed
to have put her off. After a long silence that Fräulein Zinner broke, I began
to head in a direction that could easily have led to danger.

"How do you wish to make a start?"

"You know, what interests me is the sociology of oppressed people, the
persecuted, but also the persecutors."

"Does that come from your own experience?"

"Only in part. I was already interested in the subject before I experienced in my own life what it means to be persecuted."

"A painful thing to know."

"Yes. We shouldn't speak about it. Misery is my business, but not my
pleasure."

"No one's pleasure, but everyone's plight."

"That's right. But one mustn't continually give oneself over to it. Or, at
least, shouldn't."

"But what about when we are all in the midst of it? What happens then?"

"You have a firm footing, Fräulein Zinner. You always know how things
are for you. You don't have to toss yourself into boundless seas. I'm terrible
company. It was an unforgivable mistake to invite you out this evening."

"Do you regret it?"

"I regret nothing. On the contrary, I'm grateful to you. But you must
really regret it. If you don't chase me off immediately, it's all your own fault."

"What you say is not very flattering. After we're done eating, I'd be
happy to leave and bring you back to your guesthouse."

"Have I upset you?"

"Not me, Herr Doctor, but my vanity."

"For heaven's sake, what have I done?"

"Nothing at all. Don't give it a thought. I'm an odd duck, a bit quirky. I
don't deserve anyone's kindness."

"Do you wish to play some more? The violin?"

"You can have it. I already offered it to you at the Haarburgers'."

"What am I supposed to do with a violin?"

"What should I—?"

"Play!"

"I don't play. No longer. I'm played out."

"Such pessimism doesn't suit you."

"So say you?"

"Yes. So say I. You have to start over, you have to live."

"And to whom do you say that, if I may ask?"

"To you, Fräulein Zinner. And—yes, I'll admit—to myself as well. But I think first it's my duty to share it with others."

"To each his own."

"Are you serious?"

"One must, where possible, help others to fulfill such a duty."

"Is that what you try to do?"

"Not very well. It's a good idea. But I don't accomplish much."

"But you do accomplish something. That's something. I haven't yet been able to do so in my life. But you shouldn't just give up the violin."

"Don't torment me so! There are certain things you have to bury and leave behind. What is called a guilt complex these days, Herr Doctor, should not be so easily handed over to the modern caretakers of the soul to manage. One has to, of course, bring sacrificial victims, even when they are of no use to anyone, and with victims there follows burial. One has to have the courage for it, and it's really courage, for it doesn't happen out of cowardice but through the attempt at atonement, even as a victim. Yet I couldn't say that to anyone else, because no one would understand and they would laugh me out of the room. But you must understand! Don't pretend—you indeed do understand! You know, I'm probably a bit naïve, yet I've felt that I've had somewhat of a personal relation to the great questions. In order to remain a human being, you pay a price. You are therefore guilty in simply being a human being, but you also have the chance to be a human being. That's kind of how I think of the first humans in the biblical story. If Adam and Eve were allowed to remain alive after having sinned in taking on forbidden knowledge, then that was possible only because they were required to serve some kind of atonement. Since then, it is so: whenever we feel or know we are guilty of something, we then need a sacrificial victim. It doesn't take much effort to see that, right? Don't laugh, but if I'm entirely honest with you it reminds me today of an earlier incarnation. If you would be so kind, let's not say any more about it."

All of this spoke to me, it being what I felt as well. I should certainly not have mentioned the violin, but I would have been happy to continue talking about guilt and victims, though the waiter prevented that from happening as he carried in the entrées. Both portions were served at the same time, the meat on a plate, potatoes and vegetables in a bowl, only the salad served separately in two little bowls. The waiter began to serve the food, but Fräulein Zinner waved him away. She dished it out herself, and, despite my protests, I got the greater portion.

"You hardly have any roast!"

"You'll manage it."

I had to give in, and I saw how happy Fräulein Zinner was to be able to do something for me. As she noticed how good it tasted to me, she was so happy that she couldn't contain it.

"I had hoped that it would please you. I watched you at Haarburger's and saw what little interest you had in getting hold of such delicacies and eating them. It can make one very happy to be able to take care of someone."

I didn't respond at all, but instead let it pass and just looked up in gratitude. Fräulein Zinner caught my gaze and slowly chewed little bites of her food without paying attention to mine. Perhaps she ate so slowly out of kindness, in order not to finish much earlier than I did the heaped plate in front of me. That's why it seemed best for me to eat as fast as possible, while still being polite, in order not to have to be chewing after she had finished her meal. I had never before observed someone as closely during a meal, for I had always before thought it unbecoming to dedicate so much attention to such an intimate activity. I had no idea why I was so keenly interested in how she handled her knife and fork, or even raised the food to her mouth, though I couldn't stop myself, even though I didn't feel it was right. I considered whether Fräulein Zinner didn't remind me of someone, and searched my simultaneously aroused and benumbed memory. Why do people compare people with others? I asked. Each is without compare, it seemed to me. Yet that's not true. In general, you could make comparisons when the difference was not decisive, which accounts for the masses. Certainly this girl reminded me of no one, for I had encountered no one like her before, that which was familiar sitting across from me being nothing but the strange, the unknown, which attracted me. Why was I eating with this girl? The coming together of two people unknown to each other is a mere accident, and a world collapses as a result, everything falling, everything buried, sunken, filled in, though something foggy creeps along, a secretive strangeness, digging in the depths, uncovering something, lifting the discovery high up to the light and announcing, "Look, here is what was. It appears to be an ally who lived in the long ago, but not during our time." To discover the strange in another is good fortune. It lessens the pain that lives in oneself, such discovery being the only joy.

My thoughts were disrupted by the waiter. The dessert table stood before us, set with little glass bowls filled with a soft colorful foam. I tried some, and it melted on my tongue and tasted of lemon. Fräulein Zinner looked at me somewhat absently, though she noted my pleasure. I broke the silence so suddenly with a question that it almost shocked her.

"Do cooking and housework interest you?"

"I'm a terrible cook and, to my endless worry, know nothing about running a home."

She said this with such concern; I thought I even saw tears well up. Why had I touched on something so sensitive?

"That doesn't matter," I tossed back cheerfully, and blithely went on to say, "No one needs to know about such things. When it comes time, you learn on your own."

She laughed somewhat tensely, as if a bit angry.

"Really? You think so? Your experience is amazing."

"Ah, my experience! What are you thinking!"

She looked at me, full of concern.

"I always had other things to do than housework. You don't do such things for yourself alone. You need to do it for others; otherwise, it's senseless. When my brother—"

She fell silent. The waiter cleared the dishes from the table and brought the coffee. I was pleased that we would at last be rid of him. But Fräulein Zinner's distress bothered me. The tables seemed entirely turned since the office, and on the way here, when she was so certain and I was so helpless. Did I now have the advantage? What a miserable advantage it was if all it meant was that I had transferred my troubles to this girl without becoming any steadier myself. What had I done! The entire evening had failed, a bad beginning to desires never to be satisfied. I thought about how I could manage to collect myself, or, if that was not possible, at least subordinate my concerns and prop up Fräulein Zinner. Yet what I lacked was the strength found only when I tapped the strength of another. I consciously tried to subordinate myself, but I couldn't. My dependence on other people had nothing to do with subordination.

"Tell me, Fräulein Zinner, have I done something terrible?"

She looked at me with surprise, in need of clarification.

"Perhaps not terrible," I continued, "for I wouldn't say that, just something disagreeable, something not quite right, which just isn't done."

"Don't fret so! You're a big boy."

"That's kind of you to say. I have been so regularly knocked off balance since I've been here that I fear that I am agitated by countless and often insignificant things. Instead of being reassured, I end up robbed of my last bit of confidence. But I don't wish to burden you with all that, and I am thankful that you grant me such freedom. I need a foothold, but I am left to grope and stumble or I stand before a wall that is flat and fends me off and does not buttress me. But don't think badly of me because of it! It's a halting unease that makes me say all these twisted things. That's not really who I am. For I believe I can overcome any difficulty. If you've survived, you often end up astonished at yourself; you confront yourself, curious, shy, cautious, you really question yourself, for you still can't quite believe you are the same person, whether you even exist. Sometimes I think, Yes, it's indeed so. Such moments are not at all significant, but quite the contrary, since everything is insignificant and vague, as the answer dissolves within the question. But when you simply go on living, then it's only natural that life doesn't consist of fully conscious hours but, rather, of little conversations that trickle along or small continuing activities, since the unsettled being is best suited to some kind of orderly routine. Thus when the question ceases to knock at your insides, at your very fiber, and yet nonetheless is there and continues on, there exists a mild tension that, without any great surprise, can upset you at any time and leads to an accommodation with the self-evident. Then everything becomes unquestionably interdependent. Not in an immense fashion or essentially so, but it does seem to me beneficial. Whether that is a basis for a life, I really don't know."

"But it is an accommodation. You say so yourself. One must accommodate oneself. That's what you mean to say?"

"That's what I would say. Yes, you're right. Do you recall how at the Haarburgers' I tossed out the question whether one could marry a man with my past? You responded quite vigorously to that. Do you remember?"

"Yes."

"And was your answer genuine? Do you still stand by all that you said then?"

"Every word."

"That's good. So, then, you would marry such a person? What with all the uncertainty involved?"

"Yes."

"That is absolutely crucial. Have you thought about what that would actually mean?"

"Just give me the chance!"

Fräulein Zinner chuckled heartily and caused me to laugh as well.

"Then, Fräulein Johanna, could you marry me even now?"

"Why not?"

"I'm not the man for you."

"You should let me decide that."

"I have no life to speak of."

"So you can't marry me, either?"

"Who told you that?"

"I'm free to say so myself."

"Go on! You at least have to marry in the hope of some kind of security."

"One marries for thousands of reasons. I would marry whom I liked, if he will have me."

"You mean me?"

Moved, Johanna fell silent, yet she quickly recovered and looked as if— or so I imagined—as if she were in her office handling professional matters for visitors. Johanna was completely impenetrable, together and in control, yet warm. Her quiet authoritative manner pleased me very much. Yes, I became aware of how much she pleased me for the first time, such that I was not bothered by feeling faint or by fitful moods, which always held the potential to overwhelm me, but instead could concentrate on courting her with zeal. I was free of heavy-handed flirtatiousness. I looked at her tenderly, half from the side. Her face, calm and imperturbable, as if I had said nothing audacious at all, gave me no sign as to how I should behave, whether I would be heard or not. One thing I knew: I could not stand a setback now. I nodded and spoke quietly but beseechingly.

"With me there's nothing to be had but my powerlessness."

Johanna turned to me attentively, but otherwise nothing about her changed, which provided me with the barest of openings. I talked on in almost a whisper.

"A person like me is poor and can make no promises. His existence, shot through with despair, is nothing but an open wound. Perhaps at heart he can feel grateful, but he can promise no income. It's not at all advisable to get tangled up with him. Whoever is smart will avoid him. Whoever loves him will have many bitter and weary hours. He has only himself to offer, and that is little, for otherwise there is nothing. He is faithful, not out of virtue but because of his nature. He is affectionate, even tender, but headstrong, and his intensity doesn't recommend him, as it can be horrible. He broods a great deal, and in his peculiar thoughts he develops his own path forward on which he cannot recommend that anyone travel along with him. Sometimes he is sad and almost melancholy, and then it's hard for anyone to distract or rouse him. Yet he is grateful, perhaps, and that he has said already. He also does not easily forget, and some things he never forgets, but he doesn't hold a grudge, and he fights against bad will and is forgiving. His work is probably of little worth, but he feels it is important, and he loves it. He is a widower. He loved his wife very much; he has not forgotten her, nor will he ever forget her. If he should ever marry again, he will make certain that the dead do not come between him and his new wife, nor will he stand between the living and the dead, and it will be up to the wife not to stand between her husband and those who have passed on."

Johanna listened to all of this while remaining outwardly calm, simply sitting there, not a word of it seeming too much for her and nothing seeming to disturb her, though her breathing slowed to a standstill. She didn't let herself be confused, no matter how surprised she was; I could have kept on in the same vein without at all disturbing her. Yet I couldn't expect that she would have some kind of response to what I said, no matter how much I might have wanted or hoped. I sipped my coffee and set the cup down a bit too loudly.

"Tell me, Johanna, what would you say if I really did want to marry you? In all seriousness? Will you marry me?"

"Yes."

We said nothing. I would have loved to sit next to her, but I didn't have the courage; it would have been too forward—what foolish fears! But that was the way it was. It was not necessary to switch places. I had to stay where I was, and she had to remain across from me. That was for the best. I was too overwhelmed from the success of my proposal; also, Johanna must have realized that she had been steered into giving her immediate consent. Though it seemed strange to have achieved such a forced victory, it still felt like the most natural thing in the world, there being no other outcome imaginable. It wasn't love that had brought us together, for we had not spoken of love; most likely, neither of us having even thought of it. Instead, an unfathomable desire had hauled us out of the abyss of our yawning loneliness, the two of us having been brought together from across a great distance. It had happened. We sat there silent, serious, almost like two stones, neither of us daring to think that we should embrace, our thoughts instead traveling far off into the distance across which neither of us had to explain ourselves to each other. We had said too much; now we had to remain much more reticent about what now—and perhaps always—would risk sounding highly superficial. A deep affection for my quiet friend welled up inside me, but it warned against my expressing how I felt out loud. The future was inconceivable; I did not at all feel capable of predicting any direction for the challenges that lay ahead. After a long while, I stirred myself to ask a question.

"What happens now, Johanna?"

"We will see. We are on our own and are answerable to no one on earth."

"Nothing is certain, Johanna."

"Except that we are certain. I will do anything I can for you. You can trust me."

"It will be hard for you."

"All the better."

"That is easily said."

"And slowly done. Don't worry!"

"No. I won't. I trust you, and your gentle spirit."

"Thank you."

"We should marry soon, if you don't have anything against it."

"Soon, for sure, my dear. There's no sense in waiting. I'll stand by you, and when it gets too hard, too hard for you, my dear, then don't forget that you have me, that I'm there for you."

My dearest said all this with halting warmth. Johanna soon relaxed without becoming any less serious, and effused a lovely glow. Her eyes brightened, the corners of her mouth softening. Suddenly and unexpectedly, she called the waiter over and asked him for the check. She quickly paid, having treated me, though I would have felt better if I had paid the tab. But now it was too late, so I let it happen. After the waiter thanked us, I apologized for my lapse.

"It all comes out of the same pocket now," she said simply.

I asked whether we should stay, but Johanna looked me over and decided that quiet was what I needed. I stood up, somewhat wearily, and got the coats. I then realized for the first time that I needed to help my wife, my soon-to-be wife. Maybe that's why I held the coat so clumsily, such that the waiter wanted to jump in to help, though Johanna didn't want me to feel ashamed.

"Don't either of you bother with it. I prefer to do it myself."

Thus I had to look on abashed as the waiter took my coat from me, which I thoughtlessly let happen, just as I also patiently allowed him to dress me like a display-window mannequin.

"That's very kind of you," I said in thanks. "But I'd prefer to put on my hat myself."

The waiter looked at me surprised, as I proceeded to follow Johanna, who only wanted to leave the restaurant as quickly as possible. The darkness in the street was deep and heavy, but not unpleasant, for it had gotten warmer. At least that's what I imagined, and since Johanna agreed, it must have been so. She said it was a strange country that often warms up in the evening or at night, while during the day it can often be much colder. I took my wife's arm, and she let me do so.

"Everything is different now," I said.

"How so, different? We have found each other. That's all there is to it."

"You're right. Nothing has changed. At least, not for us. We were simply meant for each other. The only difference being that we didn't know it for so long, for we did not know each other. But once it's expressed, it's self-evident, and thus we belong together. Only the others that know us will be surprised."

"That we'll have to simply understand."

"Yet how do you see things unfolding? How do we want to do this? I don't know what to do. I have no experience with the formalities of a wedding. Certainly it's complicated, what with the documents that are needed, the wedding clothes, even if it's a modest affair. And we need witnesses. We also have to invite a couple of people, you know, because of the contacts that are so important to have here. And, then, where will we live? And your job? I have my doubts when I start to imagine everything involved."

I sighed deeply, there seeming to be nothing but obstacles ahead. To follow sudden impulses was easy, and I could also make plans, but when it came to carrying them out I shrank before the mounting difficulties and didn't know how to handle them. Most likely, she was also now conscious of all the difficulties, and thus I was almost afraid that we'd never get beyond the starting point of realizing our plans.

"You know, my dear, you shouldn't worry so much. One thing at a time. I'll think about it all carefully. The formalities are simple. Tomorrow I'll make some inquiries. Then I'll be able to see it all more clearly and let you know what needs to be done."

"Isn't that the job of the groom? I'm so anxious about it all."

"About marriage?"

"Oh, not that, not if you have no fear about it. But the officials—it's a nightmare, it all is, including the practicalities. My friends are of no use, except for a few old well-meaning school buddies. And then I'm most worried about everything involved, even practical matters, you see. It's all so difficult, and I'm of no use to you. If I'm at all honest, I have to really warn you about what you're in for, before it's too late. If for no other reason than that I don't want the bond between us to break later on. Some people don't take such things seriously, saying they can just give it a try, and if it doesn't work, then they can separate. But that's no basis for a marriage. I want nothing to do with that, for I find it abominable."

"You can break your pledge. Just do what you want. I'm not forcing you to do anything."

"But you said yes."

"Yes. But you still have time to decide otherwise."

"That I cannot do. I am at your mercy, completely in your hands."

"You are a free man."

"Free? Forgive me, but that's a ridiculous word. I am never free; I don't even have any desire to be so. Freedom has been thoroughly driven out of me. It's a dream. Perhaps it's been realized by some people, but only rarely, or so I believe."

"Do you not believe in any freedom?"

"No. Or, more specifically, I am not free and know no freedom."

"Everything is just fate, the good as well as the bad?"

"It doesn't seem that simple to me. I would say that one is delivered into life, and then there is a very narrow set of circumstances in which you can move, though they are essential for each person. A freedom in bonds. About this I have thought a lot. I'll let you see in my papers sometime what I've written about it."

"That would interest me."

"What we do and what we are meant to do—together I call that destiny. There is nothing we can do about that; no one can run away from it. Fate usually involves rebellion, a blind battle against destiny itself. And there is a portion of our destiny about which we have some say. That is what one can call, if you wish, freedom. About that I could go on at length."

"Please, do!"

"This portion likely lines up with all that falls under the sphere of morals. But not with thinking and other intellectual activities. These ramble about in an odd manner, providing us with a notion of freedom, but when we examine them more closely we see just how far and to what extent they really exist. Yet this is not so when it comes to morals. There the decision lies within our own will, even if not always in action itself. If we could manifest what we decide through action in all cases, then we could rightfully speak of freedom. But actions outstrip our capabilities, our allotted human horizon. Only up until the onset of an action are we free in our determinations, not a bit further. The process of carrying out or even accomplishing an action is what decides what is determined. An action is performed only when we are allowed—when it, above all, is permissible under the laws that apply to the creature amid creation. The mass, I mean the mass of laws, appear in general to depend on the collective state of humanity, most of all on its social order, its social relations. On the degree to which the social orders are unfree, as we know. All are unfree! And thus we come up with what does not apply to everyone but, rather, to the individual, and one proudly announces, 'Man is free! Man is free!' I find that ridiculous. And you?"

"Herr Dr. Landau, what an informative exchange, a lesson from the lectern held at night on the street, on the evening of your engagement, for your attentive bride. But I'm happy to listen to it."

"Really? Oh, I'm so sorry! Have I gone on too much? Tell me, please, how I can make it up to you."

"I'm not free to decide, correct?"

"You're mocking me. But I mean it in all seriousness; you are not free. What you say is quite right."

"But I say it is right."

"No, it's a wonder, it's grace. It determines what is right. And that you have chosen me. You having already taken me on, the whole nine yards."

Johanna stopped and forced me also to stop. I bent my head down to her and pressed against her cheeks.

"You are a strange man, my dear! Very, very strange."

"Didn't I already tell you so, or at least gave you some warning?"

"That you have. You dear, dear fool, you dear wonderful man!"

"And so you can love someone like me, Johanna?"

She answered with soft quick kisses that dashed away all my foolishness. I responded to her tenderness. A homeless couple that had come together, and it was meant that they should. Was that us? Perhaps we stood there awhile, perhaps we walked on; a thin, soft rain fell in a winterlike May, but it didn't bother us. Rarely did anyone shuffle by, the footsteps disappearing. Because the darkness engulfed the walls, it was no longer a city through which we walked but a land, an open and free land, one adorned with bushes and quiet forests surrounding our dreamy existence, but a destiny blessed with happiness in the midst of it. Our shared transformation felt like floating, a forward motion on soundless tracks, the floating sensation yielding an exalted journey, the two of us hanging on to each other with hands that caressed, sometimes only our fingers touching. We did not know much about each other, but we sensed it inwardly, peace settling upon us, granting us this moment of communion. Time had erupted in fine filaments that split apart and settled gently upon our faces, us not asking how long it would last.

You want to try it with me, you want to try it with me, or so I heard, the clock singing it aloud, or perhaps I said it aloud, but most likely I didn't, for all such talk was muffled. I didn't know where I was; I thought that I was in a foreign city. Thus I was beside myself, though I also felt that Johanna was likewise beside herself and yet was aware of all that had yet to be determined. Then she let go of her stress, relaxed and, once freed, quietly began to sing to herself. I tried to make out whether it was a real song, but I couldn't tell; most likely it was a tune I didn't know that sounded as pure as glass and silver. I should have been able to see, but when I looked up I couldn't see anything. Again we held hands. I mumbled that I didn't know how to dance, but she paid no mind. She just said it wasn't anything you had to learn, as the dance itself took hold of me, not needing any accompaniment as it drew us powerfully into its spinning power and swung us in circling waves. Have you woken up? Have you finally woken up? You are a continual dreamer amid a metropolis that is never empty of shadows, where the darkness always stretches over its endless distance. Upon its slumbering flats you and your bride have been saved, as together you have reached an auspicious realm. Remember that it belongs to you, remember to keep hold of it, drink from the spring of its riches, but protect yourself from the danger of forgetting your losses, because such concern weighs heavy on the scales of memory and it can consume your hearts if you don't watch out.

We drew close to a populated street, where, despite conservation measures, the lights were turned on, the garish blue lights shining in a ghostly manner, crudely bathing the people who swayed along the sidewalk. In the street, the cars rushed by noisily and slithered through the puddles. As we looked on at all this confusion, we had to walk on, more sober and collected, slowing our gait.

"Do we have to go this way, Johanna?"

She smiled.

"It's very late, my dear. Can you see the clock there? We've been wandering through the streets for nearly two hours and didn't know it. You have to go home, and I still have a ways to go."

"Will it always have to be this way?"

"What do you mean, 'always'?"

"Always a ways to go. Is that what going home means?"

"Not much longer, my dearest! Please be patient!"

"You're right. I'm in your hands."

"If you'll let me."

"I beg you to let me, my dear Johanna."

Quietly grateful, I let her lead me through the wide streets. I heard many cars pass and closed my eyes in order to feel even more completely sheltered by the security of Johanna's protective nature. Only when I stepped over the curb of the sidewalk onto the other side did I open my eyes again. Then I felt ashamed for having pretended I was a blind man, something that had been a favorite thing to do when I was a child, when Mother or Aunt Rosa would take me by the hand and happily lead me along in this way, often for long stretches, but Johanna had either not noticed me pretending that I was blind or had simply gone along with such an innocent game. Soon we turned into a dark side street, then quickly around a corner, the flood of light behind us having been extinguished. I didn't even recognize that we were near my guesthouse, but then I realized we were. If I hadn't sensed it myself, the step of my dear one would have let me know, a hesitant and clearly noticeable faltering coming into her stride, though it wasn't really slower, just more guarded, softer.

I would have liked to stand closer to Johanna and press up against her, given how I feared saying goodbye and any inconceivable separation, worrying that any distance between us could destroy our bond, but I refrained from saying anything that could bother my dear one or raise even the slightest suspicion of the horrible anxieties that possessed me. I had to just bear it all myself. I didn't know what she felt, or how we could casually, hand in hand, say goodbye. She probably felt the same as I did, and it certainly wasn't easy. More than in the days and years past, when there had been nothing else for me, now I dreaded loneliness, it feeling for the first time unbearable. Now impatience hammered away inside me, consuming me, my frailty more obvious than ever. I was shocked at the excessiveness of the feelings that I was not capable of controlling, such that they threatened to burst from me, or, worse yet, shatter me. If I were only a bit more courageous, I would have done the only thing there was to do, not asking much or tarrying before the entrance to my accommodations but quietly tagging along to wherever Johanna was going. Nor would I have to think for long whether that was right or not, but instead I could just follow along, not saying anything foolish and always remaining by her side, rather than damning us to such loneliness. There we stood before the guesthouse, worn with weariness and yet full of desire, both of us lacking confidence as well as any solution while wondering what to do. Johanna squeezed my hand harder, until it almost hurt, and didn't want to stay or to go.

"Do you still have a ways to go, Johanna? Where do you have to go?"

"No, I can't stay with you. That can't happen here. It's impossible."

She said this forcefully, with an almost bitter passion.

"I wasn't thinking of that at all, sweetheart. You have to go home, I know. I'll just walk you there."

"In the dark? You don't know your way. It's very far, and you'll get hopelessly lost."

"Nonetheless, you have to take the tube somewhere."

"Yes. But I can't bring you with me. Unfortunately, that can't happen. We'll see each other again soon, very soon. We must see each other tomorrow, every day, always. How I'd love to stay. But, really, it won't be long. Not much more than a week, and then we'll be together."

"Well, good, just don't think of me as ludicrous. Or, indeed, I am ludicrous. But I want to protect you from anything harmful. It is and will be my job to protect you, and I will do my best to do so."

"I'm not at all afraid. Don't talk about such things."

"I only want to walk with you for a while. Then I'll be nice and go home. Here, in this neighborhood, I know my way around even at night; you have to believe me, for I'm being reasonable."

"I don't have the slightest doubt, my dear. But, please, shouldn't you be getting some rest? You had a hard day."

"Each moment with you means rest. Allow me that!"

"Okay, just until the next corner."

"From there you travel by tube?"

"Yes."

"Then I can go along with no problem. I know this way precisely. It's just straight ahead."

So we set off, and talked about the next time we could meet and what we had to get done in the next few days. Through this a lot was cleared up, it being a satisfactory close to the evening. We also managed a quick goodbye, which was necessary, it not being hard to do as Johanna caught the last train. We kissed each other softly on the lips like an old familiar couple. Then I gazed after Johanna as she bought a ticket at the booth, quickly and safely passed through the turnstile and to the escalator without looking back, the descending steps hurrying below until I could no longer see her. I left the station and scurried across to the other side of the street, where a tea stand poured forth smoke, its two oil lamps providing a pale light. A few figures lingered about, rakish souls, among them some blacks and other foreigners, also some poor suffering girls. I was hungry and thirsty and asked for a tea and a roll. The drink was watery and tasteless, the snack stringy and not very appetizing; I swallowed down only half of each. A girl spoke to me, something about a cigarette, nothing more. Since I didn't know the best way to escape being hit up for something, I served up my favorite response, which was to say that, unfortunately, I was not from here and couldn't give her any advice. That had always worked before, but this time it failed, a terrible sounding laughter rising from her and something mumbled, which sounded like a threat, although perhaps it was just harmless kidding.

I hurried off and paid no attention to what was called after me. Then I felt something hit my hat, though probably it wasn't a stone but most likely a rotten apple, nothing all that dangerous, though I hurried off twice as fast. I didn't want to stop again until I reached my guesthouse, but as I was running along I stumbled into a man who held on to me as I stammered apologies in several different languages. The stranger turned out to be a policeman, which shocked me, though he acted friendly and suggested that I be careful in the dark, once I told him that I was only trying to get back to my guesthouse. I could have reported what had happened to me back at the tea stand, but I thought it a bad excuse for my careless running and was not convinced that I had really been attacked. Perhaps a senseless fear had simply overtaken me. The policeman let me go with a well-meaning word and wished me good night.

Then I walked slowly for the last stretch and did not meet anyone else. The guesthouse was locked, but I had the house key and managed to quietly reach my room. I quickly got ready for bed, but as soon as I had undressed I changed my mind, put my coat on over my pajamas, turned up the gas fire, sat down at a little writing desk, and started a letter to Anna. She needed to know that I had gotten engaged. She deserved that from me. Once the address was written out on the sealed envelope, I got into bed. The letter to Anna provided the proper end to the day. Through it, everything I had experienced that day had been put into perspective. I had covered everything in detail; every single thing that I reported lit up another chamber of my consciousness from within. Once more, I picked up the letter. I had already sealed it, but I ripped it open and read it through, line by line, such that everything was present to me. The doors opened between all the chambers, a consistent light flooding the tiny rooms, making it seem as if they were never separated by walls. I saw myself striding through them as the victor, pleased and relaxed by the good fortune granted me. A pure new day had opened before me; wherever I turned I saw an image, any number of them, whether it be a sunny wall, a flower, a meditative garden, a glade by a brook, a hill beneath the sky, a frolicking sailboat on dusky water, the contours of a dear face, a bedecked table in a corner. Yet, when I began to examine any of them more closely, each of them turned into Johanna before my eyes. The entire world was gathered together as a flood of images and stored within me, and when I brought them all together, there stood Johanna before me. I thought about this wonder and felt nothing but gratitude and undeserved grace.

Carefully I folded the letter, got a fresh envelope that I addressed, and stuck the letter inside, though this time I didn't seal it, for if bad dreams woke me, or if the new morning brought a rude awakening, I could read the letter in order to restore my confidence. I considered whether a report that revealed so much about me should be sent to Anna. Yet it was a good letter. I was there in it, I was it, I myself—or no, it was Johanna, perhaps it was a letter for Johanna. But, in case I wanted nonetheless to send it to Anna, I had made a copy that I could keep with me wherever I went in the next days. Satisfied, I turned out the light.

It didn't take me long to fall asleep, but it was not a deep sleep. It trickled into me, finding a thousand small openings through which it pressed its dark drops. Hopes and fears seeped through and weighed down all of my murky senses. I never entirely disappeared, nor did my consciousness dissolve; instead, I was separated or burst quietly into pieces. I looked on everything, devoid of consciousness or, in fact, with a consciousness, but one that was distant and strange and didn't belong to me. I was accosted by an unruly army of clamoring questions that called out to me wordlessly, all of it adding up to an insensible interrogation. But where was I, where could I be? I couldn't move at all, but just had to suffer the fact that there was a great deal that was not me, and which perhaps belonged to no one, and which overpowered every fiber of any life supposedly run by my own will. I was not stuck in any kind of churning limbo, but for me there was also no continuous existence. I sensed that I controlled nothing, that I was at the beck and call of something else which I had to listen to and obey. That was not easy to do, for it was almost impossible to do, because all the commands simply pressed into me like a viscous fluid, all of them nearly unintelligible, while the more I tried to understand them, the more I was hindered from doing so, such that the force pushed me toward a plodding obedience, because before I could follow the demanding orders a broad swath of time covered in thick fog crept in between. Thus everything occurred behind veils and too late, much too late. The reluctance and abhorrence that resulted, as well as the awful attacks, pelted me, hurting me, but there was nothing I could do, for I had no way of getting at their cause as long as I was unable to defend myself from the onslaught. I was increasingly defenseless, although I refused to heed the demands made on me. They had no right to demand that I should give in to them, for all they wanted was to deny my basic worth and attention, and to drown me in shame. Vainly I tried to bring this miserable game to an end. Any declaration I made was like trying to strike at a cloud. I offered a single apology, but that was met only with anger. Then I tallied aloud my supposed merits, outlined my plans that stretched out a wide net full of promise, but that was dismissed, and when I alluded to the past as I summoned its shadows they were nothing but past shadows and thus remained null and void.

"What a joke," he said contemptuously. "That a man of your gifts is stuck in the same place as other refugees—that only says how deep the wound was that created your impossible social skills. An asocial sociologist, that's what you are! You need to be rebuilt from the ground up if you can't turn your life around yourself."

I bit my upper lip and stammered, "I don't know why you are treating me like . . . like a good-for-nothing. Why you are doing that . . . just like I was a criminal . . ."

"Don't be silly! No one said that you are a criminal. But the way you go about things shatters all sympathies, and you see the result yourself. A good-for-nothing, a man with a wife and children like you—in your case, that's no exaggeration."

"I would have been smarter than to let myself get tangled up with you if I had known that you were going to set in motion this unkind and unproductive game. Why did you ask me to come here?"

"You're not letting me speak. I have—"

"You promised my wife that you would leave me in peace. Again, why have you asked me here?"

"Will you listen to what I have to say?"

"I want clarity. You said to my wife that you could provide concrete help. Only because of that supposition have I come, not to have a flood of accusations wash over me."

"Concrete help—that's exactly what it is. I mean well and want to help you. I'm killing myself for you, and the only thanks I get is to be scolded! Who else has given you anything concrete, huh? I'm not like your so-called former friends whom you've told me about. What do you make of all the contacts who have done nothing but blow in your ear? And do you know why none of it gets you anywhere?"

"No."

"I can tell you exactly why. Because you always expect something. Did Fräulein Knispel call you?"

"No."

"There, you see? Did you write her?"

"No. You decided that I better not, for I might mess things up. You said so yourself. You wanted to arrange things yourself."

Herr Konirsch-Lenz sat across from me in the little ugly café where there was not a quiet moment to be had and stared at me with an expression as if he had just revealed to me the deepest secret of my puzzling existence and was now waiting for the scales to fall from my eyes and for me to accede to him in all matters and turn over the rudder of my life's miserable vessel to his control. But I only looked at him dumbfounded, hoping for a moment to gather my wits after such a stunning blow, though I soon gave up, as it seemed pointless.

"So you agree that you're a good-for-nothing?"

I didn't say a thing.

"Do you have nothing to say?"

"Not that I know of."

My mouth barely whispered this.

"I believe, my good man, that you suffer from moral weakness. Your wife could suffer as a result."

"Please, let me be."

I wanted to leave the table, but my legs betrayed me; I couldn't get up from the chair, and sank back down onto it. As if to hinder my flight, the manufacturer of Kolex wallpaper grabbed my arm.

"You treat me as if I'm not even worthy of shining your shoes, and all I want to do is help you. It makes one want to puke!"

"It makes one want to puke! You've got that right."

"Yes! Because of you! You hopeless egomaniac! But it's no use arguing with you; I won't waste my time with it! Now, you listen to me! Do you remember my telling you about Self-Help and Herr Scher?"

What Kolex had explained to me about Self-Help and Scher was meaningless. I didn't want to hear anything about it.

"Yes, I dimly remember. You told me so much that it's all jumbled up inside my head."

"Self-Help, my friend, Self-Help. Try to remember!"

"I don't know anything about it!" I said, lying.

"What's that, you no longer remember anything about Self-Help? That is indeed the organization a person in your situation must surely turn to. But I'm telling you that there's no point in expecting any kind of actual support from Self-Help, except in very exceptional circumstances, and you don't fall into that category. But the job placements you can secure there are golden, for they are done professionally. No need to rely on friendship, which you've had enough of already, and you know how far that will get you. There's no such thing as friends—that, you've learned!"

"Friends and business with friends! It all buzzes away inside my head, and it's not up to you to look after me."

"Oh, just shut up and listen! These placements by Self-Help have already helped some get back on their feet who were on the brink of despair—really tragic cases, not just harmless and self-inflicted ones like yourself. Self-Help is terrific. It was founded for selfless reasons and has been running now for over fifteen years. It runs on its own, which is something, for there are more than twenty employees there. What am I saying, twenty? There have to be at least thirty! But Self-Help has filled thousands of fantastic positions, and often free of charge. Herr Scher, someone I know well, even a good friend of mine, perhaps plays the most important role there, for he owes me. I've taken people he's recommended and placed them in my factory. I told your wife all of this—did she not tell you about it? I'm convinced that it works. Social cases. I know how to handle such matters. You shouldn't be so stubborn! I could help you and heal you; in a year you'd be cured! Then you could help me with other cases, considering your education. My friend, don't be such an idiot! And you want to be a sociologist. No wonder you're interested in the oppressed. I am as well, but I look to do something about it! With you it's nothing but your past and your sympathy for yourself. Strong people have no need to study the sociology of the oppressed; they take care of it themselves, but in a practical manner! The way you go about it is a nasty business. You have to go about it differently. You have to get cracking and do it, in concrete ways. Then you'll have the right to get involved with the oppressed and to think about their liberation. If you were my colleague, you would soon earn yourself a nice pile of money and then later could write a sociology of the liberated man. No theory, just practice. Then I'd be impressed, and all the Kratzensteins can go take a leap, as well as the snooty Dr. Kauders and the lazy potentates from whom you've expected so much. All of them will be knocked flat on their asses by you."

Konirsch-Lenz talked ever more hurriedly, his speech becoming more vulgar. He talked on and on, with me only partly listening, and even today I can hardly forgive myself for not having long gotten over it, for every word filled me with resentment. I sensed nothing but bad things for me, but I was afraid and let the wave pour over me. Sometimes I tried to break or stave off the miserable blabber, but Konirsch-Lenz cut me off right away with "Just a minute!" or "I'm talking now!" and "Listen to me!," such that I had to drink to the dregs the humiliation he intended for me.

"No, the honored sir is much too noble to begin with my wallpaper. That I know. A fussy intellectual, yes, I understand. That's why I thought of Scher. He'd be impressed with you, but as you are now he'd think you were dreck. He'd set your head straight, though; that's his job. He's quite agreeable, it would surprise you, and he's been around the block. What I say to him is as holy as a taboo. All I have to do is let him know, and he does it straight off. Perhaps he could use you as a kind of social worker. That would be right up your alley, wouldn't it? I'm thinking as a career counselor. Could you do that? As a sociologist, certainly you've studied a bit of psychology, graphology, Rorschach tests, or some such methodology?"

"I don't think I'd be well suited to it."

"You're such a shit! You're not well suited to anything! When someone isn't well suited to anything, then there's nothing he can do and he ends up on the rubbish heap. Just think of that, and to hell with you! I'll go to Scher soon, in about two weeks, no sooner."

"If it's for me, it will be a waste of your time."

"Stop being so disagreeable! I'm fed up with you, you're wasting my time—"

"Can I go now? In fourteen days I can certainly—"

"You can't do anything! Stay here! I will talk to Scher about your situation. For example, he always has a bunch of crash courses in the offing which he organizes around professions that are easy to learn, a lot of things that one can do something with. I don't know what would be suited to you; he will figure that out. Certainly not a course in engraving monograms. Or do you like monograms? Watchmaking, perhaps? Or hand-weaving? That's something for philosophers, for you can dream away while doing it. Well, then, say something! For once, give yourself a leg up! Yes?"

I didn't say anything, yet Kolex was already puffed up with a new round of his blabber.

"Well, then, I see. It's probably best that you think on it a couple of days. Then call me up. Or I'll call you, don't call me. The laurel might fall from the honored sir's forehead. Inhibitions. This we know. But there's nothing to really consider. You just get at it. Reckless, not feckless! Whoever considers too long before the hand held out to him will be left in the dust."

I was quiet and had to remain so in order to avoid bursting out in anger and causing all the guests to turn their attention to me. Konirsch-Lenz banged with a key on the marble tabletop until a waiter appeared, at which he ordered a black coffee for us both, a repulsive-smelling brew, as well as a leathery piece of cake nestled in a paper wrapper that I could remove only with some effort. I didn't want to touch either the coffee or the cake—both of them would make me sick—but there was no mercy; I had to swallow it all. Who knew what upset the man so except the fact that I continued to resist. Already he was suggesting new plans. Kolex leafed through a notebook made of his wallpaper and began to write a letter to Herr Scher. He should be the one to examine me closely, in order to sort out the rest. Yet it didn't take long for this recommendation to be written out in a hurried hand that trotted along and then stopped, at which I, pressed to do so, nodded uncertainly. Letters of recommendation were an awkward business, because dozens of them passed between hands, and Konirsch-Lenz wouldn't have had anything to do with them. The wallpaper itself simply awaited a personal touch. What one wrote was stupid flattery, outright lies, or extortion, and, in any case, the fabrication of false facts.

"Letters are nothing but lies. A banal method of pulling the wool over someone's eyes, used for ages. One no longer comes to an agreement through such things these days. You must know that best of all. And what did it get you? Not what some dirt under your little fingernails would! There you have it! If I'm sent letters that are not pure business letters, but rather private letters, then I have no use for the private ones, for I prefer not to read them at all and throw them straight away. All they do is beg, that being the point, every last one of them. This charade makes me want to puke. Letters? All I need is a rubbish basket."

The sheets of wallpaper soon unfurled their social views. I should note that the social-safety-net economy wasn't worth anything. It's awful, a spreading cancer of our time, for no one wants to work. Everyone relies on everyone else, the result being so mediocre and pathetic that you can't help turning up your nose at it. Herr Konirsch-Lenz ripped up the letter he'd begun into little pieces that he played with until they were all balled up. Then he pressed them one by one into the ashtray that, earlier, guests had filled in a disgusting manner.

What kind of miserable impression would it make, was the talk that went forward, if I were to march in with such a scrap of paper, a strong man at the height of his powers? I needed to speak up. But he kept on just the same about Self-Help, Scher, crash courses, all of it mixed up together, though when finally my counterpart shut up for a minute, I quickly posed the question of whether the courses were free.

"How could you ever come up with such a harebrained idea? Free? There is nothing in this world that is free, not even death!"

At this, a searching look fell upon me that caused me to feel lowly and crushed, a lowly cur who was trying to squeeze into some little hole. Behind me there pressed a wild pursuit hot on my heels. I had to crawl over the dead that had been thrown there, those that had been choked and beaten, deposited there, starving and in festering misery, stacked up like naked dolls and buried, their last breath a phlegmy curse. Behind me I could hear riotous shouts, then shots rang out, pointed cries, and thunderous rolling metal, sticks snapping with a groan and straw rustling that burned on a piled-high funeral pyre. Wavering commands snaked across the brittle flats as I pressed farther into the thicket. I wanted to save myself, so I had to keep to the edge, where it wasn't so dangerous, farther and farther away from the middle! Not completely on the edge, but near it, somewhere in between, where less occurred and I could wait out the rumbling that circled me. An endless coming and going of guests went on about me. Lost spirits scrambled among the cold tables, crashing into chairs that scraped along stubbornly, the plates on the table clanging, the waiters pale and impatient and threatening the refugees with outstretched arms. Many just wanted to pay the bill and get out of there, but in vain, the white caps shaking, the fluttering aprons throwing off puffs of deadly dust. It was a day of judgment, Cain had killed Abel, a cup fell, smoking, the gushing coffee spilling like blood on the dirty floor, the entreating glance of the father following, a best shirt spoiled, and sobs welling up in the throat of the approaching mother. Already a custodian was on the job, raising his sword of justice, complaining above the pieces, a waiter yammering on, blaming everyone and no one, some guests wandering about with suitcases they anxiously carried and that swayed like anchors.

I sat there tight and sweaty in my chair amid the damp arches of perdition, suffering and trembling under the punitive condemnations of the thin wallpaper, immersed in burning pain. What else could I do but allow my hearing and my sight to be offended? But, finally, the punitive condemnations faded away, the wallpaper curled and was folded, such that Herr Konirsch-Lenz once again sat across from me as a living person with eyes and a mouth, his lips moving vigorously.

"Why aren't you eating your cake?"

He asked this in a dictatorial way and pointed to a little bit left over on my plate that lay there like a heavy lump. Silently I obeyed, and forked up this last bit, turning it in disgust within my mouth from one side to the other until the factory owner had to think that I had already swallowed it. Then I grabbed my napkin as if I wanted to blow my nose and I let the bite disappear into it.

"Certainly the crash courses aren't free. One could not expect that of Self-Help. My friend, they have to run on their own, without any public funding. But they are cheap and not-for-profit. Self-Help is not looking to make money off them. The higher-ups have to just make sure to cover their costs. What were you thinking? The courses are taught conscientiously. Excellent faculty with first-class qualifications teach them. At the end you can take an exam, get a diploma, and then have a good chance of being considered for a job. In addition, as a graduate of a course you have the chance to seek advice from the job-placement service of Self-Help. The service is free and requires only a small processing fee for each placement. But you only pay once you know you have gotten a position. It's even better if you decide to become a member of Self-Help, because then you don't have to pay the processing fee."

The lecture on Self-Help kept rambling on until finally even Herr Konirsch-Lenz was exhausted. His anger had waned, he had mellowed, and so he tugged at the apron of a waiter hurrying past and ordered gin and tonics for us both. When the drinks were brought, I had to toast to my future with him. He then began to tell me about his younger days, about old socialist ideals, and the Lenz School in Mecklenburg. He became maudlin. Almost two hours had elapsed since we had gotten together, but I still had other things I wanted to get done that morning. I became impatient, for there seemed no end in sight. Ever more impatiently I shifted in my seat, such that it could not have gone unnoticed. Then the wallpaper maker asked me what was wrong. When I explained that I had promised Johanna to run an errand for her in the city, I was complimented, though at the same time Kolex was again angry, as if I had only taken up his time with my hopeless case. Indeed, if any of it was still to lead to anything he would be pleased, but as far as he could see, despite his efforts I wasn't any smarter. Then I pulled myself together and almost arrogantly responded that his misgivings were all too true. There was no turning me into a good apple.

Herr Konirsch-Lenz looked at me so severely that I expected him to erupt into anger once again. Only a consideration of where we were held him back. I wanted to quickly say goodbye, or not say goodbye, really, but just leave quickly without saying a word, but I missed my chance to do so and had to wait until he settled the bill. Outside I wanted, for Johanna's sake, to maintain my good manners and politely thank him for everything and then disappear into the bustling streets, but once again Konirsch-Lenz beat me to the punch. With feigned gentleness he asked me to walk him to his car, which sat in a side street. I was indeed on my guard, but since he spoke to me in such a friendly way, as he had done when we first met, I didn't want to deny his wishes and so followed along.

"I can drive you wherever you are going. Look, Dr. Landau, I perhaps got you all wrong and came on a bit too strong. You mustn't be upset with me, for I meant well. That's just the way I am, but you are also no hero. No one in the world understands you better than I do, not even your charming wife. Only a man can fully grasp you. I was once an idealist, even a great one, and I still have some of that in me. If I'm such a shit, how is it that I warmed to you so and took up your cause? Look, be reasonable for once! Walk straight to the next telephone booth and call up Scher or go right to Self-Help."

"Why?"

We had reached the car. Konirsch-Lenz opened the door.

"Why?" he shouted. "Why? Have you gone mad?"

"I don't believe so."

"Then you are a bum, a snotnosed kid! Then you are not worthy of having survived! Then you should have croaked like a brute animal instead of arriving like a vagabond in this country in order to live off others who have tirelessly tried to build a life for themselves here again, while you marry such a pitiful thing, bring a child into the world, then another and then let your family starve in the end!"

"How dare you!"

"Just get out of here, you . . . you . . ."

Konirsch-Lenz lifted his hand to curse me, but he could no longer find the words to do so. I also said nothing, but fended him off and spit on the ground. Then I turned around, without looking back, and walked swiftly away. Behind me I could hear him cursing continually, then at last he was in his car, myself hearing as well how he slammed the door, but I didn't pay attention to the direction in which he drove off. I was indeed extremely upset, and yet relieved. I whistled with satisfaction as I rushed through the humming streets without a plan. I was overcome by a spiteful happiness, for now I was free of all asked-for or unasked-for recommendations, and for the first time since my arrival in the metropolis I was alone and together with Johanna. With one stroke, everything else had become unimportant, all that had occurred during the course of almost four years, the revilements and debasements no longer stinging, me answerable to no one else but Johanna and myself. Since my quarrel with Jolan Haarburger until my fight with Konirsch-Lenz, I had dealt with so many people whom I had either sought out or who had reached out to me. All of them had nagged me about my fortunes and recommended that I pull myself up by my bootstraps. Woe to the powerless man who wishes to stand his ground. . . .

Everything was different now. For Johanna, it was deeply disappointing that even her old bosses in the Office for Refugees and other influential people whose friendship she thought she had made through her job had denied her the least bit of help and often didn't wish to speak to her. However, she still had a number of confidants who could not exert any influence in support of my situation or my work but who nonetheless were willing to help Johanna in any way they could. Thus we were able to survive, Johanna saving wherever she could and never missing an opportunity to do some small bit of work. What unfolded was a way of life that I never had a full grasp of. I never asked Johanna, not even later, how she managed it all behind the scenes, nor about the few people she was connected to, nor did I even know all of them. All of it amounted to a realm that Johanna controlled entirely. Even if I saw a pleasant magic performed all around me, I was never particularly struck by it; almost everything happened behind my back, and that was all I knew.

Above all, there was Betty, Johanna's second cousin, who used to be a teacher of geography and history but had been retrained, as the saying went, as a confectioner after her emigration from Vienna. She now had a little shop in South Wales where she sold chocolate wafers and other sweets, and did quite well for herself. Betty is a warm presence, always eager to help out and care for others, and is for us and the children a constant source of support. Every year we have a wonderful time visiting her in her little house, where she spoils us, Michael and Eva being her darlings whom she won over as much with her tireless patience with their games and jokes as through her sweet tidbits. Almost every month she sends us two little packages, containing not only tasty things meant for the children but also little clothes and shoes for the two of them and many other practical things for the two of us. Betty would never let Johanna pay for any of it, nor did she ever hold it against me when I ignored some of the well-intentioned advice she gave. That meant a lot to me, for relatives, especially, believe they have a right to expect that you will follow their advice or at least try to. If you don't carry it out or you don't even try to, usually you are met with the hatred of the one wishing to help, or, at a minimum, resentment, and are thus abandoned. Betty never let herself stoop to such a reaction. Thinking of her as I walked along the street, whistling, I didn't believe that she would even resent the piteous collapse of my relationship with Konirsch-Lenz. She was too fair-minded to do that, and she loved people as people deserved to be loved. She didn't seek the fulfillment of her hopes and efforts for the sake of herself but thought of her fellow men. Certainly it must have been hard for her when, once again, something fell through for me that she had set in motion, but I was never afraid that she would turn away from Johanna or me. Many years ago, Betty had been interested in teaching children and youths at risk, and had visited the Lenz School while on a study trip. There she met Konirsch-

Lenz, whose work she admired. Later, she learned by chance that he was in this country, which made her think of me, so she got hold of his address and wrote to him. This was how I was recommended to him, and now I had to think of what to say to Betty about it, or if it wouldn't do to let Johanna handle it.

With no worries, feeling almost lighthearted, I went along my way, stopping in front of shop windows, looking quickly at the piles of books displayed in the open in front of a rare-books dealer, and then moved on. On the other side of the street I suddenly noticed Otto Schallinger, who was hurrying along with a large bag. Should I call out to him? It would certainly have pleased him, but I had no desire to, and so I peeled off in a different direction. Of all my old friends, he was the only one who meant something to me, and who was still loyal. I had to admit that it was ungrateful of me, but I didn't want to change my decision. He followed me with a relentless, to me, irritating persistence, by which he sought to maintain the same distance between us. This resulted in nothing other than dim memories that ran back as far as twenty-five or thirty years. Through his contact with me, Otto wanted to retrieve his long-lost youth and reawaken it. Innumerable details of a long-lost time that were unimportant to me, and that had, for the most part, disappeared from my memory, appeared to be meaningful enough to him to be thoroughly revisited. With Sylvia, who had little interest in Otto's past and even less understanding of it, he could not talk about such things, as she expected something quite different from him. Therefore he sought, from time to time, a break from a present that wasn't very satisfying by revisiting the past with us. If we agreed, then he would show up, avuncular and carrying little presents, feeling more at home on West Park Row than we could sometimes stand. Sylvia, however, never came with him. We had long been convinced that their life together was not so happy as he tried to assure us it was, yet she was good-natured enough to tolerate his visits to us, though perhaps they didn't matter to her at all. Thus he turned to us as if fleeing to a lost paradise in order to escape the bustle of the metropolis and the country in which, despite Sylvia and his having lived here for twelve years, he never quite felt at home, although it had granted him a reasonable living, he feeling that, with us, so much of what he had experienced before the war, or at least in growing up, had been well preserved. Even our poverty, sorry as he was for it, didn't really bother him, for it even helped him to arrive at our house and feel himself amid a transformed and much more lovely youth. "Do you remember how . . ." many of his sentences began. No matter what I answered, it didn't seem to jar him from his dreamy recollections, it only bothering him now and then when I couldn't control myself and was indeed not very nice to him. Then he would gaze at me with such beseeching eyes, like a beaten child, in the hope that I would not destroy the realm he had projected. Then I had to be good to him and listen patiently to whatever he hauled out of the old schooldays, endless stories about teachers and schoolmates, and, above all, about himself. Then he pressed me to also share something of my own memories. How hard it was for me mattered as little to him as the questionable facts of my reports, for I made things up at random in order to please him, but also to spare myself and hide behind such tales.

Otto had a lot of trouble with his little Sidney, who, soon after my arrival in the metropolis, succumbed to a nasty illness that resulted in mental difficulties that required him to be institutionalized. To his sorrow, Otto had no other children, as Sylvia either could not have any more or didn't want any more. Since the misfortune with Sidney, she had changed, Otto saying that the piano had become much more important to her than anything else. She practiced whenever she had an hour to spare, because it was her ambition to pass an audition for the radio, which she had failed to do three times already. She practiced further and was supposedly happy when we sometimes suggested that Otto also visit us on a Sunday. He liked these visits the best, since Michael was now grown enough to walk and had in fact begun to speak at an early age. Uncle Otto, as he was known to our children, brought along appropriate and inappropriate gifts, as well as his camera, in order to capture Michael's curiosity about the little pictures and to win our favor. In order to be reminded more of the home he'd lost, Otto called the child Mischa, which didn't please Johanna, but there was no dissuading him. Sometimes Michael was afraid of his uncle and didn't want anything to do with him, which caused Otto to despair, though at other times the boy beamed and was trusting. Then Otto was happy, even when Johanna suggested, in good weather, that he take the child for a walk, usually to Shepherd's Field, or especially when there was a fair, which never pleased Johanna, as the child got overexcited because of it. But it was difficult to resist Otto's requests; touched by his devotion, Johanna put up with him. She also hoped that his visits provided something of a distraction for me, and thought it good that I had at least some contact with someone who shared my past, though most of all she took pity on him. Johanna was grateful when he fixed something in our little garden or in the house, be it a rickety chair or an electric cord. I found that nice as well, though I liked it less when he messed about with how I liked to keep my own garden. Also his tedious talk, which easily became too much for me, Johanna listened to patiently and did not let on whenever it became uncomfortably too much for her as well. Everything would have been bearable if only Otto had not tried to interfere with my scholarly work with his well-meaning suggestions. He felt called upon to correct some of my ideas in order that they be more easily understood by the public. His greatest pleasure lay in trying to teach me something.

"Such oppression has economic reasons and is a consequence of the bad will of the propertied classes," he would say. "Against that, my dear Arthur, since I don't believe in revolution—one sees so many of them in other countries and what it leads to—against that one can only pose good upbringing. If one only tends to the youths, which you can easily do with your Mischa alone, and instill the idea that we must look out for one another, then things will be better for the next generation, and such horrible things as what we experienced, such beastliness, will not repeat itself. If such young people come of age, they will certainly be against oppression, you will see, and they will anchor the freedom of humanity in law. Good will triumph, just you wait!"

This was roughly the smartest thing Otto had to say. He incessantly filled my ears with such bits of wisdom and regularly repeated them, such that I could hardly stand it. If I wanted peace, then I said I was tired, which didn't always work, or I kicked him out, which only upset him. Still, we never entirely discouraged his visits; they just needed to occur less frequently. A solution offered itself in letting him spend time with his Mischa, or Johanna occupied herself with Otto, while I, for shorter or longer periods, and sometimes for the entire visit, would retreat to my room under the guise of having pressing work to do.

Slowly I strolled farther along through the streets and thought about my former friends. The Bergmann-Birch siblings no longer meant anything to me, I having rarely seen them since the first weeks after my arrival. Inge, especially, had withdrawn from me, So-and-So having correctly predicted that. She seemed inexhaustible in her knack for coming up with excuses as to why we couldn't get together anytime in the next few days, and Oswald backed her up on it. That's why I soon gave up trying to cultivate contact with her and finally got over this disappointment. Much more painful was the breakup with Oswald, which I suffered from for years. Since Inge could barely stand that I had survived the war, while her own loved ones had been killed, she was unsettled by the very nature of my friendly feelings, even if I didn't think of her as at all brutal, but rather as so vulnerable that, out of self-preservation and defenselessness, she needed to wound me. I well understood Inge's sick attitude, such that I hoped to earn her affection by gently approaching her indignant pain and sad anger. That was not to be. Whatever friendly words I said to her in self-abnegation had only the opposite effect in stirring her to launch abusive attacks on me. Oswald found his sister at fault and sided with me during these skirmishes, or at least appeared to, but in the end he cleverly and secretly incited her against me. In subtle ways, he destroyed my friendship with Inge.

In subtle ways—well, was it so subtle how Oswald plotted against me, or was it nothing but nasty? He withdrew from me in a different way than his uncontrollable sister. In the first days, he extended to me an embracing friendliness that suffused me with warmth, yet I was given good advice by nobody, least of all my own feelings, in not realizing that such lavish amplitude lasts only a little while, especially when the spender is reluctant to receive anything in return. The few meetings that Oswald granted me did not betray any cooling of his affections, nor did his mood change, but soon I could hardly reach him anymore—indeed, not at all. If I went to his house after we agreed to meet, he revealed to me straight off what a pity it was that he had only ten minutes for me, as something completely unexpected had come up that he couldn't put off, though if it was all right with me, I should just come along with him. I would then do that, and after a short, hasty walk or a ride in a taxi he'd quickly say goodbye while showering me with reassurances of his friendship and with the request to visit him again as soon as possible, or at least call. If I showed up unexpectedly or uninvited, as he suggested I do, most of the time he wasn't there. If I didn't happen to find him in, then he would explain to me in detail that it wasn't the custom here in this country to surprise someone without calling ahead, for though I was always warmly welcome to visit, it would be better to arrange it beforehand.

Then I tried to reach Oswald by phone, which, unfortunately, involved a number of hurdles. Often, he wasn't at home, and his maid didn't know where he was, or he happened to have visitors, which prevented him from coming to the phone, or he had just come home or was about to leave, or it wasn't a good time because he had just gotten a headache or he was swamped with work, or, finally, it might be, as he reported with a choked voice, that he just wasn't in the proper mood for conversation. Our conversations on the telephone were often impersonal and for the most part rushed, being fruitless and soon leading to my feeling that I would soon not want to talk to anyone on the phone at all. Such paltry talk disappointed me deeply. Sometimes he employed sweet words in urging me to call again, perhaps some evening or early in the morning or the following week, perhaps the best being if Oswald could call me sometime. I would then tell him a time and place, at which he promised to reach me, though I waited in vain. And if a conversation on the telephone did occur, in which he at last listened to me with some patience and ease, at the end he would say that, much to his sincere regret, there was not much he could tell me that day, he being besieged from many directions these days, though he hoped in a week or so to free himself of all such unpleasant distractions; or he would explain that there were other reasons preventing him, there being unforeseen responsibilities that had to be taken care of, Inge's health requiring regular attention and demanding great care, or a trip that could not be postponed had thrown all plans for the coming weeks in disarray. The reasons he produced as to why he couldn't see me were inexhaustible.

So, in the first months that I was here, I often did not see Oswald for weeks at a time, and I soon began to call less often. He seemed less and less interested in my problems, declaring himself unqualified to judge my writings or my research plans, nor did he wish to talk about my experiences and my personal worries. Thus he made it impossible, for example, for me to tell him about my acquaintance and engagement with Johanna. Only after I pressed him numerous times was he willing to meet her, and on an agreed-upon evening that had been put off three times—we had already been married for fourteen days—he conducted himself in such a formal and controlled way that he remained aloof from any concern, Johanna not believing me when I said that he had been completely different before the war. He hardly ever said anything about his life or his works but preferred to talk about some book I knew nothing about, or to ask about things that meant a great deal to him but certainly much less to me. When it came time to say goodbye, his voice sounded sad, and he said how it hurt him that we saw each other so little, for he had been so happy when I arrived and to have me now in this country, yet in the past year contact with those he held dear, and that included me, had been so sparse. But, certainly, that would change soon; I just needed to have a bit of patience with him, for next month he hoped to take it easy and visit us often on West Park Row, especially since Inge had to travel to France to work on a translation.

When I left Oswald alone after that and waited for the coming months to pass, everything became more complicated. He said that he was afraid he had to confess to me that Inge had not left, as everything in France had fallen apart, so she had taken on a deadline job for a local publisher, the translation of a novel that she could not manage on her own, thus requiring Oswald's help in meeting the deadline. So his free time was entirely taken up, his sister, above all, having been made more nervous than ever with all this hectic activity, her stomach suffering as a result, and if Oswald didn't make sure that she kept to a strict and normal diet she could become quite ill. Some time later, I learned that Inge's work had gone well, and her health did not suffer that much, but now Oswald himself had a fixed contract that he couldn't get out of, and which demanded that he work ten hours a day, at least, for the next two or three months. I needed to understand the pressure he was under. Thus arose the obstacles that prevented our meeting anytime soon. That was the last straw—nothing but excuses. I had had enough of Oswald.

"That means we just can't see each other anymore!" I said emphatically on the phone.

Oswald seemed dismayed. He didn't take my words as final, but rather as a form of mistrust that he wished to dissipate, for he hated any feelings of mistrust.

"No. What are you thinking? Of course I need to see you soon. That's not the issue. Somehow that will happen. If I can't promise you when right at the moment, I'll nonetheless think about it throughout the day. You know what? Let me suggest something. I have to meet with Kauders today, and I'll ask him to let you know how soon we can see each other. He'll let you know for sure."

"I hardly ever see him."

"What do you mean, you hardly see him? That's impossible. He's your best friend here! He tells me all the time how much he worries about you."

"He says that? How nice of him!"

"Isn't that true?"

"No."

"That's impossible! He's devoted to you. He says that all the time. He even said so to Karin. One can even see the effect it's had on his work. A strong influence that can't be denied."

"Does he really not deny it?"

"No, of course not. Your basic ideas show up throughout it, and anyone who knows would recognize them."

"He wouldn't admit that to me."

"No, I simply can't believe that! I'll speak with him about it."

"Please, don't say anything! Nothing at all!"

"Why not?"

"Because I don't want you to."

"Well, if you don't want me to, then of course I'll let it be. But perhaps sometime you'll indeed let me talk to him."

"No. I beg of you, just let it go. Is there no way, then, that we can get together?"

"Ah, yes, well . . . today is not possible. You know, Kauders and what-not. I'd love to, of course. But it's difficult. I could spare an hour tomorrow. Do you have time? It doesn't have to be tomorrow. Perhaps the day after?"

"I could do it."

"Great! Should we agree on that now? Or shouldn't I indeed let you know through Kauders?"

"Please, no!"

"Is it really that unpleasant for you? Hmm. Fine. Of course, I understand. I have a suggestion. But, of course, only if you agree. You could just write me a letter."

"What kind of letter?"

"You are a master letter writer. It was always one of the greatest of pleasures to read your letters."

"What should I write to you?"

"Well, what you wish to, of course. Any kind of practical matter. About your situation. Your life. Your work. Yourself. Everything. It would interest me. You know that."

"One thing I can tell you in person, Oswald. Things aren't going well for me here. Not at all."

"Of course, I'm sorry about that. What does Johanna say about it? I must learn more about her. Write me about her! I'm so happy for you. She is really so charming. I need to get to know her better. Kauders adores her; he's almost bursting with envy. Karin, of course, can't know that. Promise me that! Johanna has an excellent reputation from the Office of Refugees. What a father she had, so highly respected! He was a wonderful doctor. You should be proud."

"So I should write to you about that?"

"Whatever you wish, Arthur. Anything from you pleases me. And write me soon!"

"But you know everything already. So-and-So tells you everything about me. You certainly see him often enough."

"You know, sometimes we talk. Mostly about work. He's like a leech I can't shake loose, but don't say I said so! I much prefer to spend time with you. You just have to believe me!"

"Unfortunately, though, it's just not going to work. Right, Oswald?"

"Of course it will. Who says that it won't work?"

"So-and-So."

"I don't believe that! I have never said that to him! Kauders is a shameless fool—believe me, a leech. He yammers on at me. Always whining. Karin gets after me, saying that he really needs me, even if I want to get rid of him. Then she softens me up and there's nothing I can do."

"He doesn't seem that bad to me. You must know a completely different So-and-So than I do."

"That might just be. No person is as transparent as glass. I'll give him a piece of my mind."

"Please, not because of me! I beg of you."

"If that's what you really want, naturally I'll respect it. I really must see you and Johanna as well."

"When?"

"Write me and say when would be good!"

"But then you won't answer my letter."

"Yes, that's right. But perhaps I will. I just might surprise you."

"I don't believe so."

"Give it a try! And if I don't write myself, then I will have your letter before me on my desk as a reminder and I'll call you up. We really should see each other next week."

He didn't expect one from me, but I wrote him a letter, a lengthy one at that, for I tried to clarify our earlier and present relationship and, if possible, to save it. Yet it all came to an end. Oswald neither answered nor called, nor did he pass on anything through So-and-So. Did he just want nothing to do with me? I stopped trying to figure it out, for there was no excusing Oswald for what he had done.

It was different, but hardly any better, with So-and-So. In the early days he was happy to meet up with me quite often, but later less so, though a casual relation was always maintained between us. Our meetings were usually short and certainly served my newly certain intention of preventing a break between us from occurring, that burden never falling upon him but resting with me, for the most part. Also, if he wanted to avoid the impression that his feeling for me had died away, then he just needed to make sure to not seem as if he didn't care, which then would not allow me to have any reason to complain about him. He was best man at my wedding, and he had recommended that Karin serve as Johanna's witness, but Betty came down from South Wales to fill that role, which annoyed So-and-So, who rudely mocked her. As a wedding present, we received from him and Karin a coffee machine, which had to be used out of hospitality whenever he was with us. He also sent us little gifts for birthdays and other occasions, which he always extolled for their usefulness. He was always so generous with Michael, just as Otto was in his own way. So-and-So was pained by, and even jealous of, the fact that I had a son, while he had not been granted any children. It annoyed him that our boy, at the most tender of ages, showed his dislike of him, which only increased with the years, the more so as Uncle So-So, which is what Michael drolly and anxiously called him, tried to win over the child with extravagant little surprises, high-spirited pranks, and grotesque gags that ended up scaring him more than winning his love. Sometimes it hurt us to see So-and-So trying to endear himself to Michael through clumsy and ineffective means. Because he felt that he looked too scary with his glasses on, he stuck them in his coat pocket, but this did no good, because he is very nearsighted, and without his glasses on has no idea what he's doing.

So-and-So made clear to us, and above all to me, both obliquely and openly, that he blamed Michael for his poor attitude. Johanna tried hard to dispel this bad feeling, for with dogged gentleness she dedicated herself to caring for and maintaining my meager ties. Thus she tried in many different ways to persuade Michael not to run straight off or cry when "dear Uncle So-So" showed up. However, it did little good, neither for the child nor for So-and-So, not to mention Johanna or me. It was obvious that he did not wish me well, and had done some things that made my settling into this country more difficult. To this end, he set in motion several ruses that, with panache or in artful, deceptive, and spiteful ways, were played out. Above all, my personal and scholarly shortcomings had to be constantly pointed out anew. I was backward, and that was the only word for it, and that was why it was not possible for me to become an academic; my ineptness at Dr. Haarburger's and in his circle had proved that sufficiently. Any further intercession on my behalf was not only difficult; it would only, in So-and-So's opinion, do me harm rather than help. I would have to live in this country for at least five years before it was possible to judge whether I had acclimated myself to it enough that any introduction made by So-and-So wouldn't bring shame to both him and me.

It's true that I couldn't prove any of this about my boyhood friend, for he went about it very slyly, though Johanna eventually believed me after I raised continual concerns that his conduct was aimed at separating me from people who knew me or had been important to me. No doubt he had also alienated Oswald, if not Inge, through his meddling. In the first years of my marriage, he had even tried to drive a wedge between Johanna and me, whereby he would carefully, albeit as my alleged best friend, who had only my interests at heart, try to point out to Johanna certain aspects of my background and qualities about me that she simply could not judge on her own. At first, Johanna felt his intentions were good, but nonetheless his talk didn't lead to much, for she saw through his game much earlier than I did. He then abandoned such means and resolved to work against me with finely-tuned weapons. My relationship with Johanna was no longer questioned, though around me and around us both an invisible, and therefore secure and inescapable, wall was erected, through whose single and hidden entrance only So-and-So could slip as a trusted envoy and middleman.

A few weeks ago, at the start of my dealings with Konirsch-Lenz, whom So-and-So hated, without knowing him personally, because of a somewhat flattering appraisal of a sociopedagogical exposé of this self-important friend of humanity, it became So-and-So's central cause to dissuade me from following my own profession, it being the only way that my practical circumstances could be set right. So-and-So told me straight out that I should give up any attempt at becoming a sociologist, while he would be happy to take up my useful ideas in his own works, for which he would amply compensate me. He even recommended that I track down the literature for him, and write up abstracts and preliminary studies that he could then make use of. He hoped to soon secure a professorship, which could essentially be sped up with my assistance. Later, he would make me his private secretary. Before then, he would endeavor to recommend me as a language teacher, while, at the same time, I should try to make it as a freelancer working for journals and newspapers. With some luck, he promised me success with short essays and aphoristic observations, which best suited me. That way, I could at least somehow manage to get along until he could keep me busy as the newly appointed Professor Kauders. When I first told him about Konirsch-Lenz, he turned the tables on me and said that I should have nothing to do with this dabbler but instead concentrate on sociology. When I asked him how he imagined I could do that, he shrugged and said, "That's your problem."

Occasionally, he liked to tell me about his personal friends, but he never introduced me to them. Usually he made it seem as if he had hardly any real friends but, rather, ones that weren't very attractive or, indeed, were repulsive acquaintances with whom he associated only because of his position, though for the most part he didn't deem it proper to put me in contact with them. I wasn't at all sure whether So-and-So was in demand as a socialite, or if he was the one pressing himself on others, though I often heard that he was plenty on the go with others, whereas with me he made it seem as if he was lonelier in this country even than I was. I knew for a fact that Karin, who was lovely and charming in social situations, had many acquaintances and understood people wonderfully, and helped not only her husband but also herself, because more than a year ago she had given up her job as a dental technician, despite Inge's ill-intentioned or outright refusal of support, and had since dedicated herself to sculpture and, along with it, in order to earn money, her work as an illustrator, which would have been impossible without good contacts.

So-and-So tried always to keep this a secret—as well as his social climbing and the increased expenses he and his wife could afford—but he couldn't entirely hide it from me. It was obvious and, therefore, also clear that he kept Karin away from Johanna and me. I had hardly seen her more than four times, for during my rare visits to So-and-So's old apartment, since I didn't yet know the new one, Karin appeared only once. Then she showed up at our wedding in a much too expensive outfit, next to which Johanna's simple lovely dress looked meager. Once we had moved to West Park Row, Karin visited with her husband, but only for a brief hour. I didn't think it out of the realm of possibility that the only reason she did come was to see the wedding pictures in which she appeared, because she asked me beseechingly to ask Otto to make copies of them for her as well. Nonetheless, Johanna thought Karin was nice, and she seemed friendly to me, and was not at all standoffish but visibly at ease with us, though I never thought she would ever be any closer to us than that. She never asked Johanna over, as she'd promised, while So-and-So probably never passed on our invitations to her. We were never invited together to the Kauders' but, rather, I always went alone, though Karin was never at home when I was there.

Once, I couldn't help making note of this and wouldn't let it rest. After So-and-So couldn't avoid explaining the reasons for the friendship's not having developed any further, I was told that in this country it was not unusual for men and women to move in different social circles. Karin was shy about this and wished to wean herself from the behavior of those from the Old Country, so, as someone just arrived from there, I should not be at all surprised that it was not easy for her to be around me. But soon after that I bumped into Karin on the street, and she was the picture of friendliness. Therefore I didn't believe a word So-and-So said. I confronted him about it and was met with evasion. First, Karin was a lady through and through, and second, she held nothing but the greatest respect for me, but the situation was indeed as he had described it to me already. Given this, there was no point in carrying it any further, and so I gave up, for I would have been met with nothing but icy silence.

Thus he succeeded in denying me whenever a personal or professional opportunity sprang up, while he nonetheless tossed me little favors, such as references for my research or helping me to obtain books, in order to try to turn me away from him without my getting upset. It was no longer a friendship at all, as we talked only about incidental matters. What indeed meant something to us, we said nothing about, just as So-and-So had done in the very first days after my arrival, during which I learned the difficult art of keeping quiet, having become smarter about it after making many mistakes. Now I asked him about neither Karin nor Oswald, whom he hardly ever mentioned, nor did I inquire about his work when he didn't talk about it himself, and even more carefully avoided any reference to what I was doing. If I overstepped my bounds in the least, then he pulled himself up as if stricken and looked at me, furious. Why he never stopped visiting me altogether was unclear to me. Perhaps he was moved to do so for similar reasons as Otto, despite the differences in their character and nature.

I could neither renew myself nor feel secure through contact with old or new friends without them feeding upon me, even if they did not intend to. My situation was iffy and also remained so, but the uncertainty of my standing was first made evident through my friends, because they found me ridiculous and did not appreciate the potential within me. That which was questionable about me became all the more questionable. That which was barely contained within itself they tore apart, dissolving it into nothingness until it was unrecognizable, and, fool that I was, for a long time I could not let myself draw near to people, or, better yet, let them draw close to me, without the last wisp of security having been wrested from me and my existence destroyed. However, it was, in fact, this uncertainty that I couldn't come to terms with, and which overexerted my willpower and led to a transformation in my condition. Before the collapse of most of my failed relations, my brief contact with the churlish Konirsch-Lenz finally revealed my outer ambitions in the face of his insanity, and I decided from then on to avoid anything that could possibly cause a person to undermine his own sense of self-worth.

It would have been easier if I had resigned myself to this much earlier, but for too long I lacked the courage, as well as the intelligence, to do so. I had been too enamored of myself—and that is wrong, as long as your inclination is to zealously seek your sense of self-worth among people you either love too little or not at all. That I came to this bit of wisdom by forfeiting my own existence! He who perseveres night and day, who lives and goes on in this way, feels the general misery of every born person infinitely heightened if he—if I—feels within himself the loss of his essence. I had hoped for too much, wanted too much that was not possible. But in my situation there was only one option: to continue on and wait for a moment of grace. Eagerness, vanity, concern for Johanna, worries about money had for so long kept me on the wrong path; I was in a panic, of which only the horribleness of a Konirsh-Lenz was able to cure me. Nonetheless, it was clear that if I let myself be consumed by fear our meager means would soon be entirely exhausted. I saw my wife and children starving, while I stood by without acknowledging or doing anything about it. Something had to happen. Not that I had to submit to the will of my foolish or heartless or two-faced advisers and supposed benefactors—no, not at all. But, still, something had to happen. I had too little faith in my unconquerable powerlessness to feel that I could handle it skillfully. Thus I was three or four steps behind the eight ball, all of which meant that the attainment of a middle-class life was unlikely. That first year was a time full of hopelessness in which, at first, something had been promised, but after that came the time in which I had to realize that a victory amid the storm was forbidden me, after which I struggled to find the right situation for my intellectual pursuits at any price and to get past all impediments.

I whistled louder and now walked much more slowly. Before me was a little park in which I saw a red telephone booth and stopped. With disgust,

I thought of the charlatans who were the cause of my forlorn wanderings, and whom I should call up in order to report the miserable fruits they had brought me. Eberhard S. was probably the most pitiful of all those I had dealt with. A tall fat man with the pale face of a child and a monocle on a little black tether. Eberhard S. now and then gave somewhat public lectures, Otto once having persuaded me to go along with him to hear this man whom he did not know personally but who fascinated him. Eberhard S. spoke on the theme of "The Sorrows and Pleasures of Loneliness," and I got myself involved in the discussion that followed. The lecturer spoke to me afterward, praising my comments, asking for my telephone number, calling two days later, visiting us, and inviting me to call on him. He presented himself as a doctor twice over, the fool presuming to be a medical doctor and a sociologist. He was perhaps a medical doctor, though a terrible one who performed his quackery with questionable cures and surrounded himself with a great hubbub, though he was certainly no sociologist. My first impression of the windbag was indeed bad, nor was Johanna impressed with him, but with a great deal of flattery and promises he lured me into his plan for a psychological-sociological journal, such that I accepted his offer despite all that my previous misadventures should have told me. I was supposed to be the general editor, at first with no salary but with all my expenses covered, but as soon as the journal was launched, which could only be a question of months, I would then be well paid. Eberhard S., who had chosen the name *Eusemia* as a "good sign" for his venture, was the publisher and editor, and wanted a propagator, author, and, especially, a recruiter to bring on talented colleagues. He sent me to printers, to news agents, bookstores, advertising agencies, and to many personalities in order to do something for *Eusemia*, during which I met with nothing but hassle and only rarely got anything worthwhile accomplished. Despite all this, by hook and by crook some issues of the ill-fated journal actually appeared in fitful starts. I could be pleased that only his name was at all involved, while my contributions remained unsigned or carried a pseudonym.

Eusemia was stillborn from the start, and for months I had devoted my working hours and free days and often nights, until I was exhausted by the effort to get the venture off the ground. I didn't receive a single penny for my efforts, and even had to contribute a substantial part of my own expenses to it. When Eberhard S. said one day with careless flippancy, and as a spur to me, that it had finally gone too far, and that I should be publicly acknowledged as the general editor, since sales of a large print run were assured, the next issue, thank God, never made it beyond proofs, because the business was mired in debt. Eberhard S. had not paid the printer for the previous issue, and the printer refused to print the new one without receiving cash payment for it. Nor did any other printer want to take on the job, which brought this senseless venture to an end, myself all the poorer for the sake of such hopes and with any number of essays and book reviews to burn for fuel. Eberhard S. couldn't pay anyone for their articles, and I had to write more than anyone else, while he continued building castles in the air, though very few of the articles were any good—nothing but wordy, pompous gibberish against whose publication I fought, or which I had to revise for content and style. In order to fill the issue, we made use of reprints when they were given to us free.

After the collapse of *Eusemia*, I felt completely lost for the first time and had to keep quiet about my disaster in order not to harm my reputation. I said nothing to anyone in regard to veiled allusions about the mockery of this venture. I told So-and-So a bit more, but as soon as he heard the name Eberhard S. he grew furious. I should have nothing to do with this no-good liar, who was not a credible person, and who years ago had plans for a journal called *Eusemia*, and in the process had pulled the wool over the eyes of many people, including Oswald Birch. So-and-So had given him, in order to support what seemed a worthwhile undertaking, an article to use. To this day, he had never received a response. Supposedly it was meant to serve intellectually starved men over there, who, presumably, lapped up vast amounts of indoctrination, to give them some scholarly and cultural-political content so that they had something to read, so that after having made so many fateful errors they could find their way again. Because of such shady dealings that good man was ruined, nor could he ever again show himself in respectable company.

I was hardly inclined to believe everything So-and-So said, and thus ignored all his warnings, for I only took them as a sign of his jealousy. I made it look as if I was convinced of the truth of his words, said nothing more about the journal, and drifted off into my misery. The concern that

Johanna raised was minimal, and when she saw how I blossomed with enthusiasm for this work she hoped, despite her fears, that it would all come to good. Therefore Johanna went easy on me, and I held her responsible for this after everything went wrong. I was unappeasable and bitter, but she spoke to me sweetly and helped me get through this deep disappointment. That, in the process of this misfortune, I had forfeited any outward chance at security she could not indeed deny, but with her help we were finally able to move on nonetheless.

Then the fourth, most desolate phase of my life in the metropolis began. Prior to this, my health had grown so bad because of the exhausting work I did for *Eusemia;* I became so weak that I would fall asleep at my desk, while at night I could hardly sleep at all. I was much in need of rest and recuperation and agreed with Johanna when she said it could not go on like this any longer. Then Betty came for a visit and was shocked at my condition. She wanted to take me straight back with her to South Wales, but since I couldn't bear the thought of being separated from Johanna, Betty invited both of us. After Johanna made all the necessary arrangements in order to be able to continue with the work she had taken in while we were away, we left for two months. By the time we returned I was feeling much better, yet I was still so weak that I would get exhausted after working for just a brief while. I have never produced so little work as I did in those days. I grew more and more discouraged, and ever more cranky, getting angry without the slightest reason and burdening Johanna, whom I, weak and powerless, would remind, with the tormenting passion of my misery at the most inappropriate moment, of what I had said to her about my faults and failings before we were married. Horribly and to my own detriment, I portrayed my worthlessness in such a repellent manner that I succeeded in shaking her equilibrium. It was certainly bad enough that I could provide her with no means of support, but now I had to rob her of her own self-confidence, myself the one who would have been to blame if she had lost faith in me. Yet she didn't lose faith, but only became uncertain, and so it was understandable that Konirsch-Lenz would have gained a bit of influence over her if he had come at her with all his guns blazing.

But now I was done with this benefactor, we having split in anger, but I was free and felt better as a result. I could hope once again. My unease had still not dissipated, but once again I felt satisfied. There was nothing more that held me and reined me in, and that allowed me to breathe easier. Indeed, I had no idea what tomorrow would bring, and yet my worries eased, it seeming to me that things could not get any worse but only better. Someone carrying a heavy bag drew away from the telephone booth across from me and hurried off with long, quick strides. I then stepped in and called home, which was not my custom. No doubt Johanna would be surprised to hear the phone ring. I had hardly said hello to her, speaking to her as cheerfully as my phone manners allowed, but actually quite cheerfully, since all my sadness had suddenly lost its grip on me, when Johanna beat me to the punch before I could explain anything.

"You had a falling out with Konirsch-Lenz. That's why you're calling me, right?"

Greatly relieved, I said it was so and was amazed that she knew it already.

"I thought so this morning, right after you left the house. You were acting so strange that all I could expect was either complete success, though I doubted that, or a complete disaster. It was all clear to me already; there's no need to explain. Don't worry about it, sweetheart! Everything will be all right."

Johanna's voice sounded confident and happy, such that my last worries left me.

"Then I want to come straight home if it's okay with you. I was worried that you would be upset. Now I'm happy."

"Come home, come home! There's also a letter here. A small contract for a book review, and the book is there as well."

"That's great."

"You see. Already things are better. We don't need any Konirsch-Lenz, nor anyone else. He actually called an hour ago. His anger seethed from every word he said. Still, he kept sputtering his apologies, saying you are the first person he's never been able to help get on the right track. He likes you so much, but it's hopeless with you, because you're stubborn, beating your head against the wall, he said, and I laughed. Then he wished me well, but that I should understand, there was nothing he could do, he was throwing in the towel. I shouldn't be angry with him. He had meant well."

"And what did you say?"

"Nothing at all. Or there was something. I said to him that it didn't matter, I wasn't angry at him, and only wanted to thank him."

"No! You told him that!"

"Yes, that's what I said."

"You shouldn't have."

"Oh, it's all right! There's no coming to terms with such people. You thank them politely and then move on."

Johanna laughed into the telephone, the receiver vibrating and humming at my ear, such that I had to hold it away. I quickly said that everything would be all right, and I'd be right home. Then we said goodbye, our spirits almost too high. When I left the phone booth, however, everything changed, all my cheerfulness draining from me, gloom encompassing me. I had to acknowledge that I was a failure. I was indeed done with my last and most overzealous benefactor, saying to myself with a smile that the wallpaper had fallen from my eyes, though the backlash from this falling out and the effect upon my circumstances were not to be denied. The fiery drive that had served my youth also made it possible for me to get through the bad years, it having continued on into my first years in the metropolis, while even in my efforts for *Eusemia* it was still evident. This drive had always been my savior, the strength that led me on. But now there was nothing left of this drive, I had nothing more, a hollowed-out existence—indeed, no existence whatsoever.

If my attitude was negative, I thought, and if I was out of good ideas, then my sense of dissolution was understandable. But that was not at all how I felt! I still felt fired with the will to go on, to do something in the service of my fellow men through an honest effort, something meaningful, something that would legitimate me. I was a mirror for much of what I had experienced in these times, myself an individual eye that had taken it all in, and to have overcome it all was a worthy endeavor! Why should I be a failure? Only because I cannot exist, since I am an expression of something, not something in my own right? Then I would have to get used to it, an obedient Adam, here I stand, not I, and yet, one, it, a name, it not being easy to say what. An existence, that I don't have, but, nonetheless, existence in itself is a powerful inner resource. I had come through; now I had to move ahead. I had been beaten, but I was not out. Something remained, something pushed on inscrutably, that inner resource. There was nothing more I could undertake, but I could just be. Perhaps I was the realization of a supernatural resolution: not an I, yet I; an I transformed by other graces.

I was shocked that I had not prayed for a long time. I needed to pray, not for something but to something. Nor even that; I just needed to pray. Could I gather myself together enough to do so? I looked down at myself and saw myself standing there remote and strange, untenable except through grace. Was I anything but borrowed grace, and thus not myself but some kind of grace somewhere, myself one who said to grace, "I am myself all the same, and yet again I am not." An idle game. I was surprised at what philosophy had previously proposed, pronouncements about the self in particular, about the personal, the triumphant I—that false equation: I think, I am. If I am, then I do not think. I am or I think. I am or am not, whether I think or not. I am, therefore I think, therefore I also think; but I am not, because I think. What pride, what presumption, what incredible defiance, from someone who had stood up against the universe in order to exist, standing there after having been catapulted from Paradise like Adam, onto the abandoned field, precipitously, as if thrown from a tower, from the Tower of Babel, its audacious walls standing against heaven and earth. That I could not do and did not want to do any longer, and yet I did not want to be pitiful, not disobedient, not without humility, repentance, sacrifice, and prayer, not without empathy, not without knowledge of my guilt and a conscience, not to alienate Being and betray it, only because there is no known Being, no certain existence that I want to embrace or possess.

I admit, such perverse thinkers were the first to deny society, their protests having denied those forms into which human existence had packed itself and secured itself among many races. Now things were different; society no longer wanted any thinkers who only wanted to serve it without becoming its slave or just preach about destruction in a seductive manner. Don't exist! So one was told aloud and secretly whispered to: Don't exist! Yet you didn't want to hear it, and so you went to the dogs nevertheless! What could one possibly say at that point? Perhaps this: Always be something less than what you are allowed to be in a pinch. Even then, it can soon occur that the next time you find yourself among your fellow men the most basic consideration will not be granted you.

"You're still here? How strange! I thought they did with you as they did with your father and hauled you away. The main thing is that it will still happen. Which is fine with me."

You couldn't say anything in response, such as, "Yes, I'm alive, but I feel terrible," for otherwise you would be severely reprimanded.

"What do you mean, 'terrible'? You don't make any sense! If you are alive, then things are good. You're not allowed to complain."

Basically, I had to agree. That someone could rise above one's lot in life seemed a foolish idea. Each gets what he gets; that I had to accept. Perhaps I was myself a miserable bit of nothing, and perhaps that was why someone had decided to shove me to the side in order to show me what I was. If that was so, then even my dissatisfaction could be thought of as a splendid piece of luck; all my disasters, all my failures had nonetheless benefited me. Thus I had to maintain a condition of continued waiting, whose intensity could not lag, the hours flowing into yet more hours, the matter not real in itself but, instead, an artificial structure through which the most difficult thing of all, order, could be pursued. Thus I devoted myself to good fortune that never arrived but remained a possibility and which could someday occur for humanity, as well as for me, in unknown ways. The kingdom that we seek has existed from the very beginning, but to bring it about was certainly a tall order, though not one that was in our control.

"You're one of the many who wish to exist. You have eaten of the fruit; that cannot be undone. Your mistake is this: that you wish to exist; what's more, that you want to have done so from the very beginning and forever-more. You concern yourself much too intensely with that. Your will to be is inexhaustible."

This I had to entirely agree with, for that was the only way I could find the strength within me to make my own determination. The wall rose up before me, though it couldn't do so forever, yet I didn't have the patience to wait to see what would happen with me. That's why I decided to wake up and walk alongside the empty wall, feeling and testing my way. Where it would lead me I really had no idea. It seemed much longer than ever before. I was surprised at how long it was.

"If we follow the length of this wall," I said, "we'll soon be outside again."

"It's pretty dark."

"It is. We know why. A new light will be installed soon."

"That has to happen. One can break a leg."

"I already told you, close your eyes for a little while so you can get used to the darkness."

Then we were in the little foyer again, the tour over. Here the daylight pressed in, and the two of them breathed easier, having been released from the darkness. I opened the door to see them out, then I remembered that they had not yet signed the visitors' book. I took out my fountain pen and unscrewed its cap.

"Please, sign our book!"

My pen was set aside and a much more beautiful one appeared, heavy, marvelous, gleaming gold. The man held it out to the lady. The pen was too much for her to handle and was hardly right for her shaky little handwriting. Then the man took hold of it, his strokes powerful, the sharp, angled lines of confident, knowing success. There, next to the date, stood "Mitzi Lever, Johannesburg; Guido Lever, Johannesburg." Frau Lever's signature was already dry, but Herr Lever's name still looked wet. I took a piece of blotting paper and laid it on top and carefully dabbed at it.

"There we are, etched in eternal memory, Mitzi. Just think, isn't that marvelous?"

"You're right. It's astonishing to think that I am now part of history. And look at all the other signatures! What do you think, Herr Doctor? How many people will write down their names here for all time in the next hundred years?"

"The Herr Doctor cannot know the answer to that. How can you ask such a dumb question?"

"The good madam was only wondering."

I said that quietly, and was rewarded with a flattering glance. Then I saw the guests out to the street and carefully closed up the hermitage. We slowly walked back to our administration building in the former school. Herr Lever looked to be totally inspired, and was very thankful, offering me a huge tip and not pleased when I declined it because of what he took to be regulations. I suggested that he could make a donation to the museum, if he wished to.

"To the museum! Why not! But you, Herr Doctor, you could surely use something and are certainly owed a great deal. It would be my pleasure. South Africa is a land of gold, and I have always earned plenty."

"Yes, so my husband has. He's very capable. And generous as well."

Nonetheless, there was no changing my mind and I only let him give me a pack of American cigarettes.

"You have to take these, Herr Doctor! Otherwise I'll be upset. You've done up everything so splendidly. There was nothing needed for the cemetery. That's old and famous. But the museum—it's really splendid. A site well worth seeing, and without compare. I will talk about it throughout the world, and especially at home. I'll send people to you. Hopefully, it will soon officially be open, a catalog will be printed—a book with pictures of the most important treasures. How lively it all is. How exciting! Aren't you excited, Mitzi?"

"And how!"

"Tell me, Herr Doctor, a question: are you insured?"

"You mean the museum?"

"Yes, the museum."

"Of course."

"Against anything? Theft, fire, water, structural damages, everything? And for how much, if I may ask?"

"That I don't know."

"Such a museum has to be well insured. You must believe me. The things it has are irreplaceable. If something happened, you have to at least be well insured."

"And you think it helps to be so?"

"Yes, just think about the material losses!"

At that I said nothing more and let the couple talk between themselves until we reached the door of the school. I waited to say goodbye to the Levers, which after they completed the tour happened at this point. Whether because of shyness, sentimentality, or politeness, the custom had always been that our visitors only rarely left from the retreat but instead always accompanied us back to the school, even when they had no further questions and only walked along quietly beside us. Only here, once you informed them that the visit was over, would they slowly say goodbye, which normally took a little while as they talked about this or that, without aim or purpose, while it lay on us to bring these pointless exchanges to an end. It almost never happened that they wanted to come into the school, because inquiries about our mounting stacks of goods or those that could be answered by our administrative offices were usually already taken care of during the tour. But the Levers had something else in mind, or perhaps not, for they didn't seem to expect anything more, but just wanted to keep talking with me and wouldn't let me get back to my work.

"I have to go now. I have a lot to do."

"Look, Herr Doctor, we're countrymen of yours. Tell us, what did your father do?"

"He sold men's clothing."

"Men's clothing? And your name is Landau?"

"Yes."

"Landau's Haberdashery? Mitzi, do you remember?"

"Yes, that's where you bought that tie, and some shirts? You also have a pair of pants from there. Very good ones."

"Yes. And on them it says HAL, a good brand. I never knew what that meant. Can you tell me?"

"The first letters of 'Haberdashery Albert Landau.'"

Herr Lever slapped his forehead.

"What an idiot I am! So simple, and yet I could never figure it out."

"Now you know," said Mitzi. "And tell me, Herr Doctor, wasn't it next to the fruit seller? What was his name?"

"Kutschera."

"That's right. Kutschera. Is he still there?"

"Yes, he still sells fruit."

"I must have a look. I've been away so long, the war and everything, and yet the good Kutschera is still there with his apples and oranges!"

"And the clothing store?" Herr Lever wanted to know. "Can I still buy something there? You must indeed have gotten the store back."

"No, you can't buy anything there."

"That's too bad. Is it closed?"

"Yes. For good."

"And your father, if I may ask?"

I didn't answer right away.

"Oh, I see!" said Herr Lever apologetically. "I'm so sorry. But it really was a first-rate store. You must at least have gotten permanent compensation."

I smiled.

"Didn't you get anything? I can't believe it. But you will, won't you?"

"No, I won't, Herr Lever, nothing at all. I don't want to, and I won't, and it won't happen."

"You don't want to? It's within your rights, and those you have to defend. Those rascals shouldn't get it. You need to pursue it!"

"I won't. It won't come to anything. Senseless, it's all senseless."

"An actual doctor, Mitzi! Just listen to yourself—you don't have the wiles of a salesman! But you owe it to your father and to yourself."

"I don't believe that. And, what's more, I won't get anything. The store was liquidated long ago. People chase after their lost property like fools, but, given the way the winds blow here, hardly anyone has gotten anything back."

"What are you saying? Do you hear this, Mitzi? Many say the same thing here. But the reason I came here was to sort out my affairs."

"I wish you good luck with that."

"Really! Do you think there's no chance of success? That would be awful!"

"Success or no success, forgive me, neither matters to me, Herr Lever. I already told you, I wish you all good luck. I just want to get away from here."

"Mitzi, he wants to leave! Just when everything is turning good again!"

I smiled.

"You're a doomsayer, Herr Doctor. You have to live again. You must. Where can you go? I'm looking for my things. Also for my brother, who, unfortunately, stayed here."

"I see, your brother," I said thoughtlessly, and again, "Good luck, Herr Lever!"

Then I wanted to hurry off, but the couple wouldn't let me go.

"It's so interesting to talk to you. It gives me a chill, but it's really interesting. Maybe you knew someone from my family."

"That could well be."

"It's likely, for your father certainly knew our family. I used to be called Lebenhart."

"Eugene Lebenhart. Ufergasse." I said it without thinking.

Herr Lever grabbed hold of my wrist hard.

"That was my brother! Mitzi, just think. Eugene—the Herr Doctor knew Eugene!"

"Just imagine. How strange, Guido. One should always speak up, that's what I say. I always think so."

"I'm sorry, good people, I did not know Eugene Lebenhart."

"Then how do you know his address?" they both said simultaneously.

I had put my foot in my mouth and saw both of the portraits before me that Herr Schnabelberger had shown me in the first days of my employment at the museum. Against the wishes of Frau Dr. Kulka, I would have to quickly explain that I had handled them. She didn't want anyone to be made aware of objects that rightfully belonged to them, and I had no right whatsoever to make an exception for Herr and Frau Lever. But I had already given myself away, and what did I care what Frau Dr. Kulka thought?

"The address? I just thought of it."

"No, don't give us the runaround," Frau Lever said impatiently.

"We have two paintings upstairs that belong to the Lebenharts of Ufergasse."

"Two paintings? My brother owned valuable paintings; he collected Dutch works. Still-lifes. They belong to me!"

"Valuable, that I don't know," I observed coldly. "And nothing Dutch. But we have two paintings."

"My husband said to you that they were very valuable paintings, old valuable originals. My brother was a connoisseur; he would have understood what he had."

"Our two paintings are not valuable," I said emphatically. "But they are originals, even if not that old and probably painted from photographs. They are of an old couple."

"Mitzi, that must be my grandparents. I begged Eugene to give them to me before we left, but he didn't want to. That's what should have happened! How did you get hold of the paintings?"

"There are many paintings that have come to us, Herr Lever. Especially paintings of family members. We have a huge number of them."

"No, I have to see them."

So I invited the couple in and to come along with me, though I said that it would be up to Herr Schnabelberger whether they could see the paintings or not.

"It would probably be better," called out Frau Lever, "if my husband had a lawyer with him! My brother-in-law had no children, nor are there any other siblings. We are the only heirs."

Herr Geschlieder said to me as we passed on the steps that it was a madhouse there today. Upstairs, I knocked on Herr Schnabelberger's door. He sat at his desk and had a tasteful woman dressed in black with white hair as a visitor. He seemed happy to see me and called out, "It's good that you've finally come!" When he noticed that the Levers were with me, and I explained that the couple still had a question, he clasped his hands together, mumbled that this was too much for him to handle, and whether it couldn't wait. I turned around with a questioning look, but the two of them stood there defiant. After a brief consultation with his wife, Herr Lever said that, since they were already here, they preferred to wait, if it wouldn't take too long. Schnabelberger mounted a mild protest, but finally, once the great distance traveled from Johannesburg was explained to him, he gave in and arranged for me to come straight to him as soon as I had accompanied the visitors to the main office. There was about to be a meeting there of all the staff, someone having appeared from the trustees in order to discuss what to do with a large load of prayer books and devotionals and how best to transport them. Several voices said right off that it wasn't possible to let the guests wait here during the meeting, but the conference was almost over, and then they could come in. The couple could stand in the hall for a little while if they couldn't go to Herr Schnabelberger. I couldn't allow the Levers to wait in the hall, nor did I want to take them up two floors to my office. Frau Dr. Kulka would surely not be very pleased if I dumped them on her, nor would the librarian, who didn't want any visitors. So there was nothing to do but ask Herr Schnabelberger whether he would allow Herr and Frau Lever to wait in his room.

"It doesn't matter to me," he said, sighing. "Lead them both in."

So that's what happened. The couple were set down in a corner, where they talked between themselves excitedly, while I was introduced to a lady, a Mrs. Mackintosh, she being the wife of a high functionary at the British Embassy.

"Well, then, my dear lady, here is Herr Dr. Landau, whom you wished to see!"

"Pleased to meet you, Doctor."

"Please, just tell him what you need!"

"If I can be of service," I added politely.

"Well, you don't know me. Someone recommended you to me."

"Yes, I see."

"Through the intercession of friends, I have learned that I can turn to you."

"I'll do what I can."

"A Dr. Kauders said to my friends that you could tell me something. That you could probably be of help to me."

"But what is the matter about, madam?"

"I've already explained everything to Herr Schnabelberger, but he insists that I must be mistaken, that I am in a museum, and not in the right place."

"Then there's nothing more I can do, madam. Herr Schnabelberger is competent when it comes to any such question, for he is my boss."

"Good that you say that, Herr Doctor. Mrs. Mackintosh would not believe me at all. But just tell him, madam!"

"My husband and I, we want to furnish an apartment tastefully, and for that we need some lovely things. We heard that you have a warehouse full of antique furniture, isn't that so?"

"We have some furniture, madam," I admitted. "But not much."

"It doesn't need to be much, Dr. Landau, just good."

"Madam, Herr Schnabelberger has already explained to you. You are at a museum, not in the place you want. You must have been falsely informed."

"Impossible, my good sir. I am never falsely informed! Someone told me that, if you're looking for antique furniture, well, then, come to this museum, where fine furniture can be bought. I love continental Biedermeier."

"Madam, you have been informed completely wrong!"

Herr Schnabelberger drummed two fingers in satisfaction on his desk when I said that.

"We'll pay for it immediately," said the lady, not backing down. "It just can't be too expensive."

"We don't sell anything," I replied firmly. "We are a museum."

"Right, a museum, I see. But you don't need it all, do you?"

I looked at Herr Schnabelberger to see whether he wished to answer for me, but, annoyingly, he sat there amused and didn't stir at all.

"You're mistaken!" I responded forcefully.

"That's right," confirmed Schnabelberger as well.

"But it can't be; I was reliably informed. Why are you hesitating? Please, do show me what you can spare! From the dead, there must be a lot!"

As if at an agreed-upon sign, Schnabelberger and I stood up.

"Look, madam, I've already told you—"

"Is that your last word, gentlemen? Are you sure?"

"Sure, madam, entirely sure, dead sure—we could not be more sure!" I said, my voice both high and sharp.

"Well, if you don't help . . ."

Mrs. Mackintosh also stood up, a tall gaunt figure, and proudly shook her head in anger. Regally, she quickly took leave of us and didn't spare us another look. We accompanied her to the door, but not a step farther. Herr Schnabelberger closed the door emphatically but reasonably behind her, then shot me a look that might have been reproachful, relieved, or amused—I couldn't tell—though probably a mixture of all three, after which he turned to Herr and Frau Lever.

"Were you pleased with the hermitage? I'm so glad. Herr Dr. Landau does a good tour."

The two said something polite in response, and said they wished to make a small donation to the museum, though they couldn't keep from sharing the reason they had come to the museum, at which they began to talk so excitedly that it was hard to understand much of what they were saying, such that Herr Schnabelberger wasn't clear on what the visitors wanted. Therefore I intervened.

"In the course of conversation, I learned that Herr Lever used to be called Lebenhart and had a brother here in the city. It then came out while we talked about our stock of family portraits, one thing led to another, and finally we reckoned that there could be one or two portraits stored here with us that would interest Herr Lever. He would like to know if there is anything that can be done about that."

Herr Schnabelberger scratched his head while thinking.

"That's not at all as easy a thing to do as you present. We have thousands of paintings, and can't just go rummaging through the entire inventory and find that the things you are looking for simply aren't here. Therefore you need to give us more precise details."

"It's two paintings."

Herr Lever indicated with his hands how big they were.

"They are my grandparents. The paintings belonged to my brother, Eugene Lebenhart, who lived on Ufergasse. That's where my brother lived. They are my grandparents, as I already told you. The man has a beard, and the woman in the companion piece is his wife."

"Well, if Herr Dr. Landau wants to make the effort to look through the catalog to see if we have anything like that, it's fine with me. But most of the paintings are anonymous. We rarely have any indications that lead us to firmly attribute names to those depicted. Usually the catalog is of little help, and we can only do something when you can give us photos or precise descriptions."

With that, Herr Schnabelberger extended his hand to the visitors and said goodbye. They wanted to say something more, but I quickly led them out and accompanied them to the main office, where the staff meeting had since come to an end. Everything was a mess, with crumpled papers and cigarette butts on the floor, and the air stuffy. I opened the window and introduced the visitors to all of the gathered employees. Herr and Frau Lever sat down in chairs they pulled up and whispered to each other while I leafed through the catalog without really knowing what I was doing, though I made it look as if I did, while after a few minutes I pulled out the cards with the details about the Lebenhart portraits.

"This must be them!"

Thus I called out and brought them the cards. Herr Lever ripped them from my hand, put on his glasses, and quietly read aloud the description, his wife nodding in agreement.

"You are fantastic, Herr Doctor!" he said, praising me. "The way you have everything in order and can find it. Those are my grandparents. Every detail is correct. It's really an art to describe all the paintings so precisely."

Herr Lever was excited and wiped at his face with his handkerchief.

"Would it be possible to see the paintings?"

"But with the greatest pleasure. If you good people would just wait here."

I asked Herr Woticky to accompany me; he was often happy to help out. While he got the storage-room key from Herr Geschlieder, I went to get my work coat. Then we opened the storeroom and didn't have to look for long, for the paintings were in the spot listed on the cards. The paintings were gray with dust and had to be wiped off first by Woticky before the bearded man and his wife were clearly visible. As we returned to the main office with the paintings and placed them on the floor and leaned them up against us, both of the Levers jumped up and looked at them.

"By gosh, look, Mitzi. There they are, as if they lived and breathed!"

Herr Lever touched the canvas of the grandmother's portrait in several places and was deeply moved.

"But they're indeed a bit damaged!" said Mitzi. "They've not been handled at all well."

"You should still feel good!" said Woticky. "You can see everything. We have paintings in which you can hardly make out anything."

I also praised the condition of the paintings, but Frau Lever felt differently and criticized their condition like a diligent housewife.

"One can certainly have it restored," her husband assured her. "A couple of scratches, and the colors have grown darker. The frame can be re-gilded. That can't cost the world."

"That certainly won't be expensive!" agreed Woticky. "We have plenty of others of cadets with big holes in them and covered in mold. As for these? Actually, a treasure! It won't take much restoration at all."

Before I could stop Woticky, he had a rag in his hand onto which he spit before bending over the painting from behind to wipe the face of the grandmother with quick movements.

"There you are!" he called out triumphantly. "Didn't I tell you so? The nose is already much brighter and shines."

I criticized such improper methods, for the painting was indeed my responsibility, but I had to admit the spot he'd cleaned looked freshly painted and much brighter than the cheeks, chin, and forehead, which Woticky had hardly touched. Frau Lever, who had looked on at the cleaning with doubtful horror, tossed Woticky a grateful look.

"So the paintings are just a bit neglected, Guido. It's just what I thought. You only have to rub them with some soft bread, which is the cheapest and the best way, and they'll be fine. But to let them get so dirty, that's a sin! Don't you have a cleaning woman here?"

"Mitzi, that's not our business. But about the dirt, you're right. I have to agree. I'd really prefer to pack them up right away and take them with me in a taxi. What can be done, Herr Doctor?"

"It's not so simple," I cautioned, and explained the first steps required for approval of such a release.

The visitors were outraged and held their heads in astonishment. They couldn't understand why inherited property that had not been freely given to the museum, which itself probably had not considered it all that valuable, couldn't be taken away without anything further needing to occur. All the employees in the main office nodded to the couple and assured them that this, indeed, was the case now, though I felt it necessary to quickly end the visit. Therefore I saw the visitors to the door and said that Herr Schnabelberger was in charge of such specific inquiries, though I asked Woticky to help me bring along the paintings to Herr Schnabelberger. Schnabelberger was anything but pleased that I had brought Herr and Frau Lever to him again, as well as having schlepped the rediscovered grandparents along with me. Woticky shoved the paintings nearer to Schnabelberger's desk and propped them up with two chairs from behind. Then he thought his duty done and left the office with a little pack of cigarettes that Herr Lever had quickly handed him. Herr Schnabelberger shifted his gaze between the paintings and the visitors.

"Well, then, what can I do for you?" he asked awkwardly.

"Those are my grandparents. The portraits belong to me."

"I certainly believe you, but everything is a bit different than you would like to think. You must file an application with the Office for the Recovery of Enemy Goods in the Finance Ministry, with a notarization of your clearance by the state police and the attestation of the Bureau of Restitution in the Office of Social Welfare, as well as fill out a property form. Everything will be checked and reviewed by the Office for the Recovery of Enemy Goods. If there are no concerns, apply for a final decision with the trustees of our museum in order to see if we have any art historical or historical objections to raise against restitution. I would think it likely that no objections will be raised by us. But, as I said, I can't be sure, for there are many things to consider. The paintings will not be released if they are valuable."

"Let me say," called out Herr Lever, "they are not for you! I know that already, for otherwise you would have hung them in the hermitage. But they are valuable to me!"

"Be happy that we don't think them valuable. Junk and worthless stuff we give away quickest of all. But I don't know. Perhaps we won't agree, and then you have no chance."

"Unheard of! And what, then, can I do?"

"That's quite simple, then you can apply for compensation."

"But the paintings! I want the paintings, not compensation!"

"Don't be unreasonable. It's not at all certain that you'll even get compensation. It is seldom agreed to, and who knows when it's ever paid out."

"The paintings! I'm not talking about compensation!"

"If your complaint is acknowledged, but the paintings are not returned, they will be photographed for you at the museum's cost. If you are turned down, we'll still work with you and let you have the paintings photographed at your cost, if you wish. Copies can also be made at your cost."

"Am I in a den of thieves or a madhouse?" exclaimed Herr Lever.

He couldn't understand Schnabelberger's suggestions, for they seemed to him unbelievable, Frau Lever also having gotten worked up over them. The two of them were indignant as they passed on somewhat unflattering words about what they thought to be the scandalous conditions in the museum, as well as commenting on the appearance of Mrs. Mackintosh.

"I believe, my good people," Schnabelberger interrupted, "the situation with the lady has nothing to do with this. I handled her along with Herr Dr. Landau, as she deserved, even though her husband is a big shot in the embassy and also in England and is supposed to be a famous critic and writer. Let's please concentrate on your situation, for we must soon close."

"Well, then, as for the Office for Enemy Goods . . . Or what's that place called?" Herr Lever began.

"The Office for the Recovery of Enemy Goods," offered Herr Schnabelberger.

"Well, I'll go there straight off. Can you give me the address?"

"But of course, my pleasure."

Herr Schnabelberger wrote out the address on a sheet with a pencil and handed it to Herr Lever.

"How long do you think it will take for such an inquiry to be answered?"

Herr Schnabelberger shrugged. "That's hard to say. Perhaps a year."

"What, a year!"

"They have a lot of inquiries to deal with there. If it goes quickly, it still might take nine months."

"By then we'll be back in Johannesburg again. We want to stay no more than a month."

Herr Schnabelberger said that he fully understood and advised turning the case over to a good lawyer, which is what he would recommend anyway, since paintings could not be taken out of the country without permission.

"Is there no justice at work in this country! It's simply outrageous! How much everything has changed here!"

"That's right, Guido, that's what I warned you about. Without a lawyer, nothing happens. You'll have to get one!"

"They're crooks, Mitzi, but what can I do? Could you be so good as to recommend one? A specialist for the restoration of property?"

"Dr. Blecha!" I blurted out. "He can do it."

"Really. Is he your lawyer?"

"No, I don't have one. He represents a friend."

"Guido, take down the address!"

Quickly I wrote it down on Herr Lever's sheet, on which the address for the Office for the Recovery of Enemy Goods was written. Now the South African had had enough and got up.

"Come, Mitzi! Those paintings hung for decades on the wall of my parents' apartment, and then Eugene had them on the wall of his salon."

He tenderly stroked the edges of the wounded frames.

"Gentlemen, no offense, but I have to say, it's a scandal. To the devil with you!"

His wife had also stood up. Herr Schnabelberger and I accompanied the incensed couple for a few steps. At the door, the Johannesburgers departed from the chief without saying a word, as he waved to me to walk the visitors to the stairs. Outside, Herr Lever turned to me, incensed.

"I won't give anything to this museum! Don't even ask me! Let's just call that justice!"

I didn't say anything in return, but I didn't turn back from the stairs as I had intended to but accompanied the couple down the stairway. Herr Lever didn't seem at all interested anymore, but his wife still paid careful attention to the paintings on the walls.

"Herr Doctor, are all of them stolen?" she asked bitterly.

To that I didn't say anything, either. Herr Geschlieder heard us and came out of his custodian's apartment. I was pleased to turn the couple over to him.

"Please, could you see these good people out?"

I excused myself and wished them a pleasant stay in their old hometown. Frau Lever had already turned away from me, but her husband stood there for a moment and looked at me gravely while quietly shaking his head.

"The city of a hundred golden towers—that's what we learned as children. It seems to me that nothing goes the way it should here anymore. Everything has changed."

"You could be right."

He reached out his hand to me.

"So, you say Dr. Blecha?"

"You can give him a try."

Herr Lever followed after his wife. I had spent over two hours with the South Africans, as well as with Mrs. Mackintosh. I had no desire to work anymore that day, for Anna had said she wanted to see me that night. We had only seen each other in passing since our journey to the mountain woods, which had happened more than two weeks earlier. She would be picking me up at the museum in less than an hour. I was pleased about that, and therefore had no desire to start in on something else. Slowly I climbed the three floors, cleared my desk, and opened the large cabinet stuffed from top to bottom with retrieved items. There was a lovely little dark-red leather purse that I had thought of; I wanted to take it with me and surprise Anna. I rarely opened the cabinet, because I hated cramming things into it, but I tried to think just what I would have to latch on to in order to pull out the little purse. Yet I was mistaken, for I couldn't find it. I would have given up the search if I weren't already bent on it. So I had to take a bunch of things out of the cabinet which I laid on a chair or spread out before me on the floor. The place looked like a junk shop; a painted porcelain vase slipped from my hands and broke into pieces, which I quickly swept up and dumped into the wastebasket. But my efforts were met with success, for finally I had the purse. I was in the process of putting everything back in order when there was a light knock on the door and, before I could say anything, Frau Dr. Kulka was standing next to me. She noticed the embarrassing mess around me with pleasure.

"So this is your work here!" she said, mocking me.

"I was looking for something, madam."

"Listen, Dr. Landau, let me be clear. Despite this strange business, I have no doubt of your diligence. I know what you have done for us. I also know that your nerves have suffered through much more than we have. But what goes too far goes too far. What is all of this stuff here?"

"Private things. They're not mine. I was given them, whether I wanted them or not. Wherever I went, I had to take them. Eventually I stopped picking up anything, and I got rid of some things in between."

"And all of it was brought here, right? In essence, a nice little private Landau Museum of Family Mementos."

"Please, don't say that so reproachfully. It's not at all true."

"Is that true? Why did you schlepp all this stuff here? You didn't ask anyone for permission and just stashed it all away here. That's not at all permissible. Nowhere in any museum would that be tolerated."

"Ah, madam, there's a lot that goes on here that would be unthinkable in any museum in the world. This stuff isn't in anyone's way, and I don't know what else to do with it."

"You have to get these things out of the museum! How could you think of bringing it all here!"

"I'm slowly getting rid of it. I don't have room for it anywhere else. I'm sorting through the things. Though I never do it during working hours. Today is an exception, because I was looking for something. This little purse! I wanted to give it to someone."

"I don't care what you do during working hours. We only care that you get your work done, not when you do it, though I would recommend that you stick to regular hours. But that's not what I want to talk about, but rather this stuff here. We can't have this kind of private museum. There's no justification for it."

As Frau Dr. Kulka lectured me, I slowly began to gather up the things around me and put them back in the cabinet.

"I won't bring anything more. It's already been at least five months since I brought anything."

"Really?"

"Yes. Why don't you believe me? I long ago stopped wanting to hear about or see any of this. You needn't have any worries."

"What's here has to go!"

"But of course. It won't be here forever."

"Will it soon disappear?"

"As soon as possible. But please be patient. It's difficult to get rid of these things. There's always something. Whether it be finding someplace to get rid of the stuff or to store it."

"When will that happen?"

In the meantime, I had put back almost everything. What still lay on the floor I casually kicked to the side. Then I closed the cabinet.

"Please, madam, don't pressure me."

"I don't mean to, but there needs to be order. It all has to be gone within a month or two."

"Don't torment me! Everything will eventually be taken care of, then one day I'll leave and you'll be rid of me."

"Do you want to leave?"

"I've wanted to for a long time, but whether or not I can I don't know."

"Completely gone. You mean leave the museum?"

"If there's an opportunity to travel abroad, I must, unfortunately, leave the museum indeed."

"You can't be serious!"

"There's no sense in talking about it, for there's no way I can leave."

"Where do you want to go?"

"Well, anywhere. At least for a while."

"For a while, that's not a bad idea. We can talk about that. Let me think if I can help you or not. An exchange would work quite well for you, and if we can spare someone here who would represent us well abroad, I'll indeed appeal to the trustees on your behalf, if you can put together practical suggestions."

"Thank you so much."

"But to leave for good, that's another story. I can't go along with that. People are leaving the country as if the earth under their feet were on fire. I don't understand why. To persevere, see it through, rebuild—that's a slogan I can support!"

I had nothing to say in response and closed the cabinet. I wrapped the purse in tissue paper and was glad that Frau Dr. Kulka no longer said anything about my things. She observed what I was doing, and I had the feeling the unpleasant encounter was not yet finished.

"I'm sorry to tell you that anything you take out of the museum you have to show to Herr Geschlieder. That's not out of distrust of you but for your own good. Just think what people might say if they saw heaps of things being schlepped out of the museum. They would talk about you, but also about us. In addition, it will create bad blood among the employees. If you show what it is you're taking out, then you and everyone else are covered."

As shameful as it was, I had to agree and submit myself to such surveillance. Herr Geschlieder wouldn't even bother glancing at my bag, but instead just smiled and nodded at me.

"There's something else I have to say to you, Dr. Landau. And that is much more critical. This is yet another instance that casts a disturbing light on your employment at the museum. That can't continue. Do you understand me? You have to give me your word of honor that such a breach of trust will not occur again. Otherwise, to my great regret, I will have to take matters in hand and bring the issue before the board."

I had no idea just what else I had done wrong, though my legs grew weak and I had to sit down on a nearby chair. My position at the museum had been difficult from the beginning, and I had exacerbated it, but personally I got along well with everyone there, many liked me, most likely even Schnabelberger, while even with Frau Dr. Kulka I had always avoided any serious confrontation. I had given my best to the museum and was not aware of any great problem with my work, and wasn't aware of having made even the slightest mistake. What, then, was the problem? Why did this feeling of doom press upon me?

"I don't understand, madam. Do you just want to get rid of me?"

"Don't talk nonsense, and just try to finally have a positive relationship with life and the museum!"

"To life? I don't see how that has anything to do with it. I do what I can. The museum has no reason to complain. Or are you talking about my relationship to the paintings? As patients, as invalids and such? We already talked about that and got past it. I have kept to everything that we agreed to."

"No, that's not it."

"Well, then, what is it? Why don't you tell me? Do you just want to get rid of me?"

"How stupid do you think I am, Doctor?"

"I'm not accusing you of anything, madam! It's all so complicated, and you shouldn't confuse me even further. I suffer, but I'm used to it. Oh, these times. You don't know what it's like. You have your husband and your children, and a nice apartment. You are secure. For you everything is pretty much assured, and for Herr Schnabelberger as well, and everyone at the museum. When you go home at night, it all makes sense. For me there is nothing but barren walls at which to stare. I feel trapped. The walls threaten to collapse about me, but they only threaten and don't fall upon me, though only then would I be free. Everything has become so haunted. Even here. You don't sense it, which is why you can walk through all the rooms at ease, whether in the hermitage or anywhere, even in the cellar. You can work in the unsorted archives, do something with them, and will feel joy in doing so besides. That's not how it is for me. I always see what lies behind, between, before me. The dead don't speak, there are no ghosts, no; yet how eerie it all is. The dead are gone, crushed and scattered, but their things speak the language of the dead, and so it will be until we get rid of the things or the shadows that cling to them. I could say a lot more about it, but I fear you wouldn't understand me and would be cross with me about it all."

As I talked, Frau Dr. Kulka had pulled up a chair and sat down across from me. She listened closely to what I had to say and was serious, while splotches of red appeared on her cheeks, perhaps from disgust, perhaps from horror, perhaps even from compassion; clearly, she felt uneasy. She had a blue pencil with which she played, leaving a line across her chin without knowing.

"Me cross? My dear Dr. Landau, what can you be thinking? But it's distressing . . . or no . . . well, yes . . . distressing, and I don't understand, you're right. But what am I to do with you? If you want to stay at the museum, you have to pull yourself together. Otherwise you're a debilitating, negative force."

"Shall I resign on the first?"

"No. You can't think that I want to get rid of you. Pull yourself together, just pull yourself together!"

"I'll do what I can."

"And, again, we're not talking about your contributions. Nor should you be hurt when someone points out your mistakes."

"For example?"

"For example, when you betray our interests to others."

"I didn't know that I had!"

"Oh, are you dense or do you not really know?"

"No."

"How, then, can the English scarecrow, this Mackintosh or whatever her name is, show up as if she were in a furniture store, unless she had been informed, you being the most likely source?"

"The Englishwoman didn't learn anything about it from me, whether directly or indirectly."

"She entered the building, mentioned your name to Geschlieder, which she then repeated to me, and with Schnabelberger she almost threw a fit because no one would sell her any furniture. Again and again, she kept demanding to see you. I have to speak to him; she had been recommended to Dr. Landau. Finally it was made clear to her that nothing but old prayer books and such stuff could be sold, and even that not to private citizens. For such deliverance, we were grateful, especially when nothing more was said about it. In addition, you are not the chief or the director, who can decide such things. Which is why it should not be the case that our visitors should be asking to deal with you."

"For heaven's sake, did Herr Schnabelberger not tell you what I said to Mrs. Mackintosh?"

"Of course."

"Then you can see, you can't help but see, that your accusations hold no water."

"But you can't tell me that you had nothing to do with it."

"Indeed, I can. I had nothing to do with it at all."

Only after long effort did I succeed in freeing myself from any suspicion that I had given out information about the museum to anyone, even foreign diplomats, in such an absurd manner. When I finally succeeded in convincing Frau Dr. Kulka of my innocence, she had something else that was bothering her.

"Okay, then, let's forget about the shameless Mrs. Mackintosh. But how did the couple from Johannesburg get the idea to ask about paintings? You certainly must have chatted a bit too much with them!"

"I'm not at all interested in the Levers."

"That makes it even more curious!"

"It came out accidentally while we were talking. You know, when Herr Schnabelberger gave me a tour of the place when I was hired, it so happened that those were the very first paintings I saw. On the back of the frames, I wrote 'Eugene and Emmi Lebenhart, Ufergasse.' That stuck in my memory. When Herr Lever said that he used to be called Lebenhart, it just slipped out. I didn't mean for anything bad to happen."

"Yet that is what happened! I know your views, and you agitate our people to the utmost. We have no interest in giving visitors crazy ideas that then result in our maybe having to hand over goods that are then lost not only to us but to the republic as well. Don't you understand that?"

"I understand, but it's not right of us."

"But then there's your own ideas about returning the goods! Of course, everything of value in the museum belongs to us all!"

"But then we are treading a fine line."

"What do you mean?"

"By taking in what the murderers stole."

"Really. . . . Do you really think so? But you're barking up the wrong tree with that!"

"Why, then, do we have laws about restitution, if I may ask?"

"Well, then, in the hope that you'll finally understand, yes, there must, of course, must be such laws. One has to offer people every opportunity. But only one chance, and nothing more than that. What's more, the law is for practical and essential items, not for paintings and many such things like we have. If we just give it away, then no one is served. In all earnestness, not even the so-called owners, and certainly not us. When I say that, I certainly mean more than you and me, for I mean the republic, the entire people. We can do something with it. And thereby we serve the building of the socialist society, and that must remain our goal."

Frau Dr. Kulka kept on talking to me for a while, telling me that we shouldn't let ourselves be led by sentimental concerns, and not just because there was often a tragic past tied to our valuables, weighty histories about which it was best not to know. What is past is past, and now we had to think of the future, of the building of peace and freedom, which depended on the common welfare, and this was the sense in which I finally needed to consider the museum and its message. Someone who handled things as impulsively as I did was a nuisance, no matter how noble his views, and while I worked with almost excessive diligence, at the same time all my efforts ended up for naught and left everything in disarray. Frau Dr. Kulka compared me to a builder who each day erected his wall brick by brick in long rows, after which I would hurry by with a crowbar and knock out some bricks down low, such that the entire structure collapsed.

I would have liked to respond, but it seemed pointless. I gave in and promised with a dry mouth not to give any more tours to anyone and to share only information that my superiors passed on to me on behalf of the trustees. I had long since decided to leave the country, but at the moment, while having to solemnly swear my allegiance to Frau Dr. Kulka, I also swore to myself, no matter the obstacles, to get out of there, even if the plans I had in mind proved untenable. Away from here, away! I almost said it aloud, but I bit my tongue and pressed my lips together, which the director took to be as good as a spoken promise, since she had cleared the air. With the salutation "Now let's be friends!," the guardian of the thievery concluded her lecture. Frau Dr. Kulka said goodbye and walked off; I could hear her high heels echoing sharply as she quickly descended the stairs.

I opened the door and wanted to call out to her, "Away from here, away!," but I just whispered it. This had nothing to do with being clever or careful; an immense pain had choked off my voice. I closed the door again and could now do nothing but wait, having realized that at any moment Anna would arrive. She shouldn't see what kind of awful time I'd just been through. Away from here, away! I paced back and forth in my little room and kept hearing the same phrase repeated: Away from here, away! It wouldn't be dark for a while, yet the sky had dimmed, the light dirty and sullen, not at all that of late summer, stale fumes pouring through the open window. I wanted to close it, but when I saw how depressing the panes that had not been cleaned in a while looked, I let it stand open—Away from here, away!—and began to pace back and forth restlessly again, picking up the wrapped purse and carrying it to the other end of the room before turning back without it, then turning back—away from here, away!—to pick up the purse again, put it down elsewhere, just a bit farther, and so on and so forth in an extremely drowsy manner. Away from here, away!

Where was Anna? Look at your watch. Don't look at your watch. No watch. Before the invention of time, waiting, not a waiting period, just waiting. Wait on, wait on! I had to sit down, without a watch, without time, just sit and wait. I was tired; my nerves were frayed, then they cramped up—I was painfully done in. Away from here! My past was to blame for it all. How was it possible to get through it without any knowledge of time? What I had suffered; what had I suffered? Just wait! I still went back and forth on whether any of the blame rested with me. About my fate, as was said, I could do nothing. Once it had arrived, it was inescapable. I should have got out earlier with Franziska, away, but there was no way for her parents to get out, and so we couldn't leave but had to stay; not leave them alone, just wait. Responsibilities had to be met, and if I wasn't able to save anyone I didn't wish to remain on the earth another day, but I should have handled it differently back then. Was there time? Only waiting, waiting it out; how could I flee? But that I stayed behind, no one could forgive me that, not those who never had to flee and never wanted to or could think what someone like me had gone through, that there were consequences that resulted which kept me from ever staying on the usual track.

Oh, what escape was there? Only to there, only to there! Why was I shamefully hiding from myself that I was changed as a result of what I had been through—Away from here, away!—someone whose past was nothing more than a graveyard, a place of rest (oh, how I felt it to be a place of rest without rest), and who had to separate himself from others, unable to join in, his perceptions different from those of others, his life one of waiting without arriving, bestowed with a different measure and grounding. He has left behind all of his dwellings, knows nothing more than the meager trove of memory, but cannot grasp anything that was once his, though he comes to understand that a remembrance exists when thought, and that it should not be remembered, but thus is a remembrance welling up, out of which something is said. I have seen what wells up inside me, not having fled it; I was there, on the spot, having reported. And thus one is no longer a part of the world that he once took to be his own. He has not fled in order to be, to be there! But, rather, that he remembers, that he exists, where he is and to see what has welled up, and by which the world still suffers.

Often, I feel like someone who has been left behind, shaking with astonishment and almost buckling before the fact that, despite everything, "I am" and "I was" are the same, the same and yet etched by time, by the tides of time, and by time's lessons. That is simply unthinkable, and nothing can change it, for not only are things missing, the cellar empty, the prayers having erupted, there was also no call that said "Hear Me!" anymore, everything unheard, no one heard any longer, no subject and no object by which I am able to recognize myself, though they still say remember, remember! Not only my family from back then—Away from here; oh, remember, was it a family?—but almost everything else is missing. What a cabinet full of harm is shut here, and almost everything missing, whereby generally people open up their gaping chasms and, however fainteartedly, still bridge them. The wall is too high and too wide, but no shoring up of memory that, out of the need to bear witness, rises up shakily, no people from back then who would also be people I know today. Sure, I know some here and there— what is taking Anna so long?—which poor memory still links to my past, but that is poor memory, the links becoming far too shaky for me to travel along. What good can it do, for example, if I find someone today who knows the city of my earlier life and even comes from it, when he is not a part of the circle in which I grew up and which held me, So-and-So, and so and so, already having left. Or, once again, I happen to meet someone I once knew in passing, but she doesn't remember anything, or she recalls everything differently than do I and can't remember anything that could mean anything to me. Such people, whom I both fear and am amazed at, make me uneasy; when I'm around them, I feel completely exposed.

Why is Anna taking so long?

No matter how well things go with people, soon a threshold is reached at which we must separate, there being no way for me to get away, and a gap in the unfolding of our already distant relations betrays what seems at first to be seamless, this being the years in which we were not together, in which nothing happened that could allow us to feel something shared. Then there is something missing between us, and I am indeed satisfied that, through careful explanation, we can dispense with every last experience we might have shared. The lack of such connections, which I mourn, is the continuity of life that separates me from my postwar colleagues. Certainly there are thousands, perhaps hundreds of thousands, who feel the same, but these loners cannot find one another, since they suffer the same life on their own. They come from many races and many places, and they have experienced different fates and must seek different partings of the ways until all are stamped by a different coin, strangers to themselves and certainly strangers to one another, and, most of all, strangers to and alienated by the millions for whom the continuity of life was never broken, because they were not hurt as badly or could save something, the possibility of visiting familiar places not out of the question, the nearness of a relative or that of a sympathetic friend, a little box of family pictures, a bundle of sacred letters, a chest of tantalizing books that were sent out—not stolen and not rotting—a childhood diary filled with sprawling script, propelled by the hope of a horizon that is arrived at.

But when all of this is gone, unreachably far away, in part no longer possible, in part no longer perceivable, then only halting memory holds them, compelling me now to remember, it becoming clear to me that man cannot live by intellect alone. In fact, intellect has been overvalued, because man too crudely engages with the sensory and drowns in it. Man beheld everything in abundance—things, devices, and the infinite set of possessions that he got lost in. Then man got used to it and knew the treasures that he observed in his mind, no longer needing to savor them, although he often desired more from them or, worse yet, longed for other things. That's when it became clear that man did not appreciate what intellect is and what comes from it. Then avid admonishers appeared who warned against such supposed plunder, saying that it was fleeting, wanting to make the precious riches seem foolish, the truth being that they were despicable, meanwhile showering the intellect with lavish praise. Many were uncomfortable with this, beginning to feel hunger amid the amplitude of their disappearing possessions, their self-awareness crumbling to nothing, as then they praised intellect with faces enraptured. Though the people themselves, however, were bereft of earthly goods they could number, they were nonetheless always taken care of, the beneficiaries of manifest actual property they had inherited, earned, and never entirely forsaken amid their meager misery. None of them were robbed of their last threads, managing to get through much that was terrible, horribly stripped of so much, denied their human rights, yet still finding a way to remain, somehow sustained, returning to vouchsafed goods, once owned, and again bestowed upon them, and yet not wanting any overabundance, no longer everything, only a little allowed again, and certainly not everything as it used to be but nonetheless welcoming some thing of it, having indeed inherited something. If this was not allowed, then they were no less shrewd at bartering, scoring something they longed for. When they remembered, the past and the present blended together, there being no essential difference between the two. If they preferred not to remember, or not much at all, things went badly for them, revitalized only by the knowledge of the wrong done them and comforted, they being the bridge over which they walked, striking out on a new beginning and prepared for a new order.

That's not what happened to me. I cannot and may not return; the bridge has collapsed, there is no ground beneath my feet, and I have no means to exist other than through the intellect. Since then, I know that intellect alone cannot encompass all of reality, which is why it is no means to exist; it is only a dangerous enticement, certainly worthwhile if one has a means to exist, but a torrid fire that dries out all your wits when you lack sustenance. Desires, memories, and hopes—they all enhance life. But life does not consist of them, nor can they alone ever amount to life, and certainly they don't contain it. It's true—I can't deny it—that I once again have so much, much more than I could ever have expected to have, or even wished for, just a few years ago, though it has all run together as one and has been tossed together into this building, which is hardly suited to it.

But what is this? Away from here . . . away! Is that what I hear? Is it sleep that it's interrupting? The rapping of time in my sleep? I can no longer wait. I must remember; away sleep, away sleep. There it is again, hard on the door. I tore myself from sleep and jumped up from the chair, shaking away the confusion. It was time, myself already in full stride, bursting out the door. Anna must be standing outside. It was raining; I couldn't dawdle. Out the room, down the hall, and opening the door. There stood the mailman in his rain poncho, patient, a compassionate man who just waved away my apology. He handed me a little package that was a book, which was why he had knocked, giving me two letters as well, all of them damp with rain. I thanked him, the mailman already heading off toward his bicycle, delivering his messages in the pouring rain. I closed the door and hurried back to my room. Anna had not arrived, but she had written, her clear handwriting before me, covered with rain, as if tears had fallen upon it. The other letter, from the city, had a fancy look about it that I did not recognize. I set this letter and the book aside and read what Anna had to say after a silence that had lasted almost a year.

Dearest Johanna and Arthur,

It's been a long while since we heard from each other. Very long, too long, or it's just a short while. I don't know. When so much is going on, it's hard to know how long it's been. The last I heard from you was the news of Eva's birth. She must be over a year old by now—a clever, wise little girl. I would love to see her, as well as all of you. Will it be possible? Patience! Alas, it's hard to write such a letter. Please be patient, and one thing will follow another. Michael must now be five. The children must indeed be growing up; one can speak reasonably with them, and they comprehend so much. What are you like as parents? Certainly splendid. Though you don't put up with any nonsense.

How shall I begin to tell you my story? I can't, or at least there's no gentle way to do so. So listen! Helmut died three days ago, quite unexpect-

edly. We just buried him yesterday, in a sad new cemetery far outside the city. There were no prior signs, no warning, no last words said; it was all over in an hour. Helmut must have had a problem with his heart that was never diagnosed. Alas, it does no good to dwell on what he did or didn't have. Suddenly, at breakfast, he was feeling fine and chipper, then he collapsed, gone in a second, not another word, never regaining consciousness. It was awful. I ran to the neighbor, who got a doctor from next door, and he arrived in a few minutes, me having stretched Helmut out on a couch, his arms dangling, his eyes—oh, his eyes looked terrible—and the doctor worked on him for a while. He said it was a massive heart attack. This and that was taken care of, and he helped me bring Helmut back to bed. What happened between his death and the funeral I cannot tell you.

I'm sure this comes as a shock to you, my dears. Oh, it's so terrible. I can still see Hermann standing before me, sweetly and movingly saying goodbye before heading off to the Eastern Front, and now Helmut is gone as well. I just can't believe it. I can't think about my situation too much, but everything has become strange for me here, even if there are good people who thoughtfully keep an eye out for me. But they are strangers to me; I have no place here any longer. And I have only one wish: Away from here, away! Last night I dreamed of Helmut, and he said, Get away from here; it's not good for you here!

Do you think, Arthur, that I could come to you both? Or is that crazy? I would be willing to do anything. The lowliest job would be fine with me, the best possibilities being the care of the blind, raising blind children, for I know Braille and everything necessary. I've been trained, and as a girl and during the war years I worked as a teacher of the blind. But there are also other things I could do. Help me, if you can. I simply must get away! At least give me some advice. I know that it's hard, and that you have your own worries (hopefully, things have gotten better), but please don't fail me now and be there for me! The language won't pose any problem. Nor is getting there a problem, that I know, for I can pull together the money. If you could let me stay with you for a short while and could send me an invitation, I can then present it and in a few weeks could be on my way, as long as everything is in order. I would love to help out, dear Johanna, with Michael and Eva.

Write to me soon! I have never waited so intensely for a letter. Include a little picture of the children, if you can, and a formal invitation.

Perhaps you'll be interested to know, Arthur, that a short while ago Peter wrote us—oh, how bitter it is to write "us"—from Wellington. Things go well for him in New Zealand, and he's very much the same dear old good-for-nothing nitwit. He also asked about you two. But enough now. And don't be angry! No, you can't be angry at someone this sad, and who remains ever faithfully yours,

Anna

I walked straight to Johanna in her room and showed her the letter. She read it while I played with Eva, who was crawling around her playpen and shrieking with pleasure. I fancied myself a proud father, to my credit. Johanna said we had to help Anna right away and invite her. Eva, who felt neglected and was protesting strongly as we spoke, was soothed by her mother as she turned her attention to her new rattle. We left the child alone in her playpen and went to my study, where we considered what we needed to do to get ready. Anna should live with us as long as was necessary. The rest would work itself out.

Then I said to Johanna that there had been some other mail as well. She opened the little package that contained the promised book of a young sociologist with the title *Stereotyping Through Prejudice*. On the cover there was a blurb signed by Kratzenstein, whose style stirred rollicking laughter in Johanna. At this I stopped trying to make out the crabbed writing of the other letter and listened to Johanna read Kratzenstein's praise aloud:

"The author responsibly undertakes to come up with answers to the most burning problems of our time through this probing existential study that fathoms the role of prejudice in causing our ills, and which is based on stereotypes. Within the intellectual confines of the scholarly appreciation of essential structures, he desires to use cool-handed methods of sober analysis to put his finger without fear or shyness on one of the hot spots of our day, but also to be a sensitive friend to man and a helping doctor who knows the worth of a real and manifest understanding of existence. After the careful exclusion of all utopian theories, the needs of all those threatened and oppressed are examined layer by layer through the piercing insight of sociology and the only possible solution revealed in the prescription of a humane democracy. I wish this impressive accomplishment great success.

"—Professor James Kratzenstein, President of the International Society of Sociologists."

We both laughed heartily at such jargon.

"If I want to pretend, all I have to do is read the blurb and not the book. I could just concentrate on the name under the blurb, for thus says the famous Professor Kratzenstein, and the work is anointed. But, I promise you, I won't be that lazy."

"We should be ashamed, Arthur. Here we are talking about this gibberish, and Anna is in despair. We're so rude and unkind."

"You're right, Johanna. That's enough. Sometimes I think the old mystic had it right in so many words, even if he didn't understand it all himself, when he said, God, the Devil, the world, and everything is in our hearts. Only the admiring praise he showers on the heart I cannot go along with. Existence—how we live it—is confusing, too much for the heart, its ordeals swamping it, and we rarely say what's clear, rarely what's true. But let's not be too hard on ourselves! We certainly have not at all grown callous. We observe the surgings of the ugly and horrible no more than the sublime, and especially the sweet and the tender, even the lovely."

"The lovely, you say?"

"Yes, even the lovely. Rarely, I know, do I speak of it. But, believe me, what human beings are capable of and once were—something of that, a possibility, a reappearance, a shadow of it can also rise up within our breasts. Separated from everything, cast out as part of the last and strongest consequence of our lost Paradise. But something of this Paradise still remains— something that survives, that stands firm and will remain firm, all of us under one law and thus the same, but with a thousand different interpretations."

"We should talk about it later. I can't leave little Eva on her own too long. What's the other letter?"

"Wait, I haven't looked at the signature yet. Just remember that we can't forget about poor Anna, even though its Resi Knispel, of all people, Resi Knispel!"

"Just a moment, I'll look in on little Eva. I'll be right back."

I buried myself in the letter and with some effort deciphered it. Johanna didn't keep me waiting long, having found that the little one was fine.

"What, then, does Resi Knispel want?"

"Let me read it. It's not very long."

I then read the letter:

My Dear Landau,

Aren't you surprised that I'm writing you? I've meant to do so for so long, really for years. I said so to Haarburger and friends in his circle, but they probably didn't say anything, and now I hear that you've ceased all contact with those people. At last, though that was some twenty months ago, I heard something about you from a fleeting acquaintance, Konirsch-Lenz. He said that you are in a bad way, that you're lonely and have fallen out with the world and with people. That surprises me. That doesn't jive with how I remember you. I asked Konirsch-Lenz to tell you to give me a call. Nothing came of it. More than likely, he didn't let you know.

Now listen, Landau, come tomorrow or whenever you can, though not Saturday or Sunday. My address is above. It concerns a wonderful project, a journal. I need you as much as bread itself. Agreed? Greetings from

Resi Knispel

Eva's voice cried out during these last words, so we couldn't talk about it, while it was also already time for me to pick up Michael, who had been attending preschool for the past few weeks, since he turned five. I rushed out of the house in the direction of Toro Road, where at the corner I was met by a wet and snuffling Santi, the Simmondses' dog, who barked a greeting and, jumping up with its front paws, soiled my coat. I shooed him away, at which he abruptly toddled off and I hurried along. The rain had ceased, only thin strands of it still dripping, the drops shining like the finest splinters of glass. How I had always loved this gentle shimmering, and before me I saw the mountain woods. I had entirely forgotten about *Stereotyping Through Prejudice*, as well as Resi Knispel, instead seeing the mountain woods, having perhaps thought of Anna, there where we walked along the border, while afterward she was across the border with her Helmut, the big, strapping man with the face of a boy.

The face of a boy called to me from the vestibule of the school, where he waited for me, hopping about and fidgeting, it being Michael, while I was a bit late. At this, I pushed away any thoughts save of him and turned to his good cheer. He was, if possible, more talkative than ever, and we were home before we knew it. At home, Eva called out, "Mi!Mi!," which meant her brother, and he replied with "Evi, Evi, hihihi!"At this, his little sister cheered. Michael got his food, pleased by the honey, but his mother had to scold him for playing around with it. Then a banana caught his attention even more, and I had to make a little man appear from the peel. Eva was fed by Johanna, the two of us having some tea and eating a little something.

After the meal, I went back to my room and wrote to Anna. She should come as soon as possible. I couldn't promise to find her a job, though both Johanna and I would try our best to help our friend in the time ahead, she needing also to see how well she liked this country and the metropolis. She just had to get here, and through her savvy life skills she would certainly soon find a suitable occupation, for everything would work out fine.

Then I leafed through *Stereotyping Through Prejudice*. The book didn't seem all that bad, though there was nothing new in it, everything following the current fashion for many statistics, results of opinion research, including quotes, but pieced together with diligence and attention to order, and in a seemingly fluid style, even if in places it fell into loose and embarrassing violations of any kind of responsible use of language. Yet another book and yet again the gaping emptiness, I thought to myself. Why was it printed and recommended? Why did someone bother to stir up so much that was already known and done? I shoved the book to the side. Today, I didn't want anything to do with it.

Then I picked up Resi Knispel's letter. I couldn't decide what I should do. This woman belonged to a world that had done me nothing but wrong; I wanted as little to do with it as it had to do with me. I was completely done with it and it all lay behind me; I simply didn't know if I wanted to go knocking on that door again. Of course, working for a journal remained, as always, an enticing possibility, one where I could have an important influence, where I could state my views, which had been denied me everywhere else, refused me as a result of stupidity or nastiness or indifference. It could grant me, if it was well-intentioned, a free hand. But could I expect that? Didn't Resi Knispel already belong to the corrupt literati in which scholarship and literature were mixed together in the mishmash of a reportage spouting off about everything but hardly grasping anything, peppered with sensations and a faux-modern style, all of it turned into a wretched journalistic stew? These cliques, with their disgusting wishy-washiness, where as a kind of victory lap I was supposed to be welcomed as a comrade-in-arms who didn't see through such mischief, though I couldn't let on about it, while despite honest efforts and novel achievements I was not seen as hostile—all of this I wanted nothing to do with whatsoever. I had finally accepted my social isolation and therefore could no longer curry favor, even if someone from there, whether out of curiosity or with good intent, lifted a pinkie for me.

But was it right to dismiss it all before I had even heard her out? I had to look into it. I just had to avoid senseless compromise, or take any promise seriously, refuse any improper impositions, as well as keep a watchful eye on the separation between my own aims and invidious requests. Either I would be taken for the person that I am, and allowed to have my say, or she would be willing to listen to me and allow me to accomplish something for which I would be responsible. If, nonetheless, it became clear that this was not what she had in mind, then I wouldn't be disappointed, but cheerfully and calmly withdraw my name from consideration before I was even offered anything. I couldn't be so dumb as to offer up all my effort and work for nothing the way I had done with Eberhard S.

That night I talked with Johanna at length about whether I should just answer the letter with silence, politely decline, or look up Fräulein Knispel. Johanna worried that I would get upset if I let myself become involved with people like this again. She was happy to see that I had achieved a partial and tolerable sense of resignation, and advised sending a friendly note to decline or writing to ask for more information. I could reassure Johanna that I now knew enough already, that writing would only draw things out, that I felt I was above all trickery, and that I would take it all in stride, even if it was a sham.

The next day, I went to see Resi Knispel. She lived in a sleepy neighborhood with expansive gardens. It didn't take me long to find the house, which seventy years ago would have been considered posh but had long since been neglected. The entrance to the uncared-for garden was open; the door to the house was perched above a flight of steps that were well worn and certainly not swept for many days. The door was closed, and to the side there were buzzers for each individual apartment, but only next to two buttons were there legible names, neither of which was Knispel. I took a chance and pressed one button and waited a few minutes. I was about to press another when I heard steps and the door opened. Fräulein Knispel stood within it.

"It's wonderful that you came, Landau. It's at least five years since we've seen each other. Or maybe even longer. Well, then, come on in!"

The wooden steps were covered with a worn carpet, the walls of the stairwell were gray with grime. Thus was I even more surprised by the apartment, with its unusually large rooms, everything modern and done in good taste, and furnished almost luxuriously. Resi Knispel led me through two rooms and then a third that was an office, a massive desk weighed down with books and manuscripts, the walls lined with full bookshelves, an open cabinet containing folders full of notes and letters, comfortable seating around a low table, cognac and glasses, little cakes and bonbons and cigarettes, and a man sitting there whom I didn't recognize right away. Only when he stood up politely did it come to me that it was Herr Buxinger, the bookseller. We greeted each other, and I was asked to have a seat while being offered everything that was there. I had to answer a bevy of questions—how I was, how had I settled in, and what I did. While I wasn't tight-lipped, I nonetheless remained cautious in responding. I also posed polite questions whose answers didn't interest me whatsoever.

Soon I learned that Herr Buxinger indeed still had his bookshop. Though he complained that I had never paid him the honor of a visit, Buxinger now had a much smaller shop inside a courtyard, where he focused less on traffic from the street and instead did mainly distribution for some foreign publishers. He spoke badly of Jolan Haarburger, calling him an unfaithful friend who had nearly ruined him. When many years ago Buxinger was in a bad way, it seemed to him the most natural thing in the world to ask his childhood friend Haarburger for a loan. The clever fox was not a willing donor, but he couldn't turn down the request, for in many ways he felt responsible for Buxinger, yet the loan did the bookseller little good, for now he owed the wily lawyer and had to dance to his tune. Haarburger got in-volved in the business, about which he knew nothing, and everything went downhill—the sales falling off, the receivables remaining uncollectable, the bills ever higher, the creditors ever more skeptical. When, finally, matters had gone too far, such that either Haarburger had to dig into his pockets once more or Buxinger had to turn over future control of the business, Haarburger did the dumbest and most despicable thing possible: he called in the loan on short notice. Buxinger didn't feel at all ashamed and could say openly that he went bankrupt, all of it a mixture of bad luck and bad intentions. A legal bankruptcy, that he could certainly handle at great sacri-fice, but not a burdensome settlement; he had to repay all of the loan, and it took a long time. And, best of all, this Haarburger, who had never made clear the length of the loan at the start, didn't want to hear anything about an arranged settlement; it was either swift payment or legal action. Buxinger then had no choice but to sell his valuable collection of autographs of writ-ers, musicians, and other famous figures. Just imagine, Goethe and Dickens, Chopin and Johann Strauss, and a long letter by Garibaldi. True, whenever one holds such a fire sale the prices are low, Herr Saubermann picking up the nicest items for chicken feed, while one even had to thank him for doing so. The proceeds from all this were not enough, such that Frau Buxinger's jewelry also had to be used, as well as anything that had the slightest value, in order to pay this nemesis, Herr Haarburger, the entire sum at once, albeit without interest, which he had to relinquish in order to keep it all on the up and up. Could I even imagine it all was possible?

Oh, yes, that I could, and I wasn't surprised at all. At this, Buxinger was as happy as a child. Of course, Resi Knispel, who still knew the Haarburg-ers, was not amused by Buxinger's talk. She said that, yes, it was all unfortu-nately handled in a shoddy way, but even the best had their flaws, one had to understand that. She had tried to talk to Haarburger in good conscience, but he turned a deaf ear to it all. Well, that's what happens, but now it was an old story upon which a lot of grass had grown. Buxinger wished to protest, yet Resi Knispel assured him that she understood his position, certainly. Nonetheless, there was no need to waste another word on it; we were here for another reason and wanted to speak about some practical matters. The bookseller agreed, and it was fine with me as well. But she had hardly finished making her useful recommendation and explaining that they wished to turn to the matter of the journal, when suddenly she switched back to Haarburger. Buxinger had to admit what he had always resented about Jolan— namely that Hannah was a gem about whom nothing bad could be said. Buxinger didn't want to hear anything more about Hannah. She had aided and abetted everything her husband had done. He had not always been such a miser, just petty and anxious, but she was a monster. Sweet and flattering, yes, she could be that, but that was all part of her craft, for otherwise she knew just how to get her way. She was the one who had really tied Jolan up in knots; otherwise, the mishap would never have occurred. Fräulein Knispel was beside herself, because Buxinger didn't have a single good thing to say about Frau Haarburger—terrible, he should stop, she's a good-hearted soul, didn't he know that? Fräulein Knispel wanted me to acknowledge this well-intentioned view. When I obviously and coolly held back from doing so, there was no end to her astonishment, for even today Hannah still asked after my wife, as she liked her very much and always wanted to know what would make Johanna feel good. I'd had enough of such talk, and so it was I this time who wanted to change the subject.

"Could I perhaps hear a bit more about the journal?"

"Yes, fine. Landau and Buxi, private battles lead to nothing, that's what I think, and at some point some kind of reconciliation will occur. Then you'll extend hands to one another as best friends."

"What about the journal?" I asked intently.

"Yes, the journal. It will be fantastic. Do you want to be a part of it, Landau?"

"I can't make any promises without learning more."

"Buxinger will be the publisher."

"That sounds great!" I said.

"But only as a straw man. He will lend his name and experience, and he'll oversee sales."

"That is, if there are any," said Buxinger cautiously.

"Go on, enough of that, Buxi! You're a killjoy. You yourself have been the one most excited about the idea from the start."

"Hopefully, then," he said politely.

"Okay, then, I will actually run the firm, but behind the scenes. I have to maneuver carefully. Once the journal is up on its feet, then I can jump in for real. My work with the Swiss press will continue, for it can only be of help, what with the contacts, the literary agents—you know, of course, Landau, that's what I do. I won't give that up. Sometimes one can make discoveries there and bring together excellent contributors. A journal stands or falls with its contributors."

"What kind of journal will it be, Fräulein Knispel?"

"You'll soon hear. Tell me, I recall, and someone said to me a couple of times, you write about all kinds of things, don't you, Landau? Sociology, suffering, misery, and such. You're at home with all of it, yes?"

"Yes, if you wish to put it that way."

"Do you already have a book out?"

"No, not out—inside, inside the desk drawer."

"That's no good. You have to bring it out! It's worthless inside the desk drawer."

"That could be, Fräulein Knispel."

"Well, then. You are sensible. And why isn't it out? Too much time spent in the ivory tower? Too learned? Too lofty?"

"I've been unlucky, one might say. But I've come to terms with that."

"Your writing needs to be snappy; I can help you with that. What with your talent! You need to grab hold of people, carry them along. That indefinable something—that's what you need to be successful. Well, Landau, do you want to give it a try—trust me for once? I'll give it my all, guaranteed."

"I don't think you'll have much luck with it."

"Let me worry about that. Bring me something and I'll read it; you'll have my unvarnished opinion. Maybe there's nothing. But if there's something to it, and I think there is, then I can do something with it. Isn't that true, Buxi?"

"But of course, Resi. You can count on it, Herr Landau. Only that which is purely literary cannot be used, no artsy novels. But, hopefully, it's not that kind of stuff, is it?"

"No, no," I whispered, half in apology, half in embarrassment.

"Listen, Landau, I have some top-notch journalists who can rewrite your dense scholarly prose so that it flows like light and sweet wine. Then I'll place it wherever you want."

"Couldn't I now at least learn a bit more about the journal, Fräulein Knispel?"

"You certainly haven't written just a bunch of heavy stuff, have you?"

"No—essays, articles, reviews, and other short items."

"Excellent. And could you write an article about a theme I assigned you or one of your own choice?"

"I would think so."

"*Primissima!* Then I can count on you!"

"That I don't know, Fräulein Knispel. I need to know more about your journal."

"Patience. I'm getting to that. As I already said, we need above all to have a staff that is experienced. In some ways, I have that already. But I need more. You need to let those who have something to say have an outlet. Do you know some people?"

"Unfortunately not. I stay out of things."

"Oh, so you're a cellar rat. Always rummaging about, yes? You need to come out into the fresh air sometime. Then you can crawl back like a badger into his den. Well, who do you know, then? Everyone belongs to some kind of circle."

"I don't have any circle. I write some reviews for journals. Of late, also some short articles on assignment—mere shoptalk, nothing important. Because of this, I haven't earned much respect. Now and then someone asks me to write a professional opinion or sends me some work to copyedit. That's about it."

"What, copyediting? Well, then, a professional, almost my equal. You have my respect. That's something. You must come across some pretty good names, no?"

"Names? Yes."

"Then let me make a recommendation straightaway. If you come across something that would interest a publisher, then show it to me. We can then talk about your cut."

"That I can't do. The author, the journal, the publisher will have put their trust in me."

"No, that's not what I mean! Often, something is free for the taking. Then bring it to me! It won't be your fault. Obviously you'll get something if I make something off it. It makes perfect sense. But it needs to be popular, though also learned. Scholarly, yet understandable to the common reader. Topical, it can even have a political slant to it—it doesn't matter whether it's right or left."

"I hardly ever come across anything like that."

"Buxi, he's hopeless. Much too serious, this Landau. But he could be a nice piece of finery to have attached to a journal. We indeed need something serious that is brutally earnest that can inspire readers simply because they can't understand a syllable of it. You could pull that off, couldn't you?"

"Perhaps."

"But only short articles by such clever visionaries, a hundred and fifty to two hundred manuscript lines for each—that we could manage."

"Would it also pay, Fräulein Knispel?"

"It's a matter of honor! Something for something. At the start, I can only promise a little. Luminaries will, of course, be paid straightaway. Do you know any luminaries?"

"Certainly not."

"Too bad. Later, everyone will certainly be paid, even well. But first the journal has to get off the ground."

"When will that happen?"

"Soon. We want to have the first issue out in four to six weeks, five to eight thousand copies, sixteen pages of text, later more, four to eight pages of advertising. For that, we already have a fantastic salesman. Buxi will help us with that. Saubermann also promised support—advertising and also money."

"So, then, the financial side of things is assured, Fräulein Knispel?"

"Just about, my dear sir. Not quite, but it's almost there. I have been waiting for this for so long, for this idea has long been dear to me, and I want to start it off on sound footing. We can't just bring out one issue, two issues, three or four, then fold up. That can't happen. It needs to be a smash hit that is able to thrive."

"How often will the journal appear?"

"Right now, once every two months. Later, every month."

"And in which language?"

"Right now it will be bilingual, every article in English and German.

When we're able, then we'll do four languages—French and Spanish, maybe Italian as well. Simultaneous publication—it's enough to leave one speechless, don't you think? After a year, we could be that far along. But, at the moment, I can't promise anything for sure; it's still just a wonderful plan."

"And what will the journal cover? Only sociology, or other things as well? What is its target audience?"

"It's like the inquisition, Landau! But let's just take one thing at a time. The journal can include everything. We don't even have to keep to sixteen pages. Scholarship, culture, politics at the highest level, literature, art, whatever there is. There can be special issues. It should be modern. Something for everyone. Maintaining the highest standards, but accessible to everyone and palatable to all. That way, it will be a success."

"If I understand right, Fräulein Knispel, in many ways it's a cat fitted out with fish fins."

"What kind of joke is that supposed to be, Herr Landau?" asked the bookseller.

"Quite simple, Herr Buxinger. The journal seems impossible, a complete paradox."

"Come on now, Landau, jokes are fine, but that's going too far. It just makes you, forgive me, look so dumb. One needs to set a standard; otherwise you lose your standing and are sent packing. But people howl at standards and are not built for them, they can't find the right kind of mouthpiece. That's why one can't sit on one's high horse, for one doesn't take anything away from the loftiest of philosophers by popularizing them. Quite the contrary. It's only then that they gain a certain stature. Look, earlier Buxi alluded to literature, but what he said isn't true. Even the best of novels can be read by the average person, because they are popular, which means realistic, and yet they still need to be considered artistic. Even a masterpiece can be picked up and really grip someone. It's always been that way, with even the most sublime works, and never did a single leaf fall from the poet's head. That's the way it is everywhere. Why should it be any different with something scholarly? Any theme can be tastefully served up. You just have to cut it down to size."

"Is that what you want to do with the contributions?"

"When it's needed, of course."

"Then I don't want to waste any more of your time."

"Don't be so sensitive, Landau! I already said, only where it's necessary, when it's to the article's good."

"It wouldn't be good for mine."

"Go on, you're not a child! Time to grow up. We'll always turn down bad articles. Even if they are well written. Don't worry! Look, we'd really love to have you work as an editor. Agreed?"

"Then I need to hear a lot more and think about it. What I really want to know is, what is the target audience? What's the purpose and goal?"

"The journal is targeted to everyone who is really interested in culture, no matter their profession, and the entire world. We want to be something that brings people together. Humane, although we don't have to lumber around like an elephant in a china shop. The idea of the West, the nurturing of the intellect, the renewal of all values and their preservation, their sacred traditions, the inalienable good, but forward-looking, worldly, thoroughly novel, a mouthpiece for all future-driven trends. Of course, democratic, but not attached to a party, we have to be sure of that; even if now and then we have to have the nerve to touch an open wound. I think just having a common goal is all it needs. We'll welcome any approaches that are tolerant in order to serve the same cause—namely, world peace and freedom. Oh, Landau and Buxi, it could be splendid. I've dreamed about it for years while lying awake, sleepless, and I will write for it myself, whatever occurs to me, reporting on anything that comes along. I certainly know what to do with a pen. But I can't do it all myself; I need many voices, a symphony of like-minded spirits. That's why I won't sign some contributions, remaining behind the scenes like an invisible conductor who only leads the orchestra. Once I reveal myself to be the publisher, there will be nothing left for me to do, though I will take much satisfaction from it—for myself, for you, for everyone."

"What will the journal be called?"

"I'm glad that you ask, Landau. A lot depends on the name, and the name is wonderful, a promising sign. It will be called *Eusemia.*"

"*Eusemia?* Do you mean that you're mixed up with the guy who under that name caused so much mischief?"

"What, you know him?" responded Fräulein Knispel and Buxinger together.

"Oh, I know the man, all right. I don't want anything to do with him or any *Eusemia*."

"But you won't have anything to do with him, Landau."

"Certainly not. It's been a good while since I got mixed up in that."

"Look, my dear sir, you always react too quickly."

"That might be, my friends, but *Eusemia*—I don't want anything to do with it. I must insist on it."

"So," interrupted Buxinger, "you're settled on it?"

"I've had enough."

"You'll have to tell me all about it sometime," said Resi Knispel. "That really interests me. He has certain qualities not to be scoffed at. But don't worry! He will have nothing to do with *Eusemia*."

"Where, then, did you get the name?"

"Quite simple. He sold us the name and all the publishing rights for chicken feed. He really doesn't have anything more to do with it."

"Not at all?"

"My, always such mistrust! I swear to you and will put it in writing, if you don't want to believe me."

"That's not necessary. Don't you worry that the name has been compromised and is a bad portent?"

"Who will be so skeptical, Herr Landau!" said the bookseller. "The main thing is, we'll do something with it. The name is hardly known and has many advantages. It's already been copyrighted, and it's Greek, distinguished, it means something, has the right tone, nor has any journal ever been called that, which is not something to scoff at. I can't imagine anything bad being ascribed to *Eusemia*."

"You're right, Buxi. It's as clear as shoe black. *Eusemia* is superb, and there's no changing it. It's not what you do but the way you do it that matters, and that we'll engineer ourselves. It will be a lark, won't it, Buxi?"

"Yes, we will make it work," he said reflectively.

"Look, Landau, we have to have courage. And, besides, we have nothing to lose. Each of us has enough bread to live on, and if it goes well we'll have a bit of butter for it, too. What do you want to write about?"

"I haven't thought that far ahead. What are others writing about? Do you have contributors? Firm commitments? Articles ready to go?"

"Of course. We have a good number. My lead article is already done; the drawers are full. But we need more, we need better. I believe in healthy competition in intellectual matters. We simply can't have enough in order to be able to choose the best. Each one wants to end up chosen, and every day the mail brings a new load. Most of them are unsolicited and average. But it all has to be organized. That's the worst problem when it comes to culture, that it's so badly organized. If it's well organized, one can run the show. That's why, Landau, I asked you who you knew."

"I can only repeat that I'll have to disappoint you."

"Impossible. You can't be serious, you're holding back. So many people know your name! When I first met you, you were as popular as a full box of candy."

"That was long ago. I'm a bit of a loner. I'm asking you, tell me who you've already convinced to pitch in, and who you're still hoping to get."

"Well, who do we have, Buxi? Let me see. Do you know Oswald Birch? Everyone knows him."

"Yes."

"You know him?"

"Yes."

"Well, then! Why then did you say that you don't know anyone? He's certainly someone! Heavy artillery! We need him."

"Do you have an article from Birch, Fräulein Knispel?"

"Half committed. But half so. I recommended that he write on the most recent research in archaeology, and he didn't say no."

"That's saying something!"

"Certainly," agreed Buxinger seriously. "That means a great deal. He dropped in to see me at the shop, looked around, bought something, and I readily buttonholed him. Nor did he say no to me. It's only the deadline that I'm worried about."

"Buxi is always anxious. No need to be at all. We just need to work on Birch, talk to him nicely, remind him, not let him turn you down. Landau, could you do me a huge favor?"

"What might that be?"

"Talk to Birch. Write him. Call him up. Get him on board."

"Why would I do that?"

"Oh, don't be ridiculous! He needs to deliver the article! And soon! It can be short. We just need his name. Birch in *Eusemia*, then in no time at all we'll be full to the gills with submissions. Tell him that you stand fully behind *Eusemia*."

"I can't promise anything with Birch. I haven't seen him in years, nor will he give me the time of day. Who else do you have?"

"An article from Saubermann. It's already done."

"Really. What's it about? Artificial pearls?"

"Actually, not a bad idea. Buxi, what do you think? But that's not it. Rather, something on cultural criticism, the outmoded museum. Very enlightening. Wonderfully written. I've already edited it."

"Then I can also assume that you have something from Frau Saubermann as well?"

"You guessed it, Landau. But I don't want to use it in the first issue. It's frightfully long, and she keeps kicking up her heels against shortening it. She is so sensitive."

"What, then, did she write about?"

"'The Principle of Moral Freedom in Institutionalized Charity.' Such a title, like a tapeworm! I like 'Moral Freedom and Charity' better. But I have to talk her into it first. She insists on using 'Principle.' That's the most important to her, but I find it clunky, vulgar. One doesn't go around talking about principles that easily these days. But the basic ideas are not at all bad. Good deeds should not undermine freedom; one nurtures those in need with a sound footing so that they can acknowledge their moral responsibilities and not simply depend on outlandish sums given them through charity. That is good neither for the giver nor for the recipient, because both are then denied freedom—namely, the rights and responsibilities of freedom. One must appreciate how easily the giver of charity can become the slave of those in need, such that it happens—and Frau Saubermann gives examples of this—that the benefactor, who, let's say, wants to go on vacation for a few weeks and who supports some poor hussy with a box of groceries once a month, has to pass, for once, on making his donation, such that the beneficiary gets nothing, yet waits for it in vain and finally spits fire and brimstone about the benefactor. That's an impossible situation. I can give it to you to read if it interests you. You can even make changes and any suggestions for shortening it."

"Who else do you have?"

"Maybe Singule. But he, unfortunately, has no time. Therefore it's not as certain."

"What do you want from him?"

"Oh, from him I have to take what he will give me. If only I can have something! He made a lot of suggestions, idea after idea. If something came of them all, there would be enough for *Eusemia* to live on for a year."

"For example?"

"He'd most like to write about microbiology. But he just can't do that, for he doesn't know the latest literature. Therefore something practical would be better, something that speaks to everyone. So he thinks 'The Influence of International Foundations on the Development of Culture.'"

"An excellent idea!" I said, unable to stop myself.

"Precisely, that's what I thought as well. But, unfortunately, he has no time. Then there is—and I know, Buxi, this will give you a fit—Haarburger."

"Not with me, Resi!" called out the bookseller, refusing to remain quiet, though he shut up the moment Knispel jokingly wagged a finger at him.

"I have Jolan Haarburger. That's important, because he's our only lawyer thus far. He's already shown me a draft that he's done. The title is not yet finalized, though it's supposed to be on a somewhat religious theme, about law and justice. I think that's wonderful."

"Is that all, then?"

"Of course not, not even close! There is also the big gun, Professor Kratzenstein!"

"That really is a big gun, Fräulein Knispel. What would he like to do?"

"You mean you don't think much of him?"

"I didn't say anything."

"He's amazing, isn't he, Buxi? A luminary! Everything that comes from Kratzenstein is clear as crystal. Whether he will be able to write anything, given his many duties, is uncertain. But he agreed to do book reviews. We already have one. *Stereotyping Through Prejudice*. It's supposedly a phenomenal work. Surely also something for you, Landau."

"I already have the book."

"You really do know everything. But he also wants to recommend many other contributors. Those that flock to the International Society of Sociologists. Frau Fixler, his secretary, is supposed to give us a long list."

"Tell me, Fräulein Knispel, if you already have Jolan Haarburger, couldn't his wife also chip in something?"

"That's sheer madness, Herr Landau! That's a terrible idea!" said Buxinger cautiously.

"But, Buxi, the merits will decide themselves. That goes without saying. Hannah is artistic and a brilliant socialite, a gathering point for intellectuals, but she's not a writer. She can help us in other ways. Do you really have no one to suggest, Landau?"

"What about Dr. Kauders? Do you have him already?"

"Anyone who is good, but I don't want him."

"Why?"

"Ugh, he's arrogant! He just makes fun of me."

"But he is a talented man, Fräulein Knispel."

"He took his time paying me, a year or even longer. I'd be happy not to sell anything to him again."

"Bills for books, Buxi—that has nothing to do with it. But he is impertinent. And though he thinks himself a great academic, he no longer is. But another suggestion, Landau?"

"You already have a lot of academics. How about anything to do with literature?"

"Oh, that I have, for it piles up like rubbish. Anyone can write poetry and short stories these days. There's no art to it. Even I can toss it off like that. What I accept really needs to be something special. Do you have something? Do you write yourself?"

"No, no, not at all, I don't have anything. But what do you think of Inge Bergmann?"

"We certainly don't need poetry, certainly not at the start. Inge Bergmann is a good egg, but a poor devil as well. I can't help her. She's always sending stories to the agency, but there's nothing I can do with them. And we can't have anything like that in *Eusemia*. Just imagine, a cultural journal, and then childlike journeys to the moon and such nonsense. Right, Buxi?"

With that I took our meeting to be over, or at least the part that concerned me. I didn't promise Resi Knispel anything, no matter how much she pressed me, no matter how much Buxinger tried to lure me in. I said that I really had to think the situation over, and that I wanted to wait until the first issue appeared. Both of them thought this discouraging and not at all nice, Resi Knispel calling it a churlish vote of mistrust. I didn't change my decision, no matter how promising the project was still being portrayed with such flashy colors. At the start, if there were indeed so many contributors willing to pitch in, the project would certainly not falter if I didn't join up right away. Resi Knispel agreed almost indignantly. It shouldn't be hard to get such a flourishing operation off the ground, but I would be passing up a unique opportunity to take part in the development of a wonderful project that would bring me fame and honor, perhaps making my name known throughout the world. I should consider what it would mean to have my article appear at the same time in two languages, and soon in four or five, which would be fantastic good fortune, emphasized Fräulein Knispel, for a recognized genius such as myself.

As neither threats nor knee-deep waves of flattery would change my mind, Fräulein Knispel asked me insistently whether the well-being of my family and my own future meant anything to me, or whether I had so many bitter experiences and disappointments under my belt as to be unreasonable enough to turn away an extended hand. Did friendship mean so little to me? It became obvious that Resi Knispel knew a lot about what had happened to me with Haarburger and many others. My misadventures had generated more vile gossip than I had realized. At first this realization upset me, but soon it no longer mattered when I recalled Johanna's warning and understood how miserable it would be to get tied up with these people once more through my own unrestrained approach. That's why I replied nicely and coolly that it was in fact the well-being of my loved ones and our future, despite all the disappointments and experiences that had occurred, that forced me to hold back. I didn't wish to upset anyone, but I at least wanted to see how things developed further before I decided for good.

Buxinger, as an upstanding person, respected my caution and said that Fräulein Knispel should be satisfied that I would take time to consider it. The publisher of *Eusemia*, however, didn't like what she called a stab in the back. Right, Buxi, she said to him accusingly, this is no way to get a journal up and running, for we've wasted a good afternoon. If all we did was waste hours and hours in fruitless conversation with each contributor, where would we end up, and if I'm to keep from wasting my own time, then I have to be smart enough not to pick the brains of overly busy people on my own sweet time, only to find out they are fools.

To this I responded, saying, Look, I was happy to come here, but not to have my brain picked, for I had explained right from the start that I couldn't agree to anything. Well, then, fine, replied Resi Knispel, but would I come to a meeting of the main contributors, from which the editorial committee would be formed, for it couldn't do me any harm to meet all the parties involved. But I didn't agree to this suggestion, either. Then was that my final word? I said it was and stood up. Resi Knispel foamed with rage. Here I was, being offered such a wonderful chance, that she found it shameless that I should turn it down, though now she at least understood what Konirsch-Lenz had said about my laziness and my destructive, nihilistic spirit. Knispel had not wanted to believe this kind of talk and had emphatically disagreed with the wallpaper manufacturer, who, incidentally, was also doing an article on his practical work on sociology, but now she saw there was something wrong with me, that I was a morbid person, an asocial, corrosive type. My horrid past, which one can only weep about, had ruined me, the result being that I would always remain unfit for any kind of positive life.

Herr Buxinger cringed with embarrassment at this nasty outburst, but I smiled at him, undisturbed, said a friendly goodbye, and promised to visit him again in his bookshop. Then I said to Resi Knispel that she could indeed be right in what she thought of me, I myself often thinking much worse of myself, but if all that was true, then she would certainly agree that *Eusemia* and I were not made for each other. In addition, I wished *Eusemia* nothing but luck. Then I thanked her for the captivating afternoon and regretted the loss of fruitful work from the hours that had been taken. I said everything as pleasantly as possible, which caused Resi Knispel to accompany me down the hall to the door in a very courteous manner, as if she had forgotten the heavy accusations she had just leveled at me. In the foyer, as I looked for the doorknob, she stopped me.

"Landau, whether you do something for *Eusemia* or not, you are quite a man. I have a lot of respect for you. You amaze me, I, I . . . You know, I liked you right away, Landau, back when I met you at the Haarburgers'. So let's let bygones be bygones. Please, don't go."

"I've no idea what more I can do for you, Fräulein Knispel."

"Resi! Don't call me Fräulein Knispel! And don't act so dumb! I once recommended that you write a novel, *The Miserable*. Don't you remember?"

"Yes, I do."

"And did you write it?"

"No."

"Write, Landau, write!"

"I'm not a writer. I've never written a novel."

"Oh, you dummy, you dear, dear fool! You drive me crazy! Write! It will be the novel of our time! Let your scholarly work have a rest. It will drive you crazy, you are meant for something much more."

"One can't turn away from oneself. One can only turn away from others. That's, unfortunately, the way it is."

"Write, write! Of course, I'll read it. I'll help you, I'll do whatever you want, if only you would just want something! I can find twenty publishers for the novel. When will you come back again, my dear?"

"I won't be coming. For now I must go."

"You can't go! Do you hear? You can't go! Not before you promise that you will come again and tell me when!"

"That's crazy. I can't promise anything!"

"You must! Do I have to spell it out for you that I love you, that I'm crazy for you? I can't live without you!"

"Let me go now!"

I wanted to open the door to the stairwell, but Knispel was blocking it; I would have to shove her out of the way. That I didn't want to do.

"Sleeping Beauty, a fable for our day. Release me, Landau!"

"Get hold of yourself! Johanna is waiting for me at home."

"Do you love Johanna, then—that proud, haughty sourpuss?"

"Don't say anything about Johanna!"

"Well, then, it will have to be both Johanna and me, but not Johanna without me!"

"Please, just let me go!"

"Landau, Landau, kiss me! You can do with me what you wish!"

"I ask only one thing: let us leave each other in peace."

The crazy woman wanted to grab hold of me and drag me off. She did so seductively, like a demon. She pulled me by the tie, it being the last one from my father's shop, scratching my hand with her long fingernails and wounding me and wanting to kiss me and bite me. I asked the madwoman to be reasonable and understanding, but all in vain. I didn't like to call out, not wanting Buxinger to witness any of this unleashed madness, but I couldn't control myself. I shook off the wild beast, pushed her away from me, ripped open the door, raced down the stairwell, and didn't stop running until I had put some distance behind me.

Once I felt I was in the clear, I tried to figure out where I was. I was disheveled, had a small scrape on my chin, which I dabbed at with a damp handkerchief, the scratches on my hand burning. My tie was askew—I loosened the knot in order to tie it afresh, and then noticed that the heavy silk was ripped, a painful wound that only Johanna's gifted hands could temporarily repair. I couldn't return to Resi Knispel. The image of my father appeared before me, Fräulein Michelup sewing silk strips with "HAL" on them, then they were placed in long cardboard boxes, each one neatly labeled, laid out on the counter and left open, the lovely ties visible and lying next to the other goods, patterns and colors arranged, Franziska choosing them, then a long rest in a drawer or in a suitcase during the years of extermination, until they found their way to me in the care of Frau Holoubek or Herr Nerad; then I hid them because I didn't want to wear them or to see them, until finally I pulled them out, one after another, three of them, feeling childishly vain because of Johanna, though she liked them, taking it as a good sign that I was willing to don a piece of the past for her. Johanna had often criticized me for not tying the ties carefully enough. She tried to show me how, fussed around with them, but didn't have much luck, me preferring to tie them the way I wished and not worrying too much about it. It took me a while to do so, but eventually I managed it, thinking it was good and asking Johanna what she thought. Johanna looked me over and laughed, though she didn't laugh too much.

"Resi Knispel must have really got to you."

"How can you say such a thing? I hardly know her, and I don't care about her at all. She couldn't mean less to me, and therefore you're wrong."

"That may be. She just looked at you so weirdly the last time we were at the Haarburgers'."

That I could not believe. I had not been rude to her, but I had not followed up on any of her invitations, and had not shown her the slightest bit of sexual interest, something that Johanna wouldn't have tolerated, though she didn't have the slightest spark of jealousy within her and always thought of my best interests. And then we were in Vaynor for fourteen days; Betty had rented a place from warmhearted people some miles outside the nosy little town where she sold her candies, us spending the first few days of our life together in a town far away from everything. In Vaynor, which consisted only of loosely gathered buildings, we didn't have to tell anyone anything about us, we were free, and indeed the people we met—one quickly got to know them—showed a sweet concern for us, such that we were happy to smile at any face we encountered while exchanging a few pleasant words as well. The people who put us up, and who supplied us with ample meals, were harmlessly chatty, but nothing they wished to know disturbed us, and nothing that they talked about made excessive claims upon us. Their worries and hopes were easily balanced. These people were like innocent children and were pleased to be able to attentively and energetically spend their days, to our pleasure, supplying us with many little pleasing things. They loved music; the piano and the violin case were seldom closed. Everyone in the house was happy when we praised their playing. When Johanna took it upon herself to show the youngest, a ten-year-old boy, a better way to bow, there was no end to his thanks. We were amply indulged with cakes and baked goods and had to empty many a glass at the insistence of our hosts.

Happily, our new friends were ready to sing us some songs from their rough and yet attractive trove of folklore. They tried to translate the words and to explain the context. Since I was pleased to take it up and join in, I won their hearts and they wanted to do anything they could for me. Thus clothes and laundry were washed, folded, and ironed, for which we were hardly allowed to give thanks. Also, I was taught on request the old language of these parts, which few spoke, but which our hosts had preserved well. The gray, weathered church was explained to us both inside and out, and we were shown the local sights where the history of the Welsh was decided in 1286. Unfortunately, the meaning of the events of the Middle Ages weren't entirely clear to us, though I understood a bit, since I was eager to know as much as I could, much more than Johanna, who was happier about my being interested than she was taken with the stories. She thought it was good for me to be healthily distracted, as if such a prolonged engagement of the mind with a distant strange people, if even in a cursory way, could help a person save himself from his own past. That, however, didn't happen, for I still remained plenty troubled, the experiences of earlier days melting into one another. Everything that I confronted in the present filled me with joy, but my inner life remained closed down to it; it was all a kind of brilliance, as if brought by a May snow, but then soon melting, running off, and gone. Johanna was much stronger, and I had to let her lead the way and let myself follow. It made sense that she knew the area better, since she had visited Betty often. And so I let Johanna lead me through the countryside, which I wanted to explore, despite the winter gray and the constant rain.

It was cold, but there was no frost, it having melted hours before. My gaze pressed through the soft mist, and everything looked as if it lived in a silent, distant dimension. We had only three days left; Johanna didn't want to be away from her work for more than a week, while I was also anxious to get on with life and didn't want to risk a longer stay, either. They were insular days, ourselves adrift, our worries subdued, as if stored behind a wall, whenever we wandered through the soft drizzle that soundlessly fell from low clouds. From Vaynor, from halfway up a somewhat steep hillside, we set aim for the valley and the old church and saw Morlais Hill across from us, though not for long, for soon we had reached the riverbed where the Taf-Fechan Brook flowed fast. On stony and sometimes muddy paths we followed it along in the direction of the current, no one to be seen anywhere, only free-range sheep standing together in little herds or on their own, grazing, looking at us curiously, and fleeing with little jumps whenever we tried to approach them or unintentionally got too close.

The dreamy background was familiar to me, for it was suffused with deep runnels much like the mountainous land back there. There stood mighty trees, their leaves gone, though they didn't look naked, since their branches crisscrossed again and again and were covered in thick layers of ivy. Various things grew about—wild meadow shoots, evergreen copses. Thus we took in a good part of the valley, but as we drew away from moss-covered grounds near the brook and toward the road, which for a little ways ran high above the Taf-Fechan, we came under the protective barrier of the high hedges. A feeling of home enveloped us, so that I dared speak only in a whisper there. Above, the landscape was bleaker; it was only right that the nearby summits we could see were called the Black Mountains, or the Fforest Fawr in Welsh. The earth fell in black folds, the black rocks stretching out; even when one gazed off into the distance, all the contours and flat spaces seemed to consist of black. The hillsides rose up treeless, whereby the modest hills carried the powerful feel of a rambling range of inaccessible sharp peaks. All that could be seen were some houses or farms and trees springing up alongside the running water; otherwise, the land rose and fell bare and empty of vegetation, only thinly covered with a layer of sparse grass. Only when your gaze turned away from the distance and looked nearer to home more closely, much more intently, was there revealed a many-layered, labyrinthine network of carpeted green, grasses, durable steady growth, and moss that looked shorn. The grazing animals had nibbled almost everything to the ground, be it the numerous sheep or also cattle, as well as calm horses striding along, lovely and awkward little ponies with thick hides and long hairy legs, their hooves draped with funny bearded tufts. They were green and black and gray and silver, together and in turns, a strange harmony that was both odd and pleasing to me. I would have gotten used to them in a few days and knew: what was here and what happened here was altogether different from what I had had back there. No longer did the mountain woods belong to me, nor that time from years ago; nor was there anywhere that was home, me realizing that I couldn't call a single speck of earth my home. I was expelled and banished, my curse a self-deception, there being no curse at all. It had to do with the acceptance of the expulsion from the paradise of my childhood and youth, my departure from there only the inevitable consequence of a force long ago set in motion. It was fine to still miss the mountain woods, as well as the landscape stretching out from them, but it was also over and done with, for now Johanna was at my side.

We walked for at least an hour in silence. What we had beheld in recent days, about the people that we knew, about the happy and the grim commotions we had endured—we had talked about that enough already. Now mighty adventures had to be set in motion, down into the depths, without direction, both backward and forward at once. But we also had to hold off these adventures; we needed to wait and blindly feel our way ahead in order that we be granted a way through, inscrutable, and yet attainable.

A reverberating whistle sounded. Not only did the old Roman roads wind through the valley, a slow, puffing train had also settled here that ran from the nearby coal-mining district to the south and right through the Black Mountains and the gardenlike meads and along Llangorse Lake and right through the middle of rich pastureland and on to the bishop's seat of Brecon. We spent a few hours there yesterday, in a lovely pub, where, as the only foreigners, we had our midday meal, the people looking at us curiously with eyes wide with surprise. Now a train from the north puffed along, a sleepy locomotive in the lead and pulling just two cars right on by us, clanging like a bunch of slicing knives, though soon it just hummed, then once again louder with a rumbling sound when the train crossed a high bridge over a ravine. Then it was quiet once again, everything fading away and enchanted, only a plaintive whistle that faded away in a wistful tone, searching for any place and footing that might be available, even if we hardly knew it and had nothing in common. We are no longer what we were, we are no longer what we were, ran the constantly receding rhythm of the train, continuing to run inside me for a while.

Soon we came to a little station, it containing an enclosed peacefulness that reminded me of a mountain hut. So remote and unattended that it felt as if it promised sanctuary, it serving the local line of the national railway, diffidently dreaming away, only a couple of times the rare arrival stopping. Pontsticill in big letters was what it said on the helplessly useless building, where not a person was to be seen within its walls or nearby. In fact, there really wasn't anything surrounding it, the station simply plunked down in the middle of nowhere, as if it were the midpoint between other destinations. The train that had rumbled past us had never, I believed, stopped at this forsaken place. The tracks had disappeared.

In awe, we walked on arm in arm, the quiet road not causing us to hurry, it feeling as if perhaps we weren't walking at all but rather that the road just slowly moved beneath our feet. We approached some houses, not even a village, much smaller than Vaynor, though it had a name, a sign saying

Dol-y-gaer. Quietly we wandered through, thus remaining unobserved. What were the people doing behind those walls? Only a child rapped against a windowpane and shouted, though he didn't meet our gaze and hardly noticed us. After only a few steps more, we had left Dol-y-gaer, this being another non-place. Peacefully there lay, as if embedded in the bottom of a large kettle, green and slate blue, a lake. Johanna knew that it was called Pen-twyn, and said that it was man-made, its waters functioning as a reservoir for many cities of the country. A little while later, we then reached two farm buildings on its shore, at which point we left the road.

It had stopped raining and was brighter than it had been in recent days. We turned left and climbed uphill, scrambling over two or three barrier hedges and eventually arriving in a damp pasture. Frequently we looked back, the lake smooth as a mirror, only looking darker from farther away, less watery, more metallic, its waters having secretly swallowed up the light, a rich denseness, viscous and filled with unfathomable depth. The little houses on its shores looked toylike, toylike, as well, the embankment with its rails, toylike above us the blank sky that pressed its whitish blue between the swiftly moving clouds that billowed up white and drifted soundlessly. The sun sequestered a hillside here and there in soft yellows, wandering out over the lake as well, its lit-up surface dazzled by its soft glittering, its rays soon reaching our slope, pushing on farther, striated by shadows that distinguished depths and heights that were gray but also patiently anticipated the unfolding wonder.

We eventually reached the top. Since we had climbed vigorously, the weather continually opening up the skies and then clearing off, and since the air in this windy land hardly stirred, we were warm. Only the stunted plant growth made it look like winter; otherwise the time of year didn't seem at all evident, it smelling of late autumn or early spring, the view of the mountains almost making it feel like summer. The soft, pearly mist, the treeless barren hills, the sloping summits and sharp peaks with their dark cliffs transformed the Black Mountains—a moderately high range that, some miles north of here, barely rose to twenty-five hundred feet—almost into a high range of triple the height and five times the length, as the peaks appeared much grander and more distant than they really were. Thus we climbed along as if in alpine meadows and pastures. Beyond lay a runnel with a little creek running through it, no more than an arm's length across, while to the left we saw a mountain that was also only a hill, yet still looked much larger than it was, and which we wanted to climb. Johanna called it Twyn Croes, though certainly she didn't know the name. It hardly took us half an hour to reach the top. I regretted that we didn't have a map, but Johanna explained the view to me as well as she could.

"When we go down again, and hopefully soon, you should have Betty tell you, for she knows better than me. She knows every corner of this country. She's proud of that, and happy when someone asks her about it. We've walked in a sort of semicircle, for we've come back some ways by climbing the heights that we didn't wish to leave. Now the man-made lake in Pen-twyn is to our north. You see the road along which we were walking; it's a Roman road. Near Pen-twyn it forks in two. The road to the right runs pretty close to the train to Brecon. The left branch climbs sharply higher and runs directly north. Without hardly wavering, it leads to Brecon. Betty is always amazed by the raised mounds of Offa's Dyke, and proudly points to them as if she had built them herself. Do you see them? The steeply rising mountains toward the left in the distance are the Brecon Beacons. They are the highest peaks of the Black Mountains. Somewhat craggy, but the view from them is nice if you're lucky. Toward the north side, from which you can see Brecon deep below, they fall off even more steeply. Farther left, where the heights are softer, I don't know my way around as well. But the valley before it—you can only guess where it is from here—it's very deep and particularly beautiful. The colors there look almost as if one were in Italy. I love it. It's called Cwm Taf, and the brook that flows there is named Taf Fawr. At Cefn—you saw it when we went for a walk with Betty on the first day here—it joins up with our beloved Taf Fechan. There you also see the hollow where Merthyr Tydfil lies, and which then grows smaller. That's the Merthyr Valley. Behind that range are the mountains of Aberdare. Straight ahead of us we can almost see Vaynor. I don't think it can be more than three-quarters of an hour away. Then there is our old familiar Morlais Hill, which blocks the view of Merthyr behind it."

"And there, where the smoke is rising?"

"That's already in the middle of the wastes of coal country. Dowlais, a poor and miserable place, an ugly town—that I know. It looks as if all the

violence of the war took place there. Nothing like that happened in Dowlais, but that's what misery can do. The area has been depressed for years,
for the men have no work and have to be taken care of by the state their
whole lives. The coal mines stretch out farther to the east, valley after valley, one after another, a brook running through each, as well as the railroad
next to it, and high-piled black mounds of coal waste. Tredegar, Ebbw Vale,
Brynmawr are some of the names."

"I'm amazed that you can remember such difficult names. I doubt that
I could."

"It took me some effort. Betty badgered me to get them right. Well, is
that enough for now?"

"Yes, Johanna. It's enough for today. We're near a border here, and
borders have always meant something to me. But this time I want to remain
on this side of the border."

"Not in the coal country?"

"No, not in the coal country. Not in any country. Just here."

"So, then, no longer in the metropolis?"

"That's unavoidable."

"I can speak to Betty. Maybe it is avoidable."

"What do you mean?"

"Well, Betty wants to help me and will do anything I ask her, if she can.
Several times she's suggested that I should move closer to her. Perhaps she
can use us to help her with her baked goods or find something else for us."

"Did you talk to her?"

"No, Arthur. But I can."

"No. That wouldn't be for me. Unfortunately. There are no prospects
here for my work. My escape can't end up landing me in complete isolation."

"I'd be with you, Arthur."

"Of course. I know. I'm so grateful you are. But I meant something else
by this."

"I understand. You have to follow your own path."

"You understand me so well, my dear. Opportunities have to be followed up on. I already know so many people, and each week I meet new
ones. There has to be something right for me. My efforts can't continue

to go for naught. True, at the moment everything is still uncertain, more uncertain than ever. But must it remain so? Is there no way for me to break through the wall? Can't I finally be a person among persons? I believe, dear, it will happen. Together with you—when you're not afraid of my uncertainty, my abyss, I can achieve something. Oh, to achieve something! I'm filled to the brim with things I want to do, books and essays to write, lectures to give, to articulate my ideas and thereby attract the interest of a small number of worthy people, as well as good friends for the both of us. Do you believe that can happen as well?"

"I will do anything you wish. I'll stand by you, whatever happens. I love you so unutterably and have limitless faith in your future, in your integrity, and your great strength."

"Don't go too far, Johanna, not too far! The darkness inside me will still shock you. My weaknesses weigh on me and can at times almost consume me entirely."

"I'm not afraid of anything, Arthur. Maybe I'm a dumb fool and have a thousand senseless anxieties of my own, but I am not a child. I'm not blind to the danger. That's why I offered to talk to Betty. She is simple and not fraught with problems, but she has the wisdom of the heart, and because of that she is kind."

"Then let us be grateful that we have her backing. But let's not ask anything of her, anything that will guarantee our life or my life in this border land. Let me sink into the metropolis. It's immense, labyrinthine, sinister, and I have yet to figure it out. But it has a mysterious neutrality, completely different from the big cities I knew back there. One doesn't belong to this city but, rather, lives with it, independent, almost free, hardly touched by it, and having nothing to do with one another. It feels as if I can never be entirely lost in its lostness. I can be unhappy in the thick of it, but there I feel the unhappiness much less than if I lived in Vaynor and climbed Twyn Croes with you each week. I have no home and seek no home. Yet the metropolis, with its couple of dozen neighborhoods—it, at least for the foreigner, is not a home but rather a habit. And not even the entire city, just the neighborhood in which one settles."

Johanna didn't say anything in response, murmuring something inaudible that still felt loving. She took me by the hand, then soon let go again and looked for a little spot where we could rest awhile. It took some time before we found a place where we could sit on the half-dry ground. Johanna took from me the knapsack—the same one that I had bought before the journey to the mountain woods—and set out something for us to eat. She did so gracefully, less energetically than Anna, she being somewhat dreamy and inward and yet, of course, confident, as if it were a matter of serving invited guests. We ate almost all the good things we'd brought along in the bag. All that remained was a piece of chocolate and two apples, which Johanna insisted that we save for later.

"Are you happy?" she asked out of the blue.

I looked at her long and hard, said nothing, laughed, and moved closer to her.

"We are very much together, Johanna. You are so good to me."

"And the dead?"

"We live from the dead, Johanna. Everything living comes from the dead. When they pass away in peace, it's forgotten, in the sense that through greater awareness we do not have to suffer a terrible shock to our consciousness. We talk about parents, grandparents, great-grandparents, and can follow a complete chain all the way back to the first people, back to Adam and Eve. But if one's parents and loved ones have been swallowed up by a distant, ambiguous, and often unknown death, then naturally we succumb to a horror that we can hardly overcome, and by which we are eventually bested, one's own family chain having been severed, and this horror can never be overcome. It weighs upon us because it is not there. Because we cannot bury it away in our souls. Thus there is no way for us to forget, for now our knowledge is meager, and with that our consciousness remains constantly on edge. For it cannot console us."

"What shall we make of it together, my dear?"

"We must live like the first human beings, Adam and Eve in the far fields after their sin."

"Yet that can't happen. That would not only be blind but also impossible."

"You're indeed right; I don't mean it literally. But we have a duty to begin again, and in this duty we are like the first human couple. What our ancestors realized, built and also misconceived is, for people like us, so beaten down and destroyed, there is nothing left but a brave new beginning to set in motion many things and plans erupting within our hearts. I don't mean by this that we should smash to pieces everything that remains and let our souls rot. On the contrary, we need to preserve what we can preserve. You know, Johanna, those I know and who know me, they don't want to hear that I call myself a conservative and feel myself to be one. When I briefly mentioned it to So-and-So, he doubled up with laughter, and then showered me with his derisive scorn. But it is indeed so, every tradition—though, of course, with this I am by no means talking about evil that's bred, the sum of which can be referred to as natural and developed over time, no, not that at all—in every tradition that really is ancient, the most inner essence of the shared existence, no matter how it transforms itself, is sacred to me. From that we should drink, absorb with every fiber, guard as the most valuable treasure, care for and preserve and share with those who come after us in ever more pure and noble fashion."

"Where, then, is the new beginning? How will it all come together?"

"The new beginning? You see, Johanna, with every heart that survives the Lord sets forth the creation once again. That is always true, and for every person. But it is hardly known and only rarely sensed. We who almost do not exist any longer feel it stronger and perhaps deeper. For the fact that we exist is a miracle. We who are no longer tolerated nor should be thought of and yet nonetheless remain, we who are not a miracle, but who are seen and thought of only as a miracle, we who are on this side and, as I know you understand, we who, no matter how much we lean back to the other side, never reach it, nor can reach it, as we can hardly recall it anymore and have only the blessing of memory in order to say something about the past, which is entirely lost. Memory, Johanna, which you honor, for I've heard you say so, that is the sacred tradition that I honor as well. It is the culmination of everything, as long as we do not lose hold of it and serve it faithfully. The new beginning that we commence with our faith and our works is indeed a repetition, yet, above all, it is a new beginning, the commitment and sacrifice to the future, the daily prayer, the journey toward a destination, and we can only know we're headed toward a destination, Johanna, for we can only hope and wish for the destination, but we don't know it and cannot reach it. It's not what is achieved but, rather, what awaits us that matters. Do you understand what I mean? Ah, I shouldn't be lecturing you!"

"I don't know if I understand it all, Arthur, and yet it says a great deal to me. You must speak, and speak freely. It's all a part of you, and it is you yourself, and I need to hear it."

I rummaged in my coat pocket and pulled out a little leather box and held it out to Johanna.

"This is for you, dear."

She fiddled with it in her hands, the clasp not opening, and only after several tries finally giving way. The pearls lay within, dull silver, sitting there somewhat embarrassed and shy, Franziska's pearls, which she never wore, a gift from her father, she once said, which I remembered now, but she only liked to wear amber or turquoise, and kept the valuable jewels in a box that she hardly ever touched. I also could see the hands that after the war had brought them and given them to me. There was no more amber, no more turquoise to receive, they were lost, but the pearls in the leather box lined with tissue paper slid from my hand into the case; I could no longer look at them. There they rested until I risked taking them with me, as Anna advised. Safely I had carried them through all the borders.

"Do you like them, Johanna? You said that you are very fond of pearls and had to leave them at home. On the morning of your departure, your mother removed them from your neck."

Johanna removed the chain from its velvet cushion and looked at the beads without a word, stroking them as they rustled and shimmered, then she poured them into the palm of her hand, a cone-shaped glistening mound piled on trembling ground. Then she closed her fingers around them, the pearls now invisible. Only from the side, spilling out from her little finger, did a little tail brashly stick out, which I observed while smiling. Johanna sensed my amusement and quickly opened her hand, ashamed, the jewels there among the shadows of her fingers a pale, shining, disorderly clump of gems. With two fingers Johanna took hold of the left end and pulled the entire chain out, grabbing the other end with her right hand and pulling it out so that before us stretched a long, gorgeous double row at eye level, and then she brought them closer to her face until the pearls lay like a satiny bow just below her nose and, opening wider, passed over her eyebrows, her temples, behind the ears, and then over her head.

Johanna bowed her head slightly, the chain shifted and clattered softly, then she stretched it out far from her face, a finger running right and left and looping the pearls around it, the center lowering to form a broad sinking point, forming a rounded bow. Johanna was pleased, that I could see, but she didn't thank me and didn't say anything, but just smiled under lowered eyelashes, her mouth open a little and uneven, one corner sunk deeper than the other, the lips barely parted, teeth not showing. I didn't look directly at her, but I didn't turn away; instead, I tried to draw closer or to look past Johanna, but that didn't work, and so I blinked. Something had begun, that I knew, though I didn't know what and didn't want to think about it, as within me it bubbled up like delirium, myself unable to breathe, a mild pain in my foot making itself known, doubtless the last effects of the injury from the suitcase that had fallen on my foot shortly before I arrived in the metropolis and which had provided me with a painful memory in the weeks since, though I had not felt it for many days. Then I remembered the last apple from back there, Anna's goodbye gift, which had rolled out of my suitcase. I couldn't help feeling that I now needed an apple as something to carry from the past into the future and which could bind the two together.

I opened the knapsack and didn't look at Johanna in order that she not get mad the moment I violated the ironclad decision made earlier. Then I had the fruit in my hand, striped with yellow and red, cool and with a soft lovely glow, a wonderful orb with sunken poles at either end. I held it, covering only half of it with my hand as protection, though I didn't intend to take a bite of the apple. Then I tried to glance at Johanna again. In her eyes there were tears, very clear and bright, though she wasn't crying but instead the teardrops were involuntary. The pearls hung perpendicular from a hand toward the ground. Our glances met, the pearls and the apple both unacknowledged signs in our hands. The hands that were free reached out to each other, but the fingers didn't grasp one another, only the backs of the hands lay against one another, betokening a bond: pearls, hands, apple.

Who knows how long we sat there? The coolness of the ground increased, the dampness rising; it was only a few days after New Year's, there being no way to ignore the season, as we felt the frost coming on. Through leather and wool it pressed and deepened, but my foot no longer hurt, only immense stiffness filled my limbs, smoky puffs of breath blowing from our mouths in the intense chill of the air. Above us the clouds moved in again, long, sinuous strains racing over summit and hill alike, though the silver-blue sky peeked through here and there. It wasn't long before the clouds lowered around us and wrapped us in thick veils and a dense enclosure soon surrounded by streams of sunlight. Nonetheless, we were bathed in light, the milky threads of cloud strongly lit through, though containing a brilliance of their own, the ridges and basins of the land soon retreating into darkness, here in the country of the Black Mountains, even the grass turning black, the lambs that slowly moved about below on the slopes now dark gray.

We had warm clothes on, but since we had been sitting for so long they no longer kept out the weather. If we didn't want to freeze completely, we couldn't stay any longer and finally had to get up, though each of us was too shy to make the first move or suggest that the other should, so we continued to sit there undecided. It could have begun raining, the air above getting more and more damp, while from the ground the dampness rose like quiet hidden flames. The apple in my left hand had turned into a frozen ball, my fingers around it so stiff that they hurt. Had the pearls in Johanna's involuntary iron grip turned to frost? I grabbed her by the hand and pressed it gently, she closing her fingers tight with her thumb stretching over them. Through such vigorous rubbing we awoke from the numbness that endangered our souls, looking more intently at each other, our gazes no longer lost in a dream but also unwavering, consciously looking into the depths, such that we knew that we would be there for each other. For the first time, we beheld each other in our shared togetherness and our foregone separateness, it becoming clear what held us together and apart, us understanding what we would have to seek and what avoid, sensing the overpowering shudder of what had been passed on to us, the undiminished power of the deep inheritance and flooding surge of an ancient beginning, the break of a new day, the wish for children perhaps having overcome Johanna in that moment much as it did me, something which earlier I only rarely felt and never yet to such a degree.

I then could have said something, or even should have, since we had run the gamut of the superficial to the intimate that day and now understood each other so well; and yet I didn't do it. I wasn't sure if Johanna expected me to; perhaps she was also not sure if I expected something from her. Yet I had to do something; I had to betray the moment and decide something. Thus I started to stand, but no, I could not, for it was not so easy, my legs being too heavy, the joints stiff. I had to let go of Johanna and swing my arms in order to lift myself up, but after a couple of tries I could get only as far as my knees. Johanna sat there without saying a word and looked at me tenderly. It could have been that she felt for me and was surprised at me at the same time; the look she shot me was a double one, sincere and direct, but also unreadable and shifting. With strong strokes I rubbed my legs in order to get the blood moving. This helped, for I could finally stand and breathe deep. Then I helped Johanna, it being easy to do so, it really being presumptuous of me to think she needed my help, for she really didn't.

"Do you like the pearls?" I asked softly, without hesitating.

"Can I keep them? Are they mine?"

I nodded. Johanna fiddled with the gold clasp, the three black pearls gleaming darkly. Soon the pearls were around her neck; for a moment I saw the lovely face of my mother before me, after which I thought of the mother of my dearest, and then of Franziska's shadow. From the place where we had sat, I picked up the papers and some rubbish, burying it all under stone, lifted the knapsack, and stuck the box for the pearls into it, wondering for a moment whether I should make the apple disappear, but then thought better of it, closed tight the laces, and went over to Johanna. We were ready.

"I know the direction in which we need to head, Johanna, but I don't know the way. Can you take the lead?"

"There is no way. We just walk on ahead. Downhill. It's not far to Vaynor."

We took the steepest path, making our way with powerful steps. Soon we were warm and took a more measured gait.

"Did Franziska wear the string of pearls?"

"Hardly, my dear. I don't believe I ever saw them on her. She liked to wear amber most of all, sometimes turquoise, as well as large Bohemian garnets, which I no longer have."

"Sweetheart, forgive me, but we had a marvelous day! We had the loveliest day we've had since we've known each other, and I am wearing Franziska's barely worn pearls. Still, will you be so good and tell me something of Franziska?"

"Franziska . . . my darling, I had a dream about her. I'm almost not inclined to share it, for it could be wrong to do so, more of an image conjured by me than a true spirit. I don't know if I should tell it."

"Don't be afraid! But, if that's the way you feel, you don't have to say anything. I don't wish to interfere. The legacy is yours, it's yours, and I respect that."

"If that's the case, Johanna, then I can tell you. I lay asleep in bed and believed that I had woken up. I was not in Vaynor, nor in the metropolis, nor actually back there. I was in no place I recognized. But I was somewhere far off, in an apartment that belonged to me. And then Franziska was there, quiet and radiant—everything about her was radiant, her clothes, her hands, and her face. But, above all, the face, and most of all the forehead above her eyebrows. That glowed the most, even more than her glowing hair and eyes, which indeed were open but looked as if they gazed through a veil. She came very close to me, pressing close to my bed. I thought that she wanted to sit down next to me, so I tried to sit up in order to show her how happy I was that she was there. But with sweeping, half-lifted arms she waved me off. Then I remained still and turned my head more strongly in her direction. She didn't sit down, but instead got very close, standing next to the bed such that her clothes rubbed against it. I couldn't touch Franziska but only behold her, my hands remaining under the blanket, and it being impossible to pull them out from there. She looked at me tenderly, very kindly, with a sympathetic and also animated sorrow. She was otherworldly, sad, and majestic, though she was also confident and not full of despair. I felt guilty before her, for she was not alive, she was just there, and I felt that anything alive had to feel guilty in the face of everything dead, the guilt of living in the face of the departed and the sublime, which we often call the eternal. I wanted to share my deepest feelings with Franziska, but I didn't want to say it aloud, I just wanted to somehow share it. Nor could I speak. Somehow I shared it with her, without words and speech, as well as without looking at her or giving her any sign; the only way she could know was because she understood me, and because I felt nothing else but this. She gazed at me intimately, not all-consuming, yet intently. Then she said, 'You mustn't worry!' I didn't worry, or at least not any longer, but then an irrepressible sadness filled me to the core, for I had left Franziska. I had left her without asking her permission, deeming it all right to be without her. That was a betrayal; I had become unfaithful. You need to know in order to understand, Johanna, that ever since the day the murderer's hand separated us, separated us forever, as she was asphyxiated and her defiled noble body was burned to ashes, I never thought of or looked at another woman, even Anna, with so much as the slightest desire, until I saw you. Then it was obviously clear to me from the first moment, and that is why when we sat with Frau Sauber-mann and Herr Buxinger at the Haarburgers' I was so bold as to speak to you despite all reason and my own will, reaching out to you in hardly a subtle fashion. Yet back to the dream. But wait. Before I go on with my story, I must tell you about a visitation that I experienced during my escape from over there and which was similar to my dream but also completely dif-ferent. During that one, I spoke to Franziska and asked her, 'Will you let me go?' Or no, it was not during the journey but after, a few weeks later in the guesthouse, just before the first time I called you and visited you in the Of-fice for Refugees. You already meant a great deal to me, for otherwise why would I have asked Franziska this question? But, nonetheless, it was differ-ent, as you will soon hear. She let me go; her voice was clearly audible, yet only her voice. I had not asked Franziska but simply posed the question. But it was Franziska's voice, clearly, no mistaking it, that answered me, saying that she had let me go, whether I existed or not. Yet now, in this dream, it was different. I had left Franziska. It had to have been so, because I could do no different, but it was, in fact, my choice; I had done it on my own. I felt the hot demands of lust that lead to adultery. Franziska knew so, for alas, she knew everything. She observed me with resonant kindness, her gaze pene-trating my skeleton and lifting it up. She spoke with a level yet muffled voice: 'I have protected you. I am now leaving you. You are free, you are free. You will now follow your own path. May the blessing of grace attend your fortunes!' I wanted to grab hold of her hands before she disappeared, a mixture of sorrow and shame and bitterness roiling inside me. But I could not grab hold, since my hands lay continually immobile under the blanket, nor could Franziska grab hold of mine, for she had withdrawn, the separation having been announced. She looked at me again in an incomparable way that I could only call benevolent, though I have never seen a look quite like it from anyone living or dead, even in a dream. Franziska moved her head slowly and gently, her eyes almost shut, as if to say 'No.' Then she lifted a hand and held it high above me, giving clearance, saying goodbye and blessing, all of it together, and then she walked away, adorned in exalted splendor. She didn't walk toward any door but rather only to the opposite wall that had no door, and which appeared to retreat from Franziska for a while, as if the room were expanding. During this she often turned to look back at me, always with a loving, departing expression, and I knew that she was not of this earth, and that as soon as she reached the wall she would step through it. I bent my head strenuously in the direction she moved, but the wall was opaque glass and Franziska walked inside it. The divider remained transparent enough, such that she turned toward me more and more often and smiled abstractly in the direction of my bed and nodded as if to indicate something to me, as if I were still a part of her realm. She remained lit up, but in her passage through the wall the distance was more shadowy, other-worldly, thinner, and, to me, disembodied and blurry. Also, it was harder and harder to see through the wall, it becoming more and more hazy, the wall fading, giving off only a vague idea of itself, and all at once, with a last look and a hand raised high, the figure stepped through the wall while turning away and leaving with its back to me. There being nothing more to see, I was alone, abandoned, lying in the room in severe, heavy darkness, my gaze always directed toward the wall, which was hardly recognizable, although gradually it appeared to be closing in from the distance and returning to the dimensions of the middle-sized room that had been there at the start of the dream. Loneliness rose up sharply within me and closed about my throat, such that I grew anxious. I couldn't see anything else, my eyes sank in a sea of tears, and as I torturously closed my eyelids in order to stop the burning stream, the thought of my mother occurred within me. Without looking at me, she sat sewing a shroud. I said *a* shroud, for I didn't know whose it was, my father's or mine. We were indeed both there, Father and I. I called out to Mother. She didn't hear and continued sewing, a bloody band painfully adorning her neck. Then I called to Father, asking him to have Mother turn to me, but he refused. I insisted that he do so in a last attempt:

'Father and Mother, I'm here, your only son, your other child, your only daughter having died many years ago in the days of limited sorrows, which now, in the days of endless loss, no longer exist.' But neither reacted to my words. Then I held out an apple as an offering, an apple like this one in my hand. No one took it, and so I set it down. Father and Mother were buried in darkness. I had to find Franziska again, so I opened my eyes wide, the stream of tears having stopped, the sockets painfully dry as sand, but nothing visible, for Franziska was now behind the wall forever. With her departure I felt eased, but extremely unhappy about where I was. Then I thought of you, Johanna, but I didn't know where you were. I was worried about you and me, and I wanted to look for you, but I had no idea where I might find you. And then I woke up. Next to me you lay in a deep slumber, no movement at all except your quiet, even breathing. Then I knew that our bond was still not complete, and yet that it could be completed, and so I lay closer to you, but without waking or disturbing you, and soon fell asleep. That's why I brought the pearls along today. I wanted to give them to you the day we got married; that's what I planned, but I couldn't then, and then I waited and waited. Now it's right, now at last."

During the story of my dream Johanna had moved closer and closer to me, and now we walked arm in arm, which was the best thing to do, given the slippery path, in order to hold each other up. Johanna didn't say a thing when I had finished; there was nothing more to say. Without saying a word, we headed toward our destination in order that we not arrive too late for dinner with our hosts. But this dream and my reporting of it to Johanna stayed with me, for its sacred truth felt salutary and manifested itself within me. Whether it's still there within me today I don't know. I cannot know for sure, yet in my powerlessness, which I acknowledge, I have been freed, or, to put it more precisely, I am more freed than before. The shadows that rise up within me and in my dreams have eased. Franziska, Father, and Mother, after many groundless attacks that have torn me to shreds, have released me from their hold. Nothing more of their fate is a part of me; it is as if I am my own person. It's as if I exist. Enough, that's enough.

I stood staggering before existence, but I was the one who staggered, and there is something there that relates existence and me to each other, perhaps never comfortably but reliably. Because Johanna is here. How far away can she be? Here she is. I can call to her, I can ask for her help. She's alive, and here am I. Indebted to a forgiving protectoress and existing only through her. And the children, their happy chirping, their liveliness, their inviolateness, and whose earthly father I remain. Their friend, they who have someone stronger than they to thank, a guardian who prays for them and can pray. Their quick daily growth under the care of their mother. She takes care of them—Johanna speaks and sings and is sweet to them day after happy day. How wonderful it is that Anna can enjoy such lovely company for a day almost every week. The children love their aunt more than anyone but ourselves, and it's best that she no longer lives so far away in the country, from which she rarely could visit. She now has a high-level position in a new home for the blind not so far away from us.

Whenever Anna is free she often comes by in the evening, spends the night with us, and then we have a lovely morning together and happily spend the whole day with one another. Now I hear the women and children. They appear to be done, and soon the call to breakfast will occur, Michael will be off to school, Eva to kindergarten. Without a doubt the boy will insist that Anna take him, while I will have to settle for the honor of ambling along behind them with Eva. I had to hurry to get ready while Johanna worked to prepare breakfast, hurrying around with clanging cups and plates in the back room, then again to the kitchen, everything soon ready. How easy it was to accept all of her sweet care, the unfolding of little daily concerns being Johanna's helpful contribution. Now I was ready and wanted to go across to the others and was already standing at their bedroom door. Then the doorbell rang, and it was certainly the mailman. Michael loved to greet him, so he quickly skipped through the hall to the front door. But this time I could tell that I had to be the one to open up, and so I hurried along beside the boy. When I opened the door, the world outside was bright and wide. The air that pressed against me was fresh, a clear autumn morning. Though it wasn't his fault that he had often brought disappointing news, the mailman is a nice man with whom I've always been on good terms. But never before had he laughed with me with such relish. He must have known something—namely, that he was bringing good news.

"A registered letter, Herr Landau!"

He handed me the receipt to sign, along with his blackened, thick, nubby pencil, the kind that only mailmen carry on their appointed rounds. With a quick motion, I signed my name and was ready to accept my letter.

"The letter?" said the man, looking at me with a smirk. "It's out there in the street."

I then looked out at the street and recognized, to my horror, the hearse that the pallbearers had previously arrived in to take me to the crematorium. I wanted to say, "It's a mistake, it's a mistake," and run off and slam the door behind me, but I didn't move from the spot. I saw how the mailman bowed to me reverently before he went on his way. His behavior confused me, such that I didn't even thank him. Then the pallbearers, Brian and Derek, jumped out from behind the hearse and opened it up such that I beheld a beautifully decorated coffin. I was not ready for such a warm welcome; who had gone to such efforts to take care of my meager existence? But I was pleasantly surprised, for the men in their handsome suits doffed their hats to me, which isn't customary here, and approached respectfully, not even daring to pass through the open gate on the tiled path that led to the front door. They remained standing outside on the sidewalk and stood there politely and humbly as if waiting for a sign from me before they would even say a word. This good behavior pleased me, though the visit itself wasn't that welcome, for I was not at all inclined to let myself in for such an unprofitable business just because of some insensible duty assigned to the pallbearers by someone, and which they wished to fulfill. The mailman was already gone and did not care about us. I saw him huddling in the Byrdwhistles' doorway as I finally roused myself to do something.

"Gentlemen, there are no dead here to haul off. You made that mistake with me once already, and I won't stand for it again."

Derek and Brian didn't react at all, and just continued standing there with heads bent. I looked them both dead in the eye and observed that, despite hanging their heads, they were both shaking shamelessly with laughter. I felt that there was something sympathetic and forgiving in their expressions, as if they grasped a deep misunderstanding, which caused them to immediately summon the kind of respect that was only proper to their lower position. I looked for the mailman once again, but what could he know as he hopped from house to house in a carefree manner, hardly thinking about me but, rather, about his work, he seeming less and less important the farther off he moved. I had done nothing for him other than sign for the delivery, but even that, even that was too much; he had my signature, meaning that I alone had to worry about what to do with these pallbearers.

"Do you have some kind of message for anyone at this house?"

The pallbearers breathed more easily and looked at me officiously.

"You, then," Brian replied, "are the famous Herr Dr. Adam Landau?"

I nodded and corrected him: "Arthur!"

"That doesn't matter, Arthur or Adam, it's all the same."

"If you say so."

This I said in a somewhat melancholy way, but I didn't think much about it.

"You mustn't be sad, Herr Doctor," Derek confided. "We are here on a happy occasion."

With an encouraging look, Brian agreed, but he seemed to disapprove of Derek's rude talk. Then he said, "My colleague is right, the news is good."

"So, then, tell me, Brian!" I said, such that he shut up, surprised that I had called the man by his first name.

Then the front door of the hearse opened, and the driver—I remembered right away that he was called Jock—got out with some difficulty and walked right up to the gate, where he greeted each pallbearer in turn. He had also left the door open behind him, and next to his seat I saw someone hunkered down in the hearse. It was a very old man who was wrapped up against the season in a winter coat, over which a long beard fell. The man looked familiar to me, but I could have been wrong; in any case, I likely wouldn't have been able to recall. But then, after a moment, I realized that it was the director of the crematorium, who had interceded personally, because I had given the pallbearers such a hard time during their last visit. Yet that probably wasn't true; the old man had likely come along for some unknown reason and had nothing to do with the task of picking up the dead. He couldn't care less about me and the three assistants, but instead just sat there unmoving, as if the whole thing had nothing to do with him.

Brian let Jock approach, and Jock planted himself between Derek and Brian and slung his arms fondly over the two of them. Did the pallbearers feel too weak to carry out their task, such that they had to rely on the driver's help? Brian, whom I had asked to speak up, still didn't speak. If the behavior of the men, who stood before me like a living wall, had not been so polite, I would have been very angry and felt there was horseplay afoot. In a room behind me, breakfast was waiting; I could hear the voices of my family and couldn't stand here in the doorway for long. I also wanted to avoid an embarrassing appearance, and to protect Anna from any kind of unpleasant business.

"Gentlemen, you know from your last visit that I was willing to follow you to the crematorium. Or not willing, to be honest, but still I went along. And yet nothing came of it. All of a sudden, you disappeared and everything was over. It all came to nothing. That can't happen again. I am still alive; everyone in this house is alive. I'm also expecting someone. Please acknowledge that you've made a mistake and leave me alone!"

The three men looked at me, disappointed, yet none said a word. Probably it was hard for them to know what to say, or perhaps they were just cowardly. I could tell that I still had to say something.

"Well, then, Brian, don't make any fuss and finally drop this business for good! I want to have breakfast and don't have any time for this."

"Oh, please, please, don't be so impatient!"

"No, really, don't be!" whispered Derek and Jock intently in order to back up Brian.

"I'm not impatient, but enough of this talk, if that's what you mean by happy news!"

"We're here to pick you up."

"That's what I in fact thought. But today you won't get me so easily. Show me your orders!"

"I don't have any orders, only an honorable duty."

"I doubt that I will honor your duty. But that's enough, off with you!"

"My colleagues and I have to put up with all you say, if that's what suits you. Still, I would really appreciate it if you would handle us a little more respectfully. It really hurts when you offend us, for we are not allowed to answer back."

"I don't mean to offend you, Brian, but if you won't listen any longer, then you have to explain in no uncertain terms what it is you want."

"Here in the middle of the street? Are you serious, Herr Doctor?"

"Well, then, come into my study. But promise me that it won't take very long."

I immediately regretted inviting the men in, but there was no turning back now and, strangely, not once was I afraid that they outnumbered me three to one. With their hats in their hands and allowing me to take the lead, the three followed me into the house and into my study. I shut the door firmly behind them, walked over to my desk, where the completed manuscript of my *Sociology of Oppressed People* lay, sat down, and pointed to some chairs, indicating that my little-desired guests should take a seat. However, they didn't respond to my gesture of invitation but stepped up to my desk as if they wanted to admire my work, though they kept a bit of a distance, which made it clear to me that they were indeed serious about being respectful.

"Well, then?" I said to Brian again.

"I have the duty to invite you to the Sociology Conference of the International Society of Sociologists at Shepherd's Field, and to take you there as well."

That couldn't be right, I couldn't possibly have heard right. The Sociology Conference. Shepherd's Field? Pallbearers sent for such a duty, nor was I even a member of the society. Who was trying to make a fool of me? I didn't know if I should be angry or just laugh, but I didn't react at all.

"Did you bring along a written invitation?"

All of the men seemed to wonder if they had. Brian squinted to either side of him at Derek and Jock before he answered me.

"An invitation, Herr Doctor? No, we don't have an invitation. But that is not necessary, for you are a guest of honor. We are only little people who know nothing. We were just given an assignment, and now we are only doing what we were asked to do. For people like us there is no talking back, unless we want to lose our paychecks. Isn't that right, Derek?"

"Yes, of course, that's correct."

"Precisely!" confirmed the one to the left.

"There you have it, Herr Doctor. We were sent, and we just do what we're told. This time we had to deal with the mailman. That was new to us. Poor Jock had to drive at a snail's pace. But what came of that? Nothing at all. And now we ask of you, let us take you to Shepherd's Field!"

"To Shepherd's Field? As I'm sitting here?"

"Yes. There they are holding the Sociology Conference. We'e supposed to bring you."

"Not to the crematorium?"

"What do you think of us! It's enough to make one cry, since you don't wish to believe us! When I say Shepherd's Field, then it's Shepherd's Field. Everything there, I've been told, is arranged for you."

"Do I have to go with you?"

"No, no. Certainly not. We have an assignment, not you. You are requested to. But of your own free will. But, as I already said, we are lackeys, and if we don't bring you it will be bad for us."

"I could write a note saying that you carried out your assignment to the fullest. I can take all the blame myself."

"Oh, please don't do that, Herr Dr. Landau! Just come along!"

"You want to put me in the coffin?"

"Who told you that? We won't put you in the coffin unless you tell us to. You have no idea how insistently we were told to only follow your lead. All we are supposed to do is give general directions, instruct, and advise. I've been doing this a long time, but I can't recall ever being reminded so vehemently about our responsibilities. You are in charge, but please don't cause any difficulties!"

"What do you think should happen? Tell me what your gut says, Brian!"

"You should sit, if you're willing, on top of the coffin. Ahead and behind you will be flowers and wreaths. Derek and I will sit on either side of you, as your honor guard. We can support you or hold you by the hands so that during the drive, if it gets bumpy, you won't lose your balance and fall. Also, the drive will be short, and the hearse has good springs. Jock will drive whatever speed you like."

"When will all this happen?"

"Whenever you would like, but if I could ask on our behalf, then as soon as possible."

At this Johanna walked in, wanting to see what was taking me so long, but when she saw the pallbearers her annoyance at my dallying seemed to disappear.

"Good morning, gentlemen. To what do we owe the pleasure of this early visit today?"

The men felt relieved to see my wife, greeting her and talking to her kindly. One could tell that they were deeply afraid that I would turn down the invitation to the Sociology Conference. That's why they made every effort to win Johanna's sympathies. She was at least as amazed as I was, though she recovered her footing much more quickly. She didn't give off any sense of mistrust but, on the contrary, behaved as if things were fine for me. Then we agreed that we probably needed to hurry, but we didn't want to rush things, and, to the pallbearers' delight, which far exceeded that of the driver, I agreed to take my place on the coffin for the drive. As soon as I said I was ready, they vied with one another to make me happy, continually asking me what I wanted during the journey. Finally, I waved away all their niceties with both hands, it having become too much. Before that caused them to despair, Johanna had the good idea to invite them to breakfast. Charmed, they accepted the invitation and promised this time not to stuff any food or silverware into their pockets.

Pleased, the guests came along with us, bowing to Anna and warmly greeting the children, who were not the least bit afraid of them. Derek remarked attentively how beautifully they had grown and developed. Places were quickly set for the three men, and still more hearty items were brought out so that we could all fortify ourselves. Oddly, I was satisfied with everything, my strong animosity, which I at least felt toward Brian, having melted away, since he had tried as best he could to soften his nature and to be friendly to the good-natured Derek, who seemed to be very interested in Anna, though he also joked around with Eva, who couldn't take her eyes off him. Meanwhile, Jock was entirely engaged by our Michael, who was proud to impress an actual charioteer with his knowledge and asked him about a hundred different things. Jock was a bit at a loss when Michael wanted to know whether a hearse was built differently from a normal car. Then the boy turned to his mother and asked pleadingly whether, in addition to the good two dozen toy cars he already owned, he could soon add a beautiful black hearse, complete with glass windows. Jock saved Johanna the effort of having to explain that such toys did not exist, because a good child didn't think about death, but how nice it would be to have other cars, such as a fire truck with a pump and a ladder. In this way, the children were happily distracted and gave Johanna and me time to discuss what we needed to with Brian. He had no trouble at all with the idea that after breakfast I would put on my best suit. He also happily assented when Johanna asked if she could attend my special day. He recommended that she put on her best dress, something becoming. She suggested that she could ride with me in the hearse, whether it be next to the coffin or along with me on top of it. Again, it became apparent that the men were to follow my orders, because Brian stated courteously that I, and I alone, could say. While it didn't fall within the purview of his assignment to say so, he thought it was not a good solution, for though the coffin was indeed solid and would not collapse under the weight, the flowers and wreaths might suffer, and that would be deplorable. In addition, in his twenty-five years of service as a pallbearer he could not recall a wife's ever having been in a hearse who was not already dead, and therefore such a thing had never been heard of before. After some consideration, we had to respect these arrangements.

Brian explained how near we were to Shepherd's Field, and that it would be easy for my wife to walk there and have Anna accompany her. If the two women left in time, they would have the chance to see me arrive and be witnesses to the certainly ample welcome that awaited me. But I couldn't stand to have Johanna walk while I rode. Which is why I had to figure out a suitable means of transportation for the women. Someone recommended a taxi, but Johanna remembered that sometimes you had to wait half an hour on the telephone, only to have one not show up. She therefore had a better idea. The Simmondses, who ran the vegetable stand around the corner, were pleasant people whose large delivery truck stood idle in the morning hours at the start of West Park Row. Johanna could speak to Mrs. Simmonds right after breakfast to see if her husband might be prepared to take them the short way to Shepherd's Field. The idea seemed to me excellent.

The bigger worry was what we should do with the children. Perhaps I should quickly take them to school and kindergarten, but Johanna was against this; we should not be celebrating while the children had a normal day of work at school. Brian looked at her gratefully and said with admiration that she was a good mother; one could see straightaway that she had all it took to provide the children with a good upbringing. Then she suggested that perhaps Michael and Eva could be left with Mrs. Stonewood or Mrs. Byrdwhistle, but they would be bored there, because the children of these women would be in school; it was a bad idea. Then I came up with the solution. If Mr. Simmonds would let us use his truck, there would certainly be enough room to take the children as well. Brian congratulated me and passed on to the father the very same compliments that he had just made to the mother.

Thus everything was settled as to what needed to happen next. Anna took it upon herself to dress up the children, who romped about in excitement. Johanna hurried over to the Simmondses', while I left the three men to smoke and talk among themselves as I hurried off to put on my best suit. Then I walked into my study in order to watch for Johanna's return from the window. Then she was there, a quick look convincing me that she had met with success at the Simmondses', and, sure enough, there followed right behind her a powerful vegetable truck that pulled up right behind the hearse. I also saw how the Simmondses got out leisurely and the two of them stood on the sidewalk next to their truck. Somewhat breathless, Johanna hurried in to say to me that the merchant had been somewhat impressed by the request and had closed his shop, Mrs. Simmonds in no way wanting to miss the excitement. When I looked out to the street again, I saw that quite a number of people had gathered, though it was not a deafening crowd as when I was supposed to go to the crematorium. Michael and Eva yelled, wanting to run out of the house, but Anna held them back, wishing to prevent too big of a scene. Johanna rushed back and forth in the house, as would any proper housewife before a family outing. Shepherd's Field—at the sound of that the children could hardly contain themselves, as for them it meant the fun of the annual fair. I didn't have the heart to smash these expectations. The idea of holding a conference under the open sky struck me as a bit austere, but hopefully they had put up a large tent, as one would use for a circus, as well as taken care to put in a stand for refreshments, so that the children wouldn't be too disappointed.

Finally, we were all ready and left the house. On the street a number of curious people had gathered, but far fewer than I had feared. The neighbors, however, were all there and looked on—that's the only way to put it—with deep respect. I didn't trust my eyes and tried to find any hint of mockery in the faces of familiar ones and strangers, or any other sign of misguided feeling, but there was not a trace of it to be found. On the contrary, they wished us well with obvious warmth and seemed proud of us, Mrs. Byrdwhistle holding back tears of joy. The ones farther off waved at us, while across in the apartment house a number stood at their windows waving handkerchiefs and little flags. I was pleased to also find there the two women with the cat that walked along the ledge.

Meanwhile, Mr. Simmonds had opened the back of his old truck and covered the flooring with many layers of newspaper, while his wife vainly basked in her fame in playing an important role at a civic event. I no longer know just how it came about, but before long Mrs. Stonewood and Mrs. Byrdwhistle and their children, as well as some other people from the neighborhood, had climbed into the vegetable truck, the delighted Eva having already been lifted up, while Michael boyishly couldn't hold back and ignored all his mother's urgings to such a degree that he got his jacket and pants dirty. Even Anna had nimbly swung herself up into the truck. Only Johanna remained next to me and waited there, not knowing what to do. Then came Jock, who stretched out a hand and assured us that he would drive carefully, he knew what this day meant. He then sat before his steering wheel, and next to him sat the old man, who, as before, didn't care about anything that was going on around him, and still looked familiar to me, though I couldn't place him.

Derek busied himself in the back of the hearse, fiddling with the flowers; he might even have shoved the coffin around a bit, but I might have imagined that. I realized that I shouldn't wait much longer, even if Brian was the model of politeness and wouldn't make the least effort to remind me to hurry. He placed himself next to Johanna and me like an old member of the family, his motions becoming more and more refined, none of them seeming at all vulgar or common, as I had felt his earlier demeanor to be. The truth was that his face possessed a mixture of noble seriousness, fatherly reserve, kind apology, and something unusual that deeply affected me. I would have been happy to shake his hand and press it in gratitude, but I didn't think it at all fitting, this kind of open bond not being the least proper to our different positions, and so I was satisfied with sharing a secret meeting of the minds between us. No matter how much I tried to resist, I couldn't help having the impression that I was standing face to face with my father, a younger version of my father, indeed, but nonetheless him, to whom I owed all honor. The man had given this impression so strongly that

I could feel my father within me. I didn't want that to go on for too long, so I told Johanna to join the others in the vegetable truck. She squeezed my hand silently, laughed at me, and went off.

Now all that was left was to get in with Brian; I didn't want to waste another minute, but I was too shy to step into the hearse ahead of my companion, not so much because I was the main person of concern as because I couldn't help seeing my father, to whom the greater honor was due, in this man. I knew that it was all up to me, and I had to decide and make my wishes known that Brian should step in first. However, I didn't want to use words and had only to think it in order to choose. Then it was made clear to me that I had to make the sacrifice and be the first. I pointed a finger at the hearse, and Brian nodded. And so I went, my father following me with an assured gravity; I sensed the almost soundless sureness of his step landing large and meaningful around me like a protective coat. At the running board I took hold of Derek's helping hand, and was struck by how much easier it was than I'd thought it would be to climb into the mighty glass cabinet of the hearse.

Brian had not helped me, he feeling certain that all was okay, and the fact that he was behind me was all that mattered. I tried to take my place atop the coffin, but that was not so easy. Coffins are meant to be lain in, not to be sat upon, and certainly not with legs straddling either side. I bemoaned my clumsiness and wanted to ask Derek if I couldn't sit on the coffin sidesaddle. I could do that, it was within my rights, but again I had to think of Brian and his words; I mustn't disappoint his pure humanity. No matter how much I wanted things my way, I couldn't have them. I was dependent on others; I was connected to them and had to do what was expected of me. It had come to be true that, to whatever extent my doubt in existence could be dissolved, something essential was attained, and I was stretched between these two extremes. Thus the most uncomfortable seat was good enough for me, the grace of life sitting upon a shrine of death within the vehicle of death.

The flowers in front of and behind me were painfully pressing against one another with their coolly swirling scents, but there was nothing I could do, some of them being askew, many of them squished. I felt bad and complained, looking apologetically at Derek and his now less telling face, while I didn't dare turn to Brian. But now, at last, I was sitting, it being hard and painful at the same time, the ridges of the coffin cutting into my thighs. I only hoped that the drive would soon start and soon end. My friends touchingly made the effort to push me into the middle of my saddle, but they didn't succeed entirely, no matter how much I tried to advise them of the best way to go about it. Finally they gave up trying to jockey me into the best spot, probably feeling sorry for me or sorry for themselves. So they left me to it, closed the glass doors, at which I heard further sounds whose meaning I couldn't quite make out, though likely they had to do with the folding up of the steps used to climb in and the turning of the lock. Then the pallbearers got in. Derek was to my left, while Brian was to my right. I wasn't feeling all that good, though the moment felt like the evening of a sacred day of rest, rather than like the morning of a weekday. I whispered the words of a prayer that was appropriate to it:

"Our Lord and the Lord of our Fathers, be pleased with our rest, bless us with Your commandments and allow us to know Your teaching. Satiate us with Your goodness, gladden us with Your salvation and purify our hearts, so that we may serve You in truth."

I had not completed this sentence before Brian knocked on the window that separated the glass cabinet from the driver, as Jock acknowledged the signal. Then I heard the motor start up, and soon we were off. I would have fallen over if my helpers had not taken mercy on me. I would have been happy to lock arms with them and give up, though I had to settle for the quiet support they extended. I would also have liked to look out at the people on the street, though given the way I had to crouch, there was no way of doing so without bending over dangerously, besides which I was too tense and wanted nothing else but a fast and happy end to the journey.

The sounds of the vehicle were drowned out by a heavy rumbling from behind. Simmonds rumbled along, but the sound pleased me, for then I could sense that Johanna was near, as well as the children. The separation couldn't last long. Then we braked somewhat sharply, but unfortunately we had not arrived at our destination, only at Halstead Way. Yet before I knew it we were already at the edge of Shepherd's Field. I was feeling very uncomfortable, because outside there was an oppressive crush full of a horrible buzzing and drowning music. This was no Sociology Conference; it was the regular fair with its usual, though today unexpected, bustle, even if upon closer inspection the number of people out at this early hour was not all that large. I couldn't resist looking intently at Brian and Derek, though to my annoyance they were not the least concerned. Thus they had managed to make a fool of me, and it rightfully happened to the failed scholar Arthur Landau, who deserved a place in a show booth at the fair. There I sat as a figure of shame, powerless in a hearse, having to wait to see what tasteless pranks awaited me.

Defenseless and awkward, I couldn't go after the mighty pallbearers, or even yell at them as I wished to. The ridiculousness of my situation in the glass cabinet was not to be overestimated. I at least got down from the coffin—how had I let myself fall for such mischief?—but it wasn't easy to do so, for even after such a short journey my legs were stiff, me feeling as if I'd been broken on the wheel. Stiffly I swung my right leg to the left side and sat facing Derek. I hoped that it upset Brian, for now I detested him; Derek seemed to me much more bearable as the less important man. But I had to learn that I had not properly sized up my companions. Derek was pleased that in turning to him I had deemed him worthy, he laughing at me respectfully and also jokingly, while from behind Brian tenderly ran his hand from the top of my head down the back of my neck, which made me shiver. Up ahead the door was opened, and outside the noise abated, something that certainly had happened at a given signal. I noticed how people had gathered about the vehicle and recognized a number of familiar faces among them.

Jock jumped out from his seat, causing the vehicle to rock, and helped the old man, who trembled as he got out but was then happy to stand on solid ground again with his own two feet. I then needed only a quick glance to know who the old man was; his movements were unmistakable. It was exactly how old Prenzel would look, my old history teacher. I recalled my terrified face when I had last seen him, how he had met me on the train platform and then had dropped me off at the guardhouse like a piece of luggage that he had found. Why was the old man in the metropolis? I would not have thought to have found Prenzel still among the living, least of all here in the metropolis, since travel from back there had not been allowed in years.

My companions in the glass cabinet then moved to open it up from the inside, but in vain they rattled the double doors. Only when Jock hurried to the back, Prenzel following slowly but curious to help his colleagues with all his strength, did the closed door finally function. At last Brian and Derek stood outside. Someone blew a fanfare, at which everything let loose with a fierce roar produced by music machines and instruments of alarm, as I worked as fast as possible to free myself from my dungeon. The pallbearers offered me a hand, but my pride refused their help. I withdrew from their too-confident grasp and staggered unassisted and alone over the running board and onto solid ground.

All around me I saw my family and all the others who had come in the vegetable truck, but also a large number of other people I knew, or at least could recall. Even the strangers who had gathered here seemed somewhat familiar to me. I probably had this impression because the strangers, as well as those I knew, aggressively tried to get within my range of sight. Yet all of them kept their distance out of a seeming shyness, such that there was an open space between me and the onlookers. Only the four men who had ridden with me in the hearse stood near me, until finally it was Professor Kratzenstein who approached, though still keeping his distance. Prenzel trudged over to me, blessed me, and took me by the hand like a little child who needed to be protected. It was touching. I believe it wouldn't have taken much for him to kiss me. Then he walked with me ahead of the others who had traveled together, bowed before the crowd, and introduced me:

"I have the great honor to introduce to you my old student Adam, also known as Dr. Arthur Landau. Many of you know him already, others will soon get to know him, but none of you really know who Adam is. Please take it all in and learn from his example. I am very proud of him, and he's earned it. I beseech all of you wholeheartedly, most honored attendees, to prove yourselves worthy of him. Make amends with him, bestow upon him what you owe him! He was always gifted, and the best history student I had. It's no wonder that he causes such a stir now in sociology."

The old man's voice quaked toward the end of his short speech, which was listened to intently and was met with resounding applause. I was delighted with Prenzel's clumsy and, above all, exaggerated praise, and bowed first to him and then to the gathering, which generally pleased them. I would have been happy to respond to the old man with something nice about his service as a high-school teacher, and then thank him several times for not having missed my special day, despite the arduous journey that had no doubt caused him many difficulties. But I never got a chance to, for Professor Kratzenstein stepped over and warmly embraced me and then began to speak:

"Fellow sociologists! Thank you, Professor Prenzel, for taking the opportunity to personally introduce your star pupil at the Sociology Conference held by the International Society of Sociologists here in Shepherd's Field, which I hereby declare to be open. However, it is you, my dear Dr. Landau, it is you whom I wish to thank from the bottom of my heart, in the name of all the gathered sociologists and associated scholars, for accepting our somewhat late and most likely somewhat surprising invitation. May it please you to be among our circle as an honorary member of the society from this day forth, and may this day bring you much joy and encouragement, as well as much gratification, as your work, which silently grew on its own, and is now finally seeing the light of day, and whose renown, ever more appreciated, spreads throughout the world, though earlier for years it brought you nothing but deep disappointment, painful misunderstanding, and even shortsighted rejection. Let that now lie behind you forgotten, and remember that the women and men gathered here carry no responsibility for the world's neglect that has caused you to suffer so much. It is my humble duty to report that all those gathered here before us knew the extent of your accomplishments from the start, and never wasted an hour in trying to knock down the wall that stood between you and the world, and actively tried to support your work, and you personally, in your days of need. It was never a secret to us who you were, and each one of us who had the chance to encounter you gave you our full attention, and for the most part also love, taking you under our wings and supporting your work openly, or, more important, behind the scenes. Never can too much come to the good, an old wise man said, and so let me state openly, dear Dr. Landau, that still not enough has come to you. I would be the first to acknowledge the deficiency in the human limits of our support for you. You, however, would kindly think of it as only the external challenges that any genius must press through in order to realize his full potential. We all know that has been achieved, and so I bid you, in the name of all present, once more a heartfelt welcome. Perhaps, honored friend, I could now ask you to come over to me. As it no doubt has already occurred to you, we have arranged for this conference to take place at Shepherd's Field for special reasons. Sociology would be worth nothing unless it applied itself to practical matters and thus studied life's problems where they live and breathe. You understand, and I hope all of us gathered here understand, how symbolic this is. Which is why I ask that next, before you move freely and openly about the conference site, you accompany me and honor the bumper-car palace with your presence, where talks about the sociology of traffic will be presented. You know these little electric cars—they're pure pleasure and entirely safe, even if one collides hard with another."

Rousing applause rose up, and I was surrounded by many people, all of whom wanted to shake my hand and clap me on the shoulders. Also, the music machines blared once more, and I was shoved along by the line of people who pushed toward the bumper cars, while the Professor continued to link arms with me. There the colored cars pleasantly ran about, little electric sparks springing from their electrical contacts that touched the wire netting, while two loudspeakers poured forth blaring noise.

As we drew closer, the electrical current was turned off, the occupants of the cars jumped nimbly out and respectfully withdrew from the course to the balustrade on the other side, where many conference participants had gathered who wanted to see me drive a bumper car. Professor Kratzenstein was polite enough to let me have my choice of cars, and so I chose a blue one. The other cars were also filled with selected guests, for during my turn none could remain empty. I would have been happy to take a seat behind the wheel, but the Professor informed me that it would be more honorable for me, as well as for him, if I turned the driver's wheel over to him. He also believed it would be more satisfying for me, for I could simply look about wherever I wished, besides its publicly marking my place within scholarship forever.

"That is a distinction, my friend, that no other can claim. I have never driven such a renowned colleague with my own hands around such a course."

"Good. Whenever you are ready, so am I."

I took it for granted that it wouldn't cost anything, at least for invited guests, but I was wrong about that. The Professor could see that I was surprised, and explained about the high cost of the electricity and for the attendants needed to work the ride. Mrs. Mackintosh, the wife of a high-ranking

584 / H. G. ADLER

official at the British Embassy, arrived with a leather bag on her shoulder and asked for some money, though I didn't receive a ticket in turn as I had hoped. That would be too official, she explained in a friendly manner. Besides, everything good in the world should be based on good faith and well-meant intentions. I wanted to pay, but Kratzenstein wouldn't let me. Then I at least wanted to pay for Johanna and Anna, who occupied two cars with my children, but the Professor wouldn't allow that, either. When I tried to press my coins on Mrs. Mackintosh, she let me know that she agreed with him and would have none of it.

"You wouldn't sell me the furniture back then, as I wanted you to. Do you remember? It's been a long while since I was angry with you, but it wasn't very kind of you. Since then I've gotten some that is much nicer. But back then I swore that I wanted nothing more to do with you, so then I don't want your money. Got it?"

Hence, I had to let it go, Kratzenstein's coins rattling as they disappeared into Mrs. Mackintosh's shoulder bag.

"An outstanding scholar!" boomed the Professor with the air of an expert. "I have a great soft spot for her. But her husband is the one to know, an embassy official and a writer and critic besides. He's just come out with another book, which he's always doing. What a fine person! Everyone says that about him."

Mrs. Mackintosh went about her business with care and speed so that the race could soon begin. The Professor didn't at all steer with the kind of elegant skill that I had expected of him, but rather in such a hilarious manner that it was twice the fun. He clutched the steering wheel tightly and turned it wildly about, such that we almost continually crashed into other drivers, slamming into them, almost tipping them over, after which it all repeated itself, us hitting other drivers sometimes slightly, sometimes harder, until my head was humming. It was lucky that the little oval cars were covered on the outside with a thick rubber pad. Once we crashed into Mrs. Stonewood, who with her two boys riding with her zigzagged back and forth awkwardly, and who was often warned by Mrs. Mackintosh to be more careful. Then there was a little while when there were no crashes, but Kratzenstein looked too long with pride at me, rather than at the oncoming cars, until we painfully crashed into Oswald Birch, who as a master driver boldly drove about on his own, the result being that his and our cars became wedged with each other and stood locked.

"How nice, Arthur, that I can wish you the best at the same time! We must, of course, see each other again soon. You are now a made man, that is clear."

"Shall I call you?"

"No, what are you thinking? Of course I will call you. Certainly. Tomorrow, for instance. It's been terribly long since I've seen you, and I need to speak to you. I've wanted to discuss some archaeological-sociological problems with you for a while."

I didn't have a chance to answer, for in the same moment our cars were separated and were able to move again. All I could do was wave at Oswald, who whizzed by at full speed. Then we hit the car of a man whom I recognized as the head officer of the train police from back there. That was unpleasant for me, for I was afraid of some kind of provocation, some kind of case being made against me. Had he traveled here with Prenzel in order to collar me and take me away? I turned around, but my old professor didn't appear to be anywhere around. Then I looked more closely at the Assessor of Sympathies and observed that I didn't need to worry, a side glance at Kratzenstein also reassuring me that nothing bad would happen. The Assessor of Sympathies even seemed to fear that I would hold his awful behavior against him now. He appeared to me to be much changed from what he had been, almost apologizing abjectly for the run-in, though he said it was not him but Kratzenstein who had been the cause of it, adding without much apparent conviction that I had been right. About what? I asked. Your political sympathies, he responded. But before I could untangle the sense of the comment and its double meaning we were off again. We then made two laps without getting hit much or bothered, though eventually we hit the car of Frau Fixler, Kratzenstein's secretary, for whom this abrupt meeting was so embarrassing that she blushed with shame. She swore that she had nothing to do with things not going so smoothly back in the days of the business between me and Herr Professor Kratzenstein. Although it was not something I would ever have requested, she promised in future to always send timely invitations to all the events of the International Society of Sociologists in letter format in a sealed envelope, not as just a worthless flyer, for she knew my address by heart. I tried to calm the excited lady, who with hands and feet was furiously trying to free her car from ours in order not to prevent our driving on.

But that was no longer necessary, for a loud chime announced the end of our pleasure ride. Indeed, the Professor asked me if I wanted another round, but I thanked him for his offer and said that I'd had enough. I also declined his suggestion that I give a brief presentation here on the race course, in front of our car, on the fundamental ideas of my sociology of oppressed people, just as it had been planned for me to do so years ago for the smaller working group of the institute.

"I need to recuperate, Herr Professor, and I'd prefer to sink inconspicuously into the crowd," I said.

"You won't have any luck with that, my friend. You stick out like a sore thumb."

"Are you trying to insult me?"

"My dear friend, what are you saying? Me and insults? Those are too completely separate and unlinkable entities! Scholarship is, if nothing else, a humble form of altruism."

I stood up and got out of the blue car, because Mrs. Mackintosh was already moving from customer to customer to collect money. That way, the Professor had to follow my wishes if he wanted to stay with me and not drive alone around the track. That was not what he intended, so he trotted along after me. Continually, people came up to me wanting to pass on their warm wishes, and often I was asked for my autograph. Suddenly I found myself in Peter's arms, his presence really surprising me.

"I flew here special from New Zealand, Arthur. I just had to. You've certainly put down roots, which is great to see. How proud I am to have been the first to help you get on your feet after the war."

"Are you also involved with sociology now?"

"Ah, sociology! I'm in advertising. The sociologists want to learn more about it from me. It wouldn't hurt you to take a course in it as well."

"It has to do," the Professor added, "with wanting to engage this gentleman as a leader in our organization. People need advertising. Otherwise the economy would grind to a halt. Thus, my friend, one has to try to model it on the basic principles of advertising technology. To pay attention to the pulse of life, that's what it is all about. This I have identified and use it to write personal testimonials to help sell the books of other scholars. That I find useful."

"I know you do that, Herr Professor. And very stylishly at that!"

"Well, then, you know. When your book comes out, I'll do it for you as well."

"Will my book appear?"

"But of course, my dear honored friend. Everything has been taken care of. I've already spoken to Singule. He will arrange for the funds from the foundation."

"Is Singule here as well?"

"Of course. We can go see him together. He and his wife are running the registration for the Sociology Conference."

Led by Peter, we worked our way through the throng and passed a carousel on which Michael rode around with Leslie, Mrs Byrdwhistle's boy. The children didn't see me, even though I waved to them. After a few attempts, we got lost and were set on the right path by the operator of a Ferris wheel, and finally managed to reach a shooting gallery, which served as the registration booth. Klara Singule offered guns to the guests, while her husband sold tickets and also appeared to be handing out the prizes. I was greeted warmly.

"It's great that you're here!" said Frau Singule. "My husband will be so pleased! It's only a shame that he has so little time. He never has time."

Yet when I looked at the ever-busy Singule, he nonetheless let everything lie and stood up.

"Landau, you managed all right after all! You're something else. It's just a shame that you're not a biologist. But you do come from Latvia, Riga, or somewhere?"

"No, you're mistaken, Herr Dr. Singule."

"I see, I see. But that doesn't matter. Your book will be printed, in Latvia or some other country, there's no essential difference. The main thing is that you are from some country. Meanwhile, in all honesty you should know that you should call me Singule. Just Singule. Don't say 'Doctor'; I can't stand it."

"That's not so important, Eduard! Let's focus on the matter at hand. We have to do something for our dear Landau."

"You have a point, Klara, that's clear. If only he were from some country. You'll take care of that, right?"

"Yes, I come from somewhere."

"Excellent. Here we have a check that should be enough to cover living expenses for one to two years. We'll also make other means of support available to you as well. And then your book, I already said, indeed, it will be printed. People have said marvelous things about it; it's been well received. Congratulations!"

"You don't in fact know my work, Herr Singule."

"Doesn't matter, doesn't matter. Why does one have to know someone's work? I know you, we all know you. That's all we need. Here, take this letter that states we've accepted it, and tomorrow send us the stuff so that we can begin printing it. In no more than two months, you'll have the galleys in hand."

Someone pushed toward the counter and wanted to shoot. Frau Singule, who during this conversation took care of all the registrations, couldn't hold back the crowd any longer.

"Eduard, you don't have time. Can't you see the sociologists who demand to be taken care of?"

The biologist then excused himself, and in saying goodbye asked that I dedicate myself to doing a study of people and how they suffered from vermin. I nodded as if I thought it a good idea. I already had all I wanted from Singule; now I could confidently ignore his time-worn suggestions. A guest who next popped up and wanted a gun revealed himself, on closer inspection, to be the good Herr Geschlieder from the museum. What a surprise it was to find someone from back there standing here. He was very happy to see me and shared with me that a large delegation from back there had gathered at Shepherd's Field. Instead of shooting, he held the rifle loosely and somewhat dangerously in front of him, such that he almost would have hit Frau Singule on the shoulder with the barrel except that the lady, as she saw that Geschlieder was talking to me, didn't admonish him, which no one would have minded, but instead kindly said that I should also try my hand at shooting, she'd be happy to provide me with six free bullets. I thanked her but said I was no kind of shooter and offered the bullets to Kratzenstein, who also had no idea how to shoot. Then I invited Peter to have a try, but Frau Singule didn't feel that was right, the free offer having been good only for me personally, and while she could go along with overstepping my bounds by passing it on to the Professor, it wasn't right to offer my bullets to a stranger, no matter how respectable he might be.

Then Kratzenstein got involved in matters, saying the man was no stranger but, rather, the future business manager and head of advertising of the International Society of Sociologists. Well, that's entirely different, the lady firmly assured him; with pleasure the man could use my six bullets. Peter happily stepped up and eagerly commenced shooting, while I carefully tucked away Singule's check and letter in my coat pocket and left the registration stand with a polite goodbye. Calling after me, Klara Singule asked that I give her the pleasure of coming to tea with my wife sometime soon, and would I be so kind as to send Johanna over to the shooting booth for a little chat with her. Peter kept on shooting, and I was glad to be free of him. I would have liked to get rid of Professor Kratzenstein as well, but he watched me like a hawk in order to stick close to me. So I had to spend more time in his company. After a while we approached the mouse circus, where I was happy to come across Eva, who was with Anna. I exchanged a couple of words with Anna about Peter, whom she had already seen. My daughter then energetically interrupted us to say that she remembered seeing a little white bunny in the mouse circus. We didn't let the child ask for too long before deciding that we would visit the mouse circus together. Anna and I vied to be the first to pay the entrance fee, then the Professor again insisted on providing the money for us all, but this time the attendant wasn't named Mrs. Mackintosh but rather Inge Bergmann, who didn't want any of our money.

"It's very nice, Landau, that you want to have a look at my mice. Such sweet little creatures, I tell you, and so clever!"

"I love the little mouse-bunny. I love her so much, Papa!"

"Is this your little one, Landau? How sweet! No wonder, coming from you."

"Yes, this is my Eva, Fräulein Bergmann. But tell me, how did you end up at the mouse circus?"

"So you really want to know, huh? But I'm not telling. Oh, don't give me that look! Because it's you, I'll tell you anyway. Mice are much better than people. And I also want to write animal stories for little sprites like Eva. Therefore I need to brush up and study a bit of animal sociology."

Inge Bergmann handed us tickets on which "Gratis" was printed. We moved toward the entrance, which was guarded by a friendly smiling train-man. I knew the face, but I didn't really know where I remembered it from. The man indeed assisted us, recalling me from the gate where I paused with my ticket before him. He was pleased that I was no longer afraid of him, which he allowed me to say, and that I had reached my destination safe and sound. This time there were no ticket puncher or punching of the ticket, for I walked freely through this barrier and into the circus, where Eva's cheering was even stronger than the last time we had visited, there being no way to draw her away from the stinking glass houses. I didn't wish to spend any more time here, but Eva begged and pleaded, so we separated from Anna, who sweetly stayed on with the children in front of the mice. Outside, the trainman saluted, at which Inge spied us, and though I would have been pleased to hurry off, she called out to us, asking if I could, if I would please wait before just disappearing.

"Well, you're a great friend to animals, aren't you, Landau? Are you going to just take to your heels after seeing the little mice? A scandal, a scandal that you aren't at all ashamed to do so!"

"I have a lot to do, Fräulein Bergmann. You'll have to indeed forgive me. My little one is still inside marveling at the little mice."

"Such a sweet child, such a sprite, and with a lot more heart in her than her father. An angel, that dear little Eva! But give me your word that you'll return! Otherwise I'll be angry with you."

"If it's at all possible, it will be my pleasure. I promise you."

"At all possible . . . Don't be so stuffy. You're horrible, Landau, horrible. You deserved what you got!"

"Don't insult my friend," interrupted Kratzenstein. "He doesn't deserve it."

"Doesn't deserve it!" Inge said mockingly, but then got hold of herself. "I hope you'll recommend us to others. Please honor me with a visit some-time again!"

Then Fräulein Bergmann had to turn to new customers. We walked on and came to the tower for the slide, one of Michael's favorite spots. Yet I saw neither him nor any other children, but instead only people of an older age, most of whom were idly standing around rather than holding a mat under their arms while climbing the steps on the inside of the tower, after which, in a tight snaking motion against the outer wall of the small chamber, they would pleasantly slide, the mat underneath them as they lay on their backs. The men who were in charge of what today appeared a lame undertaking looked very familiar to me, even if I didn't know their names. The director of the enterprise was the nice official from the border police who had once interrogated Johanna and me. His assistants, who for the most part shifted from one foot to the other and chatted with one another, were policemen, border officials, and probably other employees of the railroad as well.

"What do these people have to do with sociology?"

"My dear Landau, not so loud!" the Professor admonished. "The gentlemen have many merits, but they are very sensitive and mustn't hear you. That is the Institute for Esoteric Science, one of the most important academic institutions that is here today for the Sociology Conference."

Esoteric science. I had to smile, for I didn't have much interest in that. It made me feel queasy, but I didn't want to let the Professor see that. Kratzenstein, however, was full of praise for the scholars and their subtle field of study.

"We couldn't do without them. They work in the applied sciences, which is what underlies any study in general. Where would we be without these brave men! Everything is weighed and considered. All of it neatly plotted out, marked, and sorted, while connecting doors are placed in the erected walls. Security and stability. Just climb up, Landau, and just try sliding down!"

I didn't want to hear anything about that, for the idea of sliding made me feel dizzy, which I even admitted to Kratzenstein.

"Don't you want to climb up and try sliding down, Herr Professor? I'll wait until you're down again."

I wasn't having any of it, however, for I would have run off the moment the Professor entered the tower. But he didn't provide me with this pleasure, no matter how much he praised the installation, but instead confessed that he felt even dizzier than I did. While I felt unsure on my feet, he said he was completely dizzy, and I considered what to do, for I didn't wish to disturb his well-being by making him ill. That's why I recommended that we continue on with our survey of the fair, but at that moment the director of the institute recognized me and rushed over to me with a broad smile.

"You have finally arrived, Herr Doctor, and in such fine fashion. That pleases me no end. You can pass in and out of our tower at no cost from now on."

"That's much too nice of you. I realize how extraordinary that is."

I chatted for a little while with this gentleman and his co-workers, during which time I saw someone have his passport stamped in order to start the journey. He then whisked down from above, myself first paying attention to him once he arrived below, somewhat lightheaded but happy, for he was flattered that Kratzenstein had tugged on my arm in order to point out the sight. I looked more closely, for by now the rider had lifted himself up from the mattress he had landed on and walked over toward me shaking with joy. It was Otto Schallinger, who greeted me with a wide grin.

"So I end up meeting you at the Sociology Conference—that's terrific! How long has it been since I saw you? Prenzel only has to turn up, ha ha, for this miracle to happen! But it's quite a party. I've already spoken to Herr Birch and Fräulein Bergmann, Kauders, and Dr. Haarburger."

"So they are all here?"

"Haven't you seen them?"

"Yes, Birch and Fräulein Bergmann, but not the others."

"They'll soon find you. They're all just crazy about you. Arthur Landau is the buzzword of the day."

"Tell me, Otto, are you also now a sociologist?"

"Me? No. Or only a bit of one. I am only a fan, but one totally smitten, for I'm interested by it all. If you want to observe people and want to know what makes them tick, then you have to be half a sociologist these days."

Schallinger had a camera in a case dangling around his neck. It surprised me that he had gone down the slide with such an expensive piece of gear. Now he pulled out his apparatus and told me that he had already snapped shots of Johanna and all the children, including Michael, though he had to outsmart him. Otto also wanted to waste a shot on me, and since Kratzenstein was eager to have him do so, I had to be patient while Otto took pictures of us together and alone, the tower of the esoteric scientists always in the background.

"These are just the first unofficial snapshots," explained Otto. "The official group portrait with you and all the important conference participants will happen later. I'm hoping to make a name for myself with it."

"What makes you think that?"

"Very simple. I'll offer it to the illustrated weeklies and the daily newspapers. It'll fly out of my hands."

"Otto is right about that" was Kratzenstein's opinion.

Otto danced about me and made himself look important. Suddenly he suggested that we both make use of the tower. He recommended that we sit double on a mat, though he laughed at his former middle-school classmate when I said that I didn't want anything to do with any of it. Schallinger had to give up the idea of me accompanying him, but not on taking a second ride alone, and so he said goodbye with a mixture of sadness and cheerfulness before running into the tower once more. I didn't wait for him to come out and decided to look for Roy Rogers. On the way there, I passed the wagon of the Gypsy Fortunata, which I didn't expect to find here.

"This lady is also here?" I asked the Professor, amazed. "I wouldn't have dreamed that she would be involved with such serious scholarship."

"And how! This year we swayed between making you or Fortunata an honorary member. Of course, the choice fell to you unanimously. But something will have to go awfully wrong for Fortunata not to be in line for it next year."

"What does fortune-telling have to do with sociology?"

"You're actually asking that? You can't be serious! Without fortune-telling, scholarship would relinquish its reason for existing."

"I see, I see. That never occurred to me."

"But, dear Landau, don't feel ashamed. You cannot say in all honesty that you yourself didn't try to build a scholarly relationship with this lady. With that, you showed how useful it is for oppressed people."

"How do you know my secret?"

"We know everything about you. If we didn't know it, how could we make you an honorary member? The candidate always has to be examined from head to toe, the entire life story. For that, we have our own esoteric scientists."

During this explanation the door of Fortunata's wagon opened, and the Gypsy woman, all decked out and with a magnifying glass and a bundle of playing cards in her hand, stepped out smiling. She nodded to me in a vigorous manner to come closer, which I had no desire to do. Since Kratzenstein encouraged me with talk and gestures, I finally gave in and took some steps toward the fortune-teller. Fortunata smiled graciously, proudly walked down the three steps, and came over to me. I indeed wished to stretch out a hand to her, when I was struck by the appearance of a second figure, who happened to be dressed almost as gaudily as the Gypsy woman, standing in the door of the wagon and waving at me. This lady was exceedingly made-up, myself uncertain who the learned woman was, but Fortunata the All-Knowing took in my surprise with tireless grace.

"That is my friend Eusemia, whom you have to thank for your career. I have made this adept one my assistant and closest colleague in the institute for pansociological and metasociological deep research that I established. Does that surprise you?"

I was not only surprised; I was horrified. This development on the part of Resi Knispel I had not thought possible. I didn't answer the Gypsy woman, but instead looked around uncertainly at Kratzenstein.

"Herr Professor, is this really for real?"

"But of course, my friend! How could you doubt it? Everything that we do is serious."

Resi Knispel approached me without any hesitation and proudly handed me a prospectus for the journal *Eusemia*.

"Good day, Landau. Look, I managed to pull it off, you old toad. *Eusemia* is blossoming. You should have joined us right then and there. *Eusemia* is off and swimming like a turtle in water and is paying princely honorariums. I hope that at least you'll now decide to submit your precious articles to *Eusemia*. If you have something that's finished already, then give me a call and I'll send Eberhard to you to pick it up."

"What do you mean. . . . Is he there as well?"

"Settle down, he's not there. We know how you feel about him. But he's good enough for errands, and he finally gave us some names. Now all we need is for you to make a call. Agreed?"

"I'll have to think about that a bit more."

"My dear friend," the Professor reminded me quietly, "there's nothing to think about. We are all working together. An honor, a duty. *Eusemia* will be financed by America. Singule threw in some millions. *Eusemia* is for humanity, against nuclear war and moral disarmament, for bridging the collective isolation of mechanized existence. It is wonderful and necessary. Only then will the walls be torn down, misery will be averted, no one will have to suffer anymore. That is exactly what you want to have happen with your own oppression. In addition, *Eusemia* is the house organ of the International Society of Sociologists."

"I see," I whispered weakly.

"Please, Landau, wake up! I really should be scolding you, because you ran away from me back then like a mangy dog. But today everything is forgiven and forgotten."

"Everything, everything!" Fortunata confirmed. "Eusemia loves you. Through her you can also convince yourself that you exist. That's exactly what I told you, and I predicted a marvelous future for you."

I had to talk for a while longer with the fortune-teller and was not at all left in peace until I promised to put my knowledge and expertise in the service of the institution founded by the lady and thus soon write an article that would lay out the quickest way to bring about the freedom from oppression. Fräulein Knispel tried several times to kiss me, but whenever she tried to draw close I hid behind Kratzenstein and thereby could avoid her advances. Luckily, some people came by who wanted to talk to the ladies about matters of deep research or fortune-telling, which I used to make a quick getaway. However, I had to promise to come see them again soon. Fortunata once again prophesized my incomparable rise. Resi Knispel said in a cheery voice, "Landau, you are now famous. That's excellent. I'm proud of you. Until now, you got in your own way. But my efforts on your behalf did away with all obstacles."

Then the seers disappeared with their clients into the Gypsy wagon, the door closed, and I was left free of the researchers. The Professor couldn't keep from smiling.

"What impressive zeal! A practical woman this Eusemia Knispel, but one shouldn't believe every word she says. She seems to be quite enamored of herself and has spread a great many flattering things about herself throughout the world. The fact that she made you is, of course, complete nonsense."

We moved off and walked between some booths where the academics cavorted about. Everywhere that I appeared with Kratzenstein vain frivolity held sway. Betty, Johanna's dear relative, bumped into us and we exchanged some pleasant words. The sense of pride she had always extended to me was now justified, and I thanked her for her loyalty. Betty thought that I looked a little pale, and that it would do me good to rest a bit. Professor Kratzenstein heeded the suggestion immediately and led me to the concessions hall, where I met up again with my family and Anna. It was not in fact a hall, but all about stood some bare, dirty tables with benches in between the puddles and the rubbish. The setup reminded me of a scene in front of a mountain holiday lodge but, rather than quiet and clean, here it was loud and slovenly. The smell of cheap drink mixed disgustingly with the odor of onions, fried fish, and other cheap food that was fried in the cooking fat used in products that taste rank and give one stomach trouble, yet which in this country are sold in shops ad nauseam without any care for sensitive noses or palates, all of which disgusted me. I would have loved to just walk away, and I was already rubbing my hands with pleasure when I saw that there were not enough seats, which was why so many guests were standing, though as soon as we showed up two tables were cleared for us with exaggerated politeness. I had to resign myself to a brief stop if I was to avoid upsetting anyone. Herr and Frau Kutschera, under the jealous gaze of the Simmondses, were serving and were happy to see me. They brought apples and other fruit, and any proper snacks they had. Once again the Professor wanted to pay for us both, but Herr Kutschera would take money only for what the Professor ate, Herr Kutschera indicating that to feed me for free was the greatest honor that could be afforded him.

"Herr Doctor, I knew you; that was when you were still in high school. I always thought you had so much potential within you. If your blessed father could only see you, my dear, he would be so proud of you!"

I said that it wasn't right for me to get away this cheap. People came up to me somewhat rudely to congratulate me, to hear my voice, to touch my coat, and to share pleasantries full of hot air. Dressed in a lightly spotted apron, Herr Nerad brought a bottle of Kalakto, which is a chocolate milk the dairies over there produce, providing straws as well. I loved it as a child, but I had never had Kalakto in the metropolis. Other people I knew from the old days also were walking around. Frau Holoubek came up to me somewhat meekly, patting me and clapping me on the back. When I asked, she said that Frau Krumbholc had washed her last load of laundry and lain in the cemetery for some years already. Then Frau Holoubek and Herr Nerad reminded me what all of my relatives would have said if they knew how far I had come. These faithful souls couldn't hold back from reprimanding me for breaking off my visit so abruptly and then disappearing so suddenly without saying goodbye, for they had indeed found things after I left, all of which they had stowed away, wanting only to know when I might come for them. I had to introduce them to Johanna and the children, whom they greeted warmly and gave some sweets. Johanna thought it was too much and that the children would get stomachaches. I had finally had enough of the concessions hall and excused myself. Unfortunately, I didn't manage to slip away from the Professor this time, either. He kept right on my trail and clung to me like a brother, as if he had seen through to my intent.

"Today, my friend, you're not getting away from my clutches, you runaway!"

We came to a stand where one could try to knock down piled-up coconuts with wooden balls from behind a barrier. I was happy that Michael was not with us, for he was always after me to let him throw these balls or for me to do it. The crowd shyly stepped back; the ones throwing dropped their balls to the ground and stepped to the side in order to make enough room for me and the Professor at the wooden counter.

"We've been waiting for you for so long already!" Herr Lever called out excitedly. "Hey, Mitzi, Herr Dr. Landau is here. Give him a coconut right away!"

Mitzi walked quickly and brought a coconut from a column.

"You gave us such a lovely tour of the museum back then. Unforgettable!"

"Nothing has changed at all. You're really coming into your own! Would you like to have nine free shots?"

I thanked them for the offer, but I declined the free shots and then listened patiently to how the Levers never got their paintings, only printed photographs having been sent to them in Johannesburg at quite a cost. Which was why—how shameless!—the paintings were on display here at the Sociology Conference, Herr Lever whispering to me, asking me to intercede if I came across them and say that they really should be returned to him as the rightful owner. It would be no loss to me, so I asked where the paintings were hung, but then Herr Lever acted secretive, saying that he would leave it to my scholarly know-how, but I should at least believe that he wouldn't give a damn about sociology—"Please, no offense to you"—if he didn't have any hopes of recovering the paintings. I said goodbye to the brave couple, whom Kratzenstein kept an obvious eye on. The Professor then recommended that we visit the law pavilion. On the way there, I asked what the coconuts had to do with sociology. Kratzenstein's face grew bitter.

"Honestly, nothing at all. This South African merchant claims, in fact, that one could conduct better research in mass psychology at a ball toss at an annual fair than at a conference. I think that's nonsense. But the Levers have piles of money and pay a lot in order to be members of our society. They also pay a high rent for their stand. That's all right with us. But in fact they have other intentions—that I have long known. I'll get to the bottom of it."

The law pavilion was a middle-sized booth that I had seen for years at the annual fair at Shepherd's Field but had never yet visited, as the name of it always put me off, for it advertised sensational crimes and misdeeds of a hair-raising nature. I shared my thoughts with the Professor, but he laughed heartily and sympathetically, saying it really wasn't all that bad, for scholarship had nothing to fear or to be ashamed of. In the pavilion there was nothing at all that I had not already seen or experienced in reality. In fact, I had seen many things that were a whole lot worse. So I wandered over to the ticket booth, which had a sign on it that read "Reparations." In the booth sat Dr. Blecha, who actually was the first and only person at the conference who was shocked to see me. Dr. Blecha said right away, with agitated haste, that I should not expect any deals because of my present position, and that he didn't want to hear anything about Kauders, all of that had been decided in the negative, which even Kauders now understood as right, and what kind of dumb idea was it for me to send Herr Lever to him, Dr. Blecha. I said to the lawyer that I had just seen the Levers over by the coconuts, at which

Kratzenstein shook his head somewhat disapprovingly. Blecha looked grim and decidedly cool, saying how sensible that Herr Lever had finally given up his senseless efforts; now, at least, at his stand one could shoot properly. Then the lawyer rudely pointed a finger at my coconut.

"It looks like you had some luck there."

I deliberately ignored this nastiness and asked to be let into the law pavilion, which the Professor had already reminded me of somewhat impatiently. After Mrs. Mackintosh, the stingy Dr. Blecha was the first from the conference to refuse me free entry. I wanted to pay, but, as was the fixed custom, Kratzenstein insisted that I let him take care of it. This Dr. Blecha refused him with pointed politeness; it was only right that each should pay his own way, that being what was right in and of itself, not just for one person or another, and so it was that one should pay. Thus the Professor could let his pittance cover himself alone. I rifled through my pockets to look for change, but then I realized that when I changed at home I had left my wallet and all my loose change in the other suit. I had nothing on me but the precious check from Herr Singule and his award letter. The lawyer, meanwhile, broke into a coughing fit. I was startled, but there was no need to be, for the coughs were only covering up uncontrollable laughter over my naïveté—yes, "naïveté" was the word the lawyer used. Good faith is naïveté, he insisted absolutely. Here only cash is accepted, whereas a check, even for such a high amount, is useless to him, for the old jurist wasn't willing to just accept a scrap of paper on faith. The Professor then just wanted to give me some money, but the lawyer wouldn't allow this. Then Kratzenstein said very carefully that he only wished to lend me the amount needed, but Dr. Blecha stubbornly shook his head, saying that lending money was not allowed at the conference. At Kratzenstein's insistence, he finally acknowledged that as an honorary member of the society I should not miss the benefit of seeing the law pavilion, which was why Dr. Blecha then decided to make an exception and accept my coconut instead of the usual fee. I sighed deeply, for I wanted to give the coconut to my son, who had long wished for one. Then the lawyer had the shamelessness to say, Good then, not the coconut, it was up to me if I wanted to spoil the rascal, but he would take my pocket watch, if I preferred.

"Then I won't know the time!" I complained.

"Time is wasting away!" Blecha said emphatically.

"None of us has time," the Professor assured. "But that's not the issue. Just give the man the coconut! It will shut him up. As for your son, we'll ask Guido Lever for another one. He feels that he is in your debt and will be happy to give you one."

This talk didn't please me, and I was angry at Kratzenstein, but I gave up the coconut, which Dr. Blecha immediately began to play with. He plucked greedily at the matted tufts. But we were allowed through the cheap heavy curtain to which the greasy dirt clung. Inside, we were set upon by Hannah Haarburger.

"Jolan! Jolan!" she yelled. "The gentlemen are finally here!"

As fast as his paunch would let him, Dr. Haarburger came running up and bowed deeply.

"Here, Dr. Landau, you can marvel at the past. We have gathered all the horrors together. Nothing more can happen to you. All that is over. Pure beneficence has won a clear victory over all the dreck of the earth. The score is one to nothing. If we keep at it and don't take our hand off the wheel, we can get rid of the world's sorrow forever. We in this pavilion, however, are witness to harrowing examples of it."

Dr. Haarburger pushed a button and a bright light lit up a display booth. I saw a crane with a noose attached to it that moved back and forth above a pack of wretched little dolls in its attempt to snatch one by the throat and lift it high.

"Isn't that something, Dr. Landau? If you turn this lever here, then theoretically you should be able to grab hold of a doll and strangle it. Then it must be taken out of the game, because it's been killed. If you succeed at that, you then get the doll and a certificate. But I have to tell you, you won't be able to do it, for no one is able. It's humanity that prevents you. Just try and test your own humaneness! There's the lever, just make sure and move it slowly!"

Against my wishes the lever was already in my hand as I pushed it tentatively right and left, at which the crane roamed about, the noose rising and sinking and swirling about the dolls strewn across the bottom of the booth in a frightening array. From a loudspeaker a high-pitched voice sounded: "Adam, where are you?" Another voice answered in an even more piteous squeal: "I'm not Adam. The one next to me is Adam."

When I heard that, I felt a strong motion in my hand, the lever out of control in my hands, and so I let it go. Dr. Haarburger let go of the button, the display booth went dark, and the phantom disappeared.

"Isn't that marvelous, Dr. Landau?"

I had to agree and say that I had been beaten.

"You see, humanity won. Didn't I say it would?"

Dr. Haarburger offered to press other buttons, which would supposedly lead to other astounding things, but I waved him off. He understood why.

"What can be seen here is only what you know better than any other. But now you can see for yourself!"

"You should come see us soon!" Frau Hannah offered. "You and Johanna, with your son."

"I also have a little daughter, Eva."

"That's nice. Then bring both children. You can also visit if you need money. My husband has a lot now."

"Dr. Landau doesn't need any money," said Kratzenstein. "Everything has been taken care of for him."

"I'm so glad to hear it. Does that mean the Saubermanns? That's just what I thought. Frau Saubermann has a heart of gold."

"What are you thinking? Me and Singule! We don't need the Saubermanns, Frau Hannah. Right now everyone wants to help give Dr. Landau the resources he needs."

Dr. Haarburger stressed how pleased he was by my good fortune, though he asked me not to forget whom I had turned to when I really needed money. He would have been happy to jump into the breach. I thanked him for all his kindness and suggested that I really should be on my way in order not to disturb their work in the law pavilion any further. The Haarburgers offered to show me some more horrors, but I really wasn't curious to see them.

"Jolan, then tell our friend quickly what you did for him!"

"Humility forbids it, but truth is what we try to serve, and it's only just that we do. I picked you up at the train station because I knew who I was dealing with. Along with Hannah, I was the first there for you. I took you in like a son, recommending you and taking you around. The fact that you know the Professor is because of me. I don't mean to say that without me nothing would have come of you, but it certainly would have taken until much, much later. I say this in all humility. Isn't that true, Professor?"

"It's true," said Kratzenstein, looking as if he had just bitten into a sour apple. "All of us made him. Now he is who he is."

"Yes, he is, he is. But it all started with me."

This Dr. Haarburger said with grandeur, Frau Hannah nodding vigorously a number of times. We said goodbye to the lawyerly couple, who accompanied us as far as the greasy curtain. Outside, I threw a long side glance toward Dr. Blecha, who in the meantime had forgotten about me and continued playing with his coconut. He had already pulled off all its tufts, the fibers lying about the ticket counter in front of him, some of them clinging to his coat. We nonetheless moved on, walking only a few steps before we reached a booth where a parrot picked printed pieces of paper from a holder and gave one to any conference participant who wanted it. The parrot also wanted to give me one. However, I declined when the Professor informed me that it was only an advertisement for the International Society of Sociologists. Nonetheless, we entered, for I recognized Herr Buxinger, who was in charge of this exhibit. He was happy to shake my hand and welcome me. He being as tolerant as he is, it didn't bother him that I waved away the parrot's offer, which he warmly offered up to me, saying that I was no fan of propaganda and ads.

"That's fine, Herr Doctor. Maybe you'll be more willing to do it if you need me. In any case, I'm in my element here. I'm the sole distributor of *Eusemia*, and I'll soon start a large publishing house. Then, Herr Doctor, I'd very much like to become the publisher of your work."

Kratzenstein informed him that, given the many offers that I had, he shouldn't expect to be getting anything from me. The bookseller was so disappointed by this that I had to comfort him. When he learned that I would submit something to *Eusemia*, his eyes lit up, for with this promise he saw a guarantee of the further success of his journal.

"If you appeared only in every other issue, then it won't take long for me to make my money back and pay off all my debts with Jolan Haarburger. He still wants to get involved in my business, my old friend Jolan."

The parrot made a screeching sound and let a piece of paper fall. Someone bent to pick it up, saying, "You have to pick up your own luck from the ground." I looked more closely. It was So-and-So, who out of shyness had not even greeted me. It was hard for him that, through my sudden success, I was much better off than he was. He had not yet gained access to the long promised Professor. This made me feel bad, for an old childhood friend should never be neglected. Hence, I acknowledged him with a quiet greeting and met him with a grateful look.

"How nice, Arthur, to think that we are friends. From the very beginning I knew that you would make it the moment you got here. Did I not say that to you in my first letter after the war?"

So-and-So said this so sincerely that I couldn't disagree, especially when Kratzenstein agreed and said that we all agreed on that. I looked questioningly at the Professor, for to me his assertion seemed a bit too strong. Because he didn't want to hear any protest from me, he quickly asserted that, of course, I had certainly had some difficulties at the start, but they were nothing that any great talent would not have met. So-and-So wanted to hear whether I had seen Karin at the conference. When I said I had not, he recommended that I come along with him, for she had a very honored position as an attendant at the Wheel of Fortune. We let So-and-So lead the way, and we came to a brightly decorated booth covered with shimmering pearls and glittering jewels, all of it bathed in colored light. I was startled by so much glitter and rubbed my eyes, for I didn't want to be blinded.

"A Wheel of Fortune and sociology?"

"My dear Landau, you ask as if you were a rank beginner. Do you know nothing of the sociology of fortune?"

No, I didn't know anything about that; I had never studied this subject. Slowly I got used to the glare and could now almost look about freely. Not only did I see Karin in a luxurious evening dress—she was selling lots with numbers on them to the participants; Frau Saubermann was also here, and I had no desire to renew her acquaintance. She held sway at the Wheel of Fortune and appeared to be the supervisor. The sight of this made me sick, and I didn't want to stay a moment longer. Kratzenstein and So-and-So, however, wouldn't allow me to flee, so I had to join in. By then the benefactress had also discovered I was there and was staring at me with her eyes wide and calling out to me with delight. When she saw my reluctance, she stretched out both arms to me.

"Herr Doctor! Herr Doctor! You finally came! I've been sitting on pins and needles and waiting the entire time! So come closer! Such a joy! I'm so happy!"

Since I remained standing where I was, Kratzenstein pushed me forward. Unwillingly, I gave Frau Saubermann my hand, which she played with and caressed for a little while almost incessantly.

"You've become such a dear, wonderful man—and morally so free! The way you figured out how to do your duty! What satisfaction it brings me—how excellent it is to see you! Do you remember your visit with us? We spoke privately with each other and had such touching exchanges. Karin, dear, go on and give the Herr Doctor a handful of lots so that he makes sure to win something!"

Karin took some lots from a box and handed them to me. Then Frau Saubermann turned to the Wheel of Fortune, and at least ten of my lots won. I received some cheap cigarettes and sour candies, a little silver-plated chain, a toothbrush, a small pocket mirror made of metal, a little bowl made of pressed glass that looked polished, shirt buttons made of sandalwood, a lovely talisman made of golden yellow tin, and other useful little items. I wanted to give some of my winnings to the Professor and So-and-So, but they wouldn't take anything, so I had to stuff it all into my pockets. As if that weren't enough, Frau Saubermann handed me the main prize, which I didn't have the Wheel of Fortune to thank for. It was a chain of artificial pearls.

"That's for Johanna, Herr Doctor. The chain is long enough to circle the neck three times. I threaded the pearls myself. They were dipped in my husband's factory. Splendid wares made from a new process, which no one else has, more beautiful than the real ones. When you drape Johanna with them, please give her my best! How happy I am that this dear child has such a worthy man as you for a husband. Do you remember the night with Jolan and Hannah? I saw from the first moment that Johanna and you would make for a fine couple. You were clearly meant for each other."

Frau Saubermann dropped the pearls into a little box and apologized for not being able to spend longer with me, for she had to thread a new chain, and in record time, since a chain was needed as the main prize of the Wheel of Fortune. But the patroness took enough time to invite me and my family to visit, and to insist that if I ever needed anything I could count on her and Larry. Had I even looked for him yet? When I said I had not, she cast a disapproving look at the Professor, who apologized for this oversight and promised to walk me straightaway over to the panopticon. We took our leave of Frau Saubermann and Karin, as well as from my friend So-and-So, who during the stringing of the new chain of pearls helped out at the Wheel of Fortune. He nodded at me and then bowed deeply to the Professor. Then we were on our way and paid no attention to the good wishes called out to us.

"Herr Professor, to the panopticon? I've learned a lot from this Sociology Conference, but a panopticon here—what can that mean?"

"Sometimes it feels like you are a first-semester student and not a mature scholar. There's nothing simpler than that. In the panopticon we find the contemporary museum, which is equal to the most modern scientific achievements, for which we have the trailblazing work of our colleague Herr Saubermann to thank. Consider the word: 'panopticon.' That means everything is seen, a museum that is not just for the purpose of true learning but, rather, also speaks to the experience of the broad masses. And that is applied sociology."

I cringed when the Professor talked of the "broad masses," for I didn't like this unuseful misnomer. It prodded me to want to ask what he meant by that, but then I decided it was better to avoid a lecture from my benefactor and kept quiet until we were before the gaudy sign of the booth that said

PANOPTICON—THE CONTEMPORARY MUSEUM

in brightly colored letters. The entry price was cheap, but we didn't have to pay anything and were immediately met at the door. Herr Saubermann greeted us wearing tails, his long face beaming, and clapping his hands. I thought at first that it was with pleasure he was doing so, but it soon became clear that this was a sign to his two assistants dressed in black coats. To my pleasant surprise, they were none other than Herr Schnabelberger and Frau Dr. Kulka. He bowed deeply, and the doctor nodded delicately, yet neither said a word and needed me to speak to them first before they mouthed their spare, almost submissive phrases. Herr Saubermann, to whom I raised my left hand while continuing to wave him off, patiently suggested that I should take a little time to speak with my old colleagues, though he also longed to have my undivided attention for himself. I didn't wish to wear out his patience and thus looked for the Professor to engage Saubermann for a while. Then I told my co-workers from the museum that I had seen Herr Geschlieder already and was surprised that he was not among those working at the panopticon. Herr Schnabelberger explained to me that Geschlieder had applied. He had been turned down because he seemed too uneducated, he not having understood how Saubermann had wanted to renovate the museum. Instead, Herr Woticky was employed as an assistant.

I would happily have talked longer with Dr. Kulka and Schnabelberger, but Saubermann was being difficult and wouldn't be distracted by either my gesture or Professor Kratzenstein's efforts. Saubermann took me confidently by the arm and said that we should be good friends, to which I didn't say anything. Then he explained that Herr Schnabelberger and Frau Dr. Kulka had come around entirely to his notion of museumship and had been happy to follow his directions. He, along with these co-workers, would be happy to support my research in word and action whenever I needed them to. In addition, he was also ready to supply me with any kind of private help that I needed, and to grant this to me at any time. While normally visitors were led through the panopticon by my former co-workers, Saubermann was ready to do it himself in this case, though Schnabelberger and Dr. Kulka went along to help him. The panopticon was filled with many objects that were familiar to me from my own time at the museum. On the other hand, the treasures that Larry Saubermann had shown me at his house were not on view here. We came upon bundles of badly torn prayer books, just as we had once piled up in the cellar; here they were displayed neatly, and one was left open. Then I saw paintings that I remembered. They hung on the wallpapered walls, which I recognized as the brand Kolex, from my former friend Konirsch-Lenz, everything now free of dust, the frames repaired and everywhere useful labels that could not have been more informative.

The portraits of the Lebenhart couple hung in a prominent spot. Having in mind Lever's request, I asked why Saubermann's panoptical approach wouldn't allow them to at least hand over the paintings to the Levers so they could hang them in Johannesburg. Frau Dr. Kulka asked Saubermann if she could respond. He nodded that she could, and I was informed that, because of history, this wasn't possible, for it couldn't allow for any such return. I should understand that any dumping of stored-up treasure would mean a decrease in the true awareness of the history of those terrible years. The supposed reparation of an injustice should involve, if one understands it properly, really the injustice itself and no right to anything else. Frau Dr. Kulka didn't want to disagree with me, but that was the panoptical approach, which, no matter how brilliant my scholarly achievements might be, I had not yet sufficiently absorbed. Then Herr Schnabelberger asked to speak in order to support Dr. Kulka and note that Johannesburg was much too far off the beaten track. It is psychologically telling, I would have to agree, that the Levers ran the coconut toss in such a way that, through unusual cunning, they deftly kept the conference participants far enough from the barrier in order to prevent the possibility of a direct hit. If he, Schnabelberger, could suggest something else, he would urge them to consider whether the Levers should be involved with the work at the panopticon, in case someday they might wish to put on an exhibit in Johannesburg.

Herr Saubermann pressed his lips together in frustration. He had already made the Levers a generous offer, saying that Frau Lever could sell tickets, and Herr Lever could succeed Herr Geschlieder, yet that was scoffed at by the arrogant upstarts. The way Herr Saubermann saw it, such an upstanding man wasn't at all interested in ongoing access to the portraits of his grandparents; he wanted the paintings themselves, and that was that. There was no working with the Levers, so only under the Saubermanns' personal leadership and control would the objects see the light of day, such as here in the panopticon. Then our skillful leader added that that was enough about those paintings and we should see the rest of the exhibit. So we moved on and came to some objects that I remembered from the hermitage. One had to admit that everything was presented much more vividly. This entirely convinced me that the splendid exhibit represented the high point of the tour, for there was the coffin, surrounded by the artful figures that had so carefully been stowed away in the hermitage, and afterward had been so ignobly hauled away. Here, however, the mannequins didn't sit around the table during the Passover feast but, rather, haphazardly around and at a considerable distance from the coffin, such that one could easily walk between it and the families with plenty of room. Each mannequin could be observed from any side, each detail clear, there never having been such access to these figures before. Indeed, I heard within me a voice say, "Away from here, away!" But there was no chance of that, for my companions and everyone else standing around would prevent it, though I didn't just feel as if I were under arrest but, rather, a feeling awoke within me that said, "Stay, stay!" It was as if I were under a spell, everything preventing me from moving, a hammering sense of amazement that took away any thought of escape, such that my legs, which wanted to run far away, were stripped of all power to flee. Also before me was what I had long not allowed my eyes to believe, the mannequin of an old man standing up, though his raised hands grasped nothing, presumably not having been entrusted with the laws. Herr Saubermann seemed to know why the old man stood up, looming in all his shakiness, only looking off into the emptiness and attending the coffin, beyond which any gaze was swallowed up in the fathomless measures of past and future time. This was the end of history. It was arresting and surpassed everything that I recalled from the days of the hermitage. I didn't look at the mannequins for long, for they did not live for those who had died and the coffin reminded one that this was so, and thus I gave it my full attention. The proper state of reflection occurring within me, it was soon interrupted by an exultant voice.

"Look, Landau," said Herr Saubermann. "That is my greatest triumph. First of all, it was not easy to save this memorial and move it here at great cost and against the wishes of the local authorities and those back there, and then to restore it at even greater expense. Second, I needed all my skills of persuasion in order to convince my dear assistants and colleagues, Dr. Kulka and Schnabelberger, of the extraordinary worth and educational value of this unique object. But now they both hold the same opinion as me. The past has been saved for good, and not just brought into the present but also through some measure of care preserved for the future. So it was, so it is, so it will be."

As a special favor, I was allowed to touch the figures and then the coffin as well. I shied away from touching the mannequins and only lightly touched the grandfather. Then I drew closer to the coffin, it looking similar to the one that I had ridden to the Sociology Conference while accompanied by Brian and Derek. I quietly mentioned this coincidence, though my voice all but failed me. Everyone looked at me approvingly, as if it had taken me to reveal this to them.

"You have good eyes," explained Herr Saubermann. "It is, of course, highly symbolic. Unfortunately, I can't tell you whether that really is the coffin on which you rode here, for I don't have the authority of an expert in furniture, which among us only Mrs. Mackintosh would have. What's more, without basic archaeological training it would be hard to know. It's all such a long time ago. Do you remember? I don't, that I will openly admit. Everything was wiped out, then everything was good again. It ends up forgotten, no matter if one has the best panopticon in the world. Everything gone, for our memory is poor. But if your hard-nosed scholarly nature should be intrigued by this question, then Herr Birch, whom you know, would be the one to decide the identity of the coffin. It would certainly be worth asking. Though you'll have to agree, it's not a matter of outward truth but, rather, inner truth. And so you are right—the similarity is striking."

"We virtually buried you," Frau Dr. Kulka claimed when Herr Saubermann allowed her to speak. "You have changed so much that you either don't exist or someone totally different now lives."

"Yes," explained Herr Schnabelberger, forgetting to ask permission to speak. "You have survived completely. It's just as you want. You now belong to our panoptical museum as a coffin. You also happen to stand here before us, and you feel fine. That's all that a person can wish for."

"So it is!" the Professor asserted joyously. "Precisely! So the coffin is nothing but you as old Adam. You are separated from it as if by a wall and walk about in seeming freedom as an honorary member. A rare achievement. I believe it is even unique."

I ran my hands lightly over the coffin.

"I bequeath you this box," I said barely aloud and for no special reason. "I give it to you this very day. Where, indeed, are all the wreaths and flowers? It all needs to look good in order to serve your approach."

"A very fine remark," the factory owner and director of the panopticon agreed. "We'll take care of the flowers."

"And pearls, many pearls . . ." I whispered.

The moment seemed to have arrived to leave the museum. I was ready to leave the conference as well. Unfortunately, that was not possible, for as an honored guest one is trapped within his paradise and cannot shrink from it, but Kratzenstein was ready to leave the people of the panopticon in order to get me some fresh air. I held out my hand to the workers, and as I left the museum booth I had to sign a special page of the visitors' book, which had also been hauled out of the hermitage. Once we were outside, I heard a shrill roar that could only have come from Roy Rogers. I wasn't wrong, as the Professor confirmed, explaining that this blossoming enterprise had been transformed into an Institute for Quick-Change Artistry, which had grown in essential ways such that it now displayed the greatest achievements of the Sociology Conference. A visit was really called for. From the esoteric scientists' slide I had been lured over to Roy Rogers, and so we found our way there, where in front of the entrance most of the people I knew had gathered, they having been relieved of their responsibilites for the purposes of taking a special tour. A shimmering spectacle then proceeded, one like my ears had never before had to endure. A level of noise was reached that could hardly be taken in by my hearing. That's what I said to myself while truly dazed, though the sound did not oppress me. I also attributed this to the fact that I could already see Roy Rogers, the incomparable man with the assistants already familiar to me. He held forth with his famous skills, while the onlookers were herded into the tent accompanied by constant hoopla and boisterous calls.

Roy Rogers had found a partner equal to him who was billed as the quick-change artist of all time; he was a fast painter, a paperhanger, a prize shot, and much more that was rattled off. He was introduced as Hopalong Cassidy. He spread out a roll of wallpaper and held it up across from Roy Rogers, who tossed shimmering daggers and knives at it, though all the weapons bounced off the wallpaper that was quickly swung back and forth, and on which, through the unexplainable magic of Roy Rogers's knives, the word "Kolex" appeared in bright red. I had already been amazed to see the brand name Kolex in the panopticon, where it seemed to me ingenious, but here it had such an odd effect that the word appeared to me new and unknown and I couldn't remember it, for I had no time, as I was still breathless and besotted with the brilliance of the free performance. Roy Rogers drew his two pistols and wildly shot at the wallpaper, releasing pops and smoking clouds. Once he had emptied his guns, the word "Kolex" disappeared.

"Unbelievable!" I heard someone next to me call out. "Unbelievable! It has to be a trick, but one I've never seen before!" It was Oswald Birch who said this, and I agreed with him.

Then I looked up at the stage again, where I recognized my greatest benefactor and supporter. Hopalong Cassidy was my unforgettable friend Siegfried Konirsch-Lenz, while the lady who had helped him with rolling out and rolling up the wallpaper was Minna, his wife. By then Konirsch-Lenz had also noticed me and waved cheerily to me, called me by name, praised me to those gathered as the man of the day, and vigorously motioned for me to join him onstage. I hesitated and had little desire to follow the worthy request, but because of the entreating calls from the mouths of those above—the gathering also supporting this wish and urging me not to dally—I finally climbed up. Siegfried Hopalong embraced me and kissed me before all the onlookers, Roy Rogers doing the same. At the same time, Roy playfully threw his lasso over me, while Konirsch-Lenz kept loosening and tightening it. Then all the other artists onstage greeted me, among them two tall girls, Patricia and Petula, who were introduced to me by their mother.

Loudspeakers, music machines, and noisemakers created a wild revelry, but it seemed to me that it was drowned out by the booming applause of the conference participants in front of the stage. There was nothing I could do but bow, again and again, to the audience. I saw how they lifted Michael and Eva up from the crowd, the children waving handkerchiefs at me. Vainly I tried to shove Roy Rogers and Konirsch-Cassidy and all the members of their troupe in front of the joyous, screaming onlookers in order that at least a part of the applause go to them. That only worked a quarter of an hour later, when the pack were told to head inside the tent for the imminent start of the special presentation, at which Rogers and Cassidy carried me on their shoulders. Then the friends placed me on the stage inside, where I had to say a few words, though it was nothing more than repeated thank-yous. The relentless applause prevented a speech of any regular length. Then Herr Konirsch-Lenz unrolled his wallpaper once again with amazing alacrity, while Roy Rogers made his lasso twist and twirl as intricately as possible.

While this was going on, a wall slowly appeared between me and the onlookers. Certain that people were not paying as much attention to me, I inconspicuously stepped down from the stage at the back. Only Frau Minna noticed what I was doing, but when I whispered to her that I was planning a closing act that I wanted to think over and prepare in peace, my behavior didn't seem at all peculiar to her and she didn't pay any more attention to me. I just waited until she was no longer near me the moment she was needed onstage. Finally I looked up, and she was nowhere to be seen. I found my way to the back of the tent and looked for an exit, though I found none. The canvas was thick and was not ripped anywhere. I could have used the pocketknife I won at the Wheel of Fortune in order to cut a slit in the tent wall, but that seemed too nasty a thing to do and not easy. I would have been found out straightaway and could have been arrested for it. That's why I bent over and looked to see if there was any place where I could lift the tent and wriggle out from underneath. It was possible, but I had to crawl along the damp, dirty ground before I managed to force my way through.

Then I stood in the open air on the outer edge of the grounds on which the sociologists had met for the day. I wiped off my jacket and pants as quickly as I could. Then I heard the rattling of a chain. I looked around to see a dog lunge at me. At that, I ran away, deeper into Shepherd's Field, so that I couldn't be easily caught in case my escape was discovered. For the same reason, I avoided the usual entrance to the annual fair at Halstead Way. When I had finally run out of breath, I stopped and looked in all directions. Nothing seemed suspicious, nor was I being followed. I was left to myself and regretted only that Johanna and the children, as well as Anna, were not with me. I was concerned that they might be worried about me, while I also told myself that Johanna was smart enough to understand my secretly disappearing, which was nothing out of the ordinary for me.

In Shepherd's Field it was quiet; the ruckus of the Sociology Conference was a ways off with the tents and booths, while in the middle of the neglected field, with its weed-free grass, there was nothing else to hear. Only a few people appeared here and there, lone strollers who were not at all interested in sociology and took me to be the same as they, which they were right to do. Some young people and kids romped around, chasing after balls or enjoying themselves in other games. A tall boy seriously worked at getting his kite off the ground and was plenty proud when I complimented his agile handling of the reel and the string. From the distance I heard the piercing whistle of a locomotive and the rattling wheels of the train that raced along the rails. The metropolis was left behind, everything suffered having disappeared. There really wasn't anything there, and that's how it appeared to me. I couldn't help feeling at ease.

Only the hour itself was there, and thus it was today and it still is today. Around me everything had run together, such that I didn't know where I belonged or what I belonged to. "I'm here, I'm here!" This I called out loud. No one paid any attention, and that was good. Surely it would make it hard for anyone to sympathize, and even without this I had experienced enough ill will that I didn't wish to cultivate any more. This was why I had to deny myself so much. I will no longer avoid my fellow man; nothing is gained by remaining as distant as I have been, in having so little to do with them. Carefully I will lie low and not increase the opportunities to come together with them, but the idea that I am a crank or arrogant is something I want to avoid. No, I am neither of those, nor do I want to be at all. I have no right to be, and I have gone to great lengths to affirm the idea that I am not in any essential way different from my fellow man. And yet I still fear that I will never succeed in simply seeming harmless; I exist too much at the mercy of others and have to hear again and again what I suddenly blurt out, and, to my sorrow, I will not remain silent. This hinders me, disturbs me; there's no helping it. I have long since come to understand that it leads to nothing when I entrust myself to someone else.

Does the construct of my life work in this time? Alas, time and life. I don't want to raise old doubts. It is indeed a construct, that's the right word, and it will have to do. It is an undeveloped existence that attempts to assert itself with such a pointless new beginning, as if it were simply the consequence of a developing condition, an aging link that is connected to an existing chain that cannot be severed, which stretches visibly out ahead of me, and which, I can perceive, goes on even further, a row of continually secure dwellings, as has been extended through many generations, the magic of ancestry, father and son, myself in between, its beginnings hidden so deep and distant within unrevealable ancient times that one cannot know them, nor must know them. Up to now, my attempt to exist was an unsuitable undertaking grafted insultingly onto ruin for the sake of a bit of importance, pieced on to nothingness. That's how it seems to me. But that is said with too much bitterness and ingratitude. Nonetheless I have not become cold, nor do I lack for feelings, for in fact I am overflowing with them, even if they, too, often just die and nothing comes of them. Thus I am pulled in many directions and continually stretched further and further, such that sometimes I seem to reach as far as infinity; only the middle is missing, the familiar middle, which I can neither create nor grant myself. The threefold home of the ancestors, the countryside, and what was familiar have all been destroyed. That which was once obvious is gone, myself now wandering and living as a guest. That's a dangerous task.

What does the house on West Park Row mean, or Johanna and the children, and how do I square it with my stop in midflight? Without giving myself over to the measureless depths of sorrow, there is no way for me to manage to achieve solid footing or even affirm it, which is clearly demanded of me, for I am expected to affirm and defend just such. None of that can happen without stability. Without stability there is no way to secure any situation; instead, it becomes just a changing set of circumstances. They disappear and I can't maintain them, nor can they maintain themselves. Nothing that once was still is, nor will it still be. Everything in me is broken, I myself am broken, but amid the rubble the wall remains, and before it the readiness to answer should the question reach me. Also remaining is the expectation of the question, a groundless hope that still persists. That alone maintains the possibility of stability.

For everything else, after what I've experienced, it may be too late. If I say something, see something, know something, then it is nothing that can be affirmed; it doesn't last, no matter how much it wishes to endure and appears to be affirmed, but it is never firmly held within the mind or invoked through prayer and innocent belief. Before I know it, it dissolves, leaving me uncertain and groping in the dark. This, then, leaves me in an unbearable state, and all I can do is hold myself together. I simply have to be, because I am, and I have to do something for Johanna and the children, because I have to press on with nice gestures and a friendly demeanor and not let up. There's no other choice but to affirm myself, rather than to be affirmed by people, and certainly not by the higher authorities. No, just I myself, really just that, perhaps not to affirm myself to myself but just to affirm myself, not I myself but just to affirm something. This is indeed a surfeit of a small, humble daring, and as a result of it, all objects come into question, no longer being just this or that, but rather unaffirmed, just questions in themselves. I remain before them, becoming weak and tired as a result, until I risk the monstrous and shove them out of the way.

Because I didn't flee at the right time, I have to continually flee; no one and nothing can change that. How diminished I am as a result! A man of intellect who is nonetheless exposed, be it the man or the intellect, for either is less than existence. A survivor, condemned to cling to a signpost in the deadly snowstorm of misery, and when the snowstorm had cleared all the others were frozen, the signpost split. On the post, no destinations were legible any longer, the path itself lost, steps taken to the right and to the left, forward or behind, never once revealing the slightest trace of other foot-prints, while the feet can wander all about the traversable ground, except even the ground itself is not certain, no matter how surprisingly it holds up the weight of the one who walks on it.

But every transformation of the forgotten leads to error. No direction provides a reliable sense of things to come, and the roads of time continue to become lost in confusion; dreams gnaw away at them and mock the cer-tainty of hours. Then there are no more hours, the realms of past and future are shattered, not to be recovered or put back together, nor do they lie agape before each other, for only a demented mind would still cling to the idea of them. The run of things is twisted and destroyed; there is nothing left to retrieve.

I stand here at a loss—at a loss the peace, at a loss the restlessness itself. I pass my time in an empty present, as I turn about and ready myself. Where am I? Where today? Convoluted sorrow, which I break down, nothing of it remaining, the wind having scattered it, nor is there any more sorrow, it being all gone. I don't wish to exaggerate and portray my anxiety-ridden ex-istence in lurid darkness. Not to make it too all-important, but also to know that one has nothing more than oneself. But what do I have?

I manage, nonetheless, to remain somewhat reasonable. In my world I have tried to make sure that the guilt that never quite leaves my person has at least lessened in the past two or three years. I don't give other people much of a chance to have much to do with me anymore. My problems, whether they can be assuaged or remain unsolvable, I no longer turn to others with, and I have succeeded in extricating myself from their involvement. Thus I have robbed myself of the last opportunity to find a place among my contemporaries, to feel that I have a function as a member of society, even if it is only that of being a recognized witness to what I have lived through. I no longer hope for that, even if I should make it to fifty.

Once I had been denied almost any ties to the community, I was a relic of a person. Then I also had to relegate this relic to the inconspicuous. That had nothing to do with humility or frugality. Strangely no one expected that I would be depressed or suffer at all; on the contrary, they in fact expected me to be self-reliant, demanding that I produce something and lift myself up in the way that a man was meant to do. In no way did I measure up to such clever people, and so I don't want anything to do with how they think of me.

I have to rely much more on myself than on others. Thus I repeat to myself once more what I have come to realize: Without thinking of myself as any more important, if I am ever to exist, I know indeed that I can never let myself step outside myself; I live within my own border. It would be an implicit offense not to recognize that.

I have been forced into my isolation; I have not wanted it, for I always wanted things to be different. Rejected by all, alienated by people and their coveted status, I have been relegated to a place of my own. No one wants anything to do with me, nor do I want anything from anyone. That's why I've tried to keep separate how I survive and not follow unseemly ways. That I am essentially reliant on myself and have to worry about myself on my own—this causes enormous difficulties, such that from within everything looks so paltry, and I have nothing more than just myself, and that is ever little. Often, I ask myself whether there is anything more. That this may still be the case, despite everything, each moment confirms.

I don't separate myself from what I am not and yet nonetheless am of, that which I cannot escape or run from, for it is my imprisonment. That is neither important and essential nor unimportant and inessential. It hisses in my ears, causes horrible and sometimes also multiple sensations, pressing into me, lifting me, holding ready a thousand horrors, bowing me down and plunging me into weeks of weariness, days and nights blurring together that can hardly be distinguished from one another, because they have been mixed dully together and dipped in a stagnant brew. Then I am almost sick and drag myself around exhausted, feeling myself reduced to my own echo, such that an earlier life—this being my own earlier life—slips over me and leaves me with my senses reeling and it wanting to supply my sluggish fish-mouth with a strange speaking voice. But all of this is me myself, a tunnel in the same mountain whose shafts toss about in an earthquake.

Suddenly I am able to rally, a single movement of the hand enough to order me out of the dungeon of my breast, myself shaking and breaking into a coughing fit. Then usually better days follow, only a razor-thin fear remains and soon embeds itself as a small, smoldering desire coursing through my head from sleep to sleep, and that knows neither source nor goal.

On such days I have the desire to listen to music, uninterrupted music, almost feeding upon it. I myself have never played music, but I have always loved listening to it. Unfortunately, for many years that was only rarely possible. I never had the time, and thus music was drowned in wishes. Now it appeals to Michael. He always loved to sing, and at the age of three he had warbled many little songs quite well. Then it had inspired the boy to take up the violin. That is the newest, most important event in my house. Johanna and I thought about it a great deal, for the cost of a good teacher, which is the only thing Johanna would have, frightened us.

Carefully and quietly encouraged by me, after much hesitation his mother decided to teach him herself. We borrowed a child's violin. Johanna found the boy to be gifted and skillful. He picked it up quickly, liked to practice, and even had to be kept from practicing too much. For Michael's sake, Johanna broke her vow and picked up her violin, which she had once wanted to give to me, in order to demonstrate what he needed to hear and see, and, in addition to that, she played duets with him when he asked to, for he loved to play them. How pleased I am whenever I hear the two play while I am sitting in my study working. It makes things in the house seem nicer, easier, brighter. Eva also loves to listen and quiets down; it does us all good.

Otherwise nothing has changed, nor will much change, or, at least, I mean with me. It's different with the children. They are at the beginning; perhaps, God willing, things will work out well for them. Then, hopefully, they will get over their father, then they will themselves claim him. May they be protected and live a joyous life! May they love their mother, honor her, and thank her, but forgive their father and bear with his weakness without resentment, his affliction as Adam, the loneliness he suffers before the wall!

Michael and Eva, if you ever read these lines, which I have carefully preserved for you, then may you be blessed with the fear of the Lord, then may a buoyant spirit protect you, and everything that I have written here, may it help you find a right awareness. Your father's work, especially this book about the wall, all of these efforts, should make the experience and achievements of a tested and fragile and yet, amid his ultimate despair, an honest and hardworking person at least a little comprehensible and credible, if indeed not endearing and beloved.

Certainly you won't be living on West Park Row anymore, but I ask you, if you have the chance, to visit the site of your childhood. Perhaps the little house where you played will still be standing, and next to it the houses where you ran around with the Stonewood and Byrdwhistle children. Also, the vendors in the shops around the corner on Truro Street will still be selling their wares, there being fresh fruits and vegetables in Simmonds's shop, and perhaps there will even be a dog there that looks like Santi. Perhaps across the street at a window two women will appear and look down at you, between them a cat strutting along the sill. On the street there might be a ragman like old Ron there now, pulling his cart and knocking on doors, asking for old clothes and rags.

The train will certainly still run nearby, and you'll hear it, and I expect that at MacKenzie's they will be repairing and overhauling cars as they do now. Only the heavy smoke from the squat chimney will faintly drift smoky and dark over the streets.

You, however, should live, dear children, and honor life, and should you have children, may my blessing help you to set your sons and daughters on the right path. Perhaps then your life will seem to you an enormous treasure.

LIST OF CHARACTERS (IN ORDER OF APPEARANCE)

Dr. Arthur Landau: Born in a continental city much like Prague, he is a concentration-camp survivor. His parents were deported and killed, and his first wife, Franziska, also died in a camp. After the war, he returns to his native city and works in a museum that collects items belonging to those who perished. Eventually he chooses to emigrate to a metropolis much like London, where he meets Johanna Zinner, marries her, and with her raises their children, Michael and Eva, while he struggles to find enough support to write his *Sociology of Oppressed People*.

Fräulein Zinner/Johanna Landau: Having emigrated to the metropolis before the war, she works in the Search Office at the Bureau for Refugees. She lost her parents and her two brothers during the war. She meets Arthur Landau, marries him, raises their children, and provides the principal support for the household.

Professor Hilarius Prenzel: Arthur's high-school teacher. Early on Arthur has a nightmare of returning to his native city to visit him, only to be betrayed by Prenzel and turned in to the authorities at the train station as an alleged spy.

Michael and Eva Landau: Arthur and Johanna's children.

Herr and Frau Kutschera: Proprietors of the fruit stand around the corner from the clothing store run by Arthur's father, Albert. When Arthur returns to his native city, they are the first to tell him that his parents were taken away.

Peter: A young man who finds Arthur sprawled on a sidewalk in his native city after Arthur stumbles while fleeing a collection point for refugees at the train station. Peter then takes him to his friend Anna Meisenbach.

Anna Meisenbach: She takes Arthur in and allows him to spend a night, before having him move in with Peter. Anna's brother, Arno, went to school with Arthur but has since been executed for political crimes. She and Arthur talk of the postwar conditions in the old city and the loss of her first husband, Hermann, in the war.

SO-AND-SO/LEONARD KAUDERS: A boyhood friend of Arthur's and a sociologist who escaped to the metropolis before the war, and the first person Arthur writes to from his native city after the war. So-and-So tries to help Arthur find support in the metropolis, but with little actual success. His wife's name is Karin.

PROFESSOR KRATZENSTEIN: A very prominent sociologist and the head of the International Society of Sociologists. Arthur approaches him for help in getting the support he needs to work on his *Sociology of Oppressed People*, but Kratzenstein discourages him and does not approve of his scholarly approach.

DR. JOLAN AND HANNAH HAARBURGER: Refugees from Budapest who host a party at which they introduce Arthur to a circle of intellectuals and prewar refugees.

HERR BUXINGER: A bookseller in the circle of prewar refugees living in the metropolis.

RESI KNISPEL: A press agent from Zurich. She later tries to get Arthur to help her start a journal called *Eusemia*.

LARRY AND IDA SAUBERMANN: Philanthropic factory owners. Later, Johanna seeks work in their factory, which manufactures artificial beads, but Frau Saubermann instead condemns Arthur for failing to properly provide for his wife and children.

DR. EDUARD AND KLARA SINGULE: He is the head of a foundation but was trained as a zoologist. She is his wife and a prominent socialite. Arthur asks Singule for financial support for his work, but to no avail.

BRIAN AND DEREK: Pallbearers assigned to pick up Arthur at his home on West Park Row and take him to a crematorium, where he is to be cremated. They later return to take him to the Sociology Conference held at Shepherd's Field, at which he is to be honored. The driver of the hearse is named Jock.

HERR SCHNABELBERGER: He is the director of the museum at which Arthur works after returning to his native city following the war.

FRAU DR. KULKA: The assistant to Herr Schnabelberger at the museum. She believes the goods left behind by the victims belong to the state, whereas Arthur treats them like precious beings that need to be tended to with the utmost care.

FRAU HOLOUBEK: Once the servant of Arthur's grandmother, she now passes on goods to Arthur from those who have died.

FORTUNATA: A Gypsy fortune-teller Arthur first encounters at a fair at Shepherd's Field, and then again at the Sociology Conference later held there.

HELMUT: Anna Meisenbach's second husband, who, along with Peter and Anna, sees Arthur off when he leaves his native city by train. Later Helmut dies suddenly, prompting Anna to emigrate to the metropolis, where Arthur and Johanna take her in and help her start a new life.

HERR GESCHLIEDER: The porter at the museum where Arthur works.

FRAU FIXLER: Professor Kratzenstein's secretary.

SIEGFRIED AND MINNA KONIRSCH-LENZ: He is another philanthropist who offers to help Arthur, but only by offering to hire him to do menial work in his wallpaper manufacturing business.

GUIDO AND MITZI LEVER: Visitors from Johannesburg who grew up in Arthur's native city and fled before the war, and who later return to the city and visit the museum where Arthur works. Guido's family name used to be Lebenhart. His brother, Eugene Lebenhart, owned the portraits of their grandparents that Arthur cataloged at the museum at the start of his employment there.

MRS. MACKINTOSH: The wife of a high-ranking official at the British Embassy who tries to buy furniture from the collection gathered in the museum in Arthur's native city.

DR. OSWALD AND INGE BERGMANN: Brother and sister. He is a prominent scholar who knew Arthur in his native city, which he escaped before the war, changing his surname to Birch after immigrating to the metropolis. His sister is a poet and an illustrator of children's books. They are there to greet Arthur when he arrives by train, though Oswald had initially been unresponsive when Arthur wrote from his native city to ask for his help in emigrating.

OTTO SCHALLINGER: A friend of Arthur's from middle school, who is also there to greet Arthur when he arrives in the metropolis.

EBERHARD S.: The editor who initially gets Arthur to write for *Eusemia*, and who is disastrous at running the journal.

BETTY: Johanna's second cousin, who lives in South Wales, where Arthur and Johanna find a welcome respite from their struggles in the metropolis.

PRINCIPAL EVENTS

The Wall is a novel of sudden and subtle transitions between the past and the present, operating much like a symphonic score in its repeated themes and motifs. To aid the reader in moving through these transitions, the following synopsis is provided.

Pages 3–14: Arthur Landau at home on West Park Row, in a metropolis much like London.

14–26: Arthur dreams of a train journey back to his native city, a clear stand-in for postwar Communist Prague, where he is betrayed by a former teacher, Professor Prenzel, and detained by the state authorities.

26–33: Back in the present metropolis, Arthur and his wife, Johanna, are called in for questioning by an immigration officer, who grants Arthur a visa without any significant difficulty or restrictions.

33–35: Arthur hears a voice that threatens him and calls him Adam, saying he can never escape.

35–48: Back at West Park Row, Arthur considers Johanna, and their children, Michael and Eva, and reflects how his own memory is a "wall" between both his past and his future.

48–51: Arthur remembers the duress of war and expulsion.

51–61: Arthur recalls his return to his native city after the war and the search for his parents. He learns from the fruit vendor Herr Kutschera that they perished.

61–65: Arthur dreams that his parents condemn and reject him, while his mother sews his shroud.

65–82: After fleeing a collection point for refugees at the train station in his native city, Arthur stumbles and falls. A young man named Peter comes upon him and takes him to his friend Anna Meisenbach, who takes Arthur in and cares for him. Anna's brother, Arno, was at school with Arthur but has since been executed for political crimes. Arthur and Anna talk of the postwar suffering in the old city.

82–83: Arthur falls unconscious and has another nightmare about his parents.

83–87: Arthur comes to and Anna offers him a place to stay for the night, though Arthur cannot help thinking of her dead husband returning home to find a stranger there.

87–93: Arthur awakens from the memory of this incident to find himself again at home on West Park Row with his wife and children. In his thoughts he finds himself standing before a wall that he cannot get past.

93–102: At the invitation of his boyhood friend and fellow sociologist So-and-So (Leonard Kauders), Arthur attends a party at the home of the Haarburgers, who try to help him make important contacts in the metropolis. There he meets Professor Kratzenstein, an influential sociologist. He is also introduced to Fräulein Johanna Zinner, who works for a refugee organization in the metropolis. At the same party, he meets Herr Buxinger, a bookseller, Resi Knispel, a press agent from Zurich, Herr and Frau Saubermann, philanthropic factory owners, and Dr. Singule, the head of a foundation, and his wife. At the party, Arthur discusses his work on the sociology of oppressed people.

102–15: Arthur recalls looking at Arno's books in Anna's apartment and asking about her husband, Hermann. Anna gives Arthur some of Hermann's clothes. Arthur tells Anna that his parents and his wife, Franziska, died in the war.

115–16: Falling asleep, Arthur dreams of walking in a mountain forest with Franziska.

116–36: Arthur wakes up on West Park Row only to find that two pallbearers, Brian and Derek, have arrived with orders to take him to a crematorium in order to be cremated. Johanna urges him to do as he is asked. Arthur manages to persuade the pallbearers to allow him to walk to the crematorium. The pallbearers stay for breakfast before accompanying Arthur to the crematorium.

136–60: Arthur falls into a reverie and thinks back to his last walk with Anna in a mountain forest before deciding to leave his native country for good. He thinks back to similar hikes with Franziska.

160–74: Arthur thinks of the many families who have lost ancestors, then about his earlier work in a museum in the old city that collected the left-behind goods and portraits of the many who had died. At the museum, Arthur works with the director, Herr Schnabelberger, and his colleague Frau Dr. Kulka to sort and catalog the paintings and objects. Though he would like to see the works returned to the families, Frau Dr. Kulka argues that they now belong to the state.

174–90: Arthur's thoughts then revert to the party at the Haarburgers' and how he complained of not having a single picture of his parents. Others question why he did not remain in his native country. Marriage and moral freedom are also discussed, Arthur finding the crowd of exiles to be pretentious and corrupt. Only Johanna Zinner is sympathetic to his past suffering as she tells him of family members she herself lost. On leaving, she invites Arthur to call her sometime.

190–93: Segue to West Park Row and the present, as Arthur sits in his study, writing letters in order to seek funding and support for his work on the sociology of oppressed people.

193–203: Segue to Arthur's native city after the war, where Peter urges him to write to friends who escaped before the war in order to seek their help in emigrating. Arthur writes to So-and-So but finds it nearly impossible to express what he has been through.

203–17: Arthur reflects on Peter as a difficult person who nonetheless has tried to help him. Then, from the future, he reflects on Peter's own emigration as Arthur writes to him from the metropolis. In a letter to Peter, he recalls So-and-So's return letter to him back in his native city, when he first wrote to him in the past (we learn of So-and-So's letter to Arthur in the old city, in a letter Arthur writes to Peter from the metropolis). In that letter So-and-So asks Arthur's help in his efforts to be compensated for his family's property that was seized by the state.

217–32: Arthur then stops writing letters from home, choosing, instead, to write letters from his office at the museum. He thinks of the haunted nature of the objects he collects, especially of Franziska's pearls, which were passed on to him by an elderly survivor. Frau Holoubek, once his grandmother's servant, also passes on family mementos, thus increasing his burden. The same happens again and again with other former acquaintances, Arthur forced to stumble through the streets, weighed down with objects passed on from the dead.

232: A voice again addresses him as Adam, commanding that he return to his past.

232–34: Shaken from his reverie on West Park Row, Arthur talks with Johanna about the strangeness of time, how the present is never the present, and how he feels stuck outside of time, unable to reenter it.

234–49: Arthur then takes his children to a fair at Shepherd's Field. There he sees a show put on by Roy Rogers and his troupe, and then he visits a fortune-teller named Fortunata.

249–71: Segue to Arthur's memory of leaving his native city for good and his friends accompanying him to the train station. Present are Anna and her new husband, Helmut; the museum's porter, Herr Geschlieder; and Peter. Arthur is both anxious to leave and anxious about leaving. Once the train is en route, Franziska appears to him in a vision and releases him from having to dwell on her loss ever again.

271–300: Arthur leaves his room in a guesthouse in the metropolis to call Fräulein Zinner from a phone booth. She invites him to come to her office. Arthur rushes back to his room to dress for the occasion. Once he reaches the Search Office of the Bureau for Refugees, where Fräulein Zinner works, he climbs the stairs to her fifth-floor office but collapses on the way. Fräulein Zinner finds him and takes him to her office to recover. As he regains his strength, he tells her about his work and talks about the loss of his parents, and the past that he cannot recover or escape. They then leave to go to dinner at a restaurant. Along the way, Arthur hallucinates that his head separates from his body.

300–14: Arthur awakens the morning after his first night at Anna's while calling out Franziska's name. Anna fixes him breakfast, while Arthur is anxious about what to do next. Anna suggests that he move in with Peter. She also suggests that he write to friends abroad and try to emigrate, which she eventually hopes to do as well.

314–15: At Peter's place, Arthur tries to start work on his sociology of oppressed people, but he struggles until the return of his earlier drafts, which were carefully preserved by Franziska at the start of the war.

315–19: Segue to Arthur at work on his book in the metropolis while struggling to find support for it, especially when others urge him to take a menial job in order to support his family. Deeply frustrated at not being able to find a viable place in society, despite his constant written appeals for help, Arthur writes a short story called "The Letter Writers."

319–29: "The Letter Writers"

329–38: Arthur continues to reflect on his inability to gain support for his work. Eventually Professor Kratzenstein does agree to meet him, but all Kratzenstein is willing to do is invite Arthur to the working group of the International Society of Sociologists, rather than invite him to lecture, as he had earlier promised. Kratzenstein recommends that Arthur seek the help of Dr. Singule and Dr. Haarburger.

338–46: At Frau Haarburger's urging, Arthur visits Dr. Singule, who is of little help. All he can do is recommend that Arthur seek the help of Kratzenstein, which he has already done. Frau Singule sends him home with some chocolate for Johanna.

346–55: Arthur next visits Herr and Frau Saubermann, philanthropists who own a factory that manufactures artificial beads. Johanna, too, is invited to their home to talk about the possibility of getting work in the factory, even though she is pregnant with her first child. However, Frau Saubermann scolds Arthur for being too proud to seek out work himself in order to support his family.

355–61: Arthur then goes back to the Haarburgers to ask for further support. Frau Haarburger is upset to hear how badly the visit with the Singules went, nor does Dr. Haarburger have anything left to give him.

361–62: Penniless and destitute, Arthur thinks of himself as a fallen Adam who, in essence, does not exist.

362–79: Four years after his arrival in the metropolis, Arthur meets with Siegfried Konirsch-Lenz, another philanthropist who offers to help him, but only by offering to hire him to do menial work in his wallpaper manufacturing business, which Arthur refuses. He and Johanna return to West Park Row.

379–82: On West Park Row, Arthur reflects on how he still exists among his neighbors, who are more decent to him than his so-called friends and supporters, and decides that there is nothing to do but press on with his work.

382–89: Segue back to Arthur's work in the museum in his native city, where he thinks of the people in the portraits as patients who have survived, much to the horror of Frau Dr. Kulka, who sees the portraits simply as objects.

389–408: Herr and Frau Lever from Johannesburg arrive at the museum, having fled the old city before the war. Arthur gives them a tour of the hermitage, a former synagogue that had been converted by the occupying forces to house dioramas with wax figures depicting the customs of the people they had deported and killed. Along the way they meet Professor Hilarius Prenzel, Arthur's old high-school teacher, and the man who betrayed him to the authorities in his earlier nightmare about returning. In the museum, Arthur explains the creation of the dioramas in detail, as if he were present at the time the work was done. The Levers are amazed by it all, while Arthur feels trapped within.

408–49: Segue to Arthur's arrival in the metropolis, where at the train station he is met by the scholar Oswald Bergmann, who has changed his name to Birch, and his sister, Inge, a poet and an illustrator. So-and-So is also there to welcome him. Arthur thinks back to Oswald's reluctance in responding to his letters and pleas from the old city but forgives him and is pleased to see him at the station. Otto Schallinger, a classmate of Arthur's from middle school, is also there to greet him, along with Dr. Haarburger, who then leaves. The rest all head to Oswald Bergmann's home, where Arthur falls asleep, exhausted by his journey. When he wakes up, Oswald and So-and-So suggest that they go to a restaurant for dinner.

449–67: Segue to Arthur and Fräulein Zinner arriving at a restaurant for dinner. They talk of their lives and work, and Arthur proposes marriage and Johanna accepts. They leave the restaurant and walk arm in arm through the city, talking of their future, before Johanna heads home on the subway.

467–70: Arthur walks home and writes to Anna about his engagement to Johanna. He then falls asleep, thinking that he is on the threshold of a new beginning, but still feeling everything is in flux.

470–80: Once again, Arthur meets with Konirsch-Lenz, who continues to berate him about the need to get a paying job and to accept the assistance of an organization called Self-Help. Again, Arthur refuses, but this time he feels liberated in doing so.

480–82: Arthur thinks of Otto Schallinger, who often visits him and Johanna, finding in their home a vestige of the Old Country that he does not find elsewhere in the metropolis.

482–93: While strolling along after leaving Konirsch-Lenz, Arthur thinks of his friends and how little help they have been, beginning with Oswald Bergmann, and then So-and-So.

493–501: Arthur thinks of all the charlatans he has met in the metropolis, the worst being Eberhard S., who managed to convince him to write for his journal *Eusemia* for a pittance. He then calls Johanna to say that he has left Konirsch-Lenz and is on the way home, which pleases her. On the way, however, he muses about his failure.

501–15: Segue back to Herr and Frau Lever, who are about to leave the museum. They ask what Arthur's last name is and, upon learning that it is Landau, remember buying clothes in his father's shop. Herr Lever reveals that his name used to be Lebenhart, which causes Arthur to remember two portraits bearing that name in the museum. The Levers then insist on seeing the portraits and claim them as their own, though the museum refuses to release them. In the middle of heated discussions about this, a Mrs. Mackintosh arrives to ask if she can purchase some of the furniture that is stored in the museum, though Herr Schnabelberger will not allow it. Arthur then takes the Levers to see the portraits of their relatives. Nonetheless, the museum denies their request.

515–22: Frau Dr. Kulka comes to Arthur's office to accuse him of betraying the museum in telling the Levers about the portraits. At the end of their conversation, all Arthur wants to do is flee this life and this city for good.

522–26: While waiting for Anna to arrive at the museum, Arthur thinks of his life as one that is constantly in flight, forever on the move, and realizes that he can truly exist only within his own intellect and mind.

526–32: Stirred from sleep on West Park Row, Arthur awakens to the mailman delivering a letter from Anna saying that Helmut has died and asking if she can come to Arthur and Johanna. Another package contains a book titled *Stereotyping Through Prejudice*, which carries a jacket comment from Professor Kratzenstein that Johanna and Arthur find pretentious. Another letter is from Resi Knispel, saying she would like to talk to Arthur about a project that she has in mind for him.

532–50: Arthur visits Resi Knispel, who along with Herr Buxinger wishes to start a new journal, and she wants Arthur's help in recruiting talent to write for it. Knispel tries to persuade Arthur to popularize his work, eventually revealing that the journal's name will be *Eusemia*. Arthur says he has to think about it and prepares to leave. In the foyer, Knispel throws herself at Arthur, claiming that she's in love with him and scratching his hand as he tries to release it from her desperate hold.

550–68: Arthur and Johanna then visit her cousin Betty for two weeks in South Wales, where they enjoy the simple country people and the countryside. Despite the frosty cold, he and Johanna hike for hours over the hills and through the fields, stopping to picnic along the way. Once again, they declare their love for each other and realize that they must begin again, like Adam and Eve. Arthur presents Johanna with Franziska's pearls. Arthur tells Johanna that Franziska spoke to him in a dream right before he departed the Old Country, declaring that he was free to go, and that he now realizes that he indeed exists.

568–612: Back on West Park Row, while anticipating the arrival of Anna, Arthur is astonished when the mailman knocks on the door to announce the arrival of the pallbearers, Brian and Derek, who have orders to bring Arthur to the Sociology Conference, at which he is to be honored. They are supposed to convey Arthur there in a coffin and a hearse, but instead Arthur rides atop the coffin while Johanna and the children travel behind in the truck of a neighborhood grocer. The conference takes place at Shepherd's Field, the site of the earlier carnival, which is still up and running and now contains exhibitions hosted by all the characters encountered thus far from Arthur's past and present.

612–18: After appearing onstage with Roy Rogers, Arthur slinks to the side and escapes by crawling under the circus tent, fleeing Shepherd's Field. On his way back to West Park Row, he can only be grateful for the stability his wife and children provide him in a world that remains suspended between the past and the present, the only hope being that his children will enjoy a future that is free of such duress.

ABOUT THE AUTHOR

Born in Prague in 1910, H. G. ADLER spent two and a half years in Theresienstadt before being deported to Auschwitz, Niederorschel, and Langenstein, where he was liberated in April 1945. Leaving Prague for London in 1947, Adler worked as a freelance scholar and writer until his death in 1988. The author of twenty-six books of fiction, stories, poems, history, philosophy, and religion, he was awarded the Leo Baeck Prize for his monograph *Theresienstadt 1941–1945: The Face of a Coerced Community* in 1958. *The Wall* was completed in 1956 but did not appear in print until 1989, a year after Adler's death in London.

ABOUT THE TRANSLATOR

Peter Filkins is a poet and translator. He is the recipient of a Distinguished Translation Award from the Austrian Ministry for Education, Art, and Culture, a Berlin Prize from the American Academy in Berlin, and an Outstanding Translation Award from the American Literary Translators Association. He teaches literature and writing at Bard College at Simon's Rock and translation at Bard College. His translations of H. G. Adler's novels *The Journey* and *Panorama* were published by Random House in 2008 and 2011, respectively, and also appear under the Modern Library imprint.

ABOUT THE TYPE

The text of this book was set in Janson, a typeface designed about 1690 by Nicholas Kis (1650–1702), a Hungarian living in Amsterdam, and for many years mistakenly attributed to the Dutch printer Anton Janson. In 1919, the matrices became the property of the Stempel Foundry in Frankfurt. It is an old-style book face of excellent clarity and sharpness. Janson serifs are concave and splayed; the contrast between thick and thin strokes is marked.